A Long Healing Come Slowly

A Novel About PTSD (Post Traumatic
Stress Disorder) And Its Effects on
Suffering Individuals and Their Families

Jim Carmichael

LifeRich Publishing is a registered trademark of
The Reader's Digest Association, Inc.

Scripture quotations taken from the New American Standard Bible®,
Copyright © 1960, 1962, 1963, 1968, 1971, 1972, 1973, 1975, 1977, 1995 by
The Lockman Foundation. Used by permission. (www.Lockman.org)

This is a work of fiction. All of the characters, names, incidents,
organizations, and dialogue in this novel are either the products
of the author's imagination or are used fictitiously.

LifeRich Publishing books may be ordered through booksellers or by contacting:

LifeRich Publishing
1663 Liberty Drive
Bloomington, IN 47403
www.liferichpublishing.com
1 (888) 238-8637

Because of the dynamic nature of the Internet, any web addresses or
links contained in this book may have changed since publication and
may no longer be valid. The views expressed in this work are solely those
of the author and do not necessarily reflect the views of the publisher,
and the publisher hereby disclaims any responsibility for them.

Any people depicted in stock imagery provided by Thinkstock are
models, and such images are being used for illustrative purposes only.
Certain stock imagery © Thinkstock.

ISBN: 978-1-4897-0797-0 (sc)
ISBN: 978-1-4897-0796-3 (hc)
ISBN: 978-1-4897-0795-6 (e)

Library of Congress Control Number: 2016909612

Printed in the United States of America.

LifeRich Publishing rev. date: 10/7/2016

For Catherine, my wife.

Contents

Preface

The American military family, for all intents and purposes, is in shambles today. With an all-voluntary military and multiple deployments to Iraq and Afghanistan in the past decade, no one should be surprised about this. Active duty personnel, if they can get it, are eligible for psychological counseling. Yet if they do actually receive such counseling, their military career could end. Who counsels the mothers and fathers, wives or husbands and the children of those personnel returning home from the battlefield? What type of counsel is actually given and who receives it? Most likely the spouse and children are left to their own investigations.

This country is also rapidly outlawing the mention or open display of God or His law. Is it possible that there is a direct correlation between our desire as a nation to rid ourselves of any reference to the God of Scripture and the breakdown of society, especially its cornerstone the family? I am convinced this is so.

Spouses, you committed yourself to this veteran "for better or for worse." Are you starting to wonder when the "better" will ever come? Young teen, you may have noticed a change in your military parent and it may not be for the better. For too many, answers are in short supply. Does the hole in your soul keep getting larger and deeper.

Would it help if I told you I know how you feel? Been there, done that and got the T shirt. The T shirt is now a rag. I know many families that have gone under because of their involvement in America's wars. Perhaps you have set about on your own trying various ways to cope.

You go one more minute, and then one minute more, but the minutes just keep adding up and nothing is resolved. Are you farther from your loved one than ever? You've prayed, but the heavens seem bronzed, nothing coming in and nothing going out.

My question to you is: How is this plan of yours working? I have a better one. This novel is about hope, concrete hope, hope that you can park an aircraft carrier on. My wife and I know what it means to have one's war sweep it all away. It is also about human and divine love, the former incapable of resolving the pain and memories to anyone's satisfaction, while the latter can encounter no power greater to stop it.

If you have tried most everything and found only heartache, I have some very good news for you: you are in the perfect place, warts, pain, and all. I can assure you that God is not wringing His hands, hoping He can keep all the doings on earth from colliding and self-destructing. Military families know something that most American families do not. They know what it means to submit to higher authorities. When the powers that be say, "Get your gear together and be ready to move out at 0900," you get your gear together and are ready by 0900.

In the spiritual realm, the one true God too many people today say is a figment of our warped imagination is the Supreme cosmic Commander. It is to Him we must submit as the all-powerful, all-knowing, all-merciful. We all submit to the rule of gravity when we stand on our roof looking down at the yard below us. If you slip, gravity will rule over you. Jesus is LORD over every molecule in the universe and your body. He is equally the Law-Giver and Judge. No one can see gravity, but we know it rules over heavy objects.

Since 1997, I've been in the VA health care and mental health system. I've been in various wards for PTSD (Post Traumatic Stress Disorder) counseling, beginning in Sioux Falls, SD, then the Denver VAMC PTSD counseling center. From there, I attended the St. Louis, MO PTSD clinic, and now I'm with the Atlanta Mental Health system. I know what's being taught in these clinics and how they work. I also know why they aren't effective.

There is no cure for PTSD, but with faith in Jesus Christ there is Rock Solid Hope. As a matter of fact, my life didn't start until it took a nose dive because of my PTSD. Thank you Jesus for sending me to Vietnam and ensuring I would be diagnosed with PTSD. Thank you for not allowing those pills I took to stop the sadness. Thank you for every black hole of depression that swept over and swallowed me whole. Thank you for decreeing the torturous anxiety and forgiving my outbursts of anger. Thank you for those long years searching for the right medication, and the added years it took to find the right dosage. Thank you for all but severing my marriage, and then building it back stronger than ever. Thank you for my bride of almost fifty years. Thank you for saving me from sin.

There is only one way to live with PTSD that works: Christ's way. No, you won't find the word "PTSD" in the pages of the Bible. It's condition and promise of comfort is scattered throughout its pages, nonetheless. My wife and I know of what we speak. Be advised, you only come to full healing when you arrive on heaven's shore. Until then, the gifts God gives to His people are countless and priceless.

I have done extensive research in writing this book. If you find something amiss, let me know. I have used numerous switchbacks in this work. They are all labelled and dated.

I did not experience any "soul cleansing" having accomplished something of great moment when I typed the final words of this manuscript. Mine was not a cathartic endeavor in which some or many ghosts of the past were exercised. I no longer have any ghosts that need exercising. I don't have flashbacks or nightmares anymore. My God is able to keep the close buddies I lost in battle in the past. That their lives and deaths meant something tremendously significant goes without saying. Despite the number of pages, this book is a fast read and you will find yourself not wanting the book to end. God in Christ should receive all glory if this book helps you find the Savior.

Jim Carmichael, Ph.D.
Cumming, GA Mar. 2016

Prologue: The Letter

1 March 1967

Dear Mr. and Mrs. Wilson,

Lt. Collins asked me to write to you. I hope that was okay with you. I'm sure he'll be writing you soon if he hasn't already.

Corporal Damien Wilson sat on his steel pot with his back against a tree, having just finished cleaning his M-16. He pushed the selector on safe and laid it close to him. In these surroundings he officiated in the context of war. Behind him, a flapping gaggle of ten CH-46 medium helicopters flew some company or battalion of Marine grunts into harm's way. He felt nothing for those men as the roar of their airborne machines passed into the horizon. He'd lived in this war zone for eleven months now. The boxcar crunch of artillery made its presence known about a half click to the west. Life wasn't complete without that crashing. A flight of bomb laden F-4's from Da Nang streaked across the sky, northeast to southwest at about fifteen thousand and climbing.

The itch in his lower back roused him to personal sympathy. With his flak jacket on he couldn't really feel the rough bark of the tree through the fiberglass plates sewn into his vest. This meant that he couldn't massage the itch as an old bear does when he rubs himself against tree bark. Regardless, he pressed his back hard into it like that bear does. It helped, some.

He looked back out toward the surrounding countryside. Vietnam was often a noisy place that he had learned to segregate into dangerous and impotent sounds. Green undulating hills melted into lighter and darker tints, hues, and tones. These colors at one time provided a breathtaking conglomeration of his favorite color. That was a million years ago, when he joined the company.

In Delta Company's physical claim upon this AO, the landscape propounded to its inhabitants an ancient, serene facade. That had all become a lie during Damien's tour. This country and its green washed dyes were equivocations; themes played out upon half-truths. Tree lines, bushes, bamboo thickets, and elephant grass; the flora and fauna of Southeast Asia were seldom what they advertised. Ages ago, and half a world away, a tree line was just that, and nothing more. Now, eleven months into Damien's tour, he could no longer trust what his steely dark brown iris's told him was just rough brush. Everything was a potential trap. Vietnam had become a place in which his foe hid in, among, or under foliage waiting to kill him. All of it he had to sort through in an instant. If he sorted wrong, he was dead. He no longer put stock in the ground he walked on; for nothing was safe or sacred here anymore. Hidden or buried in the dirt were land mines and punji stakes, or worse. Charlie used everything: discarded C-Ration cans, tires, unexploded bombs, unclaimed ordinance, everything, and Damien knew that Victor Charles, wherever he was, was watching him. That little gook was out there, —somewhere. Both he and PFC Moorehouse, sitting a few feet away from him, were already sweating from the humid ninety plus-degree heat. The heat over here had a taste to it. But he would never be able to describe it back home—back in the world. They had most recently completed digging their fighting hole and both men were hungry, as hungry as one can get laboring in a sauna.

Wilson and Moorehouse couldn't have been more of a study in contrasts. Damien Wilson was built like a basketball forward, —tall, lean, and agile, quick as a deer. Moorehouse stood five feet seven inches and tripped over his feet. Damien was lightly black, and Jerry Moorehouse white. Damien's features were measured in straight, handsome lines that had drawn not a little female attention in school. Jerry had been a fat, freckle faced kid, and here, his baby fat soon melted off of him as he edged his way into life in the Corps. Damien came from the upper middle class of Ft. Worth, Texas. His father, Dr. James Wilson, was a brilliant physicist who had recently taken the position as head of the science department at Gladstone Preparatory School. After years of his wife's bantering James Wilson could now come home at night to spend time with his family. Dr. Wilson nearly disowned Damien for enlisting in the Corps.

Jerry spent his days on the tough streets of Dundalk, Baltimore's industrial blue-collar district. Jerry had no idea who his father was, nor did he care. He'd been told his old man was a thief and a streetwise punk who had raped his mother. His mother died of a heroin overdose when Jerry was five. That was when he was moved to an orphanage until he was twelve and half. He had joined the Marines from the repressive confines of a foster home. No one at Jerry's last home really cared that he'd joined the military. It just meant that they didn't have his mouth to feed any longer.

Damien's IQ was slightly over one hundred thirty. Jerry didn't know what IQ meant, not really. Damien loved Keats and Shakespeare, Hemingway and Steinbeck for starters. And Moorehouse, well, he loved Superman comics; anything with pictures. Wilson was a Baptist. He spent his final summers at his church's basketball camp. Jerry held no particular beliefs sacred. Religion had not looped its way into Jerry's existence. But Jerry was a quick understudy, amiable and free spirited, and he meshed well with this company of Marines. Despite his formative years that could have made him resentful, he worked at making friends. He was more diligent than most, which became his first order of business. Damien felt at odds, especially with some of the other black Marines and several of the white Alabama and Tennessee boys. Damien and Jerry liked each other immediately. Only their rank separated them. Jerry snored at night and, worse, sometimes on ambushes, which brought Damien's whispered wrath. Damien, however, slept light, his hand almost always curled around the pistol grip of his weapon. He'd wake at the slightest rustle or click of a twig—or for no reason.

They were different in other significant ways. Damien had witnessed enough of the Delta Company men die, both white and black. He'd killed several Viet Cong and NVA at close range. His first kill was with his K-bar—on Christmas. He'd also experienced a tragic "friendly fire" incident, and as the saying goes, "friendly fire isn't."

That was two days before Thanksgiving. When he finally rotated he'd do everything he could not to be anywhere near home on those days. The holidays would simply mock him. By now his outlook on life had submerged into the thick ooze of his own confusion, wondering if life held any truth to it or meaning for him. How was he supposed to understand all those Sunday school lessons at Emmanuel Baptist? *Love thine enemies?* Killing had become part of who he was. How does one simply stop this way of living and 'go home' as if nothing significant had happened for the past twelve months? He wondered if any place was really "safe" anymore. He'd begun to wonder if Nietzsche was right, that God was indeed dead. He started to feel that all the answers he'd trusted as a child had not simply lost their meaning, but rather never had any purpose to start with.

Trust in anything solid had gotten lost somewhere between where he sat and Da Nang. Damien had also stopped wondering if there was some plan to win this war. Nietzsche had gone insane, partly because of the venereal disease he'd contracted and partly because he no longer had any response to his own philosophy. Only God, if He did exist, knew if Johnson and McNamara had any intention of winning this elongated, open-ended conflagration.

Private Moorehouse came to Delta to escape the constant change of life without weighty relationships. He was content with the possibility of God existing or not. Here in the most dangerous place on earth, he'd found a home. Little else mattered to Jerry.

The previous two weeks had proven virulent and unrelenting to Delta Company. Each platoon had tripped one ambush each. They'd skirmished off and on for two days the preceding week with a sizable enemy force and twice they had initiated contact with the enemy. As a result, the company had suffered three KIA's and ten wounded during that span. And on last night's ambush a patrol of VC walked right into second platoon's kill zone. They found several blood trails but recovered only parts of one body the next morning.

Humans weren't the only enemy they fought. The lack of sleep and the constant tension of wondering who would get hit next cut creases into their facial features. It sank their eyes deeper into their heads. The dead weight of their packs, along with all the gun ammo boxes and rifle bandoliers, extra mortar rounds and frags, served to multiply mass times gravity to equal more weight than any of them had ever carried over distances that might break a horse, comparatively speaking. Everyone swatted the malarial mosquitoes and the other critters. They had intense disdain for the horse-size malaria pills that sent them into the bushes with their e-tools suffering from the 'Ho Chi Minh quick step." Then there were the varmints that killed or made one wish he were dead. All around them four inch black scorpions, foot long centipedes, three quarters of an inch in diameter that could bite on either end and an infinite variety of deadly snakes. They lived with dysentery and the ubiquitous heat or the incessant rain and resultant soaked clothing that could rub sores on a weary body. Annoying leeches populated the rice paddies and streams and hurt fiercely when you pulled them off. They left a hole in the skin that oozed blood and became infected quickly.

The skin between their toes split and bled from being constantly wet. When a man cut himself on the ten foot tall razor sharp elephant grass he bled, which led to infection and then a pus filled sore within fifteen minutes. The more cuts, the more infectious sores for sweat to drain into and burn. Nothing really ever healing properly. Life in Vietnam stung and burned in one way or another, and all the time.

If these things weren't sufficient to burden a man there was always the uncertainty of wondering if the effort they gave day and night was worth the cost. They held deep in their psyche the growing suspicion that America didn't care about them, and from what they read from their local newspapers, the U.S. hated them for what they did. It all conspired to sap from them what energy remained in their bodies.

With the can's lid cut open and bent to form a handle, Jerry Moorehouse raised the hot green tin can to his nose. He sniffed at the malodorous bubbling gravy bathing the beefsteak and potatoes. The heat tab cooking his meal gave off acrid, noxious fumes that burned his eyes, soldering the inside of his nose. This burning of course caused him to rub his eyes and nose with his other dirty hand. He blinked hard to clear his watering eyes and then blew on the gurgling thickened juices to cool them. He had learned to do it this way for the past few months now. In the heat, he simply endured eating. In the bush, getting to a place where you could sit long enough to shovel the food in was so often an ordeal.

Jerry stirred the contents of the can, sloshing some of the gravy over its edge so that it dripped onto his mud encrusted right boot.

"Way to go, Moorehouse," he groused to himself. He was already thinking past the main course of this B-2 Unit and into the middle of his pound cake. He loved his pound cake. So did Damien. After months in the bush Jerry found he wouldn't eat Ham and Eggs, Boned Chicken, and Chicken and Noodles, —no way, unless, of course, he could beg some spices from somebody.

After eleven months and some loose change, Damien had one full moon to go out of his twelve and seventeen. That was when he'd hitch a ride on a chopper and be out of the bush for good. At twelve months and twenty days he would be on that great big freedom bird headed home, to the land of the round eyes. So, he ate the ham slices, Beans and Wieners and once in a while, a Beefsteak ration. He had to have a heat tab for the Beefsteak. The gunk they packed in and around it was horrible if not heated. If he did heat it, it was only terrible. His mother kept him supplied with dried onions and other seasonings. She'd learned to bake German Chocolate cakes in coffee cans. She'd even filled old shoeboxes full of chocolate chip cookies and other goodies, which she sent to him. Damien was good about sharing his mom's fabulous cooking. But almost twelve months of eating the same meals, except for the few times they actually got to eat in somebody's mess hall in the rear, would drive a normal person insane. Damien wasn't normal any more. Complaining about any and everything was his right and an obligation as a grunt. It didn't alter the facts, but it felt good.

"Damien, you want my Caraway cheese? I hate this stuff." Jerry shuddered as he thought about what lay just beyond the thin metal cover he refused to cut open with his C-Rat opener.

Damien didn't look up as he spoke. "PFC Moorehouse, you know what you can do with that Caraway cheese, don't you?"

"How you gonna act, man? Don't say I never offered you nothin'. Don't come screamin' to me when you're starvin' and we can't get resupplied like last time. I'm a nice guy, Corporal...hey. By the way, when are you gonna finish telling me about your dad? Did he ever talk much about working on the atomic bomb?"

"No. He couldn't talk about it. He told me some stories, but I'm certain now that he left out quite a bit, you know, top secret things. He used to say that if he talked about that project, Mr. Hoover, the FBI Director, would personally show up at our door and take me off someplace where they couldn't find me. He is a genius, my dad. Did I tell you he met Einstein?"

"Albert Einstein?"

"Yep. Oppenheimer, Konopinski, Hans Bethe, Serber, and Teller too. All those brilliant men and so many more. They called them the Luminaries. It took all of them and thousands more to make that bomb."

"You gotta be kiddin' me. Albert Einstein? Man. Did you ever meet any of those scientists, Damien?" Jerry didn't know who Oppenheimer or Teller were. For all he knew they played baseball, but Albert Einstein? *Holy mackerel!*

"I was too little. Some of them are dead now. You know what's funny about my dad?"

"No. What?"

"Sometimes he walks out of the house when it's raining and doesn't even know it. He's just on another planet sometimes. I don't know how many times we'd be sitting at the dinner table and he would start one sentence, stop in mid thought and begin to write out an equation and then leap onto a completely different topic in the span of fifteen seconds. He just didn't have a clue he'd left us in the dust. But put him in front of a black board and give him a problem to solve and he'd be off to the races, in his own little world."

"Yeah? Like what would he write on the blackboard?" Moorehouse was half finished with his meal, and Damien had moved toward a more contemplative mood thinking about home. That brought the ache back. He wanted to get out of this place so badly he could taste it. But he wanted out alive and in one piece. He didn't care if his dad was a bit preoccupied. He'd not complain this time. Just getting there was the main thing now.

"Oh, he'd write equations I couldn't begin to understand. It was so far beyond the calculus that I did in school . . ."

"You know calculus? Wow. You must be a brain too." Jerry Moorehouse was duly impressed with the Marine sitting next to him. Most of the enlisted Marines he'd met were at least high school graduates and a few had gone to Junior College. But calculus? *Wow.* Jerry had fought the war of algebra . . . quite unsuccessfully.

"Yeah. I intend to go back to school and get my degree in Marine Biology when I get out. I'll just call it biology of the water and leave off the Marine part. The next time I play in the water I don't want to have to wade in it looking for leeches or little people who want to shoot me. How many years did you enlist for, Moorehouse?"

That was a tough subject for Jerry. When he rotated out of the bush he'd have two and half years left. Two and half years plus nine months left to be exact. It may as well be a million. "I got two and half after I rotate."

Damien just smiled. He had enlisted for three years and would have just a few months left in the Corps when he got home. "I figure I have about five or so months to do when I get back to the States." He smiled again. "I'm a short-timer." Then Damien laughed aloud as he looked at Jerry. The poor kid had forever and two weeks to go in the bush and then a lifetime to do at Pendleton or Lejeune. "I'm hurtin' for you, pal."

"Yeah."

Damien had not yet opened the letter from Michael, his best friend from school. That, he would save for dessert. He wiped his hands on his sweat stained, beyond filthy utility jacket and stirred his can of ham and limas to make the meal somewhat more edible. His eyes squinted and his nostrils flared from the fumes of his own heat tab. In a hot second Damien was just mad. He looked over at a group of Marines about thirty meters away and spoke in a normal tone at them. "Jonsie, I hope you ask me to get you out of the next working party . . ." Damien stirred his meal and fumed. Cpl. Wilson had requested Jonsie to take care of some light duty matters as a favor. For his kindness Damien was given the privilege of going in Jonsie's place on that working party. Damien even thought about throwing the can into the bushes or burying it . . . just because.

When the contents finally boiled, he stuck the spoon slowly into his can and then brought the shipment perilously close to his lips. Closing his eyes, Damien blew on it. He slurped a plump dull colored green bean between his lips and onto his tongue. At this instant, physics and boiling heat took over. In less than a split second he ejected the bean like a watermelon seed, wincing and then gritting his teeth as if trying to grind the slimy grained texture from existence. He hoped to somehow erase the fiery contact it made with his taste buds. That stinking round, green thing had seared what was left of them. With his face contorted, Cpl. Wilson concluded his response by shaking his head in utter disgust. Slowly the odious taste lessened in his mouth. He ran his tongue against his front two teeth to see if the damage would be permanent. The veins on Damien's sweaty neck protruded and his dark nostrils continued to flare. The look in his brown eyes said to one and all, *beware*.

With his tongue still smarting from the hot bean Damien set the can back on the once smoldering stove resting between his boots. Finally the heat tab had burned itself out. He prayed zealously that this meal might taste better when he attempted another bite. Lord, he hated this dismal meal, and his tongue throbbed in pain from the bargain. He just wanted to eat. Jonsie wouldn't trade his beans and weenies for love nor money. Not for Ham and Mothers. Damien would have thrown in his pound cake too—*uhhh, maybe not*. Resorting to a last ditch effort, he stirred into the can the final few bits of dried onions he'd saved from home and held his breath. Now he had to segregate the juices or any other nasty thing from touching his palpitating tongue. He wanted to eat. Moorehouse couldn't help but laugh at the faces the dark skinned Corporal sitting next to him made. Damien eyed Moorehouse's meal—*anything but Ham and Mothers*.

Things have started to get busier around here lately. But Damien always helped me look on the bright side of things when they made us do things we didn't want to do, like working parties.

Following chow, Damien once more wiped his hands on his utilities. He didn't want to soil the letter he'd saved for when he'd finished eating. He'd thought about using his rag of a towel to clean his hands but decided against it. His trousers would have to do. This was one more reason, among so many, that every Marine's jungle utilities in the company were such a mess. Melded into the numerous tears in the worn and bleached fabric was a collection of friend and foe's blood, and the past days and weeks had proven a rich environment for making one's utilities blood stained. This letter from Michael just might lighten his spirits a little. He missed their camaraderie, and especially their mischief. He'd been so preoccupied with staying alive that he didn't realize just how homesick he was until the long-overdue mail arrived on the last chopper. Damien could always talk to Michael, but not so easily to his father. Dr. Wilson seemed to not know when his chemistry, physics, or biology lectures should end and time with his son should commence. Damien needed 'guy talk' right about now —not Marine Corps talk, not Vietnam talk —but a conversation with one of his friends outside of Delta Company, even if they were half a world away and they couldn't make sense of his struggles.

Dear Damien, I haven't heard from you in a few weeks. I was getting a bit worried so I thought I'd write to see how you are fairing. Your father reads your letters to the class when you do write— hint, hint. I thought I'd let you know that no one suspects what we did at the end of last year; so far that is. I occasionally overhear a teacher talking about it. Coach McKay thinks you are somehow connected to the blocking sled, but he can't prove it. I just play dumb. Revenge has proven somewhat sweet. Unfortunately, I had to help pull it out of the creek. Oh, where were you when I needed you? It was hard getting it out.

Lucinda misses you. She has that sort of hangdog look about her. I don't know why. I hope you've had time to write her. I thought I saw Boyd Manchester looking in her direction at lunch— just thought you might want to know. Are you going to marry her when you finally get home? I think she's expecting that to hear her talk. You don't get near a basketball hoop anywhere do you? That probably is an ignorant question. The team sure could have used you on the court last season. Coach Dobbs thinks the baseball team will fare ok. He misses you on the mound, at short, at third, in the outfield, at bat, at bat, at bat . . .

I noticed you were promoted. What does a corporal do? Have you seen any action lately? I won't tell your parents if you've been in any heavy action. What's it like shooting at people or getting shot at? Have you ever killed any of the enemy? You don't say much. I guess guys aren't supposed to say things like this but I wish you were here instead of there. I miss the good times we had. I always wanted a big brother. Margaret doesn't really fill the bill. The parties seem less, I don't know, less exciting without you spiking the punch and all the other crazy things you came up with.

Do you remember Charlie Ruckles? He was killed in a car crash last month. You may remember he put the Ex-lax in the chocolate cake in Home Economics last semester. Mrs. Simmons really lost her stoic composure with the effects. It was wonderful. You remember how nothing really seemed to get to her? Two students were sent to the hospital with severe diarrhea & abdominal cramps. I think Charlie over did it, but it was so funny because Wendy Armbruster was one of the girls who went to the hospital. It was something you & I should have done before you left for San Diego.

I need your advice. Mother & father are really pushing me to finally decide on a university in the fall. As you know, father wants me to consider Texas Christian University or Texas A&M University & mother is set on Princeton or Yale Universities; at least one of the Ivy League schools. I don't know if I want to take the pre-med or engineering courses. I just don't know. Donny Rainford has already been accepted to Dartmouth University. All my friends will be leaving me in a few months. Wendy Armbruster is going to Amherst University. She really grates on my last nerve. Charlie Warden said he wanted to stay here & go to TCU. I might be able to make their baseball team or I could try out at A&M. I'm really getting tired of Ft. Worth, but nothing else appeals to me. I don't want to work for father— right now. I just don't enjoy working there.

Uh oh, here comes mother. I have to clean my room. Take care of yourself.

Your friend,
Michael

Damien heard swishing footsteps pushing through the ankle high grass in his direction, which made him look up from his letter just in time to hear Gunny Ballantine bellow, "Wilson. The lieutenant wants you."

Gunny Ballantine was a throwback from the Philistines and a distant relative of Goliath. He wore the largest jungle boots Damien had ever seen, and his hands could make a basketball look small. He carried that old, beaten and scarred club with him, which he called his "whuppin' stick." The Gunny didn't actually need his .45, but the lieutenant insisted he carry it anyway. He had trouble finding a flak jacket that actually fit his barrel chest, and he had to squeeze his helmet onto his shiny, bald head. What he gave away in looks he more than made up for in aggression.

Before returning to Vietnam, he would visit the bars in Oceanside or San Clemente, California, and "volunteer" to be their bouncer for the evening. This was his second tour in 'Nam. All in all, he'd earned the Navy Cross, a Silver Star, two Bronze stars, one with "V" device, a hand full of Vietnamese Crosses of Gallantry, plus two purple hearts. Part of his left triceps was now missing and he had welts all over his legs from the shrapnel of a Chi-com grenade. Before coming to Delta Company, between his first combat tour, and now his second in 1967, he'd done one tour on the drill field at Parris Island. That was probably the reason he couldn't whisper, and no one wanted to set in next to him on an ambush. But they all wanted him on their side when the garbage hit the fan—that was for sure.

"Great. What did I do this time, Gunny?" Wilson asked, hoping not to hear his answer.

"Nothin' corporal. First platoon has a prisoner, and the lieutenant wants you to go with him for a look-see."

"Gunny, you know I'm a short-timer; thirty-two days and a wake up. I'm so short I'm sitting on the edge of a dime danglin' my feet. And besides, I'm gettin' shorter by the minute." Damien held up his short-timer's stick he'd been working on and pled his case as all short-timers are obligated to do. He even resorted to begging, which, at this point, didn't seem beneath his dignity. "Are you sure you can't get me out of this? O'Neal isn't busy. Moorehouse here isn't either. Jonsie sure isn't. Gunny . . . I've got important friends back home, and they wouldn't want me, a real short-timer, going out there where people could do me bodily harm."

"You're breakin' my heart, corporal." Ballantine wasn't prejudiced, he hated everybody. The giant smacked his shillelagh against his helmet. "Get your gear and high tail it over to the skipper at the CP. Your piece better be clean." A Marine called his rifle a weapon, a rifle, or a piece. He learned embarrassingly at boot camp not to call it a "gun."

Damien looked at Moorehouse and then said under his breath so Ballantine hopefully wouldn't hear, "Never volunteer for anything. Oh man, I hate this place. And I especially hate this green machine . . . and lifers. *'It don't mean nothin'.'*"

Hate seemed such an easy word these days. Damien found little tolerance for these tanned diminutive people he came here to rescue from communism. That was how it started out, how he reasoned himself into this. Now after eleven months he believed that most of them wanted to kill him or wanted him to go home. He hated battling for and taking ground one day, only to abandon it the next, and then for no good reason that he could see, take it back and abandon it once again so that Delta or some other company received multiple casualties retaking it.

He hated filling body bags and sand bags. He hated the lifers, Marines who chose the Corps as their occupation, all of whom seemed to go out of their way to make his life miserable, —like Gunny Ballantine. He hated the weather, be it hot and wet or cold and wet. It really got cold over here, especially when he was soaked to the bone and the wind blew. He hated the enemy who refused to quit. He hated the Washington politicians' micromanaging this war right into the ground. Winning had long since vanished from the mental landscape of most of the Marines in Delta. Surviving replaced what remained. He hated the smell of death and he hated Ham and Mothers.

But the unexpected had slipped under the radar screen too. It embroiled him in its own web of deceit, infusing it into his being. Damien had become alive over here. This place had honed his senses. He'd become an adrenaline junkie. It took him hours to come down off of the high of firefights. He wouldn't admit it, but Corporal Wilson loved the action, the drama, and the suspense of wondering if he could cheat death one more day or moment-by-moment. His M-16 gave him a sense of authority. The frags gave him power out of proportion to reality. If he climbed into a CH-46 and saw that the crew chief had that forlorn, "Coyote-going-over-the-side-of-a-cliff" look on his face while standing amidst hundreds of empty spent brass casings Damien's heart raced with excitement. They were going into a hot LZ. This contradiction was normal for Cpl. Wilson. Damien couldn't explain it, but the high had become addictive.

He'd discovered that he could think under pressure when some men couldn't. He saw better at night over here. He sensed hidden dangers. He'd come to trust that intangible *something* that veterans learn living months at a time in the bush. This sixth sense was now so much a part of him. No amount of training stateside could ever infuse this into a man. He heard *things*. Little unobtrusive noises. *Things* all around him. Things which the FNG's, the "Cherry's," the fresh meat replacements from the world hadn't the slightest notion of.

He was now a Marine in the fullest sense of the word. When life couldn't get any worse, and Damien had reached that empty cubbyhole more than once, the brotherhood of Marines from all of America's past wars stood beside him. They urged him, and they swore at him —'*One more step, Jarhead. One more step.*' It was they, their courage, their devotion to something beyond themselves, that made him clean his rifle, hump the bush when he was too tired to move, and grit his teeth and take it. He hated this place, no doubt about that. It had stolen from him people and things that could not and would not be replaced. But it had given him qualities and perspectives so few boys his age hardly imagined existed.

Despite these infused pressures and positive commodities, the past month had made him wonder, for reasons he couldn't explain, if his luck had almost run out. He couldn't shake it.

Cpl. Wilson stood and stretched. As he did so, Damien's head felt light, somewhat dizzy. He bent over, putting his hands on his knees for balance. That action gave him heartburn in spades. C-Rats did that to him. He burped out loud. *That one's for Charlie and Gunny Ballantine.* In a moment, when the trees stopped circling, Damien bent down once more and grabbed his weapon along with several bandoliers of ammo. He always carried his two frags. He stuffed his letter into his left breast pocket and put on his steel pot, which usually made his head itch. Ready as he ever would be, Damien sauntered over to the CP utterly disgusted, because he didn't want to stop thinking of home, and this patrol forced him, one more time, back to a grunt's lot in life.

The Command Post was located in the shade, under some low hanging branches from a large tree that had been punctured and scarred not so long ago by an arty round. The previous week's skirmishes had blown the bark off of it in several places. Nearby bushes gave them the best concealment in the immediate area.

"Doc, hand me those magazines and a couple of those frags," Lieutenant Collins said to the nearest corpsman.

Lieutenant Joseph Collins, Delta Company's skipper, was a man on a mission. He'd just been promoted to Delta Company CO when Captain Stanwyck rotated out of the field and up to Battalion S-3A. Major Cronin needed an assistant. Stanwyck had done his six months in the bush, and now it was Collins's turn to take over.

Joseph Adolphus Collins graduated from Vanderbilt University with a degree in Chemical Engineering, and almost married his high school sweetheart the second semester of his sophomore year. He accomplished this latter mission over Christmas break of his junior year. He'd also gone to Parris Island his junior year, which nullified his honeymoon. But he more than made up for lost time during the summer. His uncle's cabin on the coast of Alabama a few miles out of Gulf Shores soothed Maureen Collins's ruffled feathers. Unfortunately, the Corps' demands on her husband's life had set the tone for a stormy relationship between it and her.

Joseph's senior year found him at Quantico and once more separated from Maureen. Her never ending tug of war between his desire to lead men for as long as the Corps called on him, and her genetic exigency for the sanity, security, and pay of an engineer, made life difficult on them both. Finally, her life, such as it was, had reached its apex for Maureen. She told her mother she'd had enough. She sought and obtained a divorce before Joe could secure a plane ticket home to dissuade her. So long, Maureen.

When he graduated, Joseph was commissioned a second Lieutenant. He reported for his fourteen weeks at The Basic School, and afterward, was sent to Fort Sill for Artillery School. When he filled out his dream sheet, he *did not* list infantry as any of his first three choices. Because of standing order number one in the Corps by those gutless wonders at HQ Marine Corps who *do not* get anywhere near the bush themselves, he was assigned to a rifle company and sent straightway to Vietnam.

Joseph Collins didn't look like an officer, not really. He didn't fit the physical mold that enlisted men get in their heads about what an officer is supposed to look like. He was not large like the Gunny. He didn't appear athletic under his field gear and his always-red cheeks gave him a boyish countenance that the recent fire fights and all night running gun battles worked toward scouring from him. His boots were half the size of Ballantine's, and his hands seemed a half size too small. The Lord only knew how that huge Vanderbilt ring stayed on his finger.

But Damien couldn't remember hearing Lt. Collins ever complain. He was accurate with the compass, so the men trusted him. He was very good calling in fire missions; the rounds always landed where they were supposed to land. The most recent short round was Sgt.

Marks's doing. Yet, despite these positives, Damien thought he detected an anger building within the man. He couldn't put his finger on it, but something seemed askew behind that silver bar. Lately, he'd get angry a little too often, especially when the last three men were toe tagged and medivaced out. One of the three men was Delta's XO, Lt. Kirkpatrick. With the Executive Officer gone, Ballantine was forced into assuming numerous duties not normally assigned to the company Gunnery Sgt. No one knew when the new exec would arrive. Collins had also begun to smoke more than usual. He liked Marlboro's. Too much contact lately. No sir, Damien didn't want anything to do with this patrol.

The two radiomen, LCpl's Simmons, a tall, lanky Texan—with three months and six days left in the bush, and Castillo, a medium built Latino with four months and twenty-two days to go, strapped on their radios for their pre-mission radio checks. Simmons lit up his fifteenth Kool of the day and then articulated into his hand set while Castillo moved several paces away from Simmons so Simmons could communicate with Battalion. "Oregon Mike, Oregon Mike . . . this is Delta Six . . . radio check. How do you read me, over? Oregon Mike . . . this is Delta Six . . . radio check. How do you read me, over?" Simmons had learned to talk like a radioman even without the radio.

Castillo, the Delta Company wise guy, now far enough from Simmons, checked his radio with Bull. He keyed his handset near a squat bush hoping not to be overheard by the lieutenant, "Delta Two, Delta Two . . . this is Delta Six. I need a radio check. Eenie, meenie, miney, moe, —how do you read my radio?" Bull Zimmerman, third platoon radioman, bent down and away from the Gunny so as not to be heard laughing. He cupped his hand around his mouth and spoke into his handset, "Zat you? Yo, zat you? Delta Six, I read you two by two, —too loud and too often. Bye, ya'll." To that Castillo squeezed his handset to ask, "Where's the women and booze you promised?" Bull came back, "Wake me up when dinner's ready, honey. Six out."

Having repeated this unacceptable form of military communication for the umpteenth time, Castillo looked around to see the Gunny glaring in his direction. The Gunny however didn't remove the contagious smile from Castillo's sun dyed skin and dirty face. Walking back into the CP, he said, "Radio check complete, Sir." His pseudo serious manner fooled no one. Several seconds elapsed before Simmons's radio crackled its response, "Delta Six, Delta Six . . . this is Oregon Mike. I read you loud and clear, over." Simmons acknowledged the man on the other end of the radio, "Roger that, Oregon Mike. Delta Six, out." The battalion radioman knew better than to joke on his radio; too many officers around.

Damien, the final arrival, shuffled into the CP. Three men were standing in close proximity to the lieutenant who stood chain smoking while he studied his map intently. He moved his compass over the papered surface making mental checks as he did so. Each member of the newly formed patrol rechecked his assorted ammo and grenades draped about him.

"What are you smilin' about, Castillo," the lieutenant asked, knowing the answer before he sent the question.

"Nothing, Sir."

Damien arrived in country about 8 months before I joined Delta.

"All right. Listen up. First platoon has captured what they suspect is a VC. I need to go see what they have. No, Corporal Wilson, I don't want to hear one more time how short you are, clear?" Damien nodded and showed his teeth but nothing more. The lieutenant unveiled for the three men the various coordinates on his map to orient them as to the CP's location, their route, and exact destination. "Since you all 'volunteered' for this assignment, make sure you keep your spacing at fifteen meters when we move out. I know I harp on this, but we're gonna' be in the open for about six hundred meters until we run into that long section of tall brush and bamboo at the end of this paddy. First platoon is several hundred meters beyond that thicket, so . . . unfortunately we'll be forced to stay on this dike until we reach them. The engineers have cleared this area of mines; I hope so anyway. As it stands, we have no other options, gents."

All the enlisted Marines going on the patrol were thinking the same thing: *why did they invent the helicopter? The Regimental CO and Battalion CO both have their own choppers. Why can't they go get that little gook?* But after so many months, not only in the Corps, but also in the military, they knew the answer. It was mind over matter. We the Marine Corps leadership, don't mind, and you the led don't matter.

The lieutenant paused for a second and looked at his watch. Then he resumed his instructions. "Stay on me, but keep your eyes open and your head on a swivel. I say again, don't bunch up. We're not taking a corpsman so don't anybody get hurt. But if I do go down we have two nets for support: Company and Battalion. Cpl. Wilson will assume command if that need arises. Any questions?"

"No sir," came the reply from the dirty, sweat soaked men surrounding him.

"Gunny, make sure mortars are up and ready before we move out," the lieutenant continued. Another pause, another long drag from his cigarette, and then he urged, "Gunny, go ahead and set up LaSarge's gun right there—to cover us. We're gonna be in the open forever."

Dennison's mortar crew was busy stripping increments off of the High Explosive or HE rounds. He'd use one round of Willie Peter or white phosphorus to mark the target when the call came. Cpl. Dennison studied his map, moving his compass over it. Then he looked at the yellow range card. "First check point is six hundred meters, elevation . . .seventy-two.seven, deflection zero, charge two. The ammo humpers pulled two charges off each round. Dennison adjusted the M4 sight accordingly.

He checked his compass once more, and then looked through and over his sight at his aiming point. Sixty's didn't use aiming stakes, eighty-one's did. He put the white line along the left edge of a huge tree just past the brush line. He knew exactly where first platoon was, one hundred meters to the right of the tree. Dennison adjusted the elevation knob several degrees, then he turned the zero of the micrometer knob toward the "L" or left, fifteen mils toward the setting he wanted. Next, Hal Dennison centered his longitudinal level with the elevation crank, looked at both bubbles to see if they were level. Noting the deflection bubble was just a hair off he readjusted the nut on the bipod leg and the cross level bubble came to center. This process took him a matter of seconds.

"Lieutenant, mortars are up. "LaSarge. LaSarge!" bellowed Gunny. "Get over *here*! Get your crew together, and set your gun up over *there*. You'll cover the patrol." A machine gun or a mortar tube you could call a gun.

"But Gunny, I ain't had my chow yet!" LaSarge could protest with the best of them.

"Look clown. I don't want any lip from you." Ballantine smacked his helmet several times with his club, hard enough to knock any normal human senseless. Then he said, "The Skipper wants it done now. What do I gotta do LaSarge, thump you on your melon? I will!" he barked, pointing the shillelagh menacingly toward LaSarge.

LaSarge exhaled, partly from hunger and partly from respectful exasperation; —Ballantine was eight times larger than he was. The little Indian from South Dakota had his crew move the machine gun into the most recent assigned position and get it set up. He'd seen Ballantine grab a large Marine off of a six-by truck and slam him against the tailgate and then proceeded to chew him out. The gunny went nose to nose for any petty insubordination.

Damien kind of took me under his wing. He would sit with me on some of my watches at night and he even went out on an LP, that's a listening post, one time with me when he didn't have to. I really appreciated that. I got to return the favor several times when I got a few packages from my girlfriend with cookies and stuff. He sure liked the chocolate chip cookies my girl sent to me. Thank you, Mrs. Wilson, for the goodies you have sent.

Twenty feet away two Marines, digging a fighting hole, scrambled head-over-teakettle out of their excavation. They shouted and stomped their boots, swung their entrenching tools wildly at something in the thick grass. This sudden animation scattered a large flock of perched and nesting drongos skyward from the nearby eucalyptus trees. The large bird's excited flapping, combined with their harsh jumble of metallic aviary notes, chuckles, and calls, co-opted the two men's indiscernible and foul Marine vocabulary.

"What's goin' on Gunny? You men, what's goin' on?" The lieutenant's anxious, probing voice demanded an answer.

"Sir, it was one of those foot long centipedes. I hate those things. We was just tryin' to kill it. It crawled up into this pile of rocks here before we could get it. It disappeared in there somewhere."

A slow smile spread across the lieutenant's face. This noisy diversion sliced into the rising tension growing amid the small band of men huddled near the map. Since no one got bit, Gunny turned back to his own affairs and the lieutenant returned to the immediate concern: the patrol and the promise of a prisoner. Collin's intensity betrayed somewhat his rising concern about the distance he had to cover until they reached at least *some* concealment.

The lieutenant, it seemed lately to Damien, wanted to jump right into the middle of the fire. This man liked leading his men. He was a natural skipper. But he also hated toe-tagging Marines. And lately, the former led too often to the latter. Collins checked one final time with each radioman as to his assigned frequency. He also scanned each man's ammo allotment and other equipment for his own assurance.

"I'll lead," he stated matter-of-factly. "Simmons, you're second. Wilson you follow Simmons, and Castillo you're tail end Charley. Alright, load and lock."

The four men went through the automatic process of tapping their magazines on the palms of their hands or helmets to seat the rounds. This done, they shoved the magazines into their weapons. Each man then chambered a round and put his rifle on safe. The lieutenant stepped out from under the overhanging branches of the trees, under which he and the CP group spread their gear, into the insecurity and death of Vietnam. Collins squeezed his stub of a smoke out with his fingers. The small amount of unsmoked tobacco scattered in the sudden breeze and settled in the high grass.

> Damien didn't seem to mind working with a new guy and he made sure I kept my weapon real clean. We have a gunny who likes to have surprise rifle inspections before we go out on patrol. Damien saved me some considerable embarrassment and pain several times. The gunny gets upset when our rifles aren't clean.

Simmons didn't bother counting the Skipper's steps. He knew the distance by sight, —even in the dark. When the lieutenant reached it, Simmons stepped up on the dike and moved toward the distant brush.

Two men up and out. Wilson counted in his head out of habit, 'seven . . . eight . . . nine . . .' In his full concentration and growing unease, he didn't hear Castillo move behind him so that when Simmons reached about the ten-meter point Castillo bumped Damien hard from behind. When Wilson regained his balance and not a little of his composure, he turned to confront the laughing radioman, Castillo. He hadn't heard Manny. That wasn't good. Being a short-timer had its disadvantages: a growing preoccupation with the hope that he might just make it out of this place and less concentration on "business." Damien couldn't let down now, but he had. . . for an instant.

Damien laughed a lot and made me laugh when I'd get real scared during Incoming and things like that.

"Hey. You stupid son-of-a . . . How you gonna act, Manny? You know what payback is?"

"Lighten up, man!" Castillo's jubilant grin somehow managed to disarm almost all potential belligerents. It served him well once again. Manny could go toe-to-toe in a heartbeat with any Marine in the company, except Ballantine. Nobody tried Ballantine. Damien wouldn't hesitate to drop Manny, —but not now.

Slowly, Manny's smile turned Wilson's agitation into a mocking type of corrosive smirk, "When we get back here I'm gonna kick your butt!"

"Lighten up, Damien. You're just too tense, man. Man, we probably aren't comin' back. It don't mean nothin.' You better give me your girl's address. Somebody has to replace you—might as well be me. Hey, vato?" Damien just shook his head. It was Castillo's Latino enunciation of anything English that further softened Damien's accruing mental anguish. This Latino had helped him slip mentally away—if only for a second, —from another of the endless forays out into 'Injun Country.' Damien knew they were heading toward a thick brush line and who knew what else; another ambush, another sniper, another dead Marine? Maybe Damien would finally catch one between the running lights? *Not now*, thought Damien. *Put that back in the box.*

Wilson stepped up onto the dike and began his advance into the open. Three men up and out. Castillo in the rear also knew the fifteen meters blindfolded. He finally moved out. Four advancing, exposed targets stepped on the dike to a steady rhythm. Four Marines, very alert. Damien mopped the sweat running down from under his helmet onto his face with what once had been a green towel. From months of rain, sweat, dirt, heat, blood, and the general abuse it received, it now resembled a faded, torn, stained rag. Damien sucked the salty perspiration into his mouth that slipped past his "rag" and spat it out. He blinked hard and wiped his stinging eyes with the threadbare cloth. The dirt living in the fabric mingled with his perspiration and within minutes he was having trouble seeing. "God that hurts . . . Wait up!" Damien spoke loud enough to be heard by Simmons, who called to the lieutenant, whom he could hear swearing. The small column halted and each man went to one knee, —lowering his silhouette. They were all out in the open now, and it was far too open. The smallest dirt particle in the eye hurts terribly. Damien rubbed it with his sleeve, alleviating some of the sting.

"All right. Let's move. We gotta get off this dike." Collins spat the words back at the three men following him. Simmons shook his head in agreement. Each man stood once more and advanced a little quicker along the top of the beaten paddy dike.

One hundred meters more and the turn, then some concealment. By now, Damien crunched salty, gritty mud, the foul and rancid earth of Vietnam. Castillo had watched Damien's spitting fit with amusement before his own began.

Each man wrestled in his own way with the heat and its harsh effects on man and equipment. Gravity pulled Damien's perspiration further down his neck. The pull directed the new and the old crusted dirt into muddy worry lines and small eddies of brown wet crud. The rush of water slipped past his utility jacket, which absorbed it, chafing and scraping and cutting his skin. Wet lines of body salt also had long since formed on everything each man wore. And his flak jacket held all this body heat near his rib cage. *Life as usual in the bush.* At least they weren't humping a lot of ammo and gear.

Cuckooshrikes, with their disagreeable squawks, hawked late morning meals of aerial and ground insects. They dove and zoomed in the late morning humidity. These men lived for a year within their small, broken universes rather than the broader nature that whirled and flapped around and among them. Damien's tongue began to hurt again. He should have gotten an aspirin from the doc.

He made me feel proud. I guess, because he helped me get squared away and not get into much trouble and avoid the things that can get you hurt over here.

The pace remained steady, then slowed a bit at the end of the paddy. No trouble so far. The lieutenant turned left following the dike and toward the far corner of the rice paddy. Simmons reached the conclusion of the path, then turned left. Wilson reached it and turned left. Castillo, turned to check the area behind him, and he too changed direction.

The first obstacle appeared thirty meters beyond their most recent turn and just out of sight of the company CP. Jutting upward like a hiccup in the trail, the earth pushed itself into a muddy fist. At its crown, a nasty tangle of rusty barbed wire stood sentinel. The men stopped in place and squatted as Collins worked his way over the uncooperative obstacle. *Four stationary targets.*

The wire, having snagged the leg of Collins utilities, suddenly released its spiked grip, making a ripping, twanging sound as the wire shot back into its original twisted and bent position. The leader slid several feet down the other side of the embankment,whereupon he entangled himself in another roll of old concertina. Collins, now thoroughly ensnared, tried to free his utilities from the barbs.

Simmons moved up to the fist and the wire. He also attempted to hoist himself over the wire with a smooth swing of his leg. As his leg reached its highest point, the wire attacked him with hordes of nasty, predatory barbs snagging his jungle utilities fast at the crotch. Fortunately, the wire didn't mistreat any important personal equipment. Damien caught most of Simmons' profane salvo. *Two struggling men unable to move because of this old wire.*

I'm so sorry that he was taken from you like he was. Doc Morley says he didn't suffer hardly any if that helps.

Damien half trotted toward Lance Corporal Simmons to try and assist him, when he noticed that Collins was also stuck. Just as he neared the second entangled Marine, the earth erupted and Damien vanished amid a mud-brown curtain of clods and debris.

The deafening explosion threw Damien several feet into the air. Upon reaching the height of his aerial arc, gravity cruelly slapped him back down onto the trail with a thud. Once more, the ground had misled him. The mine he never saw had severed and then discarded the lower half of his left leg into the unused, dry paddy. For a while longer his heart kept it's pace spurting his youthful red life's blood onto the trail where it flowed from his stumped leg and onto the ground around him. It spread into Collins' and Simmon's boot prints and other indentations where it congealed in pools of dark red. Simmons, moaning in agony from the impact of the concussion and shrapnel, slumped heavy upon the jumbled pile of wire.

Damien stared skyward. He said nothing. He just blinked. Towered piles of clouds drifted, observant but uninterested overhead and the argent blue sky above him faded into dark and interminable sadness . . .

I've lost some buddies over here but not like Damien. He was one of a kind. I know you will miss him very much, but please know he was one of the finest Marines I ever knew and one of the bravest. He was a hard worker and made me a better Marine, too.

This impersonal act of cruelty blurred everything. It left Cpl. Wilson's facial skin to progress from its inherent pigment to an ever-darkening gray pallor, and onward to the expected inevitability: — mortal terminus. As his life ebbed, all that remained of Damien lay in his body's fitful twitching, his lifeless limbs, and in his hollowing eyes and ashen hue. Somewhere in his impaired hearing a man or a radio squawked but it sounded rubbery inside his head. The initial heaving of his chest from the internal trauma inflicted upon the whole of his body, slowed its movement. He felt little pain.

A smudged figure hampered his remaining field of vision. Still, he detected a movement of something annexed to him; his body perhaps. Nothing could stop the disagreeable course away from this war and his world. His chest finally calmed and his eyes rolled backward. Any perceived voices and all movement ceased for him. Damien Wilson, Corporal, United States Marine Corps, human being, stopped.

Within ten minutes he lay under a careworn poncho. Castillo had already retrieved his severed leg and laid it beside Damien. Within twenty-four hours Damien would lie engulfed by the stillness at Graves Registration where the positive ID—dental records and fingerprints— would be made. Headquarters Battalion would send a message to HQMC to inform them of the Marine's name, as well as the date, and cause of death. They, in turn, would serve notice to the Inspector & Instructor staff closest to the fallen Marine's home of record. The I & I Staff would send out an officer and enlisted man to notify the family and to assist them up and through the funeral and interment. Within a week the news would reach home.

Damien talked a lot about you both and I know he loved you. I almost feel as if I know you from the way he spoke. He was proud of having a father as a professor at a private school.

Sincerely,
PFC Brian Moorehouse

One restless day, half a dozen clicks southwest of Da Nang, a mine killed Cpl. Damien A. W. Wilson. Serial number 2335730. USMC. Blood type: A POS. Religion: Baptist. Gas Mask Size: Large. On the evening news neither Chet nor David mentioned the event. Cronkite must have missed it too. It was just one of so many military deaths that week in Vietnam. As a prism changes the direction of light, death seems to as well, and this death sent a tornado careening into the lives of the remaining two Wilson's, and inadvertently, into the Lloyd's family structure, bringing it to its knees. With this death, two families teetered, as it were, on the verge . . .

One: News

>━┥◆>━━◉━━<◆┝━<

Monday, March 6, 1967
Michael turned the handle timidly on the solid oak door and entered as he had done for years. Dolores Hernandez, Stephen Lloyd's secretary for the past twenty years, looked up from the pending duties spread before her. "Hello, Michael. Come on in and have a seat. It'll be a few minutes. Your father's in a meeting."

Dolores wore her coal-black wavy hair up in a bun this afternoon revealing a familiar oval shaped face. Her smooth and attractive bronzed face had aged gracefully, during her tenure at Lloyd International Hotels. Her maturity complemented the woman Michael thought of as his second mother. During Michael's infancy, his mother, Susan, loved to bring him to the office to show off Michael's latest outfit, his newest growth spurt or trick, or to let them hear his adorable gibberish. Even as a toddler, he loved touching Dolores's face. While sitting on her lap he'd shove his stubby fingers between her square, white teeth, prompting her to curl her thin lips around his small fists and blow. These funny noises made him laugh out loud. Michael had come to know the tenderness of the dark faced woman, to smell her body and perfume so that she, like Susan, bore a fragrance he welcomed among his most enduring remembrances. Dolores had even changed his diaper when that task needed an experienced hand and his mother was preoccupied with his father.

A large, single, Akoya pearl with a pinkish hue dotted each of Dolores's ear lobes, and the matching pearl necklace set her dark blue suit in fierce contrast to her day's dress. Each added to the woman a Victorian charm and lent the impression that she thought each visitor was important to the Lloyd Empire. The whole of Dolores Hernandez conferred to the office an atmosphere of regality. Rarely had a day passed without Michael easing into the office just to experience her presence and those qualities she brought to his father's and his own world.

And so, today, Michael stood before her focusing on her left pearl earring to keep his emotions under control. Dolores's graceful neck, sat upon firm shoulders not yet slumped with the accumulated weight that each year brought to most women's lives. Dolores noted Michael's evasive look.

"Come in, Michael," she repeated, her curiosity rising. "You're out of school early today, aren't you?" Dolores's eyes always warmed to a brighter brown at his presence. She sensed something was wrong.

"Yes, ma'am." Michael's quick and distant answer with tears forming at the corners of his swollen, red-lined eyes sparked deeper concern in the woman behind the desk.

Michael Lloyd stood six foot one and weighed one hundred ninety-four pounds. He too, like his father, played strong safety on the football team. On the baseball team, Michael played first base. Those were the facts noted on the players' programs sold at the games' concession stands. What wasn't on the programs was that he kept his dark hair short, —team rules; his football helmet fit better when he kept it that length. He was a handsome kid with small, green eyes, and, like his father, was very intelligent. As is often the case, though, life is more than stats. It is pain and wonder and sorrow and joy. Today, it was this blunt force news that attacked him: the communication of his friend's death. Michael had not even thought to tell Victoria, his girl-friend.

Standing front and center before Dolores, the pain in his eyes was apparent to her. Observant to a fault, Dolores detected something else, something more than the usual blemishes accompanying the late teenage years. Dolores couldn't remember seeing the severity of such a tempest just below his beautiful facial features. *When had she last seen his coat and tie so untidy or his soul in such destitution?* Mr. Lloyd depended upon her qualities, and they paid handsome dividends when required.

"Mrs. Hernandez, I really need to talk to my father," he said as he rubbed his right index finger along the edge of her desk. She had long since given up on him calling her Dolores.

'My *father.*' *Hmmm.* It had always just been 'father,' not '*my* father', or even 'dad.' "Is everything all right, Michael?" She spoke in the certain anticipation that he would share this burden with her —at some point. With a little of *her* coaxing, he seldom disappointed. Dolores waited, a bit impatiently, for Michael's usual energy and fun and purpose to come bounding into the office following in his wake.

"Yes, ma'am. I just . . . I need to . . . uh, . . . to speak with my father."

He'd said it again, my father. This isn't good. What can it be? "Let me, um, call him for you. I'm sure he'll want to talk to you." Her eyes beckoned to him one final time. They pled to understand what loomed behind this un-Michael like demeanor.

The boy glanced up at the wall clock. Through painful eyes, clouded with the watery mists of the loss of a friend, he thought it registered 11:40. It was close to lunch.

Delores picked up the phone and punched a button. "Mr. Lloyd, I'm sorry to interrupt you, but Michael's here. I think you should speak to him." Dolores's words pulled Michael's introspection back to the reality he had wrestled all morning not to face.

Michael heard his father's muffled "Yes, I'll be right there," through the receiver. Within seconds, Stephen Lloyd opened the heavy meeting room door to greet his son.

Stephen Michael Lloyd, son of the multimillionaire hotel magnet, Marcus Josiah Fonteneau Lloyd, stood six foot two inches and weighed a touch over two hundred pounds. He weighed more when he played football for A&M and before he transferred to TCU where he and Susan were married. That was right before the Second World War. With the ensuing years he'd lost little of his muscled tone, due to working out several times a week at the health club in the basement of the Fonteneau Building. His semi- short, dark brown hair had grayed to a frosty brown since his first years at college. The graying added to his handsome, rugged features.

Three parallel horizontal lines had been etched into his forehead over the years while two deep-set vertical strokes rose above his nose.

These two creases underlined his more anxious moods, developed from the strains of life.

His eyes, perhaps more than any other facial feature, seized one's attention. Bottle green, deep set and piercing. One must pass through their forbidding regions to gain entrance to the man.

Years of stress added a slight linear ridge to the edges of each eye reaching almost into his hairline. His sturdy nose revealed signs of prolonged athletic wear and tear in college. It had become a bit swollen at the bridge, but wasn't detracting. His flat cheeks sported two slightly curved vertical lines; the longest met his jaw, and the briefest slashed the cradle of his mouth. Neither imposing upon the overall look of his face.

His mouth was a study in intellect and moderation. It projected a thin upper lip with a slight dip at the middle. The lower lip was thicker. His rugged chin jutted unobtrusively from his face a modest distance.

No single feature of Stephen's manly face dominated, and every member, line, and aspect agreed with every other to the benefit of the whole. The slightest hint of a beard shaded the areas between his nose, mouth, and chin. Many a lunch hour had been spent among the general secretarial pool discussing this handsome man.

Stephen hadn't expected to see his son until later that afternoon, when Michael would arrive and make his rounds doing odd jobs for the various departments of Lloyd International Hotels, Inc., headquartered in the Fonteneau Building in downtown Ft. Worth, Texas. Mr. Lloyd preferred that Michael 'investigate' the world of corporate business from the ground up, as he had done with his father.

During the athletic seasons, Michael divided his off school hours between football or baseball practice. Afterward, he would drive from school, Gladstone Preparatory, to the Fonteneau Building. He then made his way to the plush oak paneled offices on the thirtieth floor. Here he performed various tasks related to the overall scheme and mission of Lloyd International Hotels.

"Michael, what's wrong, son? No practice today? You're here early." Observant and aware of something negative, Stephen's eyebrows almost touched each other out of concern.

"Yes, sir, well . . . everything's o . . . well, I need to . . ." Then the dam finally burst, and Michael's emotions exploded. He grabbed his

father in a death like bear hug. Poor Dolores teared up at the sight
of something so out of place in this environment of huge corporate
mergers, evolving plans for new hotels, vast sums of stock trades, and
important people.

Upon hearing his son's confused speech and feeling the intensity
of his emotional disruption, Stephen looked for strength to buoy the
situation.

"Dolores, hand me a tissue, please. What's going on son? Uh, Dolores,
would you mind taking the Davenport file to Mr. Blackledge's office?"

"Certainly, Mr. Lloyd." Her response, stiff, dripping with
disappointment as she would have to wait for this news. She slid her
chair away from her desk and moved slowly in the direction of the two
men. She handed her boss the tissue. Although Dolores hesitated, she
left the outer office with the file as instructed. Mr. Lloyd patted and
rubbed his son's back and pulled the boy's head to his own shoulder, all
the while resisting the all-powerful tug of the "machine" he owned and
oversaw. Family always won here, regardless, and this day, Michael
counted on that quality in his father. To respond otherwise would have
wounded the boy deeply.

Several men stuck their heads out of the meeting room to discover
their employer holding his son, who was in obvious emotional distress.
They could only watch in dismay and silence. John Staddler, VP for
sales and promotions, finally spoke for the group. "Stephen, is there
anything we can do?"

"No. Thank you, John. Let's reschedule our meeting for tomorrow
morning. Check with Dolores." Stephen's eyes moved from the inquirer
to his son and then back to John, a signal for the men to leave.

A few more minutes elapsed before Michael unwrapped himself
from the warm security and familiar smell of his father's body and
aftershave. This release allowed Michael to slump onto the sofa behind
him where his energy left him, staring ahead as if into a void. His
familiar universe had changed. When he blinked the tears began again,
and with the tears came a ringing in his ears and his hands felt numb.
Mr. Lloyd began a frantic mental search for who could be in trouble
in his immediate family.

Stephen sat next to his son and said, "Michael. Please try and get
hold of yourself long enough to tell me what's wrong. Is your mother
all right?"

"Yes, sir."

"Your sister?"

"Yes, sir."

"Oookay . . . Your brother?"

"Yes, sir."

"Victoria?"

"She's fine, father. They're all fine, father!"

Stephen sensed he needed to reign this situation in before Michael became belligerent. "Well son, tell me," he said matter-of-factly, "is the *dog* all right?" Mr. Lloyd blurted the final inquiry out of sheer exasperation.

Sensing his father's growing testiness equalled only by his anxiety, Michael raised his head slowly to look directly at his dad and said, "Damien's dead."

The two words came out of Michael's mouth, hollow, like two contradictory ideas, neither of which should ever go together. Ever. Then the boy began crying again. Michael, sobbing, still wasn't certain if he believed what he just said.

"What?" Stephen asked incredulously. *Had he heard his son correctly? Surely not.* He asked once more and received the same chilling reply.

Michael repeated the words, "Damien's dead."

Mr. Lloyd's awakened consciousness refused to acknowledge what it had heard.

"What do you mean, Damien's dead? He's supposed to be coming home in a month or so." Mr. Lloyd rolled this catastrophe over in his mind. He sipped at it, tasting its brackish density. He found it repugnant as he'd always done. *Dead?* He knew what the word meant. He knew all too well what it meant from personal experience. His heart thumped in his chest and without warning, all their faces flashed by him one by one as he last saw them. This unexpected death became the provocation to reveal them, to force them into the present. Stephen Lloyd had labored since 1945 to feverishly bury the past. He didn't want or need their visit at present. But those bygone ghosts commenced haunting him afresh, without mercy, pillaging and clogging his psyche when he most needed its lucidity. *Dead.* Stephen looked around for someone to hold him.

Michael reclaimed his own emotional control with slow deliberation. The two words simply came out in a monotone, "Damien's dead."

"How do you know, son?" Stephen Lloyd's face, like his energized mind, became a study in desolation.

"The Marine Corps sent two men to the school. I was in Mr. Wilson's class when we heard a knock on the door. Then Mr. Shapiro asked Dr. Wilson to step out in the hall for a minute. The next thing we knew is that we heard Mr. Wilson yell, then we heard him crying loudly. He kept saying 'Oh, God no!' over and over again. I guess Damien was killed sometime on Monday or Tuesday, but Dr. Wilson didn't find out until this morning."

"Where is Dr. Wilson now? That was . . . stupid. Forgive me," the senior Lloyd muttered. He laid his right hand flat upon his forehead, his left hand curled unconsciously on his left hip and his mind raced over this situation. "He's probably at home now. Michael, I can't remember, what's the Wilson's phone number?"

Michael gave the number and watched his father dial the number, wait, and then say, "James, this is Stephen Lloyd. Michael just gave me the news. I'm . . . I'm *so* very sorry. What can I do?"

The boy watched his father's grave face, observing Mr. Wilson's words hit him like punches upon a losing boxer's face.

Stephen could make out Mary Ellen Wilson crying in the background. It was all he could do to get the words out, "James, I don't know if you can hear me right now, but let me take care of the meals for the next few days. Yes. Well, because I want to. I'll be by tonight. Look . . . No, James, listen to me. I've been through this before and I want to take care of anything that gets in the way of . . . Yes, I hear you. Okay. Please give my condolences to Mary Ellen. Yes, your classes will be taken care of. No, no, I don't want you to concern yourself with that. I'll call Mr. Shapiro. Okay, Right. And I'll talk to you in a little while. Goodbye, my friend."

Two: James W. Wilson

Subjectively, and for the moment, Dr. James Wilson believed that his government, the very government to which he had given so much of himself, had taken his boy and killed him. *For what*, he asked? He wanted answers. Everything James had ever hoped and wanted came wrapped in his son, Damien. Everything he'd ever done or accomplished seemed to harbor so little meaning in the deadening context of this immediate predicament. That's how it *felt*. All his academic accolades had lost their value, their meaning. Mary Ellen could not reason with him on this. Try as he might he couldn't shake the loss or make sense of it.

Mary Ellen Wilson, James's wife and Damien's mother, hurt internally as well. Mothers have more at stake than their husbands when their child dies. She had lived with this growing human for nine long months. She knew the very moment he became part of her. When Damien turned two James and she tried to replicate their first offspring; either gender would do, but were unable to conceive again. Nothing the doctors suggested or prescribed produced further progeny. Thus, Mary Ellen's world slowly began to revolve around their only heir. Theirs had been a good life for nineteen years with Damien at the core of it. The boy had excelled in almost every endeavor he tried. But now this . . .

They would never see grandchildren. Their lineage had been severed cruelly, and this void set both of them temporarily adrift. No one knowing these two stalwart pillars of their church could imagine them meandering too far past the end of the month, albeit lost amid a sea of whirling emotional debris. This news struck their relationship with the fury of an angry hurricane.

Sunday, December 4, 1904

James Washington Wilson was born Sunday, December 4, 1904, the son of a Mississippi tenant farmer. The last of seven children, James grew up laboring in cotton fields with his brothers in the middle of summers so hot he couldn't remember it ever being cold.

James was blessed with an inquiring mind and an unquenchable thirst for learning. His near photographic memory allowed him to take books home from the library without checking them out.

The First World War had barely been over seven months when James's formative education basically ground to a halt, but not his passion for learning. His teacher, Mrs. Coweta Anthony, simply didn't know what to do with him any longer. At age sixteen he graduated high school. James was offered and accepted a full academic scholarship to the prestigious Fisk University in Nashville, Tennessee.

It was during his time at Fisk that James met Mary Ellen Mathews, the beautiful geology student, who would become his wife. Actually, she was the one who pursued and caught her man.

They were married in the spring following a brief courtship. Mary Ellen Wilson graduated in 1925 with her bachelor's degree. Over the past three years, she was the sole female geologist among the exiting students of that department. She went to work for a small company testing soil samples and doing fieldwork or odd jobs to keep busy and help put food on the table.

James Wilson graduated from Fisk University in 1926 with a B.S. in physics. James had eagerly accepted Howard University's gracious offer of a full master's scholarship in physics to begin in the fall. Then, in 1931, with the depression in full bloom, James Wilson returned to his roots at Fisk. With his master's degree in hand, he began work on his PhD under under the careful eye of the world-renowned physicist, Dr. Elmer Samuel Imes.

MIT had also taken notice of Fisk's brightest science star. They offered James a teaching position there upon the issuance of his PhD. In 1935, Mary Ellen and *Dr.* James Washington Wilson packed their old Dodge Model 128 with their growing collection of belongings, and set out for the new world.

Life was good, despite the depression. James was the only black professor at the prestigious institute. Yet one minor detail went missing: they had no children to show for all of their . . . efforts.

Sunday, December 7, 1941

It had been a quiet but cold morning, that Sunday. James was slipping his coat on when the radio announcer said, "We interrupt this program for an announcement: The Imperial Japanese Navy has bombed the United States Naval base at Pearl Harbor, Hawaii. We repeat . . ."

In late 1943, Dr. Robert Oppenheimer asked Dr. James Wilson, and several other men, to participate in a super-secret project for the government as part of James' research in thermonuclear reaction in deuterium. James had shown remarkable acumen for this field, and his colleagues, as well as Dr. Albert Einstein, realized that his abilities could best be served in this capacity.

Sunday, October 12, 1947

"Oh, James. Look! He's perfect. He's got all his toes and fingers. I wish your mama and daddy could have been here to see little Damien Abraham Washington Wilson. Oh, and wouldn't mama love him? I think he looks a little like me in his eyes, but the rest of him is you. He's all you. Isn't he wonderful?"

A toothy grin spread across James' face. "He's wonderful all right. Miss Henrietta would have loved to see him. What do you think he'll be? Why he looks like a baseball player. Maybe he'll be half-smart. Just look at those long fingers. He'll pitch for some Ivy League school. I'd bet on it." James wanted at least one athlete in the family before the girls started arriving. He just knew there would be girls.

Mary Ellen had been in labor for a mere three hours when Damien announced himself to the world. She was thirty-nine, felt twenty at the moment, and was in love with this little wonder. Presently, she kissed her husband James.

"Ahem." The doctor announced his necessary intrusion on his patients, plural. "How are you two doing, Mrs. Wilson? Congratulations to both of you. What did you name the boy?"

James spoke up, "He's *Damien*, after one of my college professors, *Abraham*, after my daddy, *Washington*, after me, and *Wilson*, after the whole family. This *Damien* will be his own identity."

"What are you looking for Dr. Wilson? Do you need a pen?" Dr. Cauble asked. Mary Ellen and the doctor watched in amazement as James fumbled through his coat and trouser pockets looking for something.

"What? Oh, I've been working on an equation . . ."

Before he could finish, Mary Ellen yelled at her husband who had apparently so quickly abandoned his first offspring and wife for another love, his physics. "For crying out loud, James. Would you please let that go for five minutes and spend time with us? We have a son now."

James took a step, stumbled almost into the doctor, whom he would have surely knocked out into the hall half senseless, because of James' size, caught and righted himself, apologized profusely and hurried out of the room. He was gone in so many ways, as usual. He had always been a bull in a china shop. Mary Ellen had to continually watch James when they went shopping. He would forget where they were, absorbed in his sciences and knock this or that doodad off the shelves, a few of which cost them when the valuable made contact with the linoleum.

"James Wilson, you come back here this minute!" Mary Ellen yelled. But it was too late. James was half way to the parking lot and thoroughly mindless of the wonderful event that had just now happened to his wife and him, —a son.

Mary Ellen had learned to rest in the knowledge that, despite his great mind, and a few hefty shortcomings, James Wilson was absolutely devoted to her—when he thought about it.

June 12th, Friday, 1964

"Dr. Wilson. How good it is to finally get to meet you in person," Stephen Lloyd said. Stephen was head of the faculty hiring committee at Gladstone Preparatory School in Ft. Worth, Texas. The committee had received Dr. Wilson's incredible resume the week before. *What luck!* The timing couldn't have been more perfect. The former head of the science department there had just retired and Gladstone had begun its search process. James had also been sending out numerous feelers unsure of whether anyone wanted a man of his age teaching their children. Dr. Wilson had a tendency to talk over most human beings heads, a disadvantage Damien knew first hand.

Mary Ellen for her part had begun to need a more normal home life. She dreamed of having supper every night at 6 p.m., weekends free to spend with her husband, and no more late night committees that might find her husband in conference at the White House, or the Department of Defense, or the FBI, or who knew where else. He'd gone off once too often to Stockholm, Sweden, and Sydney, Australia, assisting those countries with some energy crisis no other human on the planet could possibly solve. Mary Ellen would settle on the North Pole if he came home every night to her. He'd applied at forty-five or fifty schools and universities across the nation. But for some reason it came down to two schools: one in Atlanta, and this one in Ft. Worth. Mary Ellen had not been to the southwest and she hated Atlanta. She wanted James to teach where Damien could enroll as a student. Gladstone was also nationally renowned for its stringent academics and winning athletic programs. Eighty-seven percent of its graduates went to Ivy League schools, and all but two percent of the remaining graduates went to the national universities. A small minority chose to study abroad at places like Cambridge or Oxford. Fifteen former students were scattered among the NBA, the NFL, and eight Major League Baseball franchises. Ft. Worth won.

"Mr. Lloyd, I have read the information you sent me, and I must say I'm impressed with this school. I trust you have read my resume and approve?"

"Approve? You're over qualified for this position, Dr. Wilson. So . . . what would it take to get you to stay and teach?"

James held all the cards. His was an impressive list of credentials to be sure. Within three days, Damien began his regular ritual of supper two nights a week at the Lloyd's and the rest at his home. Michael returned the favor so that James thought seriously about another job just to feed these two human garbage disposals.

Three: Marcus and 'The Voice'

Monday, March 6, 1967

Stephen felt the strain left by the death of his friend's son, and his son's friend. An emotional numbing so inevitable at times like these had begun to settle slowly, almost imperceptibly, upon the president of Lloyd International. Stephen Lloyd began the unpleasant process of calling his wife at home and the headmaster at school. Stephen would arrange and implement a plan to care for one more of the devastated but surviving families of this endless war.

The immediate tasks done, Mr. Lloyd placed the receiver back in its cradle and leaned against Mrs. Hernandez's desk. With his left hand now covering his mouth he stared outward into something he alone could see. The moments slipped off to wherever they go at times like these, keeping their own pace. When Michael thought he possessed a more flexible self-control, he called several times before he reached his parent. "Father? Fa-ther?"

"I'm sorry. What?"

With a deep breath Michael announced, "I want to join the Marine Corps." He was obviously in better control of his emotions now. Or *was* he? His nature lent itself to periodic motion-stopping proclamations, but not of this caliber and in this context.

Mr. Lloyd remembered Michael's announcing his desire to be a fireman. Then he wanted to play shortstop for the Yankees. He even promoted a self-serving interest in high finance. Then the medical field . . . a Priest . . . And, *what was it last year? He wanted to be . . .*

what was *it he wanted to be?* Mr. Lloyd had stopped counting. But when Michael articulated his current desire once again with such gravity, the man listened.

He'd hoped of course that Michael might pursue a career in the hotel business. Every Ivy League school waited for the announcement that the son of the vast Lloyd International Hotels, Inc., might darken their hallowed halls in the fall semester of 1967. TCU and Texas A. & M., both of which had been Stephen Lloyd's alma maters were courting the Lloyd boy coming to their schools. Four years hence, with his undergraduate degree in hand, he would proceed to graduate school and then join middle management somewhere within the infrastructure of Lloyd International, and one day, Michael would become president and C.E.O. The string needed a taut pull, but his father thought he could deliver the package to Mrs. Lloyd. Up to today, up to right now, he felt sure of it.

Michael's father did the unexpected. He walked over to where his son sat and crumpled next to him. No anger. No speeches. No determined direction to which to guide, or, if need be, force his heir to meet the generational obligations to which all Lloyd men were to one day submit. Thick silence sat between the two men, the quiet that deep emotions breed. The larger man slipped his arm around his son and held him close.

There was a vintage familiarity about Michael's request. Stephen Lloyd couldn't withstand the gathering echoes from twenty-plus years before. He remembered well the crack of billiard balls and the conversation surrounding that particular game with his father, Marcus. The smell of cigar smoke filled the room, where so often powerful businessmen and leaders of industry played this game while discussing the gathering issues of their era. That was the day Marcus lay upon Stephen what his father, Nathaniel Marcus Lloyd, had laid upon him about his duty to uphold the Lloyd tradition. Marcus must find his place in the company and pursue it with all the determination that had been bred into him. One day Stephen would be expected to occupy the head chair at the boardroom table and lead the company forward. He was, after all, a Lloyd.

With this ancestral cloud suspended above him Stephen aligned his shot so as to put the four ball in the corner. Crack. He missed. The cue ball's inertia stopped five inches from the fourteen ball resting mere centimeters from the far corner pocket. "How in the blue blazes did you miss that shot?" Marcus asked his son.

Marcus Lloyd loved this room. Of all the places in his huge house, none fit his personality or moods better. Everything meshed in here. The planets aligned in here for him. Annika, Stephen's mother, claimed ownership over the remaining ten thousand square feet of the Lloyd mansion. Some twenty feet above the two men playing pool the grand high ceiling had been buttressed together at a sharp angle by a huge oak log Marcus found on one of his properties in Louisiana. He had it cut and then trucked to his home here in Westover Hills when his game room was being built. It was a massive project, just getting the crane to lift it over the house and set in place. The log had to be cut shorter in order for it to be lifted, wedged, and bolted so that the ceiling and room could be finished. It didn't match the mahogany paneling but that didn't matter. Marcus wanted it *here*. Oak meant strength to this man. Unfortunately, he also liked mahogany with an equal vigor. He compromised and kept the two woods where he could hold a vigil on them. Annika almost lost her sanity over the project. "That big thing looks hideous!" she yelled. It doesn't agree conceptually with anything here, and certainly not the rest of the house!" Marcus wanted it, so it stayed.

Various reproductions of original paintings hung on three of the four mahogany stained soundproof walls. One, a Picasso the artist called *Les Demoiselles d'Avignon*. Annika hated it. She understood nothing of what the artist said about humanity through his brush. There was a Rembrandt, *Raising of the Cross*, a Gauguin entitled, *Whence Come We? What are we? Whither Do We Go?* Perhaps no other painting spoke more to Marcus's value system than the Frenchman, Jacques-Louis David's painting, *The Oath of the Tennis Court*. What an eclectic menagerie. It all, however, served to keep Annika away.

For the most part, Marcus had a long-standing love affair with Renoir's work. He had purchased one original, and for the rest he commissioned an outstanding local young copy artist, Andre St. Claire, to reproduce as many of Renoir's works as he thought he could. Their agreement was that Andre must sign his name prominently to them. Hung conspicuously over the mantle in his game room was Renoir's famous *Baigneuse aux Cheveux Longs*. Renoir's barely clothed model also agitated his wife for she didn't want her grandchildren to look at the woman she found disgusting. Probably a prostitute. Marcus's Texas accent wouldn't allow French to form and exit his mouth fluidly like the French. The Renoir and Picasso titles sounded European and that suited Marcus fine. Other lesser-known artists were also displayed about the room.

Assorted memorabilia were hung in no particular order to give to his guests an overview of the growth of Lloyd International from its inception in the nineteenth century. There was an old picture of the first Lloyd Hotel that had been built not far from Ft. Worth's infamous Hell's Half Acre of the late nineteenth century, the bordello and saloon capitol of the southwest. Subsequent Lloyd hotels were also photographed and framed. Several mind numbing multi-million dollar canceled checks hung prominently above the bar. One had been written for fifteen million and the other for twenty-two million. Each of these once certified checks brought a smile to Marcus's overworked brow after a hard day at the office.

On the opposing south and north walls leaned two bookshelves apiece where one would discover another of Marcus's passions, his equally eclectic collection of rare and inaugural volumes of the great thinkers and writers of the world. One could find Dickens, Chaucer, Plato, Copernicus, Shakespeare, Thomas Aquinas, Erasmus, Tennyson, Omar Khayyam, Freud, Hegel, Kant, Rousseau, Descartes, Wordsworth, Coleridge, da Vinci, Francis Bacon and St. Francis, Jefferson, Madison, Franklin, and Alfred North Whitehead, to mention but a few. He'd scour old bookstores on the trips he took.

His room had a well-stocked and padded wet bar running the length of the west wall. It resembled the one at his cabin in Canada, but was much smaller. Numerous soft cushioned chairs and tall wrought iron lamps had been strategically placed in distanced proximity to the large, thick lead-paned windows, breathing in a magnificent view of the surrounding terrace and lighted gardens.

Marcus' third obsession was his plants. The entire estate, including the library, dining room, morning room, den and the eight bedrooms was supplied with vegetation propagated in his spacious greenhouse. The residence had almost taken on a life of its own becoming a living conservatory from the great care Mr. Lloyd took with his beloved green and blooming companions. Each plant family with its multiple varieties gave to him something that even Annika, a beautiful woman in her own right, could not.

In this great and manly room of Marcus's, a burgeoning *ficus benjamina* tree had been planted in a huge terracotta clay pot in the northeast corner. Each spring it was hauled carefully outside, hosed off, and after a day outside, brought back in. In another year, it would simply be too large to remove and shower. Ficus are emotional trees, despising change of any sort. Its sturdy overhanging branches gave one the sense of being outdoors, a lovely feeling, especially on the hot Texas summer days or evenings. A dieffenbachia, two huge dracaenas, one draco, and an even larger marginata, better known as the dragon lily, brought their own ambiance and life to the room. Over here, one could find three varieties of *Pandanas veitchii* or variegated screw plant, while over there a maranta or red-veined prayer plant, then several species of impatiens someone labeled, *Touch-me-nots*.

Annika had nagged Marcus more than once that there were just too many plants for this size room. He acceded to her "suggestion," by building a special table for his orchids. Marcus was most proud of the Cattleya and Cymbidium varieties, almost as proud as he was of remembering their Latin names. For some reason the white-colored orchids intrigued him most. He had traveled extensively throughout the world to secure those particular species that he deemed worthy of his special place, near the window and on the table. Within these walls Marcus had placed all the material valuables he treasured, which, when it was unoccupied, would therefore require a safe cracker with blasting caps and C4 to breach it.

In the cold winter of 1942, and amid all the rich eccentricities of his father's special room, Stephen Lloyd stood weighing his options. This particular game provided the right occasion for his well-considered, if youthful, decision. He would have to give it an audience so that it might be seen in the full light of day. If he faltered, that is, presented an insufficient or truncated explanation, Stephen stood to lose his place in the ever-developing Lloyd Empire. His father was about to put the six ball in the middle pocket. When Marcus missed the shot Stephen set his cue stick aside in order to speak his mind.

Hearing his son's proposal, Marcus turned red with rage. He reminded Stephen that his son's dearest friend had barely two weeks before gone down in flames over the war torn skies of Europe. Marcus Josiah didn't crumple on the couch next to his son, Stephen, that day. Neither did he understand, and he growled at the thought of his son going off to war, leaving him to "mind the store" by himself. Stephen went to flight school just the same.

Michael's body stiffened against his father, and as it did, Stephen became aware, not just of Michael's size but also his breadth. Boyish features that once played upon Michael's face had blended into a visible manhood fighting for its ascendancy. He couldn't remember how or when Michael had made the turn, but he recognized the maturation all the same: the set of his jaw, the fire in his eyes, and the grit no prolonged part-time employment of "gophering" for Lloyd International could supply. Stephen Lloyd knew, or guessed that he knew, that Damien figured into this present equation.

"Father, did you hear me?" Michael's repetition of his last statement gripped his father with a primordial fear. "I want to join the Marine Corps. I want to fight."

"Why?"

With the "now or never" at stake, Michael plunged into the icy waters of his father's incisive, singular question. He must continue his course of reasoning or the "thing," his stint in the military, would be dropped forever. "Damien and I talked into the morning his last night home before he left for Vietnam. He believed in what he was going to do and why he was doing it. You and mother have been the best parents any son could have. But I'm not a boy any more. Granted, I've had some crazy ideas but . . . You know . . . No, you don't know, and I feel uneasy, well, weird, discussing it. But it was as if . . ." Michael stopped to reload. "It was as if I . . . I thought I heard Damien's voice when those two Marines showed up at school today."

Michael stared at his father's face. He noted his father's brows furrowed, the lines deepened into the well-practiced places in his forehead. "You heard his voice. Uh huh," Stephen said dubiously. Michael had hoped for a different response. But at least his father hadn't yelled at him, hadn't told him he thought he was losing his mind or something worse. What could be worse? Maybe Michael just wanted to know that his words possessed value or validity or something positive. Hearing nothing further from his father, he continued.

"I heard this," Michael paused, and then shook his head from a sudden bewilderment as if trying out of desperation to explain the unexplainable. "I heard this voice inside my mind. It wasn't my voice. I . . . I don't know how to explain it in any other words, but it's as if . . . it's as if Damien spoke to me." Michael sighed from his soul and his shoulders slumped. "I heard him say, 'come and finish what I started.' I don't know, father. It probably sounds stupid or absurd, but all of a sudden I knew, or think I knew, the direction I have to take."

With the supernatural unearthed, Michael reasserted his internal fire. "I know you are expecting me to go to college next semester, but I don't think I can, father. Not right now. Look, I don't know if you understand what I'm saying, but I think this is something I *have* . . . to do." His final two words trailed off.

There. The "thing" lay exposed like warm breath floating about in the cold air, and just as illusive. Michael sensed an indescribable and unfamiliar pride invading himself. His father, on the other hand, was experiencing a role reversal, his own father's desperate emotions. *Had Michael allowed his sense of loss to get the better of him*, Stephen wondered? They could discuss this "thing" without Michael rushing off to join this war.

Mr. Lloyd, somewhat grave, stood to his feet, inhaled, and straightened his tie. More in control of himself now, he slipped back into his office. When he reemerged he was wearing his suit coat. By the time Mrs. Hernandez reentered the room, she had hoped the scene she left earlier might have resolved itself, at least to her satisfaction. These were *her* men, too.

"Oh. I'm sorry Mr. Lloyd. Should I . . . should I see if Mr. Martel needs anything?"

"No, Dolores. We were just leaving. If there are any calls for me . . ." He hesitated. His eyes darted from object to object on her desk as if looking for something, and then straight back to the woman. Stephen Lloyd always spoke with his left index finger emphasizing the point he attempted to make.

"Tell whoever calls . . . Oh, I almost forgot, Governor Connelly is supposed to call me at three thirty today . . . Well, it can't be helped. Tell him that we have a family emergency and that I will be in the office at eight in the morning. Also, would you call Mrs. Lloyd back and tell her Michael and I will be home later, after supper. We will get something out to eat, so tell Mrs. Cassalls not to prepare anything for us."

Mr. Lloyd's judicious eyes penetrated to a level of awareness that Dolores Hernandez and he had learned to communicate over the years. "You know where we'll be." His look, disturbed yet intense, continued for a long second until he knew she grasped his meaning. Assured of his communication, he returned to Michael and the "thing."

"Dolores, would you have my car brought around, please?"

"Yes, Mr. Lloyd. Are you two okay?"

"Yeah." *Yeah, not yes.* His attenuated response worried her, for she had no idea how to interpret it.

"Come on, son. Here, straighten your tie."

"Where are we going?"

"You'll see."

The boy followed his father out of the office and down the carpeted and well-lit mahogany paneled corridor to the elevators. The door opened, disgorging its passengers amid numerous proclamations of, "Good afternoon, Mr. Lloyd," to which Mr. Lloyd returned their entreaties in full measure. Entering the elevator with Michael he pushed the button that would within moments empty father and son onto the main level of the Fonteneau Building. Reaching it, they stepped from the elevator. The lobby was sparsely populated, their heels echoing on the marble floor. Both men walked solemnly to the revolving front door of the lobby to await the car.

When the car arrived, the two men hopped in, and Stephen guided the machine away from the building and merged into the traffic. The pedestrians, street scenes, and the many tall buildings of downtown Fort Worth became a blur as Stephen's car sailed past them. The smell of new leather upholstery and Tchaikovsky's piano Concerto no. 1 in B-Flat minor filled the inner sanctum of Stephen's green Jaguar. Michael's GTO on the other hand, smelled more like McDonalds hamburgers and fries.

Dissatisfied with Tchaikovsky, Stephen turned the station to something a bit more amenable to his emotions. A mellow trumpet played, *My Funny Valentine*. Michael knew better than to change this music to something he preferred, like the Beach Boys or Mitch

Ryder, or even the Monkees. Steam rose from a manhole cover ahead. They drove past it, thoroughly oblivious to its existence and effects. Soon they headed north on 287, past the stockyards, past Mecham airport, and still farther north. Mr. Lloyd said nothing about their destination. In fact, he said nothing at all. Many unpleasant things tumbled through his mind.

After thirty minutes of Glenn Miller's *String of Pearls, Pennsylvania Six Five Thousand* and other hits his orchestra made famous, Dick Haymes sang, *I Get A Kick Out Of You*. Harry James' orchestra was followed by other less familiar musicians and orchestras. Michael listened to music he did and did not recognize. He'd often seen his parents dancing in the living room to this music. These musical strain flooded over Michael and his father at the moment stabilizing things. Good memories.

Mr. Lloyd finally broke the silence with a question: "What are you thinking, son?" He had asked the question for two reasons. First, he needed to discern the depth of his son's conviction about the military. It might have subsided, and second, he yearned to quell his own mental demons somehow.

Michael, for his part, kept waiting for the hammer to drop, for his father to vanquish his resolution to the realm of noble but impractical ideology. Still not hearing it and not feeling any agitation from his father, he settled for, "Where *are* we going?" No response.

"Now that you've had a little time to absorb Damien's death, how do you feel?" Michael's father looked straight ahead at the road when he asked this. Stephen's had question trumped his son's.

Michael shook his head. His perplexity felt real, and very discomforting. "I don't know." More silence. Then, "I've never known someone that I knew so well who died, who was killed . . . you know? I don't even know *how* Damien . . ." Michael perceived that his latent emotions would return if not checked, right now. He knew they would rise toward his throat and probably flood his eyes all over again. After a minute, Michael felt better able to subdue them, and so he said, "We went to that one funeral. I didn't know the person. You remember that lady who worked down in accounting? What was her name?"

"Mrs. Oxnam? Jill Oxnam? Yes, I remember her."

"But no one killed her. She had cancer or something. She looked so peaceful, lying there in the casket . . ." Michael's voice trailed off. He turned to stare at the cheerless, almost ready to bloom pastoral features of fenced lots moving quickly past them. Sparse buildings were set amid yellowed winter grasses; twisted trunks of mesquite trees and scrub oaks dotted the north Texas landscape. Cumulus clouds floated overhead, many resembling animate or inanimate objects contorted by the early March winds. Often, the clouds resembled recognizable human or animal shapes before the wind whirled them into something else. The backdrop was a cerulean sky, and it was never so glorious.

"Michael, what do you understand about Vietnam?"

Michael explained what he knew from his collection of copied papers, articles, and notes he'd taken from world history class, so that he felt more confident in his own opinion. He'd reached certain conclusions from school, but especially when he sat alone in his room. Damien had fought there, which is probably the main reason he collected materials on the war. Now, Michael had no friend there. He also shared Damien's growing perplexity of the war as the Marine lived it daily. This however, didn't deter Damien, and it obviously hadn't affected Michael as yet.

His father listened as Michael spoke, paying careful attention and asking questions for his own clarification. Stephen hoped that the boy would examine the idea of war according to reality and less idealistically, less adventuresome, and certainly through a less glamorous Hollywood prism.

Four: Erik T. Smit

March 6th, Monday, 1967

Michael didn't know exactly when the colors faded from the passing scenery. Staring at the moving blur before him, he asked, "Did you know anyone who died in World War Two or Korea?"

Stephen Lloyd's furrowed brows almost touched each other once more as they turned west onto Skeet Richardson Road. Their destination became obvious now: Eagle Mountain Lake, and with the change of directions, the sun lay directly in their path. Within ten minutes, the Jaguar XKE turned onto a large dirt parking lot populated by one wooden, dirt-gray building serving dual purposes: gasoline and food. The sign above the restaurant welcomed one and all: "Smitty's Place." At the back of the property, oak trees grew thick. Michael could see small parts of the lake far off in the distance, between the trees.

Six pickups, each one in various states of rust or decomposition, sat amid the dirt lot, absorbing the sun's energy. Heat waves quivered, reverberating off of the shingled roof of Smitty's and the hoods of the vehicles. As the Jag came to a stop under the shade of a well-developed oak, dust rose from the car's disturbance into a huge, moving heap. Neither man opened his door until the dirty cloud moved past.

Country music greeted Smitty's latest arrivals well before they reached the main dining hall door. The contrast between Frank Sinatra and Charley Pride couldn't have been more profound. Mr. Lloyd opened the screen door, stepped in, where he halted. *How does one describe such inert atmosphere as was found at Smitty's?* These confines had not seen the light of day in years. Fresh air would sell for a premium here, should anyone care to wholesale it.

Stephen let his eyes adjust to the change of light, peering in all directions as if trying to locate someone he knew. Michael stood next to his father, in suit and tie, feeling self-conscious, not a little lost, and not at all certain what to do next. In some way and quite unexpectedly to Michael, his father didn't look a bit misplaced. *Curious*, Michael thought.

From across the room, in an accent thick as the mouth-watering steaks advertised, came a loud, "Capt'n!" The few patrons, most of whom wore cowboy hats hiding either balding or graying hair, turned to observe the proprietor, all but running to cover the distance between himself and his two most recent guests. Within seconds everyone heard, "Capt'n Lloyd. Long time no see." The two men extended hands to greet each other, which turned into a hug.

This completely unexpected welcome transformed the boy's expression to one of deep inquisition. Michael almost felt awkward at being in such close proximity of the two men. The smaller of the two, the boy obviously did not know. None of this made any sense to Michael. Besides, his father didn't come to these kinds of places. But, for those long seconds, Michael didn't trespass on their relationship and their connection that he couldn't possibly understand.

"Oh, Smitty, this is my son, Michael." Mr. Lloyd said with a pride edging up through his white starched collar and then onto his face.

"Howdy, Michael! Pleased to meet ya; I'm Smitty. By God, you look just like the Capt'n! Spittin' image, Sir!"

"Mr. Smitty, sir . . ."

"Oh no, I ain't Mister Smitty, and I sure ain't no sir. I'm just Smitty. Just call me Smitty, all right? My real name is Erik T. Smit. It's Dutch. But ever' body just calls me Smitty."

"Yes sir, Smitty," Michael prodded. "Um, Smitty, . . . why do you call my father, Captain?"

Erik T. Smit stood all of five feet seven inches. He must have weighed one hundred thirty-seven pounds soaking wet. He looked well into his sixties, though he was only a month shy of being as old as Stephen's father. The black, tattered old ball cap rested on his head in an odd, unadjusted way covering what little hair remained on the little man's head. His tired, bluish-gray eyes danced looking at his old friend, this time with his son. Some kind of tumultuous life had scratched untidy crow's feet into the temples running away from the nook of Smitty's eyes. Even deeper lines had been etched into Smitty's face, like plowed furrows. Michael couldn't guess when Smitty had last shaved. He'd lost several teeth from careless living or lack of dental hygiene—or both, Michael guessed.

The stub of a slow burning cigarette was squeezed into the right corner of his mouth, so that when he spoke, the words exited the left side of his squinted lips. This kept the stump secure and alive. When the heat from its closing end almost burned down to his weather beaten lips he removed it with his nicotine stained and noticeably arthritic, gnarled fingers.

Smitty suddenly dropped the smoking butt to the peanut hulled, sawdust-covered floor where he crushed it, and lit another. He drew deep and then exhaled a plume of smoke into the air. His respiration produced the effect of a well-practiced cough. The lazy fans whirling overhead kept the air moving, which helped with the gathering haze, but Michael coughed anyway. The atmosphere was suffocating.

A grease stain splotched the left quadrant of Smitty's light blue cotton shirt—a bad color for this place. Small grease or dirt smirches also dotted and gathered in smears on his faded blue jeans. His boots hadn't seen any black polish in ages. *Who could this little man be?*

Smitty looked over to Mr. Lloyd for a long second. "You ain't told him, sir?"

"Told me what, Smitty?" An old timer, perhaps one of Smitty's regulars, put a few coins in the jukebox, and Merle Haggard tuned up with, *Sing a Sad Song.*

Mr. Lloyd looked at the sawdust floor, and his jaw tightened. He wished now, facing this solemn moment that he had not come with his son. But here they stood, present and accounted for. Stephen also knew more lay roasting in the fire than his past. Mr. Lloyd brought to Smitty's the uncertainty of his and his family's future. Here at Smitty's, the entrance to the furnace spread before the man and his son.

"No, no I haven't. That's why we came. Michael's best friend was killed in Vietnam a few days ago. Smitty, there are some things I need your help explaining."

51

"Ohhhh . . . I see." Smitty took closer notice of the boy this time, maybe for the first time, and there he saw the unmistakable, awful and familiar sadness in Michael's eyes. Smitty understood it from his own hard and personal experience. Michael stood searching both men's faces for clues to their relationship, but found nothing to assist him. The previous conversation proved that.

"Well Michael, let me show you around."

"What do you mean show me around, Smitty?" Michael believed there was nothing else to see here. This was an old beaten up restaurant and gas station. That's all. What could Smitty show him?

Smitty patted Michael's shoulder urging him toward the wall to the left of the door from which the boy and his father entered moments earlier. There, Michael noticed for the first time the pictures covering the walls. Smitty pointed to one of the tilted picture frames to his left, which the older man straightened. In it, both men focused on a large, four-propeller airplane, an old World War Two bomber of some kind. In the foreground of the picture stood and sat a group of men wearing heavy fur coats and those funny triangular Army Air Corps hats. Many of them carried or wore side arms. They looked young, terribly young. Although most of the men smiled for the camera, an invisible sorrow shrouded them. It lingered for over twenty years on their faces, long after the camera shudder snapped. Patsy Cline lent her own ambiance to the photographic account arrayed on Smitty's walls. She told the folks eating, *I Fall to Pieces.* All Stephen needed to hear was Jill Daniels singing, *The White Cliffs of Dover,* and he'd be lost for certain. Smitty made sure that song stayed out of his collection.

With Michael's attention glued on the first picture, Smitty pointed to another one. "Michael, this is our plane, right here, 'Beowulf's Boys.' You know who Beowulf was?"

"*Our* plane? What do you mean, *our* plane? Yes sir, I know who he was. We studied him last year in English Lit." Michael's head craned back toward his father whose eyes he caught. The boy's surprise was total. Leaving his father's face, Michael once more turned to study the picture with more care, to search for . . . his *father.* Smitty, for his part, kept talking and smoking.

"Oh. Well, I never did. Your daddy had to tell me who he was and what that feller done back then in the old days. He liked that story about that Beowulf. Your daddy didn't have to, but he let the crew vote and we took on that name, though he did suggest that'n *real* strong. The squadron knew who we was when the war was over. You betcha they did." Smitty stopped for a brief second, and then said rather sadly, "But we didn't finish the war with her. She got all shot up on the fourth mission, and we was gettin' newer planes in, and we'd get *them* shot up, and pretty soon we left off namin' our airplanes. That was toward the end, on our last couple of missions. But we flew 'er over there to Italy, though."

"Smitty, what did my father do in that plane? What kind of plane is it? I'm apparently missing a great portion of my father's life that I didn't even know existed." Michael eyed his father again. Now Stephen Lloyd, Michael's father, was a man with a past.

In short order, Michael peppered Smitty with questions, sometimes not even allowing him the opportunity to smoke or cough or address the preceding issue before another surfaced for examination.

"Well Michael, maybe we better start at the top," Smitty suggested, readjusting his tattered ball cap. "This aircraft right here is a B-24H Liberator. It was made by Consolidated-Vultee, right here in Ft. Worth. It had a ten-man crew, and your daddy was our pilot."

"Your *pilot*? *Really*?"

Smitty looked at Stephen and winked. "Yep. That stripe up 'ere on the upper rudders says we was part of the 484th Bomb Group, 827th Squadron of the 15th Air Force. Now our group insignia was a red bowtie. You can see them tail markin's right there. The bow tie was s'posed to be a hour glass, but the tail weren't big enough so they made it a bow tie.

"Wow." Michael's words came breathy and extended, projecting emphasis. "My father flew *that*?" Again, Michael looked back at his father sitting at the table alone sipping a glass of iced tea. Mr. Lloyd stared off into the distance. He didn't watch Michael or Smitty, but he listened, and Michael knew he listened. His admiration for the father he thought he knew had suddenly sky rocketed. But still, Michael could not imagine his parent, his *father*, and now his hero, flying that huge airplane.

"This pitcher must've been took before we headed off on some mission." Smitty tapped the photo with his finger. Pointing to the crew, Smitty said, "This is . . . O'Connor . . . and that's Layhee. They was killed on the mission right after this pitcher was took. Yeah, it was O'Connor and Layhee. I forget where they was from. Kansas? Missouri? Nevada! That's it. Layhee was from Nevada, and O'Connor was from Kansas. Both of 'em was waste gunners. One unlucky flak burst in the waste and they was gone."

"You mean they were killed not long after this was taken?" Michael had to absorb this for a minute. Smitty must let the boy walk this around in his mind, sizing up this type of information.

"Yep, one minute they was firin' their guns and then . . . well, *gone*." Smitty said it so frivolously.

"Is that my father, Smitty?" Michael asked. His face lit up to think of his father doing something he thought involved some form of superhuman courage not to mention strength.

"Yes, sir. That's your daddy. He was the best of the best. He always brung us back."

A new world opened and seemed to swallow the boy whole. Michael didn't let the bad grammar or the recent deaths just revisited or the twangy guitars interfere with these fresh, newly conceived moments. They were untarnished and sweet, like a newborn baby. And just as suddenly there stood his father, so young, so handsome . . . so, *a mustache?* Michael's jaw dropped a bit as he studied his father's early life. "*Wow*."

For perhaps several more minutes the boy drank in every square inch of his father's world of war. He attempted to maintain its place in the context in which he first found it. He shook his head trying to comprehend all of this: "*Wow*."

Satisfied his father was actually imbedded within the photograph, Michael slid appreciably from picture to picture, utterly mesmerized. His eyes danced over whatever the next photo offered him. Airplanes, aircrews, the dead and the wounded, the munitions of war, the ground crews climbing up into the bomber's underbellies and on the engines, destroyed and damaged aircraft, pictures of flak concentrations, charging enemy fighters, formations of bombers, P-51 escort fighters, ME-109's attacking, exploding bombers and targets ablaze. It was all there for him. But the boy could only look backward at it without feeling, without anger, . . . and without remorse.

These pictures covering the walls declared to the patrons present, the greatest days of Smitty's life. It was a life he missed and hated with equal vitality. Each aging photo revealed some aspect of the required fifty missions flown by incredible young men, so many of whom had once been Michael's age or not much older. The pride in this duty etched itself at the corners of Smitty's eyes, into the crevasses of his cheeks, around his mouth, and into his forehead like a crest of honor. And while his badge enumerated his glory days it also spoke of the price he had paid to wear it.

At some point Smitty stepped aside from his "show and tell" to watch Michael who could no longer hear him. The boy peered into the picture frames transfixed, and as if through some incantation, he stepped backward through time. It all looked back at Michael from its single dimension, now faded and dog-eared. Then, it was a new world of 1943 and 1944. This photographic "volume" hanging from the walls of Smitty's Place divulged tales of courage and savagery with unimaginable honesty.

"Michael, are ya hungry?" Smitty asked, interrupting a bombing run on the Ploesti, Romania oilfields.

"What?" Michael's dark brown hair and mist green eyes remained fixed on photos that had come alive for him. He couldn't leave them now.

"Are ya hungry? I'll have James rustle us up some ribs or chicken fried steak or, whatever you want. Capt'n, what'll you have? You boys can't leave here hungry."

Mr. Lloyd acknowledged his growing appetite, and Smitty went into the kitchen to see about the food. That left Stephen to continue observing his son engrossed in a world he'd sooner forget, but for Damien. *Damien.* Smitty returned to find the boy hovering over one of the last pictures, a B-24 on fire, breaking apart, and going down in flames from flak over Vienna, Austria. An hour had evaporated since they entered the restaurant.

"I wonder what he's thinkin,' Capt'n?"

"Smitty, if you don't stop calling me Captain, I'm gonna find someway of selling this place out from under you."

"I ain't gonna never quit callin' you Capt'n . . . And you cain't sell it no way, *Steve.*" Smitty's sarcasm hit his former plane commander square, and they both laughed. "You bought this here grand palace for me, and besides, as of last fall, it's legally mine. You give it to me. That lawyer, Levinson or Landuski or whatever his name is, he said so. He showed me the papers that he filed down at the Tarrant County court house."

"Yes, I gave it to you," retorted Stephen, "so you would have something responsible to manage. We both know you would drink yourself to death if you worked a regular job on some assembly line at GM in Arlington or General Dynamics here in Ft. Worth. How many times did I bust you to private for being drunk? Where did you get that booze, anyway? Nobody had any."

Evading the latter question, Smitty replied, "Too many, I reckon. Boy howdy. Them was the days, huh, Capt'n?"

A lull in the conversation only served to dampen the mood. "Smitty, he wants to join the Marine Corps. His friend Damien, the boy who was killed, was a corporal in the Marines. Those mud Marines..." Stephen's voice trailed off. Rising out of that barren place, Stephen wondered, "What do I tell him? Smitty, he knows which fork to use for what occasion. He's fluent in rhetoric. His manners are impeccable. He's been given an outstanding education, and his prospects are excellent. Any university in the nation would grab him in a minute. Socially, my Lord, he can mingle and converse with executives and politicians and . . . and even royalty, because he's done it. I taught him. His mother and I ensured he lacked for nothing."

Captain Lloyd paused to gather air and any pertinent information he might have forgotten germane to the conversation at hand. Smitty knew from his years with this powerful man to let him speak until he could listen to arguments and ideas other than his own. Quiet finally overtook the man.

Stephen inhaled finally so that he could exhale another question: "Smitty, I don't think he's interested in the hotel business or corporate life. He's really good at sports. I think he's a better player than I was, but until now, right now Smitty, I wasn't sure what he wanted to do. I think . . . I think there's something hiding under all that breeding, twisted in all those manners and sophisticated civility. But I have no earthly idea what. He's on just about every sports team at Gladstone, and he's been reading since age four. He'd spend hours up there in his room reading." More silence. Then, "I want him to go to A&M, maybe play football, like we'd talked about . . ." The storm brooding within Stephen Lloyd had expended its tempest.

At this point, Smitty was wondering if he was really necessary for this conversation. He was, more than he realized. As suddenly as it blew itself out, a smaller, more tempered gale arose: "Come to think of it, you weren't much of a team player in Italy were you? But you survived. Smitty, do you think we did something wrong giving him everything?"

Now, Smitty knew it was his turn. The small man measured his words as he had done so often in Italy. "Well Capt'n, I remember when we got hit over Pilsen. Ol' Beowulf almost give out on us on the way home. You remember? . . . And you was fightin' with them controls and all. Now, if I recollect, I heard you fussin' an' talkin' to the co-pilot that you run off and joined the Air Corps when your daddy didn't want you to. Well, didn't you have ever' thing too, Capt'n? Your daddy give you the whole stinkin' world, on one of them gold plates . . . and look at you now, the boss of that huge corporation. Why, how much you s'pose you're worth right now? I figger what don't kill ya only makes ya stronger, don't it . . . *Steve?*"

Another few coins clinked into the Juke Box, and Roy Orbison filled the restaurant with *Running Scared. How utterly appropriate.* Smitty tapped his foot to the beat, surveying the customers, or lack thereof, and when satisfied, he returned to the conversation.

"True. But it's that 'what doesn't kill you' part that concerns me," Stephen objected. "Our involvement in Southeast Asia is a whole lot less defined than *our* war was. The people and friends I know in Washington are very concerned that we have no clear-cut agenda over there . . . and Washington is directing the war from the White House, for crying out loud. Can you believe that? And what concerns them concerns me. You watch TV. You've seen the body count of American boys. McNamara is a first class idiot, if you ask me. And then when we heard about Damien today, you should have seen him, Smitty. He cried like, like . . ."

"He cried like you done when Lt. Lind took that piece of shrapnel through his head. Well, I remember. I hadn't ever seen a officer cry 'till you broke down. I come out of the turret to see what happened, and you yelled at me to get back up in there or you'd shoot me yourself when we got back to base. Pete Norris got cut in half and you cried, because he was the youngest kid you ever saw climb into a Liberator. That scroungy dog; I wonder what ever happened to that dog o' his?"

Michael returned to the table where the two men sat talking. An immense sadness still hung over Michael because of his friend's death, but where the melancholy had been, pride had replaced it. It welled up inside the boy, commiserate with its fellow. Damien had died, but his father had not. How can one explain or understand any of this?

Michael interrupted the two men's conversation to inquire about certain larger issues.

"Father, how many friends and crew members did you lose over there?" This was a good question, the right question, and it was the worst question of all.

"Too many. I quit counting after they gave me my own airplane and crew—after five, maybe six missions, I think." Former Captain Stephen Lloyd's eyes intensified, then deepened in their eternal greenness while his mental ruminations pulled him backward some twenty years toward those huge matters so indelicately encircling and trying to engulf him.

Michael next pulled the pin on several other potentially explosive matters Stephen would have to adjudicate, which could leave another mess he didn't want to clean up. "Did you do the right thing, father? Grandfather didn't want you to go did he? He had plans for you, didn't he?" From in the kitchen, James rattled the dinner triangle, signaling that the ribs Smitty ordered were ready for Michael, and a steak for the Capt'n. Smitty scooted his chair back and went to retrieve the food, his steps crunching through the discarded peanut hulls.

When Smitty returned, Stephen lauded, "This looks great, Smitty."

"Now you boys eat up, ya hear?"

Before Stephen could say anything more, Michael was elbow deep in the huge beef ribs smothered in sweet barbecue sauce. He gulping sweet tea like a dying, thirsty man, wiped his hands and face like a window cleaner with the forty odd napkins Smitty had brought along for this exact purpose. This starving lad's energy had thrust itself into the heat and aroma of Smitty's specialty, which made the worn-out old man beam. Stephen took a more reserved approach to his entrée. He would not leave Smitty's looking like a hog at the trough. "This is great Smitty," Michael mumbled between bites. That Michael could unlearn eighteen years of table manners in twenty-six seconds amazed Stephen, but he said nothing.

When the animated friction from Michael's side of the table slowed, his father said, "Michael, have you ever seen your grandfather mad, I mean, *really* mad? When I told him I wanted to join the Army Air Corps . . ." His words fell off into a bottomless crevasse. His broken cadence allowed Smitty and Michael to watch him measuring his next remarks. He set his fork down and chewed slowly. The old man and Michael made eye contact with each other. Then, when Stephen had the compatible words organized in their proper order, he spurred them, one fragment at a time.

Clink, clink. *Sweet Dreams*, by Patsy Cline. The conversation went from comfortless to dolorous, if that were possible. "I was in my second year at A&M. I wish you had known David Le Mont, Michael. He and I grew up together here in Ft. Worth. We both graduated from Gladstone, as you will in a few months."

Smitty's ball cap suddenly slipped off his head and flopped among the crushed peanut hulls near Michael's foot. The boy retrieved it, slapped it against a chair and handed it back to the old man, but not before Smitty lit another smoke.

"Dave was a year ahead of me, but he was my best friend. No finer guy, Dave. When he was a junior at A&M and I was a sophomore, . . . well, Pearl Harbor . . . happened." His never still, prolific eyes betrayed a hundred thoughts, all diverging at this one moment of time: regrets, adventure, fear, and its cousin, uncertainty, all of it.

"Dave dropped out of school the next day, December eighth. He didn't tell anyone, not his parents or even me. He joined the Air Corps and he wound up flying 24's too. These were the early models, D's and E's." Stephen's dialogue morphed into an awkward, even stilted configuration, and perhaps the real Stephen Lloyd began to speak for the first time since Italy.

He stretched his legs out in front of him into what resembled cloth-covered planks. His steel-bright eyes made inert contact with his shoes. Smitty saw him begin to "fly" some mission over one of the hellish targets in Austria, maybe Poland or Germany. He always "flew" when he came here to Smitty's Place. This tired, greasy steak and ribs building became Stephen Lloyd's refuge every few years, when the world of high business and its multifaceted pressures squeezed him in its vice like death grip. It was those hideous missions that called him back to its sanctuary. Dolores knew. Susan knew, too, and they let him go, to work it through for the length of hours or days it took him.

Michael's urgent need for food halted further motion, and with the cessation of nourishment, a stillness over came him. It wasn't a calm that invaded him, but a disturbing gale that filled his chest cavity. This virgin territory his father had brought to his son's plate consumed the restaurant. No artist sang; the patrons spoke in uninvited and hushed tones. The metaphysical had intruded upon the living. It was eerie and disturbing, and not a little unsettling to the boy, and it lasted but a flicker. Smitty had breathed it's death like a starving men.

Mr. Lloyd recovered, shook the flak and fighters away like so many annoying mosquitoes invading, important thoughts. He took up his friend's cause: "Anyway, Dave was killed on the nineteenth of July at Taylor River Canyon in Colorado. He didn't even make it overseas. The tail surface had failed. That's what the crash investigation reported. He didn't even get in the fight . . ."

Stephen suddenly looked in desperation for someplace to park his mind's eye, where the pain behind them would not require examination, much less elaboration. He suspected Michael would ask. Stephen didn't want to speak in much depth of those days right then. It was his wound and his alone to dress. This unexpected vignette hung above with no where to go unless someone wished it away.

Stephen's voice eventually invaded the pall, "So, I know what you are feeling son, and yes, I had to join the fight too. I felt, and still do to this day that Hitler had to be defeated. And I looked for the most destructive way I could to destroy him and everything he stood for. What I stood to lose as the son of Marcus Lloyd might never compensate me, but there were greater issues stirring inside of me, pushing me to the only action I believed right. Although your grandfather's anger didn't deter me, some of the things he said really hurt. Hindsight leads me to believe that father was fighting a subtler, but nonetheless real battle of his own. He was afraid I might be killed. Parents worry about those kinds of tall issues. Be that as it may, I thought if Germany and Japan took over the whole world, what would the Lloyd Empire mean anyway? Smitty, surely you felt the same as I? We were ready to give everything up for that cause. And more times than I care to count . . . so many times I wrestled with that when it felt as if none of it mattered." Smitty shook his head in agreement, blowing more smoke into the air and then coughing. This fit lasted longer than usual.

Michael slapped his hands on the table, hoping that this sudden action might give his words greater emphasis. "Then you do understand! That's the way I feel right now. It's the same way you did *then*. Interesting. Yes, they might just send me to Vietnam, but . . ."

"Michael. Your mother will fight both of us on this. But . . . no, *I'm* not going to fight you."

"*Your mother will fight both of us on this.*" "*Us?*" Had Michael heard his father just say, "*both of us?*" "You're not!?"

"No. I do think however . . . you should wait and go to college so you can be commissioned an officer. Trust me, it's better to be the one giving the orders than the one taking them. Right Smitty?" Smitty rolled his eyes and then winked. "But no matter what you decide, I want to tell you what no one else will. In some way I can't fully explain, I'm glad you've chosen patriotism. But the other side of the coin is, war leaves scars on you. If it doesn't kill or maim you it *will* damage you internally for the rest of your life. I still see those men I flew with. Too many of them were . . ." Measured hesitation. "I remember watching the mechanics wash the blood out of our airplane after a mission once . . . carefully picking up and scraping off the body parts splattered against the inside of the plane. There were times I thought I would lose my mind from the grief and loss I felt. I felt so responsible for every one of them that didn't make it back. I didn't think I would ever get clean again. I'm still not . . . clean."

Stephen knew it was the right thing to do—destroy the enemy. Then there was—the mental and soul-destroying pollution of knowing that you *had* killed the enemy and he had killed just as many of you. Many men couldn't live with this, but many others carried on and did. Someone artist harmonized in the background, but at this table the music didn't penetrate the mood well. "I come here every so often, because I get the shakes. I can't seem to control them. I just have to get away from things. Vietnam may well do that to you, and I can't stand that thought. The thought of looking at you and seeing no spark, no . . . no life in your eyes . . . I brought you here to see these pictures. Some of them aren't pretty . . ."

Mr. Lloyd's voice wavered, and tears began to form at the corners of his eyes. Then he stood up, all but oblivious to his surroundings: his son, his former top turret gunner, Smitty, and the last few patrons, sipping sweet tea and smoking cigarettes, most of whom seemed not to notice. He walked outside leaving Smitty to his twentieth smoke and Michael to finish his last rib. The boy had no appetite now.

Michael had just observed his father's pain he had not been privy to, indelibly inked on his father's face. The boy had now been hit with more than any two people he knew, in less than eight hours.

Outside, Stephen's eyebrows almost touched each other from the strain bearing down on him at that moment. Vagrant and self-torturing thoughts bombarded him like so many huge aircraft in formation releasing their loads, all at once, and all on him. He never thought he would face this while his son watched. *Why now?* He always seemed to be able to fight the pressure when he sensed it coming, but not now. He leaned against the wood building, put his face in his hands, and wept.

Oh, it made sense all right, and it made no sense at all. His heart swung the sword that protected his son in order to strike at the shield of patriotic logic. Stephen had long ago used this introspection to protect his own interests, his own desires. It made perfect sense then, when the stakes meant that he or someone else's son or father or husband went off to war. Yet, the possibility of losing his *own* son for the same reasons he'd enumerated aloud to his father almost twenty-five years earlier loomed larger than all the crew members and friends he lost in all the enormity of all his previous missions combined.

Stephen now understood in his gut what his father Marcus knew. The words carried the meaning his father shook at a much younger, a much stronger Stephen Lloyd. Stephen comprehended what Marcus Lloyd found impossible to express adequately or compassionately. Stephen also understood that the business did not *need* him then. It had nothing to do with that. It never did. And so, this was a battle that he, Stephen Lloyd, could not win. Marcus, Stephen's father, loved him, period, even as Stephen loved Michael. And yet, in some strange way and in the larger picture, Stephen supposed that he could not bear to lose either. Still, Michael would go, and Susan . . . *Susan* . . . His tears slowed and then stopped. It was Susan who brought a jolting sobriety to his mind. Susan would play the part of Marcus in this repeat performance.

When Stephen walked back into the restaurant he discovered Smitty and Michael deep in conversation. Smitty waxed most eloquently, even quite animated in his explanations of life in a B-24. He held the young man captive with his tales of war, heroism, and fear.

Stephen interrupted at long last, "Michael, I told Damien's father I would drop by this evening. We really need to be going, son. Smitty, thank you for your hospitality, but we have some urgent business to attend to."

"Yeah, I reckon. I wish y'all could stay, but I understand. Capt'n, if there's anything I can do . . ." Smitty's corrugated face enunciated perfectly the desolation that war brings. All the lost kids that the medics hauled out of his airplane under a blanket covering their faces . . . lived still in this old barn of a restaurant, run by the forty-five year old man who looked sixty-five. Stephen Lloyd would be leaving Smitty with the opaque contentment of knowing that his captain would be back. Stephen Lloyd *would* return, probably within the next week.

"Ya'll come back, now. Michael, you know where my place is. Come on out some time and have supper with me, okay? Bring your daddy too." Smitty began a coughing spasm lasting half a minute.

"I will, Smitty. Thanks. Thank you for everything," Michael's eyes sweeping the walls for one last look.

Five: The Trip Home

>–┤◄├–◄►–O–◄►–┤►├–◄

The moon's luminescence spread like a sheet upon the hoods of the several pickups remaining at Smitty's. What the luster didn't herald or glint off of was overshadowed and hidden. The two men climbed into the low seated sports car and headed out of the parking lot. Lonnie was the lone service station attendant sitting in his lawn chair under a harsh light bulb swatting bugs. He waved at the occupants of the fancy car moving past him and shouted something resembling, "y'all come on back." Stephen waved back as he and Michael slowly made their way out and onto the blacktop, trying not to raise more dust than necessary. The Lloyd's departure left Hank Williams unable to provide the freedom some female's cold, cold heart desperately needed. Neither could Stephen compete with the tenor of the coming spring evening. A few crickets and bullfrogs surrounding the adjacent buildings serenaded Smitty's Place and its dry board sameness for another coming Texas summer.

Michael needed to talk now more than ever. Questions, in their embryonic stages, formed, hastening around the corners of his intelligence, vied for his attention and his father's answers. He had become privy to his father's secret historic and psychological closet. Stephen's mind slowly gave birth to growing apprehensions. Each memory played about him like phantoms in a child's darkened room, his mother having just shut off the light, and with the darkness came the fear.

The hazy glare of Smitty's disappeared in the rear view mirror, now behind a stand of oaks. The winding sports car's engine and Mozart replaced Hank, and the fresh country air supplanted the quickening aroma of seared steaks, barbecued ribs and the smoky musk of the line shack called Smitty's Place.

"Why . . . I mean, how come . . . I mean, why didn't you let me know, father?"

Frustrating parental reticence greeted Michael's inquiry. Stephen welcomed the limited amount of concealment the dark car afforded him. He didn't want his son's eyes intruding upon his dismay. Mr. Lloyd's daily interchanges with powerful men from the mayor to the governor, his board of trustees to the thousands of shareholders, seldom found him at a loss for words. For reasons he did and didn't understand, talking with his son about his military past proved almost overwhelming.

What am I afraid of? Hadn't the pictures on Smitty's walls given Michael an introduction or tour into my past? I hoped I'd get lucky and might not have to say any more, yet . . . I suppose I knew this conversation would arise. I came here for this moment. But still, trying to describe to my son an elongated time of events so painful, events so horrific . . . Perhaps I prejudged that Michael couldn't grasp it. What was he supposed to grasp? What? The war . . . ?

Stephen hoped he could somehow wrest quickly from his mind the images that had waited there, mostly patient, sometimes volatile, for over two decades. Now his age was against him, and that made it harder to do just that. Smitty's was supposed to solve all that. Instead, the old place had opened Pandora's box and the fears he'd run from for far too long. They were so cleverly attacking Stephen below his diaphragm. *Was it too late to examine them with his son,* he wondered? Stephen swallowed hard. *Was it . . . ?* With his first attempt at exhumation, Stephen faltered, "I didn't . .," was as far as he got. The remainder of the sentence lodged in his throat.

The heavy cigarette smoke from several hours at Smitty's clung to the two men's clothes, their eyes and throats burning from the exposure. Stephen rolled down his window inviting the night's dry, cool air to push harshly against and across him. This winded reprieve afforded him but a few seconds more time. "I . . . uh," Stephen Lloyd said, squirming in his seat for the second time in as few minutes. He obviously didn't want to verbalize those events, but neither did he want them left with his son to figure out on his own. And neither could he leave it for Dolores to attempt to explain. She knew of the effects.

Stephen couldn't let them thrash about in his own mind any longer if he could put them to bed once and for all. He finally decided he wanted Michael to know, but that didn't make it any easier.

"Why is this so hard for you, father? I don't understand this evening." The wind howled as the car moved through the dark. *Just get him talking*, Michael thought. *Get him to say anything and the words or the stories might tumble out. Try the side door.* "When did you join the Air Force?"

Silence. Then, "Well, Michael, I didn't join the Air Force. It was the Army Air Corps back then. You have to understand the context of the world your mother and I were raised in, in the late 1930's and '40's."

Michael's father was *talking*. He was talking. Michael listened intently as the man painted a portrait of a time antecedent to the mid-1950's, long before Michael's first memories were formed. Michael's lack of information needed fine strokes, freshly painted. Stephen spoke at times in cogent particulars, and at other times, in fractured detail. So much of it proved a daunting cognitive task to both father and son. The boy didn't actually need this volume of information. Denzil Hukill and Johnny Johnson, whoever they were, didn't mean anything to him. Stephen however, thought that all of it, the men, their training, their anxieties, their highs and lows, was all-important.

When Stephen ran out of words and silence hung about them, Michael spoke. "Incredible. That's hard to imagine. I thought my math classes were tough. How did you do it?"

"I've asked myself that a hundred times. Denzil and Johnny and I would sort of crumple outside of class, completely spent. And with strength I have never quite understood, we went to the next thing. No one was more amazed than I was."

"Father . . ." Michael hesitated. "Never mind." Michael started to ask his father about last week, when Susan asked Stephen to hang that picture. How could his father fly a huge bomber, and then . . . put a hole in the wall with the hammer? *Strange.*

Fortunately for Stephen, the Gladstone campus was within sight as they turned off of Eighth Street and drove under the entry gateway. Large homes built in the grand style of the 1920's and '30s had somehow escaped demolition. There they stood sentinel on either side of Elizabeth Boulevard keeping their uninterrupted watch over the neighborhood.

They turned off of Elizabeth Blvd. and looked for parking somewhere on College Street. College was usually a narrow lane without many vehicles parked on it. At this late hour and on this of all days, both sides of the street were sardined with cars. The circumstances that brought all the familiar folks here made finding parking awkward and frustrating. Stephen drove around for several minutes before he found a place to park.

In the darkness and still of this evening, Michael made mental notes of the comings and goings of people he knew; some he didn't. He recognized the Gladstone staff, faculty, and students, both former and present. Each had come to console the Wilson's. The porch light burned brightly drawing bugs that hovered and darted and crashed into the round glass dome above the door. Mr. Shapiro acted as doorman, greeting or excusing the mourners. The day's heaviness slumped once more upon Michael again, as if it had not left but only retreated from him for a season.

Stephen looked over at his oldest boy, but the shadows created by the porch light hid his facial features. He inquired after a minute, "Are you okay, son?"

"I was. Thank you for telling me father, for taking me to Smitty's. . . . I don't want to go in there." The Wilson's apartment looked formidable.

"I know what you mean. I *know* what you mean." They were here too. Now he had to go see about James and Mary Ellen. Stephen Lloyd however, tasted the need for someone to help him.

Within thirty seconds they stood at the precipice of the Wilson's front door where they greeted Alex Shapiro. The conversations further inside the Wilson's residence were muted. James sat on the couch staring into space, incredulous to the cruel facts that confronted him. As a deacon in his church, he'd been the man to comfort the grieving. It was he who directed the words and gave the effort toward the hurting. He had no idea how to receive the same in kind. As with Job, he did not need the patriarch's "comforters" to cluster near him in his darkness.

Mary Ellen was in the bedroom with her sister and a few women from the church. The pastor stood at the refreshment table sampling the coffee and finger sandwiches, waiting, observing, ready to assist. The lights were kept low, reflecting the mood that had settled over everything and everyone.

Stephen, almost backed out the front door. The impulse to run away almost forced him into open flight, were it not for Alex who had latched onto his arm and then guided him toward the pastor. Stephen would have to stay.

The front door of the Lloyd estate opened and then closed softly as the two men arrived. The interminable silence on the ride home had finally been broken. Susan sprang from the sofa to greet two of the men in her life: her husband and her oldest son. The third and youngest Lloyd, David, was sound asleep upstairs. Both men reflected the care-worn strain of this terrible day. Susan observed the fatigue in, around, and under her husband's eyes. She smelled Smitty's too and grimaced at the acrid aroma. There were other smells present she couldn't identify.

Michael—well—she knew his hurt. She didn't know for certain whom to hug first. So, she grabbed both of her men, sweeping them into a sort of triangular hug in the midst of the large marble foyer.

Michael pulled away first and went to his room, leaving his father to sort through the details his mother usually craved. Women are talkers. They have to have conversation, words part of their internal combustion. For men, the less the glossary, the better. Susan pulled Stephen back to the sofa she had vacated mere moments ago. As he crumpled onto the cushions the air left his lungs in a sort of organic groan. He appeared so thoroughly spent, Susan let him sit in silence for several eternal minutes before proceeding with her feminine adaptation of an interrogation.

"How are they doing?" she asked, attempting not to seem *too* eager. She failed utterly.

Stephen thought to himself, *why didn't you go visit them yourself if it's so important to you?*

Further silence from her husband, then, "We walked into a room full of much less hysteria than I thought there'd be, moody silence, tears, anguish, a mangled future lost, a broken man and his heart-sick wife. That . .," Stephen's jaws tightened and then eased slowly back to exhaustion. His eyes narrowed and his cheeks rose so that Susan didn't recognize him for a few seconds. The fatigue pulled at his facial muscles and then slowly released them. He resumed what he started to say, ". . . is how they are doing, my lovely wife. Did you call them?"

"Yes, but I spoke to a cousin, Edna, I think. I couldn't hear her very well for all the noise, the crying, and all the rest of it in the background. Mary Ellen couldn't talk or wasn't able to. I left word that the food would be taken care of and then called the caterer we always use. I'll go by and check on Mary Ellen tomorrow. There were things I just couldn't drop this afternoon. This is just awful. Just *awful*."

Susan's feminine need had not yet been assuaged. Women are never satisfied with the few and often barren details men submit. She squeezed Stephen further for the fruit of the scene he had most recently vacated. Surely he could tell her more than this. She plied him for more details, but now, the emotion of it all got the better of her, and she, as all women do, began to cry again for her friends, the Wilsons.

Stephen pulled his wife close and enclosed her with his sturdy arms. Here, of all the places in her ordered world, she felt safest, amid his strength. He ingested more than a hint of her perfume, her softness, his physical need for her arising unexpectedly. In that, he could escape. Susan slowly pulled away from her husband, and Stephen took up staring into space, his surroundings becoming gradually hazy. When his mind reached what he hoped was neutral, he treaded mental air.

"Honey, what are you thinking about?" Susan attempted to interrupt his brief retreat from her. She almost felt alarmed, for he looked much too introspective, scared she thought. Alarm rose deep within her.

"What?" he said, as if shooing a fly away. At that instant, he realized his fingers were interlocked tightly with his wife's, and his grip hurt her. He of course had not the slightest inkling he was squeezing her hand so firmly.

"Oh, I'm sorry honey. I didn't realize I was gripping you so tightly. Forgive me."

"Obviously. Just now, what were you thinking? Are you okay? You looked frightened." That had to be put to bed quickly. "I'm fine. Just tired."

No one this close to the Wilson's was fine or could be expected *not* to drift off to some separate, safe or dark place to wind down and evaluate the situation. Things were *not* well in Stephen's mind or soul. He would hide like he always tried to do.

"I . . . oh, I was just thinking about the Wilson's. That's all."

"How do you think they are going to handle this? I can't imagine what they are going through. Is there more that we can do," she asked, mopping her large eyes with a tissue.

To Stephen, it felt somewhat good to finally sit and wind down. But talking . . . *Please, not now.* Susan told her husband that he needed to go take a shower. That odor starched to him wasn't ever pleasant to her cultivated senses. She couldn't imagine why the man lived the way he lived. Thankfully he entered their lives only once in a great while. In the bathroom, Stephen dropped his clothes for Susan to collect and hang on the line.

Michael came down from his room a half hour later where he lumbered into his best-loved part of the house, —the kitchen, and to his favorite appliance, —the refrigerator. He opened it, bent down to scan its contents, and not locating anything that suggested substance, called back over his shoulder. "Mother. Mother? I'm hungry. What did Mrs. Cassalls make for supper? Is there anything left?" Michael spoke from the chasm of the refrigerator so that his words were not quite audible. Susan had heard this query a thousand times. His words reverberated off the ketchup bottle, the milk carton, the four bottles of Coke, and all the other refrigerated and foil covered staples and goodies, to die somewhere in the kitchen.

Michael still needed nourishment about every twenty minutes regardless of the circumstances. He had convinced himself that he would wilt if he didn't eat . . . often. The fact that he had eaten enough for two normal human beings at Smitty's Place only four hours prior didn't matter. His hunger drove him out of his room where he left the day's sadness and cares so that he could graze in the kitchen. Nothing, not life or death, slowed his appetite.

"Michael, she fried chicken. There's still some in the fridge. It's behind the . . ." Susan's words trailed, then resumed, "behind the potatoes, I think."

Michael interrupted her directions with, "Hey, there's chicken in here, Mother. Did Mrs. Cassalls fry it tonight?"

Susan looked at her husband in amazement, mocking her son's discovery, *"Hey, there's chicken in here, mother!"* Stephen smiled half-heartedly. His wife did a fairly good Michael impersonation. Susan noted carefully Stephen's lack of emotional response. Normally, under different circumstances, her attempted humor would elicit a kiss or a chuckle from him.

"Michael, please close the door to the . . ." She heard the door shut as she spoke. Her son would keep that door open until doomsday if he had an inkling that something interesting was possibly in there waiting for him to find it, kill it if need be, and then eat it. Michael was convinced that he could find and consume whole chickens or cows much easier with it open. The boy padded back upstairs to his room. Susan poked her right index finger into Stephen's stomach and asked, "So, how are *you* doing?"

"I wish I knew. I feel a little lost right now."

Michael closed the door to his room once again. His stomach would soon be gloriously full. His mind and soul on the other hand, felt anything but settled. Food did enormous things for him and always had, but this—Damien, and now his father's past in one day—no fried chicken or hamburger and fries could chalk over this. He'd not seen his father cry, *ever*. He didn't know men were allowed to display their emotions, especially in public—until tonight, and it unnerved him. He kept playing it over and over in his mind. *Is this what happens to men who go to war?* More questions tumbled to the front of his brain like little soldiers obeying orders from places he couldn't see and from people he didn't know. For the last few hours, he'd thankfully held his emotions in check. So far. Seeing his father crying like that . . . it became more difficult now, alone in his room. Smitty's paneled walls came back into view, walls covered with black and white pictures of burning and exploding aircraft. *War must be awful*, he thought. *Is this what I want to do? Is it?*

But his understanding of war still excited him. He'd seen the movies—*Twelve O'clock High, The Sands of Iwo Jima, Battle Cry, Run Silent Run Deep, The D.I.* He assumed that he knew just how terrible it was. Those pictures revealed a brutality he'd seen in books in the school library, but they were taken of other son's fathers, not his. Even with Damien gone for so long overseas Michael felt far removed from this present war. It was 'over there' someplace. Out of sight, out of mind. Michael had occasionally heard older men speak of war. Their stories didn't do anything for him but make war seem either remote or quixotic. And when those men did speak of it, it was as if they were most reluctant to discuss what they'd been through. That didn't make sense. Why not tell what happened?

He shifted his thoughts to joining the Marines and what he thought this venture in the military would be like. It would be tough, but he was tough. He'd played football. He'd been knocked out once making a tackle. That was how tough he was. What was tougher than that? Somehow *his* experiences in the military would be different from the older veterans and their wars, maybe not even as bad. Would he bring something back with him? *What?* Hey, he might win a medal or something. He might be wounded. That would be neat, serious, but intriguing. He'd have a scar to show off. Victoria would be impressed. So would Donny. Michael put these thoughts on hold for a brief moment, wondering what his father was thinking about now.

And then Damien, his friend, came roaring into his mental processes, interrupting everything. Damien had been *killed*. He wasn't coming home to show his wounds or medals or scars. He wasn't going to walk off the airplane at Love Field as he'd walked on it to go away to war. He was coming home dead, in one of those silver boxs. Michael wasn't going to see his friend *ever* again. *What have I decided to do?*

Michael picked up the phone, then paused and listened within himself. He also wanted to make certain neither of his parents was using it. They weren't. He dialed Donny's.

"Rainford residence. This is Donald speaking."

"Donny. Hey man. You won't believe where I've been."

The conversation lasted eighteen minutes and forty-two seconds, give or take. Smitty's Place and Michael's plans for joining the Marine Corps topped the list. But it didn't go the way Michael had imagined it would, not in his wildest dreams. Donny was going to Dartmouth . . . for a reason. He thought the war in Vietnam was wrong and so did that University. Wow. They hadn't talked about Vietnam before.

"Mikey, you *can't* do this," Donny begged, and his emotions turned verbal and raw. Normally, Donny called him Michael. He only used Mikey when his life-long friend said something inappropriate, or in this case, stupid. In Donny's universe, Michael had clearly lost his marbles. Within minutes of his friend's announcement of, "I want to join the Marines," Donny was all but yelling into the receiver. "You saw your father cry. What do you think will happen to you? My heavens, Mikey, what's wrong with you!? America is attacking a defenseless nation that we attacked first in the Gulf of Tonkin. Don't you watch the news, Mikey? I remember Cronkite reporting it. They're a bunch of backward farmers who only want to live in peace. And our soldiers, they're dying by the hundreds. And for what? This war is immoral. I can't stand what my country is doing. War is the wrong way to settle things, and especially there. Our guys are baby killers. I've seen what they do on the news. And if you join the Marines you'll be just as guilty as LBJ is."

Just as Donny said, "I'm going to do everything I can to stop this war . .," Michael hung up the phone. One of his very best friends had as much as called Michael a criminal if he joined the military. *What was this world coming to?* He thought about phoning Victoria, but from his conversation with Donny, Michael felt shaken and unsettled. He thought Donny, of all people, would surely understand. *Hadn't Damien's death started something Michael felt compelled to follow? Yes, yes it had.* He picked up the phone as if to call Donny back, but when he got it halfway to his mouth, he set it back in the cradle.

He grabbed it again and dialed. One ring. Two . . . "Victoria. Hi. It's me. Let me ask you a question, if you can keep it to yourself?"

Kathleen Victoria McClure was an attractive, very attractive blonde. She had believed over the past few years she would always be committed to Michael. She had proven herself his ally many times in the past. Michael and she had been an item since the ninth grade. She'd not told Michael's parents when he got drunk out at Lake Worth. She had kept his hands in check when they drove to their favorite place to "look at the stars." She loved him and wanted this relationship to lead to what she hoped would conclude with a ring at the altar, children, and a secure future of wealth and prestige. She was even now mapping out her plans to follow him to A&M or Princeton; her grades slightly better than his. Her SAT scores dazzled, and her parent's pride knew no bounds. They, too, were excited about her future *with* Michael. They thought of him already as their son-in-law, although they contained themselves for her sake. Being connected to the Lloyd's meant unimaginable things to Mr. McClure.

Harold McClure's business, which was connected to the New York Stock Exchange, McClure and Weebank Financial, Inc., had fallen on hard times in this war economy. In Harold's world, selling refrigerators to the Eskimos in December seemed an obvious sure bet. He lived off his father's wise choices in the stock market and inherited a fortune when his father died of prostate cancer in 1961, following a prolonged illness.

Mary, Harold's wife, on the other hand, regretted her choice of marriage partners by the second year into their relationship. But by then, Victoria was one-year old, teething, and Mary was freshly pregnant with William. Three more McClure's would be born, one every other year. Mary's fate unfortunately was sealed irretrievably. She had become quite comfortable with the country club dances and civic responsibilities she had been asked to take part in via Harold. She went after them with all the vigor of a woman come to conquer the planet, anything to forget her husband.

As Victoria talked to Michael, she eyed the fourth finger of her left hand, visualizing the ostentatious ring with which Michael would surprise her, in, say, a year or two? It couldn't be too soon for her tastes and plans. "You know I can. Tell me. What's going on?"

Michael held his breath. Victoria's imagination knew no bounds. She was now more excited than when Michael first called. Hearing nothing for a long ten seconds, Victoria assumed the need to probe, "Have you decided on which school yet?" She didn't want to seem too excited, but the suspense was driving her crazy. Victoria had not been as affected as Michael had with Damien's death. She had obviously heard through the school grapevine, and her lack of concern bothered Michael.

"You have to promise. This is between you and me and the fence post." Michael's apprehension grew, apprehensive his girlfriend would turn on him too.

"Michael . . . What is *it*?" She begged, sounding hurt. That *usually* worked.

"All right. Here goes. What do you think about my joining the Marines? Donny just let me have it. He thought I was crazy."

"Michael!!!" His name came storming out of the receiver, followed by a long, icy silence.

"Victoria . . . ? Are you still there?"

In another second, a loud wail stuffed itself into the phone. Heavy sobbing succeeded her howl, and her tears were supplanted by a hard and loud dial tone.

Six: The First Miscarriage

>─┼─◆>─●─<◆>─┼─<

Stephen regarded the furniture even though Susan kept probing his defenses with questions. Out of self-defense he refused to make eye contact with her. A growing climate of fear accumulated in his mind as to what might happen if he looked directly at her. He'd let himself go at Smitty's, and that was enough. Susan wouldn't understand anyway. There really wasn't any need to involve her in past, in *His past*. But right here on the couch the past *was* as present as the present. Besides, what might happen if he started crying again in his own home seemed to him unclear, but he still couldn't take the chance of looking directly at her. Thus Stephen forced his mind to focus on something other than a dead Marine.

Michael had promised his father he would wait at least a few days before the two of them went down to the Marine recruiter. Stephen wanted the reality and the consequences of Damien's death to sink in a little longer. Time would surely clear his head and he'd agree to go on to college. Then he could be commissioned, if he still had to join the military. He'd be older then and less inclined to follow emotional ideologies. The war would surely be over in two years, three tops. Korea only lasted three. That would save Mr. Stephen Lloyd from having to inform Mrs. Susan Lloyd that her first-born son, Michael Lloyd, wanted to dash her plans for her son to pieces. *Oh boy*.

The pressures at work managing the Lloyd Empire were one thing. Stephen had grown accustomed to them. They were part of his world, his managerial blood stream. Delicately directing his son away from a war going nowhere as far as Stephen could see, was quite another. Michael had been a clear-headed child for the most part. Susan, if she were to discover Michael's plans, could and would make Stephen's home life a living hell. Men may fight the wars, but women rule the world. That axiom is universal and absolute, and the man who stands against it is a fool. It's a law that should be taught in chemistry or physics, at least in grade school.

Susan felt strangely alone even with Stephen sitting next to her. Imperceptibly—and Susan detected it as they sat together—her man had begun to shut her out. She would not let that happen. Not tonight.

"Can't you tell me anything more? Anything? I want to know every detail."

Stephen fed his wife thin, less than sufficient morsels, hardly placating her female needs. These bits would have to do for now. Stephen was just too tired to grant this woman everything she had to know. Finally, Susan surrendered to the fact that Stephen wasn't going to tell her any more. Michael had fed his hollow leg, and she *was* tired from the strain of wondering about the Wilson's and her men. They were safe where they should be, and they *all* would be in bed very soon.

"I'm tired. Let's get some rest. Tomorrow will be . . ."

Will be what? Tomorrow won't be any better.

He interrupted her movement toward the bedroom. "I'm going to stay up a bit longer, Hon. I'm not ready just yet to turn in. Go on up."

"Are you *sure*? Considering the obvious, you ought to come to bed."

"Not just yet."

"All right. But come up soon."

"Okay."

No, he wasn't all right. And no, he wasn't coming up so soon. Susan trudged up the stairs, stopped to take another look back at Stephen, and then continued her journey to their empty bedroom. Stephen went to the liquor cabinet, opened it, and reached in for the Scotch whiskey. He poured a squat, etched crystal glass half full. He heard the creaking of the floor above him. He knew it to be the sound of his wife's preparation for bed. Stephen returned to the couch and slumped once more down into its cushion. For a long second, he sat staring at the glass. He knew why he held it in his hand. He'd not touched any since VE day. Yet here he sat, holding what he hoped would dissolve this mix-master in his soul.

The smooth bite of the scotch stung as it cleared his throat, burning his esophagus on its way down. When the alcohol doused his stomach, its effects shot straight up to his head, quickly moving him toward what he wanted: relaxation, numbing and unreality. The more he sipped, the less torrid he felt. His single fear was that this scotch would betray him, that it wouldn't do what the billboards advertised. It wouldn't set him on a porch in a rocking chair, the dog nearby, and the day passing slowly and uneventful, that he'd lose all his cares. The opposite happened. His mind alerted him to the dead Marine that he had known too well, to Damien Wilson.

Forty-five minutes crept by. He couldn't escape the thought that the Wilson's had no spare sons from which to draw extras when one went down. It could have happened to Susan and him. Michael almost didn't arrive. *What if Margaret hadn't been born? And David . . . It was Michael that started the whole thing. Michael. What if he . . . didn't . . . if he hadn't come?* Susan's face suddenly hung suspended over his faculties.

Monday, March 23, 1942

Susan lay on the bed hoping to feel a slight bulge in the contour of her abdomen. It was too soon to know for sure, and she knew that. Still, contentment reigned within. Even the dark cloud of Stephen's pending departure to California that would commence his time in the service couldn't fully dissipate her inner felicity. She had missed one period for the first time in her young life. She needed the doctor whom she would see in two long days to confirm her suspicions. She was hopeful as only a woman in her situation can be that she was pregnant. She wouldn't alert Stephen, not just yet. His last day of class lay within the week. But Susan's need for substantiation seized her, throwing almost everything else out the window. Her silence would be the better part of valor, she mused.

Susan had not even called her mother. She would keep this little secret, more or less, all to herself, savoring it. It must not be a false alarm. It must be a baby, Stephen's and hers. Oh for the joy of it all. The more she let her mind run about the more she felt giddy. Stephen would be gone for who knew how long? She wanted something from him to remind her of their love.

She glanced at her watch. Stephen would be home from class in fourteen minutes and thirty-seven seconds. Susan raised her head from the pillow to get up, but in mid-raise, she felt a strange and urgent cramping in her abdomen. It spasmed lower than she needed it to, and she suspected this was not good. *Reach the bathroom—now.* With greater than expected exertion, Susan labored to cross the room, felt wobbly, weak and off balance, slightly dizzy. She reached for the door to the bathroom in a panic, halted, the pain hitting her full.

Something was *very* wrong. She reached the commode and sat, the urge to press, overwhelming. An unfamiliar inner heat and a horrid discharge oozed from her body, terrifying her as much as it stabbed her. In quick succession, numerous blood clots filled the bowl. With the immediate crisis boiling over in her mind, the urge to raise herself and look, —to confirm, seemed necessary. Under her floated a dark reddish portrait of disintegration and with it, the fetid smell of death. Pressure, fear, terror, and worst of all, acute pain: Susan's body was conspiring against her.

Susan pressed against the alcove walls and pulled her aching body, lissome frame up off of the toilet seat, grunting and straining as she did. Fully to her feet she turned to turned to confront her fears, so as to validate them. In the toilet, she stared into the most horrible sight imaginable: her tiny unformed child floated in pieces amid all that bloody tissue and dark red blobs. Her late morning breakfast moved upward into her throat. *Could this possibly get any worse*, she wondered?

Out of options, Susan put her right hand over her mouth, cradling her stomach with her left. Her skirt and underwear lay bunched and blood stained around her ankles, making any movement away from the toilet even more difficult. She had to shed them lest she fall if she moved, an insignificant movement at any other time, inconceivable at present. Susan leaned for support against the wall. Finding it, she next tried to control her breathing and her rising panic. Her vision began to blur, and she probably couldn't stand much longer on her own. She turned slightly, staring at the shower curtain's encircling, moving patterns.

A sharp, penetrating abdominal pain seized her once more, doubling her floorward. Signals from her brain forced sweeping neurological impulses within her to the point of least resistance. A low guttural cry forced its way through her throat, outward across her tongue, past her painted lips, and against the white walls of the room she occupied. It padded off the mirror, as it reached the bedroom. A second moan, more deliberate, more course framed itself in her deepest womanhood, into the bedroom and down the hall, throughout the remainder of the house where it swirled, and of itself, died an unacknowledged death. In another second, a third and final, full throated scream demanded anyone's attention. Susan had fully lost all semblance of control. Her life hung in the balance. It felt to her as if her internal organs were exiting her body. Convulsive sobs took her over.

With tears pouring from a well into which she had not as yet ever tapped, she felt a surge of pressure build once more in her diaphragm, her agonized wails renewed. Perhaps heaven or her neighbors might hear her desperation. Heaven alone could change this nightmare into a dream from which she would awaken, and when she did, she would realize it was an incubus —and nothing more. But when the scene didn't reorganize into something less painful and repulsive she urged her body against her torturous anguish toward the phone. Slithering her feet clumsily out of her bloody panties, her excruciatingly impeded locomotion left a meandering trail of blood down the hall and into the kitchen.

Reaching the kitchen table, Susan pulled herself from chair to chair, her pain almost beyond bearing. With her last gasp, she reached the refrigerator, strained to focus on her husband's class schedule taped to the refrigerator door. This required a few long, painful seconds for her eyes to focus, seconds she realized she didn't possess. Comprehension began to leave her, try as she might. About to black out, she leaned heavily against the fridge to steady her body, where her head swam, the circling room swirled about her, and the floor rose to meet her.

Seven: More Children?

Monday, March 23, 1942

"Mrs. Lloyd . . . Susan. Can you hear me?" Someone in a white coat or uniform spoke to her from a long, foggy corridor. Once more and sluggishly, the question presumed itself on her cognition, so that grudgingly, Susan fought for a lucidity so that her immediate context might clarify itself—somewhat. The woman hovering near Susan looked blonde, perhaps pretty. Susan couldn't quite make her out. She wasn't tall, but well-kept, from a hazy sort of perspective. *This woman's movements were weird, out of proportion to . . . to what?*

"Mrs. Lloyd?" From within this woman's voice Susan sensed compassion or something positive. Little else made sense.

More strained minutes floated past. Mrs. Lloyd's mind clarified to the degree that the name tag on the woman's uniform could be absorbed and understood. It read, *"Reeba. . .c"? "Rebca"? One more try.* Blinking to clear the remaining mental cobwebs and moisture from her eyes, it came slowly into focus: "Rebecca." The name lifted Susan's spirit. Rebecca was no longer a fluid, verbal phantom. She was real, and she spoke with a trained and pleasing quality. Rebecca's soothing tenor had so often calmed the most anxious of patients on her ward. *This* was to be, must be, someone Susan Lloyd desperately needed at the moment. Susan would apparently rejoin the living.

"Where . . . am I . . ?" Susan begged. Her dry, parched lips strained to form the words with their usual liquid articulation. Words, always her companions, had betrayed her and came out a throaty slur and unwelcome pain. Susan next attempted to urge her body into a sitting position, speaking to her with precise and racking pain. The one vocal syllable, "Ooooohhhhh," purged itself from her dehydrated mouth, arresting any further motion on Susan's part.

"You're in the hospital, ma'am. No, just lie quietly. You're going to be fine, Mrs. Lloyd," said Rebecca, who took her patient's right wrist in order to check the pulse rate. Susan reached with her other hand and drew Rebecca's hand to her face. Susan needed to be touched warmly. Rebecca indulged her patient.

After several delicious moments, Susan mouthed the words, "Thank you." Forcing herself. Then, "May I have . . ." forced its way out of Susan's mouth in another husky aspiration, prompting a painful coughing spasm. Determined to finish her request no matter what, the patient continued, "May I have some water?" The mere question almost nullified what little energy remained to her. Susan's head fell back against the pillow. She was utterly exhuasted.

"Of course." Rebecca reached back to the night stand where the pitcher of water sat. Beads of water had formed on the outside of the container from the cold liquid it held inside. After tipping the pitcher to the rim of the glass, she poured the contents into it. Susan's eyes remained fixed on the ceiling. The nurse then placed a straw in the glass and brought it to her patient, placing the tip of the straw against Susan's parched lips. Slowly her upper lip parted sufficiently from her lower so that Susan began to draw the water into her mouth hungrily.

"Mrs. Lloyd, please sip it."

Susan did not grasp the instructions and continued to draw heartily on the straw. The reaction of the clear liquid on her tight, sore throat caused Susan to cough and then choke. The sudden pain was almost unbearable, bringing fresh tears and muffled screams of writhing agony that almost brought her to the point of fainting.

Rebecca's experience told her Susan's urge to drink might overcome her patient. She had prepared herself for this eventuality, though. Rebecca's tone did not waver or vary. With great skill, she placed a cold, wet rag on Susan's feverish forehead while Rebecca enfolded her arms around Susan to steady her from further motion. "Shhhhhh, shhhhhh, Susan," she offered. "It's going to be okay. I'm right here. It's okay. Just relax. The doctor stepped out into the hall to talk to your husband. I will get him when I've . . ."

"Stephen!" she forced words, despite the pain, and broke free of Rebecca's comfort. "Stephen."

Stephen, his back to his wife's room, whirled around and rushed through the door. At her bedside, he almost didn't recognize the woman lying under the covers. Her tears had caused her black eyeliner to run haphazardly down her face.

"Stephen!" The words hurt to form and expel. "I think I've lost..." She winced in pain, composed herself, then, "I think I've lost..." Susan could neither complete the whole sentence of what she thought she did not remember nor could she fully contain her emotions. Finally, the words came like an erupting wellhead spewing forth its contents, "I lost our baaaabeee!"

Stephen wrapped his arms around her, embracing her -closely for the next tumultuous minutes, despite her pain. And when it seemed appropriate, he slipped his hand between the seams of the back of her hospital gown and onto her bare, smooth back. With great deliberation he rubbed her long curved frame. Susan supported her chin on his muscled shoulder, propping her head against his cheek. Stephen reciprocated by burying his nose into and among her short, soft, jet-black hair. At his nearness and touch he felt her stubborn muscles tighten, and then release as he applied pressure. It hurt, but it was a good hurt.

When he felt Susan let herself go completely, he welcomed her even more so into the full-blown security of his arms. Each shared the other's sorrow, which for the moment, knew few limits. Neither husband nor wife spoke, except for the occasional spasmed cramp, or the new ache at the reality of their smallest casualty she'd left alone in the toilet, and this painful memory brought further tears. The doctor, having just entered the room, stepped back outside to wait.

When the couple's moment bled itself out, Susan deliberately persuaded herself away from her husband and back to the sheeted mattress. She needed to look full into Stephen, to study him with great care. But it would be through his eyes Susan found her husband. A thin, red aqueous line spread along the lower edge of Stephen's sparse, delicate lashes leading to abrupt cessation at their corners. The red line coalesced into the triangular shaped whites, shading them to half red. Near the bridge of his nose, where the contour concluded softly, a reddening semi-circle spread. It dispatched tiny red fingers in search of the eternal green of his eyes. There was the curvature of his nose, long ago arced from an opposing player's helmet during a game in high school.

Stephen strained not to cry . . . for her sake, and just as probably for his own misunderstood manhood. Making a mess of it, Susan admired his struggle all the more. Small white dots from the room's light reflected off the heather green of his iris. For the first time, Susan noticed just how small and piercing his eyes really were. She cocked her head slightly, absorbing a slight painful jab near her stomach, in wonder at the sight. Despite their diminutive size, she must trust in their capacity to grasp and understand the circumstances they beheld. The dark brown nibs of his irises and the outer green surrounding them staked their own territorial rights over most of the surface of his vision.

Satisfied that he was one with her in this unparalleled tragedy, Susan spoke laconically. Her words came less throaty this time. She reached once more for the glass from which she so gingerly sipped. Satisfied she could make herself understood, she said deliberately: "I lost our baby." The words hung dead about her. Their form found no place to settle, found no one to correct them, to set them aright, no one to straighten the stick bent crooked.

Despite her empty, festering pain, Susan, for some unexplained reason, detested Stephen's obtrusion. Her frown hit its mark, whereupon, Stephen moved away from his wife, puzzled. Unable to explain this emotion to herself satisfactorily, she began searching for someone or *Someone*, upon which to place the blame. It came with the fury of a woman scorned: "If God were a God of love, surely He could have protected my body until the birth date. Surely *He* could. *God* is to be blamed!"

What do I say to this. Stephen fumbled unsatisfactorily with his wife's charges like a football freed from the runner's grip. "Honey, it's okay. Would you believe me if I told you this wasn't your fault? Surely it's not *God's*. Susan, the doctor wants to tell you some things."

Stephen knew only how to address miscues like this one, and always from the standpoint of a twenty-year-old student athlete, good enough to earn a full ride from TCU, which he really didn't need. After all, his father was Marcus Lloyd. But even Marcus probably couldn't address these types of questions that needed the most attention at this moment. Stephen couldn't understand what his wife felt, no matter how hard he tried. The headiest issue Stephen had faced thus far centered on why the shortstop had missed the fly ball in the Baylor game? Why didn't the linebacker take on the pulling guard against Tech so he could make the tackle? Whose faults were these? The coaches wanted answers. He and his teammates wanted answers. Someone was at fault. But was God really and truly at fault for this? Should anyone charge God? Surely not.

Stephen had no adequate idea *how* or *if* he should bring his manhood into Susan's world, a world he could observed only from the sidelines. He knew very little about makeup or a woman's need to shop, or why they could spend thirty to forty-five minutes coordinating their shoes with their dresses, or why they had to talk so much. The energy his wife put into these things was far beyond his not yet matured mind. Yet he always enjoyed the conclusion.

"Mrs. Lloyd, I'm Dr. Reymond." The doctor, rather than extending his hand, stepped nearer his patient. "I'm so very sorry for your loss. You probably know that you've had a miscarriage. This . . . this would have been your first child? Is that right?"

"Yes." She turned her attention from the doctor back to her husband. "Oh, Stephen . . . I wanted this child, *your* child . . . *ours* . . ." Then, ". . . because you are leaving me . . . I needed him to remind me of you, don't you *see*?" Susan's whole countenance begged for a hearing.

Once more, Susan shook the bed slightly as she cried, although she emitted little sound. That painful question of the doctor couldn't be avoided—for medical reasons. It had to be asked, just the same.

"Mrs. Lloyd, for some reason that none of us understands to our complete satisfaction, your body simply was unable to accept the new . . . the new child inside of you. How I wish I could be of more help to you in understanding this. But time will help." His words trailed off as if they were caustic, little lifeless things.

Time will help. How does this man know what will help me? I am so angry. Susan stared blankly out the window, not listening any further to the man's words . . . if there were to be more. Their sound had traveled into her ear canals to some distant, mystified part of her brain making the moment even more terrible. It was all academic now.

"I want you to get some rest, Mrs. Lloyd. We will be running some tests in the morning. But you need to take it easy for now. Your body has been through a very difficult time, and you really do need the rest. Nurse, give Mrs. Lloyd one of these so she will rest." Dr. Reymond pointed to the name of the medication he'd written on her chart.

"Yes, doctor."

Susan turned from the window to stare up at her husband. He'd been her savior in so many ways. Even she knew he couldn't make this small death go away. So, Susan looked for the next best thing from her man, hope. Stephen's expression, unfortunately, was one of absorption. She remembered seeing him on the sidelines with the same blank stare the day TCU lost to the Jesuits of Fordham, *of all schools*, twenty-eight to fourteen.

"I lost our baby, Stephen. I'm so sorry. Please forgive me." She was all but beseeching Stephen for absolution.

His dispassionate eyes said what was in his mind: he couldn't change the score. His words, on the other hand, were more affirmative. "Honey, there's nothing to forgive. It just wasn't meant to be. We've got plenty of time. We're young . . . and . . . and we're going to have a beautiful family one day. You'll see."

Stephen had earned a co-captain's position at strong safety. He'd won it by being hard on himself and anyone else who didn't play up to his potential. Just yesterday, at spring practice, he'd clobbered the cornerback when he missed a tackle, ran right over him to make it himself. Stephen came back, picked the man up and then threatened him.

Women, on the other hand, didn't accede to threats very well; he'd learned that once the hard way, from Susan. She, for her part, had to admonish Stephen to come home after practice. He had to learn to quit slapping her on the butt like one of the guys when she did something of which he approved. College ball often brought out the beast in him. He could turn into a monster if he even smelled a football field. Susan was making some headway. He had bought her flowers and cards two weeks ago. She thought she'd keep him. He had potential.

"But Stephen, you're going to leave me alone, and what if something happens to you, and I never . . ."

"Susan! I'm not . . . nothing's going to *happen* to me. I love you, Honey. You have to think positively about this."

"Think positively?! I can't think positively! Don't you understand me, Stephen? What's positive about losing our baby?" With that, all of her feminine cognitive abilities leapt through the window, last seen running down the street. The desire to hit the man she loved almost overpowered her, because he could not understand what she felt. Then she felt guilty for verbalizing her emotions so disagreeably, surreptitiously wanting to clobber him.

Susan reached carefully behind her head to retrieve one of the pillows and place it on her knees. She then leaned forward and buried her face in its white softness, because this was the one position that didn't hurt so much. By hiding, she would force the world to give back her child, or, maybe, just maybe, leave her alone for the time being. But the bed shook once more. Her dark hair was by now wet, matted with perspiration, and every trace of her apple blossom skin was tucked away from sight. Her grotesqueness hidden.

Stephen was an engineer. Engineers constructed things where nothing had been before. They are organized. They calculate costs, ensuring buildings and bridges are constructed upon solid principles of organization. They reason problems through, based upon facts and solid, time-tested figures. Then they test their hypothesis and act upon what they have deduced. Stephen's solid, logical, and formula-hyphenated world didn't mesh well with his wife's broken and subjective universe, expressed by appearance, affection and feelings. Susan held time-tested, annoying feminine emotions and intuition she could and would use on him to her advantage. He could not reconstruct in the coming days what had so thoroughly been destroyed today. With this woman, Stephen was lost. His athletic, male, logic wandered her about aimlessly.

"Mr. Lloyd, may I speak with you for a minute?" asked the doctor, motioning him to step outside the room.

Susan, without looking up from her pillow reached for and seized Stephen's arm so that she might make physical contact with him for safety's sake. She wanted and needed to inform him that she still adored him. "No Stephen, *please* don't leave me."

"Dr. Reymond, would you give us *just* a few more minutes?"

"Certainly."

Several minutes passed. The attractive nurse reentered Susan's small, antiseptic white room with its one cushioned chair, its one window, and its one picture—a tree in a field. Rebecca held a small white paper cup containing a single pill, which she handed to Susan. Rebecca apologized for intruding on them. Susan drew the cup containing the pill in it to her mouth, placing its contents on her tongue. Rebecca next handed Susan a glass of water, which Susan drank, and the transaction was complete. Assured that Susan had swallowed her medication as directed, the nurse smiled at her, winked, and left the room. Rebecca's wink communicated volumes. Rebecca wore a wedding ring. Perhaps she too had lost a baby?

Holding and being held in Stephen's arms, she eventually succumbed to the effects of the drug. As Stephen felt her grip ease, he eased her back to a position more conducive to sleep, and then tiptoed into the hall to find the doctor writing on Susan's chart.

"Mr. Lloyd, I could give you a lot of medical jargon, but that wouldn't be of much use to you right now. So may I speak plainly?"

"Yes."

"I don't hold out much hope for more children. I'm quite concerned that the damage may have been too extensive. The tests we run tomorrow should give us more information to work with."

"How did this happen, doctor? I didn't even know she was expecting. My wife didn't say a word to me."

"That doesn't surprise me," Dr. Reymond offered. He set his hand gently on Stephen's shoulder, which at this male-to-male contact invited Stephen to also let go of his own forlorn tensions. As he did Stephen lowered his head and wept. The doctor led him out of earshot of Susan's room, out of public view, and into one of the empty lounge areas on the ward.

When Stephen gained control of his emotions and faculties, the doctor continued. He explained his suspicions and the facts of Susan's condition as he had examined her when she entered the emergency room. The phone from down the hall at the nurse's station rang. Within a few seconds Rebecca walked into the waiting room where the two men sat talking. She interrupted, "Excuse me, Mr. Lloyd. I'm sorry to disturb you, sir, but your father is on the phone."

Stephen excused himself, followed the nurse back to the station, and picked up the uncradled receiver. The well-engineered Lloyd facade cracked once again as Stephen exhaled the words, "She lost the baby, father." Long, heavy seconds passed, and neither man spoke. When Stephen felt an inkling of control sweep over his searching mind, he at last was able to lay the situation before the family patriarch, his father, Marcus Josiah Fonteneau Lloyd. He then told his father he needn't come. He thought they would be okay.

The next few hours did pass, but barely. Time became a vacuous element for Stephen to endure while Susan slept. Several of the coaches, students and teammates came by to check on them—to offer condolences or help, or whatever seemed appropriate. But there wasn't anything anyone could do. Bo Griffin broke the chair in which he sat.

The athletes like Stephen and Bo could not rationalize this event from any other male perspective than winning or losing. They felt sad for Stephen. To him the score looked bad, but they knew Stephen, and he'd come back better than ever. A defensive lineman thinks about the man he is about to crash into, and then to the ball carrier, but not much farther. Bo wearied himself as to how he should think about Susan. Should he say to her, "way to go, Susan," or "it's not so bad, Mrs. Lloyd," or "hang tough?" No, he'd just slap her on the behind, and tell her to get back in there. He'd played with a broken foot and sprained knee against Tech. This wasn't *so* bad. Bo finally left his consoling, such as it was, in the waiting room. The cafeteria was down on the second floor.

Looking out the window of the waiting room Stephen thought to himself about his first day and first practice at Texas A&M. He was single then. He'd had to transfer back home to Ft. Worth when he married Susan. Only single male athletes were allowed to attend A&M. Now, TCU had offered a new, albeit familiar, sprawling world to examine with his new wife. From their hospital waiting room the campus he would soon leave felt aloof to him. It wasn't aloof of course, but it seemed to him that way.

At eight fifteen Stephen noticed a blurring movement to his left. He recognized the voice arriving with the motion. It was Susan's mother. She must have raced from Longview in record time.

"Stephen! Where's Susan?"

"Michelle. She's in 308, but she's sleeping. I think it's okay to peek in, but that's all the doctor will allow. He said not to wake her if she's sleeping."

"Stephen, are *you* okay?" asked Perry Alcott, Susan's father. The tears came afresh.

Somehow the night passed, and the new day, such as it revealed itself, presented few, if any positives. This indignant "theft" tormented Stephen, because in his protected environment he couldn't remember such unblunted pain. Marcus saw to that. Stephen remembered Ready, his first Cocker Spaniel. He died of old age on the eve of Stephen's ninth birthday. That could not compare to this, but it was all he had. The anticipation and adventure of leaving Texas to earn his wings as an Army Air Cadet faded with the night. *To what purpose would he leave his wife now*, he mused.

Eight: Father Mctammany

Monday, March 6, 1967

The situation had not changed since Stephen and Michael returned from the Wilson's. Damien was still dead, the scotch in his glass was almost gone. Thinking about and re-experiencing that first of three miscarriages caused the color red to flash across Stephen's thoughts. He was unconsciously looking at a red pillow the kids used to recline on while watching TV. *Red. Red. No, it was orange-red. Orange-red hair. Yes. Father Ed's orange-red hair. Father Ed* . . . He was the biggest red-headed man Stephen had ever known. He might have been at least a head taller than the men Stephen played ball with at TCU and A&M. Father Ed probably possessed the most uncoordinated amalgamation of facial and body features Stephen had ever seen cobbled to one frame. No priest Stephen had ever known compared in physical appearance to this giant of a man. One would have to search high and low to find a better friend, however.

Father Ed had come into their lives at one of the most difficult times Susan and Stephen had faced in their young marriage. He was there for them. Where was he tonight? Maybe Stephen would try and find Father Ed and seek his religious guidance about this, or maybe not, but what a man.

Tuesday, March 24, 1942

Father Ed McTammany tapped heavily against room 308's slightly ajar heavy door. Susan's hospital room was not large, a white sanctuary of sorts, currently half in shadow from the closed curtains. The whole visage matched her day-old mood. The morning sun had risen bright and promising, the light fighting for ascendancy through the fabric. The sun's appearance outside was unforgivably out of step with the tenor ruminating inside of Susan's soul. Stephen found little to illuminate his mood.

"Oh, Father Ed. How good of you to come," Susan offered, even though her spirits did not match her words. "Please, come in."

Father Ed, as he preferred, poked his flamethrower red hair into the room first. He did this probably more as a sign of courtesy to prepare his ailing flock for the physical menagerie that would accompany what followed. In rapid succession his sky blue eyes attempted adjustment from the hall's brightness to the penumbra of Susan's room. Next came his somewhat bent and dented nose, lending to it wild speculation as to the *vera causa* of its condition or demise, depending on one's angle of consideration. For its original and intended use he relied on the olfactories of the other priests. His mouth curved upward to reveal an *almost* full set of teeth. His ears surely must have belonged to someone else before they became his. Each ear protruded outward like strange looking doors on opposite sides of a building. They were uncarefully shaped afterthoughts to his larger-than-necessary head. His face, presented a sea of reddish-brown freckles, having adapted prudently to his facial skin's peaks and valleys, dents and dings. Father Ed had earned the sum of these negatives on the football field.

Father Ed McTammany's abrupt presentation to a world unready for him elicited so many varied responses, he had grown accustomed to the distraction he was. And he was, without pretense and preparation, comic relief set against the background of injured sheep mired in the hurts of the world they and he peopled.

Father Ed had played football—tackle, both ways, for Notre Dame. A knee injury sidelined him in the Michigan State game his senior year. He had not followed in his father's footsteps as a brick mason, but rather, he'd had taken the vows to enter the priesthood. So here, dressed in his black ministerial suit, dress Rabat vest with heavily starched white linen clerical collar, sacrament case and hat in hand, he stood, large, eager to assist, and awkward. Despite his appearance, the man's intelligence brought almost dismay when unleashed on the unruly. His was a quick wit. He was also well seasoned in his pastoral skills and almost overly charitable in his concern for his flock. Father Ed never not simply entered a room, he bruised it.

The just-entered Father Ed had become the Lloyd's priest since they returned from College Station, Texas. Susan's motionless body lay covered and parallel with the wall. Only her neck and head protruded from the covers. Physically, she communicated an absence of desire to speak with anyone not immediately connected with her, including Stephen or her parents. The nurses and doctors were exempted of course. The priest motioned to Stephen with his hat that he would occupy one of the extra chairs.

Susan shifted her head slightly, adjusting it sufficiently to observe the room's newest occupant. She sighed deeply from her gut and brought her hands to her eyes to hide them from the emotion that once again threatened to invade the moment. *Would her tears ever stop*, wondered Stephen. Susan knew she looked a fright. Still, the priest said nothing. He'd visited this moment many times, several times in this very room. Experience had taught him moments such as this, called for reserve and patience.

Five minutes elapsed with no report from the clergy sitting near the foot of the bed, the priest's silence becoming unbearable for Susan. With contorted energy she didn't know she possessed, and despite the shooting pain, the woman raised herself to a full sitting position, and the priest saw it coming. When she could accept and force back the pain's vehemence for the duration of the task to which she had set herself presently, she spoke from the brooding animus deep within her. "Why, Father Ed? What did I do? Why is God punishing me?" Then she grimaced.

From his early years of miscalculated poor judgment, Father Ed knew not to *react* to a woman in obvious turmoil and pain. Enough women had pummeled him verbally for doing so that he had learned to wait—first. He blinked, and then he began the process of standing, unfolding his frame from the chair to its full protuberance. The chair groaned, probably delighted the excessive weight had been lifted from it. He placed his hat in the chair behind him. Slowly, almost silently and most deliberately the big priest made his way to Susan's side. He said nothing, even though his eyes never left hers. Those eyes of his shone even more crystalline blue, so splendidly lucid, the closer he moved to her. It was, despite the girth of him, an wonderful, un-bruising sensation. Having found the spot he'd chosen next to the bed, Father Ed knelt, placing his thick knee and shoe toe on the polished tile floor, as he had done a thousand times on the sidelines. The other shoe balanced him. The contact with hard floor, rather than dirt or grass against his kneecap, made him wince. Now he was almost eye-to-eye with Susan Lloyd.

Father Ed stared firmly into her wide, forbidding eyes for a full five seconds, without speaking. Her face was still quite hard, pent-up emotion ready to burst forth. Father Ed peered back, fully in command of his presence. Priest and parishioner stared at one another. Then the priest wiggled his ears. The extraordinary combination of his indescribable cast-iron face, his light, dancing eyes, his never-still freckles that had to have been tattooed on, and his imposing domination of any and all situations altered the course of Susan's disposition for that singular, glorious and blessed moment.

Imperceptibly and simultaneously her previously glaring eyes widened, their refulgent glow returned. The fierce steel dots of her irises dilated slightly, replaced by a softer, rounder shape. The vivid blue of her pupils flattened in their magnificent circumference, and her high cheekbones surrendered their fisted anger. The tension drained away from her face, and she succumbed to the familiar, smooth silk of bursting joy.

Susan's down-turned mouth crept to neutral and then widened. Each corner edged upward, battling against an irresistible force, giving free access to polished white teeth. The priest's Dumbo ears had brought a smile to, and established its foothold inside her heart. Susan's hand reached to cover the giggle building behind her teeth. Her nostrils flared, and her appearance mutated into infectious laughter, which, once let loose, ached. "Oh, that's so funny. Father Ed, what would I do without you?" she loosed.

Father Ed raised his mountainous self and hobbled back painfully to his former seat to retrieve his hat. He lowered his girth slowly, once more into an ill prepared, wooden structure that seemed to wince as it received his full emphasis. He crossed his arms, thoroughly delighted at the "trick" he'd taught himself one rainy winter's day when he was eight years old.

"Young lady," he said, "don't make me have to do that again." Susan had given her mind and body full to this much-needed laughter. Her tears flowed freely this time, not from heartbreak, but from cackling mirth at his wonderful, storm-beaten facial good humor. He had not said what she feared he would say—not yet. Susan wondered if he might just saved her from this event, perhaps by saying nothing. From her pastor, she hoped to regain the knowledge that life could indeed envelope death.

Stephen didn't know quite whether to laugh or slump onto the bed from the past hours of adamantine stress. Stephen's smile acknowledged the good Father's alteration of the sum of his worst fears. Father Ed looked at Stephen and winked, "Works every time I do that."

Turning back to Susan, their priest all but pontificated, as if issuing some formal edict. "Now listen, Susan. Our Holy Catholic Church doesn't have a lot to say on this particular subject, but, if you'll permit me, I'd like to read what the catechism does tells us. And then we'll see what we can't figure out, okay?"

Having broken all barriers into her soul, the priest could do no wrong. Susan loved him for his compassion and good humor, if for no other reason.

"Would that be all right, Susan?" he inquired again.

Susan looked away, then at her fingernails. The heavy situation was suddenly gathering momentum, and it had to be attended to. The priest would not allow this the slightest freedom without examining it closely. But Susan was not prepared to discuss it despite the fact *it* was all she could think about. Stephen reached over, and taking her hand in his, said, "Susan, let Father Ed say what he needs to say." Inhaling, Susan nodded her head in the affirmative.

Father Ed retrieved a small, black Bible from the pocket of his suit coat. It was a bantam, care-worn copy, with many of its pages dog-eared or torn. Yellow tape was perhaps all that held the small, rectangular enterprise together. In his business, Father Ed had so often referred to its authority, rather than his own. Susan watched the book disappear among his big hands. Her interest rose, wondering what the book might say—to her. The man flipped through the Bible to locate the copy of the catechism's instruction he'd written out the day before on a small piece of paper.

Father Ed stalled for time, turning pages. He knew what the Church said on this thorny subject—very little. Purely from an ecclesiastical perspective however, the key to this visit would be Susan's faith. In his mind, the next few minutes depended on *her*.

He located what he needed, and the pages stilled. "Here we go. I went back over it in my study last night. When, in this case we have an unbaptized infant, the catechism tells us, with reference to the salvation of these individuals, that since the child did not reach the stage where he or she came to full term, we can only entrust the child to the mercy of God."

Father Ed's eyes didn't leave the page he held before him. He waited on Susan, pretending to see if the catechism might say more, which it did not, and he knew it did not. Hearing nothing from the bed he looked up into her delicate and lovely face. Her sparkling eyes watered, their saddening misty appearance overcame the hope she longed for but knew would not come. The lightened mood of the previous moments had gone completely. Would her priest say more? No, or else he would have. Would he banish her worst fears? No, or else he would have. No woman had ever seemed so fragile to him than did Susan Lloyd at that instant. The sun had fully dropped past the horizon of her life leaving an increasing dark hue in its place.

The priest remained motionless and quiet, praying within himself. Susan's demeanor asked, *How would she know if God would have mercy on her child? How?* The priest's answer lacked any real satisfaction for her. It did not assuage her growing panic. The Church, which he represented, would not satisfy her. The bloody mass she left in the toilet days ago came flooding back, her mind resting on the bloody tissue floating aimless and lifeless. How horrible this was! As quickly as the memory had regathered in her mind the unformed child dissolved amid the urine and blood and water of the porcelain white watery grave in which she had last seen it. How could such a small lifeless object she would never know crush her like this?

From her bed, and miles away from what had been her baby, Susan felt totally helpless to sort this out in light of her church's beliefs. She wasn't certain that they would ever coincide with her own. Father Ed could wiggle his ears until eternity dawned, but he couldn't make this ache go away. He couldn't heal her or restore her child's life. His dilemma was fixed: he dare not alter this sterile Church dogma in order to make Susan feel better. He was tempted to, though.

"How do I trust my child to God's mercy, Father?" Weariness had returned to her voice and her body. "How do I believe something like that? *I* don't even know how to trust Him for my own salvation," she blurted, wiping her tears with an agitated, clinched fist. "Just hoping I'll see my child again is not *good enough*! It's not *enough*!"

The giant priest and Susan's dialogue rose and fell for the next five minutes, mostly his. Father Ed offered the sacraments as comfort. The sacraments over, a dull gloss enveloped Susan's gaze, suggesting to the good father he should say his goodbyes. The next visit perhaps would be more cordial. Ed concluded with an appropriate prayer, and then he left the room, the atmosphere in the room more brittle than before his arrival. The priest closed the door behind him. The room that had so suddenly been vacated by Father Ed's huge presence, could not remove the emptiness enveloping Susan's soul.

As the minutes and hours ticked by Susan grew angrier, and then more restless. Stephen handed Susan his own rosary beads, the only gesture he felt appropriate. She accepted them, rolled the round beads in her fingers, staring outward but not seeing. Instead of using them for their intended purpose, she glared down at them, mocking them. They were useless.

Stephen watched as she rolled the small, dark beads upon the tender flesh between her fingers. He knew she wasn't praying the Rosary. Not this time. Her face spoke of anything but prayer. He'd seen this look on Fred's face when he dropped that touchdown pass against Southern Methodist. Susan reached over to the table to her right, and opening the drawer, she dropped the beads in. Then she closed it.

Nine: Miss Susan Alcott

Monday, March 6, 1967

Returning to the couch, Stephen slipped into unfamiliar meanderings and listless thoughts, musings that ultimately went nowhere. Recalling so much and bringing it all into the present, fatigued him on the one hand, but on the other, didn't vitiate him. He took a sip, then another, and a third. Imperceptibly, his past once again seeped and hemorrhaged back and became the present once more.

The Priest, Father Ed, hadn't any answers to speak of. He had said the things he was trained to say, that he felt comfortable saying. He certainly believed them, but he wasn't married. *How could he know the pain couples feel when their baby dies before it has a chance to live?*

The clock bonged its pronouncement eleven times. The lamp beside the couch cast its glow about the room leaving the remainder of the Lloyd homestead in darkness and retrograde. *Odd*, he thought. *Weren't more lights on? Had Susan come down and turned off . . . No. Ginny did, most likely.* Stephen had been so preoccupied with his thoughts he'd seen and heard nothing. *Strange. This is good scotch*, he thought. His neck and shoulders still ached, but the alcohol was beginning to dilute the pain. He'd write the maker of this hooch and let him know just how good it was. He must have strained his muscles sitting here, or when he drove out to Smitty's. That was it.

Question: now that the pain had almost subsided, how was he going to shut his mind off so he could go up and get some sleep? The scotch couldn't do everything. He'd also write the distiller with some suggestions. Stephen ran his finger along the rim of the glass. He was thinking too much. He stood, stretched, and heard Susan's slippers on the stairs.

"Honey, are you coming to bed?" she asked from the gray darkness of the stairs, well above him and to his right.

Perhaps it was the shadowed light that wrapped around her as she stood there holding the stair rail. She was still a gorgeous woman. This *was* good scotch. A mischievous sort of grin crossed his face.

"What?" she inquired. "You're smiling. Why?" She wanted him to share his reason with her. She wanted him to say she was lovely, and that he loved her more than anything or anyone. She wanted to hear him say it. She needed *his* comfort for the night ahead. Tomorrow would misappropriate, glom its cares on to everyone and everything tenaciously. But tonight, she wanted him near her, within breathing distance.

"I . . . you just look so pretty standing there. Like the first time I saw you. Remember?"

"I look horrible. How can you say I look pretty?" Then she asked, "Stephen, is that . . . scotch?" Her words trailed off. Disappointment welled within her. Now she knew where the compliments originated. "Stephen, *please* come to bed. Leave that drink, and come up to bed." The sight of her husband with a glass of whiskey in his hand and at a time such as this concerned Susan deeply. She could barely remember him drinking.

That women confound men is a universal. It followed therefore that Susan would naturally confuse Stephen's state of mind. She actually did want to hear how pretty her husband thought she looked. He knew that and acted upon it. He believed it was indeed true, and he knew she wanted to hear this, but she replied with an expected how unattractive she thought she appeared. Made no sense whatsoever. To Susan, her hair *was* a mess, but she loved his attention. In her womanly preoccupations, the source of her husband's adulation was purely the scotch. To Stephen, it bolstered him to action otherwise suspended by the grainy rawness of his pain that he dared not share with her. He could not tell her men die horribly in war. Everyone needs to get over it.

To Stephen, Susan could be bald, tarred and feathered, and still be attractive, be he drunk or sober. Susan wanted him to be able to look beyond the obvious and see her as she truly was. He had done just that, and it still didn't matter. Then she did what Stephen knew she would do: she adjusted her hair and straightened her robe. "I remember." Susan's response was playful, maybe capricious. Still, she did worry about how much he drank tonight, though. *Was he weaving a bit standing there looking at her? Why had he thought of that particular long ago time*, she wondered. His comment was a positive on a day that had been tainted forever with the sting of death for those not accustomed to it. She'd take what she could get, leaving Stephen to scratch his head.

Instead of moving toward her to accompany her up to bed as she entreated, Stephen dumped himself rather clumsily back onto the couch. This was *good* scotch. He turned his eyes from her to other things—back to the consuming negatives.

Susan bit her lip. Something was wrong, *very wrong*. Her husband didn't drink, and this scene appeared incredulous to her. He sat there staring ahead, oblivious to everything, including her. The moment had foundered, *but on what?* They had been talking just seconds before about his appraisal of her, and now she'd vanished from his radar. Susan didn't know what to do—or think.

For perhaps the first time in her marriage to Stephen, she felt lost. He had been so predictable. He had given her two plus decades of certainty. She could read his wants and needs like a book. Stephen Lloyd wasn't rocket science. He was a man, a wonderful and good man. He gave her purpose, and he needed *her*. He was devoted to *her* alone. He had brought her out of so many somber moods she couldn't count them all. He loved their children. She couldn't want for a better provider. He doted over her. He brought her flowers in memory of the babies she had, and those they had lost. Their intimate moments he would stretch into hours of deep pleasure. How she loved *this* man. She knew every inch of his body, even as he knew hers.

But right now, right this instant, she felt uncertain about their relationship. A dark, shadowed pall had drifted over it. It came in with him tonight. She felt its reification when he said he didn't know how he felt, that he felt a little lost. Earlier he looked scared. She glimpsed it around the corners of his eyes, heard its flit in the tone of Stephen's voice, and saw its heft upon his body when he sat down next to her. If she tried to tell her mother about her suspicions, what would she say?

Stephen hadn't come in and announced that he was dying of cancer, or he was having a nervous breakdown. He didn't need to go to the hospital that she could detect. This uncertainty was more insidious than many maladies that are so often not so obvious. The scotch spoke volumes too. Perhaps she was making far too much out of this. *Sleep on it. Evaluate it tomorrow*, Susan told herself.

She started to say something, but the tiniest parcel of a word came out. She took one more step down toward him, stopped, and then turned. The intimacy she had planned was now banished from her desires. From the corner of her right eye she saw that he'd not moved. He sat stroking his finger over his cheek, obviously deep in thought. *About what*, she worried. She knew what, but how deep was Damien's death pushing itself into her husband? Wasn't it painfully clear? Once more, she tried to speak. Then Susan closed her fears off and pushed her way back up the steps, her heart, dead weight.

Reaching the upper floor Susan allowed her eyes to readjust so that she could discern the slightly darker openings of the doors to the children's rooms. There were the familiar smells of sweaty socks, grass stained blue jeans, and the cat's litter box. Brit, the dog, had his own redolence. Regardless of the habitual and mundane things of her life, she felt alone. This wasn't the familiar kind of loneliness, when Stephen was away on a trip and would be home in a day or two. Increasing mental isolation, like the death that tramped in with Stephen and Michael, held its own pervasive and sinister qualities she could not afford to accommodate.

The long, dark hallway, which she alone occupied, benefited not a little the various moods clamoring about her heart and mind for mastery. Susan leaned against the wall, closed her eyes and breathed softly. She turned and walked into their bedroom. The moon had now risen to a sufficient angle to shine hazily through the window. The breeze pushed the curtain inward revealing a muted shaft of lumination, alighting squarely on their unoccupied bed, highlighting its emptiness. Only her side was turned down, and this too added to her consternation. An unexpected urgency assaulted her to rush down the stairs and become part of her husband's disquiet. But for some unexplained reason, and stronger than her compulsion, Susan resisted this urge. Something was very, *very wrong*, and its unfamiliarity frightened her.

Melancholy is a sickening woman, an insipid vagrant. Miss Pensive sat with Susan on her side of the bed. There she lay down onto its coolness, from which she imbibed. How long had it been since she originally lay down tonight? The clock glowed 11:42 p.m. She wasn't sleepy now. Her mind, like that of Stephen's was restless, awake, and in need of something to make it go. *You look so pretty . . . like the first time I saw you. Do you remember?* He'd said that. She remembered. Susan remembered so well that she almost felt the heat of the stage lights. She remembered those warm, long ago days when it was she, her talent, the people she had entertained, and the boys she had dated . . . the night Stephen and she had met . . . a glorious, unexpected gift it was.

Wednesday, July 3, 1940

Susan held her breath. The unheralded announcement each contestant had labored so long to hear charged the vivifying air. A very lucky Miss Someone was about to receive the title. Overhead, stage lights pricked like hot needles, their sharp, overzealous compresses against Susan's face and shoulders, growing hotter and more pointed, more stifling the longer she—the longer *they* all stood—waiting. So little breeze circulated among the final five gowned women standing so very near each other. This meant the possibility of perspiration, and with it, the loss of composure.

None of this discomfort altered the ever-smiling blondes, two brunettes, auburns, and "every-hair-shade-in-between." Certain of those women intimidated had Susan, their beauty wearying and their talent mystifying her. With each beauty contest since age fourteen, Susan had cultivated an ability to discipline her mind and energies toward the task at hand: improvement in her walk, her posture, her talent and her smile. Yet, the always-fluid, inhospitable stress remained. It awoke with her, and it crawled under the covers at night with her.

Scholarships were also at stake. This one goal, perhaps more than any other inducement, kept her returning for one more go, one more push, and one more title. The University of Texas had been her life-long pursuit, and now it lay just within her grasp—*maybe* tonight . . . maybe. Susan's empathetic nature extended toward the few girls she observed "freezing" on stage. Such emergencies, however, only created within her an inner drive to excel and not replicate their weaknesses. Along the way, Susan had come to befriend and love some of these contestants, some of whom would remain life-long friends. Nonetheless, it all came down to this night, and inside of it now, every girl remained alone. She had made it into the top ten, and now, the five finalists. Susan Alcott could only ask for one, perhaps two more things: Miss Texas, and then the unthinkable, Miss America.

The Mineral Wells Jaycee's had spread the red carpet. The past week had flown by. These gracious Texas folk had done their best to assist the girls through this exhausting three-day gala, concluding with tonight, the final night. Miss Susan Alcott had performed Debussy's *Clare de Lune*, quite well, she thought. Susan swayed and bent over her work revealing her maturity, intensity, acumen and buoyant spirit. Her mother and piano teacher, Michelle, perceived Susan's womanhood had reached an irretrievable juncture. Susan's spirit had magically intertwined artfully amid the half and quarter notes, the chords and the pedals, all of which she meshed into a symbiotic subjugation of her favorite piece. Her years of piano had peaked at the precise moment in time and space.

In the swimsuit contest the previous night, Susan exhibited her nineteen-year-old figure, alluring and full. She had also communicated her poise and above average intellect when asked by the host to hold forth on the two most socially pertinent issues of the day: unemployment and the lingering depression. Here and now, four women and Susan stood somewhere between overheated and fainting, relief and desperation, each dying to know the outcome of their efforts.

Susan could not see her mother and dad sitting in the third row beaming at her. It was easy for them to remember the little girl they had raised, nursing her bruised ego when mean Sister Georgiana spanked her hand for poor classroom posture and inattention. They bandaged her scrapes when she fell skating on the sidewalk. Michelle comforted her when Benny Leonard broke up with her for Harriett Forsner, and her daddy brooded over her mental and physical anguish when one of the hotel employees attempted to have his way with her during her second beauty pageant. Regardless, here she stood at the apex of her life, sandwiched between several of the finalists.

Perry Alcott didn't hesitate to ask himself why female competitors hold hands with each other at times like these. Instead, he succumbed to the obsequious tears coercing their way from his heart, momentarily interrupting his vision. Gravity called their liquid weight downward.

This proud papa struggled to halt this ostentatious emotional *tour de force* by retrieving his hankie for the inevitable mopping up of his male facade. Michelle looked at her husband, amazed to see him suspended freely over the precipice of such emotional upheaval. She smiled and then turned to await the judge's verdict. The 1940 Miss Texas pageant was almost in the books.

"Our fourth runner up is . . . Miss Longview, Miss Susan Michelle Alcott," Gavin Vandermeer reported proudly to the audience. The applause was hearty. Susan smiled the best-disappointed smile she could muster. She stepped forward to curtsy and then retreat. She could not have given more of herself to the past seventy-two hours. How had she not done better? Four other women had bested her, none of whose names she heard the moderator speak. Her withdrawal had came full, although internal.

Gavin reached the conclusion of all things pageant as he announced Miss Texas, Port Arthur's Miss Gloria Ann Byrns. Susan, like all the other girls, joined in congratulating her, but nothing would assuage Susan's sense of failure. No further competitions remained for Miss Longview. All the previous toil of the contests, their dozens of piano pieces memorized, their battles of nerves, their enthusiastic smiles often amounting to psychological forgery, the sometimes vicious nature of competing women, and their financial costs her parents absorbed, would now slip silently into her memory album. Nothing gave her aid and comfort. Even the pageants she had won or placed well in made little difference at this point. For this terrible and final moment, Susan must lay those times aside, not to retrieve them.

In the audience, fifteen rows back from Susan's parents, sat a young, Texas A&M athlete and engineering student. He was infatuated or smitten, as the case may be, not with the just named Miss Texas, but with one of the finalists—Susan Alcott—Miss Susan Michelle Alcott. Stephen's heart pounded in his chest as he visually grazed over her beauty.

There was a point of dissimilarity in this woman that he did not find in the others, but what was it? At some level, each woman became a similitude of her fellows. The thought seemed intellectually disreputable of course, but his eye, —and his heart, repeatedly reestablished contact with Susan. He felt flushed beholding her, his hormonal radiator cap feeling the building pressure as he watched her move fluidly, womanly, about the stage.

Susan searched for her parents, and when she found them, she embraced them and wept. In a crystalline pure trice, she understood the significance of the moment. There was nothing to do but to bleed off the wellhead of emotions she had restrained for the past days.

Stephen studied her through the multiplying lens of his binoculars. Her body was perfect, curvilinear and protrusive—all woman. All the women were attractive physically, to be sure. Susan was not the most glamorous. *What was it about her?* He liked that second runner up's blonde's hair, long, flowing over her shoulders. Susan's was short and simple, most elegant, like Claudette Colbert, Myrna Loy, or his long time favorite, Joan Bennett. Soft waves rippled around her head as she moved. She had pinned one side back with a white flower. Her makeup was muted and natural, not over done. Her lips shone bright red to accent her mouth perfect mouth and lips. She was the most attractive, the most fetching, and certainly the most confident woman on stage. Nothing else mattered to Stephen Lloyd.

Having finally stated it to himself, his architectural engineering bent seized the reigns, having fully appraised her body as structurally sound and pleasing to the eye—in every way—from head to foot. *Oh yes,* yelled his manhood.

Making such a mental checklist certainly lacked romantic vagaries, but how else did one size up a woman one wanted desperately to meet? He suspected this female might not give him the time of day. A number of women, on the other hand, were vying for young Mr. Lloyd's attention in Ft. Worth and College Station.

Ten: A Lie

❯─┤─◀❯─⊙─❮▶─┤─❰

Wednesday, July 3, 1940

"Excuse me, sir." Someone to Stephen's left tapped him on the shoulder. "Sir, we need to start cleaning up. Are you all right?"

"Oh. Yes. I was just sitting here thinking. I'm sorry. I'll get out of your way."

With the house lights turned up Stephen lingered for one second more, probing his mind to see just how his world could include this woman.

"Yes." He excused himself once more, stood, and surveyed two possible paths, only one of which he felt compelled to explore. The clean up crew was fully immersed in the business of sweeping and picking up the discarded programs strewn about. How had he edged so far—so *dangerously* far—from his playboy philosophy and his last assignment in so short a time? It was Stephen Lloyd who'd confessed to his teammates and frat brothers that marriage, if it was for him, stretched into the distant future. He couldn't see the altar from his vantage point. "Playing the field" was a far more sensible and safe approach to women.

So, how did he get *here*? Marcus had sent Stephen along with a small contingent from the marketing department by air to El Paso, Texas, to research a possible sight for a hotel. There wasn't much out there in the larger hotels. There weren't many larger hotels out there period, and Marcus wanted to see what could possibly be done to change that. It took a week to work through the process of studying demographics, contacting real estate companies, touring the various sites, and then taking their agents to lunch and dinner and for further conferences.

It had been a busy week. Stephen happened to read in the paper at breakfast the day before he left the El Paso area for home about the Miss Texas pageant being held in Mineral Wells. That wasn't *very far* from Ft. Worth. He could rent a car and stop there for the night. Mineral Wells was doable, if he stayed on Highway 80 and didn't stop except for gas and a quick bite to eat. To that end, he drove east all day Saturday.

El Paso was a long way from where he currently sat this Sunday night. That's how he had gotten *here*. Life is strange, he mused. Various competing perfumes lingered in the air. They rose into the seating, and Stephen sniffed the wind. He wondered if one in particular might be Susan's.

His first option had been to fly back home, because it wouldn't be so physically taxing or time consuming. Once at home he would tackle a busy summer discovering other complexities of Lloyd Hotels International. He'd already begun to determine how to best use his talents of architectural design to build the finest hotels in the world— ambitious, but safe.

Stephen didn't play football safe, however. He'd separated his left shoulder twice because it wasn't in his mental or anatomical makeup to wait for the play to form. They called him "The Battering Ram." During baseball season, he ran the base paths like a demon. He'd been thrown out four times in eight games trying for second. No, it wasn't in his nature to do the "safe" thing, regardless of how much the coaches yelled, and did they yell. For that matter, Stephen hadn't made captain of any team playing cautiously. He might try and bend the rules at school and home, but his parents had done a good job with Stephen, all in all.

The decision wasn't really that difficult, was it? He'd obviously lean more substantially upon the second consideration. With that settled, he felt eerily uncertain as to how to meet this woman who had touched him, who was, unbeknownst to Stephen, toying with his emotions *and* hormones. Stephen mentally calculated the odds of getting close to her, and when he came to consciousness, Susan and company had vanished backstage behind the curtain. Miss Alcott had no idea she was being pursued by wealth and privilege. She would most likely resent his intrusion into her own plans and future.

Stephen gave himself one last out. Which would it be: the uncertainty and the real possibility of rejection *here*, or, the semi-guaranteed safety of Ft. Worth? Romance or work? *Why change now*, he asked. Stephen's first step toward the stage set his second option in motion. Another step and Stephen felt more certain of himself despite the frenzied perplexities scurrying just below his baser instincts. He supposed he knew the chance he was taking, but would his father go along?

Stephen reached into the inside left breast pocket of his suit coat for his wallet. From the brown leather pouch his father insisted he carry with him at all times, he retrieved one of the business cards announcing Stephen's semi-official capacity with Lloyd Hotels.

Onto the main floor now, Stephen's plan had congealed to a more malleable configuration. Each family must pass a uniformed male checkpoint, ensuring that only the competitor's immediate relations and those offering scholarships were allowed to visit the beauty contestants—all under the watchful eye of Mineral Wells' finest, most dependable mother hens.

Stephen affixed himself unobtrusively to the rear of the line of families matriculating back stage, and the woman he hoped desperately to meet. Actually, he hoped for much more than he dared allow his mind to speculate upon right then. He positively remembered "the talk" his father had with him that Saturday evening nine distant years ago. Marcus had driven them both to look at cars, but they didn't make it to any dealerships. For the first time, Stephen beheld his father faltering with words about sex and women. Very little actual communication took place that night, but enough hopefully seeped through the perspiration of his father's verbiage. Certain salient points had lodged in the rising hormones that had begun to ferret themselves among the growth spurts of Stephen's mind and body. The locker room had become the actual male classroom for such subjects, and Stephen graduated *summa cum laude*.

He held the business card for the guard to observe, which the man took, read, and returned to Stephen. From there he passed into the staging area to find the woman who had stolen his heart. Stephen Lloyd had never seen this many beautiful women in one place, and in such close proximity to himself in his young life. He smiled as he thought of the pugilistic effluvium clashing in the locker room after practice. But in this most agreeable context, he was surrounded by perfumes of every imaginable fragrance, mingling for mastery. High-pitched squeals of joyful, nervous and excited women attacked his ears overcoming the scattered male basses and baritones commingling with their female counterparts.

Stephen caught broken bits of pitches from various university hawkers and reps., causing him to cautiously stop, listen and take mental notes when he would need them. There was still time to back away. That he might walk out of this place with a particular woman in tow must do battle with his disquieted conscience buoyed up by his days as an altar boy at church. Stephen knew beyond the slightest doubt that his intentions were anything but reputable, and yet, even his accumulating guilt did not alter his movement toward his goal.

With the intensity rising to a fever pitch, Stephen almost succumbed to it and turned to leave. As he did, a large man stepped into his path to better converse with a lovely blond, Miss Lubbock. She who seemed quite uninterested in the overstuffed and balding male blocking Stephen's exit. Turning from the older male, Lubbock put her full gaze upon Stephen. He returned her smile through a grid of teeth. The large man fortunately moved on. More parents and contestants hemmed Stephen in and he began to perspire, and his pathway of escape became confusing and intrusive. He almost yelled: "Get out of my way!", but, he did not. Stephen turned away from Lubbock when he thought he heard Susan's voice. Once last time, he hesitated. *What should I do? No. This is silly and wrong. Miss Lubbock is definitely interested. No. No. I'm coming, Susan . . .*

He stepped headstrong back into the mass of many sequined or plain-gowned women, hoping not to be cast out as the interloper he was. His mind, renewed with purpose though it was, Stephen Lloyd didn't look back at the blonde from west Texas. Maybe he should have.

He spotted her. Susan gazed full eyed in his direction. Her *blue* eyes didn't leave him, and his heart leapt into his throat. All anxiety vanished. *Oh my, those eyes of hers were blue.* For that flicker of a millisecond, she appeared, not only to notice him but also to *survey* him—and with approval, he assured himself. But within that flicker of a millisecond, an incursion of bewildered guilty panic twisted his stomach in knots, a sort of subterranean seizure. Could he carry on with his planned deceit? But why had he gone to the effort to assuage his conscience, fight through all these women to reach this point, to abandon it now? He had done much worse things in school or on the field and felt no remorse. *Get hold of yourself, old man*, he admonished his conscience. Suddenly, he trundled mentally backward ten minutes, retrieved his foolhardy plan, dusted it off, and re-memorized it. He would soon see if he believed it would work . . . in about fifteen feet. He could hardly swallow . . . or breathe. Susan was everything he imagined and more.

Ten feet and closing, slightly hidden among the crowds of families and friends, Stephen fixed his gaze completely on his prize, who abruptly turned and buried her face firmly against the breast pocket of a distinguished looking gentleman, and slowly cry her heart out. Five feet left until contact found Stephen wondering: *How do women do that? One minute they are laughing and in an instant they are a puddle of tears. Better yet, why do they do that? She'd had plenty of time to cry. Why now?* She hadn't seen him at all. He only hoped she had.

Stephen judged the man nearest Susan to be her father. No, she obviously hadn't been surveying him. He'd only flattered himself. And besides, there were now *three* of them to face, Papa Bear, Mama Bear, and black haired Goldilocks, and Mama Bear appeared from nowhere. There was still time. . . . Ft. Worth and work looked better by the second.

"Oh daddy, I tried. I really tried. I wanted to win so badly. I embarrassed mother and you, didn't I?" she blurted. Failure was draped all over her sheer, green and white striped gown. The sleeves were puffed at the shoulders and their small openings allowed her firm, slender, bare arms exposure. Her waistband snugged wonderfully against her, accentuating her feminine allure. Drawing closer, she looked even taller than her five foot nine inch frame. Oh my, she was gorgeous.

Keeping his eyes where they should be would require concentration like Stephen hadn't needed since they played Tulane, barely winning that one while having to contend with a tackle who was constantly holding him. One stinking point, and he, Stephen Lloyd, blocked the extra point. That made it a perfect season. *Stay on the field, old boy. Focus on your woman's face. The face!*

"Embarrass us? What gives you that idea? You were the smartest, prettiest and most talented woman out there tonight," her father boasted, almost shouting his bias.

Stephen had in point of fact, stood one second too long gazing. Susan's eyes pierced him once more. She had to know he existed with that look, and now he was quite sure of it. Reading the moment as best he could, Stephen Lloyd stepped forward somewhat like a bowling ball headed down the alley toward the pins. Perhaps he'd played football too many years. He only knew one way to tackle a situation of this magnitude, —head up, shoulder first. *Keep eye contact son, eye contact.*

Breathe. "Good evening and congratulations, Miss Alcott. I loved that piece of music. It's one of my favorites." *No turning back now.*

Susan assayed him, inviting his closer inspection—but not *too* close. The woman seemed demurely guarded, but at the same time, provocatively naïve. He was probably being too forward, too blunt, but . . . *my*, her eyes *were* whirlpool—"I-could-get-lost-in- them-and-drown" blue. *This* encounter would not be a fair fight.

Her sharp, red lipstick had faded over the past few hours so that it sat lackluster, even timid on her lips, not as it had an eternity ago, on stage.

"Good evening, sir. Ma'am. My name is Stephen Lloyd. I represent Lloyd Hotels International."

Stephen reached inside his coat for the card, impressed at how professional he actually sounded. Now he wasn't not quite certain as to whom he should hand it. In his indecision he extended it to Susan, but her father intercepted it. *Oops. Did I blow it?*

It read:

Stephen Lloyd
Architectural and Managerial Specialist
Lloyd Hotels International, Inc.
Ft. Worth, Texas

A phone number with address was displayed at the bottom of the card. The title didn't mean anything, but Marcus wanted his son to be "titled."

Mr. Alcott looked up from the card. "Yes, Mr. Stephen Lloyd, what can we do for you?" Perry handed the card to Susan. She received it and slowly slid her fingers across the length of it, feeling the raised lettering. Her eyes seemed lost and hazy, almost unfocused. The pungent enthusiasm and adrenaline of the competition was most likely wearing off. Stephen knew this feeling as post game fatigue. Maybe they had something in common after all.

"Our hotel would like to congratulate you, Miss Alcott, on your performance tonight. I think . . . I mean, *we* think you were the best contestant. We would like to offer you a position in our public relations department as well as a scholarship to the college of your choice." *What did I just say? Now I'm dead.*

Stephen could not believe what just hopped out of his mouth, even though he'd planned to say these very words. He had no permission from his father to make any such offer. But, it was too late now, full speed ahead. This penalty would put them back to his goal line. He'd been penalized against Tech once just like this for decking the quarterback long after he'd thrown the ball. His coach sidelined him for that stunt.

Susan stared up into Stephen's green eyes, and then at each of her parents. She seemed bewildered—hers was a "deer-in-the-headlights" gaze. Moments earlier she felt herself a failure, and now this most generous invitation. A company as large as the Lloyd Hotels wanted *her . . .* for a *position, schooling,* her *dreams,* and here it sat at her feet.

"Mr. Lloyd . . ." she began.

"No, it's Stephen," he said, almost falling into her eyes, and thus giving himself away in all likelihood.

"Stephen, I don't know what to say. I'm speechless. I thought this was the best night of my life, and then when I didn't win . . ." Her suddenly re-aroused involvement moved her once more toward tears. She turned quickly toward her mother, held her at arms length, and stared into her trying to gain some strength. A playful little smile transformed the sides of Susan's mouth.

To interrupt and further the business at hand, Susan's father redirected the focus. "Mr. Lloyd, my name is Perry Alcott." Facing the father, Stephen shook hands with Mr. Alcott. "I'm Susan's father. I hope you don't think me presumptuous, but I want to protect my daughter from, well, people who might try and take advantage of her, if you know what I mean. May I see some other identification, please?"

"Why, yes sir. Here is my driver's license. And I do know what you mean, sir." *Yep. I'm dead now.* Standing there amid all the wash and swish of gowns, of joy and disappointment, Stephen felt his heart sink with renewed vigor. He had just lied to three people. Why was it so hard to be who he was? He'd never get to meet her that way, which was his motivation, as wrong headed as it was. How did he know this was the only way to meet her? In point of fact, he didn't. Suddenly, he felt the word, "STUPID" tattooed across his forehead.

More than a few of his frat brothers would have done this. Why not *him*? But once discovered, her first impression of Stephen would be that of a charlatan, a spoiled rich kid whose motives were as rancid as the stiff, fly-covered armadillos he'd seen lying dead in and along the road this morning.

"Stephen, are you somehow related to the Lloyd's of Lloyd Hotels?" Michelle Alcott, Susan's mother, asked, hoping he'd answer in the affirmative.

"My father is Marcus Lloyd, yes, ma'am. He is also the President of Lloyd Hotels. I am his son, Mrs. Alcott. One of the tasks for which my father hired me is to search for bright, talented young people, such as your daughter, to represent our hotels." *As an Architectural and Managerial Specialist? Oh boy. That made real sense.*

With Stephen's motives working against him, he hoped he still sounded convincing . . . or not. His neck was on the line if he blinked first. "I'm here tonight to offer your daughter a career, and that includes travel, company benefits, and schooling in exchange for employment in public relations with our company." The men's eyes locked. Perry thought young Mr. Lloyd looked almost too adolescent for this role.

"Mr. Lloyd," Perry said, "I don't' mean to seem ungrateful. This offer is most generous to be sure, but why didn't you offer this to the winner, Miss Byrns?" Perry, a successful vice president for one of the nation's largest mills in America, Bainbridge, reverted to his element in his most businesslike manner. "Mr. Lloyd, have you finished college yet?" Perry wondered aloud. The two women huddled together, squeezed each other, but continuing to listen.

"Well, no sir. I'm in my second year of engineering at A&M." Stephen just blinked. "But I am employed in this capacity with my father's firm. I assure you he has given me sole permission to make the choice that I believe will benefit our company. I think your daughter fits the qualifications we are looking for. The offer is legitimate. You may call him if you wish. Shall I get him on the phone?" *Please don't ask me to do that.*

"Would you mind?" Perry asked.

It was now over for young Mr. Lloyd. The cowhide had come off the ball, and the twine unraveled quickly. Stephen's heart sank into his shoes.

"Let me find a phone. There's one on the wall across the room, but there's so much noise in here you may not be able to communicate very well. If you will give me the hotel where you are staying I can have my father call you in, say . . . forty-five minutes?"

Perry agreed, provided Stephen with the pertinent hotel information, and then made arrangements for the four of them to meet following the interview with Marcus. Stephen shook hands said goodbye, and, once out of sight, he sprinted for the nearest pay phone and dialed the number.

One ring. Two rings. Three. "Hello father, do you . . . no, I'm fine. I'll be home tomorrow. What I was going to say was, do you have any objections to our hiring someone for our public relations department?"

Marcus didn't pause to think about his answer. "Well, yes, as a matter of fact, I do. That's not the area we need any help in right now. Why? You didn't . . . hire someone, did you?"

"Uh, well, you see father . . ." Stephen had no one to blame but himself.

"Stephen, I specifically remember sending you and the team to El Paso to look for a hotel sight. I have their report on my desk. You haven't hired anyone have you? Where are you?" Marcus's tone, famous for its intimidation, had increased appreciably.

"I'm . . . in Mineral Wells."

"What on earth are you doing there? You are supposed to be here!"

Stephen leaned against the wall, dejected, unable to face his father's questions, and the predicament he alone created for three other people. The woman he hoped to know would now hate him. Beyond that, both her father and his own father would crucify him. Between them, they just might make it so difficult for him to ever find a job.

"I'm in a bit of a fix, father. No, I didn't do *that*. I need a favor. *No*, not money. I've met a girl at the Miss Texas pageant here in Mineral Wells. Her name is Susan Alcott. She's Miss Longview. Yes, I remember Cynthia quite well, but that was eight months ago. Please listen to me, father. Susan placed fourth or fifth—I can't remember which—in the Miss Texas contest tonight. Yes, and I met her *and* her parents backstage. That's right."

Up to now it wasn't going *too* badly. "But I promised her something." Stephen felt himself tumbling helplessly off of Mt. Everest. "No. No. I didn't promise her that. I told her I worked for our company—which I do—and . . ." Stephen closed his eyes and wished this all away. "I told her that my job, among other things, was to look for talented young people to work for our company." Furious silence erupted on Marcus' end.

"Son, *what* have you done?" It was that authoritative, "I'd-spank-you-if-you-weren't-so-big" tone of his.

"Father, I've met the woman I want to marry, the woman who could give you grandchildren . . ." And that was why Marcus should agree to this? Oh *boy*. More silence. Stephen knew where the soft spot lay. At least he thought he suspected he knew. Marcus knew now which anatomical organ his son was using to think with.

"*Hmph*." The old man thumped very loud on the other end. Stephen had him. He sensed it. "Tell me again what you promised her that *I* would do for *her* future?"

"I said you would . . ." Stephen began, but Marcus burst in to cut him off.

"Stephen you lied to this young woman and her parents. You are trying to build a relationship on false pretenses, and in so doing you've compromised your integrity, not to mention what they must think of *me*, THAT I WOULD BRING A SON UP TO DO THIS! LUNACY! No son, I will *not* help you! I'm *most* disappointed in you, Stephen, *very* disappointed. Where are they staying? What's the room number?" Marcus's anger loomed like a dark, threatening cloud over Stephen.

I'm dead.

Stephen's head hung just above the floor. He fingered the coin return with no real purpose. There would be no coins there. "I'm sorry. But . . . you're right, father. I was wrong. I'll . . . I'll go and somehow . . . I'll set things right." Stephen had become that green balloon someone blew up for the sole purpose of pricking a hole in it just so they could watch it screech across the room and fall to the floor deflated, a useless thing to be discarded.

"Stephen, I can't remember you *ever* doing this . . ." Marcus exclaimed, hurling another barb at his son. The world burdened the young Mr. Lloyd more than it ever had. Stephen said his apologetic goodbye to the man he respected more than any man he'd ever known, his father. Marcus said nothing, and hung up.

Stephen Lloyd had compromised his integrity for a woman. Unfortunately, his inexperienced youthful outlook didn't know the compensating value of that commodity as yet. He was about to learn. Stephen walked slowly out to the front of the auditorium, found his car in the parking lot, and drove the several blocks to Susan's hotel. What a miserable ride this was, and it didn't disappoint.

Stephen found the parking lot of the Bellaire Ambassador, and parked his car. He entered the main lobby, located the elevator, stepped inside, took a very deep breath, and pushed the button for the fourteenth floor. Finding room 1426, he paused and prayed the fastest Hail Mary in his life. Next, he raised his hand to knock. A second gust of panic gripped him to the point of thinking that jumping off the fourteenth floor might just be more appealing.

As his knuckles almost touched the door, it opened unexpectedly, startling him. Mr. Alcott, with ice bucket in hand, held the door half way open. He too was a bit startled. The two men stared at each other for an eternal second. Stephen could hear Susan crying in the background, with Mrs. Alcott comforting her.

"Mr. Lloyd, your father just called," Perry said matter-of-factly, his jaws tightening. Perry was not a small man, nor did he look meager. He stood a full two inches taller than Stephen, fully intimidating the boy. Very few men on the football field had so coward him, but this man did. Stephen began to turn an off-white, pale, nauseating sort of color. "Come in. The ladies are presentable. We'd all like to hear something from you, son." There was enough "ice" *in* the room to suffice the Alcott's needs, Stephen thought, so that Perry didn't really need to get more.

The soft glow from the table lamp, normally bathing and soothing the room's atmosphere, suddenly felt very like the quenchless incandescence of an interrogation. Two double beds with spreads to match the earth tone décor were now wrinkled. Two pillows had been piled against the headboard of one bed. The bathroom door, half shut, spoke to the black darkness of his mood. Several generic pictures, one of the Gulf Coast at sunset, the other of the Mineral Wells skyline at mid morning, adorned the wall to Stephen's left. A single wooden table covered with a mauve cloth and a padded wooden chair sat alone in the corner. Stephen guessed that Susan stayed in her own room. This was the parent's room. It would double suitably as an inquisition chamber. *Where were the manacles?*

"Mr. Lloyd," Mrs. Alcott said, finally breaking the Alcott's voluntary silence. Disappointment registered on her face and body, but especially in her voice. "I'm sorry, but . . ." Stephen interrupted, cutting her off. "Let me say this before I can't, ma'am," the words sweeping from Stephen's mouth out into the room's air, the frigid atmosphere hovering around the occupants in the room. Inhaling, he continued, "I have misrepresented myself sir, ma'am, as you know, talking to my father." Stone cold silence, and still no movement. They demanded to hear all of this. "My father gave me no such permission to offer Susan anything. I . . . um, made it up. I really misjudged myself and my father . . . I am ashamed of what I did, but not as much as my father is of me. I told him . .," and it was here that Stephen visibly winced, but he would say it. ". . . I told him that I'd found the girl I wanted to marry—your daughter. Not that it matters now, of course."

Stephen quit his *mea culpa* at this juncture. What else could he say? His opportunity with Susan Alcott squandered, but he wanted her to know just how much taken with her he'd become in such a short time. Despite having watched her one hundred feet distant, he was willing to make a fool of himself just to be near her. He really did want to give her all those opportunities of which he'd spoken. None of that made any difference now.

"But my father's concern was his own and my integrity, which I have now completely destroyed, not to mention the hurt I have brought to ya'll. He was right. He's always right. I am truly sorry for this, and I was *very* wrong. I hope you can someday forgive me."

Stephen had never felt so dejected, so utterly embarrassed, and it showed. In his life, he'd missed tackles that cost his team a game. He'd completely forgotten to write a course paper and almost flunked the class. He'd stood up Terry McDaniel on a date last year—she slapped him hard for that *faux pas*. But nothing came close to this. Still, he'd never ventured so much in order to gain so much, and then lost so totally.

"Mr. Lloyd, you have done something so reprehensible that I ought to . . ." Perry stood rigid and ready for what felt terribly familiar to him when the moment called for striking another man. For some reason beyond him, he stopped before he regretted his next actions—Michelle Alcott rose from from reflex, assured her husband might truly harm the young man, or worse. Instead, the senior of the men moved slowly, cautiously, in close to Stephen, halting when he was nearly eye to eye, toe to toe. He tipped his forehead slightly forward, mere inches from Stephen's face. Stephen swallowed hard, bracing himself for whatever came next. Mr. Alcott's lips hardly moved, "My *God*, son," and then suddenly Perry's intensity and voice rose: "There are ways of meeting my daughter, but *this . .,*" he shoved his index finger quickly toward the floor, "*this* is not one of them. *Yes*, you were wrong. Twenty years ago I'd have killed you for a lot less." Perry caught himself, pulled his head back to a safer distance—safer for Stephen, that is.

That is when he eyed or rather surveyed the beaten young man. Perry Alcott noticed something inside Stephen that registered loudly and positively. This kid wasn't beaten, no matter how badly he'd screwed up. Perry had seen that look when one of his sergeants made a mess of an attack near Soissons, costing the lives of several of Captain Alcott's Marines, and wounding several more. Perry knew the truth about the deflated young Lloyd in that instant. It lay in the set of his eyes when he understood the cost of his actions. It was what happened down there in his gut, which affected his jaw making it jut forward a certain way. It was what made Stephen stand there and take it, knowing that he'd done something terribly wrong, that he was a better man than what he displayed tonight, and he'd prove it. *Go ahead and knock, me down, but I will get back up.* It wasn't a haughty look, but a proud deportment in the face of defeat, but it wasn't defeat. A good and strong man was in there struggling with what adulthood meant.

That sergeant went on to earn the Silver Star despite some terrible wounds. Perry knew, or thought he did, that he might just trust this young man, not only with his life, but also with his daughter. Stephen had done wrong. Okay. *Now son, show me something that I know is there in you.* Yet . . . Perry wouldn't give his position away, not yet. He was a poker player, and he still had cards to play. "But I must say I am very impressed with your father. I would like to meet him sometime."

Perry straightened demeanor, breathed deeply and retreated to sit on one of the beds, tense but still observant. Stephen breathed a little easier. Perry's initial back stage observations about Stephen were and were not correct. Thankfully, no one said anything. Then Perry asked for further clarification: "One of two things is going through your mind right now, son, . . . and I want you to tell me which it is: either, you are here protecting the Lloyd name and that's all you are here for, *or*, you are genuinely sorry for what you did, and you know it will *never* happen again. Which is it for you, son?"

Susan had, by now, stopped crying. She, too, was measuring Stephen. He stood on a razor thin stage of his own making. Michelle was simply lost in her daughter's disappointment, oblivious to the event taking place in the room. She would just as soon Stephen leave.

He is quite handsome, Susan mused. He carried his dignity, humbled as it was, about him like a garland. *He lied not only to me, but also to my parents. Unforgivable, and yet . . .* He *did* hold her father's eye, not once lowering his own from fear or embarrassment. Nor had he shirked his responsibility, as so many possible suitors might have. He was muscled, mannered and courteous, and she spotted an unusual and quite attractive gentleness around his mouth and eyes. He had wronged her, and he was taking the worst her father gave out—without apparent retaliation or excuses. There was bravery here, and it drew her.

Susan had, from years of listening to her dad and watching him fail or succeed, cleaning up his binges, absorbing his tantrums, soothing his depression, learned to evaluate the cut of a man under pressure. There was so much about Stephen that appealed to her. Susan had felt it backstage. She wouldn't have known his gentleness or his strength without seeing his weakness and failure. Secretly, she was glad this had happened. Currently there was this matter of salvaging his integrity, which he had so glibly bashed upon the wrecking ball of infidelity to principle.

"Mr. Alcott, I have dragged my father's good name and reputation through the mud tonight. But I'm here, well, because I had to come. I had to set things right. What you think of me is not as important as what you think of my father. This will *never* happen again, but I don't expect you will ever find out whether that is true or not."

Humility is an inflexible teacher, Stephen thought to himself as he nodded to no one in particular.

"Susan, do you want to say something," Perry asked.

Susan spoke for the first time, rather dryly. "Daddy, if you grab one leg, I'll grab his other. Then we'll throw him out the window." Perry reached for the window latch while Michelle Alcott raised both hands to her mouth in disbelief: "Susan!" Perry unlocked the latch, pushed the window open, which brought forth the night and its sounds.

Stephen backed up cautiously, his eyes growing wide, his mind ambiguous as to what this might mean. He certainly didn't expect such a response from Susan. But when both father and daughter stood up and moved toward Stephen almost aggressively, he began to back pedal quicker. He'd never met people like this.

With incredulous thoughts flooding deflated Mr. Lloyd's mind, Stephen caught Susan's coy, slow smile forming at the edges of her mouth. Perry entertained a half chuckle as he halted his progress, turned and went to get something out of his suitcase. He retrieved a small handgun, checked the chamber for live rounds, and quite unexpectedly handed it to Susan.

By now, Stephen had no idea *what* to think. Her facial alteration had eased his discomfort, momentarily. He was actually beginning to wonder if he would make it out of the room alive. His sins might cost him everything, although he'd hoped a humble confession would have sufficed. Laying bare his soul to half cracked people was not part of the agreement when he'd conceded to this. These two cats were toying with the mouse, and the kill might be but moments away.

Susan held the weapon firmly in her hand. It looked far too comfortable there, like she'd used it in the past. Assured she had his full attention, Susan spoke slowly and deliberately, looking fully into his eyes. "Do you know what the most disappointing thing was for me tonight, Stephen?"

"Well, uh, I think I can guess, Miss Alcott."

"No. No you can't. Not really. All you saw was how pretty you think I am. You didn't look any deeper than my face and my figure, did you? There's a lot more to me than the outside. I am quite intelligent."

"I don't doubt that, ma'am," his reply was breathy, as much from terror as from anything, he backed firmly against the door where he could go no farther. Was this the end, he wondered.

"I probably have more talent in my little finger than you have in your whole body."

"Oh, I'm sure of that, ma'am. Why don't you just put that—"

"I don't want to put this weapon down."

"No, you really *should* put it down, Miss Alcott," Stephen's head nodding quickly in the affirmative.

Stephen, you have no idea how much I'm enjoying this. She had this strapping, hunk of a man, ready to wet his trousers. "I *really* want to do this, Mr. Lloyd. I want to shoot you. Dead," she blurted harshly, shaking the pistol at him. Stephen pushed himself harder against the door, terror written all over his face. Susan moved even closer, *all but* pressing her body against his. She pulled the hammer backward, click.

Michelle, could contain herself no longer, "Susan! Stop this this instant!"

"Miss Alcott, you *really* don't want to do this," Stephen agreed with the mother, his eyes as big as half dollars.

Michelle shot up and off the bed, covering her mouth with her hands. She had never seen her daughter act this way toward anyone. Perry slowly crossed his arms, proud as could be of his daughter. Stephen had to learn character, and Perry and Susan had become his instructors. With the barrel pointed a mere inch from Stephen's chest and the hammer cocked, Susan was certain she had his undivided attention, and she held it for another terrible quarter minute. Then, as suddenly as the challenge had presented itself, Susan eased the hammer back down to its original position, handed the pistol to her dad, leaned in even closer to Stephen—and smiled.

Stephen held his breath, afraid to breathe. Should he trust this unexpected show of cordiality? Unexpectedly, and with a voice that would melt any male, "Stephen, are you hungry?"

"Wh . . . *what*?" He swallowed hard. "Am I . . . am I *hungry*? Is that what you asked me?"

"Daddy, would it be all right if Stephen and I went to the hotel restaurant for a bite to eat?" There actually wasn't a question in this. It was rhetorical.

"Oh no. No, Miss Alcott. No . . ." Stephen was taken fully aback now. "No. I don't, I don't think so, ma'am. You've all been very merciful to me in light of my actions tonight. I think I'll be going. Thank you. No." Stephen mumbled as he fumbled behind him for the door handle.

It was then that Susan put her hand flat and firm on his chest, pinning him once more against the wooden door. Susan was no small, fragile woman. At five feet nine inches, she was a handful. "Stephen, most of the kids I've met from your background lack the character you've displayed tonight. I believe you *are* sorry. Personally I don't think you'll ever do that again—to anyone. And if you do it to me again, I *will* shoot you." Stephen could only shake his head in the affirmative. He had been taken to the cleaners tonight, socks, underwear, and all.

Perry finally spoke. "Why don't you and Susan go get something to eat? We'll expect you in about an hour or so. I'll be up here cleaning my pistol." Perry looked into the face of a completely bewildered and outclassed young man . . . and sort of felt sorry for him. Sort of.

"Mr. Alcott, it truly would be an honor to take Susan anywhere on any other night, but I think I should leave. I've done enough damage to last me for two years," Stephen said deflated and even more apprehensive. He was relieved though, as he kept trying to back out the door while being pushed against it. Susan's hand remained firm on his chest, going nowhere.

"Please Stephen," Susan blurted, almost afraid he would leave. "I've forgiven you, and besides, I think it *your* duty to help me celebrate my *almost* victory."

Her pain had gone from the pageant. But more importantly, what this sturdy young man brought into Susan's life would replace it. She felt she would not let him go.

Eleven: Nurse Minsk

Tuesday, March 7, 1967

—Midnight. Stephen's troubled mind tumbled and whirled past his memories of Father Ed. The scotch had soured on his stomach a bit. It was no longer having the effect he'd hoped for. The first miscarriage led him to the doorstep of the second, and the second would lead to the third. His memories normally repressed, tonight he entertained them on the sofa. Not one was positive; each possessed an almost crippling edge to it.

Depression had fully slipped through the front door and sat too near him. Susan had departed back upstairs hours ago. His plagued mindset made it difficult to focus on the objects of the room in which he sat, but he didn't care. Tonight the world consisted of Stephen Lloyd, his past hurts and "what-ifs." These deaths, like Dickens' ghosts of Christmas past, forced themselves upon him, bringing with them their unresolved tortures.

That first Thanksgiving after Stephen's return from his fifty missions over Europe merged into the present as he mulled upon it. The war had been over for three months and a couple of weeks. The Lloyds, the Alcott's, and some good friends had gathered together to celebrate and thank God for the war's conclusion and the conquering hero's return.

Stephen however, had dreaded that particular holiday. Too many of his friends hadn't come back standing upright. His centralized focus came to rest on three blanket covered men lying near his airplane,

121

and he felt guilty for participating freely in this meal. He *should* feel utter relief and exuberance for his life having been spared when so many better men than him hadn't. Europe and Japan lay in ruins. The marks of men's atrocities were being unearthed all over the world. But it was *Thanksgiving in America*, cha cha cha. Time to give thanks, to over-eat and rejoice. What the holiday had always been, could be no more. Not for Stephen Lloyd and many other men. Everyone else in the family, except Perry, who also seemed a bit subdued, celebrated. Stephen couldn't help but think of that Thanksgiving in '44 when he'd lost a dear friend in a flying accident over the Alps. The whole crew, ten men, had gone down with the ship. It lost an engine, then speed, then altitude, and then it smacked into the side of a mountain. No chutes. They were *still* missing. Their families wouldn't be celebrating this holiday.

Saturday, November 25, 1945

"Mom, will you bring in the salad? They'll all be back in a few minutes, won't they?" Susan called from the dining room. The air was ferocious with the smell of turkey and all the trimmings. Beethoven's "Moonlight Sonata" filled the room, its introduction brooding.

Michelle sounded the warning bell about the dressing. "Dear, it's one-thirty-five. How many more minutes until the dressing will be done?"

"Mother, just think," Susan offered, staring into the air, "Beethoven wrote this piece after Giulietta Guicciardi refused his proposal of marriage. That's so romantically sad, somehow. Isn't it?"

"Yes it is, dear. Very romantic and *very* sad. Susan, how many more minutes? And how many did you say would be coming for dinner? I'm getting so absent-minded these days."

Susan counted aloud, pointing to the place settings, and then looked at her watch. "Four more minutes on the dressing. Let's see, Mom and Dad Lloyd, you and Dad, and my two misguided brothers. That's six, Stephen and I make eight, and Bill and Margie, ten, and John and Amy. Twelve. Twelve, Mother. We'll need two more chairs. Drat!" Susan exclaimed, dropping a fork. As she bent over to retrieve it, a distant and ill-timed but familiar malaise seized her lower abdomen, thrusting her to the floor, writhing in agony.

"Mother!" Susan screamed as she fell, pulling a chair over on top of her.

"Susan, what is it!?"

By the time Michelle reached her daughter, blood had soaked through Susan's holiday skirt that she loved so much. Long, thin lines of red clotted and fluid fingers had already soaked into the cotton fabric and upon her legs. Her cramps made her scream and writhe in terrible pain.

"Ohhhh mother! My back . . ."

Before she passed out, Susan spoke four words, their dry deadness chilling: "I'm losing the baby."

"Oh, not again. Please, dear God, not again," Michelle prayed aloud.

"Mrs. Lloyd? Mrs. Lloyd!" Helen Minsk forced her way into Susan's haze from her finest husky, tenor voice. "Mrs. Lloyd." Nurse Minsk loomed large over her half conscious patient. Helen phrased Susan's name more in accusatorial tones than indicative or interrogative. RN Minsk had mustered out of the Army Medical Corps to find her way into the civilian medical sector, and presently into Susan Lloyd's troubles.

Minsk, was a no-nonsense woman. She usually caused no slight consternation to those unfortunate souls working under her and on *her* ward. This was *her* ward. Ask anyone. The doctors also gave her a wide berth, except Dr. Simms, who loved a good scrap with his "lieutenants." Nurse Minsk could never quite let go of the notion that she was not somehow wrestling wounded, rowdy sergeants or privates, rather than civilians. Women like Susan, pretty but weak females who had lost their equilibrium, or their children, were less than challenging. Helen Minsk literally detested fragile women. Susan Lloyd was *obviously* not a durable woman in Helen's eyes.

When women like Susan buzzed the old heifer from their sickbeds to attend to their needs, it was usually with the proffered, "Nurse Min*sk*." After a week on her ward, the patients began accenting the "*sk*," just enough for their own perverted pleasures, Helen Minsk assured herself. Her patients' immediate needs usually required a mental resilience of the nurse, so as not to curl the old girl's upper lip. If they did so, it made them quite duplicitous, along with the nursing staff, of foisting upon the hefty nurse a state of irascible bedside manner.

Susan should not have lost the baby on *this* day, or been driven to *this* hospital, so that *this* nurse, could get a chance at *this* patient. Mrs. Lloyd had interrupted *her* schedule.

"Oh, dear Jesus, not again . . ." Susan opened her eyes cautiously, gasped, hoping the reality of what she was experiencing in her lower body might be a bad dream. "Did I lose my baby? Please tell me I'm still pregnant. Please . . ." Susan was pleading with a complete stranger.

"Mrs. Lloyd, you will survive this. I've treated much worse in France, and Belgium was horrible. You are young with years ahead of you. You're going to have to be tough. Are we clear, Mrs. Lloyd?"

"But . . ."

The "bulldozer" heeled and left the room, and poor Susan's pleadings went unanswered. She couldn't believe what she heard come out of this woman's mouth. *How dare her.*

Minsk's, "I'll get the doctor for you, Mrs. Lloyd," came from somewhere down the hall. Somehow, this *woman* had never quite mustered out of the army or left roller derby.

Susan knew what had happened—again. God or someone had killed her babies. With the obvious stated, Sudan slipped into a distant but not unfamiliar seething anger, more palpable than her pain.

"Dr. Hachtmeyer, Mrs. Lloyd is awake now," nurse Minsk announced, her voice absent of any empathy.

"Thank you, Nurse Min*sk*." The doctor took great pleasure in emphasizing the '*sk*,' which always drew a raised eyebrow from the turbine driven woman. Helen headed toward the nurses station. Her nurses were ever alert to her whereabouts, and, seeing her marching full tilt in the general direction of the station, RN Corby whispered, "The tornado cometh." This SOS produced a solid effect of whirling activity at the station. Nurse Minsk also ran a taut ship.

Dr. Hachtmeyer had restricted the bulk of family and friends from entering his newest patient's room for the next few hours. Mom and Dad Lloyd remained behind to see to the guests. He did request that only Stephen accompany him into the room. Susan's tears had already streaked her mascara and eyeliner. Nothing could alter Susan's intriguing beauty and guileless charm. These dead babies were fully attempting to do just that.

Mrs. Lloyd, I'm Dr. Hachtmeyer. I examined you in the emergency room. I'm terribly sorry to tell you this, but you've lost the baby, I'm afraid."

"Ohhh." Susan moaned, gritting her teeth. Her verbalized acknowledgement, the truth officially official, contracted her red lips, and she squeezed her eyes shut. The head nurse's lack of information, aside from what she did say, hurt the more from her lack of anything resembling compassion. Susan's discolored world pained her beyond words. Her womb was torn and unoccupied. Her body was a place where her babies didn't mature, a place where they grew only so much, and then, for reasons she couldn't grasp, died. Susan's face registered everything her body, hidden under the covers, suggested. Stephen didn't cry this time, although he sat as near to Susan as the last time they rushed her to the hospital, and then once examined, up to another lonely disinfected, Spartan room.

The war had bled former Captain Stephen Lloyd emotionally dry. His ability to feel, such as it was, had been stunted, and, unlike his pre-war image, he had no more tears left to shed, not even for this. Those innocent and weightless days were gone—forever. Stephen was the same man who left almost two years before, but monumentally dissimilar from that man. The loss of this baby did not surprise him. He had grown to expect animate things to die. Just months ago human beings had been manufactured and trained for one gigantic purpose: to be thrown into the furnace of the war machine and devoured whole. Why people existed back here in the states was anybody's guess.

Through her pain and loss, Susan sensed her husband's dissonance. He wouldn't allow himself that luxury—the luxury of acceding to emotional pain—ever again. If he did, he might not return from the edge of that abyss. This disaster was *her* misfortune, not his—well, not really. Everything that the war dyed into the fabric of his soul, he had bothered about as much as he was ever going to. That's what he told himself.

She observed closely his partial presence. Stephen had chosen rather to concentrate on her hand. He ran his big index finger along its smoothness, tracing her veins and bones. Her hands had always seemed to fascinate him, although she didn't quite understand their attraction for him. He loved watching the way Susan employed them, manipulating and plying them to whatever task she set them. Her fingers bent and straightened in ways and manners that aroused him.

Stephen pulled the fleshy part of his thumb over the edge of her neat, red polished nails, feeling their sturdy edges. She was so different from him. He was the oak, and she, the willow. There were yet aspects and places of her that he had not yet known to explore.

Watching him so attentive and focused on her hands had diverted her concentration away from her own immediate and amplified conundrum. Looking closely, she became aware that his eyes looked measurably sadder, his brows, uncharacteristically bent downward at the edges more than she had remembered them. Upon closer inspection, Susan ventured, "Stephen, I didn't notice until now, . . . when did you get those crow's feet?"

"What are you talking about? I don't know." He began touching his own brows to confirm or deny her observation.

"Why there's another line here, isn't there?" Susan's long, red nail traced the deepening furrows in her husband's forehead. Stephen started to withdraw his face from her unwanted prying fingers, but she quickly reached behind his head to lock him within her field of inspection. Susan asked, "Have I upset you, Sweetheart?"

Stephen wanted to say yes, but he refrained. Upon arriving back at their apartment for the festivities, he had experienced a tinge of agitation when Michelle and his own mother fell apart at this second miscarriage. Stephen had to rush to the hospital, and his anger, the anger generated by flying dangerous missions over Germany or Austria or Poland, felt normal. This afternoon had become yet another FUBAR situation in his life. It irritated him that he couldn't sit down and eat in peace. He missed the chow hall food, well, *not really*. Stephen had spent these last few months since returning to the States rearranging the remainder of his mauled state of mind and heart in order to meet everyone's expectations. "That happy-go-lucky Stephen Lloyd we sent off to war has returned. Now we can breathe again," they said to one another. Stephen hid from everyone behind an artificial smile.

After a few minutes of holding Susan's hand, Stephen's eyes dilated, and with his mind he had vacated the room. He'd begun to fly. Higher and higher he went in that old bomber infused in his soul, and his soul smelled of one hundred Octane. It was a sweet, reassuring smell. He and that machine had become one. Its airframe and avionics, the fear, the fraying seats and peeling olive paint, those four huge radial engines roaring through the sky getting him somewhere and back, the numbing cold on his face, and the sweat and spit in his oxygen mask had completely commingled with his soul. He flew until the flak and fighters could not touch him. The ground was so far below his feet, feet half frozen in his thermal boots, boots that worked hard the rudder pedals directing them onward. His hands clutched the yoke, and he strained and fought to hold it all together so he could get them all back in one piece.

Stephen's involvement with his wife seemed miles away too much of the time since his return. He never said it exactly, but how could he feel about Susan or anyone like he used to? How do you love when you cannot or don't recollect what love feels like? How do you love when hate is so much stronger than love? Love had become lust, softened.

Stephen had learned to replace all non-essential thoughts over the course of those fifty missions, reduced them to lessen the drag on his mind. Nor was there room for thoughts of Susan on each white knuckled, bomb and fuel-overloaded takeoff. He'd seen planes forced into service and then unable to lift their huge cargoes, shudder and explode at the far end of the runway. . . never even made it into the air. He watched them disintegrate from flak over Germany, Austria, Poland, and France. He watched them take multiple flak hits, their engines trailing smoke, knew they would begin to fall behind, and be picked off by the German fighters. He'd watched them slide across the pavement as their shot up hydraulics would not allow the landing gear to go down, or the gear would give way and belly flop on the deck. There were brake screeching landings that could not be halted in time by the end of the runway which often meant possible death. Thunderstorms, down drafts and blinding squalls threatened to break his and every other aircraft apart more than once. Tires that blew on landing so unexpectedly and Stephen would have to use all his skill just to keep that beast moving down the runway, balancing the crew in the aft section at just the right moment so he could ease the nose down gently and come to a safe stop. It became a crap shoot every time he walked out to his plane.

He'd forgotten just how many times his bombers brought him and his men back safely. That was a tough old bird if you understood her characteristics and idiosyncrasies. The B-24 was notorious for its tendency to catch fire. He'd known several pilots who died in bomber incinerations. It was built with the famous high fuselage-mounted Davis wing, built to reduce low-speed drag, but unfortunately could not compensate for its increased high-speed drag. This meant it was dangerous to ditch or belly land. More than one fuselage had broken apart on impact. It's turbochargers allowed it climb higher than many flak and fighter concentrations.

He'd crawled out through huge flak holes to kiss the ground and hug his mechanics for the great job they had done patching the many holes or working hard all night so he could do his job as well as he did.

More than once, Stephen had stopped making friends and stuck with the ones he knew. Stephen's heart had shrunk, too small for another person. He had come to will himself to live, attempting to take control of everything—life was all a matter of will and control. So how could he just shut all that down and resume a normal life? The thought was sheer folly. It seemed even more ridiculous to try to explain it.

Stephen kissed Susan's hand. It was the easiest thing to do, and the safest. She coaxed this experience of his tenderness through her dull pain and heavy rolling tears. She must savor it for the days ahead. Sitting in such close proximity to him she beheld a man she knew, but slowly came to realize within her soul, she didn't. He too struggled in his own way every bit as much as she. As the days passed, Susan perceived the fermenting agitation in her husband, just as she read his resolute and humble qualities the night he lied his way into her heart and life. Had his body aborted or jettisoned some aspect of its subsistence just as her womb had rejected its precious intruders? She wondered if she had the strength to help her dear husband reach within himself to . . . *to, to do what? To reach for what?*

Susan Lloyd didn't know what lay there haunting her man. *What was it that needed reaching? What something was missing?* And Stephen kept far enough out of touch with Susan's immediate need. Oh, how she needed him to experience this loss as immediately as she had. Susan did not know, nor was she capable of realizing, the depletions that Stephen had born in his own soulish womb during his long absence in Italy. Perhaps neither husband nor wife could assist or realize the erudition of the burdens his mate bore. Time would tell.

Stephen awoke, startled, Susan's hand had unintentionally nudged him ever so slightly. Jostled into sudden arousal, he sought almost viciously for the source of his awakened state. Then he realized that he had left his wife alone, for his own separate sleep. Stephen could sleep anywhere now. He awoke to his wife crying. She had fallen into a crevasse so large and deep she felt she would never be able to climb out. Would Stephen be there to climb down at save her?

"Susan, what do you need?" The words exited Stephen all wrong, flat and abysmally dull.

Susan finally caught her breath, was able to rule her emotions sufficiently, she said, "Stephen, you went to sleep holding my hand. I need *you* right now. Oh, please honey, where do you go these days? I see you staring out in space so much. What are you looking at? Sometimes you look at me, and I think you don't . . ." She must pause in order to weigh her next words carefully. "You don't really see me, do you? It's as if you are a million miles away from me. A few minutes ago you were staring at my hand, but I don't think you were looking at it. And, how can you go to sleep so quickly? What's wrong? Do you still love me? You look as if you're lost. Are you trying to find something? Sometimes I feel as if you aren't the man I loved the night we said goodbye, before you flew away to Italy. There isn't someone . . ."

Caught on the horns of a dilemma, Stephen answered her last question, wanting desperately to avoid the others: "What? Someone else? Oh, for heaven's sake, Susan." That snapped him back. He stood and began to pace. Susan loved this man so much. His attractive, solidly hewn features still made her heart race just like they did the day he walked into her life, and just as much as when had returned from Italy. He opened the front door, removed his hat, and stood there like a little lost boy. He dropped his flight bag at his feet as if he had come home from work, surprising her to bewilderment and ecstasy. That night had been the most passionate eight hours she had ever lived or experienced. She gave more of herself to him that night than she had when he left for California, or even overseas. But the shadow of something had come between them in the past three months.

She reached for him as he passed by her bed. His jaws tightened as her pillowed voice reached into his heart, "Come sit down, Sweetheart." She patted the arm of the chair, wincing in her own pain. Stephen obediently sat where she could extend her arms around his neck, drawing him in close to her. With this impassioned suggestion, he moved further inside her embrace to once more inhale the sum of her through the fine-spun crown of her redolent hair. He closed his eyes and rested in the surety of this woman's love, but . . . but what of his own? Susan buried her nose firm against his sweatered shoulder. She, too, loved his body's natural aroma, and she imbibed deeply as the need for his strength overpowered her. Then, turning her lovely, besmirched face inward toward his neck, she tasted his skin, which yielded itself a slightly salty essence when she kissed it. For this moment, his flavor reassured her.

Yet, for as much as he held her and met her needs, she was propping him up. He didn't know if or how he would ever be able to tell her about all those things starting to consume him. At times, he wanted to shake her and yell at her: 'Do you know how petty this is? Now, get back to your navigation charts, back to your radio, back to your waste gun, back to your bombsight, back to wherever you came from. We have a mission to fly.' Then his conscience would strike him, and he would silently seek forgiveness.

Susan heard his rhythmic breathing suddenly become irregular, then ragged. She tensed against him, easing her grip only when his breaths slowed to a more even pace. Stephen's respiration resumed filtering through her hair, brushed upon her neck. His familiar aftershave added to her reassurance against the worst life had issued her thus far.

The wonderful tenderness playing out in the room closed around Susan. Without warning, Nurse Minsk entered for the regular temperature taking and blood pressure check. Susan almost expected the woman to enter with a tray of leeches. Back sprang Susan to the bitter realization that this tempered affection she shared with Stephen must be put on hold for a future intimate moment.

The room had instantly shrunk, squeezing her battered sanity tight. She screamed aloud. She pushed Stephen from her body: "No! I want my baby, and you can't give him to me. I can't have babies, Stephen!" Her wide, accusing eyes jabbed at Stephen. Someone was responsible. Someone must be guilty of this sin. Susan grabbed Stephen's sweater with both hands and pulled his face into hers, "I'm so mad. I'm so angry. God hates me! And I hate him!" With that, she rolled over on her side to face away from her husband. As she did, Susan winced once more, groaned, and her husband let her shout the words at the window. He wouldn't interfere. She had to scream.

He was however, caught somewhat off guard by his wife's outburst. Stephen knew the safe things to say, "Susan, I love you. I'm sorry about this. Things sometimes go wrong." But it was easier for him to let it pass. It took too much energy to say them.

Nurse Minsk interjected herself into this. "Mrs. Lloyd, please get a hold of yourself. This will pass. Trust me." Nurse Minsk was adamant about that. But Nurse Minsk had never been married, and Nurse Minsk could drop dead. Susan eyed this woman with a look that would drop a bull moose in its tracks. But this bull moose wouldn't allow one of her patients, especially Susan, to gain the upper hand. When Susan realized that the freight train nearing her bed wasn't going to curb her motion, the patient tightened her fists and screwed up her face into a most unflattering knot, then blurted almost hysterically, "Stephen, get 'er out of here before I kill 'er." No "h" in the third person pronoun 'her.' *Good grief.* This was so un-Susan-like, and especially in light of her otherwise daily grammatical perfectionism. Stephen chuckled to himself. He could go get some boxing gloves . . .

"Mrs. Lloyd . . ." Nurse Minsk repeated, surprised that a woman had challenged her authority.

"I mean it, Stephen. Get 'er out of here—now!" Susan would soon hurt herself if she didn't—no—if *he* didn't extricate this female wrestler from the room. He stepped in between the nurse and his wife, but had no idea what to do next except make certain the two women didn't make physical contact with each other. Susan screamed and Nurse Minsk ordered, and for a short few seconds, chaos ruled. In rushed Dr. Hachtmeyer, Praise the Lord!

Nurse Minsk growled that her patient wouldn't listen to her commands, being the staff sergeant she was at heart. Unbeknownst to any of Helen's recent patients or co-workers, a tattoo had been involuntarily imprinted on her right buttock.

Sergeant Minsk had gotten tanked in one of the nurse's tents on homemade hooch at the conclusion of hostilities in the European theatre. Several of the more enterprising, brash, and thoroughly agitated nurses serving under her command, sought revenge. Seizing up their best chance, three woman dragged her heavy, limp body into a jeep where they drove her to the nearest black market tattoo parlor half a kilometer from the German border. They gladly paid the twenty

American dollaras, observed the procedure to ensure "cleanliness," amid muffled sniggers and loud catcalls, and then drove Helen back the twenty-three miles to base, laughing all the way, where they promptly put her to bed. Nurse Minsk was transferred the following week, still unable to ascertain the culprits who made sitting a nightmare. Unfortunately, she could not prove her suspicions. The tattoo read, "Mama's girl."

"Nurse Minsk, what's going on in *here*?" the doctor demanded, observing the almost hysterical state of his patient.

"Dr. Hachtmeyer, this patient needs to get ahold of herself and calm down. I was—"

"Never mind what you *were* doing. Please leave. *Now!*" he said, pointing the way.

Susan's lament shook the bed. Her usual vigorous mind rejected this phalanx of emotions attacking her. She didn't wish them to settle, but to disburse over the whole room, upon that nurse, upon her husband, and on this doctor. Somewhat bereft of his sanity and quite bewildered at the behavior of his head nurse—but, frankly, not at all surprised—the doctor swiped his thinning hair back over his scalp. He couldn't replace Nurse Minsk. She was very dependable, *and* unfortunately she was someone's favorite at the top of the administrative chain. The doctor adjusted his glasses.

For the first time in her life, Susan hated her body. Objectively, and as a whole, it was perfect. Her beauty career had proven that. But there were things about it she would gladly trade. For instance, Susan thought that her feet were too long. Her little finger on her right hand was a bit crooked. She saw blemishes on her face that no one else did. She had a small scar on her left side. She thought she was slightly bowlegged. When Susan asked Stephen his appraisal of her physique, he just smiled in admiration. Then she would point out her "flaws," which didn't matter to him. Pleading ignorance is healthy ... and quite intelligent for a male. In Stephen's case, it was the truth. Physically, she was impressive. The truth be told—in the dark, Susan liked what she saw when she gazed into the mirror each morning ... until *now*.

His blinders made the enjoyment of his wife's body that much more glorious, and it thrilled her. But now, her body was rejecting her offspring, on a regular basis—two for two. Without warning, the unthinkable captured her attention. She faced the doctor as she wiped her eyes, and with her pliant voice, said, "Will I ever have children? Will I ever have my own child?" she asked, her voice trailing off into a void.

Doctor Hachtmeyer was a tall, thin man. His features almost seemed skeletal; his skin wrapped tightly around his skull, so much so that his veins snaked their way under his cranial skin. He wasn't homely, but he was "different" looking—odd she thought. His nose was overtly pointed, and his eyes were set deep into his head. Their only color was dark, a sad sort of overcast resonated from them. His Adam's apple quavered when he talked. Perhaps he had seen too much suffering. His teeth were yellowed, Susan thought, maybe from too much coffee or smoking. Susan noticed that he wore no wedding band, and he did have large veins protruding into his hands from his wrists. He wore a bow tie that made his head resemble a white elephant gift. His feet were long and the black wingtips made them almost clown-like when he came through the door. He was an odd man, indeed.

Harold Hachtmeyer sat on the edge of the bed, crossed his legs, and folded his hose thin arms as if they were some sort of retractable landing gear. It didn't take a rocket scientist to comprehend the worry he observed written into his patient's face. He was a melancholy man, and he could read pain. He rubbed his chin, thinking very carefully about the next few words he would say. Then he unfolded his arms and looked down at the outline of Susan's leg under the covers. He laid his right hand, or rather his right hand unfolded itself and settled on her ankle. Slowly he rubbed it as if expressing his compassion for what she thought and felt. He said nothing for another few seconds. Then finally, "Mrs. Lloyd, I can't answer that question for you." He didn't look at her at first. "I would give anything if I could."

His dark, sunken eyes settled in upon her finally. "But, I do know a physician who specializes in this field, and when you are feeling better, I'm going to put him in touch with you. I understand he's having some successes, so we're not done quite yet. Please don't give up, Mrs. Lloyd. If anyone can help you, Ol' Doc can." The doctor smiled at her, a smile that seemed to wrap itself around his face like a deflated raft does when air is injected into it. "I'm sorry about the old sarge. She's been a burr under my bonnet for the past year. Now, as you already know, you will be in bed for a while."

Susan's interminably blue eyes swung over and looked up into Stephen's as he, too, listened to the doctor. "Well, I want you to get some rest. I'll keep 'Sgt. Himmler' out of here so you can." Dr. Hachtmeyer patted her ankle. Then he unwound his torso and rose to study Susan's chart. He clicked his pen and wrote something for several seconds on her chart, which he replaced at the foot of her bed. He said he'd be in later to check on her. At that, he left, leaving Susan with her emptiness.

"I love you. I'll always love you," Stephen spoke wryly to and above his wife.

The careful wrapping of knuckles against the hard wood door interrupted the scene unfolding near the bed. "Hi, sweetheart. Are you all right? How are you feeling?" The questions from her parents flooded into the room along with their concerns.

Twelve: Deadness

>━┼━◆>━⊙━<◆━┼━<

March 7th, Tuesday, 1967

The clock chimed three times rousting Stephen from the depths of his slumber. He rubbed his eyes, mumbling to himself that he must have fallen asleep. His neck ached from leaning over the arm of the sofa as he'd been doing for . . . he didn't know how long. He'd been drooling. Disgusting. The house felt silent to him, that late night sensation that creeps over inanimate things, adjusting them to its mood. Toby the cat pattered by, stopped, looked at him and sniffed, then leapt stealthily up the steps, two at a time lest her nemesis, Brit, the cocker spaniel attack from a better vantage point. Cats were strange creatures, Stephen thought. He watched the black and white body of fur disappear above him. The cat made no noise at all.

Once more, that feeling of desperation with its deepening ache pulled at him. His sleep, however long it had lasted, had refreshed his mind to once more take up the vigil of past hurts. Stephen gave himself to his mental time-machine, not caring if it deprived him of sleep or robbed him of his last fleck of happiness. He didn't care if he missed work. Be that as it may, he would soon be getting up to perform his duties with a sleep-deprived body.

He thought about his three children upstairs asleep. There had been other children. He'd not been home from Italy very long. They would have children, he would see to that. The Texas days lingered, long and hot, and he'd been deprived of this woman for years. Susan was so beautiful and so near . . . "What do you want to do today, honey?" she'd asked him.

Saturday, July 6, 1946

"What do you want to do today, honey? It's Saturday, and Lloyd Inc. can spare you for one day. Tomorrow's Sunday. They can spare you then too," Susan informed her husband. "It's so hot out. How about—hey," she snapped her fingers. "Let's go for a swim. You haven't gone in this summer. I bet you went swimming in Italy."

"No, actually, we couldn't get the lifeguard to work the days we wanted the pool," Stephen said with his best sarcastic southwestern twang. "Besides, the colonel had other ideas like, 'let's go bomb another train yard. What do ya say, guys? How about flying through the worst flak you can imagine? Let's dodge some ME-109's for laughs.'"

"Awww. You're no fun at all. Let's go do something. Please? You've been so busy lately, and I feel so . . . so, well, so neglected." Susan extruded her bottom lip, red and lustrously smoothed with her favorite shade of lipstick, but her pretentious pouting availed her little. Stephen had other ideas as to how best he might occupy the next few hours of his day off.

"Let me show you some fun, woman," he said as he took her by the arm and brought her in tow toward the bedroom. Susan didn't resist his advances. Instead, she giggled at his playfulness. Eyeing the bed half way down the hall he felt her body go to dead weight, tugging his arm firmly as she dropped onto the carpeted hall. Her descent forced the breath from her lungs, releasing a low moan: "Oooooh." Her hand flopped outward and slapped against the dry wall, rattling the pictures. The cramps hurt so much worse this time.

"Susan!" No response. The impertinent, familiar blood seemed to know what to do and how dense to stain her clothing and saturate the carpet of their new home. Despite Stephen's prodding, Susan responded but slightly to his attempts to revitalize her. The gathering pool of blood at her hips punched him, and, for a second, he knelt there next to her.

Blood. More blood. His eyes drowned in the blood. His sight blurred and his body settled down onto the carpet with his wife lying next to him. He sat motionless, unable or not wanting to rise and call an ambulance. The changing scenes moved over him like fog sweeping in from the ocean. Susan didn't move. She, too, was no longer part of this.

There was the blood, the sudden noise, vibration and buffeting of strong air currents, mind numbing cold and swirling winds at twenty-two thousand feet. Once again Stephen flew his damaged B-24 Liberator, carrying a wounded, groaning navigator bleeding to death from shrapnel in his stomach and neck, that dead waste gunner lying crumpled and torn to pieces back there in the waste, while the other waste gunner and radio operator tended to him. Stephen's heart raced at full tilt, and he didn't know in which world he was sitting.

The present aroused him as he realized his head had been pounding on the wall behind him. He'd been back there again. He saw it all. It felt incredible *and* terrifying simultaneously. The adrenaline created a glorious rush he hated to leave, and then the sight of Susan lying on the carpet next to him, prompted: Why is Susan lying next to me bleeding? *O Lord. No. Not again.* Would he live between two worlds when blood was present? What it the blood that forced his mind to flash backward and bring the memories flooding through to the present? It must be the blood and the lifelessness of her body. He *had* heard the drone of the engines, felt the vibrations and nightmarish, numbing cold biting and searing his face. He smelled the rubber of his oxygen mask. He was at home, and he had been back *there*. *Here*, he was lost, and as far as he knew this person lying next to him was dead. How could he explain this to anyone? He felt so heavy and wired, and the anger rose.

"Oh...Ste..." Susan, when she did speak, emitted small, breathless half-words or thoughts. *Now* Stephen remembered.

"My God. Will this dying never *end*?" Stephen spoke to that invisible 'Someone' he conversed with so many times to and from targets over Europe. Somehow he'd made it back in one piece, more or less. But that was then. He didn't think about that *Someone* very much any more, hardly ever, these days. Yes, *those* days and events were always there, just at the periphery, waiting. Now it was things like this, losing another child, tense, urgent, oppressive things here in the US, not Europe, this *third* miscarriage, for one, if that's what this was.

The pressure to solve the impossible one more time flung his mind backward to that awful moment. It happened on his twenty-fourth mission. No, he wouldn't think about it, not now. He had so little energy to resist everything that went with it. *Not now. Focus.* "Focus,"

Stephen yelled at himself. He felt tired so often, but he worked as if he had limitless energy. Were these unborn children the result of his not going to Mass and Confession for the past few years? When his men started dying he quit going almost completely. Was it his attitude *about* God? Probably. He'd blamed God for so many things for so long. Now, right now, he wondered if he really counted in the larger scheme of things. But this was his wife, and she did count. Was God listening to him? Did He see? Probably not. What did he have to do to get God off his back or get him to listen in order to stop these deaths? Stephen just wanted a break from the dying. Was that too much to ask? "I fought for my country. I risked it all for someone else! Isn't that enough for *You*?!" His screams echoed down the hall and died. These were some of the lethal questions that had been and were now dogging him. It would take everything he had to put all of this back into the box.

Hearing no response from heaven provoked him to leave Susan and run to the kitchen to call an ambulance. Susan had taped the emergency number of the hospital to the back of the receiver. Flying a bomber too often filled with wounded and dead men had taught Stephen to wait for the wheels to hit the runway and allow the progress of his craft to terminate in order for the medical vehicles to pull up and deal with the bodies. *Keep flying. Keep doing your job or they won't make it.*

Assured the ambulance was on the way, he phoned Susan's parents, then his. They would meet him at the hospital. Stephen hung up the phone and returned to his wife's limp, perfume-scented body. He held her in his arms once again, forcing, even urging her to hang on. Help was on the way.

He pulled Susan closer to him until he was squeezing her, causing her to scream in agony. Finally, the doorbell rang and the room blurred. Stephen shook his head trying to unclog the cobwebs. He lay Susan's head down on the carpet and ran to the door. His trousers were also soaked in blood, adding to his insecurity. *What year is this?*

Thirteen: Dr. McNutt

>─·─·─O─·─·─<

Saturday, July 6, 1946

"Mrs. Lloyd? Mrs. Lloyd." Susan thought she recognized a Ft. Worth drawl somewhere off in the distance toyed with her mind. Seconds went by. Then two full minutes. The woman he stood staring down at began to stir, and she seemed a bit more focused and aware of her surroundings, the man spoke: "Susan. Susan, I'm Dr. McNutt." Susan blinked her eyes. "Susan. There you are. I'm Dr. McNutt. Yes, ma'am, that's me. I'm the biggest nut in here." Susan did not want to acknowledge this person's feeble attempt at humor. Not now. She knew or suspected what had happened to her—again, but didn't know why. Despite the pain, she turned away from the doctor, in search of solitude, to allow herself to be overcome with despair. Put simply, Susan Lloyd wanted to wallow in her own grief for the next few weeks, and perhaps die the death of a thousand questions. She felt an annoying tug on her right hip.

"Mrs. Lloyd, I understand this is your third miscarriage? You know, Mrs. Lloyd—can I call you Susan?" Before she could respond, he drew air and continued. "You know, Susan, when I was in France, with the Army hospital, we had this French woman . . . she used to come around and drive me crazy, she did. She wanted me to give her a shot or some pills so she and her husband could have children. She'd already lost several—kinda like you have, ma'am. Now with her, every time the fightin' would get close to her farmhouse, she'd lose another baby. And the chickens would stop layin,' and the cows would stop givin' milk, y'know? You get the picture. Guns and things like that will do that to a body, y'know? War just ruins a farm's routine. It really does."

Susan couldn't help but smile at this waddling old country doctor rambling on as he did. He possessed affability consonant with his agrarian tonality and background, probably got it before he became a physician, she hoped. He was certainly dressed like a doctor. *How did this man, this little bowling ball, ever become a doctor*, she wondered? Despite her whirling subjective turmoil, his conversation soothed the battered slice of her that needed his attention at the moment. She began to fixate on his words, and this helped her relax somewhat. *He must be making up this story*, Susan assured her mind. She didn't quite know how this doctor drew out every molecule of each syllable, as if tasting it to see if each was edible, sufficient for those listening. *Remarkable*, she thought.

And then Susan tired of his game, and turned back over on her side away from him. Susan wanted to renew her suffering and the blight that lived with her. She stared up at Stephen hoping he would help. A look of consternation had settled fully upon her face. It wondered why or who turned this McNutt character loose to pester her about things like —wait a minute. "This woman couldn't have children? Did he say the French woman couldn't have children?" Susan was certain she hadn't heard him correctly. Susan turned slowly back to face the little, round talking machine that seemed totally unflustered by his uncooperative patient. She wanted or rather needed now to ask a question germane to her predicament. "Why are you telling me this, doctor? I've never been to France. And I *can't* have children, either," Susan blurted back, a bit annoyed and still very perplexed. Dr. McNutt's amiability had perhaps turned into babbling.

"Well, ma'am, I have . . . been to France. During the war, like I said. And that French woman has four healthy boys now. Now don't that just beat all? I still get letters from her. Can't read 'em a 'tall, though. Can you read French, Susan?"

"Really? She has *four* boys? Yes, I can read French. What did you do for her?" Susan begged, sitting up slowly, as best she could. Her eyes reflected the pain in her body as she pulled gingerly to a sitting position. Oh Lord, she hurt. Despite this malaise her interest was now picked.

"Did I tell you about my Miss Daisy, Susan?" he asked, with a sudden surety of his relationship with his newest patient.

"No. We just met, doctor. How could you have told me? Please tell me about the woman's boys." Susan didn't want to alter his previous course.

"Well, Miss Daisy is one of the loves of my life." Susan let out a deep sigh; unable to understand why McNutt was talking about *his* love life in the hospital room. "I call her Miss Daisy, because I just couldn't bring myself to call her anything but that, you know, after she came to the farm to live with me. She didn't seem to mind it any—the name I mean. So it kind o' stuck. Susan, I fell in love with her eyes—the deepest, darkest eyes you ever did see. You couldn't see the bottom of those eyes. I swear you couldn't. And her hair . . . oh my. It smelled so good, except when she'd sweat, don't cha know?"

"She'd sweat?" Susan's fascination, slow at first, blossomed with this strange little doctor sitting next to her on the bed, amid some of the darkest moments of her life, jabbering away in unfettered ecstasy about this Daisy—*his* Daisy. The depth of Daisy's eyes described Susan Lloyd's quandary, which she could neither see the bottom of, nor guess.

Undaunted, McNutt continued: "Last week it would have been fourteen years we'd of been together. Yes sir, fourteen wonderful years. I . . . I think . . . I think it was about the third year when she got in the family way, don't cha' know? But she just couldn't hold on to her babies. Lost two of 'em in a row, she did. Sounds kinda familiar, don't it? Welp Susan, it was after about eight years of tryin,' she finally became—well, you know. . . She was expectin' and all. Now we have the strappin'est young 'un runnin' around the place, carryin' on and all." Dr. McNutt took careful notice of Susan's expressive involvement in his tale. He diagnosed Susan a keeper. He suddenly had her eating oats from his hand.

Dr. McNutt breathed in a hefty gust and exhaled—slowly, for effect. "My Miss Daisy died last week."

"She died? Last week? Oh, I'm so sorry, doctor. How did it happen? You must be heart broken." Susan really felt his pain, and that's what he wanted from her. He bowed his head and milked the moment for all it was worth.

"Well, Miss Daisy, for reasons I still can't quite figure out got a bit rambunctious one day. She tripped in a hole and broke her right leg. Yes sir, she shore did. There she was—a moanin' and a groanin,' lyin' on the ground, and I couldn't help her any 'cause I hurt my back. She was a bit too heavy for me to heft up and move to the barn. Fortunately, Ed Sours drove up to the house about then, and he helped me with Miss Daisy," Dr. McNutt said, his eyes like small fire crystals reliving this tale of woe.

"What did you and Ed do for her? Did you call an ambulance? You did, right?" Susan, quite concerned now for the welfare of this poor woman, Daisy McNutt.

"Well, Ed—Ed, he run quick into the house and got my rifle and brought it out to me."

"He did *what?*"

"He got my rifle, and *he* shot her, 'cause I just couldn't. We'd been together fourteen years, don't cha know?"

"Mr. Sours shot your *wife*? How could he?" Susan sat up further still, blanched from a streak of pain, but quite livid. A murder had been committed.

"Why, ma'am. Miss Daisy was my horse. Why, you didn't think I'd shoot Mary, did ya?"

Stephen leaned back in his chair laughing so hard he hurt. Susan, once this tale sank in, and that took a full second or two, threw her entire being into convulsions of laughter mixed with striking pain. The good doctor joined in, his tummy jiggling as he enjoyed the moment amid Susan and Stephen Lloyd's situation.

When the jocularity slowed and finally died, as it always does at moments of such magnitude, Dr. McNutt reached for his more somber tone, and, finding it, he spoke. "Susan, when the good Lord saved me from my sin, He gave me a gift. Now I help folks who wrestle with this very issue. We need a plan, folks. And I have one." Susan looked stunned.

"You do?" she inquired wiping a tear from her eye. "How can I ever have children, Dr. McNutt?" skepticism oozing from from her every pour. Susan was not asking a question, not really. She voiced her resignation as that of a barren woman, and a thrice-heartbroken one at that.

"Now if you do what I tell you—the way I tell you—and don't skip anything, you will have, uh . . . what do you want, Susan, a boy or a girl?" The doctor spoke and looked as if he believed every word of what he said. He knew Susan needed to hear this in this way.

"Doctor, I need a miracle, not some animal husbandry trick." Susan turned away, trying not to cry again.

"Susan, I'm not talkin' about gimmicks. If you do what I tell you, that boy—or was it a girl—will be here before you know it. I've looked at the tests, seen the X-rays. We're not out of this game just yet, my good woman." He said this with his most matter-of-fact inflection.

"I want a son, Dr. McNutt. We . . ." she began, then looked at her husband, "We want a son . . . but . . ." Susan's desires, as well as her tears, came full force once more, the evidence of failure still too weighty to avoid. When the raw emotions subsided, she placed her hand on the back of her neck, rubbed it for an elongated moment, cocked her head in McNutt's direction, —and it was obvious she had dared to think or hope, to dream for the first time in hours, — actually in years—that one day, her greatest desire might just come to fruition.

"You know, Susan, your eyes remind me of my Miss Daisy's."

"Well, don't think you're going to shoot me," Susan huffed back as she blew her nose. "I've never broken anything. Not yet, anyway."

McNutt winked and was gone.

Tuesday, March 7, 1967

Stephen heard the bathroom door shut above him. He'd fallen asleep again and didn't realize it. "What time is it?" he asked no one in particular. Four fifteen. His heaviness still hadn't let up. Above him and to his right, he heard Susan, "Stephen? Aren't you coming to bed? It's after four in the morning. Stephen?"

"I can't sleep, Honey. Go on back up. I'll be okay. Go on."

Susan shrugged her shoulders in exasperation, descended the stairs, and came and sat next to him. She leaned her head on his left shoulder, nestled herself against him, and within a minute, she could be heard breathing heavily. She needed his nearness in order to sleep. If he wouldn't come to her, she'd come to him.

Stephen had to scratch his lower back, which jostled Susan awake. "I'm sorry."

She blinked several times, and asked, "Why can't you sleep? You need at least a few hours or you'll have a very long day, dear. What's wrong?" she asked, gazing up into his face. It was now four sixteen, and he was still drinking.

Stephen sipped the last of his scotch and then wanted to know, "Do you remember when Michael was born?"

"What?"

"You remember the day Michael was born?"

"Of course I do. Why?" she asked, sitting up, rubbing her eyes. She smelled warm and good to Stephen.

"I was sitting here thinking about the babies we lost before he came."

"Why? Oh . . . " She had been able to set Damien's death aside, but Stephen couldn't. That was what this was about. He couldn't let it go, or it wouldn't let *him* go. She was the more fortunate of the two.

Susan leaned her head back against his shoulder and took his hand in hers, bringing it to her chest, "What a great day that was," he muttered. "I . . . *we* had waited so long." She, too, felt the melancholy of it.

Friday, November 5, 1948

"It's a boy, Mrs. Lloyd," the round little doctor announced, hardly able to conceal his enjoyment and pleasure at helping families who wanted nothing more than to keep populating the earth. "Nurse, mark the birth at 3:55 p.m., November fifth, 1948." Thus proclaimed, he slapped the slimy little thing he held upside down and by the feet on its bottom. His rubber gloved hands made a splat sound. This of course, made the thing cry and gasp and shake, gulping after a sufficient amount of alien atmosphere in the delivery room. Susan's collective happiness and pain knew no bounds. This child was her miracle child no matter what the country doctor said. Michael Josiah Fonteneau Lloyd nuzzled his way into her soul, a special child beyond anything he would ever know. Three miscarriages, four out of the last nine months spent in bed, and all but one doctor held out any hope for this day.

When Susan was cared for sufficiently, Dr. McNutt waddled down the hall of the maternity ward. The family gathered around to hear him announce the news, accompanied by McNutt's wide grin, "Mr. Lloyd, it's a boy," the doctor pronounced, pumping Stephen's hand for all it was worth.

"Oh my gosh, thank you, Dr. McNutt. Mother, it's a boy! Father, you have a grandson! Perry, did you hear that? Michelle . . . Michelle, where is she, Perry? Where's Michelle?"

It took a full minute for Stephen to be totally overcome by this nine-month process that had culminated with three and a half huge words: "It's a boy." Stephen had seen so much death, and now he had been part of bringing a life into the world. *Oh my.* The head nurse ran toward the crowd of people to quiet them as they cheered and congratulated each other. She didn't accomplish her mission to the full extent to which she intended, not with this group, and not under these circumstances. Grandfather Lloyd, ruler of empires and king of the hotel business, grabbed the poor woman and began to dance with her, oblivious to the sight he presented the world. He did not care one stitch. He might just buy a full wing for this hospital if he wished.

As the families hugged and slapped each other, they exchanged cigars. After several minutes of enthusiasm, Stephen slumped into the chair and wept. He wept for the joy that had come into the world, and he wept for all the losses that no one could grasp or know, but the brave men with whom he had flown. Perhaps this child would be his second chance at life—a new start. Time would tell.

Margaret Susan Lloyd sprang upon the scene at 1:02 p.m., April twenty-seventh, 1952. A Sunday. David Allen Lloyd was born at 2:23 a.m., Thursday, October third, 1957. Neither of these children forced Susan into a labor-intensive situation. The final two births were joyful works to Susan, but Michael remained her special gift from God, the God she had hated and cursed. Margaret and David were icing on the cake.

Fourteen: Staff Sergeant Smith

Tuesday, March 14, 1967

As Michael and his father had discussed after leaving the Wilson's, neither would broach the "thing," his possible military service, until the moment presented itself. Stephen had regained some of his momentum from the previous week. He seemed to sleep better, although he did have bouts of irritability that he couldn't explain. He felt glummer somehow, less accepting of the *status quo*—at the office and home, and his libido suddenly cranked up a notch, to Susan's amazement, and, at times, her annoyance. Dolores noticed a shift in her boss's behavior, which alarmed her, because it wasn't necessarily for the better. This required several phone conversations with Mrs. Lloyd.

On Tuesday, Michael met his father at the Fonteneau Building after school. From there they drove to the Tarrant County Court House to meet Staff Sergeant John Smith, SNCOIC of the recruiting station located in the basement.

"Good afternoon, Mr. Lloyd. I'm Staff Sergeant John Smith," the staff sergeant said, smiling. His name was a bit too unpretentious. He'd been kidded unmercifully all through his time in the Corps. His greeting was usually met with, "Oh, sure you are. And I'm Santa Clause. How's Pocahontas?" He had a good sense of humor for a man whose work was to draw men toward wanting to leave home, go ten thousand miles and fight in an ever escalating and unpopular war. Too many of his charges that he had signed up were beginning to return home in silver boxes, minus limbs or suffering from psychological disorders.

With the introductions over, Staff Sergeant Smith left the office to get Mr. Lloyd a cup of coffee, a hot liquid Stephen declined, and Michael usually found disagreeable. Marines could fight. Who knew if they could make coffee?

Once behind his desk, Staff Sergeant Smith turned his professional gaze upon Michael. He'd spoken with Mr. Lloyd for a half hour the day before. Smith knew the stakes, but he had a quota to meet, and it too was pressing with equal determination on him. The Staff NCO lived with this pressure from his chain of command. Stephen Lloyd was also a very powerful and influential man. Smith could very easily envision himself shuffling one stack of papers on top of another stack, and then reversing the process for several years if he didn't say what Mr. Lloyd had "suggested" over the phone. Too many days lately he hated this job.

Smith began: "Michael, I understand you want to become one of us. Is that right?"

"Yes, sir." Michael had entered the recruiting station looking for guidance. Perhaps he could be talked out of this. On the other hand, he might sense a higher calling to the Corps. The spit-shined staff sergeant sat behind his immaculate, authoritarian oak desk. A large, circular Marine emblem—the Eagle, Globe, and Anchor— hung from the wall behind him. Two flags bordered the desk in opposite corners, the American flag and the red and yellow Marine flag. It took Michael all of several seconds to feel intimidated, and now it seemed as if the government of the United States had begun to close about him.

"Talk to me, son. Why do you want to join *now*?" Staff Sergeant Smith probed. He also felt real heartburn with that question. He never asked that question, but he rarely had Mr. Stephen Lloyd sitting in his office. "What if you waited? I mean, wouldn't you want to go on to college, get your degree, and become an officer? Then, go to OCS or . . . have you considered the Naval Academy? You won't get a better education anywhere." Now, all bets were off.

Michael took a deep breath, which cleared his mind sufficiently to recall his conversations with Donny and Victoria. "Sir—"

"I'm a Staff NCO, son, not a commissioned officer. Please call me Staff Sergeant Smith." Oh my, this man really intimidated Michael. Stephen sat amused watching his son squirm.

"Yes, sir. I'm sorry, sir. Uh, yes, Staff Sergeant Smith. I see by your ribbons, you have been to Vietnam. Is that right?"

"Yes it is. Why?" He spoke more like a machine gun, spitting the words out, one after the other.

"If I could ask you, why did you go . . . Staff Sergeant?" The question came out of Michael's mouth weak, revealing in it, just who was in charge in this room.

The easy answer was obvious: "I received my orders and I went. Why, son?"

"But wasn't there more to it than that? I mean did you go kicking and screaming?"

"Well, no. I . . . I volunteered," Smith hesitated. He shouldn't have said that, and he drew within himself for a split second. While there, he heard the rattle of his transfer orders and felt the heat of Guam or some jungle in South America on his face. "I felt obligated to go, Michael. I had received a lot of superior training, and I felt that it was my responsibility to fight for my country. Shall we say, ante up?" He'd been honest, but now he envisioned the change of orders from Guam to the Aleutian Islands. The more he thought about it, the more Staff Sergeant Smith disliked people who did what these Lloyds were doing to his country and to him. It was right to stand up, no matter what the cost. He had a purple heart to prove his loyalty.

Michael continued. "The reason I'm asking, Staff Sergeant, is because a very good friend of mine, until last week that is, started yelling at me for wanting to join and fight for my country. He thought I wanted to do something *evil*. My girl friend hung up on me. It seems I'm losing my friends over just mentioning Vietnam *and* the Marines in the same sentence. Why is that, Staff Sergeant? Are we doing something evil over there? Are we killing babies, like they say?"

These were honest questions. Stephen had intentionally held his peace. This conversation hadn't gone so far a field that he couldn't bring it back in his favor. He could also have a "talk" with this Staff Sergeant if the man overstepped his bounds. And yet, Stephen Lloyd's own pride in his service for his country twenty years before this impromptu conference attempted to overrule his better judgment. It would lead to a battle with his wife's protective nature if Michael actually joined. All three men had higher chains of command.

"As you know," Smith suggested, "Vietnam is a very unpopular place with some of the American public. Not all, but some. The hippies and anti-war crowd are making it difficult on recruiting. No doubt about that. They are in the minority, but growing, and they have the ear of some powerful legislators in Washington. I think, as someone who has been there, I can say the war is being reported incorrectly. We are fighting the media, who are making us look like monsters. Our Marines, airmen, sailors, and soldiers are doing an incredible job under some very trying conditions. I'm proud to be one of them. We just aren't getting a fair shake in the press." The staff sergeant's emotions had remained just under the surface, and he had to fight every impulse to lay it out on the desk for this young man—*and* his father. The Corps needed bright young men like Michael, officers and enlisted.

Then Michael said, "I lost a very close friend not long ago. He basically said the same thing. I, too, have been given an incredible education and family that I believe are worth fighting for. I want to join. And I think that I came here this afternoon to do that."

At this point, Stephen entered the fray. This was going in the wrong direction in a hurry. "Son, now wait just a minute. You don't—"

"Father, I *do* know what I'm doing. I know what I want for the first time. I just now realized that Donny is dead wrong. And so are all these other idiots. They just want to keep taking. I think they're all convinced that the world owes them something. That's the way Donny thinks. He's going to get all he can. I suppose *somebody* has to make it possible for him to be selfish in a free country." Michael turned back to face Staff Sergeant Smith, to ask him, "My freedom doesn't come cheap, does it, Staff Sergeant?" Smith shook his head in the negative. He appreciated that this young kid, a rich kid at that, a kid who should be spoiled but wasn't, was making his job easier. Michael continued, "Victoria, she's just thinking about herself too, but for different reasons. Father, maybe for the first time in my life, I want to do something for someone else. I've been selfish too. And I didn't see it until just now. There's a price to be paid for selfish attitudes, but only by unselfish people. I don't want to be like them, father. I don't." Michael sat down.

Fifteen: A Funeral

>-I-<>-•-O-•-<>-I-<

Tuesday, March 21, 1967
The week passed with its numbing busyness. Damien's body arrived at the funeral home on Tuesday in a flag draped coffin, twenty-two days after notification of his death. After several more days, the memorial service—closed casket—would be held at ten sharp on Friday at Emmanuel Baptist Church. Michael's secret was still safe. The necessary paperwork was probably in the Recruiting Command's files by now.

Upon entering the large sanctuary, an organ played, filling the air with hymns Michael didn't recognize. He identified certain ones, but he hadn't heard them arranged or played this way. New carpet had been laid recently, its smell hanging in the air despite the feverish labors of the maintenance personnel and volunteers to get ready for the service. Being Catholic, Michael sat intrigued amid the saddened and silent cavernous atmosphere of the large protestant church, barren of the familiar: pictures or statues of Mary, the Mother of God. He saw no wood carved Jesus hanging modestly clothed on the cross behind the lectern, no priest in his sacral robe, his absolute devotion to the image of the man hanging on the cross reflected by the priest's repeated genuflection and crossing himself. No altar boys attended to their duties. He saw no hard and high ceilings enclosing vertical architecture and all things ornate that made worship for Michael safe, fraternal, comfortable.

And then he saw it, the casket, and his heart leapt into his throat. He wanted to scream, to fall on the floor and writhe about, kicking and crying. He also wanted to run away and never stop running. But then, surprisingly, he wanted to act like an adult, composed, sensible, *and* unemotional. He wanted to swear loudly and vomit. He had lived Dickens,' "the best of times," but now he had entered Dickens,' "the worst of times." Michael settled for sitting: tightening his jaws and clenching his fists.

On the high, dark mahogany walls hung tapestries of royal blue, purple, and crimson, each embossed with gold or silver lettered Scripture verses from the Bible. One verse proclaimed unapologetically, *"God is Love —1 John. 4:8."* Michael wondered at the three words. With his best friend laying lifeless not thirty feet from where he sat, how could God be love? Damien's death seemed so senseless at the moment, an act devoid of the very quality that these tapestries proclaimed God possessed. Another banner read, *"I am the Way, the Truth, and the Life —John 14:6."* It was all a lie. It had to be. These verses left Michael feeling cheated, if not angry. He hadn't admitted to himself until that moment just how much he loved Damien. He was the big brother Michael never had. The banner above the podium read, *"For God so love the world, that He gave His only begotten Son, that whosoever believes in Him, should not perish, but have everlasting life —John 3:16."*

During the gloomy days between the news of Damien's death and this moment, Michael had mused on specific issues he had not ever considered. He felt his anger resurfacing toward causes that he couldn't reach or get at. He couldn't make any connection between the God being advertised, and the brutality of the reason he sat in this hard, wooden pew. Matters of religion were seldom discussed at home. Michael's knowledge of the Bible, although taught at Gladstone as, "Great Literature," seemed completely insufficient and impotent for the overpowering situation in which he sat immersed. He didn't hear Donny to his left until his friend slipped into the pew next to him.

"Hey," Donny said, searching after Michael's eyes, but finding them elusive.

Neither was Michael certain that he wanted to return the greeting. "Hi," he answered back, but without his usual energy. Something huge had happened between them, and both Donny and Michael felt it. Victoria hadn't called despite Michael's repeated attempts in her direction. He'd heard via the grapevine that she was angry at him for talking about the military, and his plans that, at this point didn't seem to include her in the immediate, or quite possibly, distant future. It wasn't Vietnam *per se*; Victoria clearly saw that what she wanted—Michael for a husband—was slipping between her fingers. Besides her charm and beauty, Victoria could pout about as well as any girl Michael had ever known, much worse than his sister, Margaret. Damien's death had cost him a good friend possibly, and probably a girlfriend. This wasn't a good day for Michael Lloyd. To heck with them, he was going to be a Marine.

Stephen Lloyd raised his eyes from reading the order of worship and looked toward Dr. James Wilson. Stephen wasn't going to look in the direction of the casket. James' uncomprehending blank stare reached beyond this event; past all of his contemporaries, past the handful of political dignitaries, local, state, and Federal; past numerous giants of science and industry who had come to pay their respects; past relatives, past faculty members, even past his wife, and into the unfathomable abyss of this life presently hanging suspended directly over the casket in which his son lay. James, whose huge mind had wrestled with and solved enormous nuclear equations to the betterment *and* detriment of mankind, a man with an astronomical IQ, was a man who could not wrap himself around or even compete with the death of his son. He sat paralyzed physically and intellectually. He wore a small bandage on his lower left cheek, probably from inattention at shaving this morning. His kinky black hair had grayed over the years since his academic career began at Fisk University in 1926, where he labored in relative anonymity under Dr. Imes—so many good days, some difficult.

His skin wasn't a dark brown, but more of a shiny, lighter shade of ebony. His face seemed larger, rounder than Stephen remembered it when he came to interview for the position of dean of the science department at Gladstone not so long ago. He was looking for another position then. His teaching and lab work for the Nuclear Energy Department kept him beyond busy, but most satisfied.

It was his wife who insisted on his coming home at dinner *regularly*. She tried, and after years of attempts, succeeded in having him tethered to some kind of a semi-regular home schedule. Mary Ellen needed his inattentive self somewhere close by. His deep-set brown eyes had long since garnered crow's feet, eyes that had stared down unbending men of huge political endowment, the military elites who demanded what his conscience would not produce, and mathematical conundrums that would break most men, or cower them, or force their brains to seize. His large nose curved slightly toward his right ear. It had been torn and healed incorrectly from some angry, youthful pugilistic exchange. The familiar scar on the right side of his face, from his ear lobe to just above his jaw line, he wore as a badge of honor. He'd received it at the hands of jealous Mississippi white boys he'd bested in some insignificant science fair.

Stephen could tell he'd lost weight. His white-collar shirt had always attempted strangulation at his weathered, bull neck. Today it hung slightly loose. His tie knot, something he always struggled to manipulate into a tight symmetric fist, hung somewhat limp, irresolute. In so few days, Dr. James Washington Wilson had slid off his chair.

Next to James sat his wife, Mary Ellen. Poor Mary Ellen. She looked so fragile, so empty, and so very tiny. Sitting beside her husband, she always appeared slightly diminutive. Today, much more so. Her large brown eyes were puffy and red from days of crying. Her hair had been styled differently than Stephen remembered. Perhaps she had not done it herself. Her sister, a small and attractive woman like Mary Ellen, sat next to her.

Unpretentious Mary Ellen. She spoke her mind all right, and yet she was one of the gentlest women Stephen had ever known. The years had clearly worn at her like waves beating against the hard features of the cliffs, but she'd withstood the harshness that her own life presented her—for the most part. She was still a pretty woman. She too was light skinned. Today though, she seemed so lost, but for reasons that didn't exactly parallel James.' She had lost her son to the war, and it seemed, her husband to his sorrow. Now this contingency suggested her dreams had been set adrift.

Mary Ellen currently focused on and into death's infinitude, and only those who suffer alone, know its portals. Her eyes shifted from her son's casket to stare unfocused at one of the huge bouquets of colorful pink and purple carnations, mustered among the numerous floral arrangements of white cally lilies and peace lilies, pink tulips, white daffodils, hostas, pathos, and roses of every type, shade, and fragrance. It looked as if a floral company had set up shop at Emmanuel Baptist. Arrangements too numerous to count lay huddled upon the aqua carpet below the pulpit. Poor Mrs. Wilson had no idea what she was looking at, nor did she seem to care.

The large pipe organ began to play Mary Ellen's favorite hymn, *Amazing Grace.* The Pastor in his black robe sat ready behind the pulpit. Late mourners straggled in finding empty seats. Many women with their veiled hats or hatless hairdo's pressed tissues against their mouths or noses, daubed their eyes or sobbed gently. The men sat sheer, erect, and solemn faced. Some folks looked curiously about the interior of the building in which they sat, clearly uncomfortable and out of place in church. Others seemed apathetic, staring outward or at their watches. All came wreathed in their dark suits, their wives sitting next to them; thank God the body lying in the casket wasn't *their* son or husband or friend. The occasional cough or sneeze was quickly smothered in the carpet or acoustics, breaking an otherwise unbreakable silence. The aftershaves and perfumes huddled and wafted in a sort of nostalgic reminder of better days.

At exactly 10 a.m., the organ went silent. From behind him, Michael heard the padded step of order, the air moved and the slightest brushing of fabric against fabric. He looked up to observe a machine like Marine Honor Guard at close range, stepping to a silent beat toward the flag draped casket below the stage and pulpit. When they reached the coffin each man turned sharply and strode toward his position, three at either end of the silver rectangular metal box housing Damien's body. The cylinder precision of their feet ceased at the all but inaudible, "Squad, halt." Facing in toward the deceased, their white-gloved hands contrasted magnificently along the seams of their blue trousers, their red stripes running the length of the trouser leg. "Left and right, Hace. Halt. Paa-raade, rest." They stood, immobile, statuesque and respectful of the situation, the parents, the friends, the dignitaries, and most of all, their dead comrade.

For the fleck of a moment, Michael forgot his two companions: anger and sadness. He sat transfixed upon these men—three sergeants, two corporals, and a major, Vietnam veterans all. He was *duly* impressed. The pastor spoke what pastors speak, but Michael remembered little of the homily, and almost nothing of the man who delivered it. He felt ill at ease here, among words and phrases with which he could not identify, not because they came from a Baptist, but because they came at all. Perhaps nothing should be said other than to tell everyone what a great guy Damien was. The Baptists, he supposed, had their ways. This abbreviated sermon did not make it emotionally easier for Michael.

Damien and Michael had lived in different religious worlds, but that had not mattered. They rarely discussed religion. Of the words the man spoke or that Michael actually heard, the concept of the certainty of hope stunned him the most. *How could one be certain at death, and besides, why didn't he say more about Damien? Let the rest go.* Thoughts of his own possible death on the other hand, frightened Michael. Damien had said once that he wasn't afraid of death. He said he knew Jesus, whatever that meant. It certainly meant nothing to Michael. They dropped the subject, never to be retrieved again.

And then the words stopped from the man at the pulpit. The hymn singing too drew to a close. The organ played something classical, which Michael's muddled brain couldn't filter, sufficient to remember if it was Bach or Beethoven. The Pastor stepped over to the grieving parents and said something inaudible, and then greeted and ministered to the relatives.

Finally, it ended. The congregation slowly exited the church leaving the Marine Color Guard to attend to Damien. At the behest of the major, they rolled the casket back up the aisle and into the waiting hearse.

As the Lloyd's exited the church, Michael overheard James' brother, Judah, speaking, attempting to reach his much bigger brother. Judah was an ancient, worn man nearing his mid-seventies. He could flash his huge, gold, toothy smile as quick as lightening. Presently, Judah rested his hands on his round, gold tipped cane. With his balance sure, he leaned over to James, but James stared right past him. Judah then whispered to him, again, something everyone could hear. Judah's "whisper" resembled Michael's coach's yell. "Now you buck up, you hear me, James? Ain't no call to let dis drive you on, boy. You buck up, James. You a Wilson. You be prouda dat boy. He died so's you could live a free man. Damien woulda want you to be proud *dis* day. Now you g'won 'n buck up. You show de world you prouda dat boy. I'm proud." But for the moment, Judah's words only drove James further from their presence and into the vacuum of his cavernous intellect and sorrow.

Mary Ellen cried for both of her men. One was alive, but seemed to be dying. The other, the only child she would ever give birth to, lay in the casket moving past her. Damien could not of himself rise to tell her he loved her or hug her, or eat another of her pecan pies and German chocolate cakes she'd baked in red Folger's coffee cans and sent so far west. In a nostalgic moment, Mary Ellen remembered the spices she'd sent Damien for his meals, which he hated—not the spices, the C-Rations. She would not see grandchildren. *Oh, Lord.*

Michael felt the aching lump in the front of his throat move upward at Mrs. Wilson's sadness and Judah's words. Michael didn't know what to feel now. Judah was a man among men. Judah was "dumb like a fox," as Marcus, Michael's grandfather, used to say. Judah was still a robust man for his age. James *must have* come from that mold also.

James attempted to enter the limousine, but Judah once more grabbed his grieving brother firmly enough to halt him. "James. I don't 'tink you heard me, boy. You *will* get pas' *dis*. I'll hang one offa' yo' chin if'n you don' carry yo'self like a Wilson. Do ya hear me? Dat boy of yo's is a hero today. Now you treat him wit' da dignity he deserves. G'won." It sounded like a threat from the old man, but it wasn't. This was probably the manner in which Judah faced all things painful. He was a man—a proud man—and terribly proud of his nephew. He wasn't going to let his "little" brother take away from that, not one bit. Not today.

Michael backed away from the limousine and from the "sermon" he'd just experienced, and began to look for his parents. He didn't know just what would happen to Dr. Wilson in the coming days. Judah, for his part, looked as if he meant business. Over Michael's shoulder he saw Judah bend over a third time and bring his face close to James' face. "I know you hurtin,' boy. I'm hurtin' too. But we'e her fo ya.' Now you get a holt to yo'self. You carry yo' pride. Yo' son did. He wuz a United States Marine. Dat sometin' ta' be proud of if'n ya ax me."

This kind of behavior from people well below Michael's family's social status was completely new to Michael. He'd never seen a man so grand as Judah, so hard and yet so . . . so *what*? Stephen honked the horn, and Michael rant to join his family. He didn't know where Donny was. When he heard the squeal of tires—he knew. Donny loved to squeal those tires. His dad paid for them.

And thus began the tedious journey to the cemetery to say one final goodbye to Damien, car following car.

The wind played gently with the flag hanging all but limp on the tall, silver pole at the entrance to the cemetery. Tall evergreens stood sentinel at the gated entrance, all too eager at their civil greeting of the familiar stream of cars. At the head of the line the dark gray casket-bearing hearse was preeminent, followed by the black Cadillac carrying the immediate family: James and Mary Ellen, her sister, Nancy, and the five remaining Wilson's: Judah, Dinah, Mary, Peter and Deborah. Slowly, the long line of cars found their place along the cemetery route and parked. Damien, it now appeared, would be laid to rest not far from the entrance. That was good.

The hearse parked and was met by the Color Guard: uniformed Marines who knew their somber task all too well. Each man took his position as the casket was pulled out into the sun. They were trained, as best one can train for this event. In less than a minute the casket lay next to its final earthly resting place.

The family gathered and each was seated before the casket. The several hundred mourners slowly unloaded from their vehicles. They too convened, circling the family, spreading outward so that the green tent housing Damien's casket was all but orbed by the company. The chirping of sparrows and blue jays in the surrounding trees seemed an irritating distraction to Michael, who only wanted to think about the good times with Damien.

The pastor opened a small Bible and proceeded, devoid of Michael's attention.

> *"Damien, throw me the ball. I'm open. Damien! Oh for heaven's sakes. I was open. You're a ball hog, man. I was open. Damien . . ."*

". . . was loved by his fellow Marines too. One of them wrote to me, and I'd like to share a few lines . . ." "*. . . Michael, I think she likes you. She's looking in your direction. So, big boy, what are you gonna do? Huh? I'll get her number for you, but . . .*"

". . . Mary Ellen, we grieve with you both, and yet we rejoice at the knowledge that Damien is in—" "*Damien, they're gonna find out. Your dad always knows when we've been sneaking beer . . .*"

The moments ebbed and crashed hard around Michael, who felt so disjointed. The pastor's voice droned, rose, died, and then rose once again, filtering through the early humid spring air so that it could be heard by most of those gathered to say goodbye. Michael stared at his shoes and the green St. Augustine surrounding them. He recalled internally to the brevity of Damien's and his life together. That he could remember it in so few seconds seemed curious. He looked up at his younger sister, Margaret, for a long second.

Michael didn't quite know how, but he felt buoyed somehow by some unseen power. He guessed it was the knowledge that he would one day, not too distant from this moment, become what Damien had been, and Damien, too, would be proud of him. Michael would make him proud.

He saw things a bit clearer for some odd reason. He saw what Margaret was becoming, a young woman. He recalled how the boys at Gladstone had spoken of her, and fiercely jockeyed for position just to get a chance to date her when that moment arrived—next year? His eyes slipped from his sister to David, now ten years old, who happened to be picking his nose and sticking the product of his efforts into his pocket so that his mother couldn't see. The hankie Susan insisted he carry made little difference. That's why God gave me this finger. *Everyone knows that, mother.*

This heartless, almost brittle moment was one of those crystalline junctures when Michael took stock of things. From the back of his head, a seditious thought crept within sampling distance. He sipped at it—just a taste. In a year would his family be sitting in chairs situated around a green tent with him dead in the casket?

"... ral Wilson was a great Marine, and he served Delta Company, and his country with pride and distinction. I was proud to have been his company commander. Signed, First Lieutenant, Joseph A. Collins, Commanding."

Michael couldn't argue back the tears one minute more. Some distance from Michael, Donny noticed his friend turn away from the pastor's words to find a solitary space and be alone. In so doing, Michael bumped into David as he fought to reach outward toward an opening in the crowd. He politely moved beyond the fringes, only to glance at Lucinda, Damien's girlfriend. Their eyes met. She looked totally undone and neither Gladstone student spoke. Michael kept moving, lest he disintegrate. Donny Rainford almost followed his friend, but didn't. After all, he reasoned, he'd come to this funeral out of respect for Michael. He'd lost all respect for the son who would be buried in a few minutes. *Damien got what he deserved.*

Alone, Michael could now cry for his friend, whom he missed more than he imagined he would. Standing alone, he felt an arm enfold him at his shoulder. He smelled the aftershave and knew that it was his father who had come to rescue him and tell him it would be all right—somehow. Michael turned and buried his face firmly into his father's chest as he had done at the office. Within seconds the boy who would be a man shook both of them, sobbing. He was still his father's son.

When Stephen was certain Michael could bear it, he urged his son back to the ceremony to hear a short poem read by one of Damien's former teachers.

Mr. Ellis cleared his throat, then proceeded. "Robert Graves was a lieutenant in the Royal Welch Fusiliers in 1914. He wrote these words of his experiences during the Great War earlier this century. That was not so very long ago, actually. We're still fighting wars. Mr. Graves own son would be killed in the Second World War fighting the Japanese. He entitled this piece, *The Big Deeds,* and I think it is fitting that I should read it for us, gathered here, in honor of such a fine young man as my student and friend, Damien, on this day.

> *We are done with little thinking and*
> *we're done with little deeds,*
> *We are done with petty conduct and*
> *we're done with narrow creeds;*
> *We have grown to men and women,*
> *and we've noble work to do,*
> *And to-day we are a people with*
> *a larger point of view.*
> *In a big way we must labor, if*
> *our Flag shall always fly.*
> *In a big way we must suffer, in*
> *a big way we must die.*
> *There must be no little dreaming*
> *in the visions that we see,*

*There must be no selfish planning
in the joys that are to be;
We have set our faces eastwards
to the rising of the sun
That shall light a better, and there's
big work to be done.
And the petty souls and narrow,
seeking only selfish gain,
Shall be vanquished by the toilers
big enough to suffer pain.
It's a big task we have taken; 'tis
for others we must fight.
We must see our duty clearly in a
white and shining light,
We must quit our little circles where
we've moved in little ways,
And work, as men and women,
for the bigger, better days.
We must quit our selfish thinking and
our narrow views and creeds,
And as people, big and splendid, We
must do the bigger deeds.*

"I, like all of you was not prepared for this," spoke Mr. Ellis. "I shall always remember what a special young man Damien is . . . or rather, was." John Ellis was starting to lose his voice. He, too, was within inches of crying. "I'm sorry. He's still part of me, and I can't let him go just yet . . ." A long pause to collect his thoughts, and then, "But this I do know, Damien chose the bigger things and the bigger ways. It may not be today or tomorrow that I discover what they were, but one day, one day . . ." Dr. J. Clyve Ellis' emotion sent him from the spotlight where several of Gladstone's faculty comforted him. This was awful, and that was all there was to it.

The Pastor stepped forward to proclaim the benediction. "Now to the King eternal, immortal, invisible, the only wise God, be honor . . ." Michael intentionally quit listening, repressing what he knew to be true, that he, Michael Lloyd, was angry with God for letting his friend be taken away from him like this. It wasn't right. But, could anything make it right? Men die. Men especially die in war. God, he thought, didn't seem too concerned to answer him at the moment. Perhaps God had answered Michael, or maybe this was punishment for something Michael did or hadn't done. The breathtaking thing about this morning was that he had never questioned his religion, and certainly not God. He didn't have to. Now, nothing felt true, nothing seemed real.

"Detail . . . Ahh-ten-Shun! Leeeft . . . Hace. Faw-Ward . . . HARCH!"

From Michael's left, a rifle detail that he had not seen until now, caught his attention. Their snap and mechanics once more drew his regard from the immediate sad things with all of their concern and hurt to focus on man at his most proud, most respectful. "De-tail . . . Halt. Riiiight . . . Hace. Pree-Zent . . . Harms. Or-Derrr . . . Harms! De-tail . . . Ready . . ."

Each Marine rifleman clicked his rifle off safe, a movement barely noticeable, and then pressed his weapon firmly into his right shoulder to await the command. "Aim . . . Fire!"

The simultaneous crack from the muzzles brought a wince to the crowd assembled, but especially to James Wilson. His head ducked into his shoulders like a turtle does when being warned of something inconsistent with its preferred state. He stood there alone amid a sea of dark suited people, the hard slap of finality striking his mind. The sandy-haired pastor recognized the shock in James' ever widening, but unseeing eyes—no tears, just incomprehensibility. He prayed silently for the big man. The several small children attending the graveside service covered their ears, hugged their mother's legs, or buried their faces into a parent's shoulder. The smell of cordite effused upon the slight moving air making the reality of this moment the more terrible. One infant wailed at the noise, then a second.

An uninterested sprinkler's, "chuck-chuck-chuck-chuck," could be heard in the distance. The weapon's concussive discharge burst into the trees scattering the aerial wildlife to another place of safety. Several squirrels danced away to play among the spacious grounds, to frolic among headstones, to scamper up other trees. Safety for them meant scurrying away from the possibility of personal harm. All of these reactions broke upon the cemetery in an instant.

The rifle detail brought their weapons back to Port Arms, minus the command. The brass had clinked and tinkled like a tuning fork as it left the ejection ports, bounced onto the bare earth or sank into the grass. Nothing could or would alter this military courtesy, so violent in its invasion of James and Mary Ellen's private pain. The concussion made it so deliberately public. Each rifleman chambered another round, returned his weapon to his right shoulder, precisely timed with every other man, and waited, "Aim . . . Fire!"

Little David too, held his hands flat against his ears. Margaret turned and grabbed the first familiar person. Finding him, she buried her face into the strength of her father's chest so she, too, might weep openly. Damien quite unintentionally had quashed her innocence this day with a cruel swipe of his present, non-presence. She disliked these assembled sturdy fellows attired in identical crisp and cruel blue uniforms and white hats with polished brims. Men shouldn't move as if they were one, attuned to the same inner frequency. Susan felt herself begin to shake from the emotion of events that refused to consult her, bursting upon her with unfeeling frenzy. Her meandering thoughts turned from James and Mary Ellen to Michael.

The same cutting echo of discharging weapons scattered throughout the cemetery. Then the ejection and the now familiar tinkling of spent brass, the same burned powder residue dirtying the air, the same rending of the sudden breeze until the blasts once more dissipated over the vast cemetery's serene expanse. In the distance, the droning, unfeeling, repetitive, "chuck-chuck-chuck-chuck," of the sprinkler gave no notice to the mourners.

A third time, rifles went to the ready, "Aim . . . Fire!" The unwanted explosion and more infants wailed. This time several women joined them. Tinkle-cling, port arms, and the unwanted shock. "Or-Der . . . Harms. Pre-Zent . . . Harms!"

Attention shifted from the firing detail to a single Marine bugler, who, at the conclusion of his comrade's component, retrieved his horn from under his arm and pressed the instrument to his lips. With a gulp of air, he sent *Taps* fluttering and furling among the assembled and passersby. Some of the old veterans present wiped the tears from their wrinkled eyes. They stood a bit straighter, remembering rusty, cruel pasts and their buddies that had gone before them. The dust of the old things, the bitter and sweet memories recalled and refreshed, were brushed and straightened on the shelves of minds that did not forget. Only *Taps* held such haunting power.

At the conclusion of *Taps*, the NCO in charge of the firing detail bent over and retrieved several pieces of brass lying about the squad's feet. With the brass held carefully in his gloved hand, he approached the detail in process of folding the flag sharply; fold, upon fold, upon fold. The approaching sergeant reined his stride to a halt, and saluted the folded flag. When the flag had been folded into its neat, triangled bundle, white stars laying upon the deep blue field, the sergeant slipped the spent brass into the folded flag, saluted once more, did an about face, and returned to the firing detail. Assuming his position with them, he ordered, "Left . . . Hace. Faw-Ward . . . Harch." The squad made little noise as they marched upon the soft St. Augustine. "De-Tail . . . Halt. Left . . . Hace. De-Tail . . . Dis-Missed." His voice echoed and carried. None of the Marines moved out of respect for their comrade who could no longer help carry them through the long days ahead. Damien Wilson would live forever in what that blue and white and red triangle symbolized.

Several hundred pairs of eyes acknowledged the sergeant holding the flag as he handed it to the major, who inaudibly accepted it. The major performed a right face, took four measured steps and halted. He fixed his head and eyes on something in the distance. Then he performed a left face directly in front of James and Mary Ellen. He inhaled, and lowered his eyes to meet their burden. The major hated this ceremony. It represented death, yet there was such staggering purpose in all of it. Struggling with his own raw emotions, his bottom lip quivering slightly, he bent forward, one white-gloved hand pressing firmly on top with the other beneath the folded flag. He presented it with great deliberation and tremendous care to Dr. James Wilson.

The major spoke for all to hear. Only two people mattered to him. "Dr. and Mrs. Wilson, on behalf of the President of the United States, and a grateful nation, I present this flag to you in honor of your son, Corporal Damien Wilson. Please accept our deepest sympathy for your loss. My fellow Marines and I understand better than most what you have lost. Your son was a hero, and we honor him *and* you, for the sacrifice represented here this morning."

His words crashed into the mounting fierceness of the moment, for he spoke as one who knows the sting of battle. His four rows of ribbons matched that assessment. "Dr. Wilson, I have admired your work, sir, and we all owe you more than you will ever realize. It grieves . . ." the major stopped to re-gather himself and breathe, until he felt he could resume, "it grieves me deeply to present this flag to you instead of your son."

The major's tone was as measured and somber as his face portrayed. That official voice seemed small for such a large man as the decorated officer. He handed the flag to Dr. Wilson. The great man's hands trembled so much that the flag dropped from between his fingers and into his lap. Judah, standing directly behind him, gripped James Wilson's shoulder with a vice like strength, and James straightened himself as if Judah had somehow infused him with power neither man could explain. Dr. Wilson's hands sprang to the flag, and he gripped it as if it were some marvelous, treasured thing, which it of course, was.

Michael watched Damien's father carefully. A smile, ever so slight, took hold of the big man. There came the most fragile alteration in Dr. James Wilson's soul. It seemed to Michael that this it was pride, but Michael couldn't be sure. Whatever the transformation was, it was certain that Damien had given his father everything that he could give. Something was happening to Dr. Wilson, and it was quite unusual. Dr. Wilson began crying tears of joy. The difference was noticeable to many people, but it made no sense to Michael.

Stephen began to crumble deep in his inmost being. Susan was far too busy keeping David still, so she didn't observe the event or her husband. Judah stood ramrod straight behind and above his youngest brother. Donny glared, Lucinda further drew within herself.

Most uncharacteristically, this officer squatted to eye level out of respect for the great man's achievements. He wanted to do more than the required things. He needed to help the wife help her man, who all of a sudden didn't need their help. The major said nothing, but he noticed. He patted Dr. Wilson's forearm when he could finally release the flag to shake the officer's hand. The major would never recommend what he just did to any of his fellow officers and NCOs, but the magnitude of the man before him and his accomplishments, required nothing less, it seemed to the major.

Turning his gaze to Mary Ellen Wilson, the major took her hand, and spoke into her red, swollen eyes, "Mrs. Wilson, no words of mine will ever meet your need. Please accept our deepest sympathy. Your son was a very brave Marine. I know you will someday be very proud of what Damien accomplished, if you aren't already."

He read Mary Ellen's eyes for another few moments. Then the Major straightened, his right gloved hand shot to the bill of his mirrored frame cap in salute, held it rigid for a long second, and then released it slowly to his side. He did an about face, then a right face, and he strode back to the side of the casket. Elegance is sometimes measured in brevity.

Mourners filed before Damien's parents, to touch or place roses on top of the casket. Mary Ellen grieved internally for the time being, but acknowledged the warm words. Dr. Wilson rose to his feet, able somehow to greet and comfort the people who had come to do the same for him. Something powerful had happened. Judah knew it, but James lived within its might. There would be time to cry tears from this new perspective, but not now.

Within thirty minutes, the graveside service was complete. In another few minutes' car doors slammed, motors roared to life, and the motion of seventy plus vehicles of various kinds slowly departed the grounds. In another fifteen minutes, barely ten people remained; twenty minutes, and the workers were busy removing the tent and hoisting the coffin into the elongated hole in the spring dirt of Damien's Texas. The backhoe that cut the earth for the hole had been removed to the shed the day before, and the sprinklers hurled water in their wide arcs, chuck, chuck, chuck, chuck.

Sixteen:
A Dinner at the Wilson's

Saturday, March 25, 1967

"Susan, this is Mary Ellen Wilson."

"Mary Ellen? Oh, how *are* you doing? I've wanted to call you a thousand times, but I wasn't sure if I should. It's so soon after the . . . after the . . ." Susan thought the tears she had cried out were about to begin a fresh.

"I know, Susan." Mary Ellen felt the need to reassure her friend that Damien's death was still quite difficult on everyone. Mary Ellen also believed she had cried a river full over the past few days. But hearing Susan choking back her own cloistered emotions, Mary Ellen found it nearly impossible to douse her own sorrow. Now she wondered why she had called. She had felt in control when she began the dialing process, and now she felt like excusing herself to hang up in defeat.

"Are you . . ?" Once more Susan Lloyd's emotions wouldn't allow her to finish her thought.

"Yes, we're struggling with this. I miss him so much. James and I have cried together, off and on. We've argued from impatience and lack of sleep as you can imagine. Our nerves are on edge. But . . . by God's merciful grace, we are dealing as best we can. I wanted to call and thank you for what you did to get the meals here for our families and friends."

"Mary Ellen, you know it's the least we could do. My . . . goodness." Susan almost lost it.

"We do thank you both. James said so just this morning. And that's why I called. I've looked at our calendar and for the foreseeable future we're going to be having family staying with us. We, James and I, want to have you over for dinner and the only time we can make room for is this weekend. I'm sorry it has to be on such short notice like this."

"You don't have anything to apologize for." Susan thought she heard crying on the other end of the phone. "We don't need to come this soon. Really. You two need more time to be alone, don't you?"

"No, no, we need company outside the family for a few hours. It would be wonderful if you would come for dinner. Truly."

"Are you *absolutely* sure?"

"Well Susan, I'm not absolutely certain about anything except that God loves me, died for me, and is caring for me. I *am* certain about that. The rest, I'm just living day by day. I think *I* need to fix a meal for someone else. I think that would be good for me personally. So please, don't deny me that? Please say Stephen and you will come."

"Well, if you are sure. Let me see. I'm looking at the calendar now. Today is . . . today is? I can't remember what today is, Mary Ellen." Susan felt panic grip her mind.

"You sound like me. I can't remember anything either. But I have been carrying my calendar around with me just so I won't forget what day it is. Today is the twenty-fifth, Saturday. Next Saturday is the first. If the calendar is wrong, I'm sunk." Her voice promoted a joyful grace.

"Looking at my calendar, we don't have anything going on this coming Saturday. No sports. No piano lessons. We're open. How did *that* happen? What time would you like for us to come?"

"Would six be too early?"

Saturday, April 1, 1967

The drive to the Gladstone campus was quiet inside the Jaguar. Handel's *Water Music* etched the confines of the leather upholstery and dashboard, roamed freely between, over, against, and into the two passengers seated comfortably inside. Each was going separately to the same destination. Stephen said little, even though Susan attempted to coax some variation of words from him that sounded like sentences. He wanted to talk to her, and he knew on some level that it would do much for his wife's fragile composure. But Stephen was just too much into his personal turmoil over Damien's death to really notice her needs, much less care for them. He felt as if he were wrapped in clear cellophane. He could see out into the world and people could see him, but he couldn't touch them or be touched despite their immediate proximity to him. He lived in one universe and Susan in another, yet in some incommunicable way each brushed the other, perhaps they even over lapped each other. They had viewed life differently over the past week, that was all. How could he explain this? *"If only Damien hadn't been killed,"* he whispered.

"What?" Susan inquired eagerly.

"What?" Stephen felt uncomfortable that he might have been overheard.

"You said something. What did you say?"

"I didn't say anything."

"What did you *say*, Stephen? Why have you been so distant these past few days?" Susan had coaxed his head out of that shell of his and she would do all in her power to keep it out. "I feel as if you are avoiding me. What did you say just now?" Susan's belated agitation that she had been nursing began to boil to the surface. It didn't have to travel far.

"I'm not avoiding you, Hon. I don't know what I said, if I said anything. Just let it drop. Please."

"Why are you so angry? Did I do anything to upset you, Stephen? What's wrong?"

"Nothing's wrong. Why are you so angry with *me* right now?"

"I'm upset, because you are shutting me out, inch by inch. You talk to yourself, but not to *me*. And then when I ask you what you said so we can at least talk to each other, you tell me you didn't say anything. But I heard you," Susan was shouting above the radio so that Handel became a nuisance. She reached over and snapped the radio off, crossed her arms to indicate she was perturbed, and then realized that they were about to turn on to the campus. She uncrossed her arms and covered her eyes so that Stephen wouldn't see how distressed she looked. Susan had never been a woman to cache her overburdened emotions. Stephen had been there for her, for the most part, when life took on ignoble proportions.

"Oh good grief, Susan. I'm *sorry*," he said, breathing somewhat heavily from exasperation. It was easier living in a tent with four other men in Italy for a year during the war than it could be with *this* woman at times. "All right. I said, 'If only Damien hadn't died. Do you feel better now?'"

"No. And I don't understand. Why would you say *that* now? He's gone. We can't undo what's done. I wish he hadn't died too. But he's gone, and we have to make the best of it. Now come on. We're here. I don't want to go in there and upset the Wilson's anymore than they already are. We're going to have a good time. *I* need this too, Stephen. Mary Ellen certainly does. How do I look?"

Stephen shoved the words out toward the neighborhood, "You look fine."

"Mary Ellen, this is *wonderful*. I want this recipe. How did you get these onions to taste like this?" Susan was overdoing it, Stephen thought. Her overlooking the obvious was getting to him. Then she turned to Dr. Wilson, "James, how are *you* doing? Is the time off helping?" Susan kept pushing Damien's death around the periphery. Everything she did since getting into the car and walking in the front door irritated Stephen. Him withholding his thoughts from his wife and being forced to communicate them was about to boil over into this evening. He would be emotionally spent long before he climbed into bed. He felt as if his head were coming off. To add to his discomfort, pressure began building in his chest. What Stephen felt overall was not totally new, but he'd begun to experience a breaking inside of him.

Unable to contain the duress, Stephen screamed aloud: "Susan, will you please stop this!" Stephen's face became a study in intensity none of the people sitting around him had ever observed in him. His breathing came in sharp, raspy cords, and he looked as if he wanted to break something.

"Stephen, what's wrong? What did I say?" Susan's alarm was more from embarrassment than fear. Her husband had humiliated her, and she wanted to strike back. Yet, her questions didn't seem to penetrate the man sitting across from her. James leaned back in his chair as he watched his friend dealing with something even he couldn't grasp. Mary Ellen started to speak, but James motioned for her to hold her peace.

Stephen blurted his distress, "James . . . I'm sorry. I don't know what's wrong." Stephen's eyes danced, they appeared unable to focus. Stephen was not okay. He sat, staring down at the table, breathing short, jabbing breaths. James, in spite of all his current trials, set his large hand on Stephen's forearm and spoke firmly into the void absorbing his employer and friend. "Stephen?"

The touch awakened this Lloyd to something almost at the level of comprehension. It was as if Stephen Lloyd was having trouble keeping two universes separated, 1944 and 1967. He blinked, trying to stir the cobwebs back. "I'm sorry. I'm . . . sorry." Stephen felt light headed.

"James, what do we do?" Mary Ellen Wilson pleaded.

Susan was thoroughly confused and not a little hurt at this display put on by her husband. Then Susan said, "Stephen, what's wrong? I've never seen you like this. You need to start talking to me, *now*. Won't you tell me what it is? I love you."

James chimed in, "Yes. Let *us* help you."

Stephen just sat there, breathing unevenly, his head getting lighter every second. Finally, his eyes rolled back and he passed out. James caught him before he hit the kitchen floor.

"What?" Stephen started to sit up. He had no idea why he was lying on the couch, a wet rag on his forehead and a paper bag over his mouth.

A hand pushed against his chest so that he wouldn't sit. "Now, you just lay there, Mr. Lloyd. I'm the doctor around here," Mary Ellen spoke from miles away.

"What happened?"

"You hyperventilated. Stephen, are you all right?" It was Susan's voice and concern that registered in his fumbling mind. "Are you okay, Sweetheart? You had me so worried."

"I'm okay. Let me just sit up. I'll lie back down if this doesn't work."

"Stephen, what brought all this on?" James asked. "This is so uncharacteristic of you?" This scientist could be so absent from everything around him at times, and especially with the burial of his son only days earlier. But it was because of *something*, that he had carried his grief well, that, and the help of his older brother, Judah.

The three people sat huddled around Stephen who lay on the couch. He'd been down for about three minutes, unconscious apparently. This refocusing was in fact good for James and Mary Ellen. They needed to give, and tonight they could give to the Lloyd's who needed what they possessed. Their faith was buoying them in this monumental time so that giving flowed naturally. It even felt good, the first real joyful thing either had experienced in a month.

"James, I'm worried about Stephen. *Really* worried. Ever since the funeral, he's been slowly shutting me out of his life. And I don't know why."

"Hey. I'm not dead. Don't talk about me is if I'm not here, Susan." Stephen's tone was slightly angry.

Mary Ellen gathered Susan up and huddled her into the kitchen, leaving James and Stephen to talk.

"Susan, what's happening? I'm frightened. You two are the most solid, well-adjusted people I know. I've never seen Stephen snap at you like that. He adores you. And I know *you* love him. Please tell me. What can I do?"

Susan spoke of the past week, how Stephen had seemed so distant emotionally. He'd hardly said a complete sentence to her in days. There had been intimacy so much more than normal. And when they had come together, it wasn't a pleasurable time for Susan. Susan didn't know what had caused it. Was it *her*? Was it *work*? The children? She had no solid answers, and Stephen wasn't talking.

The two women continued to explore all the possibilities. Mary Ellen felt compelled to tell Susan how she was coping and about her faith, which seemed so unexpectedly yet visibly real to Susan. Susan spoke from her inadequacies, the fact that she had so little to go on, she was suddenly afraid for their marriage, and she wasn't sure if God was punishing her again for missing Mass. Avoiding the faith issue, Susan asked Mary Ellen Wilson what she thought she should do.

In the next room, the conversation was much different. Women reasoned subjectively, which required thousands of words. That's how they probed and plodded after reality until they could clutch it to the bosom. James and Stephen, on the other hand, approached it cognitively, in as few words as possible. Life worked that way for men. If they couldn't get at it through their brains in twenty-five words or less, it didn't have an answer. Advanced calculus wasn't going to work either. James had to use his scientific approach to question everything so that he might help prime the pump toward resolution. But the two men only stabbed at one tangent after another. Stephen made a few incoherent suggestions. The year 1944 wasn't on anyone's radar screen, aside from Stephen. But for Stephen, 1944 surrounded him.

Underneath it all, Stephen had the answer. He knew it the moment Michael told him Damien had been killed. That was when he saw their faces after their long absence. In his office, he felt the aircraft he had flown rise and fall upon the thrashing air currents whipped by hundreds of bombers tearing through it. He felt the exploding flak bursts ripping the air asunder. Why had it come back so ferociously? Why *now*?

Finally, Stephen sat up, lifted his weak body off the sofa, and ambled into the kitchen to tell Mrs. Lloyd it was time to go. His need was met with Susan's blunt response, "we're not through talking, Stephen. Go back in there and keep James company." Neither Stephen's nor Susan's eyes batted at his wife's abrupt response. Round two.

Stephen quit attempting to make sense of intangibles like the ones staring at him. It only made his life more miserable. There were two issues he couldn't get through. He saw the future in bleak terms, but he didn't know why. He felt pessimistic for the first time since . . . since when? Stephen knew all too well when. He explored every avenue, with the exception of one. For James, instead of plotting the empirical evidence on the board so as to map an equation to fit its equivalent, he opted to ask Stephen if he'd be interested in attending a Bible study at their church on Sunday night. He might find some answers there. Mary Ellen had also asked Susan if she'd like to go. Both Lloyd's declined. They went to church. They were sufficiently religious. The answer to their troubles would be found somewhere other than where the Wilson's wanted to direct them.

The Catholic Church had stood for centuries. If the solution were religious, the Catholic Priesthood would methodically point the way. Stephen was somewhat surprised at his terse response to James' attempt to help. He didn't mean to be so laconic, but Stephen Lloyd had always been able to solve his own stubborn problems with his ruthless examination of life. He was an engineer after all. He was rational. He'd solve it.

Susan felt embarrassed when Mary Ellen suggested her church might be of some help. The folks there had really helped James and her, she admitted. But to Susan, the term Baptist held very negative connotations. Baptists appeared so . . . so dogmatic about everything. They didn't believe the same things Catholics did. Baptists were so emotional. No, she would speak to her parish priest.

The evening ended. Actually, it slid off into the night, and the ride home was even quieter than the drive to the Wilson's.

Seventeen: A Change of Plans

❯⟶◦⟵❮

Thursday, April 6, 1967

With the world somewhat back in tow and dinner finished, Susan glanced over her calendar. She suddenly remembered that several representatives from different Ivy League schools and major universities would be at Gladstone on Friday, the fourteenth. For some reason that had escaped her memory, the universities she wanted to hear from had scheduled Gladstone much later than normal. She did recall being quite upset at this happenstance, and registered her protest to the appropriate board member, the president, who happened to be her husband. Stephen had Dolores look into it.

"Oh, Michael. Your calendar is clear for the fourteenth, isn't it?" she asked, her displeasure obvious at the possibility of missing this long-awaited academic opportunity. This important event had somehow been scheduled for a Friday night, which was for Susan, unacceptable. Michael's future however, fought against her.

"Why, mother?" Michael asked.

"I want you, your father and I, to go to the school to meet the representatives from Yale. Let's see, Harvard and Princeton will be there too. The Dartmouth Rep already came and we missed her. It was that scheduling conflict I couldn't reconcile. Anyway, we need to start talking about your schooling in a more official capacity. You're still leaning toward Princeton, aren't you?"

Michael looked at his father, embroiled in the *Star Telegram*. Their dinner had concluded a few minutes before the question floated through the air. Margaret and David had already left the dining room for parts unknown, and Ginny Cassalls was in the kitchen doing the dishes. As if on cue, Stephen folded the paper and laid it on the dining room table. He looked at Michael, who was watching him. Then he glanced at his wife, busily involved with the calendar in the kitchen. She kept tapping the pencil's eraser against her front teeth.

"Susan, would you come here for a second?" He suddenly felt agitated at having to deal with this. He gave Susan little hint of the gathering storm he was about to invite her to enter. His eyes wouldn't meet hers.

"Yes," she said, sitting next to her husband. His evasive facial expression spoke of another unrest brewing within him, which Susan noted carefully. She began to feel a little uneasy, but wasn't sure why. The reason lay behind those ball-bearing-fisted green eyes of Stephen's. Whatever *it* was, she doubtless feared that her husband would say what he would say in as few words as possible, leaving her to guess at the rest. In spite of this, Susan had lived for this moment Michael's entire life, and having reached it, her husband seemed reticent for some odd reason to move forward with it. Michael's graduation from Gladstone was a month and a half away now. *Stephen should be happy . . . or at least . . . neutral. He wasn't either. Why?* It was almost as if he enjoyed sparring with her the past weeks.

Stephen didn't want to spar or participate. He wanted to hide, but for reasons he refused to examine or articulate. He began slowly, like a pitcher's wind up. "I wanted to wait until the proper moment to speak to you about Michael's future plans. He and I have been discussing it, and I think now is the time to let you know what conclusions we've reached."

"You have? Al- . . . right." Although Susan's pleading eyes had enlarged somewhat, her breathing shallowed at the possibilities of this ominous statement. "I'm listening. I'm hoping you haven't pushed him at A&M or TCU. I'd prefer . . ." Susan sat mildly pleased that Stephen once again spoke in whole, adult sentences for her. That helped her spirits, somewhat.

"Susan. Please. Let me finish. Michael has decided not to go to school just yet." Dumbfounded silence greeted his remark.

"Well, what does that leave him? He can't just *not* go. He'll become eligible for the draft, and I won't have that. He *has* to go to school.

We've planned this for years, Stephen, for his entire life. You know that." Susan's blossoming panic grew to fear of what her husband might say next, and his eyes betrayed something menacing to her own. *What lay beneath this statement, and what could Michael's plans be,* she wondered?

"Michael—?" she inquired, turning to face her son. Her eyes had suddenly narrowed and intensified. From this, they moved to questioning, and from questioning, they melted into a pleading tenderness. And from a brief pleading tenderness to an articulate seriousness. Cautiously, she ventured the question: "Why do you want to wait, son? You know what that means don't you? Or . . . *do* you? This is no time to be idle academically. Besides, you will get so far behind. Gentlemen, let's be reasonable here."

"Mother, you aren't going to like this . . ." *Say it you coward. Say it!* Michael urged his gut to produce his manhood. "I have decided to join the military, the Marine Corps, Mother. I'm not going to college right after I graduate." Unfortunately, Michael had begun with a half-truth. He'd already joined. Regardless, the "thing," the Marine Corps thing, the thing that kills young boys lay in the open, ready for whatever Susan would throw back at him—and she would throw something, make no mistake about that. Nothing could conceal or halt it now.

Her son's announcement fully deflated the woman. Not in Susan's wildest dreams could she have imagined this. After a moment of stagnant silence, of holding her peace, her blue eyes all but dilated, where a fire commenced jitterbugging right behind her dark, round pupils. She looked from Michael to Stephen, and from a cavity within her body unused in some time; she screamed one word, "NO!" Susan stood, then pushed her way toward the den as if fighting against something heavy and frightful she couldn't see, against a monster.

Then she stopped, her arms at her sides, her fists drawn tight. She would attack this in her most parental and defiant virulence. Susan reversed her present course and stormed back through the same unseen thickness toward the two blank faced males she had left alone seconds earlier. Through her dagger-like teeth, she proclaimed to the two waiting sets of ears the words that her stomach wanted to vomit. "Michael, do you have the slightest notion what it cost me to bring you into this world?"

Be careful Susan. Don't say it, Susan. He doesn't know, Susan. You don't have to say this. Ooooh, but I do.

"Michael . . ."

You're hesitating aren't you? No, you shouldn't say this, should you? Don't equivocate, Susan . . .

"Michael, you are my fourth child, but you are my first living son." Having said it, Susan dropped her eyes to the table. When the teakettle actually blew, the water was tepid, and bloody.

"I'm what? What is there left for me to know about this family?" Michael stood up and almost squared off with both parents. "Good grief, father. Am I some kind of . . . of spineless amoeba that you couldn't tell me you flew bombers during the war? I mean, my heavens . . ." Then he looked at his mother for several long, stoic seconds of mounting pressure. "No Mother, I don't know what that means. I'm sorry if . . ."

What can I say now? I rehearsed this, but not in this context. How do I talk to my parents?

Nothing in his life had prepared Michael for this day *and* this moment. "I would have . . . I would have had three brothers or sisters?" Michael's own head of steam bled off. His shoulders dropped and his head fell into his palms. The world had given him another distasteful thing on which to chew. "But, why in the . . . Were you *ever* going to tell me?" The words felt even hollower than they sounded, and Michael began to cry out of pure frustration. It was either that or hit someone. His tears at this moment infuriated him, because his parents infuriated him. He thought they raised him to stand on his own two feet. "I won't break. Did you think I was so fragile that I couldn't handle difficult issues without coming apart at the seams!?!" His own emotions moreover, betrayed his age and his immaturity.

"Michael, you were just too young, and then after a while your father and I felt that you . . . well, that you didn't need to know." Susan placed her hand upon her son's big hand to reassure him of her love, and in some way convey to him an unspoken apology. Michael wanted to push her away, but didn't. He stared at her hand resting upon his. Hers was a touch of warmth and vitality, but he didn't want to be touched by his mother just now. How does an eighteen-year-old son come to a moment like this and respond in any way other than he had? The obstinacy he felt but had not fully conveyed was written in cursive on his furled brows.

Realizing her motherly instincts were creating ripples in their relationship, Susan spoke before Michael could. "Son, I fought to get you here, and I won't let you join . . . the *Marine Corps*? Did I hear you right?" Susan stiffened once more. That fire was back. The thought soured in her mouth. These two words tasted putrid for so many reasons. One reason lay freshly buried not too far from where she stood.

"Yes mother. You heard right. I said the Marine Corps. And . . . you might as well know. I've already *joined*." Both seized his and her battle-ax once more.

"*You . . . you . . . you* have joined? The Marine . . ." Normally, a woman can't deflate bit by bit. Neither can she weep a little at a time, but Susan disappointed both males as well as the established scheme of the universe. The air in her lungs left her, and she crumpled in the chair. Her sudden and monumental silence was deafening. Then, turning to her husband as if freshly inflated, she lit into him. "Stephen Lloyd. I am so mad at you I could spit. Have you no care for my feelings? Are you just going to let *our son* go off to the military as if he's going to football practice or something? "Stephen," and here it came, "WHAT WERE YOU THINKING?!"

She screamed this final question at the top of her lungs. Fortunately, David was at Ronny's house and out of earshot. No one was thinking about Margaret or Mrs. Cassalls. Stephen said nothing. What could he say? It wouldn't have done any good if he tried. He wouldn't contest her right to vent. Not now. She'd certainly earned it.

Turning back to face her son, she said, "Okay, young man. That's what you want? Well, let me tell you what *you* cost *me*, since you are so grown up all of a sudden. Three babies bled out of me before you came along. I lay in bed for months so I could have *you*. I almost died in the process. I don't think anyone or anything is more important to me than you two men, ESPECIALLY YOU, MICHAEL!" Susan had reached two octaves above her normal tone at the mention of her son's name.

"We just buried Damien, who, as you know, was very much a part of my life, and now you want to go, *you, my son—you* want to place your father and me in the same position Damien put his parents? Is that what you want? *Not on your life*." Susan's eyes resembled lakes of fiery gasoline. At the height of the blaze in her soul, Susan turned back to Stephen. "Stephen, what were *you* thinking? Surely you can't agree with this. There are young men dying over there day after day and for what? Does *anybody* . . . does anybody know why we are fighting over there? My GOD! Have you two lost your ever lovin' minds?!"

Once again, Susan broke from the room in open retreat, or attack, depending on one's point of view. She hurried up the stairs, fearing that she might further alienate or destroy her extreme affection for the men she loved so much, but wanted to slay in the most delicious way.

Watching her go, Stephen's demeanor remained calm, and he didn't have a clue why. With his eyes fixed on the stairs, he spoke to the boy sitting across from him. "Michael, we both knew this wouldn't be easy. I wasn't quite expecting *this*, though. I can make no guarantees about your mother. We . . . we both withheld this business about the miscarriages before you finally came. It wasn't just her idea, son. What good would it have done to tell you?"

Michael shoved his hands in his pockets and hunched his shoulders. The corners of his eyes hung limp. He felt dejected, left out of a world in which he should have been allowed to take part. "I don't know, father. But wouldn't you want to know? Wouldn't you want to know that your father flew in the greatest war in history?"

It was hard for Stephen to answer such questions he hoped would never see the light of day in his household. Stephen breathed heavily, and then he tugged slowly at his chin. "Your mother has paid a heavy price physically and mentally to have children, son."

Stephen's deep-set eyes stared blankly at the oak table separating the two men. He intentionally tried to reconstruct the past as if it were happening on television right then. It was the only way he could visualize it in order to explain it. Michael waited. He had to, if his need to know would find its satisfaction.

"When I left your mother in 1943 for Italy, we were fighting a very different war than this one we are engaged in now." The words exited Stephen's drawn lips as ponderous things. "As you know, your grandfather fought to keep me at home to help him with the hotel business. As I told you the other night, he sacrificed a great deal, but not anything like your mother did. I'll go talk to her."

"No father. *I* have to talk to her. These are *my* plans," Michael said as he pushed himself up out of the chair.

"No Michael, it's not just *your* future. What happens to *you* happens to all of us." Stephen's eyes locked on to Michael's and held them briefly. "Watching your mother go through what she did almost broke me. If you . . ."

"If I *die* over there? Isn't that what you were going to say?" Michael's sarcasm evoked a strong response from his father. Stephen unexpectedly began to feel the bite from the stress of the past month. He'd snapped at work, and several times here at home. He didn't especially enjoy striking out with his frayed emotions, laying as they did just below the surface, waiting for another victim. Now he felt impotent to settle his inner disquiet. Fight or flight?

Instead, "Don't use *that* tone with me, big boy. Do *you* understand *me*?"

"Yes, sir." Somewhat deflated, but not out of it, Michael added, "But good grief, father, I'm not a little boy anymore. You guys are treating me . . ."

"Like our immature son?" Stephen's eyebrows almost touched his hairline. *Touché.*

Slumping back into his chair, Michael ventured, "I guess . . . I don't know what to think."

Margaret entered the dining room wanting to know why her mother had yelled and then ran up the stairs to her room crying. She'd chosen not to investigate earlier at her own possible peril.

"Margaret, we're just . . . we're just trying to work through some difficult family issues." Stephen didn't move his eyes from Michael as he spoke to his daughter. Margaret was growing into her own as a young woman, much faster than her father wished. She, with her budding feminine intuition, felt the tension in the room more strongly now than upstairs.

"What issues, father?"

"Margaret," he hesitated. Two distraught women might drive a man to drink or worse. *Think Stephen. She doesn't need this. She's fifteen. But . . . she's mature for her age, isn't she? Be careful, Stephen. You're going to tell her, aren't you? Great . . .*

"Michael, you go ahead and talk to your mother like you said, and Margaret and I will talk." Margaret's presence had decided the terms and conditions for the remainder of the evening, it seemed.

Michael headed cautiously up the winding stairs to his parent's room to find his mother. Stephen, about to sit down in the living room, motioned for Margaret to join him. Margaret's suspicions were confirmed, this must be some huge deal. What trouble had Michael gotten himself into to require such a fuss? Stephen sat close to his daughter on the overstuffed brown leather sofa, just in case. The news might not go too well with Margaret, just as he had foreseen that it wouldn't with Susan.

The great room was a magnificent two thousand square foot living area, with a twenty-three foot-high arched ceiling, thick oak-paneled walls with leaded and stained glass windows. The stately antique furniture had been arranged to suit and emphasize the hard-wood floors. A massive glass-leaded oak front door had been dug out of a nearby barn, refinished and hung with pride. Susan squealed with delight as the workmen labored to hang it prior to one of the grand company Christmas parties. A brown and white alpaca rug lie sequestered on the floor, and upon it rested comfortably a heavy oak coffee table, which bordered a mammoth sofa. The sofa was flanked on either end by fixtures that spread soft lighting about the room.

Tonight the room was bathed in Tony Bennet's, *All The Things You Are*, lending to it an aura of sublime majesty, circumscribing father and daughter. This was a room built for such cumulating disclosures. These walls, the furniture, the grand size and sweep of it all, were of the sturdy type, able to absorb the most difficult circumstances, to soften and shape them to something more malleable. In the past, along with the joy of babies and birthday parties, this noble chamber had absorbed heavy things and painful news giving each its proportion and true shape. That's how and why Stephen designed it. Possibly, the accoutrements would not suffice tonight.

Holding Margaret's hand, Stephen unexpectedly observed her mother's features carved into and smoothed across her face and body. She possessed beauty perhaps surpassing Susan's at her age. She was lovely beyond what he had ever hoped she might be. He swallowed, and once more met her large blue misty eyes with his own. He inhaled, "Margaret, Michael has made a difficult choice about his future, and that decision is hard for your mother to accept. It's tough for me to handle if you want to know the truth."

"It didn't look to me like Mother's accepted anything. What's Michael going to do, join the French Foreign Legion?" she asked, half joking.

"Well, something along those lines."

"He's going into the Army, isn't he?" Her tone exited from an intense panic and dread that Stephen had not as of yet heard from his daughter. This evening had become much more difficult on him than he could have dreamed. As with his easy agitation over the past days, he felt the compulsion to escape his responsibilities, to yell, to throw something hard, to hit something. That inner force rose, then dipped in his chest and his head felt light. He wanted to scream. *No. I can't. Keep going*, he told himself.

"Not the Army," Stephen said, biting his bottom lip. "He wants to join the Marines." That substantive phrase couldn't have hurt Margaret more than if her father had cut her with a knife. The Corps was receiving a lot of bad ink this evening in the Lloyd household.

"Father, *no . . . No.*" Margaret's energized voice spoke, and her panic grew exponentially as her racing mind fed upon the images coming across the nightly television of battles going badly for the Americans. In Margaret's young, untested mind, she visualized losing her brother just like Damien.

Damien had become one of the Lloyd family members over the past years. He pestered her just like Michael did. Yet her world wasn't complete without his presence, his sweaty body fresh from some basketball triumph. He'd jockeyed for position in the fridge matching Michael's own insatiable appetite. Damien's death, still fresh and palpable, had stung her to a depth she had not yet experienced. In Susan and Margaret's eyes, nothing positive would come from this but Michael's death or maiming. And thus Margaret too began to cry, burying her head in her father's chest.

"Mother?"

"What?" Susan didn't want to talk to Michael right then.

"Nothing I say will make this any easier for you. I didn't know that you lost those babies before I was born. I'm really sorry."

"Well, your father knew. Didn't he try and talk you out of THIS?" She demanded an answer, her fresh tears postponing Michael's reply for the moment. Moist tissues lay strewn about her, and the one in Susan's hand wouldn't last much longer. Michael handed her a fresh one. "Thank you."

"Mother, I don't pretend to have all the answers that you need right now. But, I do know, at least I *think* I know that this freedom we all live by doesn't come cheap. Yes, mothers are crying tonight because they have lost their sons. But their son's gave up everything so that you and father, and Grandfather Marcus and Grandma Michelle, even Margaret, who I'd love to strangle sometimes, can live free. Mother, you can't say that you know that I wasn't born to defend what we all cherish so much, can you?"

"No, but maybe I'm just selfish, and I want my son to grow up and become an adult and get married and have grand babies that I can hold and watch grow up. I didn't raise you to get killed in some country that I don't even know where in the world it's located. You're my son, for *God's sake,* my very special treasure, and I won't give you up. I . . . I can't." The weight of this "thing" had all but broken Susan, and she burst into tears once more.

Michael leaned against the door frame, trying to experience unsuccessfully what only a mother, especially *this* mother, had carried for so many years. He was thinking beyond her and *this* moment to his time in the barrel. He visualized the black and white nightly news, and its frightened, angular perspective of war.

Wrestling to gain some semblance of control over her emotions, she wiped her eyes and blew her nose, already reddening from the repeated wiping of the tissues. More able to speak, she asked, "Does the way I *feel* make any sense to you, Michael?" Michael's silence, his lack of an adequate answer suitable for this woman's present needs caused his mother to turn away from her son. Her eyes waltzed around the room. Michael's imprint touched every feature and piece. There her eyes flitted lightly about for long, precious moments.

Susan's focus once again hardened into diligence, her reverie now dissipated. He might now enter. Susan had hoped by visually feeling the room in earnest that this "thing" might go away, and that the Michael she raised would tell her that he'd been accepted to . . . to Princeton, even A&M for crying out loud. To that end she postponed the conversation Michael wanted to have with her. She wouldn't sleep very well this night.

Michael discerned something else as he observed his mother's obtuse defiance. Sadness registered not only in her eyes, but also around the corners of her mouth, even in her shoulders. He suspected that further discussion would be fruitless. So he heeled and headed to his room. Then he stopped. Turning about, he spoke into her melancholy that he couldn't erase, and whispered, "I love you, mother." Hearing him, she quickly dried her eyes and turned to locate the source of the verbalized affections, but Michael had gone from the room.

Eighteen: Vietnam

>─┤◆>─O─<◆├─<

Monday, April 17, 1967

The strain that the "thing" brought to bear on the Lloyd family didn't depart the house for days. It was held at bay until Susan or Michael could reload for another exchange. That Monday, Susan stood in the kitchen talking on the phone. She wound the long cord around her right index finger and was deep in conversation with Bunny Blackledge, one of the company's executive wives. Michael happened by on one of his missions to the refrigerator, a mere half-hour after breakfast. In mid sentence, Susan paused and looked at him. Her train of thought with Bunny evaporated, and she caught herself focusing on this young adult rummaging through the cold food aisle of the local grocer, and she knew—she had to let Michael go. She of course didn't know how she knew, but in an instant she felt him leaving her heart and her body, not in death or in life, but in exchange.

"Bunny, can I call you back?" Susan asked leave of her friend on the other end of the phone. She replaced the receiver, but kept her focus there at his exposed back side for a long minute. Furtively, Susan sorted through her own feelings in order to assimilate the thoughts forming in her matricentric mind.

"Michael . . ." Susan heard his name tumble from her lips, but she had no lucid idea what she would say to him.

"Yes, ma'am?" he replied, although he kept rummaging in the fridge. "Mother, where's the . . ? Oh, here it is." Then he backed away from the source of all nourishment shoving the end of some food stuff in his mouth, to ask in a half discernible language, "Mother,where'sthelasagnawehadleftover,mrscassallsaidit'sinhere." Susan had long since learned refrigerator language. He finally swallowed the thing. "Mother? Are you okay?" Susan breathed heavily, staring into him.

"Son . . ." Again her attempt to verbalize the unformed concepts running wild through her brain aborted themselves. Michael looked at her more closely, consciously intent on trying to read this verbal telegram his mother couldn't quite send to him. "I spent several hours with Father McTammany yesterday," she said. The words came more freight-laden than she imagined. Susan assumed she trusted her parish priest, but that didn't alter the insurmountable obstacle she felt Stephen had left with her. Hers was a terrible misfortune, and she resented his absence. Thus, along with Michael's "higher calling," Susan felt alone and unsure of herself. "Father Ed understood my dilemma, but he told me to hear you out further on this. So, I agreed. Mrs. Cassalls and I sat up till two this morning going over it all." Susan thought once more about Stephen's physical and cognitive absence, and she did a slow burn.

Her mind felt compartmentalized consisting of two halves, each involving one of her men. There was the part involving Michael and his future absence, of not being at college but at some military training facility, and to the other half belonging to Stephen's actual physical scarcity. To this point, he had never been a non-attendee in family matters. Why was her husband leaving her alone with this? She inhaled, ingesting the air in the kitchen in hopes that Michael wouldn't leave the fridge door open too much longer.

"What made *you* decide to join the military? I don't understand, but I'm trying,"

Susan stated, attempting her pastor's ecclesiastically promoted position. The priest's counsel was as difficult to swallow as Michael's announcement had been. Still, she was aspiring to a better sense of virtue, while accommodating her son's untested desires, no matter how ignoble. Inspite of it all, Michael had already become Government Issue. Thus she martialed her iron-and-sand-willed emotions, wishing for clarity. The tears came anyway.

David entered the kitchen, then stopped. He couldn't remember seeing his mother cry, and now she was crying too much to suit him.

"Mother, where is my baseball glove? *Why* are you crying again?" These parental emotions of late unsettled him. "Michael, are *you* in trouble?" he asked. David smiled at the supposition that had just crossed his mind. "You looked at Margaret's diary again, didn't you?"

"No, I didn't."

"Honey, would you let Michael and me talk about something for a few minutes?" Susan said, blowing her nose.

This last child's ten years and the uncertainty of his mother's despondency suggested to him that he would be better served finding his baseball glove on his own. "Yes, ma'am." With that settled, and the youngest Lloyd out from under foot, Michael resumed.

"Mother, when I heard that Damien had been killed, *man*, when I heard those Marines speak to Dr. Wilson outside our class room, it was as if Damien spoke to me. I didn't even have time to think or feel anything. I just heard his voice. I didn't know if I was losing my marbles or not, but I heard his voice *clearly*. I mean, it startled me. I heard *him*— Damien. I *know* I did." Michael halted, suspecting that he tread upon the soft petals of his mother's intuition as well as her intellectual comprehension.

"And just what did . . . I can't believe this. Damien talked . . . No. This is insane, Michael. This doesn't happen. People who are dead don't speak . . . to my son. No." Her agitation had dried her tears. Susan next crossed her arms defiantly, yet unsure as to how to proceed with a conversation she couldn't have conceived of fifteen minutes earlier. Just when she felt the crush to let him go, he tells her this.

Michael lowered his eyes to the tiled kitchen floor, and in almost an inaudible voice, he said, "I knew you wouldn't believe me."

Susan rolled her eyes revealing her fuse that grew shorter by the second. "Michael . . . Oh, for heaven's sake. What did Damien *say*? What . . . what do you *think* he said?"

Michael drained the remaining air from the kitchen, even though the words came out sheepish and pale. "Come, finish what I started."

"Oh Lord, *Michael*. And on that mystical evidence, you believe you are supposed to join the military?" Her anger, pugilistic in nature, had surfaced. He had put her through several sleep-deprived nights on a voice he *thought* he heard. "Have you learned nothing living here or going to church? You are a reasonable human being, *Michael*. At least I thought you *were*. You are also a *Lloyd*. You have obligations your father and I have worked toward fulfilling for *eighteen years*. Why aren't you thinking of that *for heaven's sake!*?"

"I am."

"You *are*? *How*?" Her black eyebrows arched like a cat's back when it's incensed and ready to scrap.

"Father dropped out of school at TCU in his second year to join the military—I just found *that* out last week. Mother, he felt an obligation that was stronger than family and the entire obligations grandfather placed on him, *too*... He knew, just like I know, that it was his duty to fight for his country and the freedom of the world. Don't you *see*, Mother?"

The boy could reason from an American and patriotic stance, Susan had to give him that. His rationale wasn't all fluff. Oh, where was his father now? Susan couldn't fight a two front war with any modicum of success, and she knew it. Her attention was once again divided, and she could be conquered.

"Michael, we're *not* at war." Susan had to quit for a while. Her head began to throb under the burden of both Michael's and her apologetic, and her arms flapped impotently like a dying bird. "Michael, I can't deal with this right now. I need to go lie down. Do you know where your *father* is?"

But Michael couldn't let it go. "No, ma'am. I don't know where father is. Mother, we are at war, fighting Communism." This had to be settled now. He wasn't thinking about Susan's need to have her husband join the fracas with her or her fatigue, so he plowed ahead, despite the damage he might do. "If we don't stop it over there, it may be here before we know it. The same basic issues are at stake that father joined for, somewhat less defined, but nonetheless real. General Patton was right. He knew we'd have to fight the Russians sooner or later. Damien wrote to me that he was fighting NVA and Viet Cong soldiers equipped with Russian and Chinese made weapons and equipment. Damien believed that what he was fighting for was worth the risk. You can't say he wasn't in a war." Michael shook his head for emphasis, but he had to be careful using the words such as "shooting" and "killing." "His letters are filled with war, Mother." Michael's youthful exuberance poured from him. Her son seemed to her much more passionate about this than she imagined. Susan still clung to this unfamiliar young adult by the loosening tendons of her motherly love, but not by much else.

"Michael, I don't care what *his* letters say—"

"Mother. Just wait here. I have something to show you that I've been studying. I think it's worth your time."

"Michael, I . . ." she said, rubbing her temples. Michael had already turned and headed to his room before her third word could ascend into the air. Within a few minutes he returned to find his mother leaning against the fridge for support.

"Mother, look at this pattern." Susan limped into the dining room and slumped into a chair. Michael followed her and stood, leaning over her shoulder. He opened a notebook filled with newspaper clippings and notes he'd taken, and laid it before her for examination.

Staring back at her, Susan found facts and figures that seemed to support Michael's thesis. The clippings showed the Soviet Union's overt and covert bent toward world domination; paragraphs of various lengths cataloguing speeches and communiqués by the Communist leaders themselves. She had heard Khrushchev's speech at the U.N., where he told America, "We will bury you!" She had lived through the Bay of Pigs and the Cuban missile crisis, and she had worried herself to tears over Communism's aggressive bent. The world Michael wanted to defend was her world too, and it glared at her. Somebody's son had to stop it, but why did it have to be Damien and her son?

Beginning with the October Revolution, up to and including the Bay of Pigs, Communism's philosophical dynamic spread its clammy, all consuming tentacles before her. Susan had studied history, but not from this angle or for this reason. Michael had. She scanned articles about the McCarthy hearings, articles about former Soviet spies that had turned from their previous ideology to embrace what they once tried to destroy. These spies openly testified about other spies working in top administration posts for Roosevelt and Truman. These two men were leaders she respected, yet they did nothing to alter the current situation. One Russian spy was even a Harvard grad, Alger Hiss. Rather, the government under Roosevelt promoted and defended these men. Susan, like so many Americans, found it difficult to make the leap from a socialist ideology "out there," to one of protecting her home right here in the mid-1960s, in Westover Hills, Texas, especially if it meant giving into or letting her son head into that fray.

What was not stated and was not open to American scrutiny was NSAM 263 and NSAM 273. These were two documents, the first of which stated Kennedy's intent to assist South Vietnam *until* 1965, at which time all American military personnel would be withdrawn. The latter document was Johnson's reversal of the Kennedy doctrine, even before the assassination in Dallas had occurred. The Gulf of Tonkin had been a lie. Nothing was stated about the numerous opportunities for American withdrawals prior to 1967. No one could know however, that LBJ himself would resist any efforts by his political party to run again for the Presidency in 1968. LBJ would quit on his troops. That was yet a year away. Would the VC get in their sampans and row across the Pacific and attack California? Their ideology would.

Susan had found the world's conditions all somewhat gray and pernicious up to now. She could not imagine that her world was so terribly dangerous, or that it would ever truly be dangerous to *her*. Communism seemed just so remote—Cuba notwithstanding. Had she sat there since World War Two ended, like the proverbial frog in the kettle? Stephen was not recalled during Korea, so these types of matters had been buried amid Lloyd International. Could Communism actually be heading here in one way or another, and had her son now produced the proof she had been denying?

To Michael, an obviously impressionable and idealistic eighteen-year-old, the clues and the menace were actually knocking on the door of America. He produced other documents proving that professed Communists were actually teaching in America's universities.

"Mother, don't you see what's at stake here?" Then Michael said something disarming: "Mother, I love you enough to die for you. What you value is what I'm willing to give everything for. That's what Damien said to me, kind of. I just hope I have the courage he did."

There. The "thing"—his enlistment, the perils of the current world, Michael's impending death in Vietnam that Susan began slowly to resign herself to—received all the definition it was going to get. In so doing, perhaps it had gained some greater value and meaning. It held its place in the universe that Michael had inscribed in his mind. Susan listened to Michael from a sense of newly discovered respect. She had now *heard him*.

Deflated or resigned, and try as she might to muster it, she couldn't energize herself to fight against this any longer. She threw up one last Hail Mary, "and all this is supposed to make me like the idea of you going 10,000 miles from home, so I can be safe? I will never like this. I don't even know if I can let you go." More tears.

Before Susan responded further, Michael fired a second volley. "Mother, I have every intention of fulfilling my end of the bargain in this Lloyd dynasty. I will finish my education when my military obligation is complete, I promise you that, but not before. I signed up for three years. When that's done, it's done."

This large child vacating her dreams suddenly seemed a person of destiny. He had aged in fifteen minutes. Susan Lloyd felt conflicted, proud, yet resigned to her immeasurable loss. She stood and reached to touch his cheek for the briefest of moments before embracing him. When she tried to hug him, Susan couldn't reach her arms around his muscled circumference. Michael pulled her close to him, where they stood, mother and son, for several immortal moments. Had she given birth to this belated child for some kind of American sacrifice?

Nineteen: The Talk

>─┼─◆>─◦─<◆─┼─<

Saturday, April 22, 1967

"I'll get it, Ginny," Susan said as she took several steps into the kitchen to answer the wall phone. "Lloyd's residence."

"Miss Lloyd? Miss Lloyd?" His voice didn't connect with her memory for the first few seconds. Susan's emotional foray into the suddenly dangerous world Michael had painted for her on Wednesday, and the plans he'd worked out to solve them had gotten in the way. No one had called her that—Miss—except, except whom? She'd heard that voice before; that twang, the country music in the background . . . it was, . . . it was Smitty.

"Yes, Smitty. This is she. Is everything okay?" Smitty didn't call . . . he never called unless . . . Stephen . . . Stephen was there. Susan's blue eyes darted back and forth trying to focus on something to which she could anchor her thoughts. "Smitty, *is he* there?"

"Wull, Yes'm. I reckon he is. But it ain't good here, ma'am. I ain't never seen him like this before. It's always been . . ." Smitty's hesitation alarmed her. Then the resumption of his words were like dull, wet fists slapping against her face. "You better send Michael on out here. I don't want to worry you none, ma'am, but you pro'bly better send the boy on out here *now*. Okay? Oh yeah. I don't see his car out here. He musta got a ride."

"Yes, Smitty. I'll send Michael there as quickly as I can. And, thank you, Smitty."

"Why shore, ma'am. He'll be okay till the boy gets here. Jus' tell him to come on."

Susan lifted the receiver back into its cradle. This week, Michael had drained her energy reserves, and now this unexpected call left her momentarily paralyzed. In another minute, Susan became angry. Fortunately, Ginny Cassalls came into the kitchen to observe the long, hard stare on Susan's face, her body quivering.

"What's wrong, Mrs. Lloyd?" The urgency in her own voice alarmed even Ginny.

"It's Stephen. He's at Smitty's. Smitty wants me to send Michael. I could wring that man's neck. I am so angry, Ginny. Why did Stephen have to go out there *now*? Oooo . . . I'd love to get my hands on that man." Susan breathed fire, her eyes sparkled and flickered from the surge of emotions to that of aggression. She couldn't imagine anything really *wrong* with her husband. He was obviously being contentious. Ginny, on the other hand, considered Smitty's request as the more sensible course to pursue—send Michael. From what Ginny Cassalls could tell, Susan needed to calm down before any other decisions should be made.

"Mrs. Lloyd. Why don't you come over here and sit down. Michael . . . Michael!" Ginny tried not to yell so as to arouse Margaret, but felt she had few options open to her.

"Mother?" David's voice came from behind Susan so that David couldn't see his mother's expression. "Mother, can Ronny come over? We want to . . ."

"What!?" Susan said, wheeling about to locate the familiar voice bearing down on her. "David, what do you *want*?" she asked her youngest in a surprisingly sharp, if not unsympathetic, tone.

Upon seeing his mother's burgeoning agitation, he hesitated to repeat the request.

"David, *what do you want*?" The pressure inside Susan Lloyd seemed unbearable, and now David wanted something from her too. "What do you want, son?" Susan's question probed, but from a more controlled atmosphere.

David's answer was sheepish at best. "Can Ronny come over? We want to—"

Susan considered the request amid all the other "noise" piercing her mind at the moment. "Ginny, ask Michael to come here. David . . . oh, I don't care. Let everybody come over. I just don't *care!*" At that, Susan hurried to the living room. In the course of her sojourn to the great room with the sturdy furniture and all the living plants, the magnificent windowed view upon the sun-filtered lawn that shone through great oak branches, she slammed the door separating the kitchen from herself. She had to somehow separate the anxiety leeching her emotions dry from the makeshift calm she desperately needed. Searching the room for the exact spot to accomplish this all but impossible feat, she moved sluggishly over to the bay window that opened out onto the west side of the house, and there Susan halted. She would make her stand *here*.

The St. Augustine grasses had begun to thicken, and the early spring flowers, —the store bought pansies, were at full bloom. Hostas had already commenced arching their backs up and out of the ground because of the usually short Ft. Worth winters. Susan Lloyd's comprehension of what lay just ahead in her flower beds had been dulled by her present circumstances. On overload, this day was slowly turning to night. Stephen was absent. She was angry. David wanted something she couldn't remember. The world felt heavy, even mean-spirited to her.

"Mrs. Cassalls? What's wrong with my mother?" David asked, his innocence telling.

"Nothing, Sweetheart. She's just a little upset right now. Tell you what, why don't you go on over to Ronny's. All right? I'll call Mrs. Reynolds."

Ginny dialed Kay Reynolds' number and asked if David could come over for a little while. Then Ginny hurried to the base of the steps and called up into the bedrooms. "Michael! Michael?"

"Yes, ma'am."

"Would you come here for a minute, please?"

"Can it wait, Mrs. Cassalls? I'm in the middle of something."

Ginny sighed heavily. She was going to have to climb the stairs and speak to the older kids. She pursed her lips, lifted her foot on the first step, then the next step, etc. until she reached his room, where she found him on the phone with his girl-friend. Ginny could tell by Michael's animation that he was upset with Victoria or vice versa.

"Michael, I really hate to interrupt, but I need to speak to you, *now*."

Michael became visibly agitated with Mrs. Cassalls. "Look Victoria, I have to go. We can finish this in a few minutes. No, I have to go. Mrs. Cassalls wants me. Yes. I'll call you back. Okay? Bye."

Looking up at the housekeeper and trying not to say what he was thinking, he said instead: "What is it, ma'am?" Margaret happened by as Ginny was about to tell Michael of the family dilemma. She motioned for Margaret to join them. "Okay," she began. "Listen. Don't speak. Okay?

"Okay," they both responded, a bit concerned.

"We have an issue, and I need your help. Both of you. You father is at Smitty's. I don't have any details other than Smitty called and asked that *you*," Ginny looked at Michael, "come and get your father. Margaret, I want you to stay in your room for a bit. I need to settle your mother down. In about twenty minutes, come to the bottom of the stairs and just listen. If your mother is still angry, go back up to your room. If not, I want you to join us."

Margaret asked, "What's wrong?"

"Honey, I'm not sure. But just do what I've asked you. Okay?"

"Yes, ma'am."

Continuing, Ginny said, "Michael, go on and pick up your father. Margaret, go to your room and wait about twenty minutes. I'm sure things will be fine. Just trust me."

"I don't like this," Margaret said, as Ginny left the room. "I'm not two years old, Mrs. Cassalls."

"I know you aren't, sweet girl. This may be the wrong way to handle this, but let's do it this way."

Michael felt the grainy wood of the front screen door, its oily palm stain forever etched into the wood near the worn metal handle. Some country singer he didn't recognize, attacked his Rock 'n Roll senses. His father was somewhere inside, here at Smitty's.

He pulled the handle, which opened to the familiar stench of Smitty's smoke-filled rib shack. It was all he could do to keep from turning around and driving back home without his father. But, he dove in. Smitty sat at a table talking to the cook, smoking and then coughing. Nothing had changed in the past weeks. The little old man would surely die from emphysema within a year.

Smitty stood as Michael entered, motioning for the boy to follow him up the stairs. Michael coughed three quarters of the way across the dining room. He followed dutifully behind Smitty's slow gait upward onto a second, darker level. Michael thought he heard the sound of a man and a woman's intimate speech, rising and falling behind a door to his left. That caused him to stop.

"Pssst, Michael. He's in here. Pssst, *Michael*." The light from the room's window spread across Smitty's body as he stood in the doorway. As Michael neared the room, he detected an odor of dirty clothes and other musty and unrecognizable smells that nauseated him. The alcohol was stronger now, increasing as he came full into the doorway. Smitty, quite *non-plussed*, pointed at the man lying on the bed. His father, stripped to his shorts, lay on the dirtiest sheets and spread Michael had ever seen. He had no idea what to think. The Lloyd in him thought this entire "restaurant" should be bulldozed. He wanted to get his father off of that bed to either slap him or hug him. Maybe both. Rather, he just stood there in the doorway, observant and afraid.

"Son, it's time to grow up. This here's the war, this is."

"What?" For the second time in an hour, someone had slapped Michael on the face, literally and figuratively. "What do you mean, Smitty? I don't understand."

"I seen it in his eyes, more intense this time when he showed up early this mornin.' That buddy of yor'n, the boy that got killed? It done tripped somethin' in yer daddy that he jus' cain't quite deal with, I reckon. I didn't want to tell yer mama."

"You mean Damien's death did *this* to him?"

"Yep. Come on. Let's go on back down stairs. He's jus' drunk. He'll feel like the Devil when he wakes up." Smitty crept past Michael as he pulled the door closed. The two men retraced their steps, cutting an almost visible swath through the barely lit, stale air that hung limp in the boxed-in upstairs hallway. The two occupants behind the door had resorted to arguing, and Michael thought he heard a hand strike flesh just as he stepped on one of the creaking steps, but he couldn't be certain what he had heard. Michael needed living air, not the dead atmosphere cloistered inside this old cabin. He walked past Smitty, who had stopped to light a cigarette, and then out through the front screen into the mounting heat of the sun and a slight breeze. Out here, Michael could fill his lungs with purity.

A slow moving nausea had crept into Michael's stomach the moment he saw his father. On his way down from the second floor, it pushed firmly into his throat, and once outside, despite his best attempts notwithstanding, his breakfast ejected onto the gravel. It was involuntary. Smitty of course, had seen this kind of reaction in Italy more than once.

Gasping and choking, he bent over placing his hands on his knees, trying desperately to steady himself. The woods surrounding Smitty's spun, and the old man sidled up to the boy heaving his breakfast onto the parking lot. He patted Michael on the back, trying to reassure him there would be better days.

"Aw, it'll be okay, son. I seen this too many times in Italy. They bottle it all up, an' don't let nobody know it's all down there jus' waitin' to explode. Now, take yer daddy, for instance. He's 'bout the strongest man I ever did know. He never let it show . . . well, hardly ever. There was a few times I seen him cry, but for the most part, solid as a rock. Here Mike." Smitty handed the boy his dirty handkerchief to wipe his mouth, but Michael waved him off. Smitty left the boy for a few minutes and returned with two cold Coke bottles. He handed one to Michael. "Take a swig. Do ya good."

Michael walked slowly around the graveled lot, sipping his Coke in the late Texas spring Saturday morning. He took a swig now and then, trying to bring his senses back to conformity to something more natural, yet this proved elusive at best. He looked at the half empty bottle of Coke, then said, "Smitty, what's all bottled up in my father?"

Smitty faced a dilemma he thought wasn't any of his business to discuss. It *was* of course. Smitty didn't want to be the one to rub the boy's nose in this sort of thing. And yet, somebody had to enlighten him. Somebody had to tell him about his father's war. The wars, the Big One, Korea and Vietnam, seemed inextricably linked. Apprehensive, Smitty approached war from a philosophical mindset. When the past bothered Stephen, he turned to the bottle—at Smitty's. It was quite simple.

After Smitty returned from Italy, he stayed drunk for two years straight. He lost his wife and daughter, and had to be rescued by Captain Stephen Lloyd if he was going to be salvaged at all. The Captain put him in a hospital where he could dry out and then gave him clear title to this old shack and gas station. For the most part, Smitty had done pretty well, considering the alternative.

"Well Mike, let's you an' me go for a little walk down to the lake. I got me a boat down there jus' beyond the trees. We can do a little fishin,' an' I can try an' explain what yer daddy never done but shoulda, I guess."

"But I need to get father back home . . ."

"Not in his condition, son. He'll keep up there for a while longer. He's all right. Come on, son. I told James to look in on him." Smitty led the way down a gently sloping, winding trail someone had cut out of the scrub brush behind the restaurant, and the old man puffed on his cigarette. It seemed every physical thing about Smitty was foul, except his honesty, and for that, Michael would stay.

After five minutes Michael forgot about calling home. Within ten, he was sitting in Smitty's dirty old boat, chugging along out of the inlet and toward open water. It took the old smoking motor about forty-five minutes to push the two men across the lake to a cove. That seemed long enough for Smitty to decide what to say or not say. In the cove, willow branches hung out over the banks and the water smoothed. Smitty cut the motor. They drifted toward the closest bank until their momentum slowed and died, coming to rest at a spot where the sun seeped loosely through the thick branches depositing its rays on the flat, dark surface upon which they floated.

Twenty: Italy 1944

>─┼─◆─○─◆─┼─<

"Talkin' 'bout this ain't the easiest thing for me, son." Smitty's words came gruffer somehow, and he foresaw the drunk he'd throw for himself tonight.

"I suppose not," Michael added. Then it dawned on the boy that Smitty spoke quite freely about the war the first night they met. So Michael wanted to know what the difference was between then and now. "But Smitty, you talked to me about flying those airplanes when we first came out here. Why are you having a difficult time now?"

"Mike, I'm not sure what the difference is neither. I guess I was jus' telling the facts and stayin' away from the personal things. I guess that way I didn't have to get real involved in talkin' 'bout it."

"Wait a minute. Are you saying you can talk about the war on various levels? How is that possible?"

"Don't know. I didn't never think 'bout it till just now. Maybe you're right. Well, I'll be. Funny, ain't it?"

"If it's funny, I don't get the joke," Michael intoned.

Smitty looked to his right, out over the smooth water of the lake. He spit and watched the ripples widen and then return to calm. He was now avoiding eye contact with his captain's son. "I s'pose if we just talk about the things on the surface, like maybe, when we bombed a target, who got killed, how number three engine run rough, how the flak was light or heavy and so forth, we just avoid the feelin's of it. It's safer that way . . . Yeah, it's safer. Thanks Mike for lettin' me see that. Interestin' way of lookin' at the war. Dang, I'm plumb glad you brought that up, Mike."

"Do you think my father was able to keep it all very superficial so he didn't have to deal with it until Damien was killed?" Michael didn't wait for Smitty's response because he thought he knew the answer. "I guess Damien is the reason my father's in the shape he is. But now I have to know, Smitty. He talked to me after we left here the other night. But he didn't give me any details about the hard things, and that leaves *you* to tell me."

The water lapped against their boat as a speedboat roared past the cove, sending its rippled, juggling wake careening and sloshing off the hull for half a minute. Smitty lit a cigarette. He was thinking. He was thinking about the things he didn't want to think about, the shards of things that involuntarily invaded his mind; worried things, prickly things, events that would put a bottle of Old Crow in his hand tonight.

"Smitty . . ?" Michael said impatiently.

"Yeah? Okay. What exactly do you want ta know?"

"I want to know about some of your missions. Whatever you'll tell me."

"They was so many of 'em, and my brain seems a little addled at a time like this."

"Smitty. Please. Quit stalling."

"All right." The weathered old man blew a plume of smoke high over his head. "We was . . . we was maybe 24,000 feet over Moosebeirbaum . . . Odertal—? One of them missions. Anyways, the sky was full of flak so thick you could walk on it. I just knew them Germans had our range. I was standin' on a flak jacket and wearin' one too. Funny how I remember that. I could hear the shrapnel hittin' the airplane, an tearin' holes in 'er. I quit countin' 24's that went down after about six. I just couldn't stand it. Me and Ralph Billings was in machine gun school together. He was flyin' in the next ship over from me. I could wave at him, an' he'd wave back at me, an,' we'd look for fighters. An' then we started our bombing run an' that's when them 88's sent up even more flak." Smitty went silent. He saw it so clearly . . . and so painfully.

"What Smitty? What happened?"

A tear coursed down his face and stopped at his scraggly chin, then dropped into the bottom of the small boat. "A flak burst hit just above Ralph. It tore the top turret plumb off . . ." Smitty stopped again. "I just stood there. I couldn't do nothin.' Then their left outboard engine caught fire from another shell burst an' she fell out of formation and several minutes later, she just augured in . . . were a couple of chutes that I remember . . ." Smitty's voice had gone to hoar frost.

Michael waited as Smitty lit another cigarette. The old man's hands shook, his eyes filling with tears. It must have been a horrible day for this little old man. Another boat sped by, and once again their boat rocked to the motion of the pounding, slapping waves.

"But that weren't the worst of it." Smitty finally spoke, his voice hollow and raspy. "They was these things called shackles that held them bombs up in the bomb bays. Now, it got right cold up at that altitude, sometimes thirty below zero or more. Even with us wearin' long handles, wool clothing, flight jackets, an' even electrical flight suits, a body would like to freeze up there. Well, sometimes them bottom bombs would freeze to the shackles an' then they'd stick in the door—wouldn't drop, nope, couldn't make 'em budge. Then the top bombs would fall on top of them bottom ones and they'd be live explosions just waitin' to go off in our planes. So, on this mission, they just stuck there. The door was open and they was just stuck. Now, you gotta remember Mike, we already flew through their fighter protection—lost some 24's doin' that, an' we got this flak from them 88's goin' off all over the sky. Our plane is shakin', takin' hits, them bombs was stuck, and we just flew plumb past the target without them bombs lettin' go. I figured we'd blow up like several other crews done. So your daddy sent the flight engineer down to see what he could do, and before he could do anything, them bombs just let go. Just like that."

Smitty's excitement expired up and through the willow branches. A crane that had been wading, fishing for minnows at the far shallow end where the bay bottled against the bank took to flight, his wings flapping overhead as he quickly fought for altitude. "I told your daddy I wouldn't say nothin' to ya. An' I shouldn't, neither."

"What Smitty. What happened? You have to tell me now.

"Naw. I promised I wouldn't."

"Smitty! Something's happening to our family and I think this may be at the center of it. We need to know. You have to help my father. You *have* to," Michael said, shouting at Smitty. "You *have* to!"

The old man's jaws tightened. He took a drag from his smoke, exhaled and kept staring. "Naw."

Michael swore at Smitty. "You better tell me or so help me I'll throw you in this lake and drown you. Tell me, old man. What happened?"

Michael had never spoken to any adult as he did just now. But from his perspective, too much was at stake. "Now you tell me what happened. I'll *see to it* that my father knows that *I* made you tell me."

Smitty cocked his head and sort of twisted his mouth at an odd angle. "All right. But you made me tell ya." Smitty thought about what it meant to their relationship to break his word to the Captain. War always seemed to put men into impossible situations, and it was still doing that to Smitty. He'd be drunk before eight o'clock tonight. "Well, two of them five hundred pound bombs landed on the 24 below and behind us . . ." It looked as if Smitty had been shot. He'd kept this in as long as his friend, Captain Lloyd, had. Treason wasn't acceptable, and treason is what telling Michael felt like to Smitty. "An' that was the end of that crew. Ten men, just gone—never had a chance. I don't know why they was there. Maybe they was hit and havin' trouble controlling their plane. They jus' wasn't supposed to be there . . ."

Smitty clearly took responsibility for this catastrophe every bit as much as Stephen Lloyd had. Tears dribbled and then rolled down his rough, bearded cheeks. He sniffed, and said, "I think your daddy took it the hardest of all of us, because he was the pilot. Normally, he'd talk on the intercom when it was safe, but he was real quiet the rest of the flight. I don't think he's ever stopped feelin' guilt about that. I had to quit thinkin' about it. Couldn't stand it." Then, in a muted voice, Smitty spoke his darkest fears, "Now I thought it, again. Dang!"

Michael sat motionless, his eyes moving over the inside of the boat's dirty, scuffed silver hull. He was imagining that moment, with himself at the controls. Smitty, too, discerned that the boy was trying to think this one through, trying to visualize it, to experience it. Michael however, had no way to evaluate such events. "That must have been horrible, Smitty."

"Lieutenant Hukill spent quite a bit of time with the Capt'n, yer daddy, to help him get past it. He and the lieutenant was good buddies. I think the crew below us . . . I think yer daddy was in flight school with the pilot or co-pilot—cain't remember no more. I stopped by your daddy's tent once and seen 'em talkin'—him and the lieutenant. It ain't easy talkin' 'bout this, Mike. I ain't kiddin' ya. Can't remember when I spoke like this to nobody. My old lady, she just couldn't take it no more. I'd get drunk, an' . . ."

"Smitty, can you tell me any more? Other missions you both flew?" Michael didn't realize that Smitty needed someone to help him, to ease him back into the day that faced him back at the shack. No one would, of course. Smitty's job was to keep the pictures on the wall, count the receipts, and make sure the jukebox played Loretta and Charley and Merle. He was, after all, a little old drunk, of no use to anybody. Perhaps all the Smitty's in the world didn't really count any longer. They'd served their time. The government had gotten out of them what it wanted. Any future troubles were purely of their own making. But it was the Smitty's of America who did the terrible things very few wanted to or would do.

"Yeah, but I don't want to." The pain in Smitty's eyes ratcheted up a notch as he took a drag from his smoke, flicked the small butt into the water where it hissed, and he lit another. He turned away from Michael and stared dead-eyed out toward the lake. Across the way, two small boats were anchored off the bank, fishing poles hanging over the sides. The men occupying them sat motionless. Michael wondered what they talked about—how different their conversation was compared to Smitty's and his.

"I think it was our second Ploesti raid. We got up about three in the mornin.' Went to briefin,' ate, went to the armory an' got our guns. Yer daddy had to go to the pilot's briefin's. I remember that day, even before we took off 'cause a truck hit one of the line crew. I thought that was a omen—you know, how the mission was gonna go—and it was."

"Well, we took off. We was especially heavy with bombs and gas that day—'bout like always, I guess. Boy howdy, them skies was filled with airplanes on that mission, B-24's and B-17's, some from as far away as England—musta been a thousand heavy bombers in the air, all goin' ta the same place. I think that was about the biggest raid I was on. No, oh well. Yer daddy was busy as usual checkin' things, an' flyin,' an' all. I could see Lieutenant Hukill's plane over to our right. We was all in tight—kept the fighters off us—just a feets separated our wingtips, an' that airplane was tricky. It wouldn't just do what you wanted it to right when we reached altitude. The air's just too thin up there for it to move when you wanted it to. So, your daddy had to anticipate what to do. I could see them ailerons and rudders just a movin.' I'm of a mind your daddy done some of the best flyin' of all them pilots, and them pilots was good, if they lived long enough. You better believe he and all them pilots was plumb wore out after a mission, too. It wasn't till a month or two before we left that we had fighter cover most of the way, as I recall—them P-51's. No, wait a minute. That was the Innsbruck raid. I get 'em mixed up.

"Ploesti. Okay. It was the second Ploesti raid, an' it was low level— too low for my tastes, I'll tell ya. Our first high-level raid didn't do no real damage, an' we really got shot up. So they made us fly real low—like huggin' the ground so we couldn't get all shot up. Even then, I could see bombers gettin' tore up, some augured in from the ground fire. I was cussin' an' a prayin' an' a hopin' we'd just get out of there. I didn't want to bomb no targets that day, but your daddy, he kept 'er straight on them refineries. It seemed like it took forever to get into the target and out again. There was some powerful lot of smoke goin' up into the sky from them refineries we just bombed. We had to throw out this chaff—that's strips of aluminum foil to mess up the German radar on the way there an' back. I seen two bombers collide. It was just plumb awful. Lost some good buddies on that mission—one from our crew. He took a round in the chest . . . an' died."

Smitty, for all intents and purposes, couldn't talk about Europe any further. With shaking hands he reached into his shirt pocket for another cigarette, but discovered the pack was empty. He needed something to do with his hands, so he wadded the little paper pack into a small ball and threw it into the water. Michael was sure there was so much more to be said. Smitty remembered every plane he observed go down, how it fell, which engines were smoking, which were feathered, which were on fire. He counted the chutes, but far too often, there weren't any chutes to count. He recalled standing at the bar at the EM club overhearing some say so-and-so's plane went down on their last mission—their *last* mission, and he could see the face of the navigator or waste gunner or pilot.

That night he got drunk. No one knew where he "confiscated" the booze. When he couldn't stand up any longer, he passed out. Some of the guys found him and put him in his bunk. They didn't wake him the next day, because the mission had been scrubbed due to bad weather over the primary and secondary targets.

He'd known Lieutenant Hukill for over a year, when Smitty walked up behind Lt.'s Lloyd and Hukill who were talking. Hukill was really into his story about the previous night's mission. He'd flown what they called a nuisance raid. They bombed at one or two in the morning, which would wake the enemy up so they wouldn't get any sleep. Such missions, it was hoped, would throw off their production the next day. That was the theory. Smitty could recall Lt. Hukill's words almost verbatim, and that too surprised him. "A jet locked on to us. I kid you not, Stephen. He's locked on to us about two hundred fifty to three hundred yards behind us, and the tail gunner is locked on to him and Stephenson keeps calling me and asking if he can shoot. I mean if that jet had shot at us, he'd probably put his rounds in our bomb bay and bang; we'd still be falling out of the sky. But I told Stephenson, 'no, just hold on. If he makes any move, if he shoots anything at us at all, then let him have it with everything you have. But don't fire first.' I guess it was a kind of a stand-off. He could have killed us, and we could have returned the favor."

"Anyway, we got over the target, dropped our load—ten five hundred pounders, and he didn't fire. Not one round. Joseph's, the waist gunner, didn't see him, but the tail gunner did. I'm sure he didn't see him. Man, I cain't figure out why he didn't fire. Maybe he was just tired of the war. Maybe he just wanted to go home in one piece. Maybe he was . . . who the heck knows?"

Lazy clouds floated overhead, shading and cooling the Texas spring day for a few minutes. Smitty stared at nothing in particular out onto Eagle Mountain Lake, and since he was back in the war, he thought about some of the horrific storms they flew into and out of over Germany, Austria, and Italy. He shuddered at how lucky they'd been. Drained, he finally looked back at Michael.

"How long have we been here, Smitty?"

"Couple o' hours, I guess."

"I need to get back. I forgot to call home before we came out here. Maybe father's awake. You think?"

Smitty hauled the faded red Folger's coffee can filled with hardened concrete back into the stern next to his foot. Then he wound the rope around the motor and pulled, causing the greasy old paint chipped motor to sputter for several seconds, and then roar to life. Choking blue smoke poured from its inner workings, and for a brief second or two, Michael feared that it might not start. It did. With his hand turning the throttle, Smitty coaxed the small craft slowly out into the lake. The two men didn't speak until they reached shore, and then sparingly. Everything had been said.

Twenty-One: Drunk!

>→◦→○→◦→◦→

Saturday, April 22, 1967

Mrs. Cassalls stood at the counter in the kitchen cutting David a large slice of her incredible, to-die-for chocolate cake before the youngest Lloyd went to bed. This would be the first attempt in the three or four that it took to get him down for the night. The hour had grown late and still no men. Susan felt a stronger than normal need to attend church the following day. Today precipitated the necessity to have Ginny shepherd Margaret and David toward that end. Margaret, already upstairs for the night, lay across the bed talking to Megan Wright, trying to get some mature teenage insight into her father's behavior of late. Megan seemed the natural choice.

The Lloyd's had not attended the Church of the Immaculate Conception in a while. Susan thought it would be good for them to go to Sunday morning Mass. She surely expected her husband to come home and the following day to resume their normal routine as he had always done following his trek out to Smitty's. First, she would naturally let Stephen have a piece of her mind.

In the kitchen, David piled his fork and then his mouth full of cake. He looked down at the canine staring up at him, glued to his every move. Brit was an accomplished moocher. A long, thin membrane of lengthening drool hung from the dog's mouth, the little cocker's feet shifting from side to side. David giggled with delight at what he could do to this dog. He squeezed a pinch of his cake between his fingers and then held it up to get a further rouse out of an already intense dog.

"David. Please stop feeding Brit. You know chocolate's not good for dogs." Mrs. Cassalls was supposed to say that. The game wasn't complete until she had.

"Yes, ma'am." Ginny didn't see the small fist full David slipped into Brit's anxious mouth. That too was part of the game. The morsel was gone so fast that any evidence of David's behavior had been consumed in an instant. All floor crumbs were vacuumed as quickly. The long membrane of saliva tugged downward from the dog's mouth. A quick swipe of David's napkin removed it.

Annika Lloyd, Stephen's mother, sat next to Susan on the sofa, both women were deep in conversation. She was a perceptive woman, Annika was. She had been a beauty in her day—all the facial and physical features were still evident. She was vibrant, remarkably so, for a grandmother. She was perhaps more attractive now, because she knew so much more than she did during those hard days when Marcus and she first began their lives together. Annika was tall like Susan, and although blonde, she too was blue eyed, with a quick wit and a no nonsense bite. She derived this attribute from her Scandinavian parentage. The school children that mocked her youthful Norwegian inflection paid for it. Annika retained a small slice of her heritage when she spoke. She'd always been a fast learner, a sharper bottom feeder and fiercely protective of this boy she'd raised into manhood.

The heavy front door burst open unexpectedly. The suddenness of the sound forced a muted bark from Brit, but due to the promise of more cake, the dog half barked, fighting the terrible urge to see who had come in. His missing some of Ginny's cake was at stake here, and the tension Brit felt to do two things at once must have been incredible.

David turned his head toward the door, the fork half in his mouth, a small amount of chocolate spread over his right cheek. As the volume of the people just entered increased in the foyer, this latest intrusion lay upon boy and dog the greatest of obligations. Brit must drown out these new sounds with wild barking, while still begging his fair share of cake. David needed to greet his father. Both wanted the cake. What to do? It was a two second delay before dog and human succumbed to their basest instincts and ran to check. David's leap from the chair set Brit's nails tapping on the tiled kitchen floor to gain as much traction as possible. He could always come back to the food because David was an easy mark. The cake would wait and the boy and his dog left Mrs. Cassalls in their dust.

The sudden, profuse barking and yelling of both dog and boy respectively became the most immediate focus of Susan's ire. Her husband was but feet from her now and finally safe. She had to first contend with the interference of her youngest son and his animal. "Brit, that's enough! Settle down! Please, David. Stop running!" Brit paid little attention, and before David and Brit could reach Michael and his father, the cat crossed Brit's path. The timing couldn't have been better *or worse*, depending on whose perspective, Susan's, David's, or the dog's.

Toby, Margaret's cat, hissed in self-defense forcing Brit to alter his intended course. Brit's floppy ears rose thus registering his profound attention on this new thing. His demeanor went wild and the look of pure glee fixed itself into his body language. Brit loved chasing this cat more than he loved cake or greeting intruders. And then the canine-feline chase was on in earnest, which David joined in full flung joy. "Get 'em Brit!" David yelled as he turned the corner into the den in hot pursuit.

This brought Susan's nursed and stored anger to the fore. "David, get that dog! *David!* . . . Ahhhh, sh&t." Susan screamed and let fly with that usually unvented "S" word. It left her mouth as if shot from a canon. Susan had been so careful not to swear in the presence of her children. She promised herself she would not use it in front of them—ever. She'd promised her husband and Father McTammany she wouldn't say it. Now she was thoroughly agitated, but it was her only and last weapon she possessed.

Annika put her arm around her daughter-in-law. "It's okay. I'll go see if I can't stop this. Ginny, I need your help. David. David!" Annika wanted to run to her son above everything, but Susan needed help with the youngest boy as the most immediate concern.

Michael held Stephen upright, his right arm over his father's shoulder. Stephen's hangover was obviously still welded to him. He certainly seemed oblivious to the dog and its confusion, although the sudden emergence of light made him blink out of self-protection. Stephen stood weaving in the foyer, leaning against Michael. His eyes had that glazed look and his oversized tongue made any attempt to wet his very dry lips difficult at best. He tried to speak, but the words came coated with the dryness of inebriation. "Suz-zin. Hi! I'm sorry. I din't mean to get drunk, but I cud-unt help it, don't ya see? They're all dead . . . all of 'em, dead. Damien's dead. All of 'um. I'm ti-erd. My son . . . here . . ." Stephen slapped Michael on the chest, "*Our* son, came an' got me from good ol' Smitty's. He'z a gran' fellow, he iz."

Stephen's remaining energy had about spent itself, for the present. His clothes looked terribly wrinkled and filthy. He smelled horrible, and it was all Michael could do to stand there holding him upright. The alcohol and the breakfast it forced back up had thoroughly saturated his shirt, and both needs lent a bucolic aroma fidgeting for dominance over the arrangement of roses Stephen had bought Susan several days earlier for the way he'd behaved of late. The guileless light from the numerous room lamps emphasized his disheveled state.

Margaret somehow heard her cat scream over her own conversation with Megan and then caught the intensity of the dog's unusually wild barking spree. She knew what it meant, but usually let it go. Now she clearly heard David egging this scene of confusion into a hyper state of frenzy. The chaos was topped off by her grandmother's boisterous attempts to quell the growing riot. Margaret told Megan that she'd best talk to her tomorrow and hung up the phone. She caught sight of the event unfolding at the bottom floor, and slowed her pace to a crawl. She was afraid to confront the scene of her father and brother all in one breath. Midway, she stopped, gathered in as much as she could ingest, sighed, and quietly took several more steps to settle herself alone on the bottom step.

Margaret withheld her initial impulse—that of running to her father to look after him, to do for him only what *she* could do. A moment's reflection upon what she beheld brought revulsion for the man she adored, hate and love met between her eyes. Instead, she did nothing. Seeing her father as she had not seen him before made her tuck her skirt under her legs, set her elbows on her legs, place her chin in her hands, and become as unobtrusive, as invisible as she thought she could. She was afraid to speak what her heart felt, and she certainly didn't understand.

Annika, her grandmother, was almost finished settling her younger brother and putting the dog outside. Neither David nor the dog wanted to quit just yet. Poor, ignorant Margaret needed an explanation of these events. Something had harmed her mother this morning, and now her father looked as if he'd slept in a stagnant garbage bin. To add to Margaret's alarm, Michael would soon be leaving for the military, and Damien was dead and buried. Clearly, something so much larger than her ability to comprehend had invaded her quiet, ordered world. This fragile young woman didn't know if it could be reassembled the way it once was.

Thanks to Annika, the chase finally petered itself out. David had brought his motion to rest with a lot of help so he returned to his brother and father still standing in the foyer. Ten year old's are notoriously honest. Standing in front of and below the two men, the smell gripped David's senses causing the boy to grimace. The sight of his father's disheveled appearance captured his attention. David let fly with what everyone was thinking, "Father? What happened to *you*? *Boy*, are you in trouble. Mother doesn't ever let me get *that* dirty. Did you throw up?"

"That's enough, David. Come along upstairs," Annika suggested. "Did my father ever get that dirty when he lived with you, grandmother?"

"Never you mind. You need a bath too, young man." Annika glanced back over her shoulder at her drunken son. Her look was one of ferocity. She hoped that giving David a bath would help her keep from lighting into Stephen. He was a Lloyd, *and look at him. My God!*

Susan had to fix this, and she realized that the strong emotions vying for supremacy over her better judgment would mean nothing to Stephen at the present. She attempted to help direct the smallest Lloyd first: "David, go on upstairs like your grandmother said and get your bath. We're going to church tomorrow. Mom, use our tub."

To which David responded, "I hope father gets cleaned up. He'll really stink in church if he doesn't."

"Yes, I know, dear. We'll take care of him. You just get upstairs and take care of yourself, okay?"

"Mother, can I watch you give father a shower? This will be—"

"David? *Please*, do as I asked." Susan motioned to Annika to keep this child moving toward the stairs or she'd kill him. Ginny was busy cleaning up a potted plant that the cat had knocked over in his race to escape the dog.

"Annika? Where'd you go?" Susan inquired, "I need your help again."

"Ginny," Annika yelled, "I'm taking David to get his bath. Ginny, would you please call my husband. I think we need him."

Grandmother Annika pursued her grandson who let everyone know that Billy, another of his best buddies down the street, needed to hear about this. As they reached the stairs, Annika recognized Margaret's terror. "David, I'll be right there. You go up, turn on the water, and get in the tub in your mother's bathroom." Grandmother Annika took Margaret's face in her hands to reassure her, as only grandmother's can. "Oh, sweet girl. Your father will be all right. I love you so much. And so does your father. Do you believe me?"

Her "yes" was muffled by her overflowing emotion. Her cheeks were by now moist and red, her innocence hopefully still pure. Annika drank from those huge blue eyes into which she stared. They showed such trust. But Annika wasn't quite sure if she believed what she just said to her beloved granddaughter or not. The words felt right. "Margaret honey, I need to help your mother by looking after your brother." That was all Annika said as she freed herself from the young girl's fearful gaze to head up the stairs in search of David.

With David in Annika's tow, Susan was better able to turn her attention back to the greatest of her concerns, her husband. "Stephen, are you all right? I was so worried about *you*." Stephen gave her an incomprehensible response. His body weaved against and away from Michael. Michael would stand there as long as no one said anything. His father, moreover, was getting heavy.

"Mother, he's getting hard to hold."

"Oh . . . let's get him upstairs, Michael. I'm sorry. I'll try and help you." Susan slipped her shoulder under her husband's other arm as they both attempted to direct Stephen upstairs. Stephen unexpectedly became obstinate and dislodged their arms to stand on his own, barely. Weaving though he was, he took a step toward one of the several "moving" staircases. Stephen's inebriated brain saw three staircases, or was the handrail swaying? He decided to grab for the middle one.

To keep from falling and to show his family that he was in control, he said something that resembled, "Don' tell me whish rail ta' grab. I'll get it as it goes by. Jus' wash this." Stephen made a lunge forward to catch the handrail before it passed him. "Ya' see there. I . . .", he belched in an obnoxious show of disregard for everything he'd taught his children, "I can do this." In his fall forward, Stephen didn't realize that he almost landed on his daughter in his nearly vain attempt to keep his body upright and moving. He had no idea Margaret sat there in front of him.

Now that he held the railing, Stephen pulled his heavy, limp, uncooperative body up the stairs, his progress perilously slow. He failed several times to lift his feet sufficiently to heft his body to the next step, which almost brought him back down. He somehow caught the rail each time. Michael assisted him at every attempt. Stephen became agitated several times when he felt a hand flat against his back.

"Lea've me a-lone. I can get up . . . these stairs by myself. I'm not that dru . . . nk." Near the top he bent over and heaved, and this activity made Margaret almost sick. Fortunately, there was nothing left to come up from his stomach. After eight or nine more minutes, Stephen reached the top step. "Boy howdy, did some . . . body built some more . . ." another loud, sickening belch, ". . . stairs onto this house?"

Susan stood at the bottom stair watching the perfect husband and parent destroy so much that he'd labored for decades to build. Stephen banged into the hall walls several times, but felt nothing approaching pain. He was too numb to feel. When Michael and he had reached the bathroom, the boy turned on the light, closed the door, and leaned his father against the wall for balance. In three seconds, Stephen slid down the door into a heap on the tile floor. Michael stood staring, not sure what to make of this scene. Susan had started slowly up the stairs, and at the thud, made a dead run toward the bathroom and the noise. Michael instinctively grasped his mother's arm, halting her motion toward her husband. "I have to catch my breath. Let him lay there for a second." After another minute, Michael said, "Mother, I talked to Smitty for a long time today."

"You didn't call, and I was so worried about you both. Why didn't you call me? What did he say to you? Is your father all right?" Seconds passed, and then Susan remembered. "I want you to call my mom and dad and tell them that I need them."

"Yes, Mother. Did father ever tell you about any of the missions he flew during the war?"

Michael's question became an inconvenience that irritated her. What did Stephen's missions during the war have to do with *this*? This behavior of his was irresponsible. "What? No. Of course not.

He never talks about that time. Not to me, anyway. Michael, help me get his clothes off." When that was done, Susan ordered, "Turn on the shower and when it's warm, help me get him in and under the water." That done, "Now, do as I asked you and call your grandparents."

"Yes, ma'am."

Margaret, still reeling from the sight of her father, burst into tears and embraced her mother. "Mother, what's happening to us? I don't understand. Everything seems as if it's falling apart. Do you think father is *okay*?"

Ever since Damien's death, some *thing* had been wrong in the Lloyd household. Margaret was the most sensitive to it. The "D" word, *divorce* was not far from her mind. Two of her friend's parents had recently separated. David took things at face value. If they said it was okay, then it was okay. This entire family "play" seemed a bit odd, but to him, it didn't carry the gravity everyone thought it did.

Annika found her son sitting on the bathroom floor, his back resting against the tub. He had pulled his knees up, and he was rubbing the back of his hand against his mouth. The day's stubble made him look older and dirtier. He stared past his mother who crossed his field of vision to take a seat on the toilet lid. It was then that she noticed the pistol in his lap, half covered by his shirt. Stephen had gotten his service weapon and his hand held it firmly.

She gasped, "Oh, my God, Stephen! What are you doing with the gun?"

Stephen didn't see or hear her. He kept wincing and staring outward into something. He was most certainly not mentally present in the same bathroom Annika shared with him. She was terrified because she couldn't reach her son.

"What's going on here?" Marcus Lloyd's gruff voice invaded the moment. "Why's he sitting in the floor? For heaven's sakes son, get up!" The command fled from him with his wife's whisper.

"Marcus, he's got a gun. What do we do?" Her breathy words were sufficient to be heard by her husband.

Susan, too, spoke in hushed tones from behind her father-in-law, "Dad, is he alright?"

Marcus turned to meet her inquiry. "Susan, where did Stephen get that pistol?"

"Pistol? What pistol?" was Susan's frightened retort.

Susan whirled past Marcus to get nearer the situation. "Oh, my God! Stephen, let me have the gun. Please Sweetheart. Let me have the gun." Stephen gave no response of any kind. Susan's eyes then met Annika's, and she asked, "Mom, what should we do?" Michael had gotten just abreast of his grandfather. Marcus quickly grabbed the boy firmly to keep him from entering the bathroom. "No, Michael. Don't go in there. Go down and . . . No. Good Lord. I don't know what to do."

"Grandfather? What's wrong?" Michael stuck his head around the corner to see his grandmother, her hand over her mouth, and his mother, her arms around her waist, both women staring down at his father in disbelief. Marcus spoke firmly, "Son, your father has a pistol. Now, you wait right here. I'm going to call the police. Oh, *goodness*. Just stay here."

Twenty-Two: Col. Inhofe

>━┼◆>━•O━•<◆┼━<

Sunday, April 23, 1967

Limping back to the couch, Col. Inhofe grabbed his cane and hobbled to the front desk of the Lloyd Hotel nearest Love Field to get directions, and then he limped to the main drive to await his transportation. Michael sped around from behind the hotel, stopped in front to retrieve the doctor and headed toward Bethhaven. They had to stop once to clarify their destination and within forty-five minutes were driving onto the manicured grounds of Bethhaven, or BPH, as most elected to call it. It was preferable to keep psychiatric hospitals to one's self.

The protracted strain lay heavy upon Susan's worried, but otherwise attractive features as she paced about the main waiting room. Michael sat staring obliquely at a dark haired doctor wearing a white coat, making his rounds. Several huddled nurses, speaking in hushed tones had gathered farther down the hall. He smelled the first signs of meal preparation from somewhere down another polished marble hallway—*fish*, he thought. Michael was also the first to hear the tap-step, tap-step of a man walking with the aid of a wooden cane. He turned to read Col. Inhofe's expression, hoping he might have some positive news about his father to share with them.

The Colonel rounded the group of chairs and stopped. "He's resting. I'm treating him with Thorazine, and it appears as if he's responding to it. That's what I'd hoped." Dr. Inhofe sighed as he crumpled into one of the overstuffed chairs, flanked on either side by

Susan and Michael. Marcus had to stop by and speak to Dolores, and Annika was busy with Margaret.

Susan leaned forward and said, "Thank you so much for coming on such short notice, doctor. How were you able to get here so quickly?"

"Mrs. Lloyd, you don't want to know. But when Marcus Lloyd yells, there are people in the Pentagon that listen. Suffice it to say, I'm here."

Colonel Jerry Inhofe had been wounded in the Second World War. He'd almost lost a leg while operating on a patient as a result of incoming German artillery rounds. At the war's conclusion, Col. Inhofe returned home to a world he no longer recognized. America hadn't changed, but he had. By the mid-1960's he'd been out of medical school fifteen years and was now a practicing psychiatrist. He'd also been divorced twice. He, too, was struggling with his own demons while he attempted to care for these combat veterans with psychological disorders, as well as their families who had no idea what to do. Too many of these veterans felt as if they'd been thrown to the wolves when their repressed memories began to surface. The wives and children all too often withered on the vine from lack of information and care.

Col. Inhofe was one of the few doctors who grasped the psychosis of war, being knee deep in it, and in many different ways. And now Marcus Lloyd had called and asked him to fly down to Texas from his duty station, the Naval Hospital in Bethesda, Maryland. Marcus had enough connections in almost every section of American society so that getting a few strings pulled to have the colonel assigned to temporary duty in the southwest was a mere formality.

Michael and Susan had driven Stephen to the Lloyd International hotel nearest Love Field for a quick, preliminary examination. Marcus's driver retrieved Col. Inhofe at the airport and drove him the half mile to the hotel. Marcus had also told Michael specifically to drive to the back of the building where the manager would discretely direct them to an empty suite off of the Starlight Room, one of the hotel's main conference areas. When Dr. Inhofe examined Stephen, he was so alarmed that he called a former colleague, now working at Bethhaven Psychiatric Hospital in Dallas, to see if he had a private room available to have Mr. Lloyd admitted, stat. This is where they were now.

Massive and numerous floral arrangements and potted plants—lovely diversions for the families—had been strategically placed for maximum effect throughout the lobby. Framed oil paintings spoke of easier, more pastoral moments; clusters of living room furniture dotted the spacious visiting arena drawing one's attention beyond the building's intended purpose. A huge salt-water fish tank recessed into the wall was stocked with wild and colorful sea creatures, crustaceans and fish of various species. There were wild rock formations with live sea grasses, corals and anemones decorating the sandy bottom. Soft music played from the overhead speakers.

Other energetic nurses appeared carrying trays with small paper cups from room to room. Muted wall colors steadied the frayed or embarrassed nerves of family members waiting to speak with overworked, serious doctors. The Colonel's face grimaced as he sat. The travel and more than normal amount of walking he'd done over the past few days had tested his pain threshold to the fullest. Doctor Inhofe arranged his leg into a more comfortable position for the coming debriefing to which he'd grown so accustomed.

He already knew Susan and Michael's questions. The colonel began. "He's doing fine, let me assure you. I've seen cases much worse than your husband's, Mrs. Lloyd. You weren't expecting the gun, were you?" Then he waited, like a fielder waiting on a high fly ball to drop into his mitt.

Susan's emotional duress, held at bay for the previous hour, finally leapt from her stomach. It came up through her throat and out into the passive atmosphere of the lobby. The fly the colonel awaited dropped. Susan's eyes had become dull things from which she attempted her observation of the moment. "No, I wasn't. It scared me to death. What brought this on, colonel? Michael said it's the war, but I don't really understand how that can be. The war was over years ago. I thought . . ." Col. Inhofe knew he must guide this woman in a slightly different direction. Her visible alarm could be managed for her sake, as well as Michael's. The boy was clearly worried as well.

"Your husband hasn't talked about his experiences during the war, has he?" The colonel didn't look at the woman to whom he was now speaking, but rather chose to stare at the neat, but aged receptionist preoccupied at her desk. The Army doctor knew the answer before he asked it. The Lloyd's had the same thought processes he found he needed to realign in most of the cases he attended. The families came to him like his patients whose duress was freighted with uncertainty and whose questions were multifaceted and legion. With most of the families, as with Susan, the war ended when it ended. It was, "well past time to get on with one's life," they all said to their veteran relatives. "Mrs. Lloyd and Michael, what do you two *know* about Stephen's time in the service?"

Before Susan could speak, Michael told the colonel about what Smitty had told him. Susan listened in amazement as Michael related incredible, unbelievable stories about her husband. Susan's astonishment quickly turned to bewilderment, and she felt as if she had entered into another dimension to which she did not belong. The colonel thought that he sensed the boy's disappointment, or was it agitation? He couldn't be certain at this point. Regardless, Dr. Inhofe believed that both emotions were somehow intertwined among the boy's words and speech patterns. Michael's body language hinted at his father's withholding his life's experiences from his son, but didn't say it outright.

Doctor Inhofe remained motionless, holding his cards close to his vest—listening. He had spoken too soon with several families, and they ate his lunch, so to speak. He wondered about the same things he always did, but mostly he puzzled over the families—their complete ignorance of war's effect—now it was the Lloyd family's turn.

The veterans were a bit easier to diagnose and treat when it was all said and done. With the colonel the greater stress usually came from the family. He had to commence with the wives whose internal interests and maternal instincts resembled a mother bear protecting her cubs. He'd now come to anticipate their complete lack of comprehension of the destructive nature of war, and its prolonged effects were so pathetically lacking. Their men, however, flatly refused to talk about their experiences.

Some wives and mothers, fathers or brothers, were unbelievably selfish. Far too many felt ravaged by their men's withdrawal or binges and the future they had so meticulously constructed, awaiting their loved one's return. When he, and in some cases she, returned, a complete stranger trudged through the door into a world that could not be reconciled, the world they had most recently sworn never to think about again. The end of hostilities in Europe or the Pacific had set the table for dysfunction or divorce, and all too often, both.

Sometimes the colonel delivered a restored soldier, sailor, Marine, or airman to health—*sometimes*, but not very often. When they left his care, he wondered if the war wouldn't crop back into their lives at some point down the road, and at the most inconvenient of moments. It certainly had in this situation. Could a man be completely cured who had experienced, witnessed, or participated in hideous, often unspeakable events? Probably not. No, not fully. War had altered something fundamental about each warrior. The dilemma remained: how to get the phoenix to rise from the ashes.

These were the people Col. Inhofe saw day-in and day-out. Many came home and melted into the fabric of society, going about their business. Yet, he feared that too many would commit suicide at some moment of great stress. Many would die alone. Statistics favored the odds that many unsuspecting wives and children would be battered, physically and mentally. They couldn't understand why their returning veteran scared them so; at other times attacked the people they fought so ferociously to defend. Dr. Inhofe thought that the people who start these wars should have to live with a returning combat veteran for a year. Their anger and depression would drive these war-hungry leaders to rethink their policies. And now Vietnam was stirring up the old guard's memories, just like it was currently displacing the newest generation of terribly young men returning home from their combat tours in Southeast Asia.

Some men chain-smoked. Some pickled their livers and brains in alcohol. Some clung to the morphine-induced life that had begun when the wound's pain drove them nearly mad. Often, they became drug addicts. Some men worked like demons, always mobile, waiting for the other shoe to drop, and ill at ease when static. They avoided crowds or family gatherings. The holidays became solitary, if not unpleasant affairs. Some chased women—or men—while their spouses threw up their hands, packed, and took the children back to mother. Some simply lived with and endured it. There were the ones who managed to do reasonably well in spite of their experiences, but these veterans were invisible.

Unexpectedly, something would trigger all the mish mash quite alive inside its host veteran—a sound, a smell, a feeling, a memory, a nightmare, or . . . a death. One day the light was on, and the next, it flickered and burned out. But the families . . . the families were so pathetically thrown to the wind when the war came knocking at their unbolted door. The children such as Michael had no way to ingest this information, no experiential compass from which to approach the life sucking monster that ravaged and devoured its host's mind and soul until their father, brother, or friend was eaten hollow from the inside. Unfortunately, neither the veterans nor their families knew that the war lie behind it. This invisible gatecrasher was simply a stranger to them.

Twenty-Three: Bethhaven

Monday, April 24, 1967

"Hi." Susan's unexpected words came from behind him when she saw her husband stirring under the sheets. He blinked from the light streaming in through the window, into his hospital room, and into his eyes. Startled, Stephen sat up slowly and yawned. As he stretched, the look of confusion spread across his facial features. "That light bothers you, doesn't it? I'm sorry. Do you want me to close the blinds?"

"Please." Susan stood and drew the shades. A controlled panic shrouded Stephen. He didn't know where he was. "Susan, where am I? What time is it? Why am I dressed like this?"

"Honey, it's okay. It's all right. You're in the hospital. It's Tuesday."

Incomprehension did not look well on him. "What do you mean, it's Tuesday? What hospital?"

"It's called Bethhaven. Do you remember anything about coming here, Sweetheart?"

"No." Stephen, a bit more aware, eyed the room more carefully. It looked very plush, and there were pictures of subdued scenes on the walls.

"Where did you say I was?" he asked.

"You're at Bethhaven."

"What's Bethhaven?"

Thankfully, Dr. Inhofe entered the room, so he fielded the question. The doctor already knew what a loaded and thorny issue he had to handle right then.

The private conversation between the doctor and his patient later that morning was Q&A—preliminary background information with the patient. Dr. Inhofe asked the questions and Stephen fought not to respond much beyond name, rank, and serial number. It was a session that seemed to go nowhere. Dr. Inhofe wasn't surprised. Stephen was quite agitated at this probing. That was expected also. Stephen didn't need a reason, but he didn't want to delve into the past. It was just too painful, and it made him edgy. All those memories he wanted to keep in the past. They would talk tomorrow, Dr. Inhofe decided. He left the room telling his patient to get some rest.

Col. Inhofe met Susan in the main lobby for an after visit conference. Annika and Marcus, along with the kids, had come but left frustrated and disappointed that they couldn't see their son and father respectively, yet. Dr. Inhofe hobbled over to where Susan sat waiting. "Ooooh. I've been walking way too much. I need to sit, Mrs. Lloyd." He was in obvious pain. The wound the doctor had received during the war almost cost the colonel his leg, but the doctors in England had been able to save it, if barely. Some days the pain felt more acute than others, yet at the conclusion of each day he felt the pain and cursed the Germans who fired that round. His cane helped, unless he walked more than normal making his rounds. He was just too good a doctor for the military to let go, but neither would he find many promotions waiting on his desk. Despite the negatives, Dr. Jerry Inhofe had made light colonel by the mid-1960's.

"How did it go, doctor? Did he say *anything*? What can you tell me? When can I see him again?" Susan asked eagerly, almost hungrily.

The colonel's groan was all but unrestrained as he sat. He found that if he shifted the weight off of his bad leg, just so, he could slip into the chair easier. "Ohhhhh, it feels good to sit." The colonel settled into the chair and arranged himself so that he would be able to accommodate the discomfort better. "Well, it's as I expected. Your husband's upset for being brought here. These kinds of hospitals, regardless of how elegant we make them, carry a stigma. Men such as your husband, former officers, worry most about being branded crazy or mental cases at having to spend one second here. They believe they have so much to lose, and some do. They think they will be tarnished among their peers and their jobs will be affected adversely. You can guess the rest. They have no immediate recognition that something is wrong and must be put right."

Susan recoiled. "He isn't crazy. But I certainly don't understand his behavior the night he came home from Smitty's."

"Mrs. Lloyd, for your husband, and you too, the war has come back. I have to constantly reinforce this one idea with the relatives, and so few of them understand this. He doesn't want to think about it, but for the reasons your son and you have told me, he is being forced to remember. Can you understand that if he is going to get better, and I don't know what that will mean exactly, it's different for each case I treat, you must become part of the solution."

"I must become part of the solution? I don't understand, doctor?"

"You are critical to your husband's well-being, to his getting better, which will never be exactly as it was. It's how you respond to him when he's struggling. Many things changed as a result of being terrified for long periods of time. He may have reached a point where he considered himself already dead. I believe, although the medical community does not, that internal changes, greater than what we have always thought, have taken place inside these combatant's bodies, in their minds." The look on Susan's face was pure agony.

"Like what kind of changes, Dr. Inhofe?" she asked.

"Well, I am pushing for the government to start doing testing and research on the chemical and anatomical transformations brought on by combat trauma, for one. I also suspect physiological abnormalities, perhaps biological, even neuro-biological changes from living on adrenaline and fear. I suspect that parts of the brain have been altered, but I can't be certain until much more testing is done. Mrs. Lloyd, was your husband wounded physically during the war?"

"No."

"Okay. Then you need to know that he *was* injured, but his wound doesn't have a physical scar. War *physiologically* maims the participants to varying degrees, as I have just said, depending on their specific participation in it. I suspect that your husband must have flown some terrifying missions. I can check his record to be sure. And when you add the incident of his bombs dropping on some of his friends, and you add to that the losses of crew members he had to fly with for hours before he could return to base, well, what he and so many men like him did and went through, is just indescribable. So few of us have any idea what that type of pressure and fear does to the mind. And since the end of the war he's repressed all that guilt and anger day after day, just to function resulting in depression. I think it is a tribute to your husband's fortitude that he has done so well for so long without letting go.

"Look, Mrs. Lloyd, that man hasn't stopped loving you. I doubt he ever will. He's a very lucky man."

Susan didn't realize it, but the doctor's response to his own trauma was showing through via his present flirtation with his patient's wife. Inhofe, too, was a man battling his own physiological pain in the manner he felt most comfortable. His was with alcohol and women.

Susan Lloyd sat mere feet from this doctor who would attempt to take advantage of her if the opportunity afforded itself. The high of another drink and the pursuit of women dulled his own memories of the patients he couldn't save, and the pain that clung to him because a German artillery round killed a dear friend and all but ripped his leg off of him.

Some days during the war, usually following those horrid Allied or Axis offensives, he would operate hour after hour until he literally dropped from exhaustion. Still, the wounded kept coming until he was numb. By the time Captain Inhofe was evacuated to England he had grown to hate those young boys they placed before him, broken and bleeding men on a seldom halting assembly line where doctors attempted to and failed too often to put them back together. Psychiatry seemed the only way he could stay in the medical field, and in the military.

Fortunately, Susan had become more introspective than she normally might have so that she didn't catch the look on the doctor's face as he eyed her, even with the woman's son sitting there. Perhaps, as far as Dr. Inhofe was concerned, the fox was very busy watching the hen house.

The doctor continued, "Gaining his mental equilibrium will take a while because he doesn't want to talk about the past. Usually, what I say will not get him to open up. This just takes time. The gun, well, when we . . . I mean, when they reach that point of hopelessness following some trigger, like this recent death of your friend, it's as if— in some men—all those memories they have repressed come flooding out. A wound has been pierced, if you will, and they are overwhelmed by what they begin to remember. They experience all that guilt, all the fear, and those horrible what-ifs. It's like an avalanche, and it can crush the strongest of men. This is when you can really see the damage the war did to your husband internally."

"I would like to ask you some things, Mrs. Lloyd, if you feel up to it?" Susan had not prepared herself for answering questions.

"All right. What can I answer for you?"

"Your husband flew B-24's as a pilot. He served with the Fifteenth Air Force. Is that right?

"Yes. That's correct."

"Mrs. Lloyd, do you understand what that means?"

"What do you mean, doctor, 'do I understand what that means'?"

"Have you ever thought about what it took to fly one of those huge bombers?"

"No. I haven't. No—"

"Have you ever been near a B-24?"

"No." Susan sensed ever so slightly that this situation was somehow her fault. Dr. Inhofe wasn't being fair.

He kept up a compassionate but staccato type of questioning. "Do you know what it's like to be exposed to prolonged mind numbing cold? I understand it was sometimes minus forty degrees below zero at those altitudes. It took unbelievable strength to control a huge airplane like that, hour after hour."

"I'm certain it did. But if he didn't talk about it, how was I supposed to know?" Susan appeared on the verge of tears.

"Do you know what flak is?"

"Well, I've read or seen some films about it. I resent your line of questioning. You are making me feel as if I am the perpetrator of all of this."

Dr. Inhofe withdrew his controlled but purposeful intensity. He wanted this woman to work through the fringes of her husband's nightmarish scenarios that had suddenly been thrown out for her to absorb, then to analyze, and finally reach some intelligent conclusions so that she would respond to Stephen's situation with calm. Since that wasn't going to happen, she needed to at least taste what her husband gorged on for fifty missions.

"He . . . I mean, I . . . well, not really. I tried not to think about that, what he saw, what he experienced. I didn't *bury* my head in the sand while he was gone, if that's what you are implying? I read the newspapers, and certainly all of his letters more than once. But now . . . I just can't imagine . . . him, that is, my husband . . . *my* Stephen doing all that. But it was so far in the past . . ." Susan sounded almost sheepish, but then she blurted, "I don't think I wanted to know all, well . . . any of the details. Well, yes I did, but I didn't know what to say to Stephen. He seemed so happy to be home, and I tried to do everything I could to help him come back home. And then we had several more miscarriages, and Stephen was promoted at work. He didn't want to . . . he never really talked about the war." Susan focused on a large yellow fish swimming in the fish tank.

"It's okay, Mrs. Lloyd. I'm certainly not accusing you of anything. Please don't take it that way. I've discovered that my patient's families weren't ready for their soldiers to come home. They thought they were, but they weren't. You're doing just fine, Mrs. Lloyd, but I want you to imagine right now, if you can, what he went through. You have to ask these kinds of questions in order to put yourself in his shoes, if only for your own *awareness* of what he's been through. You can never know it to the extent that he did, but you can get just a dose of it if you try. I think it's important that you try. Does Stephen ever go to any of his squadron's reunions? Is he active in any way in those kinds of endeavors?"

"No. No, he never goes." Susan's words and sudden self-imposed guilt began to mire her and weigh her down. Doctor Inhofe allowed Susan the time to experience the void that he knew she had no way of filling. But she had to become part of it, to meet Stephen half way. Stephen's condition was not her fault, although she believed at this moment she was in some way culpable, either by silence or by fear. She didn't know which. What was she supposed to know? No one bothered to tell her. Dr. Inhofe wanted her to want to see the need of the moment more than anything—and embrace it as hers, or theirs. He wanted Susan to be willing to go to any lengths for that man suffering in there, and yet, Inhofe was trying not to be too obvious about his own feelings.

The days up ahead would weary her. They would be filled with anger, and they would frustrate her. Until the past was dealt with, and so far it hadn't seemed possible for Stephen or Susan to deal with it, their lives could not resume for one second toward any kind of normalcy. There was much she needed to research about Stephen's time in Italy.

"Tell me about lately, Mrs. Lloyd. When did you notice that life was taking a turn away from its usual patterns?"

"After the funeral I began to notice a change."

"For instance?"

Susan explained what she had observed, the trip to Smitty's, the alcohol, the impatience, and finally of Michael's going out to get his father to bring him home. Then she asked the doctor, "You don't think he meant to use it, do you? The gun, I mean?"

"Mrs. Lloyd, some men have such a keen sense of guilt over all the men who didn't make it back. They perceive life in terms of what they should have or could have done to save them so they could get back home too. And then when those men died on the way to the target or back to base, men like your husband, responsible men, well, they feel a depth of guilt they never imagined. Those of you waiting at home don't realize—and how could you—just how much guilt these men bear. You probably didn't want him to have any feelings of culpability . . ." Inhofe stopped to let this sink in. "And so, what you couldn't observe, you assumed didn't existed. In fact, without you knowing it, your joy at seeing this returning warrior home at last became part of the hammer that drove the guilt and anger deep underground. It had to. I'm not laying blame. We just never know what to expect if and when it surfaces. I believe we must start from a different place in treating these veterans, which has put me at odds with my colleagues. There are effects on men from combat trauma that need to be emphasized as a primary way of healing to the extent we can. It is crucial for the family members that they know that once this "cat" is out of the bag, life will probably be different at home. Very different. The marriages suffer so much hurt because no one is prepared to handle these angry men. . ."

The doctor stared at the floor, his gaze inaccessible and removed from the hospital. And then as quickly as he had left her presence, he returned. "Would he have used that gun? I don't know."

Susan heard a deep, male voice behind her. She recognized it immediately. It was Dr. Wilson. "Dr. Wilson! Thank you *so much* for coming."

"How is he, Susan?"

"He's resting. James, I want you to meet Stephen's doctor. Dr. Inhofe, this is Dr. James Wilson. It was Dr. Wilson's son . . . who was killed . . ." The moment was awkward as it felt for all three souls. Susan couldn't believe what she had just said, how it burst forth like that. Both doctors shook hands. James Wilson explained that Mary Ellen was sitting in the car crying. She suspected or thought she knew that it was her son's death that had put Stephen in this place. She had felt her own guilt welling up inside the closer James and she got to Bethhaven. Now she couldn't face Susan, and no one had done anything to cause this except her son. Life could be so cruel at times. When it rained, it poured.

Upon hearing of her friend's plight, Susan rushed out to the car to absolve Mary Ellen of any real or perceived trespass. Both women needed someone to hang on to.

"I want to see Stephen if I may, doctor," Dr. Wilson said.

"I am hesitant at this point. However, it might be good for him." The two men stood and discussed the situation as professionals for several more minutes.

Dr. Wilson, peeking sheepishly around the door, and tapped on it lightly.

"Come in." Stephen's cold reply and stare flattened against James' sturdy frame. A deflated "Sorry" followed.

"Hello, Stephen. How are you feeling?"

"Oh, I'm crazy. Haven't you heard? That's why I'm here. They only check *looney's* into a place like this."

"You're not crazy, Stephen. We both know that. What happened the other night?"

Stephen's eyes ran around the room searching for that elusive answer too many people kept asking him. Not wanting it found, he suggested the only possible answer: "I don't know."

Dr. Wilson sat in one of the several empty chairs. He crossed his legs to reveal a brown sock contrasted against his black suit trousers. "Let me ask you something, my friend. Do you think . . ?" He hesitated. "No, I'm sorry."

"For what? Do I think what, James? What are you sorry for?"

There came a long, heavy silence, hanging briefly about the room. This time it came from the chair in which Dr. James Wilson sat, deep in thought, wondering whether or not to proceed. Now that he'd opened this can of worms, he'd have to empty its contents. Dr. Wilson wasn't the most tactful or the easiest man to work with. In some ways, building the bomb was much more accommodating to his personality. People, from James' perspective, had too many vagaries.

Not finding any way around the question at this juncture, James Wilson decided to proceed. "What I meant to say was, do you think . . . that is to say, could it be possible, that . . . my boy's death had something to do with your being here?"

"What? *No*. Damien put me here? *No*, of course not, James. You can't put this on him. Forever more! Man, have you gone mad?"

"Stephen, you know that psychiatry is not my field. But I have learned to deduce a universal from the particulars that are given to me. Way too much doesn't add up to anything remotely satisfying—for me, anyway—about you being here. Susan and Marcus both told me that you came home drunk, and somehow brought a gun in with you. Did you intend to use it on yourself?" James waited for and hoped Stephen would supply some kind of answer. When none came, he continued, "Susan said you have been acting, what did she say, *different*, ever since you learned about Damien."

It felt horrible to James that he had to speak of his son in *this* context. He'd much rather sit at home remembering those exciting ballgames he'd watched Damien play. But the exigencies of life and the Providence from which they flowed often supplanted a man's—and his wife's—immediate needs or desires. Perhaps the grief process was part of this visit. Regardless, he was ministering to someone else, and it felt good. He needed to give.

As far as the other night was concerned, too much of it lie in the fog of Stephen's alcohol induced stupor for him to be certain of anything. He recalled the smell of Smitty's, movement in a car, a dog, some stairs, blue uniforms and indiscernible voices. Stephen scraped his top teeth against his bottom lip—a nervous habit he'd acquired over the years when answers were illusive.

James Wilson sat waiting and praying within his mind. He'd lost his son, and sleep was hard to come by. His classes at Gladstone were handled until the conclusion of the semester—if need be. Stephen thought that James would have made a good cop because he carried that look of utter authority about him from which wise and intelligent men shrank. Fools caught it in the neck. It would do Stephen no good to stretch the truth with this man: James Wilson had helped to split the atom.

"James. Why are you so worried about me? I'm fine. You should be focused on yourself. How's Mary Ellen?"

"No Stephen. You aren't well. I don't know what the problem is exactly, but you are not fine. The evidence is irrefutable. Mary Ellen is holding up. And being here is killing me. I've just lost my son . . ." the tears would begin anew if he didn't pursue this. *Concentrate man.* "Now I want to know how it came about that you are here? I've got to refocus, to stop looking at what I can't alter. There's too much at stake for me."

"Like what?"

"Stephen. Don't change the subject. What's happened? What's wrong?"

"Would you mind looking in on Susan for me?"

"Don't change the subject, my friend. Why are you stalling, Stephen? Your avoidance is more empirical evidence that things are not right."

Stephen turned over on his side so that he didn't have to face those eyes of Dr. James Wilson. James could do nothing else if Stephen chose to willfully disregard him. Finally, the silence became intolerable for both men, and James rose to leave. Stephen didn't know whether to keep feigning sleep or not, and his silence with James alarmed even him. Stephen wanted to hit something and be left alone.

James' hand rested on the door handle when Stephen offered something quite unexpected. "Something happened in me when Michael came to the office with the news about your son that day." More silence. James Wilson was a scientist of the first order. Damien had so often succumbed to his father's many interrogations. James' large size produced an audible, heavy and rhythmic breathing, which is perhaps why Stephen continued. "I labored with all my might to repress all those *things* that happened during the war. I think the anger gripped me first. And over the past weeks, that turned to depression. Of course, I fought each emotion. I learned how to, because I'd had plenty of practice when I flew all those bombing missions. I saw their faces when I held Michael as he cried in my office. They were so young, so terribly young. Why *now*?"

Stephen's bed shook as he sobbed uncontrollably. Dr. Wilson returned to the bed's side to comfort his friend, but Stephen stiff-armed him. James parried Stephen's arm in order to grab his friend, lifting him up and then bear hugging him.

Within seconds, both men were wrapped around each other, weeping, holding on for dear life lest the wheels completely spin off of the merry-go-round. One man had lost his son and a future with grandchildren and all that that meant. The other had been thrown backward upon the thorns of death and destruction and all that that elicited. The truth was at stake. No one was quite sure what Stephen had lost except Dr. James Inhofe, and he was making educated guesses. Perhaps the better question was what would Stephen Lloyd discover should he decide to pursue life?

"James. I intended to kill myself." And then to no one in particular, Stephen's aching heart cried out, "Help me. Oh, God, help me!"

It is a mighty thing to see two men embrace each other when they are both struggling with the life they have been dealt. One's religion had ill prepared him for tragedy. The other's faith buoyed him.

Twenty-Four: Two Women

The day passed like a weighty, unfeeling thing, stretched into infinity, refusing to end. Since Stephen's "situation" was not common knowledge, few visitors came to the hospital to check on Stephen and Susan. The story had been circulated at the Fonteneau Building, led by Delores: Stephen had taken some much deserved time off. For those few trusted colleagues, their visits perhaps had satisfied their curiosity but a little. That's how Stephen perceived it. They talked of everything but the obvious, and finally, mercifully, they left.

Michael came about noon on the third day of Stephen's hospitalization to relieve his mother so she could go home and get some rest. Sitting uncomfortably in the padded chair, Susan felt the fatigue settling into her bones, but guilt pressed upon her more at the thought of leaving her husband. What if Stephen awoke, found that he needed her, and she wasn't there? Mary Ellen had hung back on the periphery of the few visitors or made small talk with the staff when they had a minute. She, too, needed to stay busy, and sitting at home seemed like a death sentence. She could only wash the dishes or vacuum the carpet so many times.

In life, Damien had become part of the Wilson's home's presence, and his presence hung heavy over her heart. Mary Ellen smelled him each time she entered the front door. She saw him standing at the sink doing the dishes that last Mother's day he was home. Then there were days when she couldn't see his face. Those were the most disheartening moments for Mary Ellen. She had to force her mind to focus on each facial feature, and when each day concluded, she sometimes fell asleep on the couch from mental exhaustion.

She had not yet gathered the strength to enter his room to begin the process of sorting, cataloguing and, finally, putting his things into boxes to be stored in the attic. Annika thought it was too soon, and she said so. To Mary Ellen, clearing his room was tantamount to moving him out of her life. So, she kept putting it off. One day she would wake up and realize that Damien wasn't coming home anymore, and that frightened her. Until then, she would enjoy the experience of his once having been a powerful part of her world. Today, she had volunteered to come to Bethhaven with her husband and see what she could do there for the Lloyds.

"Susan, I'll take you home," Mary Ellen suggested. "Michael will call us if Stephen calls for you or needs anything. Won't you, son?" Mary Ellen kept looking at Michael. He would have to replace her boy. She had cooked for Michael so many times over the years. Susan had not yet told Mary Ellen of Michael's plans to join the military. She just couldn't. Michael nodded in the affirmative.

Mary Ellen had worked in a hospital briefly at Jackson College before she transferred to Fisk, where she met James. When Damien was finally born, hers was a difficult delivery. The upshot of this hard labor was that she should not try and have more children. She might die if she did, the doctor informed her. Damien, too, had been a very special child, as had Michael. Mary Ellen reached up to Michael's neck and hugged him firmly for an extra second, and then turned away, the tears rolling down her cheeks.

In the car Susan thought back over the days and weeks past—since Damien's death. Her thoughts came to rest on various times, a few specifics, and several strange conversations with Stephen that she supposed he might have wanted to direct somewhere else. Now she wondered if those things were actually related to the war, and ultimately, his admittance here to Bethhaven. Susan said little for ten minutes—the weather was good, the temperature was nice. Mary Ellen looked good in yellow. Susan flirted with another long silence.

Susan's considerations, as if they had a mind of their own, reached farther back than she could have imagined. The Korean War came to mind. Some of the men Stephen flew with in Europe had remained in the service when everyone else was leaving. He had surreptitiously been keeping up with the loss of so many B-29s to enemy MIGs. And at least one of those men, a very close pilot, went down in a B-29. Susan had noticed Stephen's mood swings, nightmares, the anxiety, but not to the extent Stephen had so recently exhibited. Neither had connected war's mounting losses with the changes that she saw then in her husband. Now she wondered. Those days didn't last all that long, and she soon forgot about it.

Unexpectedly, even for Susan, she opened up to Mary Ellen about the things Stephen and she had enjoyed before the war: swimming, hiking, going to the football games, bonfires, the intimacy. But after the war, she said, "Stephen seemed less in tune with the things we used to enjoy doing together. Actually it wasn't less, he dropped them altogether." Their friends, some of them anyway, Stephen didn't enjoy being around any more. Then there were the holidays. What was it about the holidays that he grew to dislike or avoid? Something there had been askew for years, but not so pronounced as lately.

She told Mary Ellen that he'd had nightmares for a year after he returned from Italy. Stephen would wake up screaming about a plane on fire, yelling for someone to bail out—to get a count of the chutes. He'd swear about some mechanical problem he couldn't get someone to fix on the airplane. His pajamas would be soaked with sweat by the time Susan shook him awake in order to question him. He'd be out of breath, shaking, staring into the dark. Sometimes he'd cry, blubbering like a baby, completely unaware of his emotional estate. Susan would rush into the bathroom, wet a washrag and return to wipe him with it. Then she'd cradle him close to her trying to rock his fears away. After twenty minutes or so, he'd fall limp back onto the pillow, and he wouldn't remember anything the next morning. But that was years ago. Both women needed to talk even more than they realized. Susan continued, "I told the doctor, 'he's started having them again.'"

Inhofe wanted to know the specifics of each one if she could remember them. How could she have forgotten? Susan described one night last week when Stephen woke up the children screaming so loudly. But Michael slept through it, thank God. The last few days she had felt so scatterbrained from not getting much good rest. The more Susan talked, the more she realized that her husband *had* changed. The signs were there. She hadn't wanted to admit just how much, especially during their intimate moments.

"The early years," I told the doctor, "after Stephen returned home, you know, in bed, we'd . . ." Susan hesitated. "I feel so ill at ease discussing this with you, doctor." Mary Ellen smiled.

"I understand. Take your time. I've heard this so many times. I used to get embarrassed too, especially with the wives who blurted out all the lurid details of their love lives. You can't tell me anything I haven't heard before. I'm here to help, if I can."

"I proceeded cautiously. I don't really know why. Well, our homecoming was wonderful, most tempestuous, even glorious. And over the years, that part of our lives has always been, well, very special. But lately, intimacy has become less tender, less caring. I suppose, less focused. After Damien's death, Stephen couldn't get enough of . . . you know . . ? I have felt used somehow. And I resented it, and I told him so."

"When you say, 'used,'" the doctor asked, "do you think he was trying to blunt something painful for him through your intimacy?" Dr. Jerry Inhofe knew why he was asking these questions. He had lost two good women for doing some of the same things to them. Maybe he could atone for some of it by assisting these women to understand their husbands. And then, maybe he didn't care if he atoned for it. She was good looking.

"I don't know, doctor. I suppose I was hurt at the way our lovemaking seems lately to focus on *his* needs almost exclusively. I didn't think he might have been trying to dull his pain with . . . sex. Is that what you are saying?"

"Perhaps. Well, yes. But I'm really asking you what *you* think this latest alteration in his behavior means?

Something had definitely frayed within Stephen the more Susan and Mary Ellen talked this over. Susan considered the possibility that her husband could be slowly abandoning her, even with the intimacy turned up a notch. Immediately following the funeral Stephen seemed even more restless, but at other times, apathetic. His appetite was off. He'd been gruff several times, unusually so with the children, which wasn't at all like him. He had always been a strict but fair disciplinarian, but his tone and actions lately were more than discipline. And lately, lately his eyes avoided hers. Still, their lives were so busy . . . But who had time to notice? Susan had. There wasn't anything she didn't notice about Stephen Lloyd. Anything? Anything.

"Yes," she said. "Everything you have asked me, doctor, has been there. I didn't know I was supposed to be looking for signs, but . . . I believe I was." Susan hesitated, and Mary Ellen placed her hand on Susan's hand for reassurance.

The two women were now on the turnpike passing Grand Prairie when Susan spoke about this past Saturday morning. "Stephen left early that morning . . . before I awoke. But it was when he came home . . . when he said, 'Hi Susan,' to me with so little tenderness. I remember blinking, feeling very hurt . . . you know? And . . . and I stared at him. I had to bite my lip so I wouldn't cry. He didn't call me honey or sweetheart, or . . . 'my lovely little lotus blossom,' like he sometimes does and then he winks at me. He always said, 'my lovely little lotus blossom,' when I'd caught him red handed at something." Susan smiled, remembering something precious about Stephen. "My immediate impression was . . . Oh, I don't know . . ."

"Your impression was what?" Mary Ellen asked.

"It embarrasses me to think about it now, Mary Ellen, so I've kept my suspicions to myself." Susan looked over at Mary Ellen who was taking it all in, and then Susan said longingly, "My poor, sweet Stephen." Several minutes of road noise elapsed before anything else passed between the women. Mary Ellen didn't worry about James. He was far too preoccupied or clumsy for any other woman to find him exciting. He would always love her, when he managed to put his chalk down.

Susan finally volunteered, "I was afraid he didn't love me anymore, that he'd found someone more attractive." Susan stared at the scenery, billboards, and buildings passing by, and she felt the need to focus on her nails. She wanted to somehow hide her sudden shame: the things, the persons, the features, all the feminine aspects that had made her Susan that might have faded in her husband's eyes. For the second time in her conscious life, Susan Alcott Lloyd felt unattractive.

The current state of Stephen and Susan's relationship made Susan take pause. "Lately," she hesitated from embarrassment, "lately, I've stared longer into the mirror at the woman sharing the glass with me. Twice I almost asked Margaret if she thought I was still pretty, but I lost my nerve. Suddenly the usually obvious wasn't so. It wasn't anything but a loaded question, and I didn't want Margaret picking up on . . . on things."

"On what things?" Mary Ellen responded.

"Mary Ellen, you know *what*."

"Susan, for heaven's *sakes*. You don't have anything there to worry about. I've never said this to you, but you are the most beautiful woman I've ever seen. I've always been a bit jealous of you. You're so pretty, so poised and so talented. Stephen loves you dearly. I know he does. He's a fool if he doesn't. Why would you even think such a thing?"

"Oh, Mary Ellen, thank you. I love you for that." Susan began to smile at the caring compliment from her friend. She wallowed in its caress, needing every ounce of what it offered her ego. Somewhat more sure of herself, but not totally, Susan continued her current discourse. "I'd lie there in the dark, next to Stephen, and my heart would almost pound out of my chest with worry. I wanted him desperately to hold me." Susan's troubled soul flexed back toward her former anguish for Mary Ellen's dissemination and understanding. What Mary Ellen observed in Susan's eyes amazed and alarmed her. A large, heavy fist of a tear gathered, gravity pulling at it. It rolled downward, caressing the rouged and curved lines of Susan's cheek, briefly halting at the corner of her mouth, from which it hung for a moment suspended, and then fell freely to the seat below Susan's right thigh. Splat.

"Did you voice any of these concerns to Stephen?"

"No. Well, yes. I did later though." Susan sniffed. Then she blotted the water from her eyes and cheek with a tissue she pulled from her purse. "Dolores would have told me about another woman, Mary Ellen. That woman knows, . . ." Susan offered confidently. Her eyes narrowed at the thought of just how much Dolores knew.

When Susan felt her control returning, she said, "It's funny . . ."

"What is?"

"Well, Stephen said he went to the office last Saturday, but he wouldn't look at me. He always looks at me when we talk. I love that about him." Susan's mascara had officially given up any formal attempt at keeping its designated order or her striking features in check. Her dark, reddening eyes refilled and she retrieved another tissue. "He spoke to me, but he was facing away from me as he read some papers he brought home. He said he needed to work through something. They had a big project coming up. But Sunday, Annika told me that the Minneapolis project had been settled the week before. Marcus had mentioned it to her at dinner, and Stephen would have had no reason to go in that day; none that she could think of. I remembered that so well, even though lately I forget things so easily. Apparently Marcus had been home one day too many, and that's how Annika knew for certain."

Susan slipped into a silent world where she retreated of late. For the moment, she was talked out, mentally fatigued. But she couldn't shut her mind off, and Mary Ellen let her alone with her thoughts. Amon Carter Field passed by on their left. A passenger jet began to roll down the runway for take off.

Still, that Saturday morning kept rummaging through her thoughts, so she inspected it for any new details. Stephen and she were alone in the kitchen, unchaperoned by the children. Ginny had gone to do some shopping for supper. Michael had left the house. Margaret was sleeping over with . . . with whom? Susan couldn't remember. David was still asleep or at least up in his room. She stood next to the refrigerator, her most alluring gaze fixed upon her husband. Yet her body and mind were filling with panic. She was afraid, observing his own preoccupation that he might not bid her entrance into his inner sanctum. She believed herself imminently qualified to diagnose and cure his uncertainties or his demons or whatever might interpose a barrier between them. It was then, that instant, Susan realized just how little she really knew her husband.

She certainly knew his body and how it responded to her playful touch. Susan considered stroking his mane or engaging him with several of her deep-drawn and energetic kisses. These were her private letters written with all her passion, saved for him alone. Susan filled them with all the pleasant sensations she could bring to bear. She knew where that might lead. Was that where they needed to go right this minute? Would he even go?

She knew she loved him beyond words. Love somehow meant more than kisses and passion, security, and regimen. She knew this in an instant. But did she want more of him in light of what she currently observed in his behavior? Did he want more of her at the price she was asking? What did *more* mean to her right then? To him? If Susan turned her unvoiced questions into achievement, would it destroy or divide them?

The steel-toed reality was that Stephen Lloyd had always been a private person. He was a man who guarded his own life as one guards the king's counting house. Moving emotionally close to that plateau, and even well beyond his physical arousal, Susan could detect his sensory pickets as she had gently probed him over the course of the years. She found that when she had indeed intruded within firing range of anything related to the war years, she encountered an elusive garrison laden with the weaponry that would keep him just out of her reach or into full blown retreat.

What was it that stood sentinel over his past? She couldn't know or suspect that he kept a repository filled with his own bravery and cowardice, grief and guilt, anger and elation, death and life, distress and solace, hope and despondency, low grade fevers and two years' worth of fatigue encompassing 1943-1944. These emissaries always stopped her cold. And without his permission and assistance Susan could only guess as to what she was attempting to win entrance, and then, what would all that mean to the whole of their lives? Her loquacious eyes pled with him all the more, coveting from her lover his signal of welcome to the difficult things. This Saturday morning it did not come.

The Wilson's Chevy Impala moved past Six Flags in Arlington, and it was then that Susan remembered talking to Annika that morning. "Stephen started to say something, but he hesitated." Susan's sigh was as deep as her need.

"Like what?" Annika had wondered. Susan knew that once she began a conversation with this woman, she'd best finish it.

"I was so desperate to get him to . . . to settle my fears."

"And . . . did he?" Annika inquired in her dry tone. Susan could still see Annika bending her face near Susan's to use as a fulcrum. In her mind, Susan's hesitation warranted it. So Annika began applying the pressure. "You know what I do when Marcus won't talk," she said. Susan remembered that she wasn't quite certain if she wanted to hear this. "I move in very close to him, and begin to stroke his neck. I make sure he smells my perfume . . . feels my body fully against his, and then his chemistry begins to co-mingle with mine. I ask him once more, in specific terms he understands. He sings like a magpie. If he doesn't, I take it to the next level, upstairs." Susan felt the heat of her blush rising through her blouse and warming her face. It was quite wonderfully amusing how Annika had related it. Susan's mischievous smile spread and she hoped that Mary Ellen didn't notice.

"What are you smiling about?" Mary Ellen had noticed.

"Oh, nothing."

"Like I believe that." Now it was Mary Ellen's turn, but her aim went in a direction Susan was ill prepared to confront. "Susan, tell me about your faith."

"What about my faith?"

"Well, do you have a faith in God that is capable or maybe sufficient to meet this challenge to your marriage?"

"Why would you ask me *that*?"

"I don't know how people can face huge problems like yours without Jesus. . ." Mary Ellen's Baptist heritage had once more entered the fray.

Susan turned her face outward toward the scenery, rolling her eyes in antipathy so that Mary Ellen could not see. A "lecture" on God was all she needed now. Mary Ellen all of a sudden sounded like that preacher at Damien's funeral. Susan didn't understand how God could say He loved her, and then not hear her prayers in order to fix this brokenness in their marriage. Most of the people Susan knew had worked their way through their problems and were the stronger for it. Susan's plight couldn't be so much worse than theirs.

Turning back toward her friend, Susan said, "Mary Ellen, I don't mean to sound disrespectful or even ungrateful, but I don't want to talk about religion right now."

"But I'm . . . I'm not . . ." Susan's response was firm. The curtain had descended and Mary Ellen would have to respect Susan's pain as well as her complete misunderstanding of what Mary Ellen's Jesus could do for hurting people.

The eastern edge of Ft. Worth was in sight now. Susan reinvested her energy into remembering how she hadn't responded verbally to Annika's ways with her husband, which had permitted an internal smile. The thought that a woman could so easily massage and manage Marcus Lloyd intrigued her. Her father-in-law had once been the caretaker and principle authority of Lloyd International. He had taken the company leaps beyond what his father had accomplished. Now Stephen filled those huge shoes, quite well, she thought. Marcus the multimillionaire, Marcus the . . . the little boy. An amazing revelation if there ever was one!

Susan had also brought Annika into *her* confidence. She spoke of the manner in which she had approached Stephen that Saturday morning, how her heart had grown more apprehensive, pounding upon her deepest anxieties like a drum. She had tactically placed her soft charms against Stephen's sturdy frame, smiled up at him, playfully engaged him, touched him—to arouse him, to strike at this barrier that smothered and separated them the only way she knew how.

Stephen flinched—he *flinched*! The man was truant emotionally. He *flinched*, of all things! One day his libido raged, and now it had gone on vacation. This unfortunate response broadsided her. Frustrated that her normal, hardly ever fail wiles had come to naught. Susan next labored to draw his eyes to hers so that his agitation or hurt might settle on her, might speak to her. So often when the pressures of this "thing" had set itself upon him—upon *them*—it had not overpowered him to the extent that his thoughtful eyes could not caress her. But not today, not lately, unless he wanted to *communicate* on *his* needy, sometimes unfeeling, terms.

She had reached a stalemate, a huge, rugged mountain of an impasse, upon which she would within minutes, should he not indulge her, be forced to wave her white flag of surrender. Passionless minutes ticked by with no movement on Stephen's part. Susan conceded further pursuit seemed fruitless. She had settled for hugging him around the waist, pressing her head against his chest while he read, oblivious to the whole of *their* needs. Stephen's sole accommodation had been that he rested the bottom of his chin on the top of her head.

But Stephen *had known* she was there. He felt her body against his and smelled her scent, and still, he fought with his emotions as to whether to allow her to lead him to an intimate utopia. His inner agitation won; he would keep her at arms length. He would control this. Worse, he felt her smothering him, and he didn't want her or anyone else near him at that moment. That knowledge, of course, would have killed Susan if he had spoken his desires. It felt oddly normal, this saw-toothed need, to withdraw from everything he had known and loved.

The drive time home from Bethhaven seemed to take ages. Susan had not rested on that long drive as she assured herself she would. She spent too much time talking, too much time thinking, remembering, and worst of all, assessing. Hypothetical reflection drained her; being alone was equally unbearable.

Now, Mary Ellen would have to turn around and drive back to Bethhaven—solo. She had done this favor purely out of love and concern for the Lloyds. Nothing lay behind it but that. Mrs. Wilson too didn't want to be alone with her thoughts either, but driving back would force this encumbrance upon her. Leaving Susan standing in her driveway, Mary Ellen wondered how many mothers like her were alone these days, because of *this* terrible war.

Michael pulled into the driveway at home at nine forty-five. He said he'd be home from the office by nine. He wasn't going to baseball practice that day but, rather, to the Fonteneau Building when he left school. It would be good to be near his grandfather, to talk and get his advice about his future, to hear *something* encouraging. Grandfather Marcus usually said the right things when life closed in on Michael. Neither Michael nor his grandfather wanted to entertain the employee's inquiries regarding Stephen, so they both avoided the topic as much as possible when people were around. The boy didn't need to be hounded by questions about his father. Grandfather Marcus gave Michael some filing work, which he took care of much faster than Marcus had anticipated.

Now Michael had time on his hands. Unwillingly, his thoughts turned to his former girlfriend Victoria who had dropped him like a hot potato when he mentioned joining the Marines. She was *so* pretty, and *so* female to boot. They'd had some great times, but now he considered how self-serving she seemed. She was after a Lloyd, no matter what the cost, and she hadn't come to the funeral, which irked him. He'd invested so much of himself on her, just to discover there really wasn't much to her beyond her looks.

And then there was Donny. He had read Michael the riot act for wanting to support LBJ and his ilk. Michael's "best friend" was also egotistical; he didn't know what was truly important. Sometimes Donny-boy could be such a ratfink.

Michael bid his grandfather goodbye, left the office and went to spend the late afternoon at some park nearby. An hour later, there sat

Michael, on a playground swing. Fortunately when he arrived, most of the mothers had already taken their children home. He wanted to be alone to think things out. It felt good to swing on a real swing set once more. Its to and fro helped him escape the adult world into which he'd suddenly been plunged.

Eventually, the swing's inertia was overcome by his weight and gravity. His motion slowed and his heels scuffing the dirt as he came to rest. The days of children's games had ended, and he knew it now. He wondered if life meant more than college and marriage in their essential compounds. Life meant . . . life meant *what*? In sports, it meant meeting the next snap of the ball head on. It meant watching the play unfold, reading his keys, deciding if he was watching a pass or a run unwind, and then doing what he'd been trained to do—with an *attitude*. He could choose to meet the other team on their terms or they could meet him on his. Maybe his love life, past friendships and coming graduation really existed around the periphery of the urgent rather than the significant, the meaningful.

Michael realized or suspected that his future was now sealed for the next few years. The ball had been snapped and he could let it run over him. He could meet it or he could absorb it in order to come to terms with it. Still, what he must do and what he wanted to do deliquesced into him like butter on a trout in a hot skillet. He couldn't evade this enlistment that he'd felt so strongly about several weeks before. Was that voice he was so cock sure of actually Damien's? Was it something he'd imagined, like his mother suspected? Instantaneously, he felt stupid for his impulsiveness, and he wanted the future back that might have been so he could sit on the swing a bit longer.

At present, this boy-man wasn't facing the coming days at all boldly. He wanted his father back too, just like he was before he heard about Damien. For the briefest of moments, sojourning as a child a bit longer appealed to him. Several years ago, growing up meant he couldn't wait to alight upon this very moment, to graduate from Gladstone and . . . go to college. But here it sat, the luster of his promised adulthood looked and felt tarnished, and so much less appealing than he'd imagined; his closest friends—pulling away willingly. So many things wouldn't roll back around any more. Michael sat on the swing as long as he possibly could in the deserted park not far from where his grandfather and father worked.

"James, you're too quiet. Are you all right?" Mary Ellen asked because she was worried about her husband. She must focus on others; the heart of Christianity or the essence of her belief system in God was to be had in doing. She'd certainly lived a life of faith, setting her own needs, feelings, and hurts aside for the sake of others in her family, church and neighborhood. Ministering to the Lloyd's felt spiritually natural. Yet within the well of the essential Mary Ellen, there burgeoned a compulsion to stop everything—to go off and cry, for days if need be, to get into the tub and soak for a month, to be alone and pity herself, to let God hold her and hope He would not banish her for lack of duty's sake.

Another way of speaking the "faith" language was to say that her life was not her own. Since she belonged to the Lord, He would see her through this. He'd promised. But until the Lord's return, which she looked for daily, she must keep on keepin' on. It was the mundane that was so difficult, and the arduous was unbearable at present. Believers could and should expect the occasional rough spot. But this, this wasn't simply a rough spot. The Wilson's were experiencing the immediate, stabbing, paralyzing effects of their only child's death. Still, He, God, didn't want an old mopin' woman advertising His kingdom. It wasn't good for business. It was up to Mary Ellen to set a straight course if life were to get back to normal. He, God, desired laborers for His vineyard. It wasn't God's doing, this death. He had little to do with it, and there was the rub. Where in fact was He on Damien's last day, last few minutes, last few seconds? And then, in her more enlightened moments, when the sun poked through, briefly, she remembered that Jesus and His Father had experienced separation—

That's what she'd heard preached from the pulpit as far back as she could remember. What she actually felt was billowing sorrow reaching to the heavens, wisps of pernicious rage, bottomless guilt, the consuming need to blame someone, even God, if that helped, and an increasing need to withdraw. Somehow, she must set all these sickening feelings aside. It was unbelief on Mary Ellen's part to grieve past a set number of days. That's what she had said to so many folks when they faced difficulties and death, and Mary Ellen had believed every word of it, maybe . . . until now.

But just who set the number of days until one got back to normal, no one had told her. It had always been so. Everyone knew it. Valerie

Kendall at church said the Scriptures were very plain about this matter. Mary Ellen should be rejoicing by now, or at least by the end of the month. Her son was in heaven with Jesus. This was the meaning of Christ's victory over death. At the funeral, the pastor was, all-in-all, up beat. He didn't want to concentrate on the negative beyond its due, or the severity of the pain Mary Ellen and James felt. The days would pass and life would return with the simple truth overcoming whatever grief remained for the Wilson's to ferret out. They would get past this, *but it was up to them.*

Judah, too, had been emphatic. "You a Wilson, boy. Buck up, ya hear?" Everyone had put on that plastic smile for them or had approached the Wilson's from the position of Stoicism. No one at church quite knew *what* to say, except that Damien was in heaven.

James himself had heard other voices. The ones that called him a . . . well, he wouldn't say what they had called him. Everyone knew, they said, that Vietnam is a white man's war. LBJ was killin' all the black boys and savin' the white boys. It was a racial conflict, pure and simple. James *should be* angry because he'd let his son be used by "the Man." He wondered what Dr. King would tell him. Maybe James and Mary Ellen should be happy. Damien was in heaven. Maybe they should be angry. But heaven *had* invaded James' heart at the graveside.

The fact was that the Wilson's sat obtuse, impaled upon thoughts they couldn't control as they drove west along the turnpike toward home. They hurt beyond anything either of them could have imagined. There would be no grandchildren, no daughter-in-law to pamper. Damien's never-to-be wife would not become the daughter-in-law they could not welcome. There would be no more basketball games at whatever college James decided to attend when he returned from Vietnam. Their son *wasn't* coming home—alive. Ever. A bronze grave marker circumscribed the ground above where Damien lay six feet below, covered with half a ton of earth. Soon the grass would grow back over the rectangular spot that had become his decaying body's perpetual resting place.

James voiced what he'd hidden away for a month. "Robert said the government used our son, and we ought to be angry about it. The pastor said we must put this behind us. Damien's in heaven, he said. Judah says to 'buck up.' I just want my boy back. I can't teach anymore—that desire has left me. Who knows if it will ever return? I can't even reason with this. My own soul torments me over what can never be. And now the Lloyd's are in trouble. Oh, Lord. Stephen is living in the past when he was back in the war flying those airplanes. And I lucked out. *I sure did.* I was too smart for all that."

James' derisive tone pecked at Mary Ellen's raw sensitivities. She told James to stop it, but he kept impaling his mind on the javelin of things he couldn't change. "I helped to create a behemoth to kill thousands of Japanese so our boys wouldn't have to land on the home islands of Japan—estimated casualties during that invasion: one million soldiers and Marines. Mary Ellen, I don't know when I've *ever* felt so low. I thought I had a handle on it at the graveside. I was certain of it. Why can't people just let us alone and let us hurt? It's as if it's all wrong to be hurting, . . . you know? I feel as if I've lost my way. Is that wrong?"

"I don't know if it *is* wrong. I don't know either," Mary Ellen moaned, leaning into James sturdy frame. She was already in tears. James' usual absent-minded constitution hung suspended for the time being. He somehow managed to becalm her ache and refocus her needs by discussing his own. James and she had not in so many words expressed their feelings to each other, not this openly that they could recall. Neither had said much to the other in the past few weeks, but plowed through the house blindly as two organisms going about their business, numb and disinterested. They did not lay blame at the other's feet.

There it sat on the coffee table. James had not picked it up once. Mary Ellen had absentmindedly dropped yesterday's *Star Telegram* on top of it, almost covering it. James bent over and firmly grasped it between his fingers. Its leather cover was careworn and the pages were dirty from use. "Mary Ellen, sit down here for a minute. We need to spend some time in here, listening to God and stop listening to everyone else."

Mary Ellen was drawn to her husband's request like a dying woman to an oasis. She had needed his leadership and she instantly knew what had been missing.

"James, read the twenty-third Psalm to me."

"Good choice. Let's see. The Lord is my shepherd; I shall not want.

2 He maketh me to lie down in green pastures: he leadeth me beside the still waters.

3 He restoreth my soul: he leadeth me in the paths of righteousness for his name's sake.

4 Yea, though I walk through the valley of the shadow of death, I will fear no evil: for thou art with me; thy rod and thy staff they comfort me.

5 Thou preparest a table before me in the presence of mine enemies: thou anointest my head with oil; my cup runneth over.

6 Surely goodness and mercy shall follow me all the days of my life: and I will dwell in the house of the Lord for ever.

They had mustered no desire for each other physically. Intimacy, when considered, seemed wrong, so out of place. Tonight, that would be rectified. They had and needed each other more than they realized. The Lord was slowly putting things in their proper order.

Twenty-Five: Maj. Perry Alcott

>—i—‹›—•O•—‹›—i—‹

Friday, April 28, 1967

"Daddy, I'm about to go out of my mind," Susan expressed her disquiet sitting at the kitchen table close to her dad. She held his hand tightly, looking him in the eye, she once more near the precipice of tears. She hadn't always been able to draw strength from him. Perry Alcott's white hair and aging broad shoulders lent to the kitchen and Susan's soul, an atmosphere of wisdom, strength, experience and proportion. He would surely know how to evaluate this.

Perry Alcott had retired a major in the Marine Corps in 1919, by the time the Treaty of Versailles had been ratified, and the Kaiser's once grand German army had been thoroughly humiliated. That's what he told himself. That's what they all told themselves.

"Now, you listen to me, Susan. Stephen's a good man. He's tough. Like all of us he's suppressed quite a bit from when he was in Europe. I know I did. I thought I would go insane at times during and after the war." Perry's words emptied into the kitchen with its hanging pots and pans, modern conveniences and appliances, its warm space and welcoming atmosphere. He had filled it with meaning, and at times, not a little uncertainty.

Perry's drive from Longview, Texas, was gotten through, mostly in silence to meet with his daughter. Michelle had learned painfully from long, bitter experience when to leave her husband to his thoughts and not to take his barbed jabs and criticism personally. She had to for her own sanity. What he said to Susan would be critical to their daughter's well-being. But what would he *actually* say to Susan? She had asked him on the phone about his own experiences in the Great War, from a personal perspective. She recalled seeing his many emotional outbursts as she grew up with him prior to and throughout the depression years.

Perry eyed his daughter, looking deep into her soul. He knew what to tell her, but how? Still, he felt agitation and not a little apprehension rising within him of having to prick this barbed balloon for her. It wasn't that he didn't think about the war, he thought about it all the time, maybe too much. He still wondered how many times he'd ordered his men to do things that cost them their lives. But speaking openly to others, not familiar with war was poles apart from conversations with some of his buddies who had gone through the same experiences as he. His neighbors and acquaintances hadn't the slightest idea of how to understand those times or him, why he was the oddball in his neighborhood, seldom seen outside in the front yard. Perry had long felt ill at ease in social settings. Small talk drove him nuts. Michelle, on the other hand, was Miss Social Butterfly, desperately in need of gatherings, meetings and anything that provided human companionship and conversation, anything that got her away from the cloistered life at 419 Barclay St.

People who hadn't been to combat wanted *someone* to fight to secure their freedoms, but then they didn't want to hear about or be affected by what they had required those someone's to do on their behalf. Those someone's could talk about the war in the garage or along the bar railing, but don't bring it into the parlor where the polite company held its soirées.

The older he grew the more life infuriated him. Perry feared that the questions Susan asked him had as much to do with him as it did with Stephen. She wanted a world free from war and *especially its effects*. Stephen being drunk, Stephen with a gun, Stephen in Bethhaven, were effects.

"Susan, do you remember when I had that trouble with Bainbridge in 1934?"

"Yes. I thought it was so unfair of the company to treat you like that," she offered. "Mom was angry for weeks, wasn't she?"

"Yeah. Your mother was upset . . ."

Perry had to coordinate a sales conference in New York City at the height of the depression. He had come up quickly through the ranks of Bainbridge Mills after finding and losing numerous positions on the railroad, at the Foundry and at a dry goods store in Chillicothe. Finally, he'd seen his opportunity with Bainbridge Mills in a newspaper ad. Beginning in 1931, he'd passed in and out of middle management in rapid succession. By September of 1934, Perry Alcott had advanced to Vice President of Sales for the Eastern United States. He was a "born leader," one executive had noted, unaware he'd led men in battle and to their deaths in the trenches and rolling hills of France. Despite the economy of the times, Bainbridge was doing quite well in the industry, producing quality rayon products, such as bedspreads, which became an instant success and money maker.

That New York City sales conference became a watershed for Perry, but not for the better. He'd run into his old Regimental Commander at a bar in Manhattan, where the conversation turned malodorous. Certain decisions the Colonel had made during the battle of Soissons had cost the then, Lieutenant Alcott, a gaping hole in his leg, the C.O. of Perry's company and four enlisted Marines their lives. Alcott, nose to nose with his former superior, accused Sours of inexcusable and inept leadership in and around Beaurepaire farm, the place where Perry had been wounded—the first time.

July 19, 1918 had been a memorable day for Lt. Perry Alcott and the men of the 55th Company. Lt. Alcott had been wounded the first time in March by German artillery. But this day, he'd receive his second and third wounds in rapid succession. The rifle round went in and through his right thigh cleanly, but hurt beyond words. He had to get his men in position as soon as the artillery he'd called for cleared two very effective German machine gun nests in the rolling gorges behind Beaurepaire Farm. The 219th German Infantry was well dug in to the 55th Company's position. The Germans had tried valiantly to address the growing Allied threat to their immediate front, the terrain favored those on the defensive. This particular farm had been built in a large compound style, the main house in the middle, a tall, grand white rock wall surrounding it. At least it *was* a high wall until the Allied artillery began to pound the area.

Lt. Alcott stood as best he could, the corpsman tended to Alcott's bleeding wound, and everyone waited for the rounds to be first be fired and then land. Out of nowhere, Colonel Sours drove up in his staff car, jumped out and began issuing orders to the effect: "Keep these men moving, for God's sakes, Captain Cooke! Get 'em moving!"

The captain of the 55th Company, 2/5, 2nd Division, was a man named Elliott D. Cooke, a fine officer. Sours' unwanted bravado would inexplicably and unnecessarily expose the skipper, the company gunny, and the whole first squad to those Heinie gun positions before they could be taken out. Thirty seconds was all Cooke wanted for the incoming rounds. Capt. Cooke, no small man himself, healed around to confront the colonel and inform him that another thirty seconds would make all the difference. Sours would have none of it: "Get 'em moving Captain or I'll have you relieved!"

Lt. Alcott, still being treated, was promoted on the spot to C.O. of the company. Lt. Alcott, not hearing the artillery scream to his rescue, yelled, "Follow me, Marines!" Limping badly and in great pain, one of the two German machine guns put a round through Perry's other leg, in his calf. The corpsman who had just bandaged the Lt., seeing the new skipper go down, ran immediately to attend Alcott, got the wound to stop bleeding by winding a long cloth gauze around his calf tightly. Alcott kept trying to get up to lead his men, but the corpsman was just as insistent, demanding Alcott lay still so he could be taken to relative safety and medical attention. Perry yelled at the corpsman to tie both wounds tight since he was not going to allow his men to move forward without him. Lt. Alcott took four wobbly steps and collapsed.

The Gunny and three Pfc's, along with the skipper, went down in rapid succession attempting to comply with Sours' orders. The Lt. would not participate further in the final push of the Meuse-Argonne Offensive, regardless. Along with a bronze star with "V" device, Lt. Alcott was promoted to captain while recovering in the hospital. Perry's war was ended.

Standing nose to nose with Ed Sours in the bar, Perry's fists were clinched and ready to strike, when the walked in. The bartender, an experienced man at his trade, knew early into their conversation that these two men would go to blows sooner or later. These two men didn't like each other. The argument had stirred up a hornet's nest of unresolved issues that had lain dormant within Perry, and probably Ed Sours.

There had been numerous signs along the years that all was not what it should be with Perry Alcott. Little things—words, tones of voice, looks askance—any one might actualize big reactions. Things like tripping over the dog so that he spilled the garbage in the middle of the kitchen floor, or that inevitable kink in the garden hose restricting the water's flow forcing him have to stop what he was doing and untwist it, just drove him nuts. Not being able to find things when just moments before he noted, "I put it right *there*! Where in the world is *it*? *Michelle* . . !" There was the time when the checkbook didn't balance, and he lit it on fire. Michelle invited guests for dinner more than once, but instead, Perry wanted the evening alone with his family. She spent twenty minutes coaxing him to take part in the evening she'd carefully planned and looked forward to having. Perry usually came to regret his responses.

Perry didn't know why he exploded like he did. He didn't plan to go into a rage at the worst possible times, but he did. He didn't plan to stay angry and then withdraw from everyone and everything for three hours to two days. He didn't mean to stare angrily at Michelle. His ill temper had so little to do with her personally. Then he'd apologize and everyone in the family would hold his or her collective breaths until the next explosion. The pattern repeated itself year after year, episode after episode.

Perry reminded Susan of one of the worst confrontations he and Michelle had. He was in the back yard raking leaves when an old Jenny flew over. The sight and sound of that dilapidated puddle jumper sent shivers down his spine. He dove on the ground instinctively, remembering being strafed by German aircraft. That event cost him fifteen of his men during an attack on some hill. He got up, grabbed the rake, broke it, threw it over the hedge, and then walked over and sat at the base of an old oak tree, lowered his head and cried.

That had been a difficult day for Michelle as well. She had work for Perry to do, and the sudden cessation of his assigned chores agitated her to no end. She marched over to Perry and inquired as to why he'd stopped work. *What was the matter with him?* Then she huffed at his unexplained tears, and demanded that he get back to the chores— *right now*. She had laundry and fifteen other things to do on this fine Saturday and needed his help in getting the house in order. Their dinner guests would arrive at five thirty. He told her to go stuff it, or something to that effect.

Actually, he said things that she never would have imagined should come from her husband. He'd never talked like that around her, much less to their children. Michelle gasped and Perry went stomping back to retrieve the broken rake. He examined the broken ends, was too mentally addled to repair the tool, and then threw both pieces into the neighbor's yard. Michelle was more than bewildered by this behavior. She had attempted to understand scenes of this nature that had unfolded before her too often. Perry stormed over to where she stood and chewed her out for all he was worth. Michelle, thoroughly taken back, cried of course. It took her a half hour to recover her composure. Perry was now finished with the yard and his chores. He picked up a fallen limb and threw it as far as he could, and then he drove to the bar not far from the house. Later that evening, he came home soused. Michelle cancelled the dinner. Susan remembered.

Questions that Michelle should have asked were left alone. Perry didn't bring his work home, nor was he permitted to bring his war home, but he did just the same.

Wednesday, May 16, 1935

Instead of leading the conference in New York, he spent the weekend holed up in his hotel room drunk and abusive toward the hotel staff. He threatened to fight anyone who tried to talk him out of his intentions of—getting and staying drunk.

The company founder and president, D. Aldwin Salazar, a World War I veteran himself, sat Perry Alcott down in his plush office following the conference, and "suggested" that if said behavior ever happened again, said employee would find himself out of said job. Said threat was not a pleasant thought in this depressed economy.

But Perry couldn't let it go once the genie had been uncorked. His drinking took on a new life. He started bringing home a fifth of cheap whiskey every third night, just to "take the edge off." Perry also became abusive toward Michelle and the boys; Susan, the youngest, stayed out of harm's way. His performance dropped off at work, so much so that he was demoted, a suggestion made by Mr. Salazar out of respect for his service record in France. Perry's next step would be the employment line.

Perry was let go on June twelfth of the following year. His behavior at the office had reached an apex of belligerence and sarcasm. Perry stayed drunk for almost a month after he left Bainbridge, and Michelle threatened to take the children and leave. Someone had to work outside the home to put food on the table. Michelle couldn't do both her job and her husband's.

Mr. Perry Alcott had a decision to make that tore at his soul. He was angry and he had no way to deal with it, nor was there anyone to whom he might confide. But he was in love with Michelle. She was the first good and beautiful thing that had happened to him in his life. The children were a plus.

It was perhaps the hottest day in 1935 when Perry, a dozen roses in hand, rang the doorbell of his own New York City home. When Michelle answered, he asked permission from the woman of the house if she would accept his most sincere apologies for his actions of late— all of them. He was not a man to make promises, but he relented this one time. "I promise that I will not touch another drop. Ever." Perry Alcott was as good as his word.

But he had left a ravaged wake of pain and heartache, especially with his boys, which took him years to set straight. They had to sell their house and move back to Longview, Texas. The children had to enroll in schools that didn't welcome these transplanted Yankees with open arms, even though the Alcott's hailed from Longview originally.

Susan began her distinguished career in the beauty pageants in and around Longview soon after moving back, culminating with the Miss Texas pageant of 1940.

"Do you know why we moved back to Longview, Susan?" Perry asked.

"Not exactly. I've always thought it was because the company had chosen someone else for a position it promised to you. You fought it and they fired you for making trouble. That was the reason, wasn't it? Daddy, I was glad we came back. I really didn't care why we left. You eventually got your old job back anyway. Why? What does that have to do with my situation now?"

Perry looked deeply into his daughter's eyes. He was thankful that she had not understood the circumstances of their leaving New York. That was thirty-two years ago, but it was still very fresh in Perry's mind. "We left New York, because Mr. Salazar fired me."

"*Fired* you? *Why*, daddy?"

"Well, he fired me for a lot of reasons, but it was the war mostly. I see that now."

"The war? What do you mean *the war*?" This single phrase was beginning to wear on Susan. Was Stephen, and now her father, trying to find a scapegoat for their own failures? How could *war* do this? How could the *past* do so much damage to so many?

Perry continued. "What I mean is, when I ran into Colonel Sours in that bar in New York City, as soon as I saw him I got mad. Just the sight of him and I wanted to kill him. I believe he caused some fine Marines to get killed and wounded, because he was too impatient, or something, and I . . ." Perry hesitated.

This was new information to his daughter that had affected Susan's life so many years ago. Until now, she hadn't found need to make sense of it. That's when Damien's death flashed across her mind. She saw her husband leaning against the tub, drunk, with the pistol in his hand. *How to make sense of this?*

"Susan, the gist is that I started drinking to forget all the pain and anger. I believe the war was at the heart of it. I don't understand how what happened in 1918 is still haunting me in 1967. But it's the reason that I almost lost your mother and you kids." He turned a pale shade of scarlet from the embarrassment of this self-disclosure.

Susan somewhat remembered her dad drinking, the yelling, the fear, and his abuse. For some reason she couldn't recall, it didn't last that long and then it stopped. There was the sudden move back to Texas with the readjustment from the northeast to the southwest. Her brothers and she had done reasonably well, considering how her mother had trooped on. But the specifics given to her then remained aloof. The move, the new school, friends and old acquaintances smoothed over any adversity.

"What do you mean you almost lost us?"

Susan held his eyes with hers and wouldn't let them go. Written in that hazel color she perceived that her dad felt the shame of his actions. The recent events with Stephen had repercussions for Perry's life too. As Susan had kept her father posted on the phone about Stephen's progress in the hospital, Perry felt that old impertinent pressure building within him. His natural tendency the past few weeks was to avoid his son-in-law. He knew Stephen's heartache, and he didn't want to be dragged back into all of that. It took too long to extricate himself from the last go round. But Stephen's troubles had a domino effect on Susan, the children, the grandparent's lives, and Grandpa Perry felt trapped and energized simultaneously.

"Look Squirt, here's how this works." "Squirt" was his pet name for Susan. It was *the* sobriquet they both needed at the moment. That *name* brought back so much of what was good about their relationship. "Those of us who went off to war want our lives to be smooth and peaceful when we return."

"Why is that so important to you daddy? Everyone has rough places they go through."

"Susan, take the most chaotic situation in your life you can think of and multiply it by a factor of one thousand or ten thousand. Doesn't matter. Make it go on, not for thirty seconds or two minutes, but half a day or a week. Then add the deaths or maiming of people that are very important to you, men you trained and shared letters and chow with. Add total devastation to everything around you—trees gone, the landscape barren, burned flesh, noise so intense you think you will go insane, dirt turned to a sea of mud, blood, hunger, rats the size of dogs, fatigue, fear so palpable you can taste it, and then just make it go on and on, until you don't care anymore, about anything. Living and dying are all the same. You begin to realize that you have no control over anything. You can't remember when or where you were born. And you can't say when you will die or how."

"I remember a particular day. It was sunny, cold . . . puffy clouds overhead. The artillery from both sides had stripped the land of every tree. Everything was colored gray. There was no grass, just mud— oozing, stinking mud. It had rained all night, and I was standing there shivering, soaked to the bone. I was hungry, very hungry. We were standing in the trench, mud up to our wazoo's . . . and the Germans started shelling us—*again*. When they found the range, I saw men blown up into the air, their arms and legs and heads going in all different directions. They were there one minute and gone the next. We couldn't do anything but take it."

"For some reason I started counting the first rounds that came in, one after another. On the twenty-second round it dawned on me that I had no control over my life. I never had . . . That shattered me. I had thought up to that point that I could do whatever I set my mind to. Nothing could stop me. But it all changed that day, for me, anyway." Perry's stare dissolved to the point that his mind seemed to be swallowing every hurt he'd suffered in the war. "They shelled us for five days straight. Then we got on line and attacked, what was left of us."

"I learned that control is an illusion. Everything just happens and you can't stop it. No amount of yelling or ordering or anything will stop it. It just goes on and on and on. I still hear their screams for help. And every time I went to get my wounded men, the Heinies would shoot their machine guns, and more men would go down. I was told to hold my position, so I couldn't shift my men to flank them. Somebody was always ordering me to do something impossible, which we did, but my men died by the ton. Their futures were cut down as if a man's future meant absolutely nothing to anyone or anything. Those were great men I and others sent to their deaths. We had to stay in our trenches, what was left of us, and listen to their screams—Samuels, Jackson, Billy McGuffin, Ronald Beesly and Haddock. They were the bait. They died of their wounds—horrible wounds—in agony and thirst . . . alone. And I couldn't stop it. I had men to lead. I always wanted to lead men, and that desire became my curse. After several months, most of the men had been killed or were in the hospital recovering. Pretty soon everyone was a stranger." Perry's eyes filled with tears. But he didn't succumb.

Silence. Five minutes decamped in the kitchen. Perry's shallow breathing meshed with the air in the room. Behind Perry's eyes, a war raged.

Thankfully, Susan's father extricated himself to speak, "Susan, you have some idea of how the war has affected me. I tried a few times to explain it to your mother, but I finally gave up. She couldn't grasp it, bless her heart. We vets don't want anyone, not even our spouse, messing up that illusive moment of tranquility for us. We might not ever get it again. And we will fight to keep things on an even keel. We all have this idea of how things are *supposed* to run. To achieve and hold a still moment is a matter of survival for me. Your mother, to put it bluntly, is selfish."

"Selfish? Is that what you think *I* am, too? Daddy, I've stood by Stephen until I'm about to drop from exhaustion. I'm doing this, because I love him."

"No. You want *your* life back the way it was. That's why you called your mother and me. In reality, you are just as much the focus as Stephen is. Your mom and I have been through this for years, and I don't think she still understands it. I'm not saying you don't have a right to be happy or that you don't love Stephen. You do. But you have to figure into this equation that you are living with a wounded man, a man who has a wound that won't be healed. It might be easier if he lost an arm or a leg in the war. Then you could *see* the wound, and understand that his arm will never be put back. On his difficult days, you could always say the problem is he doesn't feel whole. He lost an arm. He can't rake the yard like you want him to."

"But it's different when your spirit or your mind is broken. You can't see that part of a man. Stephen had no visible wound to blame. So, when he started acting strange here lately, you didn't know how to evaluate his behavior. You couldn't figure it out. I bet you never even suspected the war had anything to do with it. So you got mad at him, because he wasn't acting the way he was *supposed* to act. He had broken *your* peace."

"You can live with your fists clinched and in total denial, or you can embrace this as part of who *you two* are—now, and tomorrow, too. I don't believe you will never be able to go back to how it used to be. Your husband's war is here, and that means it's your war, too. You can live thankful that Stephen was man enough to go and fight. And you can grow in your understanding that war changes the men who conduct it. Or, you can fight the effects of the war for the rest of your life, be miserable and feel cheated, and then quit. It's tough any way you look at it. *His pain* must become your own. Michelle couldn't really accept that. But she's one in a million because she stayed with me. Many marriages after the war couldn't withstand the pressure, and so they crumbled. Susan, I think you are a very brave woman. You have met every challenge that I can remember. Here is another dare for you."

Susan was visibly upset at his suggestion that she was protecting her own best interests, that she was selfish. He wondered just how much she'd heard of what he'd said. "What doesn't mom understand, Daddy?"

"Your mother doesn't grasp that inside of me there is a monster living and feeding. I don't know what else to call it. I have to constantly stay energized to keep it away from her. I have to fight so that I don't think, don't remember, and don't associate things like smells or sounds. And I failed miserably because that thing is there and isn't going anywhere. When this thing grabs hold of me, my moods aren't toward something positive, but they're toward self-destruction."

Perry's argument produced a sort of face-off between Susan and her dad. He wasn't angry. In fact, he seemed rather composed for the dreadful things he'd just articulated.

"Have I ever told you about the poison gas?"

"*Poison gas*? No, Daddy. What about poison gas?"

"I guess it is time for me to tell you, for yours and Stephen's sake. The Germans would shell us with mustard gas from time to time. I saw too many men die *horrible* deaths from it. We would get in any low place we could find when they'd shell us with high explosives, but not with the gas. I remember replacements pulling their gas masks off thinking the shelling was over and the attack would begin. But the gas clung to the low places with us when we thought it was gone. We told 'em. We warned 'em. They were just babies, and they inhaled the gas by the lungs full. Dumb sons-of-a . . . They lay in their hospital beds coughing their lungs up and died anyway. I can still hear their screams wanting someone to put them out of their misery. I wanted to shoot them. I can smell the gas still. Mustard gas, now that was the worst. That gas attacked your skin. It loved wet skin: eyes, armpits, the groin area. It burned its way into us. The blisters . . ."

His was the warrior's tale, told a million times by a million men. *Just the facts. Just the facts.* "I have to fight not to think about wounds I didn't think could possibly be inflicted on men. I didn't think a man could keep running if he had no head. But I saw it happen. I learned not to stick a bayonet in a man's ribs, because the blade would break off sometimes or get stuck in ol' Heine. That was because while you were preoccupied trying to work the bayonet back out of him, with one foot on his chest you might just get jabbed yourself." The tiniest smile spread across Perry's face. Susan suspected he'd done just what he was describing. How awful, she thought. How terribly crazy.

"I taught boys how to kill the enemy. I told them that if they did *what* I said, *when* I said, they would go home safe. That promise got broken real quick. I have to labor to stay one step ahead of the wrong decisions that I made that cost people horribly . . . and the right decisions that cost them anyway. I couldn't win no matter what I did."

"Who knew that it would stay with me? We were so young. We went to France thinking we'd live forever. What *nonsense*! The Corps expected me to fight, and if I came home that was fine. They'd gotten from me what they wanted." Susan sat wide-eyed, her skin turning pale at her father's grotesque vignettes. She couldn't imagine *her* daddy sticking a bayonet in the ground, much less a human being.

Perry looked and felt old, much older than his sixty-eight years. He had never once spoken to Susan of these things. She was always too young, and the war wasn't a polite topic. The stories disturbed her mother terribly when Perry and some of his war buddies passed the suds around the kitchen table in the evening. Their tongues loosened and the stories flowed like water from a dam. There didn't seem to be any regret in their tone. They spoke as young men, when the killing was sweet.

Perry once spoke of a particularly nasty fight with a German patrol one afternoon as the neighbors from next door, Harry and Ruth Radley, stood leaning on the fence. Ruth, a rather heavyset woman covered her ears, and then lumbered ponderously toward the back screen door and into the house. The poor woman almost ripped her back door off its hinges in order to get away from this beast, Perry Alcott.

Corporate men didn't discuss such things at the office either. It was permissible to have one's brandy in the evening at home, and if need be, to mull over the caustic memories of mortal combat on one's own time. It was not acceptable to bring them to work on Monday or Thursday. What's done is done, they said. The war is over. "Now, best you mind the store. Do you understand, Mr. Alcott? See that you do."

The problem is that it wasn't over. For all of these reasons and more, it had to be suppressed with vigilance. In a sense, Perry was continually at war. He fought to keep it away from his family, and he fought to keep it from his employees and from his bosses. He worked at repression probably more than any other matter in his life. He grew so tired of it all, and he saw no way for it to simply go away. Life had not become so simple and polite for Mr. Alcott. He didn't want pity, far from it. He did want understanding, especially from Michelle. He'd earned the right to talk about it and yet he couldn't. There were times when he wanted or needed to speak of those days for his own sanity's sake. He also knew that Stephen needed to talk. Perry made a vain attempt at suppression of an opinion over the path that his grandson had chosen.

Buoyed, Perry said, "Now don't get me wrong, Squirt. I'm proud of what we did in France. If we hadn't gone over there, who knows how the world would be different today? It wouldn't be for the better, you can bet on that. It's too bad that the men who lead their nations into battle aren't forced to fight themselves. I'd have loved to see huge old Hindenburg and Ludendorff square off against Petain and Joffre, and then Pershing and old Lloyd George for good measure. Winners take all. All the soldiers would stand on the sidelines and cheer, and there would only be a few casualties. Only buffoons want war in the first place. With those old heavyweights, the war would have lasted about three minutes. Tops.

"But it doesn't work that way. Young men have to carry the water and bear the scars for everybody they represent. I'm still bearing those scars. You have to get this fact in your gut, what happened to Stephen *then,* affects you *now.* It affects you in ways you can't imagine. All of that pain and incredible sorrow has awakened, and you both must fight it together, or your marriage, if not your soul, will die from it. This is the cost of freedom. It's not just fighting and then the war is over. The End. Every soldier brings it all back.

"Some vets are fortunate that there are people in his life that are there for him, and won't judge him. They can look past his fits of rage, his valleys of depression, and his drinking to numb the pain. I can see Johnson and McNamara don't grasp what they are doing, and brave boys are paying the price. They're going to come home, the ones who make it out alive, and they will have psychological problems just like we did, and just like Stephen is having now. Maybe this war will be different, maybe a lot worse, because so few people back here seem to want them over there. Nobody understands it, anyway.

"Susan, it seems to me that you have to decide what it means to be married to a combat veteran who's seen some ugly things. You can segregate your lives into only the good areas. You can spin your wheels trying to close off the unwanted parts, and I'll guarantee you your marriage won't last another year, if that long."

"Oh Daddy, don't say that."

"Look, you can't live any longer as if World War Two belongs in a big coffee table edition that you can open or close at will. That war is still going on in the lives of millions of men and women across this globe. The Korean vets are still struggling too."

"So, what do I *do,* Daddy?"

Stephen looked at the ceiling. Susan still didn't grasp his words. His eyes lowered to the stove, and in a monotone, Perry spoke once more. "You have to realize that everyday, on a subconscious level, Stephen wakes up with the war. It goes to work with him. It goes to bed with you two. It plays along side the kids." His monotone ended. "But it *never* goes away. And regardless of your determination for there to be only good times, this monster is here and he ain't leavin'! I'm not telling you that life is as bleak as it can get and there won't be anything to smile about. You have to treasure the good moments. You must look past his anger and how lost he seems right now in the hospital, to its cause. Don't take *anything* personal."

"I get mad, because I can't find the tools in the garage or there's rust on them. The correlation is, if you can't find your grenades or your weapon is dirty somebody dies. I get mad at what I see on the TV. The correlation is, certain things I don't agree with really upset me. I get mad at your mother. The correlation is, when those under my command didn't do what I told them the way I told them, it many times cost a man his life. I get mad when people interrupt me or won't let me finish a project. The correlation is, completing the mission comes before everything. If you keep me from my mission, men may die. I get mad at just about everything that doesn't go the way it has to go—in my mind, of course. The correlation is *always* death." Perry's neck veins protruded outward and his face reddened.

"But the source behind my wrong headed emotions is the war. There are times when the only emotion I feel is rage. That's the bottom line. I'm sixty-eight years old and I can remember it all, like it was yesterday. I stay angry, but somehow I'm able to keep moving. When your mom takes my anger personally, we both lose. It's the anger that I have to vent that, and when it releases, it cannot be taken personally. I have learned to apologize, though—a lot. That helps her, I hope. Michelle has come so far in her understanding, and I love her for that. And remember this, too, Susan. Stephen and I have done very well in this life despite the war. Oh yeah, one other thing. Which would you rather choose: to speak German or Japanese by force, or live with a man who has festering psychological issues? That, it seems to me, is your current choice."

Susan stared at her father for long seconds more. She'd not thought of this quite in those terms. Then she stood and hugged the man she adored. In another few days Susan would bring Stephen home. Things would be different. She would see to that.

Twenty-Six:
Dr. Inhofe's 'Meaning'

Saturday, April 29, 1967

"Doctor Inhofe?" Susan ventured a question she hoped she wouldn't regret. "Would you mind telling me . . ?" Her eyes fixed on the doctor's pant leg, then back to Inhofe's eyes. She did not want seem too forward. Michael remained in the background, but near in proximity.

"Tell you what, Mrs. Lloyd?"

"I hope you won't think me morbidly curious, but . . ."

"Oh, my leg. I guess I can do that. Today, I think I can. Tomorrow, who knows?"

"Do you think me wrong for asking? My father-in-law said you were hurt in the war, but he didn't give me many details. I talked to my dad yesterday about his involvement in the First World War. He'd kept it *all* from me. The way he talked about it, it was horrible. I'd like to hear your story. You don't have to answer this if you don't want to. It just seems as if everywhere I turn these days, I am running into men who turn out to have gone through some war. It's the strangest thing. It's stranger than strange. It feels as if I'm living in the *Twilight Zone* or something. I'm almost afraid to go anywhere now."

The doctor, a man who looked amazingly like John F. Kennedy, hesitated. He suddenly didn't know if he wanted to appease her curiosity. Dr. Jerry Inhofe kept his personal life out of his counseling, or tried to. He pursed his lips and took a deep breath. "I don't normally . . . In terms of specifics, why is *my* story important to you, Mrs. Lloyd?" the doctor was now stalling. He'd changed his mind.

"It's important to me, because I've been so sheltered. I see that now. I didn't tell you before, but I participated in war bond drives, and I even did some months as a donut dolly. Marcus wouldn't let me do more. I watched the newsreels at the movies and kept up with everything I could that was happening in Europe, especially Italy. But now it seems that I missed something, that dimension where men actually meet each other in battle. I want to know, and I don't know how else to tell you or to find out. I was kept thousands of miles from all the death and destruction. Am I making any sense?"

"Yes, yes you are, Mrs. Lloyd." Very few of his patients or their spouses ever asked him about *it*—his leg. "Are you sure? It isn't pretty. I have to warn you." He looked for some sign of Susan's resignation from her inquiry. Seeing none, he said, "Here goes." At that, he rolled his pant leg up carefully, and exposed Susan and Michael to his gruesome wound. Their look was indescribable. Then he said, "It took me several years to piece together what happened to me." Colonel Jerry Inhofe attempted to keep the necessary information on a superficial level where he could control it—emotionally, of course.

Rolling his trouser leg down, he continued, "Apparently, I was operating on a Major Green or Greenwood." The colonel shook his head as if this cranial motion might produce the name. "He was so dirty. I think he had a chest wound, and I was in the midst of cutting away his field jacket and fatigue shirt to expose the damage. When all of a sudden this screaming shell ripped a hole in the top of the tent and landed directly behind the nurse assisting me. Her name was Elizabeth—Lizzy. She was Captain Bob Frazee's wife. Lizzy Frazee, what an awful name."

Jerry's eyes went dead—so much for the superficial level. His hands rose to cover his face, and his shame. His head slammed back into the soft, high backed chair. He couldn't keep from bawling, his body convulsed as he remembered his time in Hell. Susan and Michael reached to support him from empathetic reflex, a subtle vicarious living through his sorrow.

"Is everything all right?" A small woman stood beside Susan, intent on assisting the woman's husband in any way possible. The receptionist's sudden and unexpected involvement surprised Susan. "Should I get a doctor for your husband, ma'am?"

"Oh, no, he's not . . ." Susan let it drop. "I think we're fine. He is a doctor, but he's . . . everything will be fine. Thank you so much."

"All right. If you're sure."

"Yes. We're okay."

By then, the doctor had begun the process of composing himself. He took out his handkerchief and blew his nose. "Whew. It gets harder every time. So I don't think about it. I work and I drink. I drink a lot—too much." The doctor breathed deep as he wiped his eyes, and got himself into a state where he could finish or get to his point, quickly. Michael edged closer, intent on hearing this. The only war he'd ever actually seen was on the big screen and the nightly news on television. A mangled leg was never part of the short TV segments, which the producers implied when he watched Vic Morrow on the weekly TV series *Combat*.

"Are you okay, doctor? You don't have to finish this." Susan almost pled with him to stop. Every one of these men she knew had cried. The meaning of war and it costs weren't quite as illusive to her now.

"Yes. Yes, I do. I think for your sakes, I do. Perhaps for mine as well."

"Well . . . the shell hit and Lizzy's body absorbed the brunt of the impact. I usually stood where she was standing, but the light that time of the day was better on this other side of the table. I must have turned to get an instrument or something." He stopped again. "It was Lizzy's body and the wounded major who saved my life. The blast threw me through the side of the tent. There wasn't enough of either of them to scrape together. They just disappeared, . . . and I'm still alive." The last words exited like the thrust of a bayonet's cold steel, piercing into the hard wood surface of the coffee table separating the doctor from his patients.

"After I . . . after I had gone through all the surgeries and therapy, I had to face the fact that I couldn't stand on my feet for hours doing surgery like I used to. I could hardly stand at all. So, I had to accept that part of my life was over. It was devastating for me. It was like those doctors went ahead and amputated some part of me I couldn't see. In case you are wondering, I have powerful connections. That's why I'm still in the service. It's the only reason. So I went back to school and became a psychiatrist."

"And your wife?" Susan needed to hear about this woman.

"Her name was Elizabeth, too. I could handle being home for about six months, and then we divorced. When I wasn't studying or in class, I was drunk, abusive, chasing women, and angry. Worst of all, I felt guilty. Lizzy and I didn't do . . . we didn't do anything my wife would insist on a divorce for. I wish now Lizzie and I had . . . well, you know." Michael was present so he didn't press it. "I was in love with Lizzy. The woman I married, Elizabeth, didn't mean anything to me anymore. Neither could I work my way past all the men I didn't save . . . and the one . . . the two who saved me. My wife remarried not long after we divorced." Jerry's eyes searched for some safe place for them to light, and, finding none, he went back to the "bayonet" of regret he'd left stuck in the coffee table.

As Susan listened, quite absorbed in a moribund, fascinated sort of way, she couldn't help but notice the strange and quite unexpected similarity between her husband, her daddy, and this man. It wasn't the physical characteristics that were homogeneous. This doctor had the same grim, forlorn appearance imprinted on his face that she had witnessed on her daddy and on Stephen.

"I met Vickie in Las Vegas, at a psychiatrist convention in 1952. We got married and had a son. She left with Billy when she'd had enough. I'm not easy to live with. I tell myself I'm a social drinker. But I'm an alcoholic, a drunk. I, too, am still angry. Please don't quote the proverb to me, "physician, heal thyself." The doctor felt wrung out. Susan suspected that Inhofe was eyeing her surreptitiously, and she would have to be careful around him. Susan felt that she should ask another more important question to put his mind in the proper frame: "What is your diagnosis, doctor? I love that man in there, and I want him back, as whole as you can give him to me."

"May I speak plainly with you?" Doctor Inhofe addressed his question both to Michael and his mother.

"Why yes. Yes, of course." Susan said.

"All right. When he's ready he must begin to talk about the war, at his pace, not yours. That's going to be difficult on both of you, because you want him well as soon as possible. Now, let me define 'well' for you both. 'Well,' as it applies to these veterans means that they have begun to talk about their experiences more openly in an environment that is accepting, so that they can deal with the past honestly. But 'well,' does not mean *cured*, like when you get over a cold so that you can resume all your normal duties. I've found that the greater the trauma the greater and longer the effect on the patient. An important aside you must always remember is this: many veterans came home emotional wrecks. They weren't as lucky as you have been, Mrs. Lloyd and Michael. They couldn't hold a job. They went straight to the bottle and didn't quit until they died of alcoholic poisoning or worse. They never married their high school sweetheart like they promised. When their parents had enough, they kicked the vets out and told them not to come back. You have your family, Mrs. Lloyd, and you have your dad, Michael. You both have had all the security and love he has provided for you for over two decades, and so much more. I have had patients that have never been presented the opportunities, or the years and the children, as you have had. That has to stay somewhere in the forefront of your mind as *all of you*," he paused for effect, "begin this treatment process. If you went with me through one day's rounds at the hospital, you would thank your lucky stars for how fortunate you two have been. Okay?"

"Doctor, do you think my father will . . . I mean . . . get well enough that he can go back to work?" Michael asked, his concern growing the more the colonel spoke.

"Michael, I know what you're asking. Son, time heals a lot of wounds. You have to care for your dad, and he's going to be very difficult to live with for a while, perhaps for the rest of the time you know him. You may never quite get used to his outbursts and various types of behavior, which I must tell you, are going to be very unpredictable, at best, for a while. But you'll learn that more times than not, he doesn't mean what he says when he's agitated. He would take it back or not say it if he could. I know this from personal experience. If he doesn't apologize, let it go. Don't hold grudges. Remember, it's the effect of the war that's yelling at you. It's a body that is chemically, physiologically, anatomically, biologically, and perhaps in other ways altered from prolonged stress and fear. He *couldn't* come back the same man. Not possible. And when you are ready to quit, remember, if he could change his behavior, he would. Trust me, he would. Hold on to the good days. Savor his humor. Tell him you love him. And when you are alone with your mom, Michael, tell your frustrations to her or to your grandparents. Didn't you say one of them was in the Great War?"

"Yes, sir. My grandpa."

"It's heartbreaking to watch so many wives and children who just can't compensate for or tolerate the adverse changes they see in their husbands. Also Susan, you must help him discover the meaning of his experiences during the war. I'll explain that in a minute. There's something else you need to know. Stephen doesn't have to think about being angry. He already is mad. Anger is one of the changes that the war created in these men."

"What do you mean, he's angry?" Susan had heard this adjective from her father too. That her husband was still furious over what happened years before didn't seem logical. When life attacked Susan, whether from the children's behavior or some other reason, she would boil from within for a few minutes. Then she'd be over it and on with her life.

The doctor continued, "What I'm saying is this: war provides an environment in which men experience prolonged exposure to danger, being afraid not just for a few minutes, but for hours and days. They are angry because they can't hit back or keep death at bay. There is a sadness that grips them that you most likely won't ever be able to comprehend because, too often, their friends died right in front of them. These awful events altered these men to such an extent that they are not the same fundamental men that you said goodbye to prior to the war. They still feel guilty, and their guilt leads to anger, and anger to depression, and then they become afraid that they have ruined everything they have labored to build. And that's just to mention a few symptoms.

"As I keep saying, physiologically they are changed men. They also lived off of the rush of adrenaline. There is no drug quite like that. The fight to control situations, because fighting meant the total loss of control. And when you realize the control you thought you had over matters is an illusion . . . well, I have known too many men whose whole belief systems collapsed when that *one* conscious item was blown to bits on the battlefield."

"Do you believe in God, doctor?" Susan questioned.

"I think I used to. I don't know any more. I lost some things too. What do *you* believe, Mrs. Lloyd? Does God exist for *you*? You are going to need more than just yourself in this."

"Well, I am a Catholic, and I go to church."

"That's not what I asked. Do you believe in *God*?"

"Of course I believe in God."

"What does it mean to Susan Lloyd to believe in God when her husband lies in a hospital bed because of the past, and the future is suddenly quite uncertain?"

There was a long pause from Susan. Then she ventured an answer that left her grasping in the dark. "It means that . . . that God exists. It means that He's . . ." No one had ever asked her that. She felt as if God was again punishing her for something, but she dare not say that aloud or in front of Michael. She'd been Catholic all her life. Her parents had, and her grandparents before them. She believed what they believed. Catholicism was a family matter. Belief was not the *main* thing. If one believed in God and did their best, God could not ask more than that, *could He*? Susan had always done her best. But now her unvoiced answer did seem a bit thin. In this context, so much was riding on fundamentals and core values. Susan had no idea if she had any actual answer. Had she merely been living on her parent's faith all her life? Of what did *her* faith consist?

"Mrs. Lloyd, in order for you to get your family through this sanely, *you* have to develop something that *you* can hang onto. And you haven't sold me that you have that, regardless of what your religious background is. It has to be solid. My colleagues have each come to certain conclusions about how to approach these veterans. Some directions we have tried and abandoned. We will try one philosophy and if that fails to achieve the desired results, we look at another. I can assure you that long hours in study and discussions, writing papers, argumentation and thought have led us to embrace certain standards and beliefs, if you will. Most of us defer to something other than the accustomed forms of religion. For instance, if Buddhism is of value to a patient, then we encourage them to take that approach. If psychotherapy helps, and many of my colleagues prefer it, then we take that tack. If in the final analysis, chucking it all and moving away to the mountains works, we tell them to do that. In other words, whatever assists in the healing process—that is what we pursue with our patients."

"We are also developing various drugs. Some of these medications have also helped our patients tremendously. Others have not. What I'm saying is if one approach doesn't work with your husband, there are many different ways we can proceed. But all of this will take time. Does that help?"

"Oh, yes. It does very much. Thank you."

"As I said a minute ago, I am of the opinion we have to help your husband find the meaning or purpose to his trauma."

"The *meaning*? I don't understand." Susan pled for clarification.

"Well, your husband must reconcile the war in terms of not only what its real meaning *was*, but what it *will be* for him. I believe that there is so much positive human potential in this approach. *Your* participation is equally crucial. Both you and I must help Stephen learn how to turn his tragedy into his own personal triumph and human achievement."

"What do you mean turn the tragedy into triumph? How? I feel so ignorant."

"Obviously we can't go back and change the war and the terrible things that happened there. But, we *can* change ourselves. The meaning for any given situation, whether we are talking about cancer or combat, is that this event that has and is causing us so much heartache *can* have a meaning if we mentally assign significance to it, real significance. Whatever the assigned meaning we give it will make it possible to change *us* for the better. Do you see that?"

"Not exactly."

"We must provide a positive mental atmosphere, for lack of a better phrase, for Stephen to rise above himself and his past. It's the past that is dragging him down, so much so, that he can't think and so reach beyond himself in order to become useful once again."

"Okay."

"Mrs. Lloyd, Victor Frankl was implicit in this. There is the possibility of investing meaning even in suffering and death. This is *my* approach. I've seen it help some of these men and their families."

"Hmmm." Susan had not as yet thought of her husband's dilemma in such terms. Michael remained silent although he was clearly thinking about these concepts. She asked, "So you have had success with this approach?"

"Yes. But here's the kicker. No one, not I or even you, can give Stephen the exact meaning for what he went through."

Dr. Inhofe anticipated the next retort from Susan. It always seemed to come. "Wait a minute, doctor. I thought you just said that we couldn't help Stephen find the meaning for the war. Can we or can't we?" Susan was suddenly bewildered, and bewildered was not what she needed. Dr. Inhofe had given her hope, and then just as quickly, he seemed to snatch it from her grasp with his doublespeak.

"I understand your dilemma, believe me. What I mean is this: there is a meaning out there, which is meant *just* for your husband. You can suggest things. You can coach him along when you sense the time is right. But in the final analysis, Stephen is the only human being who can discover it for himself and embrace that particular purpose as his own. But *at least* we can show him that there is a meaning for his life, and no matter how bad it gets, the meaning is there. Life retains its own purpose regardless of the situation or conditions thrust upon it."

"Suffering, in terms of significance, is different from, say, work or love. And, believe it or not, the person who suffers has the *advantage* over the worker or lover, if I may use those words. Stephen, with the right guidance, should be able to mold even his sufferings into great human achievements. This is the greatness of the human spirit that I've discovered. Let me give you a personal example."

"Oh, I wish you would. This sounds so complicated to me." Michael shook his head in the affirmative as well.

"As I said earlier, when I knew I could no longer perform surgery— and I lived for that—because I was so good at what I did, when they told me I wouldn't be able to stand for very long, if at all, I was lost, hopelessly, pitifully lost. I have two ex-wives and a son to support, who wouldn't talk to me. Doctor J. Edwin Stanley put a copy of Viktor Frankl's, *The Unheard Cry for Meaning,* into my hands. I had to read Freud and Adler, Maslow, B.F. Skinner, Pavlov and so many others when I was in school. I'd found problems with many of the ideas these great minds had chosen. But in Frankl I discovered a man who thought like I did. Frankl helped to put my life in order, because I saw what he, of all the others, were saying. I knew Victor Frankl's thinking could make a significant impact, if I would but avail myself of his ideas, fully. Now, I'm on the pathway to finding my most creative human potential."

"You see, Michael, it finally dawned on me that, as a surgeon, I had no satisfying contact with the person I was helping, except the few moments before and after surgery. And that was key, *no satisfying contact.* When I was able to grasp that, I knew I could move on with my life. I loved being a surgeon—up to a point, of course. That took a long time to admit to myself. But, because of the nature and extent of my wounds, under Frankl I was able to coalesce with hurting people in ways I could never have done before. My life, such as it is, has a whole new meaning for me. It means something for me to step into all of the brokenness in people's lives and see them rethink the effect of their pain as well as their beliefs. Surgery never could heal my broken spirit. Not once. I now help others to discover their potential so that they, too, can heal on the inside, *some of the time*—any way. This is much more creative and much more satisfying, to me.

"When veterans reach the point Stephen has, it means that they have exhausted their resources to repress all the pain. That's because they have been unable to give it any appreciable purpose, and therefore they believe their past, with all the memories, must stay out of sight. For many of them, in terms of the bigger picture, the war meant the defeat of the enemy. That *is* truly significant in itself. But when they shut their eyes at night many times they cannot place a value on the particulars, like the individual deaths, which always seem to be very random. One man lived and another man died. They want to shield you from their war by keeping it out of sight, and they don't want to have to take it out and examine something that they cannot reconcile rationally. Does that make sense?"

"I think so, doctor," Susan added. "Not very long ago I thought the war *didn't* come home with Stephen. But I'm beginning to believe I was completely wrong. He would have nightmares, but wouldn't share them with me. And then finally . . . Oh, I have some stories to tell you. But when the babies finally came, there was just no time to do anything about the past."

"Trust me, the war came home with your husband. But, he had no way to make sense of it on his own, nor was he given any tools to do so. How was he supposed to attach a meaning to all that without the tools, Susan?"

"I . . . I don't really know. I never thought about any of this. This is so new."

"Let me tell you," the doctor continued, "I reached a point as a physician in Europe that I could no longer experience my patient's pain. It got to where it didn't bother me that the man I'd just spent an hour operating on, piecing delicate muscle and tissue together had died just like that. Another wounded private or captain or someone would fill the table in his place, and they just kept coming—night and day, often seven days a week, month after month, until I was numb. Lizzy, my nurse, was the only color in my life that wasn't the shade of death. I think she was the only thing I ever really loved . . . you know?"

"I remember leaving the states determined to do my part to save our boys, and then . . . I grew to hate them, to hate their agony, to hate their wounds, to hate their robbing me of even five minutes of sleep, a meal, a smoke. I didn't care if the chow was hot or cold, I just wanted to be left alone, to get as far away from . . . from *them* . . . as I could, and they just kept coming through my surgery like cars on an assembly line, and I became another guy putting parts on chassis so they could go back out there and come back in for more refitting when the Germans broke through them again and again and again."

He had finally finished his evangelistic spiel. Colonel Jerry Inhofe sat still, suddenly quite fatigued and disturbed, as he glowered back into that hole that ate men alive. He had not, to his knowledge, ever spoken with a patient's family exactly as he had just done. Both Michael and Susan observed that same beside-the-tub stare of Stephen's several nights before, engraved on Dr. Inhofe's face.

"I am *so* sorry, Susan and Michael," he eventually remarked. "I don't know why . . . that came out. I'm so careful not to get involved to that degree. I'm embarrassed. Please forgive me."

"For what?" Susan spoke, hurrying to quell his fears. "You obviously needed to let something go, and I am glad we were here for you. So this must be what Stephen is feeling right now?"

"Pretty much."

Twenty-Seven: Canada

Thursday, May 11, 1967

It had been eighteen days since Stephen was admitted to Bethhaven and four days since Stephen was released. Today, prior to leaving their Westover Hills home, a dour cloud had tarnished their upcoming drive to Amon Carter Field where Michael's parents would catch their plane for Vancouver and then drive deep into Canada. That knot had settled firmly in Stephen's sternum, its pressure had become a familiar part of his life since Damien's funeral. When it grabbed the reigns, like now, he knew it wouldn't let up for a while. The inmost pressing began with Susan's routine and newly irritating manner of packing. For that reason, she had postponed it until the last minute, a mere four hours before they were to leave for the airport, in her preference for attending to other things.

The thought of them missing their plane drove Stephen almost up the wall. David's constant need to ask questions created the conditions for the perfect storm, waiting to derail the Lloyd's. Stephen's emotional estate, which he blamed on Susan and her youngest son, made it the more difficult for him to do the simplest, albeit necessary things. Relieving Susan of some of the family cares would have helped the situation progress forward. Instead, Stephen went downstairs and sat, fuming. Susan sat on the bed next to the suitcase, bewildered, almost in tears. Should she call Annika?

While in the den, Stephen became anxious at being among all those people at Amon Carter. Of late, he had come to dread crowds with their herding mentality. Now he had to face another confluence of humanity in a building and then on the flight.

Dr. Inhofe had asked Marcus, when Stephen was still under his care, if he knew of a place Susan and Stephen could retreat to in order for them to work through some of these issues. Marcus suggested they use his "cabin" in Canada. The doctor concurred. Next, he phoned and spoke to Stephen and Susan about it. And so, that became Stephen's sole mission. There could be no detours and no problems. He would grit his teeth and shut out the crowds at the airport, and probably Susan if the situation called for it. When several or all these things came together badly, he either lashed out or he sulked, and then his animosity turned to depression, and depression overcame everything else. Of late, he had said too many hurtful, hateful things when he reached this state. Yet, in the end, he had not intended or wanted to say any of them.

Down stairs, Stephen's patience had finally run dry. The dog even avoided him. He went to the liquor cabinet and poured himself a squat glass of Scotch. When Susan discovered that Stephen was downstairs drinking this early, and prior to the flight, she became thoroughly disgusted about the whole enterprise. It seemed somehow irresponsible to her. Michael's graduation was coming up in June, which meant they had just so much time to work through this issue of Stephen's, and the pressure on Susan was intense. Michael had to graduate, Stephen had to get better, Margaret had to relax, and David needed to play catch with his father. The upshot was that Stephen internally evaded his family that morning, and Susan aged.

Stephen's eyes turned to slits, and his jaw muscles squeezed and alternately released. Before they had set foot out of the house the man was thoroughly upset, the family in turmoil, and Susan ready for a Florida beach—alone. Margaret cried alone in her room because her father was lost, internalizing her father's anger. Stephen's poor little girl was so frightened at what she couldn't understand, and Susan couldn't explain it to her because she didn't understand it or was not yet convinced. David ran outside to play, electing not to tell his father goodbye. Susan believed that Stephen's behavior didn't bother him. It did of course. That was the irony of it all. Stephen Lloyd could not help it, change it, or control it, which made him that much more agitated.

He had to get to the airport so he could get to the cabin. Susan was suddenly in a real hurry, and her 'normality' had become irrational to Stephen. Susan had packed, phoned and packed, and fussed and packed. In fact, she was intentionally dragging her feet because she was somehow abandoning her children to their own awful fate. Yet Susan was just being Susan. She had been Susan for the twenty-five years Stephen had known her, but today this regulated, acceptable behavior of hers was unacceptable.

Michael drove, and Stephen sat emotionally numb in the back seat. Susan looked at the airline tickets for the twentieth time, the ride conducted in dreary silence. The sole conversation occurred between Susan and her son, and that was sporadic at best. Stephen's eyes darted from passing object to object as they rode from Ft. Worth toward Dallas. His immediate reason for living lay in reaching the cabin. After that, he hadn't a clue, because he didn't want to know anything beyond that. Dr. Inhofe and his psychiatry could go take a flying leap. Why did Stephen feel so little attachment to these people who loved him so much? How could that happen? It was true and real nonetheless.

A dull, reclusive thud moved in front of Stephen's eyes. He subtly hoped that the plane might crash even before they took off. Of course he didn't think about what would happen to his wife and children if it did or all the people who would die. Tomorrow wasn't worth waiting for, and there was no other way to put it.

Sitting in the aircraft waiting for takeoff, he thought once more about Susan's endless altering of her wardrobe, her packing and repacking, the dozen or so calls she "just had to make" before she dared to set foot out of the house, the "one more thing" she had to remind Michael, Margaret or David about, all of which irked him. There was that last minute phone call from Susan's mother-in-law—his own mother, to whom he didn't want to speak. Collectively, these things tightened around his middle. How many times he'd gone through this without the slightest bump on his part, he didn't know. Life had changed recently in drastic ways. The plane didn't crash and Stephen didn't talk.

In Vancouver, and with all the emotional hoopla of the flight behind him—he wanted to punch that idiot in customs. An hour and ten minutes after landing he sat alone in the rental car with his wife. Susan drove and Stephen stared blankly out the windshield as the miles sped past them. He'd seen it all before. The farther north they traveled, the more clouds moved in to weld out the sun. This particular overcast caused Stephen to want to be alone even more. He wanted this thing inside of him to find someone else's life and family to destroy. He wanted to love his wife again. *Fat chance*, he thought. *What is love? What does it feel like?* He'd forgotten, but there he sat, a crumpled, bloated, yet empty piece of humanity, useless in the main, hurting and incapable of articulating his plight to the woman he felt so little for, yet loved so terribly. At some point, he didn't know when, he realized that he couldn't remember the smell of her perfume, even though she was but feet away. So much had gone out of his life.

Stephen's vacillating disposition served only to erode the remaining bits of Susan's usually buoyant spirit and excitement about such trips. Every few minutes she would force herself to refocus on their purpose for leaving Texas. The original intent had been for them to talk, to get away for a little while, or to escape, depending on whose perspective ruled the moment. During the drive out of Vancouver, Susan thought several times about letting Stephen out along the side of the road, turning around and driving back to the airport. Back in Vancouver, she would catch a plane and fly home, or somewhere—anywhere.

This auspicious beginning of the adventure—or purgatory—didn't bode well for its conclusion, because it pointed with razor sharp edges at the future with only anxiety and frustration at its core. Yet, Susan, in some unexplainable way, felt that she was being drawn north, despite her emotional misgivings. She couldn't shake that sensation. But with each passing mile Susan's nagging sense of desperation and loneliness also increased. She knew no former military pilots or their wives, and thus she had no one with whom to talk. Stephen sat brooding and irascible, too much within himself to alter the complexion of the trip. Susan's mother had offered little or no help understanding her father or her husband. Michelle had never wanted to know.

The beautiful but impersonal miles sped by. They took Marine Way to the Trans- Canada Highway 1 southwest, over the Fraser River that dogged their heels, past New Westminster, the turn for Abbotsford, the turn off to Chilliwack and the mountains that border them. Stephen finally nodded off, and Susan felt even more alone. Once again they crossed the Fraser at Hope, then Puckatholetchin, then Dogwood Valley, Alber Flat, Yale, Stout, Spuzzum, and after that, the towns and villages lost all meaning. Klakamich, Nicomen, and at Spences Bridge, Highway 8 began and wound south. With Arrowstone Provincial Park up ahead, the Trans-Canada Highway turned east, and the Caribou Highway 97 commenced. Susan had begun to worry if something went wrong with the car, there was hardly any place to find assistance. Fill township appeared, then 70 Mile House where they lunched and fueled the car.

The snow-capped peaks, meadows, pines, and exquisitely cold fresh air couldn't alter the next unpleasantry Stephen faced. He noticed that the attendant filling the tank stared one second too long at Susan. In Stephen's mental state he began to think himself into a volatile situation that didn't exist. The attendant pumped the fuel, took the money from Susan, and went inside the station. That was reality. Mentally, and because of Stephen's accumulated agitation over the past several hours, he visualized the attendant speaking gruffly with Susan, or perhaps he thought he'd scraped his rent car with the pump handle. These same types of negative phenomena had begun to occur with alarming regularity the past few weeks. Solely in his mind, Stephen flew out of the car, first insulting the man, then grabbing him, which led to punching and kicking the man; beating him into the concrete or being battered and bested by a man he had never laid eyes on until now.

"Stephen!" Susan interrupted his illusory pugilistic match. She saw his mouth twisted, speaking unverbalized words, and the words filled her with misgivings.

"*What?*" His voice was strained and terse. "What?" He needed to pound something, if only in his mind.

"Are you all right?"

"Yes. Put it in gear and let's get out of here."

Nothing Susan had said or did today seemed to affect Stephen in a positive way. The previous three weeks therapy with Dr. Inhofe had at least brought her husband around to communicate with her a little more, but their words and moments together often became strained or distant—very distant. A one-sided conversation for eight hours in the car was not what she'd hoped for. The soft goodness that had once been their relationship had turned to rough, flakey crust. If pressed, Susan Lloyd couldn't remember any of the towns she had driven past.

Highway 24 branched to her right, east, but she continued north. One Hundred Eight Mile Ranch came and went, Wright, Enterprise,

141 Mile House, Sugarcane, Williams Lake and past that, nothing until Quesnel.

Invading her solitude outside of Quesnel, CBD Radio One news anchor informed her, "In Viet Nam today, the fighting over the past month has proven lethal for American and South Vietnamese forces. A combined group of U.S. Marines of the First Battalion, Fifth Marines, along with five Battalions of ARVN Rangers located approximately ten miles south of Da Nang in the Que Son Valley, have been engaging a formidable but well-entrenched NVA Regiment. 'American and South Vietnamese casualties have been especially high,' said one Marine spokesman. According to official reports, a staggering one hundred-ten Marines have been killed, and four hundred seventy-three were wounded. Enemy dead was counted at only fifty-seven. In other news—Toronto Mayor . . ." Susan turned the radio off.

"I wonder where the Que Son Valley is," Susan asked herself, looking out over the dashboard. Lately, she'd been hearing names like, The Rock Pile, Saigon, Da Nang, Quang Tri, Dong Ha, Nha Trang and Hue City. Such strange names these were. And each double or triple worded town or village somehow reminded her of places like Dusseldorf, Anzio, Budapest, Bucharest and Turin, she had heard on the radio years ago. What Stephen had done over so many European cities had somehow trapped him inside a mind that was still at war, not only with him, but it felt as if it were with her too. If it was with her, perhaps it was also with the world around her, and a world their son would soon confront.

Oh, these were lonely miles she traversed. They seemed lonelier still as she drove past Woodpecker, Crysdale, Stoner, Red Rock. Doggedly, Susan repotted her mind in the soil of the jutting mountains, snow capped and majestic. And then Red Rock's speed zone appeared up ahead. Disconsolate, the weight of her burden had by Red Rock all but overcome her.

Ten minutes later, Stephen mumbled, "Prince George is up ahead." This announcement broke her unhallowed and crowded alienation. "Look for 16 going west."

"Stephen, I'm tired. I'm the one who's been doing all the driving. I'd like to stop here for the night." Susan might as well have been doing unpleasant things at home, like sewing, driving the kids to practice, or doing the wash. She wanted to be swept up in this glorious scenery of which she'd observed so little. To her, this trip and these past hours had become a great waste of time and money.

"By all means, stop. I couldn't care less."

Susan had agreed, at the doctor's insistence, following almost three full weeks of immersion into Victor Frankl's mind, to take the fraying remnants of her soul and her shell of a husband, and fly north into Canada. Stephen had discovered no significant purpose for all the men and crews he'd watched go down over the skies of Europe. None. Remembering only made him more convinced there wasn't any meaning to be found.

If for no one else, Susan had felt the need to escape the daily doses of the Huntley and Brinkley Report, and Walter Cronkite's, 'And that's the way it is.' She could certainly do without the national news reporters and photojournalists whose lives and experiences seemed to mock her misery, especially since her eldest son had so recently announced his intentions to —not head off to college —*just yet*. The nightly news at six and ten o'clock focused repeatedly on several unresolved issues: the war in Southeast Asia and how it had turned into a quagmire with its horrible body counts and its disgruntled returning veterans actively protesting the war. Russia was always rattling her saber. These were good for lead stories. The cosmos appeared to be heading for the brink one more time.

Domestically, the student protesters took over college administration buildings almost at will, draft dodging card burners fled to Canada, and the President's Great Socialist Society, he assured a wary public, would spur economic recovery. In truth, Johnson's stratagem wasn't great, and it wouldn't lead to anything resembling recovery. It only helped to stir unrest in the country's soul. Taxpayer handouts to the poor kept the impoverished dependent on the government. Maybe *that* was the goal.

The tempestuous cauldron, which was the civil rights movement, stirred the heart of this country one way or the other. On the nightly news, America was treated to unrelenting doses of vicious police dogs and powerful fire hoses turned on the colored populace in Mississippi and Alabama. Such fear and courage served only to inflame America's fraying central nervous system, if not ripping and tearing the heart out of the south itself. Lately, television nearly dragged Susan under.

In 1962, the world stood on the brink of annihilation at the turbulent shores of Cuba. In 1963, John Kennedy was lost in Dallas. Nineteen sixty-four trailed slowly behind the riderless horse clopping down Pennsylvania Avenue. America increased her resolve by sending regular troops to Vietnam. She had left behind the illusion that we had come to simply "advise" the South Vietnamese. Each year the war escalated and more boys came home in those terrible silver coffins than the previous year, without the hint of a plan to win. Nineteen sixty-seven shoved the war into the Wilson's and the Lloyd's front door. Damien had been killed there, Susan's husband was broken, and her son was headed west, too far west. She had to get away.

This trip to the Lloyd's cabin had been prescribed by Dr. Inhofe to somehow salvage a deteriorating mood deep within the bowels of their marriage. "When you make the reservations, fly only as far as Vancouver. Drive the rest of the way. It will do you both good," he, Dr. Jerry Inhofe, had said to Susan. Such adventures had apparently not helped Dr. Jerry Inhofe's two marriages, Viktor Frankl notwithstanding. Observing her husband as he limped along during their sessions, or rather in spite of him, she resolved to stay the course. "If the opportunity presents itself, then talk. We've spoken at length about how to broach the subject of the war, and made suggestions you can make that may lead to discovery. That's also an assignment I gave to Stephen."

But he, Stephen Lloyd, didn't want to talk, and he made it known that he had little intention of taking suggestions, thank you very much. Driving farther north Susan made repeated attempts to speak about these things, three in all, but each time she came up nursing her growing grudge. One by one her suggestions slammed into Stephen's steel plated resistance.

All that Thursday in the car, she had plenty of time to mull over her father's advice and their doctor's counseling sessions. Susan had felt confident that things would work out that morning she sat with her daddy in her Westover Hills kitchen. The doctor had instilled even more positive conviction. But these past hours flying northwest from Texas, and now driving with Stephen into the heart of Northwestern Canada, had untied the laces of her composure and self-reliance. Everything this day seemed so overwhelming. Making it worse, Michael was just over a month from leaving for his Marine training and his graduation from Gladstone was too close to be withdrawing like this. Susan reached into her purse to pull a tissue from the small packet she kept. In spite of these issues fighting against her, she was determined to save herself, her sanity, and her marriage, if at all possible. *Hurry Susan.*

To Stephen, currently sitting in the passenger's seat, the doctor's words didn't seem ambiguous. "Stephen, we've talked about finding meaning for the war. I know right now it seems that there can't possibly be any. Your mind and soul has suffered severe trauma that you've repressed for so long. But there is a meaning to your pain. Trust me. If your life is going to turn out well, you have to find it on your own. No one can do for you what only you can do. I hope you find it like I did."

Funny, Stephen thought. *What meaning has Dr. Inhofe really found? He's a loser and a drunk. Instead of cutting people open with a knife, he's dissecting them with his mind and someone else's philosophy, and for a huge fee. He's figured out how to keep from drinking himself to death—so far. Some meaning. This trip is hopeless. There is no meaning; no way out. Sartre was right. I wish I were dead.*

The doctor's closing words to Susan had been, "These days away from the children and everything familiar can be the most blessed of your life, or they can become some of the most futile. It's what *you* make of them—for both of you. Remember Susan, *you* too need to find meaning for what you are going through. You will become the poorer if you miss this opportunity regardless of what your husband does or doesn't do. I'm not suggesting that you will discover everything there is to find over the next weeks. But you can begin the process. I hope you can experience this with him. Assist Stephen to discover the purpose of his pain. That may mean your life should go in a completely different direction from the course you are now on. I don't know."

Susan had looked shocked at the doctor's suggestion. "You mean, leave the hotel business?"

"If that's what it takes, yes. Or, you might take the hotel business in a completely different direction. There are an infinite number of possibilities here. If you discard one, examine another. But don't give up. You *can* find it together."

It would be a long night in a Prince George hotel. Susan only hoped she could rest. She also hoped that Stephen might dream about something humorous to alter his disposition for the coming day when they would arrive at the cabin.

Friday, May 12, 1967

"Are we anywhere close?" Susan begged. Their destination these two days on the road was the Lloyd's cabin, built especially so that the Lloyd men could get away from their wives, children, some of the business, and life in general. The Nechako plateau was a vast area of rolling hills, spawning numerous lakes and rivers. It was forested mostly with pine, some spruce, and fir. They had passed many lakes to this point, and these immediate hills were filled with glorious aspen stands. This was the Boreal Forest in all its wonder.

The Carrier-Sekani Indians lived here. The moose, mule and white tail deer that roamed at will had drawn them. Some woodland caribou had been seen lately. The carnivores, such as grizzly, black bear, wolf, coyote, lynx, martins and wolverines, all ranged over the area and could be observed, but usually through binoculars. When Stephen began to accompany his father the last few years before his military service, he loved watching the otters play in or near the rivers if he could sneak up on them. Lolling in the back of Stephen's mind were the snowshoe hairs, porcupines, squirrels and beaver dams, which meant an abundance of beaver and muskrat.

Stephen knew it was time for the lakes to thaw and open for the waterfowl, ducks, loons, and Canadian geese in abundance. The birds of prey were here as well, loitering high overhead, observant of the slightest movement below. The Lloyds could always count on the small lakes to be filled with trout, kokanee or sockeye salmon and mountain whitefish. The burbot, with its big mouth, awaited a large mouthful of bait—and a big hidden hook—attached to an eager fisherman's line.

"Keep going. You're headed in the right direction." Yellowhead Highway 16 was a continuation of the previous day's ride, only this time Stephen was awake. Prince George by this time lay far behind in the mirror. Numerous roads branched off in various directions, but there was now less civilization heading west. Mile followed lonely mile. No conversation, just their thoughts to accompany the two isolated people.

Stephen's tone this morning was not seeded with impatience, but rather indifference. Susan also detected the fringes of agitation, which ringed it about making his few words that much more sardonic and piercing. Stephen was not unaware of the gorgeous British Colombian wilderness rushing past him nine miles southwest of Vanderhoof, although it hardly made any appreciable impact on his senses. Each sensation fed the tributaries of his changing moods. Thus, what should have been a breathtaking drive became an annoyance—for Stephen, but not Susan. Each pine forest, rock formation or mountain range, along with large, dotted, groupings of yellow, deep purple, pinks, blues and white wild-flowers, mocked him with their ubiquitous loveliness and tranquility, reminding him that he possessed none. *Susan, Someone made this.*

Susan clutched firmly to her breast the hope of a new day to start afresh. She had awakened, determined and renewed, thinking seriously about her husband's military occupation for what it actually had been: part of a huge American Air Corps that had suffered horrendous losses to keep her world free. His Bomb Wing and Squadron were tasked with bombing Nazi Germany into submission. During those long days of his absence, Susan read everything she could on what Stephen might be doing on a particular day of flying. She had seen a picture in *Look* magazine of planes like the one he flew, picked one of them as his plane, and then scissored it out of the picture. It was that very plane she would tack onto her bulletin board to sequester it completely out of its context of danger. In so doing, she could keep him safe—somehow. It was denial, but it had worked for her.

She had yet to take that immense mental leap from calling what she thought her husband had been doing, *flying,* to the cold realization that Stephen's squadron alone had bombed and killed hundreds, perhaps thousands of people: German soldiers, perhaps their families, the aged, the sick, mothers and their children and infants. He had participated in destroying their homes and livelihoods, not once but multiple times, and at the risk of his own life, every time he left the ground. He, and countless Allied men like him, had given everything they had to destroy the German war machine, its people, and the infrastructure so critical to its success.

This process of recognition would require more time for Susan as well as her husband. They both had miles to go before they thought about the past on the same wavelength. Flying was all she really wished to know about those days—and that Stephen was incapable of leaving the war over there. Stephen had been a bomber pilot. Bomber pilots drop bombs and bombs kill people and destroy things.

Isle Pierre Road broke off of 16, then the sign for the Norman Lake Road, one mile ahead came into view. Stephen gave Susan no advanced warning, "The exit is coming up. You better slow down." Susan had to bite her tongue not to respond. Breakfast had tasted cold sitting across from a seemingly unemotional husband at the hotel restaurant. Her success rate with Stephen was becoming abysmal.

He really didn't care if Susan turned at the exit or not. She could keep driving until they drove off the edge of the earth for all he really cared. Into this second day of travel, Susan didn't know how long they had sat so distantly close. Hardly ten words had passed between them, and if Stephen hadn't pointed out the turn to her, she would have missed it. Well, he *was* paying attention even if he didn't appear to be.

Susan slowed the car, irritated at her husband's thoughtlessness to say, "Why didn't you tell me it was right here?"

"Sorry."

"Sorry? Stephen, if you don't start talking to me, so help me . . ." Susan had to bite her lip again from saying something they'd both regret, and her heart beat quickly from the sudden rise in her emotional energy. On and on Norman Lake Road continued, no signs of any other roads manifested themselves. And then, "Take a right here."

"*Here?* Stephen, it looks as if this road doesn't go *anywhere!*"

"It does. Just turn and drive."

Gritting her teeth, Susan turned on to the one lane, rough dirt road heading west. The tops of the tall pines on either side of the rutted and graveled passage waved in the stiff wind. Each registered its protests against the strong winds aloft, their dark green needles and bark colored pinecones holding on tightly. Clouds had chased the sun into hiding several days previous to their arrival, pouring gloom onto what Susan anticipated might prove a better day.

To make things worse, a cold rain began to fall, and its addition to the atmosphere inside the rented Cadillac caused a chill to run the length of Susan's back. She turned on the wipers. The sound of wind and rain, tires on muddy gravel, and the steady swishing of rubber on glass invaded the Stephen-imposed silence.

This "road" meandered for several more miles. The huge pines on either side of the road created a cavern like canyon through which the car passed. Susan finally rolled her window down just a bit inviting the living freshness to invade the interior of the car, where it amplified and caressed the growing need within her. The road began to wind slowly to the left, and there, as Susan navigated the turn, an immense fenced pasture spread before them. At about her two o'clock position, a massive log cabin protruded, surrounded by an innumerable army of pines standing majestically in formation, each tree placed perfectly next to his fellows. Heavy moist gray clouds had already begun to descend upon the structure, and within minutes the building lay partially concealed. A long, rumbling boom of thunder echoed in and among the dense packed tree covered hills and slopes.

"Is *that* the *cabin*?" Susan asked, adjusting her posture in her seat. "It's huge! O Stephen, this is gorgeous. You never told me . . ." She wanted to say it took her breath away, but refrained.

Stephen didn't acknowledge or bother to share her discovery. With the forest on their left and the fenced range spreading outward for more than a mile on their right, fat cattle grazed in ankle deep grass, dotted with yellow and blue flowers. The Lloyd's owned several thousand acres, much of it grassland sufficient for many more head than were visible.

From some untrammeled place within her, Susan sensed the ache of hope, despite the past hours of Stephen's silence, despite the glorious mountains she couldn't enjoy because of her mental state, and despite her misgivings of leaving the children. How utterly unexpected and welcomed was this trespass. Perhaps hope does spring eternal, as melodramatic as it sounded and felt. Would this view of the sky and expansive land, green and fertile, and so at peace with itself serve to quell the legion of concerns that had constructed a suitable living space within her? She hung to the remoteness of hope and warmth, faint as these felt.

Still, she could let Stephen out at the cabin, fully in view now, and drive off. She could, but she might not. If that contemptible thought—leaving her husband at the side of the road—had invaded her once, it had tapped on the glass pane of her mind a hundred times in flight, and then periodically on the road north. In Stephen's reticence to talk to her, as all women need to talk and be held in meaningful conversation, she also prayed for time to think about many things, about her wedding vows, "in sickness and in health . . ." She could think about life without him, if it came to that, but Susan dismissed such thoughts out of hand. She took her vows seriously . . . *until lately*.

In the final analysis, there was no life without this man, but there surely hadn't been much lately *with* him. She would muse over his ranging sensitivities and care when she needed him, such as when the babies wouldn't come, because they had never really formed inside of her. He had brought her flowers on the anniversary of each death—three reminders each year. How caring, how thoughtful he was. He had been there for her—always. And when the babies did finally come, he shared the diaper changes, the very early morning feeding times, the colic, the measles, Michael's broken finger, Margaret's first boyfriend and her tumultuous breakup, David's hamster that died and the somber burial in the backyard, complete with wooden cross, and the vacations with all the laughter and good times . . . all those wonderful years together she would remember and treasure again. Stephen was one man in a million, one of a kind. He was. This would pass. It had to.

More disturbing questions would challenge her to tiptoe slowly but perceptively back through the years of their marriage. *Had there been any warning signs of this? Had there?* Yes—the times he'd leave for Smitty's. She'd covered this. *Did that count though?* He hadn't gone far, but he stayed out of her sight for days. And Stephen never talked about what happened in Europe, so she couldn't or didn't feel the need to try to connect with all that. She'd found him many times just standing out in the yard, alone. She could see him shaking his head and talking, but to whom? She didn't like his impatience over . . . *over what?* Over lots of things, or was she being fair to him? Yes, well . . . probably not. There must have been other signs she'd missed completely. She walked in on Stephen crying on the phone years ago when she heard that someone he flew with had died—no, he committed suicide. That's right. She'd left him to that, alone. She didn't want to hear about it. How insensitive of her it was. Her work was cut out for her.

Stephen's complete silence about the war was a sign, wasn't it? And he avoided the reunions. What else had she missed? She had lived her life absolutely blind to what he kept from her. *Why?* She hadn't wanted the carefully constructed order of her life upset. But it had been of late, and she knew she was now fighting for the survival of that life.

Stephen's tranquility was also in disarray. These issues led her in two separate directions. Why had she been so blind, and why had he kept it all from her? Now, she was going to have to face those questions, and she worried equally that he might not participate. God, she loved this man . . . *in sickness and in health. Susan, do you take this man to be your lawfully wedded husband—? Do I still take this man? But he has so much pain we both have to deal with. The whole dynamic of our relationship has changed. Hasn't it? I have to own up to what this means. I have to. I can't duck this. I too pushed aside or was able to come to grips with my own miscarriages so many years ago as the case may be. But I still hurt when I think about losing my babies, my poor babies. Now the war Stephen had left 'way over there' so long ago is right here for both of us to deal with. I have to look at this war. But I'm so scared. God, do you hear me? Are you still angry with me? I'm so alone. What does all of this mean? That's what Dr. Inhofe had been probing for weeks. Do I still need Stephen? Does he need me? Stephen isn't the only one who needs space and time to think.*

Twenty-Eight:
Mary Ellen's Need

>━┼━◀▶━•━◉━•━◀▶━┼━◁

Friday, May 12, 1967

"Can we go visit Damien today, James? I want to place fresh flowers on his grave." Mary Ellen's need to be near her son overwhelmed her. He was there waiting for her. James wasn't certain how long reality would take. Mary Ellen was the most sensible woman he'd ever known, not that he'd known many. When he could put his math and science down long enough, he might become agitated at her stint in unreality. He'd give her more time, although he had no real choice.

James put his paper down and looked up at his wife, still in her bathrobe and slippers. He said nothing. Mary Ellen wondered at the unopened missive from her brother-in-law. "You haven't opened the letter from Judah. How come? You know he means well," she said.

"Yes. I know that he means well, but I . . . I can't answer what I know he wants me to say. He wants to hear that I'm doing just ducky. He's going to say to me, 'How are y'all doin'? James, are y'all buckin' up?' I'll answer it. I will. Just not today."

"All right. I won't push you." Mary Ellen came over and sat in her husband's lap. She laid her head on his sturdy shoulders and put her arms around his big neck. He smelled good in the morning. For reasons that Mary Ellen need not understand at the moment, she began to cry, slowly at first. Her sorrow had been building again over the last few days, and this morning she expressed it by the size and number of her tears. Her inner turmoil turned to torrents within minutes. "I miss him so much, James," she whispered in exhausted tones.

James believed he had cried enough. His life had felt flat too long. Today, he wasn't going to lose his way. He'd said good-bye to his son. He was proud of Damien. He was going to buck up. He didn't question this strengthening of his inner man by the Spirit of God. He wasn't forgetting or getting over it, because some of the folks in his church had urged him to show God's victory. However, any positive inertia on his part felt foreign, it had been so long since that old absentmindedness articulated itself, thankfully. Mary Ellen's and his colleagues evaluation of him, simply did not register with James nor did they gain a toehold about his mind.

"Mary Ellen!" James raised his voice in expectation as he lifted her from his lap. He strode into his office, sat at his oak desk, opened a file drawer, retrieved a piece of paper and pencil and he began to write furiously.

"What?" she responded, drying her tears as she followed him into his office.

"Mary Ellen, if I square the medium, put that over one half, carry the—"

"James, what on earth are you talking about? *No*, James. *No*! Now you put that away."

His protest met her own with equal vitality. "I've been working on this equation for months for NASA, and the way to the solution jumped out and bit me just now. Why didn't I see it before!?"

"James Wilson. *Don't* you dare leave me alone today. Do you hear me? You still have some time off coming. And we're going to go out and decorate Damien's grave. Are you listening to me?" She of course knew he was not, so she headed into the bedroom to change clothes. James Wilson was going to the cemetery whether he liked it or not.

"Sure thing, Mary Ellen. If I can figure out how to . . . Hon, this won't take me but a minute. I have to run with this while it's still fresh. I'll be right back," he called over his shoulder to his retreating wife, the final two words almost unrecognizable. Mary Ellen knew what he just said.

"*James*! Ja . . . mes!" she screamed from the middle of the closet. It was no use. She had lost him—again. She'd had to share him with numbers and concepts all their married life. But Mary Ellen wasn't crying anymore. She'd suddenly focused on the old James so quickly that she didn't realize his climb out of the "slough of despond," as John Bunyan had described it in his great work, *Pilgrim's Progress*. James had brought her out as well. Somehow the Cross was tied in to this moment just passed. Mary Ellen felt lighter, less encumbered, but she couldn't quite connect her husband's part in it. She missed her son . . . missed him in the worst possible way. But now, now it would be all right. She got a chill. The *Cross*!

Mentally occupied with this divine intervention, Mary Ellen walked down the hall, and without thinking, started to say something as if Damien was in his room and she wanted him to take out the trash or come and hang up his coat. It was an unconscious exercise she'd performed a thousand times. She halted short when she realized that it was not her son there laboring diligently over some problem so far beyond the calculus she'd taken in college. She was about two feet into the room before Mary Ellen Wilson grasped that this room wasn't Damien's room any longer. She knew it now, fully and thoroughly. It was the strangest feeling. She had almost called his name, expecting him to answer her. Her mind had said, *'Damien,'* but the words wouldn't form in her mouth.

James looked up from the problem he was well on his way to solving, but she could tell he was too mentally distant to grasp her slightly altered position in the universe. Mary Ellen capped her mouth with her hand in moribund surprise, her disappointed joy thorough. James was busy tapping and rubbing numbers from the white chalk against the dark board—he'd moved to the board from his desk—to realize what had just happened to his wife. It felt so natural to Mary Ellen to walk down the hall and find her son lying on his bed reading or talking on the phone. What didn't feel natural at that instant was finding her husband occupying Damien's room, standing in front of a chalk board, books crammed in every available space, on every shelf, a large desk cluttered with papers and chalk dust, dried mud on the carpet that he had no idea he'd brought in on his shoes. A half-eaten sandwich from "who-knew-when" lay on a paper plate. An empty Coke bottle was also half buried under the papers.

Mary Ellen had bought a plant three weeks before especially for his desk in memory of Damien. It was now dead. He'd not even thought about watering it. He didn't know it was there. It didn't matter that he was going through grief himself. He'd have let it die anyway and been surprised when Mary Ellen pointed out that it needed watering. Her better judgment told her not to buy it. Brown leaves hung limp from its dead branches. Several had fallen off and were crushed by his inability to recognize their presence. "Yes, Hon? I'm almost finished here. Just a few more minutes." Dr. Wilson turned back to his first love, the marks on a board.

She turned and walked back into the kitchen, the place she felt most at home. If she were to get to the cemetery Betty would have to take her, and she was in no mood to drive there on her own. James was gone, as usual, but *now* it all would be okay.

It was now a good day; indeed, a fine day. Gravestones and markers spread before Mary Ellen as she walked toward a particular place she dreamed of at night. Betty trailed behind a few steps allowing her friend to draw within herself or do whatever it was she would do. Betty was there as an observer and friend. Finding the place, Mary Ellen laid the flowers, a dozen yellow roses, her favorite, next to the bronze marker. The St. Augustine had almost retaken the fresh gash in the ground made by the backhoe. On the marker, in raised lettering, Mary Ellen knelt to rub her finger along her son's name, then along his birth date. She halted for a long second at the death date as if to expunge it, if at all possible. Mary Ellen touched his branch of service, USMC, his place of service, VIETNAM, his year of service, 1967. Tears came afresh but not so terribly hard this day. She needed James, but he was in love with his numbers. Betty stepped over to lay a hand on her back, to steady her, and let her know she was there if Mary Ellen needed her. Mary Ellen just wanted to tell her son that she'd not forgotten him. It was a silly thought, a luxury she indulged, and one of the few to which Mary Ellen actually gave way.

The raised cross, quite unexpectedly, if not imperceptibly, imbedded but raised on the head marker drew her attention away from her sorrow. She had seen crosses all her life, in churches, on tombstones, in books, and in pictures. Today, it came to have a fuller meaning than it ever had. The meaning of the Gospel itself stared up at her through those two short perpendicular lines. It was hard to explain. Until now, this very minute, it had been a *symbol* of Easter. Looking down at it, she sensed the substance of its work. Oh, it was inspiring to be sure. Something was different about Mary Ellen when she stood. Damien wasn't dead, in the true sense of the word.

Twenty-Nine: Quill Du Pont

Friday, May 12, 1967

Mr. Quill Du Pont, the "cabin's" caretaker, stood on the steps at the conclusion of the long driveway. He held an umbrella in one hand and leaned on a cane with the other, waiting for the car to stop so he could greet his guests. Amid the large droplets splashing on the windshield and car body, Susan noted that he was a slight man, almost fragile. Despite his physical appearance, an inner smiling glow shone from within his soul. How odd these two, the physical and the non-corporeal commingled. Susan took heart from the whole of his reception. When the passenger door opened, he welcomed his old friend and employer, extending to him an umbrella to ward off the weather, which Stephen declined. Quill made note of his boss, understood immediately *what* stood before him, that pandering to Stephen would only agitate him. So, Quill limped around to the driver's side to introduce himself to Susan as she exited the vehicle.

He was a lovely man, she thought, trying to gather an unobstructed view of the caretaker as his umbrella moved about his head. Susan was drawn to him—to his warm, easy charm.

"Susan, you're more beautiful than your pictures. Lovely pearls you're wearing. My Emily loved pearls. She would have liked you, I think." The old man winked. His smile was wide and generous. Susan pulled the sweater over her shoulders. She'd worn a sundress from Texas, not thinking clearly about the weather in Canada whilst trying to see to all the last minute details. Susan had not thought lucidly about too many things lately. Now she began to concern herself about the clothes she had packed. Stephen gave no suggestions.

"Why, thank you." She rubbed against his compliments like a cat against its owner's trouser leg. *Hang the clothes*, she thought. Stephen's sullen mood had left her famished for attention, male or otherwise. Quill's kind, tangible words renewed her with the sense that everyone or everything wasn't lost, silent, and angry.

Mr. Du Pont lived in the small cabin one hundred yards up the hill and almost directly behind the main lodge, which the pines and fog currently hid from view. A golf car made life so much easier for Quill these days. Susan would spend some time talking to this diminutive male specimen if Stephen didn't oblige her, and fairly soon. As she looked about this immense and glorious country, Susan decided she might just stay after all. Marcus had phoned ahead as he said he would to have Quill make the preparations for the two guests. Marcus also informed him of Stephen's condition and the purpose of this visit. Their stay would be—indefinite.

Quill Du Pont had been widowed several years, and thus he welcomed his old friend, whom, he could tell, was presently struggling with the inner demon about which Marcus had spoken. Stephen's dull eyes registered volumes. Mr. Du Pont, all seventy-three years of him, had seen plenty of pain in his life. His often tumultuous troubles didn't alter his affection for the Lloyd's, over whose northern assets Quill had kept yearly vigil since 1928, minus his military hiatus from December 1941 to the conclusion of the war with Japan, in 1945. The old man loved the gracious solitude of Canada, his birthplace, with its unparalleled beauty. But with Emily's death there was an emptiness in his Canada. He missed Emily, his bride of fifty-seven years, far more than he could say. She'd died three years before from cancer. These days, Quill cherished the moments when the few sporadic guests came for a visit— even if it was the Lloyd's home. He missed talking to a woman.

"Come, Susan. Let me show you the place." Quill held his elbow out for Susan to take. The old man paused, then turning to face Stephen, he spoke from his own inner strength, saying, "Stephen, Roger will get the bags and drive the car around. Right now I want to show the place off to your Missy here. You need to come with us and get out of the rain." Mr. Du Pont winked once more at Susan, who smiled out of sheer desperation to alleviate her sadness and take upon her countenance something other than worry. Quill thought she might be even more beautiful when she wasn't so anxious, like she was.

Stephen gave a subtle hint that Quill's words had in fact agitated him. Susan matched his slow, measured pace to accommodate Quill's hobbling disability. Stephen stood for a few more minutes as their left behind "orphan," plodded along twenty or so yards behind this odd couple, getting himself wetter by the minute. He followed in the aimless fog of his delayed post-battle fatigue—that's what the doctor had called it.

The rain, coming much steadier now, pelted the umbrella, and Susan huddled close to her new friend. Even in the rain she smelled his age, camouflaged somewhat by his Old Spice. His dress attested to the fact that he was probably not the launderer Emily had been. With each step Stephen took, up felt down and down seemed twisted sideways. This place he loved so much as a younger man bore in on him, perhaps more so than Texas had. Susan's composure, as it came into near proximity of the old man's serenity, threatened to crumble almost to the breaking point. How could she possibly allow Quill to see her let go of her burdens right in front of him? She'd just met him. Susan, simply put, felt that she had to shoulder harder against this.

Stephen's austere silence left him in a sort of self-imposed exile. His callous disregard for everything, including his soggy discomfort, didn't cease with the downpour. His inner rage urged him to walk slower, to absorb more rain, so that when he reached the front porch, his saturated clothes, like his depression and mislaid self, drooped about him, dripping and arctic. Susan refused to embrace the misery that looking behind her would bring as her escort and she climbed the steps up to the large porch. She had so little to give to rectify it. If she looked back, she would lose what composure she had managed to salvage from the driveway to the cabin. This ascension to the lodge bred life, and Susan reveled in leaving her passenger to look after himself for a few minutes.

The front porch, as sturdy as the pines from which it was hewn and shaped, was an elixir. Something solid held her upright. Quill shook the umbrella and folded it. He then pulled back the screen door and depressed the latch handle. Pushing against the heavy pine door, he opened it and set the umbrella in the holder with the other umbrellas.

Holding the door open, Susan stepped into a cathedral splendor and elegance of massive proportions. Quill didn't introduce the various aspects of the Lloyd's northern home to Susan; the cabin introduced itself to her.

"This used to be a much smaller hay barn back in the late twenties. The man who owned it had some bad debts he couldn't pay off. When your father-in-law found out about it, he bought it, along with the five hundred acres. It wasn't until about 1934, smack dab in the depression that Mr. Lloyd began to slowly fix it up. He started the additions in . . . '36, was it? We built the last bedroom in 1949."

To the left, the fireplace gave off a welcoming glow with its clement salutation. Quill flipped on the wall switch and the room, if it could be called such, came alive, like a gargantuan thing extending itself to reveal its sumptuous resplendency. A magnificent crystal chandelier hung suspended some thirty feet from the corpulent center beam, the circumference of both the beam and chandelier that hung from it, she could only guess. Its light cast a pleasurable radiance about; a warm yellow glow illuminated the hall's warehouse dimensions. The luscious smell of smooth, yellowed and tanned pine log walls hung heavy about her. Susan felt almost like whispering. After several delightful moments, she finally murmured, "*Oh, my*, Mr. Du Pont . . . *I—*"

"Oh no, Susan. Just call me Quill."

"What?" The woman couldn't take her eyes and mind off of the size of this room. Susan still wanted to whisper.

"Call me Quill." The old man loved to watch his guests take in all in.

Susan's eyes followed the walls up, up, up to the full height of the log ceiling, some fifty feet above her. Five round beams, each immense in their individual size and perhaps fifty feet long held the cabin's frame together. Twenty feet, perhaps more, Susan calculated, separated support beam from support beam over her head. Fifty antelope heads, forty-two deer heads, numerous game birds, many with their wings extended as if in flight, headless antlers galore and several bear heads decorated the walls. One head must have been a grizzly; it was enormous and menacing, its mouth wide in mid growl revealing large, apical white teeth. There were twelve moose heads, all resplendent with the type of antlers curious to that species of mammal. Dispersed among the wild game heads were mounted trophy game fish of various types: brook, rainbow, lake, brown, bull trout, kokanee, yellow perch, pink, chinook, sockeye salmon, whitefish, a dolly varden, many with their mouths opened wide as if to bite a Kit-A-Mat, a Gibbs, or some other type of artificial lure.

Yet it wasn't a barn, this—this living *thing*—was *the* common room. It's magnitudinous dimensions absorbed her. She felt insignificant, a mere miniature amid giants. Perhaps, if she'd been prepared for this, Susan might also have spread her troubles about her so that each one could be observed from the perspective that this room brought all things for judgment. Curious, but she felt momentarily reluctant to consider all the disparaging particulars that had accompanied her here. The opportunity to do so had not passed, but she would muse over them later, not now.

The dome so high overhead deadened the rain that had accompanied them. It was as if it was raining in Montana. What sounds she could hear coming from the open door interjected a soothing pattered rhythm into the glorious circumstance and sanctuary Susan had entered. Stephen had still not come in. She bit her bottom lip, trying not to suggest, pry or, worse, to needle him. She did nothing.

Standing as if alone for those few, odd minutes, and except for the busy fire, Susan drank in and was absorbed by the tranquility and immensity, the stillness of this wonderful oasis. Sanguine inertia radiated outward among these logs, for that was the intent of this recalibrated architecture, quite vigorous enough to ease her hurt the way all things pleasant and enormous have the potential to ease unpleasantries. It took a full quarter hour, but the weariness in her mind and heart palpitated composure. Those rays of hope that had abandoned her in Texas bled slowly into her soul once more. The pressure that squeezed at her face lessened.

Susan hugged herself, closed her eyes, and breathed deeply. Quill continued watching her from near the door. He thought of how pretty she was. The aromatic smell of coffee, brewing the past twenty minutes wafted in front of her nose. This delicious smell homogenized with the wood, and the possibilities, like this grand place, felt limitless. Susan ventured a few steps further from this sudden surge of strength that dared her to become part of the room, part of the living, once more.

"Coffee, Susan?" His was an ancient voice whose tone and words dispersed oddly amid the room. He requested permission to serve her.

Quill's words did not echo, nor did they die. They simply evaporated, not from lack of resolve, but from . . . the size and distance.

"Oh, yes. Please. I'd *love* some." Her words exited less like escaping things and more like living things; her spirit was being renewed. But then, and against her wishes or resolve, several unpleasantries caught up to her from yesterday's long drive and this morning's vexing, though shorter, trip from Prince George. Stephen was one of those unpleasantries, and it felt awful. She turned back toward the open screen door and spoke to the man she had left sitting on the porch and out of her sight. "Stephen, please come in and get out of those wet things." As suddenly as the glory came, it bled off.

Hearing no answer, Susan repeated her request, once more to no avail. It wasn't that Quill Du Pont didn't know about this issue that had come his way, or that he didn't care about Stephen. To the contrary, Quill had to deal with this particular issue all his life, but always from the inside looking out. The old man said nothing as he disappeared into the kitchen, prepared the coffee, and returned with two large mugs.

"Marcus said you like yours black, with a spoon of sugar. Am I right?"

"Yes. Thank you."

Quill handed Susan a rather large coffee cup with the Texas A&M logo on it, noting her delighted surprise, —Susan still needed to touch her Texas roots, where her children were. As he leaned toward his guest, Quill added, "He'll be all right." Quill said this nodding in Stephen's direction. Once more he winked. Susan had begun to live and die with his thoughtfulness and charming regard for her.

"Thank you, Mr. Du Pont."

"Quill. Just call me Quill. I'm so sharp, you understand." She sighed deeply, missing his attempt at humor, but not her husband's lack of it. "But we do need to get him in here so he doesn't catch his death."

"Thank you, Quill." Susan stopped attempting to hide her moist and anguished eyes from the old man, not that she could. It took too much energy to suppress her fears that her husband was suffering, and that her life was in the throes of spinning out of control. Susan felt so incapable of bringing any of it to some acceptable resolution. Lately, she'd awakened with this mysterious dark *thing*, worked at avoiding it all day, and then went to sleep feeling herself a failure. Susan held her mug with both hands, at the very least to absorb its warmth, and at most, to have something of home to steady her nerves. Susan hadn't realized until she held the cup that she was shaking.

The old man limped over to the door, opened it and stepped onto the porch and Stephen. He said something to her husband Susan couldn't make out, at which point, Stephen rose and followed Quill inside, through grand hall, and toward the stairs to the bedrooms. Quill returned to his female company alone.

"He's all right." His calm amazed Susan.

Quill sipped from his own mug, waiting and evaluating, as he leaned on his cane. He was more of a tea drinker. He knew the massive structure had so much more to speak to his guest. For the next long minutes his passivity welcomed Susan to the world he lived and breathed. Susan was one of only three women that had ever come here—Emily, Annika, back in 1934 and again in '39, and now Susan Lloyd. He knew much more about Susan than he let on. He perceived, for instance, that she longed to be free, not only from these obvious burdens, but also from the ones that she hadn't yet come to recognize. The years had shown Quill the wisdom in permitting his hurting guests to feel their way along. The questions and the answers would come in their own good moment.

After a few more sips, a delectable sensation swirled about Susan with what seemed to infuse within her even more of a renewed vigor. This inner awareness enabled Susan to at least believe that an attempt to come to terms with her life was possible. Thus, she ventured a more judicious observation, or, as a woman, a subjective critique of the room. She began with the almost six foot tall Frederic Remington bronze. Its prominence was almost breathtaking as Quill flipped the spot light switch illuminating four male riders sitting atop their mounts waving pistols in the air, the quartet hell bent for leather. It was entitled, *Coming Through The Rye*. She, like all the guests, had to touch it, to test it.

Then there was the furniture: the two main couches with accompanying chairs, which Marcus had strategically spread over what must be a half-acre of living space. Susan wanted to ask Quill the room's dimensions, because she was starting to feel more at ease. In spite of this, she didn't want to interrupt the room's life with her own frivolous chitchat.

Each chair or couch, unusually large and overstuffed, matched this room. Men had obviously built these for other men to enjoy, the comfort and size perfect for resting tired bodies that had hiked the hills in search of elusive deer, or waded the frigid streams and lakes to pull the big ones out to give something to Jacques, the on-site chef, to barbecue or pan fry. Jacques was without equal when it came to trout, or anything else for that matter. The French Canadian had yet to appear.

Separating the many opposite facing sofas were equally large and accommodating coffee tables. Resting heavily in the centers were other, smaller Remington bronzes. The one closest was *A Moment of Great Peril.* The bronze depicted an angry bull attacking a rider and his horse. Various current and outdated magazines: *Field and Stream, Argosy, The Hunter's Almanac,* and other masculine titles Susan didn't recognize or desire to pick up and peruse lay strewn about the table's surfaces. She saw no copies of *Better Homes and Gardens,* but she expected none. Covering the floor under this nearest coffee table was a full reddish brown bearskin rug; the head faced outward, and its mouth wide with teeth, ferocious and menacing. Susan counted seven other secluded, but smaller living areas. The furniture, consisting of four or five chairs, was equally extravagant and arranged symmetrically around coffee tables in each separate area. An animal skin of some sort lay under the tables of each ensemble.

Built about three quarters the length along the north wall, perhaps thirty feet long, stood a glossy, imported mahogany wet bar—from Italy, with a four-foot high mirror behind it, running the whole of its span. If Susan closed her eyes, she just knew she could imagine Doc or Chester or Miss Kitty, perhaps even Matt Dillon from *Gunsmoke,* maybe Paladin from *Have Gun, Will Travel,* Hopalong Cassidy, Roy Rogers, Tom Mix, Gabby Hayes, Gene Autry, maybe even the Duke, leaning against the rail, a piano player tickling the ivories.

The mirror behind the bar made the already huge room appear even more grandiose, and a gold plated foot rail ran along its base. This "monstrosity," as Annika had called it, had been built for the consumption of libations that would surely follow a strenuous days outing. On the counter beneath the mirror stood numerous varied bottles of imported whiskeys, bourbons, vodkas, rums and gins. The wine cellar Susan hadn't yet seen in the spacious, temperature controlled basement was equally well stocked with domestic and imported wines purchased from Marcus's travels in America and Europe. Perhaps three hundred hunters or sportsmen could occupy the sum of this room and still there would be plenty of space without feeling crowded. The most that had ever visited the "old place" at any given time numbered seventy-three. A staircase ascended diagonally behind the bar, which intentionally hid it from view. No one came north of the Canadian border without the appropriate invitation.

Conspicuous by their absence, Susan saw no toys, no ball and bat, no dolls, no board games with their pieces and play money, no idle adolescent messes, and *no* television. That one-eyed monster was truant by design, for which she was most thankful. There were no frills whatsoever, no plants, hanging or otherwise, to be watered, only the necessities mandatory for the specially invited male population who temporarily sheltered here during the summer months. In terms of practicality, Susan felt that there was so much wasted space. But in terms of her pressing needs—the one's with which she'd entered, maybe it wasn't large enough.

A welcomed lightness swept over her, and she felt her pressure equalized. Breathing the delight of it all, Susan noticed the second floor. "Quill, there's a whole second floor up there," she announced, once more thoroughly amazed, her mouth agape. Midway up the west wall, some twenty-five feet above the bar, the semi-exposed second floor commixed with its surroundings, and this discovery beckoned to her. On that level, all nine bedrooms, each with its own bath, lay unseen and unused for the last seven months. An attendant railing gated off the upper balcony over which one could lean to gaze down upon the imaginary guests mingling below. The banister sequestered the sometimes-tipsy habitué and friends from landing kersplat onto the unforgiving bar or the smooth pine floor below. Conversations, either from high above or down below, were muted from uninvited ears. Raised voices, shameful nuisances, ribald humor, were rarely out of place in this sanctuary of masculinity.

Imperceptible at the stair's conclusion, perhaps due to the lighting and time of day, a second, less comprehensive sitting room than the one in which Susan stood, had so often invited the enthusiasts to dawdle in the multi-volumed library, an eclectically diverse collection of books or simply for more intimate conversations. There was also a second, smaller wet bar Susan would discover there. Perhaps the most disturbing thing to her was how much she failed to observe of her immediate surroundings upon her entry. Her burdens had obtruded upon her visual intake.

This was a man's world into which she had now transgressed. A woman's touch, frilly draperies, cream colored doilies, mute-hued cushions, other feminine amenities and peculiarities, were as conspicuously absent as the children's things had been on the main level. Built into the being and openness of this structure was an invitation for the owner and his guests to visit, relax, let-go, and enjoy. With the ingestion of this world came inner calm that always repulsed the cares that the Lloyd men usually brought with them from so far below the Canadian border.

Susan had heard many times about this northern hideaway of Marcus' and Stephen's all her married life. But its secluded beauty, welcome, and manliness had to be experienced to understand why the men relished coming here—without their women. Thus, standing in the midst of this seductive wellhead where failed business mergers were finally counted as loss, and successes were lauded and soon discarded or built upon. From all of this, she drank deeply. Susan looked once more into the expressionless eyes of the deer and moose heads, the birds that simulated flight, but would never quite achieve, and the fish that feigned attacking their prey. She thought about how their troubles had long since ended. A large picture window had been built into the wall behind her, facing west, revealing the open range where the one hundred fifty or so head of cattle they had passed an hour before, or was it longer, roamed at leisure.

Susan felt a sudden chill come over her, despite the sweater draped over her shoulders. The warmth from the oversized fireplace invited her to draw closer. As she approached the crackling, hissing, orange-blue-green of the flames, Susan was quite unexpectedly put in mind of Daphne Du Maurier's book *Rebecca*. Her eyes darted about as she saw it all—*a bit melodramatic*, she thought. Yes, but wonderfully so. The whole edifice invited her to become melodramatic.

"Quill, have you ever read the book, *Rebecca*, Daphne Du Maurier's novel?"

"*Rebecca*? No. Can't say I have. Why?" Quill wondered where she could be going with this question.

"I was . . . I was thinking about it, just now. It was as if I could see Maxim De Winter, he was the main character, standing right here where I am. In the book, the scene I'm particularly thinking about, Miss Du Maurier describes a large grated fireplace like this one." Susan spoke into the fire, not turning to face Quill. She enjoyed immensely being lost in this glorious room with her cozy remembrance of that wonderful novel, not to mention the warm fire. "I loved the story. Mr. Hitchcock made it vibrant and alive for me in his movie, *Rebecca.*" She turned to face Quill who was leaning on his cane.

He'd stood too long. But her thoughts forbid her from squandering the present glory. Her cravings were selfish and felt that way too. "Do you mind if I sit?" Quill asked. Several oversized chairs had been arranged not distant from the fireplace for just such a need.

"Oh, *I'm* so sorry. I . . . I've been so selfish." She flushed red, felt the embarrassment of looking after her own main concern, which, of course she was. "No. Forgive me. I was lost in the moment. It felt wonderful, too."

"Good. So, what about this book, *Rebecca?*" he exhaled.

Susan hadn't really expected Quill to allow her musings to take flight or to entertain any actual interest in them. In spite of the book, she began to wonder after Stephen. "Is he okay?" Interestingly, she did not pursue this diversion, this immediate interest, or climb the many steps up to the second floor and go in search of her husband. Selfish indeed.

"He's fine," Quill said assuringly. "He's been here many times. When you are settled in, we'll talk. Right now, I'll venture he's exhausted. It's so hard to fight what he's been fighting without it wearing a body and mind completely out."

"And you know this *how?*" she probed.

"Oh, I know."

A pregnant silence lingered, then, assured as she could be that Stephen was . . . that he was safe, Susan returned to the story, permitting her thoughts to leap ahead of her words to her exact but unknown destination—the fireplace—before which she stood, and once more she was drawn in to that earlier moment, even before that, to when Max introduced his new bride, the second Mrs. de Winter, to the staff in charge of looking after Manderley, her new home. Manderley was a gargantuan house standing in the English countryside of Cornwall.

It was replete with east and west wings, a huge open hall connecting them, where the fancy dress balls of the past took place attended by the surrounding city dwellers and tenant farmers, anyone and everyone. And not so very unlike the one in which Susan now stood, but for the flagged stone of Britain's Cornwall region cut to form the structure and soul of the house rather than these large, sturdy pine logs, did Manderley exist.

Quill could barely keep up with her intricate twists and plots, speaking as if she were there that moment, but on her guard for Mrs. Danvers. Susan realized however, that she had left Quill with too many disparate details to make heads or tails of this "story." Susan spoke of the Manderley staff: Frith, the butler, each of the servants, men and women of lesser English rank charged with the care and upkeep of the house.

The shadowy, slight contours of this black widow named Danny Danvers had become the perfect foil for Du Maurier's readers: the whole of the woman's small, round face, her bottomless eyes, arched brows, her diminutive, round mouth framed by thin lips, the hump on her nose, her icy, killing words, the death black dress, and the woman's petite hands, so proper, clasped at her stomach. Mrs. Danvers! Yes. This thing—this stressor that stood in the way of Susan and Stephen's happiness—now materialized. The actress, Judith Anderson, *was* Mrs. Danvers. And Mrs. Danvers was real. She wasn't a metaphor. She wasn't a character in a novel to be discarded when one put down the book to look after one's other duties. Danny was here, albeit in another form. Oh, but she was here.

Then, turning to face Quill, her eyes wide and awake, Susan took up her story in earnest. "In the novel, Mrs. Danvers set about destroying any possibility of love Maxim might find with his new wife. To horrible old 'Danny,' this *new* Rebecca was an impostor, an interloper, someone she had to destroy. And if she could dispatch the latest copy of her former mistress, Rebecca, then Maxim could be had, too, for bringing the fraud.

The real Rebecca was somehow still alive, laughing at Maxim and at all the other men, even Crawley.

"Who's Crawley?" Quill interrupted.

"He's Maxim de Winter's best friend and manager of the estate," Susan answered. "Mrs. Danvers hated and terrified the new Mrs. de

Winter. If Danny couldn't keep Rebecca's memory alive at Manderley, no one would live there. I, too, feel so terrified of Mrs. Danvers." Susan's mug dropped to the wood floor, but didn't break. Quill bent down and attended to the dropped mug, which was fortunately empty. Looking back up at her, he said, "Susan. Susan, hold on. I'm lost here. Who's Mrs. Danvers?"

"Oh, I'm sorry, Quill. I'll explain the story to you when I feel like I have more of a handle on it."

"Okay. It sounded like a good, scary story to me. I like a good Hitchcock. Look, nobody's going to hurt you, Susan. Not here. You will love this place. I assure you."

Unsure what to say further, she exhaled timidly, "I hope so."

The Texas she had left so early the day before had been hot and muggy. Here, the world stood in wait for Susan: fresh, cool, and so compassionate in its embrace. Her own needs were as complex and seemingly insurmountable as the land and home in and on which she stood. Quill continued to permit his guest to absorb and to be absorbed by her surroundings, to invite it to take hold of her and consume her. It didn't disappoint, never did. He basked in this exact moment, when his guests took their initial awestruck, jaw dropping crash into the universe he oversaw. This brought him pleasure beyond words. But they didn't usually talk about someone named Mrs. Danvers, whoever she was. Seven months of the year, Mr. Quill Du Pont had exclusive and uninterrupted squatter's rights.

It would have been quite easy for Quill to leave Susan and Stephen to their problems, but Quill was not that sort of man. The glow Susan had observed streaming from Quill Du Pont's being would not permit such an exit. Susan felt as if a nap were in order before dinner.

Thirty: The Brooding Storm

>━┼◆>・O・‹◆┼━<

Friday, May 12, 1967

"Oh, you startled me," Susan blurted into the vast expanse of the room over which she stood gazing. Stephen's hand softly touched and then alighted on her shoulder. She turned to greet his smile, a welcomed relief after weeks of agitation and despair. The feel of his hand on her concerned her at first, and then she recognized its warm, familiar tenderness. His touch always had brought the sun out in her troubled moments.

"This is incredible, isn't it?"

Hmmm, Susan thought. The short nap Susan had taken reinvigorated her.

For Stephen, the 'thing' had just let go, and he was now freed to come near and stand there beside her. Stephen asked the question as he leaned over the rail to enjoy, with his wife, the wonder of such a place. Susan eyed her husband coyly, and then turned once more to resume her submersion into fascination with the room. "I'll be right back," he said. She didn't long for him to stand too close to her, neither did she delight in his abrupt absence. His nearness and restored mood left her conflicted, if not confused.

Stephen hurried over to the cabinet housing the record player, opened it, and filed through a stack of records. With great care he chose the ones he wanted, and slid several of the unpackaged LP's onto the spindle. Then he flipped the switch, and down dropped Tony Bennett's rendition of *Laura*. The mood turned to velvet, infusing something life giving and nutritious into both people. For all her troubles of late, immersed into the expanse of the cabin as she was now, Susan almost felt as she did the moment when they first kissed—*almost*. A dazzling excitement lifted her; raw romance surged within her replacing the other hurtful things, which she kept, for the moment, at arms length. Stephen would have to move closer in so many ways.

Stephen's return to the rail possessed his easy, carefree form, but his wife was so infernally conjectural as to how he could live a week in such a foul mood, and then, like Dr. Jekyll and Mr. Hyde, transform himself so utterly. He whispered in Susan's ear, "I'm so sorry for the past week. Dance with me?" He took her in his arms and moved her about the floor. A moment later, "Thank God, it finally let up."

She pushed back from Stephen. This question, her husband's dual personalities, nettled at her and she wanted some answers before she could enjoy this. Just an hour ago, Stephen sat, picked and brooded over the lavish dinner, resplendent with candles, music and wine. Stephen hardly took notice of her. Unfortunately, the meal was set before them later than Mr. Du Pont had ordered. Was that it?

"Stephen, did the meal being late make you so unpleasant? Was it because dinner was late?" Susan felt there was much more to this— *there had to be*. Jacques had often found himself at the receiving end of a disapproving scowl or a short paycheck, and a lecture from the old caretaker. But when his guests pushed back from the table to enjoy an after-dinner wine or Scotch, having let the day escape, the French Canadian had more than made up for his tardiness with meals that were fit for royalty.

"No," he offered. "The meal being late or early, didn't matter. I can't explain why I've been so angry lately. Something literally grabs me here," he pointed to his abdomen, "and squeezes me. If it doesn't let up, I stay angry. I can't make it stop. Sometimes you don't have to do anything and I'm either depressed or angry. Don't you believe me?"

"Stephen, there *has* to be more to it than that."

Her eyes filled, not only with tears from the life they had escaped below the Canadian border, but from the absence of Susan's familiar world. Susan was partially coming to terms with the possibility that her life, in some inexplicable way, had changed. This nebulous uncertainty left her with so many misgivings to sort through, and her Stephen lay at the heart of most of them. She had never cried so much in her life.

"There isn't," he said, resigned to the misunderstanding that had become part of their relationship. One of Stephen's best friends had lost a leg in the war flying fighters. His wife refused to acknowledge his artificial limb, would not look at it. They divorced not long after his return. His war, as all wars do, had killed more than bodies. It killed minds and families and marriages.

Stephen pulled Susan closer to him and led her around the library to the luscious rhythm and lyrics of Tony Bennett and Nelson Riddle's orchestra. She felt unfamiliarly awkward so near his body right then— he had been so remote and impossibly hard to touch and reach for too long now—distance started to feel normal. Yes, he had hurt her deeply. Sinatra followed Bennett and Rosemary Clooney followed Frank. Perhaps it was the wine, the music, or both. His smell and his strength helped her to ease closer against him, and they moved as one soul to Vernon Duke's, *Autumn in New York*. Stephen's magic was back if only for this moment, and this knowledge let her breathe somewhat less encumbered, despite the fatigue that had begun to reclaim her. Susan kept moving with Stephen as he led her about the upper floor, each commingling with the other. Mrs. Danvers had failed for the moment.

Quill and Jacques had long since departed the cabin for their homey accommodations up the hill. Susan once more relished the spaciousness of the library. It was surprisingly comfortable, and it fit well with her mood that began to thaw with the music and her man. The sum of the whole piney warehouse was theirs. By the time Frank intoned, *April in Paris*, Susan was snuggling and giggling, giddy with joy. The moment too, for however long it lasted, belonged to her . . . to them. She would take what he would give her in this fragile moment; and Stephen would take what she would give him tonight. Tomorrow, she would ask, and tomorrow—tomorrow, he *must* talk.

Saturday, May 13, 1967

Stephen's focus didn't arrive completely with the sun's first gladdening but pale, frosty blue rays. The sheer, manly fabric of two of the bedroom's large single windows filtered out most of the eastern Canadian sky. Slowly he came awake with what he hoped might lead to a better day than its predecessors. He didn't feel the pressure in his gut—a better sign to begin this day. The four tongue and grooved pine walls of the bedroom held several pictures, reproductions of Van Gogh's, *The Night Café*, Rembrandt's, *The Resurrection of Christ*, and Édouard Manet's, *Boating*. Above the bed hung Morisot's beautiful impressionistic work, *Young Girl by the Window*. At the foot of the bed stood a small table. On the tabletop sat an authentic Carl Kauba bronze of an intense looking Indian bedecked in full war bonnet headdress holding a rifle. The artist entitled it *War*.

Above the door hung a noble buck's head, the body of which Stephen had killed on his second hunt years ago. Dark eyes stared blankly into the space of the room, and its horns were curved and sharp like the many proud deer displayed on the walls of the main floor. Two large five-drawer antique dressers lined one wall. In the corner another overstuffed chair with accompanying lamp waited vacant and still, their intended purpose seldom fulfilled. The room had a large walk-in closet, the door of which hung slightly ajar this morning. The queen bed and night stands were the only other pieces in the room. On either side of the bed, a rug made from deerskin would greet bare feet instead of cold, smooth wood. Stephen had chosen this room because it was one of the several with a fireplace. Susan had wondered who the decorator was—probably Marcus. Nothing matched.

Blinking several times, Stephen caught sight of the clock—7:02. The second hand clicked the newest moment as if it were beating against some invisible foe . . . click, twenty-seven, click, twenty-eight, click, twenty-nine, click, thirty. Stephen saw the room clearly now. Without permission, his life jabbed against something harsh, refusing to manifest itself so he could at least see his opponent to protect himself . . . jab, thirty-one, jab, thirty-two, jab, thirty-three, jab, thirty-four. Not a good sign.

Something seemed amiss. What was it? He felt his stomach growl. His eyebrows squeezed together when he didn't smell the coffee brewing. He didn't smell bacon and eggs, which he expected to greet him. Without any coaxing, what wasn't happening on the floor below had become a newest agitation, and *this* became the fist tightening in his gut in this infant day.

"I pay that cook to make breakfast, not just dinner." There it was for Susan. Was it back? Oh God, she hoped not. *Please don't spoil this day too.*

Stephen's mind and body, with its needs and wants, protested against the swelling psychological knot. *Turn it off now or you can't stop it*, his mind barked at him. Stephen blinked hard as his jaw muscles tightened—today they felt sore—and from those first waking moments the battle within him was joined. *No. No! Not now! Not a repeat of yesterday and the day before, ditto and ditto again. It's too early.* He had no fight in him, not that he really fought his invisible adversary. He just got steamrolled and Susan caught the brunt of his brooding.

He turned quietly over to face his waking wife. Had she heard him just now? Maybe her beauty or nearness and the sweet love they'd shared hours ago could quell these demons come back to play. He lay there watching her, fighting, yet languorously hoping to savor the previous night's wonder, chemistry and heat, to smell her body again, to taste her, and to love her from where he lay. The morning's drowsy moments made this woman most appealing, the antagonist trying its best to put a damper on his desires and the day. In another minute, affection resonated from his sleeping wife that felt irresistible to him. Her extraordinary passion lingered in his thoughts, subduing momentarily his gathering clutter of darkness and anger. He felt his heaviness abate briefly, replaced by a sort of airlessness. The full urge to be playful had crept into the scheme of things, thankfully. Stephen reached to brush back her hair so that he could enjoy her insatiable eyes, presently closed.

His touch awakened her. With the instinct of an aroused woman, she took his hand and kissed it, placing a value of the enduring pleasure of its caress, and the man she attached to it. As Stephen edged closer, Susan blinked, her mind suddenly eager at his closeness, her raw smile inviting him. She was now fully awake. Quite unexpectedly, Stephen observed unfamiliar lines drawn into her face. These were not deep crevasses to be sure, but recent borders and furrows nonetheless. Vertical strokes had etched into the skin above her upper lip where it had once been so smooth. There were slight horizontal indentations creasing the sides of her eyes and above her brow. Her neck hinted at the worry streaks ranging around it. *When did these appear?* The porcelain fleck of her girlish, beautiful skin appeared less intense, less something . . . More dry, less lustrous . . . He didn't know.

Susan was aging. He couldn't imagine it. She had always been perfect, her facial features and her body. He wondered just how much he'd put there in the past few months. Still, Susan was the same woman this morning as she was last night.

She noticed his slight reserve. She saw it in his eyes, worrying her immediately. So many things vexed her lately. In their marriage, she wanted to be rid of this man and what he'd introduced into their relationship. Susan was now laying blame. And when that emotion subsided and the guilt arose, she wanted him more than she could say. She despaired over her physical appearance and Stephen's now, this minute's, visual apprehension. She knew he was analyzing her. Susan didn't come to this time in her life to have to face all of this at once. None of it was ever in her plans, those secret dreams she had as a girl about the man she would one day marry. She didn't think about aging or that her prince might help to dissipate her happiness. War and all it wrought had been the farthest thing from her mind in those days.

Susan raised her body to sit upright, to read him more closely. She had slept for hours and dreamed hungrily of this second, but she had awakened to discover that it might not hold the fragrant vision she wished. Still clutching his hand to her breast, but more tightly, she voiced her soul, "Oh darling. Do you still love me? Am I still beautiful to you?"

His answer didn't arrive swiftly enough to satisfy her the instant she asked it. This delay caused her to worry afresh, though his reply was thoughtful. "Yes, you are now and forever, the most beautiful woman in the world."

Susan almost panicked because of his hesitation. Had her worst fears materialized? Was she less attractive to him now, regardless? Would he begin to look elsewhere? Susan urged Stephen closer to her. The moment took its well-practiced course and passion.

Thirty-One:
Going Through the Motions

Saturday, May 13, 1967

"Michael. It's Donny."

Surprise. "Hi." Michael's response was weak, perhaps limp. He didn't want to talk to Donny, but they'd been friends for so long, he couldn't just drop their relationship without trying to revive it. "What's going on, man? Where have you been?"

"Out of town. We went up to Dartmouth. I heard about your dad. I'm sorry, man. How is he?"

Michael didn't quite know how or what to answer Donny, because he hadn't talked to either of his parents for several days. Delores had phoned to say they had arrived safe, but that was about all. He thought about the trip to Amon Carter and how silently hostile it had been. Today Michael had wrestled with the guilt of wanting his father out of the house for a while. His mother had been emotionally stressed by everything that was going on. Michael had almost gotten into several verbal jousts with his father before they left, something he couldn't have imagined months before. He knew, too, what his sister was worried about. But when his father did return would he be pleasant? Depressed? Angry? In need of more space? No one knew.

Michael had watched his mother cry, sitting disconsolate and alone when his father blew through the house. At times he seemed to be looking for a fight, and then he'd apologize. Margaret made excuses for her father when her friends came over. David left the house, choosing to avoid any form of confrontation. Brit and he would go chase the next-door neighbor's cat.

Dr. Wilson had called to check in, to see how things were faring. Mrs. Wilson had baked a German chocolate cake for the Lloyd children and brought it by. She would still cry when she mentioned Damien's name, but Mrs. Wilson seemed to be getting over her son's death. That's what it looked like. It was just so hard.

Michael wanted to say, "Donny I'm so scared for my father. There's so much I don't understand." But it was best to avoid the mention of war with Donny.

He changed the subject to something a bit closer to home. Michael wasn't certain if he wanted to know the answer to the question he was about to ask, but his curiosity was killing him. "Have you seen Victoria? I was just wondering . . . you know."

"Man, are you sure you want to know?"

"I don't know. Yeah. I guess."

"She's seeing Will Towers. I thought about calling you several times, but . . . you know how it is."

"Yeah. Will Towers, huh?"

"Yeah. Hey, you want to get some guys together and play some ball or something?"

Michael missed practicing baseball. He'd gone over to Robert's house and they threw the ball around for a couple of hours. But Michael was just going through the motions. He'd rather spend time with his grandfather at the office. He'd run errands and avoid the people who wondered how things were going. They knew to steer clear of Marcus Lloyd with their questions. Michael would get in his car and drive here and there, but without Victoria, there seemed no point in it now. *Will Towers, huh?* He'd sat up late Thursday night talking to his sister, of all people. He heard her crying after his parents left for Canada. Margaret was frightened. She didn't know what all this meant and she wanted Michael's opinion as he stood in her doorway, watching her.

As for Donny, Michael's former best friend, it was what *wasn't* being said that agitated him. A primary ideological wedge had been driven between them. Donny and he were avoiding the obvious and it stunk. This 'blankety-blank' war had, and was even then, cutting a swath down the middle of old friendships. "Hey, I gotta go. Call you later, Donny."

"Okay."

Michael put the receiver back on the hook. Nothing felt solid under him anymore. *Where had it all gone?* He knew Damien didn't mean to cause him so much personal pain, but he had. He picked up the phone and dialed long distance. One ring.

"Hello?"

"Grandma, is grandpa available? Can I talk to him? This is Michael."

"Michael? I'm so glad you called. Have you heard from your mom and dad today?"

"No, ma'am. Not today. Have you?"

"No. Here's your grandpa." He heard her say, "It's Michael."

"Michael. Hey son. How are you? Is everything all right?"

"Well, that's what I called about. Mother told us about you being in the war and I don't . . . I mean, I'm starting to understand some things about my father's time in the service, but I miss my father. I'm afraid I've lost him for good. I just need to know everything's going to be all right. It *is* going to be all right, isn't it, grandpa?"

"Michael, you trust me, don't you, son?"

"Yes, sir."

"Your father's in good hands. *I* raised that girl—your mother—and if anyone can bring him around, your mom can. Now you just hang in there, ya hear?"

"Yes, sir. I mean, I lay in bed at night and . . ." Michael was about as close to tears as any eighteen year old is supposed to allow himself to be. Perry heard quivering uncertainty in his grandson's voice. His own war was plying its pressure on former Major Alcott, USMC, Retired. And this was his grandson. He couldn't let this boy down.

The conversation went back and forth a few more minutes until Michael felt fatigue setting in, and he thought he could actually go to sleep. Sleep was at a premium in the Lloyd household these days. Margaret wasn't sleeping much either. Grandpa Perry had said the necessary things, and this eased his disquiet for the moment. But Grandpa Perry wasn't offering any of the things Michael wanted desperately to know.

"Thanks grandpa. I appreciate it, thanks."

"Sure. You can call me any time. I'll be talking to you, son."

Thirty-Two:
Hail Mary, Full of Grace

>─┼─◆>─○─<◆─┼─<

Saturday, May 13, 1967
Susan and Stephen lay side-by-side touching for several more minutes without any ceremonial words passing between them. Breathing came in heavy draughts. The air was made warm by the full and fresh bouquet of the moment. It would be displaced by the day, but not presently. Susan took her husband's hand to interlock her fingers with his. "Am I still beautiful to you, Stephen?" Her question revealed the fragility of her soul.

There was no hesitation this time. "Yes. Yes you are." He didn't elaborate like she wanted, but neither did he slight her. Their eyes held each other and neither blinked. The honesty was real and the unfettered sincerity welcomed.

"Would you do something for me this morning?" she asked.

"If I can? What would you like for me to do for you?" He knew what she wanted.

His slight smile came soft and reassuring all the same. Susan ventured further. "Please talk to me. Let's see if we, together, can't make some sense of this. Okay?" Her eyes contracted, pleading in their resolution.

"About what?"

"You know what, Stephen. The war, memories, meaning. That's why we're here. You know all this." *Careful Susan.*

313

Perhaps love's varied expressions, no matter how glorious, are not meant to last—in this life. Perhaps. Frail humanity cannot hold on to them but for a few fleeting moments. The sturdy male body Susan clung to rolled over on his back. His familiar cue for continued intimacy, the need to play more, to feel the softness of his wife and be touched by her had now dissipated. He needed for her to leave the past out of this completely, at least for today. Stephen's desire for pleasure had been overruled and cast aside by her need to talk.

He swore into the ceiling. "You women would rather talk than eat."

"No. No!" Her words were almost breathless imperatives, if not pleadings. Susan labored to be heard, to keep her husband's sudden anger subdued—and her own. "Sweetheart, you know that's not true. We enjoyed each other last night and . . . and now, this morning. I do want you near me, and I can't give you anymore of myself. But our lives involve more than just sex. I need some things *too*, and they're not simply physical. You aren't the only one who's hurting, Stephen. Don't you see that? When you get angry, you take it out on me and the children. But when you're depressed, I am too." Susan's mind slowly twisted into a knot, sluggish lassitude creeping over her again. The day had not yet begun, and the fatigue of all the preceding days piled back on to her.

Then came Stephen's almost inaudible response, "Yeah, I know," and another long silence. He knew very well that her needs were as real as his own. At times he didn't care. What he did not grasp were the broken aspects of *their* life, the ones Humpty Dumpty's men couldn't put back together again. And his needs, as such would not remain silent forever. Each had its own moments of release at everyone's expense. Stephen was the vessel in and through which they lived. Hitler and Tojo and Stalin had slung putrescence, destruction and death across the globe. It clung lethally to those closest to its demise, as it now did to Stephen, and in turn, to his family. The agitation pressing on him earlier had returned, and it superseded any desire his wife might have.

Stephen scraped his teeth against each other in an angular way as he stared at the ceiling. "What do you want me to tell you exactly?"

"Well," Susan had rehearsed this moment for hours in the car, but now she felt adrift, because she didn't think they would actually get this far so soon. "Well . . . to start with, Dr. Inhofe said we needed to talk about . . . things . . . the war. I want to know . . . why you are so angry. Are you mad at me? Did I do something to upset you? If

I did, please tell me what it is, and I'll try not to do it any more. I promise. I love you so much, honey." Susan's questions spilled out of her relentless spirit, like Niagara spilling over the falls, yet none were actually about the war, and that was confusing to him.

Stephen started to get up, but Susan pulled him back onto the bed and slid her upper torso on top of him. She hoped that she might pin him down literally in a manner that would entice him to communicate. She kissed his cheeks. "Are you upset with me?"

"No. It's just that . . ." The words trailed off, and Stephen felt the need to avoid her eyes. Is honesty always the best policy? Can or should he expose her to this? He fought to keep her out of it. The damaged European women . . . Stephen had fought to keep his wife from experiencing any of that.

He struggled to put his arms around her. Holding her required Herculean effort, more than he thought he possessed. That inner knotted pressure was coming back with a vengeance. "It's just that . . ." More fumbling with dark ideas and Stephen kept avoiding her glance. "I'm just angry. I don't know why." A tear formed at the side of his left eye, filled heavy with unintelligible emotion. It ran quickly down the side of his head, dispersing into his hair.

He had no desire whatsoever to indulge his wife with this particular conversation. Why couldn't she let him have today, to avoid this topic, postponing it another twenty-four hours? He felt too brittle or jagged. Like it or not, Stephen was probably going to have to fight to keep her questions at bay, and he didn't want to fight right now, not with her, and not with himself.

"I'm sorry. Go ahead," Susan whispered, her breath sweet and living and filled with everything good . . . almost. She didn't attempt to withdraw her words or soft features from him. He knew the power of this woman's body and soul over him.

He pulled the covers around her, and each could feel the other's heart beating in the closeness of this moment. "Susan, you didn't do *anything*."

"Are you *sure*?" Stephen reassured her with a nod. *She was missing it, completely.* Somewhat pacified and not wanting to challenge his answer, she continued. "Well, would you please tell me . . . about Italy, about what you did, about what happened to you? I saw the newsreels and read the papers. I kept track as best I could. But it's not like being there, is it?" He didn't respond, and his breathing shallowed. Susan wanted to lead him into that bomber, through those flak filled skies, and to wherever else this might take them. She believed it could or must be gotten at one step at time, like with chess or checkers, one jump following the other.

"Didn't Dr. Inhofe get you to talk about . . . what you did there? I'd like for you to tell me. I really want to know. I know it's difficult for you, but we can work through it together. Can't we?" She kissed his lips to see what it would take to move him to talk. This was a price she was willing to pay, but he didn't affirm or recognize her effort. Susan kept looking down at him for some sign of life. Those long, dormant, emotional memories of his seemed to be punishing him, she presumed. He lay very still, first looking into her large, man-eating eyes staring back at him. Then he looked away. He made no sign as to his intentions. She could only wonder what his eyes had seen. He could only guess at her determination to find out. He started to pull her to him, but released her. He suspected she would give herself to him, but he would wind up right back here, back at this infernal question, and he would feel guilty for satisfying his urge, and she would remain left out, ignorant, and used.

He wanted to return to his initial waking thoughts, but he read in her eyes that she would not be put off. His breath was deep, as if attempting or needing all the air in the bedroom to continue to speak to her. "I wish it were that easy."

"It might be easier than you think," Susan said. There was a lustrous sensuality mingling with her words. The tone of her voice was reassuring, and she hoped that he would not move, but remain and speak to her. From the doctor's instructions she knew she was treading on a wound that might not ever heal satisfactorily. Stephen's arm tightened around her, drawing her to him in a less than subtle attempt to suppress her will. She would give, but not relent. Not now. Silence, again, covered them like the sheet, and their dual breathing was the only sound in the room, not counting the clock. He brushed back her hair because it tickled his nose. "I'm sorry," she said, in a kittenish, playful smile.

There came from his chest and throat a heavy sigh. "Okay." He couldn't concentrate on her questions with his wife this close. Stephen gently hoisted her back over to her side of the bed. "Let's go back to the morning we left for the airport, to start with. You started packing late, as usual . . ." This wasn't the way she'd planned this, yet here it was. Stephen kept the war out of it, again, and he was missing it.

Without thinking, yesterday's cold solitude infringed upon the moment, and reminded Susan of her own repressed hurt. "Stephen, I had to get the kids taken care of, and then make sure everything was in order. And you certainly didn't help me. You just sat there and stared. I had to pack for both of us. I never had to do that before. And then . . ."

Stephen's agitation returned as Susan reeled off charge after charge, which was met with counter charges. What he had felt compressing within him minutes ago, returned with a vengeance. "Good grief Susan, you asked me to talk to you. And then you accuse me of not helping you. Well, I could barely function. Don't you understand that? Right now, the way you are charging me with this . . . it feels like the world is squeezing me to death. The second you started pressuring me, something inside of me started to tighten, and suddenly I'm angry. In a minute I'll want to hit something . . . hard. I want to be left alone. I can't help the way I feel. Then there's that stupid cook, Jacques. Quill won't get rid of him. He's always late. And yesterday, that clown at the gas station . . . he just took his sweet time, and I needed to get *here*." Stephen rolled away from her onto his side, shaking, he was so angry. The thing crouching outside of his peripheral thinking leapt aboard his thought processes and pounded at his temples. With it came fear, but this was more desperate than the foreboding of the past several months.

"Stephen, please don't turn away. I'm sorry. Dr. Inhofe said that . . ."

"Dr. Inhofe said this, and Dr. Inhofe said that. Who cares what that shrink said? Just leave me alone, Susan. Please quit asking me, will you?" He flung the covers at her and stomped over to where his clothes lay.

"No, honey . . . Please don't leave! I'll just sit here and listen. . . but we *need* to talk. I need for you to *talk* to me," Susan screamed as she pulled the covers up around her. Her husband kept dressing, and Susan bawled into the sheet, trying to muffle her pain that no one within two hundred feet could hear. *"Please don't go. I'll let you talk. I'll let you not talk. I won't interfere. I promise,"* she panted. Round eight went to the damage of the war. The Lloyd's, neither of them could put anything on the scoreboard.

Through his anger, Stephen couldn't hear his wife any more. So long as Stephen held his position, he was in control and control was everything. The second he relented, he had no control. He would become small and weak, fragile, and then broken. He certainly wasn't going to talk to her about the war, not today. The harder she tried, the farther he slipped from her. Susan's words began as soothing as honey, they had flowed over the scab of the wound, gently tugging at its edges, but finished so harshly, threatening to expose what lay beneath. Through her tears, Susan watched her husband's eyes searching for something unseen. She didn't know what his mind raced after, but she sensed that he was in a desperate situation, paralleling that of her own.

He sensed something creeping *into* his soul, not *around* the edges of it. Stephen sat up in the chair with only one shoe tied. His eyes spread wide with desperation. When Dr. Inhofe and he were alone, the doctor had almost pricked it. Crying, that was it. If he began to cry, he believed he might never stop. On the same level, Stephen didn't realize that what he'd told the doctor was untrue. He didn't feel emotionally dead inside. Anger was an emotion, and it wasn't dead. He felt sadness and remorse. He felt a hundred different things. He felt passion or arousal toward his wife. But love? No. Were all the intimate times purely lust? He *had* to leave the room. He *had* to escape. Too many things nagged at him.

He finished dressing, and then ran downstairs leaving his wife to mend her own tears. It was then that he smelled the bacon cooking. As he opened the door to leave, Stephen pulled Jacques into the large room. The Canadian had just that moment put his hand on the outside of the front door handle, and Stephen, blind with his own anger and fear, glared at the lanky cook with a hideous seething.

"Pardon, Monsieur," the man said as he stumbled into the room. Stephen, without thinking, grabbed both lapels of the man's shirt, pushed him hard against the door and, with teeth gritted, forced the words forward into the man's face, "Our meals will be on time from now on! I pay you to have the food prepared on time! Is that clear?"

Jacques' eyes widened to just under the size of half dollars, gulped the words, "Oui, oui Monsieur."

Susan stood at the top of the rail watching the scene play out, the two men having met at the door, Stephen's agitation with her taken to the next level with the cook. Forlorn in the extreme, Susan covered her face and wept. Jacques, cognizant of some sort of domestic 'situation' into which he'd been pulled and almost beaten, caught movement above him, looked up to observe Mrs. Lloyd crying. Removed his hat, he lifted his best French Canadian flavored English toward the woman, "Bonjour, Madame. Would you like to eat now? I had to go back to ze cabin for something."

His was reasonably good English, and would have been charming at any other moment. He gazed back at the heavy door, and that last strained moment with his employer. Late? Jacques was always late, or rather, these Americans were so often too early. Jacques observed the man who paid his salary, and who had almost pounded him into the door, continue his steady pace beyond the drive. In several more minutes Stephen would be well out into the dew-covered field. Jacques looked back up at Mrs. Lloyd who was now descending the stairs. When she reached the picture window, Susan halted and stared through it following her husband's figure growing smaller by the second.

Jacques braved the question once more, motioning to the kitchen, and said rather weakly, "Breakfast, Madame?"

"No. No thank you, Jacques. Nothing for me this morning." Susan didn't think about the effort Jacques had expended preparing it or that the food that would be thrown out, because there was no one to eat it. She felt spent, and it was barely 7:50.

"As you wish, Madam." Jacques went into the large kitchen to clean up. When he finished, he quickly walked to the door trying not to disturb his guest, tipped his hat, backed out silently, and closed the heavy wooden barrier behind him.

She stood alone, oh so alone, touching the glass with her right hand as if to reach out and pluck her husband from his discomfort. Slowly, her left hand rose to cover her mouth, and she shook from holding it all in. Before she could run upstairs, the moment's earlier conversation saddled her body into the throes of convulsion, and its resultant tears would not be halted. Her own sad weight pulled her to the cold planking, the same floor upon which Quill and she had walked the day they arrived. Susan's emotional gravity pulled her toward the floor so that she now sobbed from a squatting position, her head leaning against the log wall. Susan did not know she had this many tears to cry out from the wellspring of her desperation.

In the middle of her anguish, she reached heavenward and cried out to someone she hoped would hear, someone who might see her desperation and be merciful. "O God. Help me. Why has my life come to this? What did I do to deserve this? Help me. Help me. Please. Help me." And then, as if all the liquid within her were gone, she stood slowly to gaze once again after the man she loved, but he was nowhere to be seen. Drying her tears, Susan looked up toward the second level where she had danced with her husband hours ago, and that lovely memory made his exit more painful.

She stood there holding herself for warmth. Her back pressed against the chilled log wall, and out into the warehouse. The sturdy, smooth, and rounded pine logs received the weight of her body, buoying her. She was a small thing now, engulfed by a huge paradox, a Catch-22 the size of the room into which she felt compressed. Was this what combat was like? She sensed just then that she was impotent to alter her circumstances. Never had that happened to her. She was always so capable for every task. *She* had met the challenges of the talent and beauty contests with the force of her being. *She* had overcome childlessness; beaten it on its own terms and won. But this . . . *this*. Never had success been dependent on someone else. . . and she had *no control* over her husband, what he might or might not do. And the panic crept over her, a dismaying consternation with its own potency, and Susan felt bested. Not merely bested, but beaten, squashed into the ground. She was over her head. He might never come back . . . *o but he would, he must . . . must he? Come back, my Stephen. Come back to me.*

Her nose ran but there were no more tears. She looked out *there* once more, but Stephen was still gone. What was there to see anyway, but a huge, empty house several million miles from her children and someplace resembling happiness? She blew her nose on her nightgown, which made her feel that much more invalidated, unlovely and lonely. The handkerchief she kept in her pocket wasn't there for her when she needed it. Susan shook from the cold. The embers from last night's fire had long since given away their heat. Jacques should have at least been here to make a fire. Jack London's, *To Build a Fire*, rushed through her memory. She wiped her cheeks, daubed her eyes and spread her gown over her feet. In a few seconds Susan shook uncontrollably from the cold.

Dear God, I'm desperate. Help me. Please save my marriage. Save that man out there. Please God. Are you there? Is it that I just don't have enough faith to believe? Just what am I supposed to believe? Show me . . . O God. Blessed Virgin Mary, hear me. Speak to your son Jesus for me. I know I haven't been to church in so long . . . but I promise to . . .

She recited a Hail Mary, which she desperately hoped was full of grace. For several minutes Susan mouthed words until her mind alighted on another inconsequential nuisance of a thought. Then she said the "Our Father" twice, and at the conclusion of her prayers, Susan felt a little less inundated by her own thoughts. Was that what her faith was all about, saying prayers over and over so that she would feel less pain, less afraid, perhaps feel God's nearness? What would His closeness feel like? Was faith something she knew she knew? Was it emotional or rational? But in point of fact, she knew she didn't know. And just where was God in this disintegrating life of hers? Her marriage, except for the babies, had experienced few trials to test her metal until Damien was killed, or was it the metal of her faith that God jested with her about? Were they somehow connected, and if so, how? Susan's questions seemed endless, and no answers came. There was probably no one to ask.

Susan had been so absorbed with her misery that she hadn't felt how cold not only her feet were, but how stiff her body felt. Goose bumps danced on her bare arms. With the reality of her cold body came new fears to displace those with which she'd just dealt, only these fresh storms battered her the more severely. That former question lashed at her soul once again. How, or better, *why* would God let this happen—to her? She believed in her heart that she was a good person, so undeserving of such divine cruelty. God must surely know that. What right had God to throw her into such mental disarray? Susan felt sure she could produce any adequate proof of her own moral virtue should God require it of her. She'd been happy not so very long ago, so was God punishing her again? Was it not *He* who took her babies, and now *He* was taking her husband? She thought she might go insane if Stephen didn't return immediately. It wasn't fair.

With this frank admission, the tears held in reserve for such times followed the curves of her cheeks. The first, then the second splashed onto the wood upon which she stood. The third and the fourth fell before she marshaled the emotional resources to halt the spigot. Susan led her weary body back up the stairs to their bed, now hers alone, where she packed the covers around her. Here, she would huddle in her misery . . . and wait for Stephen. Once more she cried until no sound came, and her loneliness closed about her like a prison.

Thirty-Three: Cheslatta Falls

><-!-<>-<O-<<>-!-<

Saturday, May 13, 1967

By the time Stephen had things a little better under control the dew had soaked through his loafers and into his socks. He hadn't gone down to get his boots, he just left, and he left angry. Now he was also half a mile from the cabin, and fully out of sight of his wife. His wet feet agitated him even more so that he looked up into the sky, uttering something he was glad his children didn't hear. He realized that he had only two choices: go back and face his wife and apologize to Jacques, or keep going. It was about that time that Stephen looked up to see the bull staring at him, a mere thirty yards away. He hadn't paid any attention to where he was going, and was only mildly aware that he was walking through a field dotted with cattle.

This two thousand-pound bull appeared to be fully engaged with him, which caused Stephen's anger to suddenly go limp. He didn't know how to read this huge, menacing animal. Fortunately the bull kept chewing his cud. In another second, he sniffed the air, snorted, flipped his tail, and then turned to saunter slowly away. He seemed disinterested with the human that just crossed his path. A plus, all things considered. The fat, red and white Hereford, would take charge of a less occupied and grassier area, to Stephen's relief.

"Why am I so angry?" Stephen prodded himself to answer—rather, dared himself to venture a guess. He, in fact, believed he knew the answer. He saw it, even experienced it while sitting in the chair in the bedroom. It was guilt, plain and simple. The bombs had hung in the bomb bay, and Captain Mark Sampson's plane, limped accidentally under his, just when the bomb shackles let go, releasing 10,000 pounds of high explosive ordinance, two five hundred pounders of which crashed right through the right wing and fuselage. The impact disintegrated what seconds before had been an airplane with a ten-man crew. He had killed every one of them. It was his fault. No, it was really Will's fault. *He* was the bombardier. *He* toggled the bombs. It was also Consolidated's or some unknown manufacturer's fault. *They* designed and built the shackles. It was equally the government's fault, because *they* approved the design. But, when push came to shove, it was *his*, Captain Stephen Lloyd's fault. *He* was the pilot. It was that simple and that complex.

Blind rage flared to red, and before he knew what he was doing, Stephen picked up a large stone and threw it at the retreating bull. He hoped it might turn around, charge and kill him. Then his guilt would be assuaged. Guilt was a weighty, live thing. He'd buried it following the investigation—he'd been cleared of course. The Air Corps knew about the shackles, but sent the bombers up anyway. Some consolation. He'd killed ten men, because shackles weren't a sufficiently high priority. They were just shackles that held tons of high explosives. If their proper functioning wasn't that important to the brass hats back at HQ, why should *he* worry about it? Maintaining that drivel was the coward's way out, and he knew it. He wasn't a coward.

In the final analysis, war was one large conundrum. It lulled men into worse case scenarios from which they would never be able to extricate themselves. In that sense, wars never end until the last possible effect carries no more weight with it. But every war lives on in incalculable ways, and certainly in the lives of those who participate in it. Was it bad luck? Luck was planned into everything, you know, those things that happen that no one can explain. The ball bounces this way and then that way. Nobody knows where or how it will bounce.

He'd begun several letters to the wives and parents of the unlucky crew, but couldn't get past the, "Dear Mr.—Dear Mrs.—" If only he hadn't known anyone from that crew, but he had. *Oh, God help me.* He'd folded and stuffed and pushed this horrible state of affairs away with all the other losses so that he would never find it, even if he tried. Now it was back in his face, smothering him, destroying his marriage, his job and his life.

Stephen fell on his knees crying for all his life was worth. He begged for forgiveness from men who could no longer forgive him. He begged God too for forgiveness, for the crime of waiting so long to ask. He begged the trees to hear his confession. One last time he begged the bull to kill him. That's when he heard, or thought he heard, off in the distance, a multiengine radial airplane. It must be behind the clouds.

Stephen came to a lethargic awareness that his face was partially covered with mud and wet grass, the instinct to fight and kill, ridiculously high. Some delicious power had heightened his body's senses, and he felt stronger than he had in years, to the point of invincibility. His hands, feet, nose and mouth tingled. He felt like running, but where? And why? And then he knew he had been there. For that fullest instant he *saw* his left leg swinging in front of the pilot's seat. He could see, even *feel* his escape kit pinned to his knee pocket, the yellow life vest about his neck. He felt the seat's cushion under him as he sat, and behind his back, the parachute pushed against him. His hunting knife was strapped to his ankle—it was all there.

In an instant, Stephen saw himself sitting securely in his seat, his check list began: 1. Open the bomb bay doors. 2. Remove the pitot head covers. 3. The pilot and co-pilot climb up and into the bomb bay doors and proceed to the cockpit. 4. The flight engineer turns on the four fuel selector valves. 5. Two valves on the right side to control fuel flow to the two right engines, two valves on the left side to control the fuel flow on the left two engines. 6. The fuel tanks had to be checked for how much fuel each had on hand. 7. Pilot and co-pilot adjust his seat. 8. Pilot and co-pilot adjusts his rudder pedals. 9. Remove the controls lever up, in the locked position. 10. Stow the strap in the overhead. 11. The locking lever was checked in the down position. 12. The locks were completely released so that the pilot could move the yoke in each direction. 13. The flight engineer assumed a vantage point from which he could watch the ailerons move in unison with the yoke's movement. There had to be free movement. 14. The elevators were checked, up and down on both left and right surfaces by pulling the yoke toward the pilot and then toward the front of the plane. 15. The pilot moved both the rudders and yoke simultaneously, and then rapidly for freedom of movement. 16. The co-pilot had to ensure the ignition switches and master ignition switches were both in the "off" position. 17. One of the ground crew pulled the propellor through completely two full revolutions. 18. Fuel had to be cleared in the combustion chambers of the engines. 19. The power to start the engines could come from the batteries themselves plus the auxiliary power unit. 19a. A battery cart on the ground could also be used to provide power to start the aircraft. 20. The generator switches on the generator panel are kept off, . . . and so it went. After flight training, Stephen could do it in his sleep.

Turkey In The Straw—he always whistled it when they entered the flak, and it too became part of the mental clutter, this annoying ditty helped settle his increasing fears. And just as quickly—the entire palpitating panorama of aircraft and war faded, and then was gone.

But the emotions of it remained, racing through him at break neck speed. It *was* gone, but he had . . . He had what? No one would believe him. It didn't matter, because he felt all but out of control. He was just as fully aware that something extraordinary had occurred with *him* at its epicenter. Worst of all he wanted it back. Stephen wanted to bottle what he felt. But it was gone now. The memories of the investigation and the sound of that distant airplane, the hundred octane smell tripped something in his mind. How very strange and powerful. When the adrenaline wore off, he'd feel drained. His former guilt had mingled with his flashback, and he felt sick from their power over him.

The sun disappeared behind gray clouds for the length of time he'd 'flown.' He felt spent, fearful, and excited all at once, and his heart kept dancing in his chest. Try as he might, Stephen couldn't calm himself. Where was Susan? Susan . . . He'd left her alone, pleading with him not to leave her. No, he didn't want her *here*, and yet he yearned for her, to hold him and to be held by her. He had to catch his breath, but when he stood, his mind circled, and back down on the grass he sat, cradling his head, his breath still not fully under control. His stomach growled unexpectedly. He hadn't eaten in . . . since last night. Jacques . . . *he was late with dinner, remember?*

Several drops of rain splattered upon him. In the distance, the crack of thunder echoed through the valley, bouncing among the white trunked cedars, the poplars, blue spruce, and huge pines. Within minutes, the rain came in torrents. Within minutes, he stood there soaked, the second time in a week. He hadn't planned this day well, or at all. That was just it. This thing pressing against his chest forced him to react, not think. He hadn't been able to plan for any of this. On the other hand and for some odd reason, he was glad to be drenched. His depressions planted the seedlings with a hope that he might catch pneumonia and die. Then he'd be done with this. Pulling himself up against his weight, which felt ponderous, Stephen began to walk again. The direction didn't matter. Lightening struck and cracked through the dark sky overhead. He dared it to hit him. Life felt once more out of control.

His guilt felt heavier than his waterlogged clothing and his slipping muddy shoes. Finding a covering of pines, he stood shaking under them. The wind pushed at him, urging him to find some other place to be miserable. Stephen Lloyd remembered what it felt like to hate, for he hated his very existence.

Stephen barely noticed when the rain began to let up. He kept walking, up one hill and down another. At times he'd stop to rest, more from hunger, but often from his soaked leather shoes that weren't made for hiking, especially wet. His back ached, and the thought that he had probably reached the end of the trail took root. Around three-thirty, the skies broke and the late afternoon sun poked its rays out through the forest he inhabited. However, the sun's renewed warmth didn't penetrate the forest floor where he labored.

Unfortunately, he knew where he was. The fragrant, recently washed air kept prodding his senses, but he refused its comfort. The elements and the man himself had made Mr. Stephen Lloyd as miserable as possible. He walked aimlessly, yet no matter how he tried, he couldn't get himself lost. He was soaked to the bone, shivering, feeling fragile from hunger so that he didn't think as clearly as he might have otherwise.

When he approached a rise in the forest wall, he heard the din of rushing water and his heart leapt. The moment had come for Stephen Lloyd to decide. On the other side of the trees he could hear it clearly. He'd forgotten about the cliff and the river. Stepping through the thick branches, and still wet with the rain, he came to the ledge at Cheslatta Falls. One hundred fifty feet below him flowed the thundering waters, first over the edge of the falls, then headlong down, down, ever downward into the river valley so far below him. He'd fished that river many times. He hadn't come this way in several years, and now he stood facing his desire. He'd asked the bull, then God, and then lightening to kill him. With little effort, Stephen could actually be done with this. He squatted at the edge. He was no longer cold.

Stephen surveyed the vast river valley. As he did so, he felt a clarity come over him. His body would strike the rocks initially at about fifty or sixty feet below him, and then he would tumble and bounce, crushing his skull completely and any other bones the rocks hadn't already shattered. If he made it to the fast flowing water, his broken body would be unable to keep him from drowning. He wondered if the first impact would hurt, but abandoned the thought. Stephen sat letting his legs dangle over the edge. Maybe the rock upon which he had put his entire weight would give way. There would be no choice to make. In seconds he would be dead. *You can do this. Lloyd . . . you're a pile of garbage. The world would be better off without you. You are slowly destroying your wife. I hate you and so does God. You're a murderer. You have lived all these years, well past what you deserve. You should have died, not them. You never gave them a chance.*

Something moving above him in the distance caught his attention. Stephen shielded his eyes with his hands from the low hanging sun. He suddenly wanted to see what had disturbed his intention. It was an eagle riding the currents. "Incredible," he whispered, and then he returned to the business at hand—killing himself. Then a second disturbance of his mental faculties roused him—Michael. "How will his son handle this?" And then Margaret's voice interrupted him: "Father, what do you think of my boyfriend? What college do you want me to attend? Why would you kill yourself? I love you so much, but now you're dead, and I wanted you to be here to give me away when I got married, but you're gone." In his mind's eye he saw David, startling and clear, sitting on the couch, watching TV. Brit sat in his lap. Both boy and dog looked quite content. Susan said nothing. She stood with her arms crossed, a look of intense disappointment and anguish on her face. Beautiful Susan. Marcus and Annika entered the fray, each asking questions of this dead man, Stephen Lloyd.

Stephen's need to be rid of his troubles couldn't compete with all these people. They demanded that he live. Annika would lose her mind. And then there was Susan. He felt her smooth body against his; felt himself aroused and swore at his weak passions. That look from her eyes pounded against him. *I'm so sorry Susan. I'm just lost. In time you won't miss me. The world is better off without me. I've lived longer than I should. Kiss the grand babies for me. I love you. I love you.* What did that mean, really, "I love you?" What is love?

Stephen edged closer to the lip of the rock. He felt quite calm for a man that was about to destroy so many people's lives. "Stephen." From behind him, he heard Quill's voice. "Nice view," the old man spoke from the distance, but not out of hearing. "Think that's a good idea, son?"

Stephen didn't turn around, but asked, "How long have you been there?"

"A little while. I knew where to find you. I thought about it too, but I sat over *there*," Quill pointed several yards from where Stephen sat, "when I couldn't take the pressure anymore. If you intend to do it, over there is a better place. I think you'll die quicker. No chance you'll end up a paraplegic. A friend of mine tried to kill himself by jumping off a bridge. Ended up with a broken neck. Now he's dead, but what a pain taking care of him for the last seven years of his miserable life . . ." Quill Du Pont let the thunder of the falls and the rush of the distant river carry the conversation for the next few minutes. "Old Sam, now he did it right. He got his .45, stuck it in his mouth and pulled the trigger. By the time Sam got home from years in a POW camp, his wife had gone and gotten remarried."

"What do you mean remarried?"

"She didn't know if he was alive or not. Never did tell you about my time in the service and after the war, did I?"

"No. Not that I recall."

"Ever hear of Bataan?"

"Yeah. Who hasn't?"

Quill stood just inside the tree line. He figured that if his voice registered panic, Stephen might jump. "When MacArthur left the Philippines, it all went down hill. Before the Japs got us, we were down to eating the mules. No ammo. Nothing left to fight with." The old man surveyed the great expanse laid out before him. His age and the pickup truck ride he'd taken to find Stephen had tired him. His legs ached shifting gears, and now he leaned on his cane. His eyes became reflective pools, deep and moist. So many ghosts passed by in review, and so much pain. "Guys I'd done several hitches with . . . bayoneted when they fell out. No chance to escape. Some of the guys from my unit were taken to work on . . . did you ever see that movie, uh, *Bridge on the River Kwai*? That was all Hollywood. The prisoners died by the thousands and none of us helped the Japs build a bridge. Never saw any of those men again. I was sent to a POW compound for a few months, then to another one."

Quill appeared frailer standing near that ledge mere feet from the bigger man. He reached into his wallet and pulled out a picture of himself before the war, and moved a bit closer to Stephen. It was of a large man wearing a football uniform. "That was me. I was a tackle for the University of Montana before I joined the Army—ROTC. Hard to believe, huh?"

Stephen took the yellowed, line creased photo in his large hand, and stared into it incredulously. "What happened?"

"Well, it started with the malaria, then the dysentery. I was so dad-gum weak. I drank rancid water and ate various . . . *things* to keep alive. I weighed a hundred and two pounds when the war ended. I got to where I wanted to die more than I wanted to live. I was on one of those Jap ships headed to Tokyo when our own flyboys torpedoed the ship. I still don't know how I ended up on a door in the ocean. The few of us that survived were rescued two days later by another Jap ship, a destroyer I think. Just skin and bones, I was. When we got to Japan they took us to a POW compound. I was given enough to eat to keep me alive, but not much more. Then the flyboys dropped the bomb and the Japs started chopping off the heads of the captured flyboys. Still can't eat rice."

Stephen's appreciation for this man soared. "I had no idea, Quill. But you said you sat over there and thought about . . . *this*?" Quill had this view, Stephen had Smitty's.

"I've been to this cliff six times. I was going to fling myself off every time. I meant to, believe me, because I hurt so badly inside. I hated myself for living when so many better men than I didn't make it. Some days I would throw up until there was nothing left in my body to heave. Helen, she didn't understand, bless her heart. I was so angry all the time. But she never left me. I never did feel like I fit in back in Montana. I had to get away from everything. Your daddy offered me my old job back, so we moved back up here."

"What kept you from jumping?"

The old man studied the terrain carefully. What he had to say was critical. "Look out there."

"Out where?"

"*There!*" Quill's arm swept across his front, indicating the vast wilderness spread before them both. "*There*. What do you see?"

Stephen breathed deeply. What should have been an awe-inspiring expanse of trees and river, roaring sound and smell, colors and hues of breathtaking glory visited his senses, only in black and white. He couldn't see, because his mind was so disturbed and his body so troubled. The pressure had only intensified over the course of the preceding hours. Now his rib cage ached. It felt deflated, out of shape. He really didn't want Quill here. He wanted to be left alone. He wanted to kill himself, nothing more, nothing less.

"You can't see it, can you?"

"No. Not really. How did you know?"

"Like I said, I've been here six times to do just what you still want to do. You're Catholic. That's right, isn't it?"

Stephen nodded in the affirmative. "Why, what are you?"

"I'm . . . well, let's just say I'm a Christian. Leave it at that."

"So, what does religion have to do with anything?"

"Everything. You believe in God, son?"

There was a long silence from the man sitting next to Quill Du Pont. "I don't know."

"I know *that* feeling. When I came home, the only real emotion I could express was hate. If there was a God, I hated him. It took me ten years to gain back thirty pounds. And the first guy that tried to talk to me about God, well sir, I sure thought about trying to take him out, if you know what I mean? I just didn't have the strength to fight—like I did when I played ball. I cussed him a blue streak, though. When I felt well enough, I got drunk. That almost killed me. You know, it was as if . . . it was as if I couldn't die. I know that sounds crazy, but . . . I really began to believe I was doomed to live, a great big offensive tackle shackled to a little, weak body. Yep, I've been here six times."

"So, why didn't you jump?"

"Well, I stood right over there. I could feel the rock ledge under my shoes and just as I began to lean forward, I suddenly *saw* the beauty of this valley, this river, the forest, and these hills. I saw it all, and I still can't explain it. It was surreal. Then I rocked backward . . . kind of awe-struck. I mean I *saw* it in colors and sounds, even smells that I didn't know existed. The thought that all this didn't get here by itself suddenly was the only thing I could think about. I also knew that I couldn't destroy myself because I was somehow connected to . . . to all this. That's when I knew this special place had to have a Creator. I came here to *finally* do it, and suddenly I didn't want to. I wanted to explore it, and that meant I had to live. Some decision, huh? Anyway, I walked all over these hills and I ended up back at the cabin. Your dad had left two days before—before the weather closed in.

"There was my Helen, waiting for me. I think she knew every time I headed this way that it might be the last time she'd see me alive. She always knew when I had to leave, when things were closing in on me." Quill had grown melancholy, his words heavy with nostalgia. "Oh, son, that woman loved me."

"Do you miss her?"

"I do, but she needed what I couldn't give her. There were times when I thought about asking her to go back home and remarry, because I was so cold emotionally. She would give me that 'you've got to be kidding me' look, and go in the kitchen and bake me a black berry or apple pie, or, well, you know. I didn't cry when the cancer took her. I closed her eyes, but I didn't cry. Imagine that? I didn't cry over my wife. No tears. I think . . ."

"What?"

"No."

"What? I want to hear what you're thinking, Quill?"

"Well, the relationship I had with my platoon was the deepest . . . " The old man hesitated. His wound had been closed for years and he didn't really want to fester it again. For the past several minutes, the conversation had moved from the non-emotional, superficial level, to a degree that only combat survivors can reach. The words are not specifically or necessarily different, but the souls of the men begin to speak to each other in ways and means that each man understands, is comfortable with, and desperately needs to communicate. Quill was no longer Stephen's employee, but a fellow survivor of Hell.

"I know why I could never return her love in the same proportion she gave it out to me. I . . . I, well, I loved those guys, Donaldson, McGee, Johnny Newsome, Leonard, Hall, Berry, and Captain Johnson. I watched them all die, and I was so weak . . . I discovered, a bit too late that there is a love you have for your buddies, and it's different than the love you have for your wife and kids." Quill looked at Stephen to see

331

if his words were registering. They were. "When I came home, going through the long recovery period, I realized that I didn't love Helen the way I did before the war. It felt as if someone severed part of me while I was a prisoner all those years, and, try as I might, I couldn't give myself to her or anyone else ever again. I mean, I gave her what I could, but it felt . . . and still feels as if there's part of me I have to hold back from folks, like at church. It's as if I need to save it for something ahead. And then when I try to express that part I hold back, or to even look at it, there's nothing there. Does that make any sense?"

"Yes. Since the funeral, I haven't felt as if I fit into my family."

"I know what that feels like," Quill said.

Quill chanced another question as he stared out into the distance, "Stephen, do you ever get a pressure in your gut that seems to take over, and you're at its mercy until it lets go?" The old man knew the younger man's answer before he asked it. Stephen needed to know other men had walked in his shoes too.

"Yes. I can feel it right now."

Silence. The roar of water over the cliff carried the conversation for a minute more. Quill picked up a divergent theme to see how it might be greeted. "Have trouble sleeping?" Stephen nodded his agreement. Quill continued. "I started going to this little church down the road. You pass it before you get here. I felt really strange going, I have to tell you. It had been years since I'd darkened the door of a church. Are you okay with this, Stephen?"

"I don't know. I hurt so much . . . and I feel so guilty." Stephen felt at great risk now. Sudden hot tears welled in his eyes, for it finally seemed as if another human being understood. Stephen's face felt round and heavy. Quill surmised that the heart of the man was surfacing, and no one could stop it—nor should they. Stephen spoke as if he wanted to live. "I flew B-24's out of Italy—Fifteenth Air Force. On one particular mission . . . my bombs hung up in the bomb bay, then let go and killed a friend of mine and his ten man crew." That was as far as Stephen could get before the tears and the grief overwhelmed him for the second time in one day. The old man stood awkwardly, leaning heavy on his cane. He was more concerned at the moment about how close Stephen was to slipping over the edge and to his death. He moved closer to the younger man, years his junior, laid his hand on Stephen's head, and let him cry it out.

"I know. Let it go, son. Just . . . let it go."

Stephen felt as fragile as Quill looked for those long, difficult moments sitting on the ledge. He hadn't eaten in many hours, so he wasn't able to think clearly and his emotions carried him like the water carried the sound. The day's care with its agitation and grief, his wet clothes, and the blisters from his shoes that were not made to walk in wet had drained him of most of his energy reserves. Quill reached into his coat pocket and retrieved a sandwich he'd forgotten Jacques had made. Susan had given it to Quill should he find her husband. "Tell him I love him so much," were Susan's parting words to the caretaker. He knew right where to look once he was alerted to the situation.

The angle of the sun was now well below the treetops, and the air grew much cooler. The breeze smacked into Stephen's wet clothing, and he shook once again. He looked like death warmed over.

"Come on, Stephen. Let's get you home. We can finish this tomorrow."

Thirty-Four: Avoidance

>─┤─◄►──○──◄►─┤─◄

Saturday, May 13, 1967

"Help me get his wet clothes off," Quill said to Susan. The old man wrestled with Stephen's shirt while Susan untied his shoes and pulled them off. Quill was exhausted from his drive and then the hundred-yard walk over rough ground to the falls where he found Stephen. He felt even more tired from helping the bigger man find his way back to the truck. What little help he could give to assist Stephen up the stairs had almost done him in. At times like this, Quill hated the size of the main cabin. The day's light had dwindled to an almost extinguished ember causing the Canadian spring air to cool rapidly. Stephen sat trembling involuntarily in the chair next to the tub as it filled with hot water. Stephen's glassy eyes refused to focus. Susan held her questions and agitation, until Stephen was clean, warm, clothed and fed. She noted also from her husband's expressionless stare that his anger had subsided. For this one small favor, she was grateful. Perhaps God had heard her after all.

The steam from the water ascended like visible helium wisps, forming condensation on the walls and around the tub. Once the mirror fogged, Susan turned the tap handles and the rushing water stopped, all but a drip . . . drip . . . drip. Somehow, Susan and Quill had encouraged Stephen to his feet so that they both could tug at his britches. Stripped to his underwear, Quill suggested to Susan that he would wait in the kitchen. He wanted to speak to her about some things, but it could wait for now. As he closed the door to the bathroom, Stephen unexpectedly and halfheartedly mumbled, "Thank you, Quill." Quill winked, and left the man and his wife alone. Susan wondered if the heated vapors had to some degree resuscitated her husband's limp body and mind. He stood in the middle of the bathroom now, slightly animated but mostly unconcerned. He looked terrible. Dried blood, dirt and grass stained his face and matted his hair, and his stomach growled.

Stephen kicked his underwear onto the floor, and with Susan's help, lowered himself into the stinging water, which felt like needles driving into his hairy legs and bottom. He made hissing and o'ooing sounds the further he coaxed his body into the tub. The water rose to the safety drain, and some drained out, gurgling as it went. Susan wanted to tell him to quit acting like a baby, but she didn't, not after this morning. At last, he eased his weary, naked body full into its warmth. The smell of his dirty skin being scalded into submission brought back memories of his mother bathing him when he was a boy. He'd gotten dirty then too. Stephen's flesh kept tingling even after several minutes, and his toes ached as they thawed.

For the past twenty minutes while Quill and Susan had worked on Stephen, Stephen had unintentionally not looked at his wife. He felt too miserable to focus on her, because he was mired deep in thought. He heard Susan turn to leave, and he didn't protest. She left the door open, returning with a stool, which she placed next to the tub. It was then that she noticed the dried blood, compacted dirt, and grass on his forehead that the rain hadn't washed away completely.

For several agonizing minutes she sat and stared at him. No words passed between them, and Susan fought her impulse to make a fuss over her husband's blood and torn, dirty skin. She was relieved that he was home and safe, but that knowledge didn't overcome the anger also resident within her. Should she say something? Was no apology forthcoming? This was virgin territory for them both. In some thankful sense, his being back here was enough. This was all that mattered to Susan—*for the moment*. But in another, much more frustrating sense, which she'd spent the entire day cultivating, his being here wasn't enough. He had walked out on her this morning. His evasion and argumentative tenor, along with the ease with which he disappeared following the pleasure they had shared galled her. What she thought and felt was every bit as important as his problems. *Hello, Mrs. Danvers. I will stand up to you. Count on it.*

Finally, but with little emotion, Susan asked, "Can I wash your back?" It was a slippery, but cautious question. It was also one intended to test the waters of their marriage.

"Sure." To Stephen, talking felt like lifting a bulky, pernicious thing.

Susan talked about insignificant things as she soaped his back, the water sloshed in the tub. Stephen felt the growing familiarity of pressure returning into the nether regions of his chest. This time its source was shame, and he felt the full brunt of it. He knew he'd worried her. He'd left angry. He'd done everything wrong. He'd reacted like a good bomber pilot trying to save his life and that of his crew, fight or flight. He chose the latter, and now he wanted to die a lonely death for his crimes—even came close to it, but he'd not tell her that.

This 'entity' had him firmly in its grip, and he still had no hard reference point from which to mentally address it, or speak to Susan about it. He had some hunches, but nothing solid. Stephen thought he had an ally in Quill. The old man spoke from an understanding they both shared. Still, he didn't want to talk about the war—not with his wife, regardless of what they had come here to do. Susan had come here for that. Stephen, had come because that was the mission. Now that the mission was over for him, what was he supposed to do?

In the midst of his mental gyrations, the slight hint of Susan's perfume and warm breath caught him off guard. It softened the agitation of self-inflicted resistance that had built within his mind and body from this morning. He sank deeper into the water. "Oooooh," he breathed aloud. He'd bought another few seconds of nonverbal, non-communication.

Susan's "I love you," was part question, part indicative.

But to Stephen, responding in kind created the sensation of his heart bursting. He was spending far too much time alone in his own head lately. With all the strength he used when he sat at the gym's bench press, Stephen whispered, "I know. I love you too." Tepid words.

"Do you really *love* me, Stephen?" There could have been more to this question, like, why did you run off from me this morning? Why did you hurt me so deeply? Why couldn't you just answer some of my concerns? Why is it so difficult to talk to me, but she didn't need another argument right now. With her question, a cloud filled the bathroom.

A man who has been married for half his life to one woman doesn't feel ill at ease when his wife observes his naked body. But at the moment, with her needs or demands the same as when he left her, Stephen recognized that he didn't want her near him. He wasn't sure why, he just didn't. One or both of them seemed oddly out of place. He felt crowded, and he couldn't help what he felt or wanted. Stephen certainly couldn't help the fact that Susan wanted what she wanted. Talking was a decided vexation. Besides, how could he tell her that she irritated him? He loved her, but love wasn't the issue, or was it? He wanted to be left alone. She wanted his words and nearness more than life itself. Susan was beginning to realize just how much she derived her identity from her husband. His identity, however, had taken some serious hits of late, and being left to work this involuntary state out in his mind was crucial to Stephen's well being. A prying mother hen was not part of that process that he wanted to deal with at the moment.

Damien's demise had forever altered the present and future. Because of that untimely death Stephen would have to face his past. But please, not right now. Surely Susan could understand that. No. No she couldn't. If Stephen had changed, then probably their marriage had also changed. But what was the form it would take, or rather, was it taking? He had no way of knowing. He just didn't want to talk. He didn't want her to touch him either, even though she was scrubbing his back. All these questions were so close at hand, and they had to be addressed. But he couldn't—not even now.

Stephen had begun to live in a world that coincided with what lived in him, a life of reaction, not cognition. There was a huge difference. In the corporate world that he knew and traveled, reaction would destroy him. It would asphyxiate everything that he and his forbearers had built. In the world of combat, thinking would kill him.

"Susan," Stephen forced the word out of his mind like an abscessed sore, a deep, pus like thing that hurt thinking about touching it. "I can't talk . . . right now."

Emotions, framed by the words Susan's innermost being had chosen during the day's lonely vigil, poured forth. "Oh, Stephen, I was so scared. I thought I wouldn't ever see you again. Don't you know how much I love you?" That said, a negative ardor balanced the whole, "Don't you *ever* do that to me again."

Susan's last words felt to Stephen like day's old repressed fists battering at the barrier he'd erected around himself. They bounced off of course, but left his head pounding. Out of survival, Stephen pulled his arms over his head, as if signaling to her 'get out of here and leave me alone.' Stephen heard his wife crying and then the door shut. She'd granted his request, thank God. He was alone now, and once more he'd hurt her. That seemed to be the best he could do of late, hurt his wife. Still, he refused to explain to her the issue he faced from his past, and since he wasn't talking, he couldn't halt their effects. Since he couldn't restrain the past as it interfaced with his immediate life, he had no way to meet Susan's present need. He couldn't meet his own need for peace. For the moment, he sat in the tub, alone . . . and silent.

After a while the water turned lukewarm and ceased to sooth him. Only the sound of his breathing interfered with the quiet and occasional sloshing. Susan's presence, if it had done nothing else, had made this silence acceptable, if not wonderful. Sitting alone with his thoughts had also turned this bath into a miserable experience. His life was coming apart, and now he knew it. He imagined that he was in danger of losing the very things that had made life bearable to him: his wife, family, career and his reason for being. Within the scope of seventy minutes, Stephen had gone from half conscious shivering, to warmth, then anger, which seemed inevitably headed toward despair, and finally purposelessness. He'd not tried to drown himself yet, but the thought eddied around the edges of his mind.

Sunday, May 14, 1967

In the morning Susan didn't avoid Stephen, but she didn't go out of her way to cover the hazy and jagged matter separating them. Thus she resolved to take the day and spend it rewinding her unraveling soul. Stephen would surely not do much, she hoped. Susan felt sorry for herself as she dressed. As she looked into the mirror, she decided not to apply any makeup, not that she needed much. Susan had always been fortunate that way. The woman staring back at her had no other woman sympathetic to her plight with which to discuss her husband's and her misery. That woman was ferociously tired. During the night Susan had slept sporadically. She often turned over or felt behind her countless times in order to touch Stephen. Resigned to his soft fits of sluggish respiration and her own infrequent catnaps, Susan fought with Mrs. Danvers over the soul of her husband and herself. She succumbed to fatigue around 3:45.

At breakfast, Quill said he was going to church and then to visit a rancher friend of his. He would return later in the afternoon. Stephen paid little attention to this pronouncement. He ate quickly and headed out the door without saying goodbye to anyone, his barriers had already gone up. His departure surprised Susan, and now the day was beginning to wallow once again. It bore its weight like a beefy, truculent thing. With the men gone, Susan sat alone at the table in the huge warehouse, picking at the scrambled eggs and bacon on her plate that had gone cold. She pondered anew how her life and marriage could have come to this.

Jacques returned to clean the dishes only to find that Susan had already done them. She phoned the children and cried joyfully at their voices. They were so very far from her. Each shared the current events surrounding their lives, and Susan's heart ached, because she was not present to savor any of it. She spoke evasively about their father, but gave Margaret and David her assurances that all would be fine. Michael reminded his mother about his coming graduation in June, an event that had been emblazoned on her conscious mind since he was born. He was concerned that his parents' purpose for coming to Canada might not have run its course by then. Susan, too, was anxious about this, but told him not to worry. It would all work out. With that, she hung up before Michael heard her cry.

Then, fighting her building anger, Susan returned to the sofa and wrote each child a letter that she would not mail. She read four pages from Hemingway's *To Have and Have Not*, a novel she brought with her. Susan found it difficult to concentrate. Hemingway's existentialism depressed her. Now she wondered why she had picked that particular work.

Around noon, she ate lunch alone and then walked over to the huge picture window to gaze out upon the pastoral setting far below and in front of the cabin. Well out into the field, she observed the lazy cattle swishing their tails at bothersome flies. Once, she caught sight of Stephen doing something down near the drive.

Later in the day, the orange, yellow, red and velvet sunset coaxed from her an exclamation point, "magnificent!" Susan thought of the melody to *Canadian Sunset* she'd spent hours learning on the piano when she was nine, or was it twelve? It would be nice to have a piano she thought, but the men didn't see the need for such things. Tuning it would definitely be a problem here. Had none of the men played? Susan hugged herself as the day closed around her and she felt its solemn chill. She dined alone, but for Jacques's presence in the kitchen. Stephen was a no show and Quill hadn't returned either as he said. She could only wonder about this.

Concerning Stephen, he had spent the day avoiding his wife as well as his own thoughts, preferring rather to be alone, to find something to keep his hands and mind busy. He tinkered with this and that in the barn, and then walked the fence line to check for loose or broken wire. It was nine-twelve p.m. when he opened the cabin's main door. Susan had left a light on downstairs. Stephen slipped behind the bar where he found an unopened bottle of Canadian Club. He poured a crystal glass half full, and took a seat in the nearest living area. This was the first time he'd been quiet all day, but he didn't want to entrap himself by sudden idleness. On an empty stomach, half a glass of Scotch whiskey would unwind him or make him sick so that he couldn't think. In point of fact, neither happened. Stephen sipped the libation slowly but steadily until the glass was almost empty and the numbness had begun its advance toward subduing his thinking processes. He climbed the stairs lightheaded, his steps unsteady and cumbersome. As he neared the bedroom door, Stephen thought that he heard his wife crying. It would be easier to sleep in the next room. That was the last lucid thought he remembered.

The week matriculated slowly, wearily. When Susan attempted to confront or converse with Stephen, she found him once more argumentative or nonverbal. He produced excuses to tend to business that he assured her were most urgent. Despite her verbal protests, often bellicose in nature, Stephen left her to sort through alone what he refused to confront. He had not called the children by Wednesday. Dolores had been told to refer all matters to Marcus Lloyd, which she did.

On Thursday, Stephen came out of his tight-fisted shell. Susan had no idea how to evaluate this man or what to say to him when this transformation occurred. He'd waked her two nights in a row in the middle of his bad dreams, counting chutes or calling out bogeys at various numbers on the clock. She had to shake him awake to stop the nightmares. She'd hold him and rock him back to sleep, wondering about her own feelings for him. In the morning Susan followed her husband around the place, asking about this saddle or that type of hay or feed.

Susan saw the barn cat scamper after a big rat to which she screamed hysterically and all but jumped into Stephen's arms. After Susan had been calmed sufficiently, their laughter burst asunder the almost week-old tension and avoidance. Stephen spent the better part of ten minutes apologizing for his behavior. She accepted his words at face value, but she too felt distant. He took her hand and Susan let him walk her out into the field, but away from the cattle. It took a half-mile before he said anything. Stephen was somewhat evasive about his nightmares when she asked, but he owed her that much. The blessed rat had forced their difficulties toward the center of their relationship.

Stephen couldn't have been more dear or charming on Friday and Saturday. He seemed so at ease with life. A transformation appeared to have taken place and Susan drew close to him, wanting to drink him in. They slept late, loved deeply, talked, slept, loved again, and laughed. Finally they opened the bedroom door about 3 p.m. It was a glorious day, what was left of it. Stephen smiled and Susan felt a warm glow all through her soul. The world seemed conquerable.

Thirty-Five: The "Thing"

$\rightarrowtail\cdot\text{\textbardbl}\cdot\blacklozenge\!\!\succ\!\!\cdot\bigcirc\cdot\!\!\prec\!\!\blacklozenge\cdot\text{\textbardbl}\cdot\twoheadleftarrow$

Sunday, May 21, 1967

After going to church and visiting his friend, Quill returned to find Stephen arguing with Susan over something that seemed to the old man very insignificant. He heard their bedroom door slam and Stephen came rushing past him in a huff.

"Is everything okay?" Quill ventured, knowing the answer but attempting to be polite.

Stephen mumbled something as he sped past the old man, mainly because he was far too eager to leave the proximity of his wife. The afternoon ground on, and Susan stayed in the bedroom. Stephen dug and replaced a fence post. When he realized that he dug it in the wrong place, he threw the posthole digger out into the field. He set off to be alone in the tree line, swearing at everything.

At seven p.m., Susan descended the stairs. She hoped that the hindmost part of her tenth day in Canada would produce an acceptable evening. She needed a better one than this day had portended, but frankly didn't expect she'd find it. Her dressing preparations had wearied her because of her husband's volatile exit earlier in the day. In what mental condition would she find him tonight, she wondered? Susan applied her makeup with apprehension one minute, something just under the screen of joy the next.

No one stood below on the main level to observe how fetching she looked. Susan Lloyd was an elegant woman, as graceful this evening as the night she first laid eyes on Stephen. This particular black gown clung to her as if the designer had her in mind when he set pencil to paper. It accented her eyes as much as her figure. It, or she, or both, had stopped Stephen in his tracks the moment he saw her wearing it that first night in Houston. All the men with whom Stephen stood conversing halted stock still at the sight of Susan. That was several years ago. Within three minutes she had these powerful men, two generals, several top corporate execs, one engineer, and a graduate student infatuated, probably in love with her. With her intellect, Susan kept them looking at her face, not the usual places men's eyes played about her physique, no little accomplishment to be sure. There was so much of her to observe and enjoy, even from a distance.

That night she held her prestigious audience spellbound for forty-five minutes engaging them on a host of subjects. Stephen watched her from his vantage point, admiring his woman. And when they were alone, he kissed her passionately and told her just how much he admired her. His words were to her love, real love. It was the best night of her life. Susan languished in the memory of that night for several minutes more.

When that powerful thought faded, her spirit felt a bit less buoyant. Susan stood and slipped on the black sequined gown. She pressed and smoothed it around her hips and waist. She liked what she saw. On the periphery of her mental state, Susan Lloyd felt that their chances at marriage were slipping away. What else could she or should she try? Neither her mother nor Annika was present to coach her. Susan took one last look in the mirror. Her lips shone, her nails were immaculate, her hair perfect, and her teeth white and straight. She wondered if anyone would notice. The goblet was perfect, but was the vessel empty? As with the Spartans, she would either return to this room with her shield...or on it. She left her dressing to go stand at the top of the stairs.

Her descent of the long stairs above and behind the bar appeared methodical to the casual observer. It was anything but. Susan felt too restless for that. Having reached the mid-way point, she breathed deeply, and all but bounced to the main floor. An uninvited thought, positive and glorious, filled her mind with possibilities: it would be a good and fine evening. At the bottom step, Susan was confronted by the smell of Jacques' usually late banquet, drenching her senses.

At nine o'clock, she was hungry and her stomach told her so. Tonight, the Frenchman had planned well. The house and its aroma, the amenities, which Jacques brought to it, held a promise of sanctuary to her emotions that had been stretched and drained. But the room was void of people save Jacques and her. It was nine o'clock and there was no one with which to share herself. Once more Susan wrestled to overcome and subdue her anxiety. Sudden fatigue attempted to drag her under its carriage and trample her.

She waited another fifteen minutes for Stephen to appear at the top of the stairs. She wanted him to look upon her, dazzling below him, and to realize what a fool he'd been. She wanted him to apologize, take her in his arms, hold her and speak to her all evening. She wanted him to dance close to her until her legs ached, to finish the evening with wine and take her to his bed. Instead, Susan sat alone. She felt old, unpretty, and unwanted.

At 9:17, she heard a knock at the door far across the room, uncrossed her legs, stood, and went to answer it. Quill waited in the porch light swatting the bugs. His suit coat and tie hung loosely on him, both were old and long out of date. He held a bunch of wild flowers in his fist, several of which hung limp around his old hand. He hadn't much hair to comb these days, but he did the best he could with the little he did have.

"Please come in, kind sir," Susan welcomed him with a refreshing smile and a quick curtsy she didn't know was left inside her.

Quill handed her the flowers blushing and said awkwardly, "They reminded me of your . . . of your eyes . . . and, um, your smile. *Dog-gone it,*" he muttered under his breath. He wasn't good at sentimentality, but he'd rehearsed it word for word for the past half hour. He didn't want his compliment to bear the roughness it just had. But like an old fool, Quill would rather stand there and look at Susan. The warmth he brought out of her more than made up for his compliment. Susan knew when a man wanted to look at her, even if he was old enough to be her granddad. "You look so pretty, Susan. I...I didn't mean to stare." He hoped he'd not been too obvious.

"Yes you did, and I love you for it. I'm feeling a little *underappreciated* today, if you know what I mean—" Susan said this while whispering in his ear and looking at the top of the stairs in hopes of finally seeing her husband. At her terrifying nearness, Quill turned even redder.

At 9:34, Stephen came loping down the stairs to acknowledge Susan and Quill's presence. Their two worlds, Stephen's and Susan's, had not even jostled one another, but slipped innocuously past each other with barely the hint of recognition. Stephen said nothing about her gown or the effort she'd taken to please him. Now she believed he didn't deserve her industry. He was unaware or unconcerned about those long, careful minutes she'd spent before the mirror, applying her perfume and makeup, fixing and unfixing her hair the way he liked for her to wear it, and all the while fighting her inmost demons. Stephen was lost or his compass was broken. Susan couldn't change these things apparently. Quill noted the instant the air rushed from Susan's spirit. The old man held Susan's chair, indicating his desire for her to sit so he could act like a gentleman.

Stephen ran back upstairs. Within several minutes the music of Mantovani flowed like fine wine over the table and the people settled there. It helped. Quill told some of his jokes—old standby's, a few of which were actually funny. He couldn't have been more surprised or pleased when Susan laughed. He'd do just about anything to amuse her. Quill thought she was prettiest, most vivacious or extraordinary when her heart gave way to merriment. This was his real bouquet. His sense of humor had been his best and only gift to Helen. It wasn't until the final few weeks of her life that she understood this. Quill's humor was all he really had to give her. Her actual recognition of his humble present, so long unnoted, made Helen's leaving the more difficult.

Stephen kept his distance in spite of Quill's humor. He'd not worn his suit and tie, but slacks and a shirt because he didn't feel like wearing what Susan had laid out for him. His wife's choice of his dinner clothes had irked him. He was trying to join in, but found he couldn't. Tightness gripped his chest, and he almost felt eager to duel.

Thirty-Six: Camp O'Donnell

When Jacques cleared away the dessert dishes, Quill asked a question midway through the melody of, *All The Things You Are.* Quill's expression seemed reserved. His eyes looked away from his guest's and into his wine glass. "It's hard, isn't it?"

Susan looked over at Quill, wondering if she had heard him correctly. "I'm sorry?" she asked. Susan noticed that he wasn't smiling. He blinked several times obviously deep in thought. "What? What isn't easy?"

"This . . . this unhappiness that sat down to eat with us. This *thing* that came with you. It isn't easy living with it, is it?" Quill waited for the somewhat familiar question to settle, to locate its target. "Would you tell me what you're thinking right now, Susan?" He suspected she was quite vulnerable and needed to talk about more than the weather. Perhaps in conversing with her, he might help her to understand what few others could or would. These were the thoughts and passions of this old man; a hermit gone to seed in central British Columbia after his Helen had died. Quill's feelings, as he observed this magnificent woman, were not prurient. He was just lonesome for female companionship and a little conversation with someone other than Jacques or Raymond, which also surprised him. Quill hadn't realized just how much until this evening.

"Mr. Lloyd told me Stephen had been seeing a psychiatrist before coming here."

"Yes, we were," Susan acknowledge. "I hoped the treatments would last longer—you know, so that Dr. Inhofe might tell me more about how to . . . how to help Stephen. He gave us the name of another doctor in Ft. Worth. But somehow Dr. Inhofe's schedule and the direction of our time were changed, and through a little coaxing, here we are. Here we are. But where are we?" Susan halted, because she felt specific emotions rushing toward her throat and gathering behind her eyes, demanding to be heard and seen. Quill saw that, too.

"I see." He looked at Stephen, saw him staring into space, preoccupied. "So . . . Susan, how do *you* feel?"

Quill knew women lived in the world of feelings and words—lots of words. She took a long minute to answer, because she wanted to note how interested Stephen was in what she would say. Susan feared that her words might set off another powder keg, the concussion of which might do her in. "I'm frustrated and hurt. I'm angry. Quill, I'm not quite sure what to do. It was before we came up here my daddy actually talked to me about his experiences and the effect the war had on him. Stephen's doctor also shared some of his experiences in the Second World War, and a little of what happened after he came back. But my mother flatly refuses to discuss those early years she and my daddy shared after he came home. It's almost as if these veterans, like Stephen, are *afraid* to talk about it." Susan looked squarely at Stephen, daring him to say something, anything. He declined her challenge, so she continued. "It's like they think they'll *die* if they say anything. You know? First my daddy, then Dr. Inhof talked to me, and the way it was with the doctor . . ."

Quill sipped his tea. He thought and remembered, and then inhaled deeply as his eternal eyes met Susan's again. Those eyes had seen more than any human should have to. Each retina, wrinkle and scar had known horrors and wounds, sorrow and pain, all of which lived just below the surface of Quill Du Pont. Susan, of course, knew none of this about Quill. If she had, she would have asked Quill to lay it out for her days ago. Quill only knew to bide his time.

Susan touched his weathered hand softly, coaxing him to speak. Her caress startled him somewhat, though he knew she was about to place her hand on his. His hands and fingers were scarred, bent, and mangled. Why hadn't she noticed them before, she wondered? Susan Lloyd hadn't realized how preoccupied she'd been until that moment. She forgot he wore gloves during the day, but he wasn't wearing them tonight. Why? And his nails, he hardly had any. His hands were ghastly looking, broken and knotted little sticks. Only a few fingers actually worked with any degree of effectiveness.

He caught her surprise and revulsion, but by now he was used to it. He even expected it. Despite herself, Susan attempted concealment, unsuccessfully so. Helen had lettered herself as to how and where to stroke his 'claws' when she wanted to ease his demons or to urge him in a direction conducive to their relationship.

"I'm sorry. I didn't mean to stare, Quill." That wasn't true. No one having seen Quill's hands couldn't help but stare.

"No, that's all right. I'm used to it. I didn't wear my gloves tonight for a reason."

"What reason?" she wondered.

He breathed heavily. Talking about this was never easy for him just as Susan had said before. He spoke so little about it. Here at the cabin, there wasn't anyone with which to discuss the war. Oh, there was his old Army buddy, Hal McKinney, in Prince George. But they didn't see each other very often any more. Hal had a bad heart, and he too lived alone now.

"No, go ahead and look. Touch 'em. It's okay. I get bored up here, so these mangled claws usually start the conversation when folks do come. It also gets me out of a lot of work." He winked at her. Susan, too, held her breath in order to assay the moment. She, like Helen before her, had wondered which parts of his hands still retained little or no nerve damage. Quill would have enjoyed her touch and attention more if he could feel her soft hands. Susan's expressions resembled that of Helen's too when he returned from the Pacific.

It wasn't pity in her eyes that he saw. It was more like wonder and empathy, maybe incredible tenderness. He saw Helen in Susan as she examined his hands, turning them over, running her index finger along what used to be his nails, and rubbing her finger over the broken, unhealed bones. More than the Japanese had distorted them. The shrapnel from a Jap artillery round had imbedded itself against several nerves. The doctors feared what surgery might do. It didn't matter that she couldn't possibly understand that he had weathered a storm of unimaginable proportions, dished out with typical Imperial Japanese brutality and deprivation.

Helen finally stammered awkwardly to the place where Quill trusted her enough to allow her to touch his hands. She, too, had felt disconnected

348

from Quill after years of waiting for him to turn in her direction, to let her in, even as Susan felt this evening toward her own husband. To that exact moment following the war, Quill's hands had been curious oddities to Helen. It was a sunny day in October 1949. Quill's defenses must have been down that day. There was something in Helen's eyes that spoke to his pain, something in the way she poured over each scar and broken bone that wouldn't heal properly. That day became the first step to something more in their relationship. It wasn't much, but it was more. The way in which she carefully and lovingly embraced his imprisonment through his hands stated that she loved him no matter.

While Quill found himself alternating between these two women, Helen had, in some ethereal sense, returned to him. She sat close for the preceding moments and hours in the person of Susan Lloyd. Quill felt that, for whatever reason, he would open his rusting heart to Susan, as he should have with Helen, but never did. This was for her. He owed Helen, and he would pay her through Susan.

Looking at the overall presentation of Quill so proximate to her at the table took the form of a disquieting experience. His sunken face, bottomless eyes forced by age and experience deep into their sockets, his hands broken and distorted from war and the beatings, and the long, slow the onset of arthritis, were laying claim to him. Time and the medical field had been incapable of repositioning these features to their original settings after such a lengthy imprisonment.

Quill bore other brands and scars from the too numerous and unnecessary slappings and pounding's issued at the hands of his Japanese guards. They were all too eager to appease their own inferiority and please their superiors. His nose, too, lay at an odd angle, and it didn't receive air well. His breathing was always labored and thick. His thin neck broadcast a nasty serrated scar his shirt collars couldn't fully hide. Both of his arms had been broken, and neither of them could be set immediately or properly, which made physical work agonizing and difficult. He still had numerous broken ribs that had healed at offensive angles, only to be rebroken by angry, over-zealous guards. To this day, certain movements were excruciating. His right leg wobbled, although his pride and learned survival skills willed him to walk.

He forgot things completely. He kept his pad and pencil near him at all times, except when he couldn't remember where he laid them last. His thinning brown hair hid a few of the scars on the back of his head, the brunt of which came after he'd passed out from the beatings. The ravages of uncontested parasites added to his breathing and bowel difficulties.

Several times, the guards or his fellow soldiers gave him up for dead. After lying still for far too long, someone would come to gather his broken body for burial. There were just too many men dying every day to notice or care about one particular individual. But from some place known only to Quill Du Pont, he'd painfully prop himself to sitting, gather what little senses and strength he possessed, and stand upon insecure legs, bow, and slowly drag himself back to his labors or his mat to collapse. No one knows, least of all Quill, how he survived. Maybe he just refused to quit.

All the indescribable torture and starvation, the murders committed by the camp guards, their cruelty and hatred for men who would surrender rather than die was not without its price emotionally and psychologically. Playing football, he knew how to hit a man so that he didn't get up for the remainder of the play. But that was the nature of the sport. It was mutually shared and respected by both teams. In captivity, however, no respect was accorded these beaten Allies, and, as with so many captured men, hate finally conquered and ultimately sustained Sgt. Quill Du Pont. He dreamed about beating these fierce little Nips beyond recognition, then slowly mutilating their bodies as they screamed for mercy. He would show them none. Adding to his extreme discomfort, his government had deserted his fellow combatants and him, so that he harbored a smoldering grudge with FDR, MacArthur, and men like him.

While in the Philippines prior to the war, he'd cheated on Helen during a drunken liberty, and that ate at him while a prisoner. The girl was a pretty little Filipino whore. She meant nothing. That's what he told himself. But adultery is adultery. In captivity, when the Japs were at their cruel worst, Quill toyed with Helen's imaginary indigence at his infidelity. The resulting heated conversation he replayed in his mind day after miserable day, enabling him to go one minute more— for the first year. He willed himself to argue with her, and then he shut Helen out so he could watch her, the sharpness of her disappointment, and the sting in her tone, her turned down eyes, which made the fire flicker in him day, by day, by day, by day.

Helen's was the poisoned prison of faithfulness, because she had loved him since the first grade, since the first day of school. In captivity,

Quill focused on the Helen he had left, the Helen of his mind's eye, and his part in hurting her. If he survived this, Quill knew he couldn't keep it from her, thus he began to believe that he deserved everything he received at the hands of these inhuman Japanese. Yet with the passing of the endless, never free years, his strength and his will to live ebbed and all but gradually evaporated, save a little. It was this final ace, his wrongdoing and the ongoing arguments with Helen that kept his hope from inching away from him. Nightmares overcame his short, fitful naps, and he'd awaken screaming her name, begging for forgiveness.

He remembered the first time he saw his own scrawny figure reflected in a pool of dirty rainwater. The man staring back at him was emaciated, a skeletal shadow that terrified him. That man's eyes had become dark circles set amid hollow cheeks and cracked, leather-dry lips. He could count his broken ribs beneath the ragged shirt he wore. His head felt dizzy the whole day now. From the fog of that picture came the realization that he was *that* man, a dead man walking, a dead man sleeping. Little would matter the moment he could no longer remember Helen's face to tell her what a scoundrel he was or to sip at the smell of her perfume. His energy to argue would finally deserted him by tonight, surely by tomorrow at the latest, and he could die.

But he had to live to tell her, didn't he? Then nothing else mattered. Life would soon desert him and he'd be gone if he didn't steal himself into a frame of mind that would beat these captors. It was several days following this incident that, somehow, the Filipino guerrillas smuggled a few of the prisoners some rice and pig meat. Quill ate ravenously. One more day, he'd go one more day.

"Susan," he hesitated. He was suddenly afraid. "Susan . . ." once more he made an attempt to speak.

"Quill, what is it?"

"Susan, do you remember an event during the war called the Bataan Death March?"

"Yes. *Why?*" she asked cautiously. Looking at this little man, at his hands and face, she knew, yet she knew nothing. "Oh *no*. Not you? That's why your hands . . ?"

"Yes, ma'am. General Wainwright surrendered in mid-April 1942. I was in captivity for over three years."

Susan couldn't speak for a few minutes. Then she said, "Go on. I want to hear this."

"Susan, I don't know what it was like flying a bomber into what your Stephen did, mission after mission. Only he can tell you that. I can't imagine it. I don't like to fly, myself."

"Oh, but he *won't*, Quill. He *won't*." Susan looked at her husband whom she thought or hoped was listening to their conversation.

"Susan . . . Susan. Listen to me, please."

"All right," she agreed to an uneasy truce.

"Stephen and I share something that you probably . . . well, you will find hard, if not troubling. And much as I dislike talking about it myself, I want to try and explain it to you as best I can. I know what he's going through. I never did talk about it with my Helen. I couldn't or wouldn't, and that brought her so much grief. She desperately wanted to know . . . just like you do. Not talking about it is *very* normal." He paused, feeling the emotions rumbling below, daring to exert their power over him. Susan noted that he was on the verge of tears, and that he might not be able to resume what he had begun. Once more she stroked his hand, attempting as best she could to ease his pain. "My Helen . . . she did that when she saw it coming. Thank you."

"There were signs?" That was what Dr. Inhofe had said, but she'd forgotten.

"Oh yes. You'll learn to read them on Stephen as Helen did with me. Susan, apparently Stephen's war has decided to make itself known now for some reason. What we each went through, we had to repress or we would go insane. We had no time to grieve over our losses, which were considerable. So we shoved it all down there and kept going." Quill said nothing about Bataan in terms of specifics . . . for now. "You can't demand that your husband just start talking about his experiences. It doesn't happen that way. He has to trust you."

"Trust me? What on *earth* do you mean, *trust me*?" Susan was all but incensed.

"No, Susan. The kind of trust I'm talking about is different than what you're thinking. I'm talking about a life and death kind of trust. You're thinking about him showing up every day at 6 p.m. for dinner, taking the kids to ball games . . . that kind of thing. You trust him to pay the bills. The kind of trust *we* mean is completely different. It's defined on a level we didn't know existed until we were put in situations they make movies about. He had to trust his navigator to get him exactly over the target and back home. He had to trust his gunners to keep the German fighters from shooting him down. He had to trust the mechanics that his plane was airworthy—every time, every mission. He had to trust that his parachute riggers did their jobs or he'd hit the ground hard if he ever bailed out. I had to trust that my buddies would keep me on my feet, bandage my wounds, and feed me when I couldn't feed myself . . ." Tears rolled down Quill's cheeks, for the last statements were as close to his war as he wanted to approach.

Once more she stroked his hand, and he let her. There had been Damien, her father, her husband, and Dr. Inhofe. Now Quill Du Pont. All these veterans in the span of days or weeks had crossed her path. It seemed every place Susan turned lately she bumped into little men and big men, all of who were broken in some way by war. Was it a coincidence? It was strange. It wasn't fair. Were there no normal human beings left in the world? Quill was the little broken man of the group. He had no one to care for him or brush away his loneliness anymore.

"I know you don't know the answer to this, but I'm going to ask it anyway. Susan, do you know what it's like to be so scared that you throw up?"

She thought for a minute. "Yes, I do. When I competed in the Miss Texas pageant, I felt so queasy and scared I vomited. I didn't tell my parents. Yes. I've been scared." She felt certain she could compete with these fractured men.

Susan saw the smile forming ever so slightly on Quill's small, wrinkled face. "No, I mean *scared*, dear." Quill leaned in closer. "So scared you believe you are about to die—as a matter of fact, you reach a place where you already are dead in your mind. After a while I quit vomiting. I just wasn't scared any more. It took too much energy. I bet many times your husband got up to go fly, he got scared. He may have seen some of those bombers explode right next to him from the flak. He may have had men killed in his airplane. I saw some planes lose their engines, which meant they would fall behind the formation and the Jap Zero's might pick them off. He flew through storms that would make you so air sick you couldn't believe. And he never missed a mission, I bet."

It was then that Stephen interrupted. "To the contrary, Quill. There was once when we turned around." Susan turned to look at Stephen, amazed and thankful to see he was following and maybe going to take part in this conversation.

Quill resumed his discourse. "He was sick and exhausted, and scared, and yet he flew, day after day, betting or knowing that he might not come back. After a while, maybe he wondered why he did." Quill turned his attention to Stephen and said, "You felt guilty for landing again . . . and coming home safely, leaving so many great guys behind, didn't you?" Stephen shook his head in agreement. "There are no adequate words to describe such heroism."

Someone was rubbing her nose in it—again. Dr. Inhofe had spoken in the same vein, but now Susan was *hearing* it. The woman felt small and alone, and the house or cabin slowly enveloped her once more. Stephen would have to fill in the details. Dr. Inhofe had laid a foundation, her father had added on to it, and now it was Quill's turn to build on to that. Maybe she *did* need to be surrounded by such men, broken or not.

"Um, Quill . . . You asked me if I knew about Bataan? The Death March?"

"Yes."

"Is that why you know about where my Stephen is right now? Why he's struggling so much? His doctor was wounded horribly in France or Belgium. I can't remember which."

"Yes, ma'am. I don't really want to go into what . . . into my war experiences and all, but I know what's going on with Stephen—I think I do. I wasn't in the Air Corps. But I figure he came home and tried to pick up all the pieces that he'd left just like you expected him to. And like a loving, obedient husband he did. He went to work with an Irishman's frenzy. Didn't he?

"Well, yes. What else should he have done? The war was over. That was all in the past. I supposed he'd forget about it." *The war was over. That was in the past. I supposed he'd forget about it.* Those concepts felt alien to her now, at least as she heard herself say them. "But then the babies came, and he went back to school to finish his degree, and then went to work for his father. And now he's the president of Lloyd Hotels International." Susan patted her husband's arm, although Stephen didn't acknowledge her affection or her pride. It didn't seem to mean anything to him at that particular moment.

"Susan, how was he supposed to deal with all that death and destruction? He thought that if he opened that spigot he wouldn't be able to shut it off . . . that he would literally die. Besides, would you have understood? Probably not."

Susan had placed the words 'death and destruction' in the same sentence with the man, Stephen Lloyd. Yet there was still a disconnect between her mind and the real thing. Was she so preoccupied with getting pregnant, having children, and doing all the things married couples do that she missed his . . . his *what*? Quill watched her eyes shift and dart back over the years. Stephen never talked about it. He *never* talked about it. She felt a faint trace of her own culpability from having entered this discussion. What *was* the war like for *her* husband? She was now building a suitable set of tools from which to unpack this question.

Susan unexpectedly made the turn toward reality. With these men's assistance, she had begun to define the war into bite size pieces on which she could chew, and just perhaps, digest some of it. It might become something more than an abstract concept or past event attempting to make contact with *her* cosmos. A newsreel is one-dimensional, but life has more sides, and for her to trek into the worst that man can inflict upon himself, Susan might discover that no man or woman who engages it comes away unscathed. Did she want to do that? Yes. Perhaps she *was* getting it—somewhat. These are damaged people until the day they die. That seemed obvious now. Each person seemed to handle it differently, but all are touched radically. She *had been* ignorant. She didn't mean to be, but her kind of ignorance kept her safe. She *hadn't asked*.

Susan wanted to hear about the war now. She could and would listen now that Quill had 'smacked' her across the face with it, and it stung. Susan returned the old man's all- knowing gaze, and her purpose for being here closed about her. Reality is a cruel taskmaster. It can also bring in the light. *She did want to know, but more than she thought she knew.*

"Susan, I have a theory about what happens to men under the prolonged stresses of war. Now, mind you, I can't prove any of this yet, but I think it's got some merit to it. I had aspirations of becoming a doctor once. I took some premed classes at the University."

"What is it? Please tell me, Quill. What do you think?"

"I think that in some way, our mind and bodies had to compensate... chemically and internally, so that we literally came home different people in some kind of basic, fundamental, organic way from what we were before the war. It's more than psychological alteration.

Thirty-Seven:
War and Sovereignty

"Dr. Inhofe said the same thing, Quill."

"He did? Well, I'll be. As prisoners of the Japanese it dawned on me quickly that my life meant nothing to them, because they had no respect for prisoners. We went moment by moment for three years wondering if we would see the sunset. Something like twenty thousand men *alone* died at Camp O'Donnell. God knows how many died walking *to* the camp. The Japs didn't care. From all that fear, anger, hatred and revulsion, I was and am axiomatically changed. Now, I can't in any way prove this idea, of course. But I believe it's true nonetheless. I was a fun loving guy before I left for overseas. I loved chasing the girls, driving fast, playing ball. You know all the things we did as kids without a care. But when I came home all I wanted to do was avoid everything I'd lived to return to. No one seemed to care back here that we'd been imprisoned for three or more years. The government just turned us loose after the surrender. I brooded and kept to myself. I was afraid to be around people. I drank once but it almost killed me from all those parasites and things still in my body. Thankfully Mr. Lloyd offered me my old job back, and I couldn't wait to get as far away from society as I could. I slept with a pistol under my pillow and a knife near me for years even after I became a Christian. The old me died in that POW camp.

"I have done some reading in medical journals, but it's all so new—these studies they're doing now. You may not believe this looking at me, but I was a tackle at the University of Montana. I weighed two hundred pounds—all muscle I might add." Quill puffed his chest out, which made him cough. His ribs hurt too. "Excuse me. You think that's funny, don't you? It is, kind of. I came home weighing just slightly over one hundred pounds." Susan shook her head in dismay. "My Helen used to try and coax me into conversation about the camps and how we were treated and such, but I'd retreat faster than a turtle sticking his head back in his shell, if you know what I mean."

"I'm starting to, Quill. Did you act like Stephen is acting now?"

"I was worse, a whole lot worse." Quill winked at Stephen, and Stephen nodded in appreciation. "I wasn't fit to be around for years. Stephen's been struggling for how long? Several months? I came home hating Japs. I hated beyond anything I ever imagined a person could hate. I was consumed with hate. I hated God for not stopping the murder. I hated FDR and MacArthur for deserting us like I said. I hated anything and everything. I remember blaming Helen for . . ." He felt ashamed *still* for what he wasn't going to delve into. That had been a horrible day in their marriage. "I'd never leave a scrap of food on my plate Helen fixed for me. She used to get so mad at me for licking the plate . . . yes, I licked the plate. You bet your life. They starved us like rats, and if it wasn't nailed down, we'd eat it just to survive."

"We had this chaplain, Captain Sullivan, if I remember right. Anyway, he went into captivity with us. He was a real trooper, the captain was. Well, one day, some of us had gotten fed up with the Japs beheading us, beating us unconscious and treating us like garbage. Some of us asked the Padre, 'Where is your God now, Chaplain?'

"He didn't miss a beat. He was dipping his spoon into that gruel they served us when he said, 'Where He always is, on His throne, ruling over His universe and this camp, ensuring that His eternal purpose in Christ is carried out. To be even more specific, King David asks the question in Psalm 139, "Where can I go from (God) your Spirit? Where can I flee from your presence?"

"His answer is very illuminating and comforting to *me*. David says, 'If I go up to the heavens, you (God) are there; if I make my bed in Hell, you are there.' Men, God is right here."

"None of that made any sense to me and the other men. Corporal Hal Farley, a drinking buddy of mine, he spoke up, angry as he could be and said, 'You mean God was right there with that guy over there they just bayoneted to death and *that* fits into God's eternal plan?'

"Captain Sullivan said, 'Yes sir, the murder of that man surely does. I'm glad you understood me, Hal. That couldn't have happened if God had not willed it to happen.'"

"Old Hal shoots back, forgetting or not caring he was talking to a captain, 'You mean . . . *no way. How?*'"

"Sullivan said, 'Do you think that man ever heard the plan of salvation in his life? Probably. He might have gone to Sunday school when he was little.'"

"Hal said he saw that guy, Larry Nabors, attend Sunday Chapel a number of times. The chaplain asked if he became a Christian. Hal said, 'Nah. We'd go bar hoppin' when we could get shore liberty.'"

"The chaplain said, 'The Gospel of Luke talks about some men who came to Jesus complaining about how Pilate had killed some Jews so he could mix their blood in his sacrifices. The Jews wanted Jesus to condemn Pilate's actions, but Jesus didn't. Instead, Jesus said, 'unless you repent, you will likewise perish.' In other words, we who are left knowing that death could come at any time, when we see things like the death of our fellow prisoner, we shouldn't protest and hate the Japs. We are still alive for one reason. We didn't die so that we might repent of our sins and seek forgiveness from God or something worse might happen to us. Will you repent now? If you don't, something much worse might happen to you. Hell awaits those who refuse to repent and seek God's forgiveness by faith. I'm not mad at the Japanese. They can't help themselves. They've refused God's love in Christ. I love the Christ who died for me.' None of us knew what to say.'"

"Then the captain said something else that shocked me. He said, 'That man over there lived every second he was ordained to live. He wasn't robbed of anything. You know how I know that?'"

"Well, all the fellas shook their heads no."

Sullivan said, "You may have heard of the Apostle Paul in the Bible?"

"A few of us said we had."

"Paul wrote to the Christians living at Rome and told them that God had raised up this really mean king in Egypt for one purpose: to show His power over Pharaoh so that God's great name would be declared throughout the whole world. In other words, God created this horrid man Pharaoh and hardened his heart so God's people would be brutalized and stuck in captivity. Are you listening? And after four centuries, God would visit His people and all but destroy Egypt with plagues and kill Egypt's first born. God told Moses that He had heard Israel's cries and seen their hardships and would keep His covenant promise with Abraham, Isaac, and Jacob. God knew what Israel was going through then and He knows our pain now. So Paul says in Romans nine, 'I will harden whom I will harden and show mercy on whom I will show mercy."

"You all may also remember how Pharaoh sent his whole army chasing after Israel? Moses raised his staff and God parted the sea so that His people could cross over on dry land. The Bible tells us that God judged Pharaoh. The LORD killed his army and all the first born in Egypt. Why? First, Pharaoh killed Israel's firstborn, and second, God wanted to demonstrate His power in Pharaoh, and that His name might be proclaimed throughout the whole earth. So, Paul asks this question for guys who think like you do in our situation. 'Why does God still find fault with us if God hardens men's hearts and they act according to God's dictates?' Paul then asks this: 'Who resists God's will? Who are you o man who answers back to God? Will the molded thing say to its molder, Why have you made me like this?' In other words, 'Why have you hardened my heart so that I respond contrary to your will, God?'"

"God's answer is most instructive and it's not what we want to hear. 'Has the potter—that is, *God*, no right over the clay—that is, *us*, to make out of the same lump one vessel for beauty and another for menial use?'"

"Of course. He has every right to do with what is His, which is anything. The Scriptures attest that God is in the heavens and He does what He pleases, which is always right, I might add. He has a right to harden these Japanese guards' hearts so that they are very brutal to us, and that is His right. Remember, the wages of sin is death. If a man refuses to repent of his sin and turn in faith to Jesus to save him, he should expect nothing but hell because that is what he deserves. If he doesn't, it is only because God is being merciful a little while longer. And then when that man dies, the brutality of the Japanese will seem like child's play compared to the torment of an eternal Hell. There is a cause and effect where sin is concerned. Whatever a man sews, he will reap. The Japanese sewed brutality and they reaped the A-Bomb as a response. Jesus says repeatedly, in Hell, there will be weeping, wailing and gnashing of teeth for all eternity, and, in the Lake of Fire, no less. So, what Moses *and* Paul are telling us is that God will, in *His* infinitely good and wise time, bring judgment on these Japanese and all who refuse to trust in Jesus.

"Behind me, Charlie said, 'I don't get it, Chaplain?' What's that got to do with us?' Old Charlie Whitherspoon wasn't the smartest guy in the company.

"Everything, Charlie," said Sullivan. "Tell you what: imagine, if you will, that if you built a tractor engine from scratch. Okay?' We all understood that, so many of us came from farms. 'Now, this may sound crazy, but just imagine if that tractor engine could talk and it said to you, "Hey, I wanted to be a locomotive engine. How come you made me into a tractor engine?"

"Charlie trumped up again and said, 'Tractor engines can't talk.'"

"We all laughed. I told Charlie to shut up."

"I said you have to imagine this, Charlie," the chaplain said almost laughing, "but what would *you*, the builder, say to that tractor engine? Would you say, 'Oh, I'm sorry. If you want to be a locomotive engine, you should be one. I'll change you right now.' No, you would say, 'I made you for one thing, to plow that field. You are mine and there isn't going to be any argument.'"

"You see, the Bible says that God is our Creator King and Governor. He made each of us for *His* purposes, for His good pleasure and glory, or for evil. It also tells us that He is perfect, all-wise, unchangeable, and He knows absolutely why He does what He does. He has numbered every hair on our heads, named all the stars and not lost one. When calamity comes to a city, God says it is His doing. He withholds water just as He uses water to overwhelm and destroy people and property. The deceived and deceiver are His. He makes fools of judges, He loosens the bonds of kings, and overthrows the mighty. He pours contempt on royalty. He takes away men's understanding. In His hand is even the breath we breathe. All things were created through Christ and for Christ. Jesus is before all things, and in Christ, all things in heaven and earth hold together. God even made the wicked for the day of evil. The Bible even goes so far as to say, for all things are Your servants.

"So, Paul says in real blunt terms to each of us here, 'Who are you, O prisoners of the Imperial Japanese, to question God your Creator and Sustainer as to why you are a prisoner?' It is God's will that we *are* their prisoners. Paul had *learned* contentment in all circumstances by being put in terrible circumstances repeatedly. Isaiah tells us that it was God's eternal will to crush and cause His very own sinless Son to suffer and die at the hands of wicked Romans and Jews to save His elect from sin. And as far as I know, none of us is perfect in all our ways. This God is the King of the entire cosmos. So, in that sense the discussion is ended.

"Now, God says, glorify me in your captivity. Well, gentlemen, by the power of God's Holy Spirit, that is what I am going to try and do. Jesus bought me with His precious blood to be His own special treasure. I won't glorify God very well and I don't like being here. I *hate* it here. But I'm here because God is pleased to put me here to minister to you. I am not here because I'm unlucky. The only thing that keeps me sane in the midst of all *this* death and suffering is the living and eternally true Word of God and my place reserved in heaven. Jesus came here and lived. He knows suffering more than all of us because as God, all the curses due His elect fell on Him. As God, He was able to bear up under it. The Bible assures me that I have a faithful High Priest who is absolutely able to sympathize with every one of my weaknesses, and He prays for me.'"

"Charlie said he wasn't going to ever like it being a prisoner of these murderers no matter what the chaplain or that Bible said. Almost all of us agreed with Charlie. Some of the guys thought the chaplain meant he wasn't going to resist the Japs anymore. Well, I just didn't know God in those terms. I don't think I'd ever really thought about what God was like."

"Several men walked off disgusted saying how unfair God was. Anyway, the chaplain asked those of us who remained how we knew what God was truly like? We all said we either knew or thought He wasn't like that. Then Captain Sullivan asked us a real corker of a question. I'll never forget it. He asked, 'If we're all just having a run of bad luck—you know, being captured, perhaps fate or chance or the Devil has put one over on us—then how are we ever going to make any sense of out all *this*? What meaning can Bradley's death this morning, or the guy they shot yesterday, or the men who couldn't make it any longer possibly have?'"

"Bill Sontag piped up and said, 'I don't think anyone in the States even knows we're alive or here, or even *cares* if they do.'"

"We all kind of looked at each other, unsure how to answer, but feeling pretty much the same. We all just felt lost. I was coming real close to giving up at that point."

"The chaplain then remarked, 'As I said, God knows we're here in this prison, Bill. But, and this is huge—if He doesn't know about or hasn't determined this time and place for each of us, then all this we've endured has *no* meaning. And that means there is *no* God, no hope, no future. None. The look on Bill's face was one of pure bewilderment. And it doesn't matter whether we charge these guards, die with malaria, escape, or are set free. Life has no meaning, no purpose if God isn't invested in every moment or molecule of all this.'"

Quill sighed from the memories, and he broke from the story to tell Susan something pertinent to his point. "I heard one man say once, 'If we can make no sense out of the universals of life, like there is a God and there is truth, love and beauty, then how can we expect to make any appreciable sense out of the particulars, like being a captive of the Japanese? Seeing men die and endure torture, watching airplanes go down by the dozens, and now watching a man you love go through these difficult moments and not know why. If God hasn't decreed this and every other particular moment from eternity past, then it *has* no meaning. Let's just all give up, lie down, and die.'"

"Susan, the Bible assures us that *all* things, the universals and the particulars, work together for good, to *those* who love God, and are the called according to His purpose. Because I love Jesus, whom the Bible says is God and Lord, I believe He's called me to be here with you to explain some of this suffering you two are going through. Right this moment is His perfect will for me, and I will praise God in each and every one of my tribulations for His name's sake, to the best of my ability. And if He's called me to speak to you like this, even in this pain, this is the most meaningful place and event on earth, and by His enabling grace, I will respond. I don't want to talk about some of these things, but I do. He decreed that I say them, so I say them willingly. I'm not talking about mechanical determinism where we're all puppets controlled by some impersonal force. If that were the case, we could not be held responsible for our actions and God's commands would be absurd."

Quill returned to talking about his life in captivity. "So what's the purpose for my being in this hell hole, Chaplain?" one man demanded. "I can't say as I love God like what you just said."

"Jesus tells us we are light," Sullivan shot back. "Paul said that when he was weakest, he was strong because Christ's power dwelled in him. That means that when Paul experienced God's grace in the worst circumstances, eternity had invaded his circumstances. Here, I'm experiencing just a taste of heaven. I don't want to be anywhere else. Besides, I deserve *much worse* than this. The Bible says that before I trusted in Jesus to deliver me from the bondage of sin, I was a rebellious lawbreaker deserving God's justice. However, He has spared me to share His great mercy with sinners like myself and you guys. Even these Japanese if they let me. That's what I do know. There's an interesting verse in Exodus. God said to Moses, 'Who has made man's mouth? Or who makes him mute or deaf, or seeing or blind? Is it not I, the Lord?' The Bible says that God even caused David to number Israel and thousands died as a result of David's sin, while at the same time it says that God does not tempt anyone to sin. So gentlemen, let me ask you, how does a man become right with God before he dies?"

"I never will forget that conversation," Quill said. "They shot the chaplain two days later. The Japs had started putting us in groups of ten men. If one of the ten men escaped, they shot all ten. One of the men assigned to his group made it past the wire and the chaplain and eight other men were lined up after they caught him. The camp commander beheaded the guy that escaped, and they made the whole camp watch. Then he began to shoot the seven other men in the back of the head, one by one."

Quill stared into the great room, seeing that moment for what it was, murder. The next words trickled out, one upon another, "BANG, plop. BANG, plop. BANG, plop. I was sure I saw a smile come across the chaplain's face right before Tanaka shot him. With that pistol aimed at his head I saw him look up to heaven, and I thought for sure I saw him say, 'Thank you.' That was a very low day for me. I couldn't believe *that* could be God's will. I hated God all the more. Sullivan was a *good* man."

Sitting at the becalmed table, Quill realized he had lost his battle. His capture poured out of him like water from a boot. "We had this one guard. We called him, 'Old One Eye.' We'd start messing with his . . ."

Quill stopped, realizing that he'd punctured his own protective shell. His face manifested total surprise, turning into bewilderment, and he avoided Susan's intense interest. Helen had not been privy to this much information in their thirty years of marriage. "I'm sorry, Susan. I never ever meant to go that far. I know where this will lead . . . for *me*, anyway. Stephen is why you are here."

"Quill, won't you keep going? This is . . . I think I'm *starting* to understand more about what you all have been saying. Stephen's doctor shared his story with my son and me. I knew that while Stephen was away that he did dangerous things; that he was involved in events where men died. He hadn't avoided it somehow—you know—what I saw on the newsreels and read in the papers. But his letters were evasive now that I think about them. I didn't want him in harm's way, but I knew he was. I thought I'd go insane when I didn't get a letter each week. Can you believe me?" She took Quill's face in her hands and kissed his cheek, which made him blush three shades of red. Her words had come as an apology long overdue. This little man had also suffered for her. Then Susan began to softly touch each scar. His renewed tears greeted her acceptance.

While attending to Quill, Susan heard Stephen slide his chair away from the table, rise, and walk in the direction of the great stairway. Susan called after him, but he kept moving away, out of her reach. He ascended the steps and disappeared above her. From up overhead, they heard Stephen open the bathroom door, and then close it. He had exchanged the openness and conversation at the table for retreat and seclusion. He would not come down until the sun rose.

"I knew this would happen," Quill said, his head down, trying to avoid Susan's stare. Quill had opened his own wound and the refuse flowed. She didn't want it to stop as ugly as it was. Not now. She knew where Stephen was if she needed to get to him.

Susan and Quill talked the night away, deep into the early morning hours, until fatigue overcame Quill and his lovely guest. Susan's world of beauty and motherhood, of wife and lover, of comfort and ease had been shaken to its foundation. Perhaps now peers could be laid for a solid groundwork of understanding. Stephen wouldn't wake up to the same woman that had helped him into the tub days earlier. Stephen had become a hero to her: a quiet, silent man of valor. He had lived a lifetime that she was only now just beginning to appreciate, and needed more than ever to hear and digest.

Her dad, Dr. Inhofe, and now Quill Du Pont had built upon each man's supporting layer. Susan must carry on the work, one tedious shovel-full at a time. She was becoming aware, albeit slowly, that she had brushed shoulders with men who had saved her world, making it safe so that she didn't have to know any of this. They had done these things for her, and they had paid a price she couldn't possibly imagine even though she was beginning to see it.

Quill had interwoven spiritual doctrines and concepts among his tales of triumph and tragedy, mostly tragedy, and each story assumed its own lifetime. It dominated the conversation until the world he created for her began to require some sense be made of it. It was the sense part that Quill had made as his life's goal. Quill spoke of God's intervention at enabling him to control his hate toward those Japanese guards, seeking forgiveness each time it reared its ugly head, of the depression and anger that still at times almost overpowered him, of his Bible readings and favorite verses, and of the Gospel itself. A sense of Susan's own need for cleansing grew with an immediacy within her mind and heart that surprised, not only the weathered old man, but also the woman. The divine plan had now been laid before her, and she wouldn't rest until she had wrestled with it. Her religious journey had been nothing like Quill's—not alive in the way he spoke of it. The priests and sisters hadn't shared Christ *this* way.

Thirty-Eight: The Promise

> ⊱—⊹—◯—⊹—⊰

Monday, May 22, 1967

"Hi," came Susan's breathy and joyful, even halcyon, welcome. He felt the palms of her eyes caressing, softening his granite hard spirit. Her smile warmed him so that for the moment, little clouded the freshness of this awakening. Both mortals lay near each other, warm under the covers. She had gotten three hours of sleep, been awake for ten minutes, and lucid for the past three. She waited for Stephen to show some sign of life. As his sight converged at the point of clarity, his senses came on line gathering in the scent of the woman so close to him, a woman overtly eager to be near him. Something was quite different about Susan, of that he became immediately aware. Stephen closed his eyes again and in so doing, he experienced his wife's calm contentment descending upon him. It was now 6:31.

The decisions Stephen had made after leaving the table seven hours before waddled across his thinking. He was at peace with it all now. He had thought it all through. Any foreboding or apprehension he might have possessed about these things, Susan's immediate and ample regard soothed. As Stephen was apparently thinking about something, Susan waited for her husband to rejoin her. Hours ago, Quill had helped her unclutter and put right her mind. She needed a new view of the world as it is, not as it should be or she wanted it to be.

Oddly, this instant felt like virgin territory to Susan. She would rest in the expectation that her Stephen, although wounded in some dreadful way, was not beyond her ability to cure, or at the very least, to help get him past this and begin afresh their future together. She *was* getting it. Quill had been worse than Stephen, and look at *him*.

Quill had given her a lot to ponder. Lying beside her man made her tremble a bit as she thought about all the unknowns. Quill had retained his sense of humor in spite of the war. He worked. He had somehow realized the ways in which he hurt his wife, and he tried his best to make up for his deficiencies. He thought deeply about life and his Helen. He was a man of faith. He had stayed with Helen regardless, and she had not abandoned him. Yes, Quill had problems, but he was still going about his life. Stephen, she determined, could as well. Her marriage vows, which Susan had reviewed for those silent hours in the car long days before, might bear their teeth later, they might gnaw on her body, mind, and soul, but Susan loved this man, and she knew he loved her. That was that. No further discussion was needed.

Stephen Lloyd's most recent culpability slowly claimed him, deep and unwieldy. He felt it behind his eyes, in his heart, and down in his stomach. He had hurt and worried, even exasperated this woman beyond her capacity to carry it. She must surely hate him by now. Of that he was certain—but there she lie, smiling and receptive. Why? He had been a pain in the neck, or worse, for several months running. He wanted to turn away from her, and he wanted her to hold him and make it all better. He wanted his pleasure with her, and he wanted her to hate him. As long as he said no, he was in control.

Oh, he'd apologized until his apologies were worthless endeavors, just noisy and empty promises. He had resolved as he lie there, so help him, not to allow himself to become so agitated today. Maybe he'd even talk to her a bit. Perhaps, but that was hours ago. Now he was at peace for the first time in months, because he'd settled it in his mind. That felt good.

From behind the safety of the thin flesh shield that separated his perception from his earlier escape from reality, Stephen felt Susan's warm breath, and then her lips kissing his eyelids. She wanted to apologize to him. There was so much she hadn't understood, but so many really good people had at least given her some perspective from which to approach Stephen. Each piece of the puzzle formed a part of the whole so she might actually patch it into something meaningful—with enough time. They had plenty of that.

Overriding his perceptions, Stephen tested the waters by peeking out from behind the asylum of his short lashes. Finding his wife still welcoming, if not accepting and insistent, he urged the other eye to participate.

"Hi." Susan extended a breathy felicitation once again. With this, Stephen felt that it might be safe to reveal himself to whatever came next. Susan didn't seem . . . he knew what she could *seem*.

"Hi," he returned from the caves of his very small but piercing sight. "Susan, I'm—" Before he could coax the third word for her perusal, she kissed him with all the passion she could bring to such a context. Almost from reflex, Stephen pulled her to him, tightening his reins. Something wonderful and grand was exchanged, and he did not want any of this to escape. They had not kissed with such depth of passion in years.

"Susan, I know I keep—" Again she kissed him. Because Stephen understood trust at this level, she spoke on a level and in a manner commensurate with his need—and he trusted it was for him alone. Susan spelled and defined her acceptance of all he was, is, and would be, from that unabridged dictionary of hers. Their inner eyes feasted even more heartily, each upon the other. The mutual environment for everything they had or would face together, Susan ensured. Breakfast would wait. Susan promised herself Stephen and she would see the colors again.

The invitation echoed from the kitchen to the far end of the over-spacious main room, "Come in!" Jacques and his hungry guests were sequestered around pancakes, eggs, bacon, juice, fresh fruit, and plenty of hot coffee. Quill closed the front door and hobbled across the sun-bright cathedral-like expanse of the main living room to the source of all things that smelled wonderful and tasted the same. Jacques was in his element, a room that boasted elegance, wonder, and sustenance.

Quill studied the smile resident upon Stephen's face. Susan sat very near her husband absorbed in the man she had brought back to life. Together, they looked like honeymooners. Quill tried to contain his smile. He set his cap down on the table and waited for Jacques to fill his empty plate and cup.

"Good morning," Stephen suggested to the old man. "I feel good today."

"I think so," was Quill's apt retort.

A Long Healing Come Slowly

Susan's full heart brought a twinkling glow to her eyes. The sparkle had returned, and Quill felt a little jealous that one man could so thoroughly bind the affections of this woman for himself. He, too, had been part of the restoration process of which he was sitting in the middle enjoying. He missed his Helen, and he flatly refused to kiss Jacques. He'd as soon kiss that mule out in the barn.

After he'd taken his first sip of tea, Quill asked, "Well, what do you folks have planned for today? You want to ride the horses? Walk? Go into town? What can I arrange for you?" There are moments that are the essence of life, that breathe of their excitement or magic. Their lack of burden, if only temporary, is pure pleasure, and these four people sat amid such a moment. Of course, great moments seldom linger past one's ability to reap from the morning's glory all that it offers or promises. Stephen was counting on this natural law of diminishing returns. The black hole would reappear, it was just a matter of his misfortune, yes, probably even bad luck.

Susan attempted to exploit to the full her buoyant frame of mind with all her might. She ate little, preferring to hold her husband's arm and rest her head on his shoulder. She felt like a silly schoolgirl with a crush. Nothing mattered to her. Squeezing the seconds so that she could lengthen them, she, too, suspected that they wouldn't last. Mr. Hyde and Mrs. Danvers would return. But she had right now. It was full and rich, and she would take it. The children were fine. Michael and Margaret were finishing their finals—without their mother present, and she loved this man—better, he loved her. Hadn't he affirmed it so?

"Susan tells me you two sat up quite late last night, talking 'shop.'" Stephen's inquiry was significant, because from it, this day would explain itself. Things needed to find their level with a man, and Stephen couldn't rest before he discovered that equivalent. Mentally, Stephen searched the day's terrain and his relationship with Susan for obstacles that might trip him up and cause the pressure and agitation to return. Finding none that he could see in her immediate proximity, he said the old man, "Talk to me about what it meant."

"You sure?"

"Yeah, I think so."

Quill put on his poker face, for he was about to play his ace. "Make me a promise." He spoke with certainty, although he felt his suggestion

369

might backfire and condemn Susan. Quill knew what last night had done for Stephen—the exact opposite of what he feared might happen in mere moments.

"If I can." Stephen offered.

"Not good enough. You gotta promise." Jacques stood against the now cold oven, arms crossed, towel over his shoulder, staring at the main focus, Stephen. Susan lifted her head from her husband's shoulder, looked first at Quill, and then at Stephen. Stephen's poker face emerged to counter Quill's. They had both spent hours shuffling the deck during the war. They had equally stared at each other in a hundred different faces in a thousand different hands of five-card stud. The stakes, whatever they were now, were high, perhaps the highest of Stephen and Susan's life, and the silence was deafening.

"Tell me your proposal first." Stephen bluffed. He was stalling. Quill had played this game more.

"Nope. Promise."

More silence. Stephen shifted away from Susan to look at her. His guess was that the promise had to do with her . . . something with her. Perhaps talk with her about the war. Quill's eyes never left his competitor.

Stephen blinked first. His tongue slid between his front teeth and his eyes half closed. This would hurt. "Okay. I promise. Now what did I promise?"

"You have to talk to your wife." He'd guessed correctly. "You have to tell her two things. First, you have to tell her the worst day of life as a bomber pilot . . . and then the funniest thing that happened to you."

A little conversation wasn't going to resolve the past sufficient for them to move into the future, leaving nothing behind. It wasn't going to be, 'and they lived happily ever after,' or that simple. It was however, a beginning and something on which to build hope. It would reveal to Stephen that if he could take one step, no matter how small, he could take another, and then another.

Quill had played his hand. He had no more cards up his sleeve as far as priming the pump was concerned. Marcus had counted on Quill's ability and experiences. It looked as if both men had gambled and won. Susan held her breath and prayed. Stephen's eyes dropped ever so slowly to his lap. The emotions that had drawn so close to the surface of late betrayed him once again. The river began with tears sliding over the contours of his face and onto his lap. His shoulders and head bobbed silently up and down. Within ten seconds those sobs turned to convulsions and he grabbed Susan in a death like grip lest he fall to the floor and shatter. Quill watched, vicariously experiencing Stephen's pain. Quill knew what the man felt and what he would say to Susan, which story he must tell her. If the good part was to be got at, they must pass through the valley of the shadow of death together. Now was the time.

Quill lifted his slight weight from the chair and motioned with his head for Jacques to follow him. He smiled at Susan whose own large, beautiful eyes spoke her appreciation to her frail old angel. In several seconds, Susan and Stephen sat alone in each other's arms.

Thirty-Nine: The Confession

Monday, May 22, 1967

"Are you going to be okay, honey?" Susan prodded, assessing the situation so close to her heart.

"Yeah. Yeah I think so," Stephen sniffed, wiping his eyes and cheeks with his hand. He reached for his hankie and blew his nose. He stared out into the vacant room. The sun streamed through the layered sets of windows reaching to the full height of the east wall. It was such a magnificent room the more Susan looked at it. In certain ways, it was as breathtaking as the rugged country in which it nestled. Until this trip Stephen had never tired of looking at it, into the field where the hapless cattle grazed and the view beyond. Hopefully they were getting fatter for the day Quill would sell them. Their tails swished amid the pine-covered hills beyond the field and the distant peaks bordering the horizon, usually snow capped. It was breathtaking. Stephen saw that old bull he'd met the other day when off by himself. He had a high head. Stephen smiled at the old boy.

"What's so funny?" Susan stroked his hair, visibly intent on whatever he might say. He enjoyed her attention, enjoyed it immensely.

"Nothing. I was just looking at that bull, thinking about *his* life."

"What on earth for?" This wasn't the direction she wanted their next moments to go. "Now you promised Quill that you would talk to me. And I'm going to hold you to it, Mr. 'Corporate-Executive-and-Former Hotshot Bomber Pilot.' I want to hear about your worst day first, so we can get to the funny things. You did laugh over there, didn't

372

you?" Susan's sarcasm helped the anxiety building within Stephen for it looked as if panic were gripping him. She saw it in his eyes, fearing that he might just go back on his word, regardless. She knew Quill had taken a risk with their relationship, and something had to give. Susan couldn't say after this morning that it was headed nowhere.

"Actually, no. The colonel forbade us to laugh. There were laugh guards stationed everywhere. Anyone caught laughing had to fly twice as many missions."

"Stephen, tell me about . . . about . . . about how it was. Please. I want to know. Besides, we might even find a meaning for it." Susan gripped his sleeve, begging him to talk about what was wrapped around him, squeezing him to death. "Tell me!" Her tone surprised even her, for it was clothed in desperation of so many types. Her eyes seemed larger than normal. But then nothing in their lives lately seemed normal. "I'm so sorry, sweetheart." She spoke as if from a faint pout. "Forgive me. I'm just afraid that if you don't tell me now, you never will, and something will happen to us worse than . . . And I couldn't bear that. I don't think I could live without you, Stephen." Susan's eyes searched him, darting from side to side, as if she were rummaging into his soul, turning the pages within him. He toyed with her need, somewhat aroused by her intensity, her beauty, and her proximity, yet unsure what his own intentions might be.

If I tell her, I'll regret it somehow. My control will be gone. I'll probably start crying again, and maybe I won't be able to stop this time. Maybe she'll hate me. Why wouldn't she? I can't tell her I killed ten of our own men. Nobody would accept such a hideous story without hating them—not even Susan. But if I don't tell her something, I'll lose her. This is just too much. I could talk about that mission when Steve Lind bought it. That was pretty bad.

Stephen's silent refrain reached a crescendo. "You're afraid to tell me about something, aren't you? You're afraid I'll . . ." Susan reached for Stephen's farthest shoulder from her, and pulled him to face her. But he wouldn't make eye contact with her so that the obvious separated them. "I won't hate you, darling. Would you trust me with whatever this is? I won't hate . . . look at me, Stephen." When she held his eyes with her own, she said, "Nothing you did in the war is terrible enough for me to hate you—She already knew about the bomb shackles— Do you believe me?" *Why won't he trust me? I gave myself without reservations this morning, and I thought he understood me. Oh God, help me. Help us both. I love him so much.*

Silence and misty eyes looked back from the man. *How can I tell her I'm a murderer? No woman can stomach that. I will ruin her, too. There is so much for me to lose if I tell her.* Susan clasped his hand in hers, hoping to arouse the pleasure of their morning's intimacy, and what specifically *that* time spoke to him about *this* very moment,

"I love you beyond words. I will always love you, Stephen Lloyd."

Do I trust you, Susan? Do I?

For sustained seconds, neither man nor woman focused on anything but the other, reading and studying each other. Stephen was an easy man to like, but of late terribly difficult to love. Susan kept saying that phrase without hesitation, "I love you." She fortunately suffered from so much of the latter and lived in the former. The former was a matter of course for her. But a man's past is never an idle thing. It weaves and bobs in and out of one's consciousness. It seldom varies in its proximity to one's thoughts. Perhaps it was her pressing him for something. It might have been the entire context of the past months, and certainly Stephen himself didn't plan for such events to unfold. Someone must know, but from behind Susan's dark, lustrous hair, nestled amid her scented neck, in some kind of strange way, Stephen's blue eyes went flat, and he saw the flak, heard it, and smelled the cordite. He once more experienced the raw emotions of abject fear of flying into it, but also the unavoidable knowledge that is exactly what he would do, and he would probably die for it. All this and so much more is what he felt at that moment. Into the spinning, random shards of red-hot steel he flew as he began to speak.

"We were over Germany . . ." His words were oppressive beasts with the freight of easily detected guilt, if one looked for it. "For the life of me, I can't remember the name of the target, but our squadron was the high squadron for this mission. I remember that."

Slow at first and a bit couched, the words soon began to roll and tumble, then more fluid from behind the psychological barricade he had built, brick-by-emotional brick, and year-by-repressed year. The more he coaxed the scene into a verbal portrait for Susan, the more he feared painting it. Despite his reticence, it cascaded out of him and onto that canvas from behind his own fabricated obstruction, until that ancient moment and this present one synthesized, and the bombs that had frozen to the shackles finally released, and he heard and felt the explosion beneath his aircraft. Captain Stephen Lloyd knew exactly what had happened—what he had done to his good friend and nine other men that never knew what hit them—ten Americans that would never, ever be found. There wouldn't be enough body parts or airplane left to find. It was all so ghastly and lucid, and he stared out there ahead of his aircraft in heart stricken disbelief. It was as if he wasn't describing it now, but *living* it once more.

Susan sat spellbound, listening and watching his neck muscles twitch and tighten. His hands went to fists. His arms became steel bars of rigidity. He was there, at that moment in history, and Susan understood that her husband sat in the middle of it. She fully noted what it did to him. Every muscle's response to the murder he alone had committed registered on him.

Then, everything he had eaten came back up, spewing over the table, over Susan, and over him. From the rancid and offensive smell very little had begun to digest in his stomach. The force of this experience bent Stephen double, sending his head floor-ward. At the same instant his body wretched, and as he did, he shoved the table out of his way. Within about twenty seconds, he was heaving air, for there was no more food to expel. The horrible stench of half eaten eggs and bacon was nauseating. Hearing someone lose it, adds to the overall experience—and not for the better.

For twenty-two years, Stephen had covered over that wound with a scab so thick nothing could penetrate it—*nothing*—until now. It had been a bewildering process to reach this point, and one he would have to carefully evaluate, when he was more stable.

Susan was so taken aback with this anatomical response that she sat there for a second, and then placed her hand on Stephen's back as he sat doubled over. She was almost in a state of shock observing this. But he'd said it, and it was out now—not just the food, but the matter, the horrible, terrible truth. How he hated to vomit, but this was beyond any sickness he had ever encountered.

He heard something slide, then bare feet on wood, and the rustling of something to his right. For a long moment, he couldn't grasp the cause of the mess he'd created, or understand its stench. Slowly, feeling returned to his mind and senses. He sat up, looking at his own half-digested meal. Reliving or exhuming the past was exhausting work. Sitting in it like this, the room began to spin. Another few seconds and he felt a wet cloth covering his face, wiping him down. He had now reached the lowest possible valley one could imagine, but at the same time, he felt lighter, freer. How *odd*.

As Stephen rested, he attempted to gain some semblance of clarity. His body wobbled slightly and shook in the chair, and Susan wondered what else she might do. What did this mean? Only some kind of powerful emotion could produce such a response. To Susan, the ridiculously obvious, wasn't, not yet, but she was getting there. And despite her own grappling with the scene recently unfolded, she couldn't allow this thing, this 'Mrs. Danvers' as she was beginning to call it all, to just get away. Susan would care for Stephen first, then clean the mess, and afterward—yes, afterward—rein it all in.

The whole weighty affair lasted several minutes. "Good grief, Susan. What happened here?" The voice was Stephen's, but it sounded like a man gargling in something thick. He spit onto the floor.

"You threw up. Are you okay now?" Susan didn't know why, but this whole unpleasant experience didn't unsettle her—didn't make her sick. It certainly smelled bad enough. She supposed all the childhood bouts with flu in the middle of the night had immunized her against turning away from her family when they were in such need. But he had told her. He had said it. It couldn't harm their relationship any further. Susan couldn't explain the sensation of relief she felt. Stephen was all that mattered to her.

After a few minutes, the strangest look registered on his face. And then, from somewhere in the lowest parts of his being, came a slow laugh. It was the most incredible sight and sound to ever greet Susan. Stephen sat in his own vomit, laughing. The joy escalated into something resembling, well, she didn't know rightly what. And if she didn't know better, she'd think he was a man who had been set free from something. A cancerous tumor had been lacerated and drained from his psyche. More would follow in due course, she assured herself.

"Stephen, I thought to myself," Susan said, "I was going to tell you I knew about the shackles and this very incident."

"You knew?" Stephen stared into space. He'd kept this in for two decades and thought he had to keep it away from her. And now he discovered she knew. "When did you find out?"

"I'll never tell you. I love you Mr. Stephen Lloyd. That's all that matters to me. I love you."

Forty: He's Gone, Susan

>─┼─◆>─·─O─·─<◆─┼─<

Monday, May 22, 1967

"Come on up and sit a spell. I need some company." Quill offered a rocker apiece to Susan and Stephen. They had trudged the one hundred or so yards up into the tree line to find the old man's cabin and Quill sitting alone. He sat a lot these days it seemed. Walking didn't agree with him anymore, and he was just now getting over the effects of that long drive and trek to find Stephen, although Quill didn't complain.

"You're not too busy?" Stephen inquired, a smile welded onto his face. Quill's veranda was spacious and grand, with an even more spectacular view. The old man had entertained thoughts once of bulldozing the main cabin below his, because it partly obstructed the panorama. Sufficient rockers filled the sitting area for the couple to find a comfortable spot.

And then Susan did it. She made a suggestion that set Stephen off. Susan sat in the chair to Quill's right and Stephen got comfortable in the rocker to the old man's left. After a minute, Susan wanted Stephen to switch with her. She didn't want him to sit in the sun. Thus Stephen went from freedom to bondage to his anger in a millisecond.

When she'd become comfortable in her new chair, Quill observed, "Well, by the looks of things, I'd say this place agrees with you, Susan."

"Oh yes, Quill. It does."

Stephen kept rocking, trying to keep his equilibrium in harmony and out of public view. Unfortunately, the emotional debris from Susan's urging at the change in sitting arrangements began to block

377

the flow in Stephen's mind and his peace dissipated. It registered in his eyes and jaw, but Susan was busy soaking in the valley below and really tasting the air. Quill had been whittling on an old gnarled stick with an even older jackknife. The shavings from the branch lay scattered about his feet. Somehow, over the years, Quill had learned to hold a knife in his broken hands, but it was painful to watch. After twenty minutes of steady carving, Quill could barely hold a fork for days. He'd learned to pace himself.

Quill motioned behind him to his living quarters and said, "Hey. Come on in here. I want to show you both something. I carved a bird for you Susan, and I want you to have it. It's a little something for you to remember me by. Let's see, what did I carve for Stephen? Oh yes."

"Stephen, do you want to see?" she asked, standing at the door of the cabin.

"No. I think I'll stay here," Stephen answered somewhat coldly. He didn't look at her, and he hoped Susan hadn't observed the storm once more gathering in his soul, behind his eyes and in the way he clinched his jaws, not that it would have mattered. It was best and safest to ride it out. She left her husband alone with the certain knowledge that he had been transformed, and she felt in her heart that she had been part of his metamorphosis. This was the way out for them both. She would love this man forever. Yet Susan had begun to look through her subjective and feminine lenses more objectively, so that she might see what was real. Her world could not be altered so quickly, and for such incidental matters as switching rocking chairs.

"Okay," she said. Quill opened the screen door for Susan and he followed her inside. He turned and said to Stephen, "I won't steal your girl just yet," and winked. The screen squeaked as it closed.

Stephen listened to their voices beyond the door. Both were preoccupied, enjoying the labors of a man no one expected possessed such skill. Quill seemed happy explaining and showing his work. In a few minutes, Stephen stood and moved down the hill, kicking rocks and stirring the dirt as he weaved in and out of the trees. His mind felt dark and his course unambiguous.

"These are incredible, Quill. How did you carve them with *your* hands? Stephen, you have to see these carvings." Susan raised her voice to ensure her request was not missed on her husband. "They're so skillfully made, and . . . Stephen?" Looking puzzled at Quill, she said, "Now I wonder where he went? Stee-phen? Maybe he went back to our room."

"Yeah. He'll be back directly. Let me show you how I carved this feather. My hands make doing anything like this very painful, that's why I'm so proud of it."

The minutes passed and before they realized they had liquidated an hour. No Stephen. Quill was the first to suggest he go take a look and see where his other guest might be. Susan thought she'd go check up in their room. He was probably sleeping. Maybe he was tired. "We'll meet you back here in fifteen minutes, Quill."

"All right."

The two departed, Quill boarded the golf cart and headed toward the stables, and Susan to the cabin. She hadn't thought to call Jacques in the kitchen from Quill's cabin. She opened the large screen door and smelled lunch cooking, a roast with carrots and potatoes. She strode into the kitchen to inquire of Jacques if he'd seen her husband. He hadn't. He'd been busy in the kitchen. "I'll just go upstairs and look for him," she said. Susan climbed the stairs and stopped at the top step. She called, "Stee-phen?" No answer. "Stee-phen." Then she checked their room. He hadn't been there. *Where could he be?* This was a mystery. Okay, back down the stairs to see if Quill had located the missing husband.

On the front porch of the main cabin, Susan surveyed the pasture and magnificence of the surrounding mountains. What a breathtaking view. It must be difficult to live here year round, she mused. She turned in the direction of the stables. *No one in that direction.* Where *was* that man? From down the hill she saw Raymond running toward the far side of the stable. That was odd. Susan strode quickly in that direction. Perhaps Stephen had fallen and hurt himself or . . . *or what?* She would go and take a look, just to quell her rising apprehension.

Susan reached the corner of the stable nearest the cabin when Quill turned the far corner. He raised his eyes at the same instant Susan came bounding in his direction. She noted that Quill was wiping his hands with a rag. They were red. Now, full-blown panic gripped Susan. "Quill? What's wrong? Is it Stephen?"

What was he going to tell her? Regardless, he couldn't allow her to see Stephen, not like that.

Susan began to run in earnest in the direction from which Quill had just come. Quill, although physically smaller than Susan, halted her forward motion by placing his body in front of her and his hands on her shoulders. "Susan. Don't go around there. You don't want to see him like that. I can't let you. Raymond, get a sheet. Now!" Quill yelled back over his shoulder.

"Yes, boss. I'll take care of it."

Susan strained to get past Quill, but he wouldn't budge. "Quill, what's happened to Stephen?" Panic and emotions poured out of her, because she didn't know what had happened, but Susan knew it involved her husband. "Quill, I *have* to see."

"No, Susan. You don't want to see him that way."

"In *what* way? What way?! Would you please stop being so evasive? So help me Quill, I'll hit you if you don't tell me what's happened to Stephen. Was it an accident? Is he hurt badly? STEE-PHEN! He may need me. Please Quill, I have to go to him! I have to!" Susan pled for all she was worth, but to no avail.

Still holding her firmly, Quill looked directly into her piercing blue eyes. He spoke slowly and deliberately. "Susan. Stephen is dead."

At this pronouncement, she stopped pushing against Quill. "Dead? My Stephen is . . . dead? No, no, . . . no. Not *my* Stephen. We were just talking to him an hour ago. No! Tell me you're making this up! It's a sick joke! That's it. It's not possible! He loves me! He wouldn't die . . . How did it happen, Quill? I want to know. How did it happen?! Who killed my Stephen?!"

Quill stared at the ground for a long second, but kept himself between the woman and her husband. It would be easier to lie. He'd done it in the Philippines. He'd say something like, *"No, Joe isn't dead. He's still on that work detail."* But Joe had been strung up by his arms and beaten to death, or bayoneted, or beheaded for trying to escape, or he lay dead in the makeshift infirmary from some disease or starvation.

Removing his broken hands from Susan's shoulders, he laid the facts before her. "He's dead, Susan. He shot himself." The woman blinked, fully uncomprehending. Her arms and shoulders went limp. Her mouth twitched as if she were attempting to form words from a foreign language. "Susan, did you hear me? He's dead. He's gone."

"He *shot* . . ? No. My Stephen couldn't have. He loves me! He wouldn't shoot himself. *NOOOO!*" Susan's scream bled out of her anguished soul. Now she began once more to push to get to the body, but Quill wouldn't budge. "I have to see him." Through clinched teeth, she urged Quill to get out of her way. With all her might, Susan shouted, "Let me see for *myself*, Quill!"

Now, the old man would let her see. "Okay." He had forestalled her so that she could begin to absorb the situation. Looking behind him, Quill noted that Raymond had just finished pulling the sheet over Stephen. "Okay."

Quill stepped aside and took Susan's arm. She leaned heavy against him, and he leaned hard on his cane. Together they turned the stable corner. A dirty sheet lay on the ground covering a body. The long protrusion under the sheet was about Stephen's size. It *could* be him. Those *were his* shoes sticking out. But no, it wasn't possible. Stephen loved her too much. He loved her forever. He'd said so this morning. He wouldn't leave her.

Susan stood above the sheet for a long second, and then dropped slowly to her knees, near to his head. Once more, she looked down at the boots sticking out from under the sheet. Coming to terms with this, *right* this minute, was not the issue, confirmation of the body under this semi-white shroud was. It might possibly be her husband. Reluctantly, Susan pulled back the sheet covering his face. His hair came into view, then his forehead. She smelled his shampoo. His eyes were open wide, staring upward and distant. Lower, she pulled the sheet until his face and the right side of his head lay exposed. His mouth was half open, covered black with powder burns. Blood trickled out the side of his mouth. An upper tooth had been chipped from the recoil of the pistol.

Susan placed her hand under his head to cradle it at the same instant Quill said, "Don't—" Too late. She had unfortunately discovered the exit wound with its oozing blood, brain matter and chipped bone. Susan looked down at her left hand covered in dripping warm, red liquid. She attempted to scream but no sound came forth. Her perception was fully muddled. She couldn't quite grasp that the remains filtering between her long fingers belonged to Stephen. Susan pulled her husband's limp head against her and began rocking back and forth. Neither Quill nor Susan thought about the fact that they had disturbed a crime scene. It didn't enter their minds.

Forty-One: The Call Home

>─!─◆>─•─⊙─•─<◆─!─<

Monday, May 22, 1967

"Yes. Tell him it's Quill Du Pont, in Canada. I'll wait. Thank you."
Dolores returned to inquire if this was an important or urgent matter,
or, could it possibly wait? "Ma'am, it's very important, and no, I'm
afraid it can't wait. Good. Thank you."

No one in their right mind wants to call a parent and tell them their
son is dead. But to tell them their only son has committed suicide . . .
Quill didn't really want to think about what he was going to say. He
was just the caretaker from Canada. Still, he had to do this, and he
rehearsed nothing. His thumping mind kept going back to the picture
of Stephen Lloyd lying face up. Stephen's hand was still wrapped
around the handgun, probably out of reflex when the round ripped
through his mouth, directly into his brain, and out the other side. It
landed somewhere out in the field, spent and harmless.

"Hello, Quill. How are things up there in Canada? It's starting
to get—"

"Mr. Lloyd. I have no idea how to say this. I'm sorry, but, . . ."
There was a pause, unmeasured and raspy.

"What is it, Quill? Is everything okay? Is someone sick? When are
they coming home?"

"I don't know sir. No one is sick. Your son is . . . your son is gone.
He's dead, sir." Quill's hand strangling the phone had already gone numb.

"Dead? Dead?! What are you telling me, Quill?" Marcus shouted.
"I know he's having some problems with the war, but he's not *dead!*

That can't be. Quill are you sure about this? This must be a mistake. It is a mistake, isn't it? Was . . . was he in an accident? Was there an accident?! Oh, God. *Dead*? You were supposed to help my son, not let him die!"

Dolores suddenly stood from behind her desk, her hand stuck over her mouth. Tears had begun to slide down her face from the fear that what she was hearing might just be true. She simultaneously reached for a tissue and to grasp her boss's sleeve to make him look at her and tell her what the man on the other end of the line was saying. Marcus slapped at Dolores's hand fending her off. He was trying to listen, gather information, and stay on his feet. He had begun to turn pale. Several men from the meeting in the large room reserved for company business drifted into the outer office as the conversation grew in intensity. Fresh looks of concern drew over their faces as well. They, in turn, looked to Dolores to fill in the blanks.

Quill had to give this to his employer in one giant dose, and, as he suspected, Marcus couldn't swallow it. Once more, that hard approach to life's pain that Quill had learned as a POW came to the fore. *You just tell them. Let the chips fall where they may.* But it wasn't always so easy with these pampered civilians. He tried to break it slowly, gently, ease them into it. He didn't, of course. In one real sense, as far as Quill's submerging emotions were concerned, this was another dead soldier he was talking about, just one more body to bury. The more Marcus Lloyd shouted his questions, the more Quill withdrew. Former First Sergeant Quill Du Pont had long since lost his ability to experience empathy about these matters. "Sir, First Sergeant Du Pont reporting. We have six dead, fourteen wounded, and the enemy has broken through at points seven and nine." It was so easy to give the facts, so long as they weren't cluttered with *feelings.*

In the scene playing out in his mind prior to his phone call, he'd imagined their gasps, their crying, and their useless hand wringing. Quill's seldom-dormant impatience reconnected with him. These people were so pathetic, because they had never seen the darker side of men who are so eager to destroy each other and themselves. Yet, this was his employer on the phone and he was a good man. Some people, he guessed, shouldn't have to see the darkness. Perhaps this is the reason men like Quill existed. Still, they needed to know the hard-bitten truth.

"Mr. Lloyd, I don't know any other way to say this except to tell you. Stephen committed suicide. I'm very sorry, sir." All the old and familiar guilt flooded Quill. He felt sick and angry. It wasn't his fault. He wanted to strangle Marcus Lloyd. It wasn't his *fault*!

Marcus let go of the phone and somehow stumbled over to the couch, dropping like a bag of rocks onto it. His face was drawn, the matter tearing through his mind, fantastic! "Mr. Lloyd? Can you tell us what's going on, sir? Can we help?" Marcus was beyond hearing, beyond comprehension. His mouth moved as if he were communicating with some invisible person—Stephen perhaps.

Dolores picked up the phone. "Hello. This is Mr. Lloyd's secretary, Dolores Hernandez. Um, can you tell me . . . uh, can you tell me what's happened, sir? Mr. Lloyd is, well, he's having some trouble grasping what you told him. You'd better tell *me*, I think."

It took Quill almost a full minute before he was ready to respond to anyone in any civil manner. He wanted to kill someone. He wanted to say, 'you tell that boss of yours it's not my fault,' or worse, much worse. Then Quill thought to seek his God, like that of Nehemiah, in a short, quick, burst: O my God. Give me grace. Finally, Quill managed, "Miss Hernandez, as I said, this is Quill Du Pont up in Canada." His voice was more steady.

"Yes. Mr. Du Pont. What's happened? Is it bad? Tell me everything you can."

Quill laid it all out for her and finally hung up. Both people had pressing matters to which they must attend. Delores sat down to absorb the terrible reality being forced upon her own world. She would now have to tell Annika. Annika would have to inform the children, and life would change at Lloyd Hotels International, Inc., in unforeseeable ways. She took a deep breath, noting that Marcus Lloyd was still in a state of shock, but currently surrounded by the department heads. Delores began agonizing over her task of breaking the news to the men present at the meeting. She knew they should not say anything, release any information until told to do so by Mr. Lloyd. That was as far as she thought her authority extended in this matter.

The call to lure Annika here would probably try every good grace living within the heart of Dolores Hernandez. These people had been her family for the past several decades. Was it about to end, she wondered? There were so many unanswered questions.

"Mrs. Lloyd? This is Dolores. Your husband would love to see you. Would it be convenient for you to come downtown, you know, as soon as it's convenient? No, things are . . . things are in a little disarray around here, and I could . . . I could sure use your help. Yes, Mr. Lloyd is having a difficult day, and I know he could use your insight to help him sort through it." Annika's curiosity had been aroused and she wanted answers for this rather odd call in the middle of the day. Annika thought that was the reason they paid all those execs—rather too well, she mused. Dolores had almost stumbled over the enormity of this horrible news on the phone to Mrs. Lloyd, but she hadn't lied. She knew how to get what she needed, and no one ever questioned her abilities. "No. He's in a meeting right now, but it will be over momentarily. Yes, ma'am. We'll look forward to seeing you."

Mr. Blackledge saw Dolores slump back into her chair and sob uncontrollably. Tye Blackledge, a thin, nervous man with thick glasses, would not permit the situation to get out of control. He stepped over to check on Dolores. His voice was suddenly shrill when he phoned his own secretary to get her to come to the main office. He needed help. He couldn't allow anyone in here right now, nor could he let the phone go without someone answering it. Lloyd International must proceed as if everything were normal.

Of the several men in full support mode surrounding Marcus Lloyd, Alvin Snider went after water, tissue, and whatever he thought appropriate. He would hopefully anticipate what had not yet been voiced. Charlie Billings suggested they call the emergency room at the local hospital to see if they would have someone stand by, just in case. That was approved. Next, Charlie looked at Dolores. He wasn't angry with her, but she was a puddle, and her emotions showing like this made him ill at ease. "Charlie. Charlie, make reservations for . . . for how many of us ought to go, do you think?" Tye Blackledge asked.

"Go where?" wondered Charlie.

"To *Canada*. Where else?"

"Oh man, I didn't even think about that. My God, I wonder how Susan is?" Charlie Billings rubbed his chin as his thoughts broadened to encompass the whole Lloyd family. This kind of death is incomprehensible in the ways it colors family members, not to mention company matters.

"Charlie?"

"What? Oh, I'm having trouble concentrating. Sorry. I don't know. Help me think, Tye."

The men filed through all the possible candidates in their minds that could immediately drop what they were doing and fly to Canada. "I think four should go," Tye finally dropped into the somber mood flooding the office. "Will, me, Sandra, and . . . can you leave, Charlie?"

"No. Someone has to stay here and take care of things. Mike Simpkins. That's four. His team will just have to double up what they're working on."

Monday, May 22, 1967

Ginny Cassalls set the receiver down gently onto its cradle. She sat down in the chair, laid her hands in her lap, and stared into space. She felt sick. Then she lifted her left arm and placed it on the table next to the phone.

"Mrs. Cassalls, have you seen my ball glove? I put it down in the den last night, and I can't find it now. Do you know—? Mrs. Cassalls? Are you okay?"

The question roused the maid out of her stupor. She looked David in the eye in a way he had never seen. She was most serious indeed. She said to the smallest Lloyd who was wondering what he had done to deserve such a look, "David, would you go get your brother and sister and tell them to come here for a minute, please? And you come with them, too. Okay?"

"Yes, ma'am. Did I do something wrong?"

When she didn't answer, David rushed off to find Margaret and Michael. Fortunately, Michael was headed down the stairs in search of nourishment and Margaret was busy searching for her purse. Margaret could be heard from her room, "Mrs. Cassalls? Have you seen my purse? I can't find it anywhere? David? What did you do with my purse? You went looking for my gum, didn't you?"

David didn't have far to look when he heard his sister's accusations. He yelled up to her to come down. Mrs. Cassalls had something she needed to say. Margaret was ready to brain her little brother when she reached the bottom step. Mrs. Cassalls ran interference for the youngest Lloyd and herded the children into the living room. They could tell something was wrong. Ginny Cassalls avoided eye contact with a vengeance.

"Mrs. Cassalls, what's wrong?" Margaret asked in a panic. "Are my parents okay? It's my parents, isn't it?"

Long, furtive seconds crept by, and Mrs. Cassalls withheld her words. How would she say this? She adored these children and couldn't bear to harm them in any way. "Children, it's your father." She couldn't say it. There was no energy to speak. Michael stood and hovered over her.

"Mrs. Cassalls. Is he—?" Michael squeezed his eyes shut as he pursed his lips. With a deep breath, he finished his sentence. "Is he dead?" How Michael came to ask the question, Mrs. Cassalls couldn't guess. She nodded somberly. Margaret rushed at the poor woman who was overcome with emotion, and the two females clung to each other, weeping. David went into his own panic mode. He pulled on the women, and then grabbed his big brother who was finding it hard enough to control his own emotional equilibrium to answer David's pleas for clarification.

Their father couldn't be dead. David only knew one person who had died in his whole life: Damien. He hadn't yet begun to grasp what death was, except that Damien didn't come around any more. What else could death mean to a ten year old? Did this mean his father wouldn't come home anymore, too? That couldn't possibly be, could it? David could not embrace a world without his father.

Michael's arms tingled and his body felt disjointed. The room had lost its oxygen, and he felt as if he were swimming in a vat of gelatin. The crying females and his screaming brother made it hard to think. He had no idea what to do. He, too, couldn't imagine a world without his father. It wouldn't be worth living. Suddenly the thought came at him with a cruel blow to his needs. He would be leaving for the Marines in a month. *Why* had he joined? *Why* now? This surely trumped Damien's death and that voice he thought he heard. Michael cursed that voice. He cursed his situation and he got angry. He hated Damien for dying. It was probably Damien's fault that his father was dead. Oh God, he hated Damien.

Michael stormed up the stairs and into his room. His rage began to know no bounds. He ran at his bed and grabbed the mattress and flung it into the middle of the room. He picked up the chair in front of his desk and threw it at the wall where it crashed, sinking partly into the dry wall. He grabbed the chair for another go when he heard Mrs. Cassalls yell, "Michael! You *stop that* this instant, young man!"

Ginny stood there breathing heavy. Margaret was still attached to her, crying her heart out. They could hear David crying below. The poor little guy wasn't even certain what was happening, but he knew his father wasn't coming home. Michael's lungs heaved, and he wasn't through throwing things. He wanted to hit something hard, again and again and again until he had no more strength. But whom would he hit? Better, what? Michael sank to his knees on the floor of his room, bent his head and wept. There would be no father to watch him graduate.

Monday, May 22, 1967

As is always the case, such news meant to stay within the inner sanctum of a company like Lloyd International, Inc. cannot be contained. Small birds carry it throughout the cubicles, from one person to another. Inter office channels will not play by anyone's set of rules, regardless of the need for privacy. This was news and it had to find its sustenance in word-of-mouth communication. Dr. James Wilson also caught the scent, its power all but doubling him over. He'd lost two important men in his life in the span of a millisecond. It was the rumors that irritated him the most. He'd heard that Stephen had been shot in a hunting accident. An hour later, James heard Stephen had been killed in a car crash. Next, Stephen had shot someone. James wanted the facts and nothing more.

"Hello, Mrs. Hernandez, this is Dr. James Wilson, Damien's dad. Doing okay, thank you for asking. I would like to speak to Marcus, if he's available. I've heard too many things, but I suspect that something's happened to Stephen. I don't know what, and I would like to . . . No, that would be fine, thank you . . . Yes, I'll wait." James Wilson's heart raced hard in his chest. Mary Ellen held his hand as both of them stood in the kitchen glued to each other, worried for Susan, and almost certain something dreadful had happened to their friend's husband. "Oh. Is Marcus all right—? No, Mary Ellen is fine . . . He's busy? Hmmm. Well, Mrs. Hernandez, would *you tell us* what has happened? We've heard so many terrible things. We . . ." There was a pause, time for Dolores to weigh her options. This man deserved an answer with what he'd been through, but she asked him not to repeat any of it any further, to which he acceded.

"He *did*? Oh, *my Lord*." James Wilson stared into Mary Ellen's eyes. He searched for a way to tell her while he held his hand over the mouthpiece.

"What?" she asked. "*What?*"

James swallowed and then relayed the information to his wife, "Stephen's dead. He killed himself." Mary Ellen crumpled onto the nearest chair. Dr. Wilson continued with Dolores. "Yes. When? I understand fully. How is Susan? Okay. What about the children? Do they know? Good. Grandpa Perry is on his way here, and Michelle is already on a flight to Prince George. So, Mrs. Cassalls has told them? I suppose its best that they know. Is there anything we can do? Mrs. Hernandez, has anyone flown up there specifically to see about transporting the body . . . uh, Stephen back here? Oh, they're leaving tomorrow? Is it possible for me to get on that flight? Yes, would you check? Perhaps I can help in some way or do something. I *need* to do something."

James felt weak suddenly and somewhat light headed. He knew that Damien's death played into this in some horribly tragic way. Damien's death linked Dr. Wilson and Mary Ellen to this tragedy. Maybe he shouldn't go. In times of great turmoil, the body often did strange things. It followed illogical signals given it by the mind that caused it to cope in its own way. Without the hint of warning, James felt the need to relieve himself. "Here Mary Ellen, take this." He rushed to the bathroom, almost not making it to the toilet.

Forty-Two: Looking Back

>─┤◆├─◦─○─◦─┤◆├─ ≪

Monday, May 22, 1967

Quill had done what he should and could do, for the time being. Constable Jardan, a thick-necked man with full mustache and bushy eyebrows, had left thirty minutes before after questioning Susan, Quill, Jacques and Raymond. The ambulance attendants had already loaded the body into the back of their vehicle. They would be rolling down the driveway and out of sight within a few minutes. Quill leaned heavily against his cane. Death was never an easy customer to deal with. He was too old for this, he told himself. He'd lost too many friends, too many close comrades in arms.

That old film, *Death Takes a Holiday,* came to mind. But *he,* Death, never did. Watching them put Stephen's body in the back of that vehicle, that cold, official vehicle, irked him. He suspected that his inadequate conversation to Lloyd International had plowed a wake in Ft. Worth and all points on the compass. Several households and a large company would be affected. He wanted to go to sleep and wake up to discover this had been a nightmare. He could handle nightmares.

He couldn't physically handle all the details that Stephen's suicide had created for him. Somehow, God would grant him the strength, but Quill wished that he were younger. His shoulders could carry heavier burdens then, but not now. He knew that Susan would struggle to leave her bed tomorrow. He was thankful that Susan's mother and company representatives were on their way.

He limped up the hill to the main cabin to look in on Susan. She could see her husband after the autopsy, maybe tomorrow, late. Regulations, as indecent as they were to Susan and Quill, had to be followed. The constable had been quite clear on that fact. Although he sympathized with Mrs. Lloyd's plight, being an American, he had his procedures to follow. He did set the official inquest, regulations as well, in two days. The constable balanced Canadian statutes with his sympathy, recognizing that Mrs. Lloyd needed to get home to her children as soon as possible.

Quill opened the front door, and spotted Susan in one of her favorite sitting groups, —the one nearest the fireplace. She'd tucked her legs up under her and stared blankly into the huge hearth. She'd elected not to turn on a lamp. She'd been crying and she couldn't bear the light—or for anyone to see her like this. The huge room was almost as dark as her soul felt. Quill had said to her that her children had been told. Susan wanted to talk to them, but the moment she began to speak about it she only cried the louder.

Quill struggled over and sat opposite her, attempting to sit in such a fashion as not to exhale loudly or make his hip hurt more than it did. That proved fruitless. He'd been standing too long, answering questions, providing details, and showing the authorities this or that bit of evidence. He recognized the pistol. It was Stephen's. There were dozens of rifles and handguns stored in various places. Stephen would have had no trouble killing himself by such means. It would be tomorrow when Quill remembered when he found Stephen at the falls and spoke of his friend 'doing it right, sticking a pistol in his mouth.'

Susan interrupted the silence. "I wish . . ." she began, stopped, and then made another go at it. "I wish my children were here." That was as far as she got. Her weeping came with renewed vigor. Quill thought it best not to sit too close by and comfort her. He knew why. He had to detach himself from this unreal, or all too real, scene playing out about him. He also wanted to protect his own self-interests. Standing outside was where he preferred. On the other hand, he'd gotten very close, not so much to the Lloyds themselves, although that was true, but more so to the needs he saw in them. This he could do without hesitation.

Talking, too, did no good, because it felt familiar and so wearisome. Quill hated it when some of the folks at the church came by after Helen passed. They quoted Scripture to him or recited well-meaning platitudes attempting to soothe his hurt. None of this made him feel better. He wanted to tell them how inconsiderate they were, of how little they knew about death. It was some time after Helen's burial that Quill realized just how much ranchers knew about death—they went through it with their horses, cattle, dogs, hogs, you name it, and sometimes family members. In his mind he apologized, but the nearness and conversation was too burdensome all the same. He'd smile and pray they left as quickly as possible.

Sitting here with Susan, Quill said nothing except asked her if she wanted a cup of coffee, which she declined. The phone rang and Jacques informed Susan her mother wanted to talk to her.

"Hello, Mom? He's gone . . ." Susan rocked again with painful sobs. It was her mother and finally she could let go with someone familiar.

"I know honey. I love you. I'm in . . . Susan?"

As soon as Susan could get hold of herself, she replied, "Yes, I'm here. Somehow I'm still here. Good old Susan, she's always *here*."

In spite of her own self-loathing and pity party, Susan drew strength from her mom's voice and motherly words. Michelle was already in the Vancouver airport, but they were having some airplane trouble, and she didn't know when she would arrive in Prince George.

Quill heard parts of this phone conversation. Alone with his thoughts in the dark, grand main room, he mentally abandoned the two women on the phone to retrace the last moments he'd had with Stephen. He hoped that his dead friend might have embraced something of what he had said on his porch. Introspection along the lines of self-recriminations came fast and furious for Quill. What Marcus had said to him still hurt. This wasn't his fault. But Stephen was dead all the same. What had he said exactly to Stephen? Bits of this and pieces of that slowly came together to form an incomplete picture for examination. What *did* he say? Stephen was agitated. About *what*?

Monday, May 15, 1967

Quill's memories began to play like a broken record in his head of the times he spent 'counseling' them on the porch of his cabin. That particular 'session,' Stephen Lloyd wanted to be spared just one hour without *some form* of caustic turmoil. Susan also labored not to throw up her hands and admit defeat. Ever the optimist, Susan held a bare thread of hope that their time and insights gleaned from Dr. Inhofe, might begin to bear fruit if given the proper attention they deserved.

She spoke to her husband who didn't want to listen. "Dr. Inhofe said that we must try and see if *we*, and at some point *you*, can make the trials mean something, like *he* did. Each trial *has* a significant meaning, and it's waiting there to be discovered. Remember, he said he was wounded. You should have seen his leg. He said he couldn't perform surgeries any longer, so he became a psychiatrist. Now, he spends time with his patients helping them search for what they can do to help others, although he didn't get very far during *your* counseling sessions. He did say he was more fulfilled now than he ever was as a surgeon. Isn't there something you could do in the hotel business to help less fortunate people? There must be something. Dr. Inhofe couldn't tell you what the war was supposed to *mean* to you, but he believed you could find it if you searched for it. I think the struggle you are going through now can be a . . . a stepping stone to something good, or even great. Won't you even try, dear?"

Quill also remembered observing that Stephen felt more overwhelmed than ever. He could tell Stephen wanted Susan to back off and give her husband more time. The man needed space and distance. He needed quiet so that things could settle. Susan, on the other hand, wanted her husband 'fixed,' and the sooner the better. Hence, her almost immediate pushing for talk. And then there were those pressures from Texas, their son's graduation and leaving for the service.

A melancholy mood had once more settled in upon Stephen; a fine early morning mist with nothing to burn it off. Without the good doctor within 2,000 miles, Stephen could do whatever he wanted with Dr. Inhofe's counseling and suggestions. Inhofe's world wasn't so cockeyed significant. It took *him* years to find his way, and the doctor couldn't even stay married. He drank heavily when he wasn't solving all the world's problems. Stephen defined success a bit differently than that good old doctor did. On Stephen's face was plastered that, 'I don't buy what he's selling, and I don't really care, I only went along with this to get away from him' look.

The fact that Stephen had given up diffused his wife's eagerness, and thus Susan was left not knowing what to say. She saw more clearly than ever that they had come all this way, thousands of miles, leaving her children and behind to fight *together* matters she considered quite significant. Stephen obviously thought otherwise. He'd come to Canada to put space and time between himself and that hospital room, those irritating counseling sessions—even his wife if need be—to get away from *every* form of pressure. She looked forlorn at the prospects of a return to Texas. She stared out over the distant field with its grazing cattle and the tree covered hills beyond it. Try as she might, Susan's impatience to get on with this healing process, to get it going, made her restless and often unable to enjoy the quiet and glory of her surroundings. Her own needs were screaming at her for attention, and she could only focus on her husband who wasn't cooperating. This was one of the days when she struggled to smell the roses . . . and the pines.

Quill even remembered asking that day, "Can I interrupt you two for a second?" It had been a bit unsettling for Quill to burst into a marriage undergoing difficulties as this one was. That Stephen was Quill's employer added to his hesitation. Yet Quill's guests needed his help, so he reached into this familiar turbulence to say, "Helen and I went through this very thing for years." But instead of his joining Stephen's side, he directed a question her way. "Hasn't life hurt *you* lately, Susan?"

"Well, yes, but . . ."

"But what?" Stephen seemed somewhat intrigued that the old man would begin with her. He had begun that day to insulate himself from the coming fusillade of barbed suggestions. But Quill didn't throw any at him.

"Haven't you gotten the raw end of the carrot too, Susan?"

Could she possibly answer this in front of her husband? It took great effort on her part to answer it honestly and aloud. "I suppose so, but . . ." Susan was certain that she wasn't the problem. She didn't need fixing. She did need *something*, though—perhaps understanding, to be heard, and Stephen wasn't in the mood to listen or try to understand her. The man she'd married and been in love with for so many wonderful years had abandoned her sitting barely five feet from her. Susan thought she had caught an intonation in Quill's tone that there might be a problem or need on her end too. She did like the thought that someone considered *her* feelings. Faithful Quill once again caressed a wounded aspect of her life that needed it. What had she overlooked about herself in all her years as self-appointed female physician to the Lloyd household?

"In one sense, what you two are dealing with here is from the same source. The war has come home to Texas, and you *both* are smarting from it. Right?"

No kidding, Sherlock, and both people responded in the affirmative.

"Stephen, I asked you about your faith yesterday. As I recall, you told me you were Catholic. That right? You do go to church?"

"Yes. We both grew up Catholic. Why? We don't go as much as we should. Why do you keep asking me this?" Stephen wondered why he felt as if he had to apologize for his religion. His response to the question was a bit gruff. For some reason questions about faith or religion agitated him, especially now.

Quill racked his brain. What *had* he said to Stephen in response? Oh yes. "We have some common ground to work with, as far as I can see. I don't have to use so many terms you don't understand or aren't familiar with. Right? I didn't realize it either when I got home from the war, but there is a direct connection between the troubles you both are facing now with the past and your beliefs." Quill knew he had to be very careful not to push Stephen off the porch with questions he suspected this man didn't want to examine, much less answer.

For Stephen at that moment it was far easier to be angry. It wasn't easier to try and find some relief by delving into God. "If you say so," the man exhaled, because the connection was about as clear as mud. Stephen looked as if he wanted to crawl back into his shell. The war had convinced Stephen that there weren't sufficient or adequate answers to his past in the church. Quite frankly, he'd abandoned his church and faith in Italy, although he went through the motions for his wife's sake when he returned. Quill was amazed that Stephen didn't get up and leave, so the old man pressed forward. It was interesting how vets like Stephen avoided the very issue that could help them if they would just look at them from a another perspective. Theologically, Quill knew this avoidance.

"In order to get to the heart of what I had to look at, let me ask you both to answer a couple of questions. Is that okay?" Susan said yes, but Stephen didn't respond. Agitation and its partner, withdrawal, squeezed him hard. Quill continued, "and if you can believe me, I want you to trust that I've been right where you sit, facing the same daunting hurt with no resolution on the horizon that I could see. Okay? You said you believe that God exists. Well, if he exists, what kind of God is He?" Stephen remained nonverbal and noncommittal, and his jaws flexed taut, then relaxed.

Susan thought hard, but came to no satisfying resolution. Her muddled thoughts were based more on guilt rather than coherence or fact. With another attempt, she approached the issue of God from the side door, the one that she always entered. "I'm a Catholic. I consider myself religious. Of course I believe God exists." But in her heart, Susan believed that God was punishing her for something she had done, and this trouble in their lives proved it. She couldn't just come out and *say* that God had something against her. The safe response was, "God is love, that's what He is." Stephen sat there calculating the coming trouble from his lack of an answer.

Susan waited for her husband. Hearing nothing, she said, "Stephen? You believe in God, right?" Her question crashed against his deafening, terrifying silence. "Stee-phen . . ." When Susan was irritated or puzzled she elongated his name in two syllables for emphasis. That was another thing that irritated him. Susan could protract the first vowel so that he felt his name scrape sharply against his inner ear and the inside of his tightening chest.

"I go to church with you. Isn't that enough, Susan?" Stephen answered from the tone of rudeness and perhaps resignation, which left him feeling trapped. It caught Susan in the diaphragm, hard.

"*What*?" she sprang at him. "I thought you . . . *No. Why* did we go to church all those years? It sounds to me as if it meant nothing to you. *Why* did you go, Stephen? *Why*?" These weren't really questions, they were accusations. It might have been better at this juncture if they had given the matter a rest and gone for a walk, or at least sat in silence mired in less cumbersome issues. God was speaking in the storm, regardless. "I'm thoroughly confused now, and hurt too." So much of what Susan Lloyd had thought that was solid in her life, might be an illusion. "I don't believe you, Stephen. Did the war cost you your faith, too?" Quill could see it. She was beginning to get it, now.

Stephen should have thanked Quill for bringing Susan to admit just how little she knew about the *real* cost of war. There were the obvious things, the nightmares, the impatience, the depression and the anger. But there were also small, seemingly insignificant ways in which the war cut into a man's ability to think about his past and face the present. One day those events, still very much alive and surrounding him, all but rubbed out many of the basic elements such as religion that Stephen had taken for granted in his formative years. He never really had "faith." He had church.

So many combat vets said they cast their faith or beliefs into the caskets or rough-hewn trenches of their fallen comrades, preferring to live without them. Creeds and convictions had little or nothing to say about the slaughter. What could his Catholic faith, which he had not taken all that seriously growing up, tell Stephen about the randomness of death on every mission or the fantastic ways men could be blown apart? There was nothing in his logic with which to believe what other men believed. By 1967, little of his former religious life remained or was recognizable. Time and repression had dissolved it.

Gradually Stephen *had* quit going to Mass or Confession while serving in Italy. He'd found himself going out of his way to avoid the Catholic chaplains. Every aircraft that augured in, that succumbed to enemy fighters or that disintegrated when the flak hit it left him less and less certain that God existed. If God did exist, maybe it meant that God didn't care or that He had no power to stop the slaughter. God could very well be a myth, as far as he knew.

Quill remembered observing the beautiful woman peering into and through Stephen's silence that had become as deep as the ache in her heart. Stephen's latest responses were completely beyond the pale of her imagination. If the truth were told, her answers were also hypocritical. Susan had doubted her own faith more than once when the babies died. With her uncertainty went God's very existence. With God's disappearance came the guilt. But that was years ago. She'd gotten her faith back, hadn't she? She was very much part of her church and its activities—*when she went*. Still, those days had come to her mind on the porch.

The old man had to let them both draw close to the end of their ropes before he resumed. "Susan, you have to admit, Stephen has been quite open and honest with you and himself. That's so important. I'm convinced by my own experiences on Bataan that we have to be brutally honest if we're going to give those events their proper and correct evaluation. And God's rich mercy has enabled me to do *at least* that."

"Hmmm . . ." Susan mumbled. Stephen, for his part, allowed the old man to mutter on. He'd rather sulk, and his agitation had become a distraction for Susan. The knot squeezing in Stephen's diaphragm was hard.

"I don't care if I get to where either of you thinks I need to be. I am where I am. And I think I'm beginning to be at peace with that, really at peace." His words trailed off. But Quill remembered wondering what Stephen's words could have actually meant? Perhaps Stephen was in the process of taking his own route, resolving it somehow or other, or maybe he had now found a meaning he could live with and hadn't told anyone. Maybe he was seeing the light. Maybe.

"Susan, your hurts are important also. But you didn't answer my second question. What kind of God *is* your God?"

Susan turned away from Quill's gaze, ashamed, confused and, most of all, uncertain. What she thought and felt seemed more ominous or wrongheaded. After a long silence, she turned back to Quill to say, "I think God is punishing me for hating Him when I lost my children. I thought He was so cruel to me. When I thought about it, He could have stopped it. God could have. Why didn't He, Quill?"

"You have held that in for a long time, haven't you?" the old man remembered asking. His tone had seemed to soothe her unraveling emotions.

"Yes, I have." For Susan, this confession of sorts did feel good to finally admit. "Probably too long. I don't know what kind of God He is. When life is good, I love God. He's wonderful. But when it hurts . . . when it goes all wrong, like now . . ." She didn't need to finish her thought.

"I know about the part when it hurts, Susan. Let me ask you this: what is *your* individual basis or authority for making your evaluations about God when life is so hard? Is it church dogma? Your priest? Is it the pope, perhaps? Your parents? What? This may be one of the most important questions you will ever answer."

"I don't know, really," she had answered. "I don't always agree with the pope and some of our priests, although I try as best I can to obey what they say."

"Until now, am I right?" Quill smiled at her.

"Until now, yes. And when the babies died . . ."

"*Now* you are being honest. In every church that I know of there is a hierarchy that hands down decisions to the laity. Right?" She nodded in affirmation. "The church's business is men's souls, redemption. My question is this: what happens when we disagree with those who are set over us, but we may not know where to go to prove our assertions? Do we grumble? Do we leave the church? What do we do?"

Both Stephen and Susan had stared blankly. They didn't know.

Continuing, Quill said, "The Methodists have their Bishops. I know of certain bishops who have disagreed with other bishops. The Baptists disagree with their leaders, Presbyterians with their Presbyteries. So where does a regular church member go when these human authorities who all say they speak for God, disagree with each other, and especially when their decisions might affect our eternal destiny?

"Let me give you a for instance regarding your own church Susan. Let's take papal infallibility. From Church history we know that certain Roman Catholic popes have radically disagreed with and changed the policy or dogma of the former popes. The ecumenical Council of Constance in 1409 in Avignon, France, set itself up above the pope. Even today, Rome cannot be absolutely certain if a current pope is a descendant of the papal line from Martin V, who is supposed to be a direct descendant of Peter. In 1417, this papal schism—France vs. Rome—finally ended because of the decisions of Constance. Three popes all claimed the papacy simultaneously. Gregory XII said he would resign if the other two claimants did. The Constance council deposed the other two popes, Benedict XIII and John XXIII. This council even brought seventy charges against Pope John, every charge known to man, it stated.

"I bet you were unaware that in 1958, when Cardinal Roncalli became the pope, he took the name John XXIII. That's important simply because when he took that name, he officially branded the first John XXIII an Antipope. Rome actually removed this first John from Catholic papal history. Most Catholics are woefully ignorant of their own history." Both Susan and Stephen preferred to remain quiet on such matters, for Quill had spoken of *them* as part of that crowd.

"The point I'm making is that, from the fourth to the eleventh centuries, papal infallibility was a given. The pope spoke infallibly for God. However, Rome has conceded that many of the papal elections during those early centuries were corrupted and consequently invalidated by the contemporary secular political forces. The church leadership as well as the pope himself were egregiously corrupt and wicked. This means that the bishops who voted for each new pope should have had their ordinations invalidated because they did not meet the condition of "outstanding and habitual goodness," as well as "perfect chastity" within themselves.

Thus, those bishops should not have cast a ballot, and the pope's election should have been nullified. We know of course they weren't. Frankly, the doctrine of papal infallibility, for all intents and purposes, has carried now actual weight where it matters. Pope Paul VI cannot legitimately claim papal infallibility. Papal infallibility is truly an oxymoron. And if that is true, then the Roman Catholic traditions carry no authority either. And this brings us back to my last question. Now that we understand the false foundation of authority upon which the Catholic church stands, where are you to go to find an infallible authority to shed light on your toughest questions? And if the pope is *de facto* illegitimate in his proclamations, where do might you go to receive objective, authoritative guidance?

Susan ventured aloud, "Sometimes I get this sense about things, and many times I'm right."

"Ever been wrong on an important issue when you "felt" right about it?" Quill asked.

"Well, yes."

"What did you do then?"

Susan said, "I apologize. Well, sometimes I do."

Quill remembered that Stephen just sat there, mulling this over a bit longer without commenting.

Quill offered a little theological sarcasm to lighten the mood. "I can just hear God now. 'Gee folks, I'm sorry. I meant that you have to do this instead of that. You have to believe this instead of that. I meant well. Sorry.' The Lloyd's didn't discuss dogma. Theology was a priestly concern. Quill continued, "Let me give you a for instance. And please don't think I'm picking on Catholics, because I can give you illustration after illustration for other religions if you want. I'm the kind of student that wants to pull things out and see how and why they work, see if they can stand up to objective truth. Sorry. Well, purgatory is a Catholic doctrine that I have studied, just to be better informed. And I was quite surprised at what I found. I have a Catholic friend that told me when her husband died the priest said at the wake that her husband was in heaven with God.

"She was an astute woman, very intelligent, except where it came to her church. She just didn't ask things that I suppose I would have. Anyway, a disturbing thought crossed her mind one day. She told me she didn't know why she asked it at the time, but it seemed important to her, and she had to know the answer. So she went and asked the priest why, at her husband's funeral, had he prayed for her husband's soul if he was already in heaven with God? She said that stumped him. He'd never been asked that question nor had he asked it himself. Another problem for my friend was this same priest said in a class not a month before her husband's death that *only* the Virgin Mary and the saints go straight to heaven when they die. Everyone else must be purged of his or her transgressions in purgatory.

"I asked her what Christ's death was for if *we* have to purify ourselves? The Bible speaks clearly that if the concept of purgatory were true, this would automatically nullify the atonement of Christ. Wouldn't it? Scripture is emphatic that man *cannot* purge himself of his own sin. How would we know when enough was enough purging? Holiness is God's work. Also, the Bible says that it is appointed once for man to die, but after death comes the judgment. There is no second chance for purging *if* the Bible's right.

"My Catholic friend felt the full weight of a dilemma for the first time in her religious life. She was born a Catholic, and she couldn't view life from any other perspective. She felt panicked. So she kept pressing her priest hoping he might resolve this to her satisfaction. Apparently, the priest tried several times to side step the issue, and when she wouldn't drop it he finally admitted, grudgingly, her husband was in purgatory. I guess he was just trying to be kind to her.

"She felt angry with him because he had to lied to her. How could her husband be in two places at once? He was either at that moment being tormented in fire for who knew how many millions of years, or he was in heaven with God. And she didn't know *how* to know the truth since the priest had lied to her. Her church had even been selling indulgences to pay for its building program and this would, by her giving financially, make her husband's suffering in purgatory shorter."

"Susan, the Bible speaks repeatedly against man's attempts to place a price tag on salvation. It only perverts the Gospel when we do. Scripturally, indulgences are indefensible regardless of how or why they are used.

"She had another dilemma. She was terrified of death now that her husband was gone. She was also beginning to have her own health issues to deal with. I offered the Bible's comfort to her, but she was inconsolable. It was heartbreaking to watch.

"I did ask her if she knew where the concept of Purgatory came from. She said no. I told her it came from the Councils of Florence and Trent in the fifteenth and sixteenth centuries. She said that she knew a few priests and some of the sisters who didn't even believe in purgatory. Their belief was that it wasn't a real place but more of a condition. But even if it is a condition, the cross of Christ is still nullified.

"So I asked her. Why had these authoritative Councils introduced purgatory, something not previously taught? Why then had the churches been teaching it for centuries as fact when it was just introduced in the fourteenth century, and *they* were supposed to speak for God. So what did this mean when these other priests and sisters were also speaking for God as heaven's authority and they *now* disagree with purgatory? My question, at least to me, seemed obvious. Who's right?"

"I know that *her* Church says purgatory can be found in the Bible. We both looked at the passages they use as proof. But when we examined the verses even she could tell that they were very poorly interpreted and taken out of their context. I showed her that Scripture says that for the true Christian, to be absent from the body is to be immediately present with the Lord. In other words, we have two sources claiming authority, the Bible on one hand, and the Catholic Church and its traditions on the other. That is to say, the conclusion to which the Catholic Church comes is completely opposite on this important topic and opposed to the conclusion to which the Scriptures truly come. Someone is wrong and someone is right.

"We know that they have found some writings on the catacomb walls about the concept. But, scratches on catacomb walls are a far cry from authoritative. Then, all of a sudden, in 1438 at Florence, Purgatory as official dogma was introduced to the Church, and along with it, indulgences sold to shorten a man's time in purgatory in order to build their grand cathedrals, *etc.* Either it's a real place based on an authoritative source or it isn't. And what happens to all those people for the first fourteen centuries who never heard of it? Are they in purgatory or not?"

Forty-Three:
Growing Up Catholic

><+>·O·<+><

Monday, May 15, 1967

"Quill, *honestly.* I've haven't thought about this since I was in Catholic school. And then it seemed too far into the future for me to worry about," Susan remembered, leaning back in the rocker, her facial bewilderment giving air to her lethargic spirit. "I don't know how to answer this on a personal level, or where people actually go when they die. I know that I go to church, but I personally haven't felt the need to question anything—not really. I *am* a good Catholic. I know that. I love the services. I sit in awe sometimes . . . all the ceremony and . . . I go to confession so I can take the Eucharist. Dogma doesn't interest me. And I really don't know what's in the Bible, although we own several."

Quill shifted the weight of his story to a related question, "Susan, are you afraid to die? Do you think about that time you know you're going to face one of these days? Will you face it as a church saint or sinner?" Quill could plainly remember the distressing weight he saw that these next questions placed upon Susan. "As I understand it," he had said, "if you aren't a saint, according to Roman Catholic tradition, you're gonna be in purgatory for a mighty long time. You will be tormented in fire until you have been purged of all traces of your iniquity . . . unless your church isn't correct about purgatory." He knew his last statement might possibly be taken as cruel or incorrect or unthinkable, especially in light of what this woman was already going through. Clearly, Susan was in over her head. The questions she hadn't considered, she should have, but the business of life had dampened any need to dwell on such things.

"Personally," Quill had offered, "I look forward to my death. Scripture and the Holy Spirit dwelling in me guarantees that I will be with the Lord Jesus forever when I die. The *moment* I die, the Bible says I will be made perfect in holiness so that I can pass into glory. And on Judgment Day, Christ will openly acknowledge and acquit me of all sin so that I can enjoy God's perfect blessedness in heaven. So you are *not* excited about dying?"

"No. I'm terrified of the thought. Quill, how do *you know* for sure? I have no such certainty." Stephen continued to rock in his chair and gaze about the surrounding hillside.

Susan the Bible is very specific about salvation and that you can know for certain that you have eternal life. The apostle John wrote in 1 John 5:13, These things I have written to you who believe in the name of the Son of God, so that you may know that you have eternal life. Quill knew that in so many mainline churches a person simply had to walk an aisle, pray a prayer, and ask Jesus to come into their heart. 'Step right up and get your life insurance policy right here, folks.' So much of it was superficial and pathetic, because they were relying on the act of praying the prayer or walking the aisle. He'd talked to too many folks that had prayed the sinner's prayer and been baptized, but now had no more dealings with the church. What the Church had promised: a good life, prosperity, and the like had not happened. The statistics showed that hundreds of people each year made professions of faith and were baptized. Unfortunately, several years later, far too many had left the church disillusioned.

While in the Army Quill had felt sorry for 'those religious guys' in his outfit. That was before Bataan fell. And then he went into captivity. Those goody two shoes went to church. They didn't do what real men do: get drunk and fight. And then he began to understanding just how meaningless his life was. It didn't take him very long to see the truth of his wasted life. But as a believer, Quill began to see that nothing is wasted in God's eternal administration, not even his own wilderness wanderings before, during and after captivity. He kept hoping that Susan and Stephen might see their dilemma through his proclamation of the truth and follow on questions, as well as their meager answers, or the complete lack thereof.

"What does your church offer you in the way of comfort regarding death?" he had asked.

"Quill, I hate to say this, but I've resigned myself to going to purgatory, if it exists. But mostly, I don't want to think about it. So I guess I have no comfort to speak of." Susan's lack of facial expression didn't symphonize with her words and her tone, much less her fears. Quill was and was not surprised. It's incredible, if not arrogant, how people believe they alone determine the time they die, and Quill had been among the most arrogant. This conversation reminded him of the parable Jesus taught about the rich man who said he would tear down his barns and build bigger ones, because his life was going so well financially. Jesus however, called him a fool. 'Don't you know your soul is required of you this very night?' No, he didn't.

"Look," Quill had said, "I'm not saying that our gut isn't right sometimes about the decisions we make. Many men have pointed us in the right direction. Nobody denies that. What I am saying is that each of us has been divinely thrown into various situations that puts us far beyond the ability of a gut feeling, an opinion, or well meaning advice, even a papal edict to know just what to do or think, from a purely human standpoint. Perhaps like this situation? Would that be fair?"

"You mean, Quill, you think God created this situation we're in right now, Stephen's predicament and my own anxiety? How is that right? It makes no sense."

"Susan, I mean more than that. I mean He decreed it to come to pass, and so it has. I realize that it makes little or no sense to you, just like it once did not to me. Apart from God's saving grace you only observe life and experience it from a purely logical, albeit fallen, human perspective. The person who has not trusted Jesus's work on Calvary cannot accept God's truth. In fact, he hates it. But when God's Spirit saves you, He brings light and understanding. He blesses us with desires we didn't have before. He counsels us and guides us, applies the finished work of Jesus to us. Because the Holy Spirit dwells in us, what we are going through begins to take on purpose and significance. Trials become an incredible opportunity to discover the nature and the work of God in our lives. I'm not suggesting that many of our trials are enjoyable. To the contrary, they can be very difficult. The Book of Hebrews says Jesus Himself learned obedience to God from His suffering. And King David said, 'It is good for me that I was afflicted, That I may learn Your statutes,' and, 'And that in faithfulness You have afflicted me.' The apostle Paul said he was the chiefest of all sinners. All true knowledge comes from the Bible and in the Person of Jesus, who said, 'I am the way, and the truth, and the life. No man can come to the Father but through Me.' So, in order to understand reality truly, we need some type of special revelation from *outside* of our human experience that's infallible and utterly trustworthy.

Quill recalled Stephen's interruption. "Come on Quill. There too many contradictions in the Bible."

"Stephen, there are places in Scripture I can't reconcile—not right now, or maybe in my lifetime. Can you name one?" Hearing silence, he continued. If there seems to be contradictions, that doesn't mean those issues *can't* be reconciled. Let me ask you how you plan to reconcile the issue of purgatory and all those centuries without it being taught or it being taught and various ecclesiastical *authorities* disagreeing with one another as to whether it even exists? And *if* Scripture doesn't teach it and the Catholic Church didn't teach it officially for fourteen centuries, what does that tell you? And if this teaching came thirteen centuries after the Apostles died—and they didn't teach it, then we can't say that the Apostles had anything to do with its teaching, can we? And if it plainly contradicts the atonement of Christ, which it does, why would God want it taught?"

"I know, but—" Stephen tried to interject a theory he had, but didn't make it.

"Now wait, Stephen. I read the Bible by what is known as the Analogy of Faith; Scripture is always the best interpreter of Scripture. That means that we are to interpret the difficult passages by those that speak clearly on a particular topic. That's a good rule of thumb. The Bible speaks in sentences and paragraphs that anyone can understand. It reveals God as a logical Being. Scripture says it's impossible for God to lie. That means He won't contradict Himself as opposed to the men and councils who have down through church history. In Genesis one it says that we are created in God's own image and that's the reason I can say we think logically. Otherwise, we couldn't communicate with each other about anything. God certainly wouldn't be able to communicate with us in ways that we would understand. So, if a certain passage *seems* to say one thing contrary to what I have thought all along or appears to be unclear on something, then I go to the verses that speak plainly about that particular topic. That also means I have to know what the Bible says. I have to read it. You and I know, as we get older and wiser, we change our opinions about things we were certain of when we were younger. God doesn't grow old and become wiser. He knows everything immediately and perfectly that there is to know. Oh, and God doesn't make rocks so big He can't move them. That's contradictory on its face. So, when the Bible speaks, God speaks.

Quill had taken a breath. He wanted his guests to ponder what he'd just said. After a minute, he continued. "There's a verse in Galatians that says—let me see if I can find it. Here it is. I was just dealing with this last week, that's how I remember it; chapter three, verse eight: "The Scripture, foreseeing that God would justify the Gentiles by faith, preached the gospel beforehand to Abraham, saying, "All the nations will be blessed in you." But referring to the original covenant statement that Moses wrote in Genesis 12:3, "And I will bless those who bless you, And the one who curses you I will curse. And in you all the families of the earth will be blessed." So, Paul writes in Gal. 3:8, *The Scripture*, foreseeing that God would justify the Gentiles by faith, but Moses says the Spoke in Gen. 12:3, "All the nations will be blessed in you." That's why when I quote the Bible, I am in fact, quoting God's revealed, authoritative will. Where the Bible speaks, God speaks.

"You can accept my supposition as authoritative or reject it," Quill remembered saying. "And that's fine. But you need to know why you disagree, and it has to stand up to the scrutiny of God's truth. The Bible states I don't know how many times that it is the inerrant, infallible, and absolute Word of God. God has given me His Spirit and some great teachers to help me understand what He has done for me and demands of me. Scripture says the secret things belong to God. But, in the final analysis and especially with what you and I have been through Stephen, we both need something objective and infinitely beyond our fallible intellect to provide wisdom to understand what we can't resolve or find any meaning for, humanly speaking, like war.

"The Bible is my anchor. There have been days and weeks when I couldn't open its pages I was so depressed or angry or . . . or just sad. But what I'd learned when I could read it helped get me through those tough days so that when it did let up I was able to pick up where

I left off. And God didn't stop loving me when I went through those times, because nothing can separate me from His love. King David had difficult days. In Psalm 119, he understood that God would revive him in His Word and covenant love. That's why I'd started memorizing it.

"Then another tidal wave would come along, and I'd get pushed from pillar to post and have to go through it all over again. But it was the God of the Scriptures that anchored me. My God held me up. He knows my condition better than even I do, and, as a Christian, He never shoves that wretched condition in my face, because He dealt with it in His Son's cross-work. Jesus and the Holy Spirit continually pray for me. God's Spirit is even *now* making me holy like His Son Jesus is. God Himself declared me righteous in His eyes when I believed His word. Jesus' blood has paid for my sin *once and for all* time and eternity. He loves me, because He chose me to receive His infinite grace from all eternity past for His good pleasure and for my salvation, based solely upon His own free choice. God is the only free Being in the universe. Man is not free to choose God. We're born thoroughly dead in sin, and dead people don't choose anything. No amount of the Spirit's *influence* can make me choose God. You and I are born spiritually incapable of loving God. The Apostle John, in his gospel says that I didn't choose Him, but He chose me. By the Spirit, I know these things in the deepest part of my being. There is more meaning in these doctrinal statements than all the fame or fortune or whatever people are looking for.

Looking back, these things seemed like a foreign language to Stephen. But Stephen had said something that surprised Quill. "I don't know if my church knows how to speak to the emotional and psychological injuries, the suffering and guilt inflicted on the survivors of combat. I tried to talk to a priest once about some issues that were really hard for me to understand, but he didn't know what to say. The ones who did know about what we had gone through only offered us the sacraments. I guess to them that was supposed to solve *all* my problems. Then I could go off on a mission and die in a state of grace over some target. It seemed so unsatisfying, or empty or *something*. I think I finally gave up believing there might be more to religion and the Church than what I observed. I kept going though, but I don't know why."

"Stephen, I haven't found very much help in my church either now that Pastor Franklin is gone. Some of those folks really didn't want me coming into their congregation looking so sad or depressed, so hopeless at times. Church was supposed to be a happy place, not for sad or mad people like me. We don't want any visitors seeing unhappy faces they said in so many different ways. Well, I wasn't a happy man after the war. Besides, happiness is not God's goal for me, obedience and holiness is, and those realities are found only in Jesus. I've known more than one clergy who didn't understand why I lived in the past like I do. And that's one reason why I have been forced to look beyond these church authorities like bishops and popes and presbyteries and preachers, to one solid foundation that, as far as I'm concerned, is eternally secure and accepting. I cling to the God of the Bible. *He* feeds something inside me that no one else can." Quill did remember saying this. That was a load lifted.

He remembered saying other things too. "Stephen, let me tell you something else about what's inside of us that's broken. I like to use the snowball illustration. Picture a snowball sitting on the side of a mountain. The snowball is the war. Sometimes it just sits there. Those are the days you relish. Other days . . . when life gets tough, that snowball begins to move over the side. I've tried for years to keep it from not going over the cliff and dragging me with it. I worked with my carvings. I took walks, not so much any more. I tried to relax. I did whatever I could to keep that huge white ball up there. But most of the time, I was worn-out from failing to keep it up there. You know? People out *there* don't understand what we live doing. They don't. I remember one day writing about my experiences in the war. A friend of mine asked me what I was doing. He said I *had* to quit thinking about the past. Let it go. Stop being so sad. Refuse to let it get me down. So I tried that. And I tried that, and I tried that, and I . . . Get the picture?" Stephen nodded in agreement.

"Helen would make me mad. I couldn't find my drill. My truck had a flat tire when I needed to go someplace. My knife was dull and I couldn't sharpen it because my hands hurt too much. The toilet would get stopped up. That bull out there would get out of the pasture and wander all over, . . . tore up Bill Henry's shed three months ago. That danged snowball wanted to come down, and I couldn't let it. I'd get angry and threaten to shoot Helen, the bull, my truck, the toilet . . .

after a few years of that, I quit trying to keep it up there. My friend, Bill Henry, let me have it when I was sad one day. I got about this close to his nose and I said I couldn't quit being sad today. I was ready to keel haul him. Bill doesn't come around anymore, and I don't miss him. One day, I decided to let the snowball, *the war*, go all the way to the bottom. I didn't feel better . . . and yes, that was wrong. But for once I felt I was being real with the world. "I'd tell Helen that I was angry or sad over some issue, and I didn't try and hide it any longer.

"I knew that I wasn't *always* sad, but *some* days I was. That's key. I'm not always sad or angry. I do have good days, many more now. I had to let the anger out, not hold it in so it could eat at me. Holding it in caused Helen and I to argue. Anger was going to do to me what it wanted anyway. I'd just get away from everything and let it go. Even as a Christian, God doesn't stop the sad or mad from happening to me. He could, should that please Him. He is ever present with me among those things.

"I'm discovering that every time I'm tempted by a bad emotion, God makes a way of escape for me. Something external will alter the situation or my inner turmoil will subside unexpectedly, or it draws me to prayer. As King and Lord, it pleases Him that these emotions come forth so that He can show me His power over them in my life. At seventy-three, I still get angry and depressed. It returns, not as often, but it *always* leaves, praise God! When it comes, Jesus controls the duration and intensity, and then removes it from me. *Always.* I think Helen began to understand that toward the end of her life.

"There's something else I had Helen try when I'd have a bad day. I told her to go about her business as if I was having a good day. I told her to pay me no mind, but to pray for herself and me with everything she had. I told her that when she sensed my mood change for the worse, she needed to leave and go into Prince George and shop or go see some of her friends, or, or even go someplace where she could read the Scriptures for herself and me . . . just get away from me so I couldn't affect her day for the worse. That took her a while, but she told me it was freeing to her. But she had to pray for me. Then it was just Jesus and me and I was free to hear God myself. And it was Jesus and Helen. That's not a bad place to be.

"Yes Susan, I still get quite depressed some days as you have seen. Thoughts of suicide occasionally run through my mind, even at my age. But the thoughts come around so much less as I've gotten older. I don't think about those days very much at all, any more. That is the blessing of the Gospel. And I attribute that to the Lord Jesus. God has made me so much more aware that *He knows* I'm broken inside. He led me into captivity, and He watched over me there, and now His Spirit lives in me to help me go through the tough times to teach me obedience and holiness. That's how Jesus learned it. Paul had learned over time that when he was weak physically, he was in fact strong because of God's grace that was given to him. His weakness was his glory.

"So I don't try and hide all those "run away" emotions anymore. If you ask me how I'm doing when I'm having a bad day, I'm going to tell you the truth. I'm depressed or I'm angry. God has mercifully granted that I've had some good days while you've been here. But my relationship with God hasn't been altered one bit simply because I've been tempted with suicidal thoughts, or I've been so sad I cried some of the day, or got so agitated I wanted to hit someone. I didn't. But because those days come around, I experience eternal mercy breaking into time in my life. The Apostle Paul said nothing could separate me from God's love. My faith is *His* gift, but it's *my* faith too. He is at work in me for His good pleasure from before the foundation of the world and continues through eternity future.

"So all of this, My Savior and my war, is who I am. One day, my war will be no more. My life is more real and more meaningful now than it has ever been, because God graciously reveals Himself in so many aspects of it. It pleased God to lead His Son into the wilderness and suffer, and it pleased God to crush Jesus, the Son of God, on the cross. Who am I to blame God if He is pleased to crush me at times? No, I don't like to suffer. Jesus didn't want to either. Remember Jesus' requests in the Garden of Gethsemane? Oh God, take this cup from Me. Jesus also said to His disciples, 'in this world you shall have tribulation. But be of good cheer. I have overcome the world.' I'm learning to bring my sinful thoughts captive to the obedience of Christ like the Apostle Paul says.

Tuesday, May 16, 1967
The noon dishes had been cleared. Quill sat staring out into his empty cup. The high sun was busy filtering through the pines, through the

windows and down into the room. Stephen and Susan had fought that morning, but it wasn't that intense, fortunately. There they sat, on opposing sides of the table, somewhat dejected.

"You know Susan, Helen finally understood that whatever I was going through would pass. She began to see God's hand in it for good, and she'd wait it out, but she'd pray for me. Now here's the great part. God put us together, my brokenness and incomplete holiness. God's will was that she stay with me *because* my condition was what would bring about her own holiness and obedience. My troubles were God's gift to her to make *her* more Christ-like. Camp O'Donnell was God's gift to me to do the same thing in me. Jesus learned obedience from the things He suffered. Pain and suffering was the road to glory.

"In the early days of our faith, I'd get angry and hurtful, and I knew I hurt her. But she was learning to wait before she said something back. I know now that God had wrapped her in His grace. She knew I'd come back at some point to apologize. She must have fought some real inner battles over me . . . but my relationship to Jesus was never in doubt. *Jesus*, not Helen, is the author and finisher of my faith. Paul says that nothing in this world can ever separate God's chosen people from His love. Over the years, we both began to rest in that knowledge, even though I was depressed or feeling particularly guilty or angry or sleepless. Too often, I'd forget about God's promises at the worst of moments, but they were true, nonetheless. His promises held me while I struggled. God has always kept His covenant promises to me.

"I think it was later in the afternoon that same day . . . and Susan had been asking me about Camp O'Donnell and God's presence there, and both Susan and Stephen seemed to ask it at the same time: 'Hold it, Quill. Hold it. You said this the other day that God was present there. Well then, why did He let so many people die, and so horribly?'

"So I had tried to clarify it a bit more for them. 'Life,' I had stated, 'is about a lot of things. It's about marriage. It's about Little League baseball. It's about elections. Granted, but this life, if it is anything, is preparation for the next life. At any time of the day or night, on the TV or radio, you can hear the Gospel proclaimed. You hear it each week at church. You read Bible verses in books that have nothing to do with God. Our dollar bills and coins have, "In God We Trust," printed or stamped on them. This creation shouts *God* all over it. Yet, when difficult times come, we are completely unable to connect God with the trouble. I bet by the time you two were twenty years old, you had heard God's message of salvation in Christ dozens, maybe hundreds of times. But, each time you heard that message might have been your last. If you would have died after the first time you heard it, you were responsible to heed its warning, to turn from your wickedness and be saved from God's coming wrath. The creation makes man inexcusable because it speaks about God and His power and invisible attributes. Your friends, just like you know God exists. Yet, you have continued headlong into the danger completely oblivious as if God had never commanded all men to repent. Don't you see His mercy to you?'"

"The Bible says, 'For the wrath of God is revealed from heaven against all ungodliness and unrighteousness of men who suppress the truth in unrighteousness, because that which is known about God is evident within them; for God made it evident to them. For since the creation of the world His invisible attributes, His eternal power and divine nature, have been clearly seen, being understood through what has been made, so that they are without excuse. For even though they knew God, they did not honor Him as God or give thanks, but they became futile in their speculations, and their foolish heart was darkened. Professing to be wise, they became fools, and exchanged the glory of the incorruptible God for an image in the form of corruptible man and of birds and four-footed animals and crawling creatures.'"

"Do you hear what this apostle is saying? God's very wrath is right now being poured out against all of you ungodliness. Stephen, I don't know about the men with whom you served, but the infantry I served with were about as crude a bunch of men as you can imagine. But we all heard the chaplains preach at one time or another. We usually received Communion. And then we too took the Lord's Name in vain without even thinking about it. We lied and we stole things. We lusted and we hated. Men suppress the truth they hear and observe by doing further unrighteousness. Worse, Paul said that this truth about God is evident to them because God Himself *made it evident to them.*

"And every bomber that went down or every man that died on Corregidor and Bataan was a warning to us who survived, to you and to me Stephen, that the next one might be us. . . and we needed to repent or something worse would come on us. If that isn't bad enough, because we refused to acknowledge God's sovereign right over us. We, in our unrighteousness believe we are wise. We are sure we know more than God, who knows everything. And being "wise," Paul says we became fools for believing we aren't as bad as we are or that God is a snake or bull or a bird. We know He exists because we have been created in His *moral* image. We don't honor Him for keeping us alive. We don't realize that every good thing we possess came from Him, even the breath we breathe. It is all a gift of His mercy. We exchange His glory for something else of no real value or worth, for something that honors *us*. I did that. The heavens declare God's glory, but we look at them and move on to other things, so much more "important."

"We come back from a bombing mission thinking we're lucky. The guy in front of us steps on a mine, and *we* live. We were just lucky or good. *We* can't be fooled. But we know better. But the Bible says there is a God who will one day call us to account for taking *His* glorious character and works and rubbing them in the dirt.

So, here you are again, one more chance to hear God speak to you about your rebellion and a hope He offers you beyond the grave. And since all men have sinned, none of them is righteous, no, *not one*. Maybe a better question to ask is, Why did anyone make it out of the war alive? The Nazis were sinners. The Japs were sinners. The French, the British, the Americans were all sinners. The Russians were sinners. And Ezekiel said the soul that sins shall die. Why did God allow those men in the camp to die like that? If you think that was bad . . . or Auschwitz or Buchenvald or any other concentration camp you can name, they were all a picnic compared to the coming wrath and judgment of God. Those camps only lasted a few years. Yes, they were hideous . . . so many people murdered there. God's eyes roam throughout the earth, beholding the evil and the good. The creation screams at the men who do evil and good: the All Powerful God, the Lord of redemption and justice exists! Turn to Him and be saved all the ends of the earth! Everyday, people die, and the people who remain are incredibly ignorant of the fact that unless they repent, they too will likewise perish.

"Genesis three tells us why life is war, why life hurts, why life is not fair, why men kill each other, why men die. When Adam sinned, all men were imputed or counted as dead in sin at *that* instant. Men choose the darkness rather than the light. And since we love the darkness, that is, wickedness and evil, we refuse to submit to Jesus's rule in our hearts. Susan, Jesus was also present when your babies died. But did you ever think, 'My baby died, if I don't repent, I, too, might die horribly like that baby?' No. I bet not. He was present when those bombers went down and yours didn't. But Stephen, did you ever say to yourself, 'my buddies just got killed. I have this moment to turn from my sin and trust Jesus's work on the cross?' I bet not, and neither did I. I'm not judging *either* of you. I was just as guilty and blind. He shielded your plane Stephen in order to give you and your crew one more opportunity to turn to Him and be saved from this wicked and adulterous generation. That's why you are *here, today*. You're alive because *He* kept you alive. You are alive to hear the Good News one more time. But you are also that much more guilty if you refuse Him who calls from heaven. Don't you see?"

Both Stephen and Susan had looked stunned. They seemed to be completely uncomprehending of Quill's dire warnings. Quill had laid out the way of escape that had been clearly been laid out for them to grasp by faith, yet they were blind to it, because it could only be spiritually understood. Quill's words seemed not to have penetrated farther than their ear lobes.

After a few minutes, Susan had recounted her reasons for rejecting Quill's assertions. "Quill, I go to church. I love the Mass and I love the Lord Jesus. I just don't understand what you're getting at." Susan had rebuffed her host's perceived accusation that she had spurned God anywhere near the degree Quill seemed to suggest. She was a good person. *Anyone* could vouch for her morals. She had not cheated on Stephen. She had not killed anyone. She was a good mother, *anyone* could see that. And Stephen: well, he was a great employer and friend to many in the Ft. Worth community. He'd given vast sums of money to various charities. He had grown up in the Catholic Church. He'd attended Confession and Mass faithfully until Italy. Yes, he'd had some doubts, but those would be ironed out in due course. Okay, he might have purgatory to face, but he would weather that.

"Quill, I *am* a good person. I know it. As God is my witness, I am a good person, and I don't like your insinuation that I'm not!"

"I completely understand your resistance. I, too, didn't believe the Bible's insistence that I was *not* good. But then, I knew I had done everything the Bible said it did and so much more. Let me ask it this way. Have you ever lied?"

Susan looked at Stephen for help, then back to Quill. "Well, yes. I have told a *few*."

"So if you lie, what does that make you?"

Stunned, Susan swallowed hard. "I . . . well, I guess it makes me a liar."

"Ok. Have you ever stolen anything?"

"Everybody has stolen *something*. So yes, I once took something from the store."

"If you steal something, what does that make you?"

"It makes me a stealer . . . I mean a thief," Susan said in a huff.

"Okay. You have lied, so you are a liar. You said you stole something. That makes you a thief. Have you ever lusted?"

Susan's eyes went to the floor. She knew she had been found out, but she wouldn't venture anything out loud. Stephen's eyebrows raised, but he knew he, too, had lusted after one of the secretaries at the office on more than one occasion. He certainly would not tell his wife of the pretty Italian woman that lived off base that made eyes at him. He'd visited her house on more than one occasion. That information stayed in his tent.

"I'll take that as a yes. Jesus said that if we lust after a woman or a man as the case may be, we have committed adultery with them in our hearts. So, by your own admission, you are a liar, a thief, and an adulteress. Have you ever taken the Lord's name in vain?"

"Oh my. I did, and just last week. But I asked forgiveness right away," Susan offered, rather embarrassed to have to admit it.

"That makes you a blasphemer. God says He will hold us guilty if we treat His name so thoughtlessly. Okay. By your own admission, you are a liar, a thief, an adulteress, and a blasphemer. Have you ever hated someone, Susan?"

"Well, yes. I hated Marsha Tipton for taking my boyfriend once."

"God says if we hate our brother *or* sister in our heart, we have committed murder. So, let's add all this goodness of yours up. You are a liar, a thief, an adulteress, a blasphemer, *and* a murderer. Is that right? I haven't added something that isn't true of you, have I?"

Susan truly looked and felt guilty, now that Quill had put it this way. Yes, she was guilty before a holy God, and *she knew it*, and now, so did Quill. "It's okay, Susan. I flunked it too," he said as he winked. "And Stephen here, he flunked it too. The wages of sin is death. The Bible says if we break *one law*, we are guilty of breaking *all* of them, not just the one. The law is an unbreakable unit. If you run a stop sign, you break *the whole law*, not simply a single law. So think how many times a day you break the *whole law* of God. Now multiply that times seven days a week. Then multiply that times three hundred sixty-five days a year. Now multiply that by how old you are and you will see that you should be in hell right now.

"Stephen," Quill added, "every man the Japs beat to death or shot or bayoneted or decapitated should have been me. *I was guilty* before a holy God who had demanded repeatedly that I turn from my sin. We so often grade sin. We say, murder is a ten, but a white lie is a one. But white lies put Jesus on the cross just as much as murder. The Good News is that Jesus took my curse for breaking His law on Himself at the cross. He became sin or like sin—remember He was sinless—and, for doing those things I was guilty of, He transferred or imputed to me His righteousness instead. I deserved His curses for breaking His law. Instead, He took my curse on Himself and died in my place. I was made righteous by faith and He became sin. God gave me new life, and then opened my eyes and *gave me* the faith to trust Jesus's work on my behalf. There was no longer any need to be good enough so I could merit salvation. I had nothing to offer God but my sin and guilt. He offered me His holiness and redemption. Jesus died on the cross and satisfied completely God's justice. God's just character demanded an accounting or reckoning for our sin. Somebody had to pay the price. Jesus said He would and He did.

"No Susan, you are not good—not in God's eyes."

"No," she agreed. "You're right. I guess I'm not."

Forty-Four: Guilt?

Two days before Stephen died, Quill remembered his knee bothering him something awful. How time had flown. "Let me sum everything up," Quill had said, "with this question. If you were to die right now, and stand before God, and He were to ask you why He should let you into His heaven, what would you say to Him? Susan, what would you say to God?"

Quill could tell this was also a fearful question to Susan. She'd ducked it in various forms for years, but had by now formulated her own response. "Well, like I said a few days ago, I've been . . . I mean, I've lived . . . I've *tried* to live a good life. I think the good I've done would outweigh my bad. I think I've earned the right to heaven. That's what I would probably say. I've been baptized as an infant and I take the sacraments every time I go to church. But I don't think anyone can really know for sure he's going to heaven. *Can he?*"

Quill had spent the past few days telling Susan that he knew without the shadow of a doubt that *he* was going to heaven, and now she was asking him if it was possible to know for certain. Incredible. Susan had agreed that she was a Hell-deserving sinner. Chuckling to himself, Quill had an inkling of what Pastor Franklin lived with when Quill first started attending his church. Quill once more wanted to ask Susan to elaborate on what she believed now about purgatory. She told him she believed she would end up there, but that only meant she was guilty of sin. *The folks outside of God's saving grace are incapable of seeing their inconsistencies,* he thought. He had quoted more than once,

1 John 5:13, These things I have written to you who believe in the name of the Son of God, so that you may know that you have eternal life.

Quill didn't respond verbally to her answer. "Stephen? How about you? What would you say?"

Quill had guessed correctly Stephen didn't want to play this game today. He kept looking out toward the bull that had come into view. For long seconds he said nothing. Then, "I don't know," he had blurted. "I feel way too guilty for . . ." His jaws tightened and his eyes caught Susan's for the first time during their conversation. "You're right. I think I know God exists, but . . . God couldn't . . . He couldn't possibly forgive me for what I did. I can't even forgive myself. I lived and so many better men than I didn't. I don't know why I should have married Susan, and . . . all that."

He remembered Stephen simply had no answers, not for himself, not for Susan, not for Quill, and certainly not for God. He hadn't looked for any, because from where he stood, there probably weren't any to be had. His answer was equally amazing. Quill remembered thanking the Lord for His mercy, giving him eyes to see.

Quill had asked both of them what kind of God they believed He is and why they went to Church to worship Him on Sunday. It amazed and bewildered Quill that people go to worship a God they can't define, like Susan and Stephen had done, for years. They had no true coherent idea what His nature was like, or why He was angry at them or that they should be terrified of Him. The God that he had read about in the Scriptures is a God who revealed Himself in His objective, propositional revelation: the Bible, and in His Son come to earth to assure His people that their death, which He had also decreed from all eternity, could be a threshold to something incredibly wonderful, or, eternally horrible if they reject His gracious offer of salvation. Nothing seemed to be communicated to Stephen about his time in B-24s. Jesus had told His disciples that to them only had He revealed the kingdom's mystery, but that everyone else would "see," but not perceive, "hear," but not understand so that they would *not turn* to Him for forgiveness. They had the prophets and Moses, and they spoke about Jesus. Listen to them!

Quill winced when he thought back at mentioning the cliff. "It was after I made that sixth trip to the cliff where I found you, Stephen . . ." Susan's eyes grew wide at the word 'cliff,' in the same breath with her husband. This thought terrified her. ". . . and that the pastor . . ." Quill had kept talking, but didn't realize what he'd said.

"Wait a minute. Wait a minute," Susan interrupted. "What cliff? You didn't tell me about a cliff, Quill. Stephen, what were you doing at a cliff?"

"Great, Quill. Thanks. It's nothing, honey. Really. I just wandered over there and sat. I had a lot of thinking to do."

"*Nothing*?!" Susan could tell by Quill's face that there was more to this than Stephen's mitigation of the facts. "You mean . . . *you tried* . . . Stephen were you . . . were you going to . . . to jump? *Stee-phen*!" Susan's enunciation contained those two four-lettered syllables, the prolonged 'e' he hated to hear coming out of his wife's mouth. "*Why?*" Susan shook her head in disbelief, as well as from hurt. "*Don't* you love me? *Don't* you love our children? Then why, Stephen?"

You will never understand why, Susan. How can I possibly explain this to you? You have been so sheltered all your life. You're so fortunate. But I can't explain it in any understandable way so that you will grasp the depth of my sorrow and guilt.

Susan's face and eyes remained fierce in their own mode of protective rage as she glared at her husband. Then she stood quickly to her feet, folded her arms from the energy their anger had lent her. Next, she prowled around the porch as if ready to pounce. Unable to withhold her rage for one second more, Susan vented, "*Ahhhhhhhh!*" Now, she swore with all her might, and as quickly as it had come, the emotions died for lack of adequate resupply. She was a woman surrounded by men she couldn't for the life of her possibly understand. Stephen's gaze remained on that bull several hundred yards away. Susan returned to the rocker from whence the tornado rampaging inside her had ejected her, and then lowered her body back into it, fully spent.

Stephen then said, "Okay, I'll tell you, Susan." As if wakened from a stupor, Stephen's words came grudgingly and agitated. "I was . . . sitting on the edge of that cliff . . . with my legs dangling over it. I was feeling the full brunt of my guilt for surviving. It was so unfair. And I went from anger to a state of depression that was overpowering. I believed I had nothing to live for, not for you, not for the kids, *nothing*. The world had never looked so bleak and empty. It didn't matter to me that you love me. I know you do. But *nothing* mattered. I was an impotent murderer who'd escaped his crimes and it was time to pay up. That was the only important thing. Somehow I had to finally pay for what I'd done. I was a useless, murdering son-of-a . . . The world would be better off without me."

"*Stee-phen!*" Susan's exasperation had reached a crescendo, and she sprang to her feet again. Her unbelief couldn't have been more total. But it was here, if it pleased the Holy Spirit, that Susan should have listened and prayed for Stephen. It was here that she, if having been regenerated, could have rested in God's mercy and grace, that He had saved Stephen when she was completely unaware of the danger. God had saved Stephen for his fifty missions, He could do so at the falls. But she did not listen, nor did she pray. She did not rest in God's mercy to her. Instead she reacted according to her flesh.

Stephen's retort was equally sharp. "Well, you just had to know . . ." A long, pregnant pause ensued. When he was certain Susan wouldn't interrupt, Stephen resumed. "But . . . I remember sitting there, thinking about all those men . . . I don't know where that bird came from, but I saw this eagle, and I started watching it fly and soar so effortlessly. It was beautiful. When it flew out of sight, I inched my way closer to the edge, and then I thought of Michael. I heard his name in my thoughts. I saw his face, then Margaret's, and then David's, and my father and then mother's face, and . . . then I heard *your* voice. I saw all of your faces so clearly. You and the family and that eagle were what kept me from jumping, I guess. And then I heard my own name being called from behind me. It was Quill. I thought I had imagined my name being called until Quill said it a second time."

That was when Quill chimed in. "Susan. I made six trips to that cliff."

"Men! You all are *absolutely* crazy. *You know that*? I never will understand men. How could you even think of killing yourselves? Don't you know what that would do to your families? When will you ever think of *anyone but yourselves*!? My heavens. You both should be ashamed. Where's my pistol when I need it?" Susan crossed her arms and stared out into the trees, her body tight, her mind wild with agitation. A wisp of breeze lifted her hair gently, which she brushed forcefully back in place. Once again, God had spoken through Stephen about His mercy to her, and Susan was oblivious to it.

"I can get you one." Stephen volunteered.

"Don't *tempt* me."

"I rather thought you wouldn't understand." Stephen smiled a bit sheepishly as he looked at Quill. Perhaps for the first time in an hour, the younger man looked as if he felt better. Here too, God had been merciful to them both, yet they completely missed it. This had been good for Stephen in a sadistic sort of way. He hadn't died from all his tears or from this confession, after all.

Susan was attuned, but only to her natural feminine instincts for personal and familial survival. "What's there to understand? To orphan and widow your family, does that make *any* sense to you?" Susan demanded from her husband. "Honestly. You two deserve each other. Quill, please tell me what you started to say, before I *club* this man," Susan verbalized heatedly, pointing her right index finger like a pistol barrel at Stephen, even more agitated at her lack of comprehension, which Stephen knew didn't exist for his wife. And then there were the other concerns: How does a man live with himself when he believes, regardless of what others might say, that he and he alone is responsible. Is perception truly reality? Who would want to live with a man who believes himself a murderer? The man doesn't and neither would his family. At some point they would wish him gone. That was the rub for Stephen.

Quill interjected, "As *I* started to say, I was feeling very low and guilty. I'd been to the, ahem . . . cliff, and couldn't do it . . . not even the sixth time. So I came on home, pathetic and angry with myself—very depressed. And then one day—I think it was in July—the last guy I'd ever expect to show up, came calling to visit me, —the pastor of that little church down the road you all passed. I made it known that I wasn't into religion of any kind, especially his, whatever that was. Well, he listened patiently and then left. That was just fine with me. The next week, he shows up again. I didn't talk much. He finally left. Showed up again. Then again.

"After a couple of months, I got up the nerve to ask him. It wasn't really a single question I dumped on him, but my whole anger at God. I let him have it with both barrels. I cussed and I fussed, and he just let me talk. Then he said, 'thank you,' and left. Boy, that was a strange experience, let me tell you. I expected him to give it back to me in spades. But he didn't. Reverend Samuel Franklin, what a man. I just couldn't see God's mercy staring me in the face: six times the Lord turned my desire for self destruction to impotence, and this man, this pastor, on call to do God's bidding . . . for me.

"Well, he held his peace, waiting for God's timing. Well, he kept coming around, and after a while he'd worn me down by not sayin' *anything*. I really was glad, too. I thought preachers were supposed to talk a lot about religion and things. I never liked any of 'em I'd met. Well, before long I started asking him some pointed questions. And then one day he answered me plainly. He was a very patient man. I'd never met anybody like him. Come to find out, he'd fought in the trenches in France—1918. Been wounded three times. He said he almost died from mustard gas. He'd bayoneted more Germans than he could count, even when they were disarmed and begging him not to, and he knew just how I felt about my guilt. Over there, he went blind with rage. He said he did things to the Germans he couldn't talk about. It was just too horrible for him. Once, I actually listened and heard his story, he and I were able to get down to it, and my life hasn't been the same since.

Today, this is what I would say to God if He asked me why He should let me into His heaven: first . . ."

"Quill, you already told this to us."

"I did?"

"Yes, you did."

"*No*. . . But I love to say it . . ." Quill smiled. "Doggone it!" Everyone got a laugh out of Quill's absentmindedness. The old man meant well.

The porch lay quiet under the weight of Quill's words. The wind that had picked up in the last few minutes had started to swirl. It played about the pine needles high above the porch, so that the trees creaked as they swayed and a cone plopped on the ground. A squirrel shinnied down a tree in front of the porch. The small critter stopped at the cone and sniffed the air. Satisfied all was well with his world, the rodent sat firmly on his haunches and dug into his dinner, almost as large as he. As he remembered it, Quill's head rang from his elongated 'sermon.'

Still, it had felt wonderful sitting there. Out into the west and millions of miles away the earth rotated past the sun. So much was as it should be. The smell of this pine forest intoxicated each of the occupants on the porch. God was speaking in other ways, the old man thought. None of the Lloyd's troubles had come to any resolution.

Forty-Five: Sin and Belief

>─┼─<>─○─<>─┼─<

Wednesday, May 17, 1967

Quill did not appear for breakfast, nor was he present for lunch. At two thirty in the afternoon, Susan began to worry, even though she had only known him for a few days. She asked Jacques about Quill, but he would not give her a straight answer. He did however, hint at it around the edges by his evasive comments. She had come to count on his presence as much as his wisdom to assist her to steer through the rocky channel of combat's after effects about which she had known so little.

"I think I will walk up to your cabin and just check in on him myself," she suggested. This caused Jacques no little consternation. Quill had sworn him to silence until his desolation wore off. It always did, and Jacques had grown accustomed to Quill's bouts with depression, but he didn't want Mrs. Lloyd to enter his darkness while facing her own.

"I don' think Quill wants any company today, Mrs. Lloyd," Jacques countered, hoping the woman would reconsider her present course. "Really, he hasn't felt well today." But it was the manner or tone the cook had used that piqued her attention. Jacques was hiding something. Of course he was, and she didn't *need* to insert herself. Quill had too often over the years inserted himself in other hurting veteran's lives, only to discover the cost was heavy. His fatigue of late led to this depression, and depression led to a depth of soulish gloom that might lay the old man low for days.

"What are you keeping from me, Jacques?" she finally asked.

"Nothing. He's not feeling well to-day, that's all."

"I have nursed plenty of children and adults back to health in Texas. I bet I can bring him around." At that, she rose from her chair and headed off through the vast lodge, pulled the great oak doors open, ventured across the porch and down the steps, around the side of the lodge and straight up the hill to Quill's cabin. Jacques had ridden the golf cart, and this is how she came to Quill's cabin.

When Susan reached the porch, she ascended the steps and walked toward the screen door, where she hesitated. Something was amiss, she could feel it, but she couldn't put her finger on it. Cautiously peering through the screen, Susan could just make out a dark, solitary figure sitting quite still in the worn lounge chair. No interior lights had betrayed the man inside. The shades were drawn so the room was almost shrouded in darkness, except for the light invading the room through the screen door. The overcast sky allowed even less light to penetrate the room.

"Quill?... Are you all right?" she asked. timidly. Hearing nothing, she put her right hand gently on the wire mesh screen, attempting in her own way to touch his world. The solitary figure remained motionless and mute. "Quill?"

"Mrs. Lloyd, please. I'm fine. I didn't feel like being around anyone today. You have enough issues right now. I'm just tired, that's all. Please, I'll be ok. Thank you."

"It's Susan . . . I want to help . . . if I can. May I come in? I won't force you to say or do anything. I've enjoyed our talks and I'd like to . . . to help." Susan perceived Quill's disquiet turn to restrained agitation with his following response to her. "Ma'am, I'll be okay. I'd just like to be alone today. I do appreciate your concern."

Unable to decide what to do, she did nothing. Perhaps the old man knew he had caused *her* even more pain the past few days, and thus he spoke softly and sympathetically, "The Lord is carrying me now. He's the only one who knows this dark place. There are days that He has set aside for me to go to that place with Him. I too am filling up the sufferings of Christ. Shall I not go? He takes me there by the hand. He determines the intensity and duration of that place, . . . and then He brings it to a conclusion. It works that way every time. I always grow spiritually from it, but it's a dark place, and today, it's almost debilitating. I'm in good hands, though, but thank you for caring, Mrs. Lloyd. I'll see you when it's over. Good-bye."

Those last words of his had wearied him. He didn't want to explain anything else to anyone. Quill studied her silhouette from his enshrouded mind. Her shoulders finally slumped and her head bent forward, pressing itself against the screen, where it bobbed quickly up and down. Susan wept, and then ever so gradually, her shape collapsed upon the porch, finally resting on the wooden portico, a blubbering mess. It was all Quill could do not to let her remain in that spot, so alone and so terribly confused, with no one to point the way. He forced himself to set aside his eclipse, rise, and limp toward the door and the woman.

When Quill returned from the bathroom, he nestled slowly, almost gingerly back into his chair, his hips aching. Susan had gone upstairs to bed. Jacques was last seen carrying a tray of food up the steps to her room. Several minutes later, down he came with the same tray, the food untouched. He paused at Quill's chair and asked, "Would you like this, Quill? Mrs. Lloyd wouldn't open her door. I hate to throw it out."

"No. I'm not hungry either. Thanks." Jacques returned to the kitchen. And after a few noisy minutes left to return up the hill to the cabin. That left Quill once more to his own thoughts of that day on the porch, and his dark cares ran their course.

"How does God's Gospel I just spoke about compare to what *you* believe, Susan?" he asked her earlier that evening.

Susan had no reply. Stephen couldn't quite fathom the picture Quill had just painted of realities in the spiritual world the old man understood.

"So, what did that psychiatrist fella tell you, Susan, about how Stephen was to go about finding meaning for the past?" Quill asked from curiosity.

"What? Oh, he said that Stephen must determine his own meaning for the trauma. He was the only one who could, although *I* can help. And once he found it he would be wise to allow it to change him." Quill's dubious look showed.

"That's what he said, huh? Do you agree with him?"

"I haven't had sufficient time to really evaluate it. I've been so busy trying to keep my family, Stephen, and myself together that . . .

426

I honestly don't know. It did sound good when he first talked about it. Now, I don't know."

"It seems to me . . ." Quill halted his thought in place. He had a tendency to go overboard, to talk too soon or too long. There weren't that many folks to talk to up here though. "Do you want to talk about this any more, Susan?"

"Yes. *I* do. We *obviously* aren't getting anywhere the way we are going now." Susan eyed her husband. Stephen didn't glare at her, but wished she'd stop prodding Quill on.

"I want to help you two so much, because I know what this feels like. I know what it does to two people. Okay? It seems to me that this doctor, as well meaning as he is, and I have no doubt he means well, has offered you some kind of limited, impersonal help at *best*. He's offered you a bandage to put on the cancer eating away at Stephen. Certain types of information can help us to think differently about difficult times like these. But it can also move us in the *wrong* direction. What if Stephen decides robbing banks or raping women are the most satisfying things he can pursue? It may harm other people, but it makes Stephen happy, because he finds fulfillment there, as warped as that is, in doing those kinds of things."

"That's ridiculous. No one thinks like that. Dr. Inhofe seemed happy to me," Susan reacted, defending the man who had been so kind to her family and her.

Quill rebutted, "Yes it is ridiculous, but didn't Stephen say the man was a drunk? He may help some folks, but what about his *own* home life? How many times did you say he'd been married? Getting drunk and chasing women seems to satisfy him."

"*Several* times he's been married," Stephen said, certifying the doctor's failings.

"Using or abusing women may be fun or all right to *him*, but what about the women he leaves devastated? The children? Remember, he may have found *his* meaning in a new occupation, but he seems satisfied being a horrible husband and person. What about the meaning they've found to their lives after he's labored to wreck their lives in his self-fulfillment? Unfortunately, it sounds to me as if he's trampled over a lot of people to find what makes *him* happy and fulfilled . . . I could be wrong.

"From my perspective he hasn't dealt with Stephen's, much less his own, basic problems. The Bible says God exists, and He is a Moral

Governor and Creator. He exerts His holy, moral will on His creation, which presently is in a state of rebellion against Him. His will is that all men everywhere repent, turn from their sin and guilt, and trust in Christ for salvation, as I've already said . . . probably too many times now. But I'm convinced that receiving this grace is what gives meaning to every aspect of our lives and fills the horrible void inside of us, which always helps others. And then, in due time, the Lord may begin to answer some of our questions. Believe me, God is actively present in this process. Your doctor friend hasn't dealt with that at all, because in his world, most likely, this doctor doesn't see that his world, as broken as it is, is still part of God's moral universe. If the doctor can diagnose and work on what he *perceives* is wrong, his patients may be made better, but only temporarily. But he isn't dealing with mankind's most basic dilemma: God's wrath and condemnation against man's transgressions and guilt, his alienation from God, all of which inevitably leads to death.

"I thought when I was a POW that my greatest trouble was captivity. If I could stop living with gnawing hunger and thirst that made my tongue swell in my mouth, malaria, dysentery, and things I still don't know about, if I could just get out of that hellhole, I thought, I'd be free, full, and quenched.

"I came home at the end of the war only to discover I was still a prisoner of the effects of my captivity. The Bible says we're all born prisoners or slaves if you will, of our lawbreaking, whether we ever go into actual captivity or not. Unfortunately, if all we believe about our sin is it's a mistake or a goof up, we remain prisoners of sin. Sin is not merely a conscious awareness of doing what we choose not to do, but it's believing we have the ability to do right and not do wrong. And if that's what we think sin is, then we don't understand what the Bible says about sin. You probably want me to stop talking about sin, and not just anyone's violations, but yours and mine. And if I stop, then I show how completely blind to who and what I am. Sin separates us from God, from ourselves, from each other, and from the creation. The Bible says, 'Therefore, just as through one man sin entered into the world, and death through sin, and so death spread to all men, because all *sinned*—' It also says, 'And you were dead in your trespasses and sins,' which again emphasizes that we entered this life as spiritually dead, God hating sinners. Until you have settled the issue of your own sin and God's wrath against it, you remain in darkness.

"We cannot see ourselves as the sinners we are apart from the Holy Spirit showing it to us. It's heinous nature is hidden to us, but we *can see* the effects of it and we feel the guilt, don't we? Transgression reveals the madness and evil intentions of our hearts. We have no fear of God, we don't see ourselves as slaves to the passions of sin. Disobedience to God violates the very first commandment. We will love and worship anything but God. As combat veterans, we can be so consumed with our sin and guilt that we give *them* our constant attention, or our worship, if you will. The prophet Jeremiah said, "The heart is deceitful above all things, and desperately wicked: who can know it?"

"Wait Quill. I don't hate God!" Susan finally burst into Quill's monologue, attempting to set him straight.

"Susan, do you remember several days ago when I asked you if you had ever lied, and you said yes? And I said that makes you a liar. Remember?"

"Yes . . . I remember."

"Let me read something else to you. This is from the book of Galatians, chapter two, verses fifteen and sixteen. Paul, speaking as a Jew wrote, "We are Jews by nature and not sinners from among the Gentiles; nevertheless knowing that a man is not justified by the works of the Law but through faith in Christ Jesus, even we have believed in Christ Jesus, so that we may be *justified by faith in Christ* and not by the works of the Law; *since by the works of the Law no flesh will be justified.*" According to the apostle Paul, how does a person become right with God? By trying to keep the law of God, or by trusting *only* in Christ Jesus?

"Let me see that," Susan demanded. Quill gladly handed her his Bible. She reread those verses several times. Quill prayed silently for the Spirit to open her understanding. "Hmmm. But Quill, I *do* trust Christ . . . I asked Him again yesterday to help or save me or something."

"Susan, you also told me that you don't have any assurance of a relationship with the Lord. Remember me reading what the apostle John wrote, that you could *know* that you have eternal life, only by believing in what Jesus did for sinners?"

"Oh, I forgot."

"Susan, you can "believe" in Jesus until the cows come home, and never *really* come to saving faith. To believe in Jesus means to believe in what He alone did in *our* place. He came to take *our place*, to take upon Himself what we are incapable of *being* and *doing*. God demands perfect holiness. He demands that we love Him with our whole mind, soul, body, and strength. The first man, Adam failed to do that. The last Adam, Christ Jesus, the God-Man, did what no man after the first Adam could do. Does that make and sense? The first man Adam, and every man since him has failed to keep God's law. Christ alone succeeded. When we trust Christ, we trust what *He alone* is and did. He was tempted in all points as we are, but He did not sin when tempted. When we believe in Christ *that* way, God declares us righteous, every bit as righteous as His Son is now. By faith, it is His Son's righteousness we bear. As the sinless God-Man, He has something to offer God on our behalf, Himself.

"Man cannot atone or die for his own sins so that he can be forgiven. Why? Because man is a sinner. Man is a defiled cosmic rebel against God. God only accepts a perfect, unblemished sacrifice, mentioned so often in Leviticus. Jesus is fully Man, minus trespasses since He was born from a human mother, born under the rule of the law. He gave up none of His divine attributes in His incarnation. The Spirit of God is divine, not like Joseph, so Jesus is not tainted with human sinfulness. He *alone* is therefore able to shed His blood *once for all time* acceptably and thus atone for sin. He is that perfect sacrifice God requires. This is where the Catholic church with the Mass gets it all wrong. Hebrews 9 makes if very clear that Jesus offered Himself *once, for all time*, not to be re-crucified every time the Mass is held. In your church, Susan, the elements actually *are* Christ's body and blood. Not so, says the Bible.

"Thus, when He went humbly and obediently to the cross, He hung there on behalf of *everyone* who believes in *His* atonement *for* them. He bore our sin, shame and curse, *and* He satisfied God's justice—if you sin, you die. 'It is finished,' Jesus declared on the cross in His body. In your church Susan, Jesus's work can never be finished because each time the Mass is said, Jesus is once again crucified. He also turned away God's wrath toward sin so that we who believe might be reconciled to God, and thus redeemed or delivered from the bondage of sin. In Him is everything we need for salvation.

"You might remember the exodus story in the Old Testament. Israel had been slaves in Egypt for hundreds of years. They could not free themselves because their bondage was total. But God came powerfully and *He* delivered them from bondage to Pharaoh. That's what happens when we trust Christ. We need trust Jesus one time, and only once in order to be made free from sin.

"Every Sunday, many people walk down the aisle when the invitation is given or pray a prayer to invite Jesus into their hearts. Then two weeks later, or a month, or six months later, where are they? They no longer attend church because what they did when they walked that aisle or prayed that prayer was not *from* humble, saving faith. It was an attempt to find *relief* from their pain or crisis, or get the "goodies" God is dispensing. Far too often, their lives get worse. So they live lives disillusioned with the whole religion thing.

"Wait. What you just said to me Quill was that I had to *trust* Jesus. I've done that *hundreds* of times," Susan admitted. "Why, I did it before breakfast today. I just don't understand."

"You just proved my point. You still keep confessing that you aren't any closer to *knowing* if your faith is real or not. Susan, what exactly are you trusting in? Belief for many people means nothing more than relief from pain or circumstances. That's not true faith. True faith is knowing you need forgiveness more than anything else, *first*. Faith involves humbly submitting your will to a King. It means you agree with Him that you deserve death for the ways you have broken His commandments.

Susan looked incredulous. "What kind of nonsense is this? I'm not a prisoner of sin, Quill."

"Do you sin, regularly?"

"Yes. But I ask for forgiveness too."

"But you said you are afraid to die, Susan. I ask for forgiveness too. The difference is, God has actually delivered me from the punishment and the penalty of my sin. When I break God's law now, I do so as His child. You, on the other hand, appear to be asking forgiveness as an alien lawbreaker who still deserves God's just punishment. "Do you know if God's Spirit lives in you and is there with you at all times, guiding and teaching you true truth, and actually forgiving you in order to restore fellowship?"

Susan didn't answer.

"Do you see the difference? Do you know what repentance is?" Quill probed a bit deeper.

"I think so."

"What is it?"

"It's . . . well, it's like being sorry you did something wrong. No. I suppose I don't."

"Repentance is a gift from God, just like faith is. It is a change of view; we suddenly recognize that we bear personal guilt, we are defiled and helpless to do anything about it. In other words, we gain a true knowledge of sin and ourselves as sinners. Moreover, we have a change of feeling about our wrongdoing, so that we have genuine sorrow over our sin. We feel remorse and despair, you know, "Woe is me! I'm doomed!" Finally, we sense a change of purpose. There is an actual turning away from sin so that we seek forgiveness and cleansing. In Catholicism, repentance became penance, an external action. Biblical repentance begins internally by the Spirit of God.

"You two came up here to Canada seeking answers and relief, and you two still don't seem to have any solutions. I didn't have any either, at first. Scripture tells us Christ is a King. Kings demand their subjects submit to his will. That's repentance. Jesus gives you the option now to bow your knee in submission to His authority over you. But when you die, not having submitted to Him, He will force you to acknowledge Him as King and then cast you into Hell. In saving faith, God makes our dead soul alive first, grants us true repentance, which will always accomplish what God demands it accomplish.

Stephen couldn't take it any more. "Why do you keep harping on sin in every breath you take, Quill? I'm sick of hearing about it. Just *shut up*, for God's sake."

Susan was taken aback. "Stee-phen Lloyd! Quill, you can talk to me."

A sheepish look crept over Stephen's demeanor, although he *was* by now sick of Quill rubbing his nose in it. And yet, he knew what the old man said was true about him, and he still didn't understand the answer of how to be rid of it.

Quill held back until he was certain that he should proceed. "Stephen, as far as God's will is concerned, your biggest issue right now is that you are a sinner who won't admit it, not to yourself and not to God. You think that something you did during the war has made you a "sinner." The Bible says we were born sinners before we ever did anything good or bad. And until you you can admit that, you have no hope.

Forty-Six: Deaf and Dumb in the Kingdom

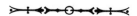

Thursday, May 18, 1967

"Let me show you something, Susan." Quill remembered that morning like it was ten minutes ago. He had brought some paper and a pencil with him, along with his Bible. "You might want to look too, if you're of a mind, Stephen. This has helped me no end in making sense of the war for me. Pastor Franklin preached and taught about five unifying themes or cables that are present throughout the Bible. We find them originally in Genesis one through three, and then again in Revelation twenty-one through twenty-two, verse five. They connect everything in between. The first and most important cable is the 'kingdom of God,' and in order to understand what that is . . . I'll give you the only other Bible I could find, Susan, so you can look these passages of Scripture up for yourselves. Okay?"

"Quill, I'm not too acquainted with the Bible," she admitted, a bit sheepishly.

"That's ok. I had to learn where things were as well. I didn't know come here from sick 'em the first time I opened the Bible either. I'm not going to make fun of you."

"Well, okay, if you promise not to." Susan felt *a little more* self-assured that this experience wasn't going to become so upsetting she would wish she'd never attempted it.

"In the New Testament," Quill continued, "better yet, turn to the index here in the front and look for the Gospel of Luke; it's in the New Testament." Once Susan found the index, she located the New Testament, and then Luke.

"I have Luke."

"Now, find the nineteenth chapter. Yes, right there. Now, would you mind reading verse 12 for me?"

"Okay. Verse 12. "He said therefore, a certain nobleman went into a far country to receive for himself a kingdom, and to return."

The "he" is Jesus speaking. Okay now, let's make sure we know what this nobleman is telling us about the word "kingdom."

"Quill," Susan interrupted, "Why is this cable so important? What does this have to do with our situation, Stephen's and mine?"

"Great question. The reason this has helped me over the years is that it *anchored* me to the unity of eternity and time. If it goes on history's timeline, it's important, like those three years as a POW. We all believed that those years were stolen from us. These cables showed me that those years were an integral aspect of the overall whole of my life. After I came home, life just seemed meaningless. I mean, if a guard got mad or he didn't get mad, if they grabbed a man, tied him up and then bayoneted him, what did it matter? Life had no meaning. If one man escaped and was recaptured, they shot ten men. If we lived or we died, it *just* didn't matter. Nothing mattered any more. *Nothing* seemed as if it was connected to *anything else*. I was a rat on a treadmill going nowhere. My hatred for those Japs kept me going. After we were released, what was I supposed to do now?

"We were starting to hear things at O'Donnell. The Americans were moving closer to the Philippines, and that gave us some hope. But the Japs were also hearing the same things, and they kept starving us, kept beating us, kept killing us. There was malaria and dysentery, elephantiasis, cholera, the lack of anything nutritious, completely unsanitary conditions, and there were blocks of days that I can't remember hardly anything.

"Funny thing happened when our troops finally did arrive. I had been sick with malaria, shaking I was so cold, hallucinating . . . but then one night, the Japs just *left*. There we were the next morning, locked up but no Japs in sight. It was all so stinking anti-climactic. I was skin and bones, glad beyond description to be free, but psychologically in bondage to my hatred of the Japs and lost. And there was nobody around to hate or get even with. I was sick and I wanted to die. I felt like death . . . weighed about one hundred pounds.

"Those little bast- . . . um, sorry, the *Nips* came home with me in ways I couldn't imagine. I dreamed about them; either they would kill me or I would spend the whole dream running after them. I couldn't catch 'em. And then I'd yell out at night, seeing one of the guys hung up and bayoneted by the whole Jap Army. I grabbed Helen by the throat several times, about to beat her to death thinking she was a Jap, and she would scream my name and I'd wake up. Of course, I'd apologize profusely, avoid her for several days, too ashamed of myself . . . I *hated* myself. I *hated* the Japs. I *hated* MacArthur for running out on us. I just *hated*. Hate was all I could do really well. My body still hurt from the tropical diseases. In a sense, my body came home, but my mind didn't.

"At that point, the future, it appeared to me, would be nothing but war. If we weren't in a war, we soon would be. Life was simply *war*. I have a few relatives who are still fighting the Civil War. Then there was the Great War. It was supposed to end all war. It was so terrible. I lost a bunch of family members either to that war or the influenza epidemic that followed it. Then came the Great Depression, and then Pearl Harbor and— *wham! Another war!* Five years later, Korea, and now Viet Nam. There was nothing for me to look forward to except *more war*. Life was just a conveyor belt taking us from one war to the next to the next, and promising us nothing but misery. And then we die. That was the prospect as I saw it. I had no hope, and I finally packed me and Helen up and came up here. The world could go jam its head into a propellor blade. I just didn't care." Quill smiled slowly to himself.

"What, Quill? Why are you smiling," Susan wanted to know.

"But coming up here was God's plan for me all along. God wanted me totally miserable. He wanted me up here to meet Pastor Franklin. I wasn't actually running *away* from war like I thought. I was running *to* Christ . . . and I didn't even know it," his smile widened. Now, Quill bore that same peaceful countenance the day Susan first laid eyes on him. I needed a sovereign God and King, and here He revealed Himself as such.

"Pastor Franklin said the Bible could be divided up into five themes or cables: the Kingdom of God, the Covenants, the Mediators, the Temple, and the Land of Promise. These themes were clearly visible in Genesis chapters one through three and again in Revelation twenty-one through twenty-two, verse five. Once I understood the concept of kingdom, then he showed me how to find it on almost every page of the Bible. He started in Luke's Gospel, chapter 19, verse 12."

"Let me explain the context of Luke 19:12. As you just read, Susan, it says that this nobleman went to a far country to receive for himself a *kingdom*. What do you think that means, 'he went to receive a kingdom'?"

"I have no idea," Susan offered. "Well, a *kingdom* . . . let's see." Susan ventured her guess, "A kingdom is a land or a group of people . . . isn't it?"

"Well, if kingdom only means the land or the people, then the nobleman had a real problem on his hands. He had to "hire" a construction company to dig up the dirt from that far land, gather all the people together under guard and haul them back to his own country. *Right*? But I don't think Jesus meant that. What it does mean is the nobleman had to leave his country and go to that *far country* to receive the *authority* so that when he did come back to his *own* country, he then had the enforceable power to call his servants to account for the money he had given them, and demand to know how they had used it. Up to that point, he didn't possess the authority to demand any type of accounting.

"Amazingly, I read not long ago that something exactly like this parable actually happened in Palestine some forty years before Jesus was born. In forty B.C., the Parthians invaded Syria and set up a man named Aristobulus the Second on the throne as their king and high priest. A man named Herod the Great was ruling then over Judea. But in order for him to defeat Aristobulus, he had to go to Rome to get the *authority* from the Roman Senate to raise an army and restore Roman rule in Judea. Up to that point, he didn't have the right to rule. Well, in thirty-seven B.C., Rome gave Herod the Great, King of Judea, the authority he needed, and he subsequently raised an army and defeated the Parthians.

"So when Jesus told this parable, some of these people hearing Jesus would have had some understanding of that war because it hadn't happened all that long before. And even now they were still living under Herodian rule through Herod's descendants. So, the point of

Luke's parable is that, according to Jesus, to receive a kingdom means to receive the authority or right to rule over something. And once this nobleman had the authority he needed, he then could call his servants to account once he returned. This is a *big* deal. This nobleman who became king, according to Jesus, actually did call each servant to account. That may not mean anything right this minute, but it will, so bear with me. I need to set this up by adding a few more details. Okay?

"Okay. If you say so." Stephen said, a bit too sarcastically for his wife, who rolled her eyes in disgust.

"According to Luke, three major things happened prior to Jesus telling this parable. First, Jesus hid the truth from the disciples minds about His mocking and scourging, and then His death and resurrection. Second, Jesus healed a physically blind man. That blind man called Jesus, the Son of David. David had been the king of Israel a thousand years earlier. Third, after Jesus healed the blind man, He went into Jericho, and when He saw Zacchaeus, the tax collector, He called him and said He needed to dine with him. Something happened at Zacchaeus's house that day, which corresponds to the previous two miracles. The Bible says, "and Zacchaeus stood, and said unto the Lord: Behold, Lord, the half of my goods I give to the poor; and if I have taken any thing from any man by false accusation, I restore him fourfold. And Jesus said unto him, This day is salvation come to this house, for so much as he also is a son of Abraham. For the Son of man is come to seek and to save that which was lost."

"Zacchaeus, at some point in the meal, trusted in Jesus to deliver him from his disobedience and make him a *true son* of Abraham. Everybody hated tax collectors because they cheated their neighbors while becoming rich off of their pain and toil, and even worse, they collected taxes for Rome.

"Now there's an important connection between the disciples, this physically blind man, and Zacchaeus. Jesus withheld sight from His disciples, but He gave the first blind man *physical* sight, and to Zacchaeus, Jesus gave *spiritual* sight. This tax collector saw just how spiritually blind to his sin he was. Jesus, with kingly power over physical and spiritual blindness, gave "sight" to both men, but withheld it from His disciples. In so doing, He was showing His royal authority over all things. He was also destroying the works of the devil, which was blinding men to the truth.

"Jesus called Himself, "the Son of Man," which is a reference to the ultimate, eternal Son of Man mentioned in Daniel, chapter seven. What Jesus was getting at was that this Son of Man, as both Daniel and Jesus called Him—wait, let me turn to Daniel seven . . . here it is— This Jesus, "was given . . . dominion, and glory, and a kingdom, that all people, nations, and languages, should serve him: his dominion is an everlasting dominion, which shall not pass away, and his kingdom that which shall not be destroyed." Jesus, according to Luke, is both David's human, kingly Son—the first blind man—and, He is also the predicted King mentioned in Daniel who possesses all authority to rule over the cosmos, the second blind man."

Daniel speaks about "kingdom" and "dominion" also, as being eternal. David's Son would also possess an eternal throne and kingdom.

"Quill, what's this got to do with me finding meaning?" Stephen asked, and not a little bit frustrated, lifting his agitation onto Quill. "Would you please start making sense?"

"Stephen . . . please. I'm trying to follow this, for heaven's sake." Susan interjected, her agitation showing openly.

"Stephen," Quill continued, "I didn't get it at first, either. What both Luke and Daniel are getting at is, when we think about Jesus Christ, we must think wider than just our war. Our war keeps us tied to one particular event, even though it lasted for a few years. That or those events must be placed within an eternal context. And within that context, we discover a King who has ruled over all of them to His own glory and His people's good. Stephen, when you arrived, you were chained to all those missions, but especially to that one event, weren't you?

"Yes."

"You still don't see it, do you?"

"See what, Quill?"

"Jesus, the King of the Kingdom, places our woes into a unified, eternal whole, not to lessen them, but to give them their proper perspective from God's vantage point. Now each and every circumstance, good or bad, has meaning, not that we assign our purpose to it, but God does. He was there with us personally. That knowledge in and of itself didn't "cure" him, but once he digested it, lived with it, meditated on it, he could look at the past from God's perspective, which is true reality. He couldn't change the past, but the past was suddenly connected to the present and that gave him the assurance his future would be in heaven with Jesus. Jesus was there in the past with him, and Scripture says He can never leave us nor forsake us, and, Jesus is the same, both today and tomorrow. The shrapnel still lodged in his back, the buddies he lost, the fear he still felt . . . all of it fit into God's larger purposes, and I desperately needed that perspective.

"True reality, huh? Sure. This is as clear as mud to me," Stephen argued back, and Susan became increasingly concerned that her husband might walk out any second. *However,* what Quill was saying might be pertinent for her own disordered life. It might be worth the effort to her, which was equally as much the point.

"Nothing worthwhile is easy," Quill offered assuringly. "I stuck with it until God made it plain. I had no other place to turn, Stephen, and I don't think you do either. I was headed toward self-destruction, and as I think back on those lessons, I'm mighty glad the Lord kept me working at it. But it was as difficult as asking God to open my eyes so I could see. You can do that, can't you, Stephen?

"Now this nobleman turned King is Jesus, who also was given all authority while on earth, just prior to going back to heaven. The nobleman, who is Jesus, now has the authority to bring men into judgment *when He returns,* and that judgment will also include the Jap guards . . . I was guilty of my own transgressions just as they were of theirs. Seeing Christ the King in the Bible, I became concerned about my own sin. At the conclusion of the parable, we read, 'I tell you that to everyone who has, more shall be given, but from the one who does not have, even what he does have shall be taken away.'"

"So," quipped Stephen, "how is this impending judgment supposed to help me give meaning to the war?"

"Stephen, you're staring right at it, the meaning, I mean."

"*What?*"

"Stephen, everything in your life, good and bad, has brought you to *this* point. You could have been in that crippled bomber under yours when the bombs let go, but you *weren't.* The guilt you've carried has led you *here.* I hope you can hear what I'm saying because these words are life, man."

"They are . . . ? *Life?*"

"Okay. Just keep listening. Well, the bad news for those who refuse to believe is that this nobleman, turned King, is coming again to judge all those who have refused to have this King rule over them. Worse, this coming judgment means . . . let me find it . . . Revelation twenty, verses ten through fifteen, ought to make the most skeptical or foolhardy think twice about not turning to Christ in faith. "And the devil *that deceived them* was cast into the lake of fire and brimstone, where the beast and the false prophet are, and shall be tormented day and night for ever and ever. And I saw a great white throne"—remember, only king sits on thrones—"and him that sat on it, from whose face the earth and the heaven fled away; and there was found no place for them. And I saw the dead, small and great, stand before God; and the books were opened: and another book was opened, which is the book of life: *and the dead were judged* out of those things which were written in the books, according to their works. And the sea gave up the dead which were in it; and death and hell delivered up the dead which were in them: and they were judged every man according to their works. And death and hell were cast into the lake of fire. This is the second death. *And whosoever was not found written in the book of life was cast into the lake of fire.*"

"The apostle John also speaks about our works being judged. The Bible *expects* believers will do good works as a result of their faith. Good works are who we know we are His. Paul said that even our works had been determined before the foundation of the world. So, the Bible anticipates that Christians will do good works because the Holy Spirit has been given to us."

From a testing tone, Stephen asked, "What if I don't decide to trust in Jesus?"

"If you decide *not* to trust in Jesus, you have already sentenced yourself eternally to that fiery lake, unless at some future point you choose to turn from your sin and trust Him. There can be nothing worse, Stephen, because there are no second chances after death. These verses say nothing about a purgatory that is supposed to purify a person, so that when he is purified, then he goes to heaven. Neither is there any reincarnation. None of that is found in these pages. The Bible says it is appointed to men once to die, and after that comes judgment. God's word is unalterable.

"However, the *good news* is that Revelation, chapters twenty-one and twenty-two speaks of eternal bliss with Jesus; a new heavens and a new earth will appear coming down from heaven. It is there that we who have trusted in Jesus's work and not our own, will spend eternity ruling with the Lord God. No more pain. No thoughts about this life, no sorrow . . . no death. We won't even regard those whom we have loved but rejected God's grace.

"Let's see if I can recap this so we can know what we've discussed. Luke tells us that God's kingdom primarily requires a king who rules with authority over a domain, that is, over people and land. The domain is secondary, but nonetheless very important. Luke reminds us that ruling kings are also judges. In order to escape judgment, we must trust in Jesus's provision for escaping all of this. This coming King and Judge suffered for us when He lived here, taking our curse that we deserved, on the cross. By means of our King's own substitutionary atonement we can now be forgiven. At the judgment, we shall also hear Him declare us righteous.

"How is knowing all or any of this, Quill, so important? How can it have any significance for my problems?" Stephen asked, almost belligerent by this point.

Quill now understood just how dark and heavy was the devil's deceit and the veil over Stephen's heart, perhaps the Lord's doing as with His disciples, or just like Zacchaeus's had been. "Stephen, unless God opens your mind and heart to hear Him speak through His word and through me, these concepts will continue to be foolish and make no sense. It's as if you have been listening for relief from your guilt and trespasses on a particular radio frequency all your life. What you need to happen is for God to tune your heart to His frequency so you can hear what He is saying. Does that help? You probably had something like that happen when you were flying in Italy?"

"Well, yes, that makes sense, I suppose. So let me get this straight. You are speaking to me on 107.7, but I have been listening on 96.4. Is that correct?"

"Yeah. That's pretty much it."

"So all I have to do is ask God to change me to 96.4?" Stephen asked.

"Your hearing has to be, shall we say, re-tuned by Someone outside of yourself, by the Holy Spirit. What I mean by that is, Jesus spoke to large crowds many times when He preached. Still, He kept saying, "He that has ears to hear, let him hear." He knew there were those who heard Him speaking 'words,' but they had not idea what

He meant by those words. For example, in the last chapter of Luke, there were two disciples who were really upset because Jesus had been crucified and their hope for Israel becoming a political power seemed all but gone. They couldn't figure out what it all meant, kind of like you, Stephen, even though Jesus said many times He would suffer, be beaten, crucified, and rise again, because death had to be defeated. The crucifixion made no sense to them. But then, while the men walked and discussed these things, Jesus appeared, yet He kept them from recognizing Him. He kept their eyes blind. He asked the men questions about the recent events involving the crucifixion and such, but, still, they were unable to make sense of it. Jesus finally scolded them for being slow of heart, not believing everything the prophets foretold bout Him. So, He proclaimed the Himself as Messiah (King) from Moses's writings. And then over supper, He broke the bread, blessed it, and then passed it to them.

"Now here's the point. As soon as Jesus broke the bread, their *eyes were opened* and they suddenly *recognized Him!*" Up to that moment, Jesus was a stranger to them, even though they had seen Him do miracles and heard Him preach. Once their eyes were opened, they understood the Scriptures that He had been explaining to them. Otherwise, they were deaf and blind to all spiritual truth. *Jesus* opened their eyes. They, like Zacchaeus, didn't know they were spiritually blind.

"Hmmm," Stephen replied. "So you are saying I'm deaf and blind to what you've been talking about?"

"Yes, I'm afraid so, my friend. I keep telling you the same things again and again, and you still don't understand. I'm not trying to insult you. I too was deaf and blind to these things once," Quill admitted quickly. "But listen, we *all* are born blind and deaf to spiritual realities. Pastor Franklin spent months going over the same old ground with me. But then one day, *wham*! I *saw* what he was saying. It all made sense because God opened my eyes. God brought me all the way to British Columbia—and me thinking I was escaping from everyone and everything—and once here, Jesus spoke through this preacher to my dead heart, and I *saw*. I *saw* my own wretchedness, but I also *saw* Jesus as the only remedy.

"So far, it seems, the Lord has not chosen to do that for you, Stephen. However, just like with Helen and me, He has brought you both up here to at least listen to me. Tell me if I'm right: down in your gut, you're saying, 'Quill, just tell me *how* to find the meaning. Don't give me this "trust Jesus" stuff. If there is a meaning to the war for me, just tell me what it is for crying out loud! You can probably remember "trusting" Jesus many times during the war, when the sky was filled with flak or fighters. You probably prayed before each takeoff and landing, for it to go well . . . and here you are. You weren't praying to Buddha, right? Am I close?"

"Yes, that would be fairly accurate."

"Stephen, before you can find real meaning for your life, you have to be given spiritual sight and that sight is based solely on absolute truth and submission to that truth. Okay?"

"Okay."

"But before you can find real meaning, you must humbly submit your will to Christ—repent—acknowledging God's kingly right to rule over you. If God demands submission, which He does, He will surely give it. He rules over us to bless us and bring Himself glory."

Stephen sat there stupefied. He could understand aerodynamics and drag coefficients, trigonometry, physics, how to start, fly, and land a four-engine bomber, even how to run a corporate giant like Lloyd International. He had not the slightest idea what Quill Du Pont was saying to him. What could humbling oneself have to do with finding meaning? "Quill, I'm sorry, I feel about as humble as I can be, still, I don't see the correlation. It just doesn't make any sense to me."

To this, Quill asked, "Do you agree that you have sinned against God and you deserve God's judgment for your sin?"

"Yes, but I'm not *that* bad. Not as bad as *you're* making me out to be. And besides, what does my sin have to do with finding meaning? What do you *mean*, Quill?" Stephen was right back where he began weeks before.

"The Catholic Church uses the words 'venial' and 'mortal,'" Stephen continued, "as if they are clubs to get the population back under their thumb. For me, the Church lost a lot of credibility over Europe. They kept saying 'believe,' so I'd 'believe.' Believe *what*? Catholics, Protestants, Orthodox, Atheists, Agnostics . . . died by the hundreds believing or not believing. I believed until I couldn't believe anymore. There was nothing to believe in after a while . . . not in the Blessed Virgin. I'd partake of the Eucharist . . . so I could die in a state of grace and change nothing in my life. Chuck Noland, one of my co-pilots, was a "believing" Catholic, like me. He took a piece of shrapnel through the head on a mission. Willie Sutton was a 'believing' Catholic. We found enough of his body to put in a paper bag when that German twenty millimeter round cut him in two. I came to *believe* that cleaning a man's brains out of a cockpit will take a long time and you can't really scour it all out. Those pieces of brains will be there the next time you hop in the pilot's seat, and the next mission and the next. I believe that if you fly six hundred bombers through a heavy flak concentration, a certain percentage of them will go down and a bunch of people will die. Yes sir. I believe. I believe if you can drown out the pain with enough whiskey, you will probably be sick in the morning! If there is anything beyond what I can see, I suppose I *don't* believe like you do."

Forty-Seven: Quill's Purpose

After lunch, Quill sat by himself, licking his wounds as it were, a bit embarrassed and or frustrated. He wasn't quite sure which, having taken the brunt of Stephen's long held vitriol that had, up to today, been left unsaid. Packed and ready notwithstanding, the man was still completely blind to spiritual truth for all Quill's efforts. Quill's saving grace was the knowledge that only God can open blind eyes. His job was to speak the truth.

Susan, on the other hand, would not leave the immediate topic alone. With Stephen outside and busy, she asked, "Quill, did this kingdom concept begin in the New Testament? It seems so, from what you have been saying and reading to us. But I can't figure out why you went from Luke nineteen to Genesis one?"

"I took you to Luke nineteen first, for a reason. I wanted you both to hear from Jesus's lips how *He* defined the term. We next went to Genesis one because there we see the moment God began to reign over His cosmic kingdom . . . at the very beginning. Jesus came as a royal Creator. On the last day of creation, God made Adam in His royal image, which meant Adam was given authority—an earthly king—to rule over the creation as God's representative. Being created in God's image also means that Adam had true knowledge of God, piety toward God, and justice toward our fellow men. The kingdom or rule of God begins in Genesis one and runs all the way through the Bible to the end of the book of Revelation, where it ends with man ruling with Jesus forever and ever.

"Remember the nobleman in Luke nineteen? Well, in Genesis one, when God says, "Let there be light," God spoke with kingly authority into the darkness, "and there was light." When He said, "Let the earth sprout vegetation, plants yielding seed, and fruit trees on the earth bearing fruit after their kind with seed in them;" and the next thing we read, *and it was so.*" Among so many other things, God was teaching Adam about the culture and how he, as God's royal representative, and by the wisdom he'd been given bring forth unimaginable treasures God had implanted in the universe for man to discover for the betterment of man and for God's glory. Man was free to discover, experiment with and rule over the areas of medicine, teaching, flight, farming, fashion, building, music, art, metallurgy, you name it. Adam was to teach his children to rule each area as God taught him so that one day, the whole earth would reflect that image and glory. I think this is one of the reasons the Genesis account is so short compared to other ANE creation myths. God gave Adam a pattern for creativity, discovery, experimentation and rule. Moses was writing theology primarily, culture secondarily, not cosmology.

"Not what?"

"Cosmology. Genesis 1:1 and other verses tell us God created everything. Cosmology is the study of how everything was made. Genesis one, verses twenty-six through twenty-eight says, 'Then God said, "Let Us make man in Our image, according to Our likeness; and let them rule over the fish of the sea and over the birds of the sky and over the cattle and over all the earth, and over every creeping thing that creeps on the earth." 'God created man in His own image, in the image of God He created him; male and female He created them. God blessed them; and God said to them,' "Be fruitful and multiply, and fill the earth, and subdue it; and rule over the fish of the sea and over the birds of the sky and over every living thing that moves on the earth."'"

"There are three very important words in these verses: 'image,' 'dominion,' and 'blessing.' In verses twenty-six and twenty-seven, God declares that He created Adam and Woman in His royal image and likeness. He says so four times. To be created in God's image means first of all as I said, to know God *truly,* but as a creature, to have *piety* toward God and to act with *justice* toward men. As such, Adam was created to *have* dominion, that is, to function as a ruler over every creature and over the earth as its royal head and representative.

Adam was able at first to rule in complete, willing *submission* to His Creator and King. In verse twenty-eight, God *commands* Adam to do five things, 'be fruitful, multiply, fill the earth, subdue it and then rule over" the creation;' from the indicative, "have dominion," in verse twenty-six, to the imperative in verse twenty-eight, "rule!" And with the statement and command comes his status: Adam is royal.

The first three commands, "Be fruitful, and multiply, and fill the earth," have to do with marriage as their procreative responsibility, and the last two imperatives have to do with Adam's mediatorial occupation: a monarch. All five of these commands refer more specifically to their function. As a king, he was to raise godly descendants whose dual purpose would be procreation and subduing, *and then* ruling over the cosmos creatively and culturally as laid out in the pattern of the six days of creation.

"Let me read that again." Susan took the book from Quill and studied it carefully.

"Wow. It says all *that*? That gives marriage a much more serious purpose, doesn't it?"

"Yes it does," Quill answered. "I'll show you how it all fits and flows from the Old into the New Testament. I just want you to see the original "job description" God gave Adam. It hasn't changed, either. When do you think Genesis was written, Susan?"

"I don't know. I never thought about it."

"Well, think about it for a minute."

"I don't know, Quill."

"Moses wrote the first five books of the Bible just after Israel left Egypt, within a forty year period, but before Israel entered the Promised Land, in the desert of Sinai."

"*Oh*. I didn't realize that. Thanks."

"Sure. For just over four hundred years, God's people had been slaves in Egypt. As a side note, and while I'm thinking about it, redemption primarily means freedom from slavery or bondage. When we come to Christ in faith, He delivers us from slavery to disobedience—to sin, and Satan."

"Interesting."

"You bet it is. So, the Egyptians believed their king was the living image of the gods. Adam was created as God's living image, yet Moses makes it clear that Adam was a *created* being, he was not divine. It is important for us to see that in this opening account of creation. Israel was given a different, yet true, perspective about man than what they had grown up believing and seeing in Egypt. Not merely Pharaoh, but all men are living images of the true God, Jehovah. This was radical theology. Egyptians were not a proselytizing nation. They lived and died in Egypt, along the Nile, but the Nile had attained godlike status since they believed life came from that river. Yes, they did conquer other nations, but not to make those nations Egyptians. They went to war for protection. Israel, on the other hand, was to expand Eden, or now Canaan, outward until His glorious image filled the earth as Adam was told to do. Each Israelite collectively had now become corporate 'Adam,' so to speak.

Susan wondered if following this was even possible, but she made it seem as if she were keeping up.

"We have spoken about three words so far, 'image,' 'rule,' and 'blessing.' The third word is in Genesis one, verse twenty-eight. It's the verb, *blessed*. "And God *blessed* them." God put this couple in Eden in a *state* of blessing, so that imaging and ruling were done as natural, loving and joyous activities in a world unspotted by sin. Man's original occupation was to reflect God by ruling over all things, expanding the temple or Garden outward until the divine glory image filled the earth as the seas fill the earth. He could do so magnificently, obediently, and happily because he was a covenantally *blessed* person. Today, this same Great Commission is found at the end of Matthew's Gospel.

"If we look at Romans six, verses twelve through fourteen we can see how things turned out once Adam broke the covenant and fell into sin. "Therefore do not let sin reign in your mortal body so that you obey its lusts, and do not go on presenting the members of your body to sin as instruments of unrighteousness; but present yourselves to God as those alive from the dead, and your members as instruments of righteousness to God. For sin shall not be master over you, for you are not under law but under grace."

"Rather than ruling over the creation and Satan, the creation, Satan and death began to rule over Adam and everyone descended from him, including you and me, Susan. That is the history of the world to the present. We are *the ruled*, rather than *the rulers*. As sinners ruled by sin, we start wars. We kill and we hate each other.

"Yes, we do."

"Finally, let's go to the very last chapter of the Bible, to Revelation twenty-two, verse five, to see how it turns out. The last clause of verse five says, "and they (believers) shall reign for ever and ever." This statement forces us back to the very beginning, back to Genesis one, verses twenty-six and twenty-eight, where Adam was authorized or made fit for his primary function—a king who would rule as head of the creation, with true knowledge of God and piety toward God, as well as justice toward men. He could do so willingly, in complete submission to his Creator and King. What the apostle John tells us is that redeemed sinners in Christ, we will one day finally be able to fulfill what God meant for Adam and every "Adam" after him to do all along, rule forever."

Forty-Eight: Bound By Oath

✄—┼—◆>—☉—<◆—┼—✄

"Susan, learning the bigger picture with all its important little pieces was like finding life for me. I realized that if I couldn't make any sense of this, I was done. I had no hope at all because I had no way to gain perspective of what so many of us had gone through. Somehow it all fit into a bigger picture—And all I had to do was ask God to show me. In the Philippines, we were all merely lab rats in a cosmic laboratory being experimented on by a mad, demented scientist running the asylum in an arbitrary way? In captivity, it certainly seemed so. How do you explain those barbarians who kept us hostage and treated us so inhumanely? And then, once released, I was doomed to hatred and alcohol. Or, was there some way of seeing it all as it really is? The Army was not into anger management. They too used us and there we all were: angry and on the warpath with no one to kill. My life was anything but *blessed*. I felt cursed right down to my soul, and I needed help.

So, God created man to rule, but since the fall of man into sin, Satan, death, and sin rule over him. But the end of the story says man will one day occupy his original role, that of king, but forever this time. That's simple enough to see. What we start with, we end with, a royal, blessed image bearer. So, the Bible moves from man as a ruling king, to man as a ruled king, to man as a king who rules forever."

"What is so important," Susan interrupted to ask, "about Adam ruling?"

"To be created in God's image, which is a royal, creative image among other attributes, means nothing less than reigning over all things as God does and then relating to and ruling those things justly and creatively. It means to be productive here and now, which goes to the heart of work itself. My labors now have great significance because they are connected to what I will be one day, a royal ruler. All right, I've covered the entire Bible and left out an awful lot that I could say about the kingdom, but that gives you a wide angle lens. We were meant to rule with Christ as His blessed image bearers, and one day, we will.

"There is so much more to the kingdom, but at least you have a wide angled lens to see it from. That brings us to the covenant. God as King and Creator, relates to His domain by means of a covenant. There is one main covenant from which all other covenants spring. That is the eternal covenant of redemption God made or cut, if you will, by the Persons of the Godhead. There are a lot of definitions of what a covenant is, but the Bible itself gives us the best definition. Pastor Franklin started with Hebrews chapter thirteen, verses twenty and twenty-one. Let me read that. "Now the God of peace, that brought again from the dead our Lord Jesus, that great shepherd of the sheep, through the blood of the everlasting covenant, make you perfect in every good work to do his will, working in you that which is well pleasing in his sight, through Jesus Christ; to whom be glory for ever and ever. Amen." In eternity past, God bound Himself to accomplish our salvation, and He did so without out help.

"The reason I like these verses as a starting point for defining this covenant of redemption is because it gives us the big picture and connects to the kingdom. In these two verses, we learn that God's covenant is eternal, it involves death through the shedding of blood. It talks about Jesus's resurrection, and the resulting peace we have with God the Father. It speaks of Jesus as our great shepherd, who makes us perfect in every thing we do so that we *actually do* His will and *are* pleasing in His sight. And when it is all said and done, Jesus receives the glory. It means God initiates the covenant and binds Himself to its completion.

"There's more there, but you get the picture. In eternity past, the Father, Son, and Holy Spirit put a plan in action to, at the very least, save all who believe in Christ from the penalty of sin, which is death. Scripture also reveals that at that time the Godhead covenanted with Itself, God wrote the names of His chosen people in the Lamb's Book of Life as to whom He would save, so that in time, space, and history, they would actually trust in Him for salvation. In time, Jesus would actually live and die for them as well so that they surely would believe, their number being as many as the stars.

"Once we enter creation and time, God covenanted with that very creation, which is mentioned by the prophet Jeremiah. Its total restoration is in Revelation twenty-one and twenty-two. Romans eight tells us the creation is currently groaning waiting for our redemption— you know, tornadoes, hurricanes, earth quakes—so that when the King or authorized nobleman returns for judgment, He will bring a whole new creation with Him. Genesis is written in covenant-treaty form, but I don't want to get into that right here. Covenants involved witnesses, oaths, curses and blessings, *etc.* In other words, when God covenants to do something, He binds Himself by life and death to do that very thing. When the Son wrote our names in His book, He swore to deliver us completely from law breaking and death. He gave us His Holy Spirit as a down payment, guaranteeing our full acceptance before God at the resurrection, when He openly declares us righteous. But that's up ahead.

"The Bible tells us that man sinned. But just as surely, God had already sworn that He would make a way of escape from the death we deserved as sinners. Once Adam rebelled, God spoke Genesis chapter three, verse fifteen, which says, "And I will put enmity Between you and the woman, And between your seed and her seed; He shall bruise you on the head, And you shall bruise him on the heel."

"Two battling kingdoms are represented in this verse, Satan's and Christ's. It was spoken of from the standpoint of the serpent's seed who are all those who refuse to submit to Christ, and the woman's seed, Jesus Christ and those who will believe, but primarily the Seed refers to Jesus. This battle will last for all time until the judgment. It also involves the two types of wounds. The serpent will bruise the "heel" of the Lord Jesus. Jesus will in fact die on the cross, but since death can't hold Him, He will be raised from the dead on the third day, never to die again. Satan however, will finally be defeated once for all, the "head" wound, as John spoke about in Revelation chapter twenty.

"Wait. Now some of this is vaguely familiar. So you say, or the *Bible* says, that Christ and Satan will be at war for all history?" Susan pondered out loud. "I'm missing something here, Quill. Why this covenant now?"

"Back in Genesis two, verses sixteen and seventeen—sorry, I got a bit ahead of myself—in Genesis chapter two, verses sixteen and seventeen, God had said that if Adam ate of the fruit of a particular tree, he would die. Satan provided the inducement via the serpent. Well, Adam did indeed eat, but Adam should have ruled over and judged the serpent as commanded. Now God was obliged to bring the covenant curses to bear on the transgressors of the covenant, that is, you eat, you die. But remember, back in eternity past, the Godhead covenanted to redeem man from sin when this first crime occurred, by means of a blood sacrifice. That sacrifice pointed to Jesus, the great shepherd of the sheep in Hebrews chapter thirteen, verses twenty and twenty-one. Remember?

"Yes."

"Okay. Since it was not time for Jesus to come as that sacrifice in Eden, God began the long process of teaching His people what atonement, substitution, and sacrifice meant. In Genesis chapter three, verse twenty-one, we read, "The Lord God made garments of skin for Adam and his wife, and clothed them." God Himself killed an animal—I think it was probably a lamb or lambs—killed them and shed their blood, and that substitutionary blood of an innocent, unblemished animal atoned for their sins and satisfied God's justice. The animal died in their places, and that sacrifice pointed to Jesus. That's what happened at Calvary, Jesus received the punishment we deserved and imputed or transferred His righteousness to us so we could be forgiven. After Calvary, Jesus was raised from the dead, and Scripture says we were also raised with Him. We celebrate and remember these events every Easter, but Easter started here, in Eden.

"But what about the resurrection you mentioned? Who was resurrected in Eden? No one died except the animal?"

"Great question, Susan. As Jesus once said to someone else who began to understand His words, "You are not far from the kingdom." In the Old Testament, several people were raised from the dead. So, for all intents and purposes, Adam and Woman were as good as dead, weren't they?"

"Well, I guess so."

"God had said, 'The day you eat, you shall die!' I mean, that settled it. Scripture later says Adam eventually died *physically*, but the most immediate death he suffered was *spiritual* death. No longer could he look at the creation and associate it with the Creator. Adam and Eve hid from God and became blind to the things of God. Suddenly, they had no desire to please God because they couldn't, nor did they want to. That's spiritual death."

"They needed to be born spiritually alive from above by the Holy Spirit, as Jesus spoke about in John three. Once regenerated or made alive spiritually by God, then they could believe in what God said back in Genesis chapter three, verse fifteen, which I believe they did. Adam, by faith, renamed his wife *Eve*, meaning the mother of all those *spiritually* alive. Everyone after Adam who also believed in the promise of the covenant, that Seed who would come through the woman, subsequently received eternal life. As for Eve, well, after she gave birth to her first born son, Cain, she showed her faith in the promise when she said, "I have gotten a man, *the Lord*." She said by faith, 'this son Cain, *is* the promised Seed, the Messiah! Redemption is at hand!' We know that God was speaking in Genesis chapter three, verse fifteen about a time a long way down the road, to Mary and Jesus. The Bible never speaks about *the seed of the woman*, only the seed of the man, except right here. And since Joseph was not Jesus's actual father—the Holy Spirit was—Jesus's human nature was sinless and protected from all defilement. Thus, from conception, Jesus became the unblemished, atoning Lamb who takes away the sin of the world. The Bible speaks a lot about sin *and* atonement.

"We call this covenant promise in Genesis chapter three, verse fifteen, the first proclamation of the covenants of *grace*. The next covenant is with Noah, then comes the covenant with Abraham, then Moses, then David, and finally, the new covenant spoken of by the prophets, Jeremiah and Ezekiel. Each covenant builds upon and adds to the previous covenants. And you remember these verses, 'This cup which is poured out for you is the new covenant in My blood.'"

"You mean, the Supper we celebrate in the Mass, began here in Genesis three?"

"Yes, but it began much earlier than that, in eternity past, remember from Hebrew thirteen? So, just as we have spoken about the kingdom, man as ruler, man as ruled, and man finally as ruler forever, so we see the covenant stretching from eternity past, connecting eternity with time, and time finally gives way to eternity future. Each succeeding covenant adds more information until Jesus says all is fulfilled in my death and resurrection.

Forty-Nine:
The Mediatorial Covenant

"Here's something important Genesis two tells us, and this leads us to the third theme or cable. Adam was to *serve* and *guard* the Garden-Temple. This made him a mediatorial priest. A mediator is someone who stands between two parties at odds with each other in order to reconcile them. The disagreement comes in after man sinned. According to Genesis two, verse fifteen, we learn, "Then the Lord God took the man and put him into the garden of Eden to cultivate it and keep it." The two verbs translated, "cultivate" and "keep," makes it sound as if Adam's primary job was a farmer. We know already he was a king. However, every time those two Hebrew verbs, 'cultivate' and 'keep' are used *together* in the Bible, they are used in the context of the priests performing their duties in the temple. A better translation would be, the priests were to *serve* the temple, and they were also to *guard* it against anything unclean, like talking serpents. Remember, in Genesis chapter one, verses twenty-six and twenty-eight, Adam was instructed to rule over the animals *and* creeping things. In other words, Adam and Woman, along with their other royal duties, were to *serve* and *guard* as priests in the Temple or Eden.

"God created man as both a king *and* a priest. Adam actually was a priest, instructing his sons about substitutionary atonement, but only Abel followed his father's instruction by becoming a shepherd. Abel and not Cain, offered acceptable, blood sacrifices. To add one more "mediatorial" office, Genesis chapter two verses, fifteen, nineteen and twenty-three tells us that Adam spoke for the creation, by naming the animals and his wife, making him a *prophet*, also. Adam served God as a mediatorial king, priest, *and* prophet. So, Adam and Woman, as blessed, living images of the LORD God, were to rule the cosmos as royal priests and prophets, that is, as God's mediators. The Bible is filled with these three mediatorial offices, kings and priests and prophets, right?

"This is where the idea of priests began?"

"Yep." Quill crossed his eyes and asked, "Ain't this fun?"

Susan rolled her eyes. "Can we continue or will this take all day?"

"It'll take several years, but I'll keep it short for you. So, let me run the table. What we want to do is see how the Bible connects Genesis chapter one, verses twenty-six and twenty-eight, with Genesis chapter two, verses, fifteen, nineteen, and twenty-three. The concepts of image, rule, blessing, and king, prophet, and priest are fulfilled in Revelation chapter twenty-one through chapter twenty-two, verse five. The last part of Revelation chapter twenty-two, verse five reminds us that man began as a king, and he shall finish as a king—prophet and priest—ruling with Jesus forever, remember?"

"Do I have a choice?"

"No. If we look at Genesis chapter three, verse sixteen, we find God telling Woman that, now as a sinner, all women will have pain in childbirth. Worse, since Eve encouraged Adam to eat as well, "Yet your desire will be for your husband, And he will rule over you." There's that word, "rule" again. Adam, because he was not deceived first as his wife was, must now "rule" over his wife. Why is that? Because transgression entered through her first. Rather than submitting to his headship, she suddenly wants to rule over him. That's why marriage is so hard. We don't treat each other justly as God's image bearers. "And yes, Adam was complicit. He should have taken his headship role more seriously and protected his wife, by ruling over the serpent and pronouncing judgment on it.

"Now wait a minute, Quill. I don't want to *rule* Stephen. That's not fair."

"Susan, the issue is the mitigated curse. Rather than rule as a co-equal with Adam, Woman now became subservient to Adam, her husband, because of the wicked influence she exerted on Adam to eat sinfully." Quill asked, "Remember, rather than rule, Adam and Eve are now the "ruled." Death, sin, sickness and Satan began to rule over them.

What did God say would happen if they ate of the forbidden fruit, Susan?" Quill asked.

"Hmmm. I don't remem . . . they would die. Oh, *now* I remember."

"Death and curese, or obedience and blessing? They deserved to die. But God graciously granted them eternal life because they believed the promise, and in so doing, became righteous. I'd say that was more than fair. It was just and gracious since their substitute, the animal, died in their place, but also pointed to Jesus."

"Okay. You win."

"In Genesis chapter four, verse seven, Cain is told that his anger against Abel wants to *rule over* him but he must *rule over* it. He didn't. He killed his brother Abel anyway. He was *ruled* by sin and death resulted.

"The concept of ruling is all-important to God because He is a kingly Ruler. He maintains that idea from Genesis on. Husbands are to rule their wives *lovingly*, as Christ rules and loves the Church. We, the Church, are to submit to His headship over us, but we do so more and more willingly because the Holy Spirit lives in us. And if a person dies for someone, that proves His love, doesn't it? We are to love our wives to the point of death, if need be. We are not to be ruled by sin or Satan, but to rule over *them* by the freedom and power God alone supplies.

"I *never* saw it that way before, Quill." Susan clearly had much to think about, including her relationship with Stephen. She *had* attempted to rule her husband. She did not understand the degree to which her husband was broken. His track record had been excellent up to now in such matters. Still, so much needed to be done at home so they could leave for Canada. Susan had fumed and nagged Stephen over his lack of help, to shame him if need be to get him to help her. Her agitation had ruled *her* so that she in her turn, tried to rule him. Getting Stephen fixed with so little time in which to accomplish that feat, Susan pushed and yelled and almost lost her sanity.

Not once did she cry out in desperation to God. Susan had no previous experiences of trust from which she could call on Christ for His care and help. Nor did she want to. Her religious world was kept in isolation from every other area of her life. She had no actual covenant relationship with Christ. Michelle had not asked to help her pack, and neither had Annika. Jesus had shaken her security and stability so that she might focus on Him, and still she looked to herself where she found only spiritual bankruptcy. She was clearly guilty, but it was hard to admit to herself, much less confess to God. Quill saw it on her face.

"After Genesis three and four the image concept continues to be important. In Genesis chapter five, verses one through three, we read, "This is the book of the generations of Adam. In the day when God created man, He made him in the likeness of God. He created them male and female, and He blessed them and named them Man in the day when they were created. When Adam had lived one hundred and thirty years, he became the father of a son in his own likeness, according to his image, and named him Seth." The image of God remains very important to God. The apostle Paul reminds us what it means to be 'in Christ.' Romans chapter eight reminds us, "For whom he did foreknow, he also did predestinate *to be conformed to the image of his Son.* As we grow in grace, the Holy Spirit applies what Jesus did for us that we might reflect His image more and more."

"The next aspect of the covenant of grace in Scripture is Noah. Once God judged the earth with a flood, Noah became the next or second Adam, the second lord or king of the earth. In the world-wide flood, God began His creation again out of water, which reminds us of Genesis chapter one, verse two, where the Holy Spirit hovered over the waters, ruling over the chaos. Genesis chapters six through nine gives us a look at two more aspects of the covenant of grace. First, God swore to Noah that He would never again flood the earth. We see that covenant sign in the rainbow when it rains. That ensured the earth would continue so that the Gospel could go forward. Also in Genesis chapter nine, we see something familiar we've read before. In verse one we find, 'And God blessed Noah and his sons, and said unto them, Be fruitful, and multiply, and replenish the earth,' and in verse seven, 'As for you, be fruitful and multiply; Populate the earth abundantly and multiply in it.' You remember. Those are two of the five commands God gave Adam, and I think implying that all five were still in effect. By Abraham's day, God says that *He* and no one else will make His people fruitful and multiply them.

Today, Susan had her own copy of the Bible that Quill brought with him. She was unaccustomed to looking up Scriptures, so Quill assisted her. "Genesis is the first book in the Bible, but don't hesitate to use the table of contents until you are more familiar with where the books are located."

"Thank you for being patient with me," Susan said, apologetically.

"I've had to live in this book for self preservation. You will get used to things. I have faith in you. Okay, let me tell you why those last verses we read are so important for men like me and Stephen, and also for the families of these folks. Matthew chapter twenty-eight, verses eighteen through twenty is a restatement of this first Great Commission or mandate in Genesis chapter one, verses twenty-six through twenty-eight. Go to your table of contents and look for the first New Testament book, which is Matthew. Then go to the last three verses of chapter twenty-eight. You go ahead and read them, Susan."

"I feel a little awkward, but I'll try." It took a few uncomfortable moments before she located the right verses. You said verses eighteen through twenty?" "And Jesus came up and spoke to them, saying, "All authority has been given to Me in heaven and on earth. Go therefore and make disciples of all the nations, baptizing them in the name of the Father and the Son and the Holy Spirit, teaching them to observe all that I commanded you; and lo, I am with you always, even to the end of the age."

"Good. To make disciples is to make image bearers. What does Jesus say was given to Him?" Quill probed.

"Um, all authority . . . in heaven and in earth," she answered.

"He tells us He is the cosmic King of Daniel seven and the Son of Man in Luke nineteen." Susan's surprise was total.

"Jesus, the royal Creator, had that authority in Genesis one, didn't he? And in a certain sense, so did Adam. God authorized Adam to serve Him by ruling over creation and to see culturally what God had buried in the cosmos for him to discover. But here in Matthew twenty-eight, we see Jesus, the nobleman who, before He goes to the "far country," receives that authority so He can be seated next to His Father. And, at some future time, He will return here, to his former country in order to judge His wicked servants, Satan's seed and His blessed servants.

"Oh my. I need to think about this," Susan exhaled. "It is, but it isn't that complicated. I can learn this."

"Yes, you can. But here's why this is important for those of us who wrestle with the trauma of war, veterans *and* spouses. I know too many men who went into captivity with me, survived, came home, got married, worked for thirty years and then finally quit *everything*. At retirement, they no longer had any purpose. Actually, they lost any hope of purpose in those camps and Hell Ships . . . took everything out of them. They became shells of men. Some went nuts and ended up in the psyche wards. I can't really blame them. I've felt that. You see, apart from Christ, life is truly meaningless. Remember, I was miserable not long after I moved here. I made everyone else miserable, my kids included. I was so empty. Your father-in-law offered me a job as caretaker, but because of my hate and no way to release it properly, I visited those falls six times.

"Why didn't you jump, Quill? Why *six* attempts? You know, that would have hurt Helen . . ." Susan was thoroughly intrigued at the way men—*desperate* men—think. Her Stephen was just such a man, and she was still trying to understand and fix him.

"Once Pastor Franklin showed me *Christ* and what *He* offers me, my life took on meaning. I couldn't simply sit around here, nail a board or two back up, or find purpose in mending a fence. I knew too many men who needed what I had been given in Christ. There have been times when I'm overwhelmed by the pain my buddies still suffer.

I've met a number of Korean War vets who wrestle with the same types of issues I do. Helen used to type my letters for me to those guys. My phone bills were off the charts, but those men needed what I had found. Captivity? I thank *God* for it, not because it was such a good time—it was horrible—but because it *broke* me, so God could then raise me to new life from the living death I woke up to each day. In *Christ*, my life has real purpose.

"You've seen that I *still* get depressed. Susan, I can't tell you how worthless I feel most of the time. Helen and I once drove to Vancouver and I didn't talk to her the whole way. Some days, talking is like lifting something way too heavy over my head. I just can't. Jesus didn't fix the war's brokenness for me. If He had, I wouldn't need to trust Him as much as I do. The only way we can please God is by faith, day after day, moment by moment.

"Besides, over the years, I've begun to sense His nearness more in those dark times, and what I sense of Him is just a quick taste of what heaven will be like." And then, as if switching gears, Quill added, "Too many of those veterans are dead now. Some committed suicide, some, the diseases took their course and medicine couldn't fix them. Some trusted in the Lord, but too many tuned me out. I think . . . I *hope*, they saw Jesus's light in me. Sometimes it wasn't so bright . . ." Quill's eyes were now full of tears, remembering. His had been a hard life during and after captivity, but now it was a fulfilling existence. Each day he awoke to the knowledge that God had specifically made that day, and Quill Du Pont was part of an eternal plan.

"*Uhum*," he coughed. Susan had reached to touch his hand, to share this moment, to let him know she was there, but he had withdrawn it. Instead, he wiped his eyes with his sleeve and continued, "Noah too offered sacrifices," Quill said as he reached for his hankie. He blew into it, wiped his nose, and returned the white cloth to his back pocket. "And he even spoke prophetically toward the end of Genesis chapter nine, the second aspect of the Noahic covenant. Here in verses twenty-four through twenty-seven. Noah speaks prophetically—remember Adam named his wife and the animals *prophetically*, so also Noah declared prophetically that salvation would come through the tents of his first born, Shem. In other words, for the sons of Ham, the Canaanites, to be saved, they must come humbly *into* Shem's tents. Salvation will come through the Jews. The Noahic covenant. I mean, there's so much more to this, but at least you can see an overview of it.

"Then comes Abraham. Abraham became rich, and he too was a *type* of ruler or king, if you will. Abraham offered sacrifices. There's your priesthood. Then God tells Pharaoh that Abraham is a prophet. Within the Abrahamic covenant, God promises him who had no son that Sarah would give birth to a son—they were both well past childbearing—and royal descendants would come from him. This points back to Adam and Noah's royalty. God is keeping that concept fresh. Also, God promised Abraham a land. Hebrews eleven tells us that Abraham understood this land was not the physical land of Canaan in which he then stood. It was a heavenly land. Remember Revelation twenty-one?

Susan nodded in the affirmative.

"Then we move to Moses, the man who prophetically recorded the first five books of the Bible and spoke as God's prophet to Israel. Moses too offered sacrifices. There's something interesting in second Old Testament book, Exodus, chapter nineteen, that we need to look at. Do you have it? Now read verse six.

"Okay, verse six says, 'And you shall be to Me a kingdom of priests and a holy nation.' These are the words that you shall speak to the sons of Israel.' "Do you see it?" Quill asked.

"What, 'a kingdom of priests'?"

"Yessir-ee. If we turn to First Peter, chapter two, verse nine. I'll read this one. "But you are a chosen race, *a royal priesthood*, a holy nation, a people for God's own possession, so that you may *proclaim* the excellencies of Him who has called you out of darkness into His marvelous light." Do you see the three mediatorial offices, Susan? Believers are royal priests and prophets."

"Wow. The same phrase!"

"Yes. Jehovah called Adam the first royal priest. Noah, the next Adam, also performed sacrifices. Abraham did as well. Next Israel, or corporate Adam, was to become a nation of royal priests. But they, too, failed to live as such. Now, Peter, who by the way is writing to both Jews and Gentiles, is telling *them* that they have become—in Christ—what Adam and Noah, and Israel, each failed to be. In Christ, God's people are what He has designated us to be originally. Tonight, you can also look up—now make a note of these other New Testament verses: Revelation chapter one, verse six, chapter five, verse ten, chapter twenty, verse four and chapter twenty-two, verse five. Each of these verses speak of God's people as royal priests. Oh, I almost forgot. In Genesis chapter fourteen, Abraham meets a priestly king named Melchizedek. I don't want to get into his character and purpose, but I believe God is keeping this royal priest and prophet concept moving forward toward the New Testament.

"The Mosaic covenant was given to God's kingdom of priests to show them how to behave as a His people. God gave them the Ten Commandments, the law. But He gave it in such a way as to show Israel His merciful grace. First, God delivered Israel from slavery—He redeemed them for obedient service. Next, He gave them His glorious laws, laws that put other nation's legal codes to shame. If you compare say, Hammurabi's laws with those of Moses,' there is no comparison. God's laws are moral, just, and merciful. But right after God gives his laws, He then sets up the priestly system and the sacrificial system to show them how to find forgiveness when they break His laws. God knows we can't keep His law, so He installed a system that pointed to the sacrificial lamb and King who takes away the world's sin. What mercy. I'm just giving you the high points.

"After Moses came the Davidic covenant in Second Samuel seven. David was a king, who also offered sacrifices and spoke prophetically in the Psalms. In David, God promised him a Son and an eternal house. So, the Bible is filled with the three mediatorial offices of king, prophet, and priest. In Christ, I am part of that three office mediatorial ministry. In heaven, and because of Jesus, I have been given great status. I, too, am a royal priest and prophet.

"The final covenant is called the New Covenant. The prophet Jeremiah, in chapter thirty-one, verses thirty-one through thirty-four, says, . . . I'm sorry Susan. I should have let you find it. When you do, be sure to mark it so you will know where it is. Why don't you read those verses?" Susan turned to the Table of contents, found Jeremiah, then found chapter thirty-one. "Behold, days are coming," declares the Lord, "when I will make a new covenant with the house of Israel and with the house of Judah, not like the covenant which I made with their fathers in the day I took them by the hand to bring them out of the land of Egypt, My covenant which they broke, although I was a husband to them," declares the Lord. "But this is the covenant which I will make with the house of Israel after those days," declares the Lord, "I will put My law within them and on their heart I will write it; and I will be their God, and they shall be My people. They will not teach again, each man his neighbor and each man his brother, saying, 'Know the Lord,' for they will all know Me, from the least of them to the greatest of them," declares the Lord, "for I will forgive their iniquity, and their sin I will remember no more."

"Rather than the external written law, chiseled into stone tablets, God will now write His laws on His people's hearts. The clauses, "I will be their God, and they shall be My people," is an oft repeated phrase of the Mosaic covenant. It is personalized and fulfilled in Revelation twenty-one, verse three, . . . you might want to put something in Jeremiah thirty-one so you won't lose your place. Turn to Revelation twenty-one. I'm not in a hurry. Go ahead and read that. "And I heard a loud voice from the throne, saying, "Behold, the tabernacle of God is among men, and He will dwell among them, and they shall be His people, and God Himself will be among them,"

"And again in verse seven."

"And I will be his God and he will be My son." "Now that's amazing, Quill. I think the implications of this are even more incredible. What God spoke to Israel in Egypt is found here at the very end of time! There is a glorious unity to it all, isn't there?"

"Oh, you bet your life there is. I won't read what Ezekiel thirty-six says, but it is quite similar. I'll write it down for you to look at. Jeremiah, chapter thirty-one, fits right here in the upper room. Let me turn to that and read it. In Luke 22, Jesus sent Peter and John ahead to prepare the Passover meal.

"When the hour had come, He reclined at the table, and the apostles with Him. And He said to them, 'I have earnestly desired to eat this Passover with you before I suffer; for I say to you, I shall never again eat it until it is fulfilled in the kingdom of God. And when He had taken a cup and given thanks, He said, Take this and share it among yourselves; for I say to you, I will not drink of the fruit of the vine from now on until the kingdom of God comes.' "And when He had taken some bread and given thanks, He broke it and gave it to them, saying," 'This is My body which is given for you; do this in remembrance of Me.' And in the same way He took the cup after they had eaten, saying, "This cup which is poured out for you is the new covenant in My blood."

"What Jeremiah and Ezekiel prophesied was fulfilled as the disciples were reclining at table with Jesus. When we partake of the Lord's Supper, we remember Jesus's sacrifice on our behalf. We look at everything our Lord did for us—and we are His people for whom He died, He delivered us from sin—and we should also search our hearts for unconfessed sin, not morosely, but in anticipation of His future return. This final covenant of grace, the New Covenant, is founded upon every covenant that comes before it. We first see it when God killed the animals, shed their blood, substituted the animal for Adam and Eve, and covered their nakedness. All of that comes forward in the upper room and is fulfilled in Jesus.

"So, we have talked about God's kingdom, His covenants, His mediators. Two more, and they won't take that long, but they too are so full of incredible insights . . .

Fifty: Two Final Cables

>━┥◀▸━○━◀▸┝━≺

"Alright Mrs. Lloyd, the last two cables. I see you brought your notes. Good. Remember, it only took me years to get all of this straight, so nobody, including me, is expecting you to put all of this together right now or in the next few days. Are you ready?"

"As ready as I'll ever be. Go ahead."

"The Land of Promise is actually easy to understand. There are three parts to it. First, we have Paradise or Eden. Next, the Bible speaks about the Land of Canaan or Promise. Israel left Egypt for *that* land, but they, like Adam, disobeyed God and were cast out of the Land. That leaves us with the last Paradise, the New Heavens and New Earth found in Revelation chapter twenty-one, verse one. But we need to compare Genesis chapter one, verse one with Revelation twenty-one, verse one. Moses wrote in Genesis one, verse one, "In the beginning God created the heaven and the earth." The apostle John wrote in Revelation twenty-one, verse one, "And I saw a new heaven and a new earth: for the first heaven and the first earth were passed away; and there was no more sea." This verse at the end of the Bible fulfills the first verse of the Bible.

"Why is the land cable important? As a prisoner, I got lost in the vast emptiness and chaos of death. The sun came up and with it came death. The sun went down and with it came death. I was convinced that I would never see anything but death. No matter what land I stood on, things died. Survivors who made it to freedom died of their wounds or the diseases that the doctors couldn't cure. There was nothing but

Jim Carmichael

death. But that's not what the Bible points to. Life is moving toward a conclusion, and yes, there are wars death all along the way. The Bible commences with, "In the beginning," and it ends with, "And I saw a new heaven and a new earth." The Holy Spirit has been impressing that truth on my mind and heart. I am on my way to that land where there is no more death, as Revelation twenty-one, verse four says.

"Quill, *how* do you know this for certain?" Susan almost begged him to assure her.

"The patriarch Abraham knew it the way I know it. Listen to this in Hebrews eleven, 'All these who the writer has been talking about died in faith, without receiving the promises, but having seen them and having welcomed them from a distance, and having confessed that they were strangers and exiles on the earth. For those who say such things make it clear that they are seeking a country of their own. And indeed if they had been thinking of that country from which they went out, that is, Canaan, they would have had opportunity to return. But as it is, they desire a better country, that is, *a heavenly one*. Therefore God is not ashamed to be called their God; for He has prepared a city for them.' That city is New Jerusalem described in Revelation twenty-one.

"I can see that city, the New Jerusalem, just as clearly as Abraham did because God gave us the same Holy Spirit to seal it on our hearts. I'm on my way there, and I am ready to go.

"The final cable is the temple, Susan. The temple or even the tabernacle is best understood in a short clause: "I (God) dwell in Your midst." It's real simple. Matthew chapter one, verse twenty-three boils it down to one word . . . I'll wait until you find it. Matthew one. Yes, verse twenty-three. "Behold, the virgin shall be with child and shall bear a Son, and they shall call His name Immanuel," which translated means, "God with us."

"From heaven, Jesus descended into the cosmos He had made in Genesis chapter one. Genesis three, verse eight gives us the first indication of the meaning of "Immanuel." It says, 'They heard the sound of the Lord God walking in the garden in the cool of the day, and the man and his wife hid themselves from the presence of the Lord God among the trees of the garden.' Notice the phrase, 'the Lord God walking in the garden.' The Lord Jesus, Jehovah Elohim, Immanuel, had been dwelling in fellowship daily *among* Adam and Woman.

466

But in verse eight we are told that Adam had just sinned and hidden himself. Jesus has now come in judgment, walking back and forth as Judge, in the wind of the storm.

On each day of creation, God built another aspect of this cosmic temple until He was finished on day six. On *that* day, He created the man and woman, the *summum bonum* of creation, its highest good so that He might dwell among us.

"The next inkling that we have of God dwelling in our midst comes in the wilderness, after Israel's redemption from slavery. After Pharaoh let Israel go, God once more hardened his heart, so off the king and his chariot army went to bring back the Israelite slaves. But the LORD God had other plans. Susan, would you read Exodus fourteen, verses nineteen through twenty?" 'The angel of God, who had been going before the camp of Israel, moved and went behind them; and the pillar of cloud moved from before them and stood behind them. So it came between the camp of Egypt and the camp of Israel; and there was the cloud along with the darkness, yet it gave light at night. Thus the one did not come near the other all night.'

"Good, thank you. God had been in the midst of Israel all along, from Eden to Sinai. But once more they saw 'Immanuel,' in the pillar of cloud and fire. God dwells among His people as Jesus's name indicates. Now once Israel was fully ridded of Pharaoh's army, drowned in the Red Sea, God had Israel build the tabernacle. The tabernacle symbolized the cosmos in miniature, with the Ark of the Covenant, God's footstool, at the heart of it. Once it was built, God filled this moveable tabernacle by means of a cloud in order that He might continue to dwell among His people.

As Israel neared Canaan, Numbers chapter two, verse seventeen tells us that the tabernacle was placed in the middle of the twelve tribes of Israel. That moveable tabernacle remained with Israel for years, reminding them that the God of the universe dwelled among *them* and that they were to be a holy people to Him, otherwise, He couldn't dwell with them. The next time we see this visible representation of 'Immanuel' is when God had King David's son, Solomon, build the static temple in Jerusalem so that He could once more fill it with His presence.

"About a thousand years later, Israel went into captivity for serving idols and chasing after other countries, rather than worshipping the true God who had 'Immanuel*ed*' among them. Seventy years later, God sent Ezra the priest and a remnant of Israel in captivity back to Jerusalem to rebuild the ruins and proclaim the God of Israel to the surrounding nations. Later, Nehemiah the governor also returned with a small group of people who rebuilt the walls around Jerusalem. Once the walls were up, the people began temple construction. Unfortunately, God's downcast people became unfaithful once again, so God sent three more prophets to get the people back to building the temple so that they would have that visible representation of His immediate presence among them.

"After Jesus was born, the apostle John made a very important statement in John chapter one, verse fourteen. He wrote, "And the Word was made flesh, and dwelt among us, (and we beheld his glory, the glory as of the only begotten of the Father,) full of grace and truth." That verb "dwelt," is the word "tabernacled" or "tented." Jesus, at His birth, came and did the same thing He did in Eden, at Sinai, and in Palestine, He 'Immanueled' among His people. Now, after Jesus had ascended to the Father, after Pentecost, the apostle Paul wrote to the Christians at Corinth—and this is really interesting, Susan, Paul wrote, "Do you not know that you are a temple of God and that the Spirit of God dwells in you? If any man destroys the temple of God, God will destroy him, for the temple of God is holy, and that is what you are." With Jesus in heaven praying for and guarding the Church on earth, we His people have become His living temples.

"And finally, when time is no more, Jesus fulfills everything the temple stood for, this time for good. John wrote of this incredible event in Revelation chapter twenty-one, verses twenty-two and twenty-three, "And I saw no temple in it (*i.e.*, New Jerusalem), for the Lord God the Almighty and the Lamb are its temple. And the city has no need of the sun or of the moon to shine on it, for the glory of God has illumined it, and its lamp is the Lamb." No more temple.

"Incredible, Quill. And to think these cables run throughout the plan of God . . ."

"Yeah. It is pretty amazing, isn't it?

"This has been quite a discovery," she remarked. "You have given me so much to think about. Perhaps we ought to stop for tonight.

"Good idea. See you in the morning."

Friday, May 19, 1967

Quill did not come to breakfast at his usual time this morning, and this prompted Susan to a renewed sense of concern. At least Stephen sat reading a local newspaper with her. She knew where he was, but now, where was Quill?

"Jacques," she asked, "do you think Quill is okay? Should I go look in on him?"

"Oh, I think he will be down in a little while. I will keep the food warm for him, regardless. He seemed to be resting all right when I left him several hours ago."

It was then that Quill came through the great doors. His limp more pronounced than it had been since Susan and Stephen's arrival. His gate was painful to watch. At one point, the old man stopped to rest his aching body on one of the comfortable chairs. Susan could stand it no longer, she stood and walked toward him. Stephen joined her.

"What can we get you, Quill?" she asked.

"Oooo. This old hip hurts some days more than others, I guess. Today, it's throbbing something fierce. Ask Jacque if he wouldn't mind bringing me my breakfast in here? I just don't think I want to walk any further. I took my pills earlier, the ones the doctor gave me for this. I have one more to take after I've eaten and then I'll be good as new."

Stephen was already half way to the kitchen making signals to the cook before Quill had finished his request, and Susan helped Quill settle into the cushioned chair. She drew up the coffee table for Jacques to place his plate of food upon so that he could eat. After another five minutes had passed, Quill had forked his first bite. Ten minutes after that, Quill had taken his last medication.

"Mighty fine, cuisine, Mr. Jacques," Quill stated. "We eat quite nicely around here, I don't mind telling you folks. Stephen, what do you have planned for today?"

"Well, at the insistence of my wife earlier this morning, I am going to put pen to paper and describe some things about Italy for her. It might be easier for me that way. Lord knows I haven't talked about anything much that I was supposed to, to this point. I also have some phone calls to make later today. I need to speak to the kids."

Susan was careful not to shout for glee that her husband was attempting to fulfill her wishes; sort of getting back into the saddle. Quill understood the situation so much better than both of his guests.

The 'storm' had relinquished its grip on Stephen, for the moment, and for this, he was thankful, if only for Susan's sake. She needed a good day. But the old man also knew that nothing had been resolved on the Lloyd's end so that when it invaded once more, Stephen might not be able to withstand its onslaught. And if he were defeated another time, God only knew where that would take Susan. Stephen asked leave of his wife and friend, and headed upstairs to his chore. When he reached the library level, he stopped and turned, then leaned over the rail to observe his wife and his friend. "Quill, you've been spending a lot of time with my wife the past few days. Don't be getting any ideas about running off with her."

"That's exactly what I was planning on doing," he shouted back. Then, fixing his gaze on Susan, Quill whispered, "Would you please run off with me?"

Susan sat drinking her coffee, absorbed in something Quill could not ascertain, staring into the abyss. "What? I'm sorry. I was thinking about some of the things you talked about last night."

Once more Quill said, "I asked you if you'd run off with me, and Stephen said he didn't want you to." Quill blushed as he said it.

"I just might if that block-head husband of mine doesn't start working through this with me. The time is slipping away. The children need their parents. My son is leaving shortly for the military, and . . ." Her eyes filled with tears, to which she refused to give way. Not today. Seeing no clean napkin in the immediate vicinity, she ran her sleeve across her eyes. Quill handed her his hankie, which was at that moment, still unused.

Susan sat on the porch watching the rain, still amazed at the beauty surrounding her. Steam rose from the backs of the cattle, brute animals who preferred to stand and be cooled by this gift of heaven. Quill was able to move around later that morning; his pills had done their work. He had some chores that needed his attention and this sent him into Prince George. His return was a pleasant surprise to Raymond who was expecting a letter from his aunt. He had inherited some property about twenty miles away.

Exiting his pickup, Quill spotted Raymond coming toward him. "Sorry Raymond. No letter. I'll make sure you get it when it arrives."

"Thanks Quill." The disappointment registered on his face.

"I know he's anxious about that piece of land," Quill muttered to Susan.

"I have a question," Susan asked, scanning several pieces of paper containing her recorded observations of her tutor's lectures. "I'm looking at some of these notes—oh, and you still haven't written all of this down for me.

"Let me see your set of notes," he said. Susan handed him the pieces of paper upon which she carefully wrote. After reading each page, he offered, "I'm impressed. I don't think I want to add to this list, except to make a few corrections here . . . and here . . . and right here. Change this word to 'land,' and here, write 'authority.' Here, you might use the word 'covenant.' My hands won't let me write legibly any more. I lied. I couldn't write it all down if I wanted to. It's up here, in my melon," he said, knocking on his head.

"Here's a concern I have for you. Knowing all of this can become nothing more than a lot of 'unused information,' for lack of a better word. I mean, I have shown you more than most folks know about the Bible, but without submitting your will to Christ's, none of this matters. It only makes you more guilty before God.

Once more, silence on Susan's part. "Susan, would you mind if I prayed for you, right now?"

"No. Not at all."

"Okay. God of all glory, I ask that You might open Susan and Stephen's eyes to behold Your glory, even as You did for the two disciples You encountered on the road to Emmaus. They were blind, but You gave them sight. They could not see, but You did open their perception to behold Your Son. O Lord God, I ask that You would save this marriage by Your power. Assist Stephen and Susan to know Your salvation. It is in Your holy name I ask these things. Amen."

"Quill, that was beautiful."

Fifty-One:
Trouble in the South

Wednesday, May 24, 1967

The two days following Stephen's death whirled about Susan, Quill, the team from Lloyd International . . . and Dr. James Wilson had finally arrived. Mercifully, the inquest had not lasted long, and the death was officially ruled a suicide. Everyone present at the time of death were exonerated. Dr. Wilson too had come all this way to help, but his misery only compounded itself when he attempted to speak with Susan. He wondered if she connected Damien's death with that of her husband's. Perhaps Susan hadn't put the two together in any comprehensive way, and blame, if there should be any, hadn't entered her mind. Perhaps that would come later. Perhaps. Someone was surely responsible. Seeing her friend's misery, Susan reassured Dr. Wilson that there was no need to bring Damien into this. She told him that he must concentrate on his own grief, and that James was most considerate for coming to see about her, but Mr. Du Pont had helped her immeasurably. If the truth be told, James needed Canada more than Canada needed him.

Will, Michelle, and Sandra stayed close by Susan. Tye and Mike took care of the legal matters, signing the official papers and making certain all was in order prior to their departure from Canada. Charlie, the man who stayed behind, kept life on an even keel at corporate headquarters, signing this and that as Mr. Lloyd's official representative.

Marcus and Annika sequestered themselves between Susan's and their own home, dealing ineffectively with their own grief and yet, trying to help the children with theirs. Annika cried for two straight days, so she was more of a hindrance, and Marcus, when he was home, walked around the house and grounds, unaware of his own existence or location most of the time. Ginny Cassalls tramped through the days as if in a fog. Stephen's body was already en route south by late Wednesday evening. There was nothing left for any of the Lloyd International folks to do but fly home.

Quill too wondered what to do next. He had to face the possibility that Mr. Lloyd might sell the property. There might be too many painful memories if he kept it. Quill heard the phone ring, which Jacques answered.

"Oui, Monsieur Lloyd. He is right here. I'll get him for you. Quill, it's Monsieur Lloyd."

Quill nodded, raised his frame from the chair with a groan and limped his way from the porch into the familiar surroundings of his own cabin. "Thanks, Jacques. Mr. Lloyd. How are you doing, sir?"

"I'm not doing well, but I'm dealing with it. I don't want to, but I have to. Now, we need to talk about the place up there . . ." This is what Quill had dreaded, but it came so soon.

"Sir, with all due respect, are you sure you want to talk about this right now? We're fine here. You have so much on your plate to look after. The place isn't going anywhere."

"Maybe you're right . . ." Marcus's voice trailed off, and Marcus had too much energy to burn off sitting and waiting on his son's body and his daughter-in-law, Dr. Wilson, and the rest of his employees to return. Annika was still a mess. Perry and Michelle, who had finally arrived, had their hands full keeping the children busy and no time to grieve sufficiently themselves. Ginny Cassalls stayed in the kitchen, sometimes cooking meals that didn't need cooking. Half the time she didn't know why a sauce was on the stove or why two hams had been cooked and were sitting on the table. In fact, she couldn't remember cooking either of them.

Father McTammany had stopped by the Lloyd residence to see about the funeral plans, to help where it was needed. Susan was due in this afternoon at 3:12, and Perry would meet the group. He'd told Marcus not to send the limousine. He needed to be with his daughter. The others that had gone up to Canada had left their cars parked in the lot.

The passengers deplaned far too slowly for Perry—and for Quill. The latter had begun the day looking for several items he wanted to take with him but couldn't locate. The former discovered a flat tire moments before leaving for the airport. Each event had lit the fuse and heightened the intensity. Quill felt rushed by these Lloyd International people, and Perry by the flat tire. By the time Quill reached Texas, his negative emotions had snowballed, rolling all the way to "the bottom of the hill," plowing over everything vulnerable in his life. Perry was almost at his own valley when he reached Amon Carter. Neither men rarely attempted to stop it anymore once it began to roll. Quill found his trust in God enabled him to bear these moments, but sometimes it didn't show. Perry had no such assistance. Susan observed Quill's moods alter with the miles and remembered Stephen's mental state so often the last month, before . . . From her vantage point, he was wrestling under the weight of his bent mind. Quill would win of course, and oh, how she counted on that. And there it came, the faintest hint of a smile on Quill.

And so, she leaned a little closer to Quill, hoping that what possessed him would quieten her inmost tempest as she sat waiting to exit the plane. Quill Du Pont, Dr. Wilson, Sandra King, Mike Simpkins, Will Thompson, Tye Blackledge, Michelle, and Susan comprised the final group of passengers leaving the aircraft.

Susan had worn a black dress, black shoes, a black hat, black veil, and dark sunglasses Michelle had brought with her for Susan. Her outside visage matched perfectly her inner mood. To a casual observer, she was a woman in mourning if ever there was one. Sandra had been quite helpful in being there for her; another woman's presence outside of her family was appreciated. Michelle sat quietly the whole flight patting her daughter's arm or hand mumbling things that made little sense to Susan, but might have on other occasions. These signs of parental affection annoyed Susan after several hours, and Michelle apologized more than she should have.

Perry felt strangely unemotional as he stood there looking through the heavy glass watching for his daughter to step off the plane to begin the progress through the most difficult event a wife can encounter. It bothered him no little bit that he felt so little passion. He wanted to feel empathetic, if only for his daughter's sake.

Susan halted on the top of the steps as she exited the plane, which is the moment the Texas sun slapped her, and she immediately began to drip inside her dark clothes. The wide brimmed straw hat she wore helped. The aluminum stairs down to the tarmac rang from the contact with her high heels. Susan stopped at the bottom of the ladder and waited for Quill. His cane gave him sufficient balance thankfully, even though he took it slow descending the steep stairway to the tarmac. On the positive side, an attractive stewardess held his arm while he navigated the stairs. He was obviously in some discomfort, but he made the bottom step. Susan and the others helped him from there to the gate. At the gate, the wheel chair that had been ordered for him arrived.

"Daddy!" Susan shouted, but the shrieking sound of jet and propeller driven aircraft with their engines on full throttle all but drowned out her call. A break came in the noise and she called once more, "Daddy!" Perry caught sight of Susan and Michelle about the time Susan's words reached him, and thus, he ran to meet his daughter, wife and her guest. It was at that moment the reporters from the *Star Telegram* and *Dallas Morning News*, as well as many other regional and national papers, and some from as far away as Paris, London, Rome, DC, New York, Chicago, and LA blew past him. Other media outlets, *AP* and *UPI* had also caught wind of this story a month earlier, and it had NEWS written all over it. A possible death or suicide in the Lloyd family was a sensation and they would get the scoop if one existed. How they never discovered Stephen's whereabouts was anybody's guess.

The *Dallas* reporter inconsiderately shoved Perry aside to get as close as possible for a good picture, completely unaware of his identity as Susan Lloyd's father. Now Perry was having real difficulty reaching Susan. Quill, Michelle and Dr. Wilson, along with the other Lloyd employees, closed ranks around Susan and Quill in an attempt to fend off these persistent media interlopers. Unfortunately, Quill's wheel chair had a slightly bent wheel making it difficult to steer in a straight line. That was all they needed. They had to get their luggage and find the vehicles so they could leave this madness, jostling, questions, and prying eyes. The much younger Lloyd International folks formed a 'V' and plowed through the reporters while they hurled their questions at

Susan like spears. Quill's hips began to ache more so, but his protests were drowned out by the growing chaos and speed of this huddle.

"Mrs. Lloyd, would you tell us about the death of your husband? Mrs. Lloyd, is it true that he committed suicide? Are our reports correct? Mrs. Lloyd, any comment? Mrs. Lloyd? Mrs. Lloyd—?" Susan was ill prepared for such commotion and questions, and she certainly had no ability to deal with it right then.

Unfortunately, the reporters in their obnoxious eagerness to get a story at *any* cost, added more curious onlookers and the small band had grown from the gate toward the parking lot. Perry grabbed a reporter by the jacket and threw him up against the wall, forcing his forearm hard against the man's throat. Mr. Alcott's eyes glowered down at the smaller man wriggling against the pain, trying harder escape the grasp of his mad captor, a much larger man than he and very hostile.

Perry Alcott spoke between gritted teeth, "You better tell your other reporter pals to back off or I'll start breaking some heads. You got that?" Perry shoved the reporter farther into the wall, if that was possible, and then went in search of another media numbskull to crush, which didn't take but a second. By now, the former major was in full combat mode, a feeling he hadn't experienced in years, and it served him well as far as he was concerned. The just accosted newsman, from his spot on the floor, started yelling 'freedom of the press.' Perry was beyond hearing or caring that the man's rights had been violated, or that Perry might be sued for his actions.

The Lloyd employees had so far and somehow kept the newspaper people at bay, they kept moving their grieving group closer to the main entrance. Sandra King gave her keys to Charlie and told him to make a run for the parking lot and bring the car around as quickly as possible. Dr. Wilson, a bull of a man, had already knocked over two reporters, stepping on a third. He seemed to be enjoying this, intellect and all. All his pent up emotions had found a release point. Perry finally caught up to the group surrounding his daughter, but the obnoxious reporters continued to ply Susan with questions, seeking any response her. Mike Simpkins had earlier, very thoughtfully removed his coat and placed it over Susan so that she could not be photographed.

Heads are going to roll on this one, Mike screamed across to Tye. The person responsible for the leak to the papers would be fortunate if they only found him or her at the bottom of the Trinity River wearing cement goulashes. Marcus was livid when he found out.

Perry got one last exhilarating shot in as Will and Tye were last seen stuffing Susan and Quill into the back seat of Sandra King's green Chrysler. He hadn't had this much fun since France. A reporter had stopped in the doorway to insert a bulb into his flash attachment, when Perry collided with him from behind sending him head first into the glass door. He slid downward the entire length of the glass and onto his face, out cold. Perry didn't stop to apologize. Now Perry would have to find his own car and try to follow the car Susan was in, wherever it was.

Perry could see that the remaining reporters had disbursed in search of their own vehicles and news vans. Fortunately, Perry was parked closer than the media people. He jumped in his car, sped toward the entrance, where he brought it to a screeching halt in such a way to block the newspaper and media personnel from exiting the airport parking lot. It took a policeman a few seconds to spot the lawbreaker and begin waving his hands frantically to get Perry moving. By then Perry was out of his car, the hood was up, and Perry's head was under it. He appeared to be checking something under the hood. Something among all those rubber hoses, electrical wires, fan belts and fan, breather and other paraphernalia was not working right and it had to be checked out. Right this instant.

Unfortunately for the media, the news vans and reporters began to converge at Perry's location and they wanted out. They had a story to report to Mr. and Mrs. America. Horns honked and tempers flared. Perry was threatened with legal action repeatedly. But for some reason his distributor cap had a malfunction, as he told the officer, "the 'ranafrance' had come disconnected at the 'siz-wheel' and it will take me a few more minutes to reconnect it." Perry winked at the officer, whispering that he was Susan Lloyd's dad. Fortunately, the security officer hated the media almost as much as Perry did. It was all the guard could do to keep from laughing out loud. Officer Jack Langford stuck his head under the hood to see if he could determine if the 'ranafrance' was really broken or just disconnected.

"Yeah," he interjected to Perry, "I had one of these thingamabobs come loose on me once in France, during the war. It must've taken us fifteen or twenty minutes to get it back on the road. Might take *you* longer." Having concurred with Perry's diagnosis, Officer Langford stepped over to the irate media in order to attempt some sort of smoothing of their ruffled feathers as best he could. Other security guards arrived to inspect the broken 'ranafrance,' and one officer, after fifteen minutes of pulling this wire and checking that fluid level managed to get the car to start so that the unfortunate man with engine trouble could be on his way.

Fifty-Two:
Welcome Home, Mother

Wednesday, May 24, 1967

Susan was greeted at the front door of her home by the crush of eager, yet tearful children, with their converging conversations that blended into a cacophony of sounds making little sense except to a mother. Her sadness and joy commingled as she bent down on David's level to embrace him. Her youngest finally let go. His mother was home. Susan, too, was home, such as it was.

The house felt as if it greeted her, but more like a sad glove. Despite the overall welcome, her husband would not cross its threshold for her again. Stephen was everywhere she looked. She could smell him. His things hadn't been removed from when they left, his jacket, his hat, the furniture he'd bought, each object became a knife simultaneously stabbing and slicing her heart, even though she must set aside her own grief for the immediate needs of her children.

Brit would not be outdone, though. He squirmed his way into the inner circle, tail wagging to beat the band, to get to Susan in spite of all the legs and feet surrounding him. He had a habit of wetting the floor when he became excited, as he now did. Ginny knew what was happening inside the huddle of bodies if Brit were involved, and she had a towel already in her hand. There would be no sense in scolding him. Today it didn't matter.

Annika and Marcus Lloyd held back. Mary Ellen rested securely in the arms of her husband. Michelle, Ginny Cassalls and Dolores stood on the periphery watching and waiting for their turn to hug, speak, and cry with Susan. Quill stood alone just inside the door, almost forgotten. Marcus spotted him finally and went to greet him. The two men stepped unnoticed into the den to discuss matters germane to the events of the previous week.

Flowers and potted plants had been arriving on a regular basis for several days straight. Brit was beside himself each time the doorbell rang. He accentuated his own over inflated persona ensuring that the invader understood that he would be killed out right if he or she even thought about coming inside his oversized dog house. After the tenth trip to the Lloyd residence today, the flower woman, one Janice Conwell, her name tag read, handed Brit a dog treat. From that moment onward, Janice could have stolen all the jewelry, silverware and other valuables: she could have driven a moving van up to the front porch absconding with every stick of furniture the Lloyd's owned. Just keep the goodies coming.

When dinner concluded David needed to show his mother the pictures he drew during her absence and the new way he caught the ball in his glove. Margaret, too, had much to discuss with her mother. Michael preferred to spend time with his Grandpa Perry. He possessed questions and emotions demanding release, and anger, anger was at the top of the heap. It had taken him days while he waited for his mother to return from Canada before he felt confident enough to address this type of situation.

After a bit, Dolores left, preferring to spend time with her family. She felt assured that her second family was now safe, minus one. She cried all the way home. Dr. Wilson and Mary Ellen accepted the invitation to stay and eat. They were part of this now. They had no child to go home or to check on. Aside from the massive amounts of food arriving each hour from their church, Ginny had made twenty-four desserts. She didn't need to cook anything, but cooking was her release. However, the poor woman couldn't remember if she'd added the right ingredients into the mixing bowl. A chocolate cake, like the two hams, she couldn't recall even making. Hemorrhaging distraction had enveloped her mind and each piece of the luscious cake was sliced off at the price of a tear. She too felt numb, unable to function in her usual, efficient manner. She had to stop in the middle of cutting Michael's piece, her hand shook so badly. She did forget one egg and the baking soda, and David noticed. "Mrs. Cassalls, this cake tastes funny."

Brit sat eagerly at her feet and hopelessly in the way, begging some errant crumb, a dropped cracker, a piece of this or that too close to the table's edge. Ginny wasn't aware that she was feeding the dog enough scraps lately to make him gain weight. Neither did she know that Brit had vomited his last meal next to David's bed. His little stomach wasn't used to such rich provender.

David wasn't helping matters either. He, too, kept sneaking Brit table food beyond the dog's usual allotment. Dogs take advantage of every opportunity when sadness preoccupies their people. Brit ate well and then dumped it from either of his ends on the carpet. The doorbell's ding-dong sent an electric discharge to Brit's brain, charged him into a frenzied state of barking while his feet scraped the floor for traction. *This might be the woman with the green things . . . and dog treats.* It was. The dog returned triumphantly for more cake. Within mere moments, drool from his time at the table had wrapped itself around his head when he ran to see about his treat. At the moment, the little moocher sat staring up intently into the face of Ginny Cassalls.

Quill assured Mrs. Cassalls that her cooking was superb, rivaling that of Jacques, the best chef in all of British Columbia. Ginny barely heard his remarks, and Marcus Lloyd relayed the compliment to Ginny, who nodded and sensed an unspoken need to head into the kitchen for something. She didn't know for what or for whom.

"Toby! Margaret, Michael . . . Toby's eating the ham! Oh . . . Lord . . ." Ginny sat at the kitchen table and cried. Margaret ran to her rescue to grab the cat, whose stomach was by then retching, the animal fully in the throes of ridding itself of this gourmet meal.

"Mrs. Cassalls, get the door quick!" Too late.

Susan looked at her dad, who stood laughing so hard he almost fell over his wife sitting next to him. The levity of the moment, at the expense of the Lloyd livestock and Ginny's labors of love, was exquisite, a tonic Susan and the family desperately needed. The events broke the mood sufficient to enable her to take a few bites she had resisted during the meal itself.

481

Quill excused himself, pushed back from the table, took hold of his cane, and started for the stairs. Marcus nodded to Michael hoping he would understand that Quill might need some assistance getting up the stairs. Unfortunately, Michael was preoccupied and Grandfather Marcus rapped on the table to get his attention. Quill was by now at the first step. Michael jumped up and made an excuse that he had to go upstairs, stopped and offered to help Mr. Du Pont if he needed it. Quill thanked the boy and extended his arm. Up they both went, slowly, feeling each step. Quill did not look at all well, but perhaps it was the trip. To Michael, he smelled like old people usually do. They seemed to need their clothes washed, or deodorant, or a bath, or all the above. The boy showed his manners, regardless.

Susan had asked Quill prior to leaving Canada to speak at the funeral. That was the main reason for his presence so far below the border. At first he refused, his insides tearing at him to be in control by his obstinance, regardless of whom it bothered. But Susan somehow convinced him that he was the only man who could put to rest all the talk that she knew would whirl about this death. She had not counted on the media, but she should have. Now Susan would have to live with the whispered conversations that Stephen had been mentally unbalanced. That was the reason he'd been in a mental institution or somewhere out of the public eye.

Dr. Wilson sat next to Mary Ellen, half way into a good cigar, living with his own struggles and unaware that his moment of pleasure, the first in a while, impinged upon Susan's and the family's grief. Mrs. Cassalls kept blowing the smoke away, hoping he might get the hint. To add to her consternation, Marcus too lit up another of Cuba's finest, and then suggested they adjourn to the patio. Ginny began opening sufficient cross ventilation to scour the nasty odor from the dining room. Mary Ellen snatched the foul thing from her husband's fingers, scolding him beyond the need of the moment. It was then that Mary Ellen noticed, not his mismatched sox, but the brown shoe on his right foot. The other was covered in black patent leather. He'd returned from Canada looking like that.

This type of death meant something more where the children were concerned. Susan could bear up under it she had thought, but sitting at the table, she realized she had deceived herself. As Susan unwound from the flight and the crush of the unexpected reporters—Marcus was fully aware of this dastardly betrayal by one of his employees and was looking into the matter. He'd already hired a private investigator— Susan Lloyd felt herself start to unravel.

In Canada, she'd kept some powerful emotions at bay. She didn't know exactly what, but something forceful lurked just beyond the perimeter and out of sight. She sensed its nearness with her mother sitting so close.

The dam burst at 8:43 p.m. Susan broke down completely, because she believed she was safe to do so. Margaret next joined the chorus, but David ran out the door to see if anyone was still outside playing. He didn't want any part of this.

Fifty-Three: A Conversation

Wednesday, May 24, 1967

Quill lie on his bed in the Lloyd's guest room. He hated flying, always had, and in the quiet of this spacious room he felt as if he could finally relax a little. He'd remembered opting out of the aviation test when he went into the service, preferring instead to keep his feet planted firmly on *terra firma*. Aviation, when he entered the Army, was too undependable for his tastes. There was way too much bailing wire and bubble gum holding those crates together. He'd taken a semester off from college in 1933. The money wasn't there, so he thought he'd join the army for a hitch, see something of the world, and return to the university when his enlistment was up. Then he'd have some money in his pocket so he could hit the books and the gridiron. He never made it back to college, because they shipped him out to the Philippines. He had however gotten married before he sailed, and in 1937, been promoted unexpectedly to first shirt. First Sergeant Du Pont looked forward to a little adventure. He found it in late 1941.

A tear formed at the edge of his left eye, built to sufficient size and weight so that it slid down the side of his face. The salty liquid felt cold against his skin. He was too old to push his fears around like he used to, and he had to tell himself at the moment to let them go. Despite his own best advice, the whole wretched panorama of Bataan invaded his mind. He smelled the dirt peculiar to Camp O'Donnell, he tasted the stagnant water the Japs gave them to drink. Why couldn't it leave him in peace? He felt the slice of the bayonet across his flesh with its searing pain, heard the scream erupt from his mouth, and longed for death to overtake him.

How could he ever forget the agony of brutal men beating weaker ones? Most had become defenseless shells of skin stretched across protruding bones, flesh covered walking stalks that crumpled when struck with rifle butts or the angry boots of the Japanese. Their knee joints had become larger than their thighs and calves. He remembered cursing those men who took chances they hadn't the strength to carry through by attempting escape. Then he'd have to watch as the Japs lop their heads off.

The first years after his return home, when Quill slept, he dreamed about walking, about never being able to stop walking, walking until he awoke screaming, half insane. His hips and knees hurt him for days. With his walking dreams he felt the sun cooking his head, arms and shoulders, and the thirst parching his lips until they bled. His stomach growled, and that horrid Jap guard kept striking his swollen stomach with a sharp stick until weakness and pain drove him face down into the dirt. No matter how many times he fell from that stick, his weakness and exhaustion, once more he found himself walking, striving to get away from it, never able to stop walking. He quit walking only long enough to fall down, heard the fat Jap's fetid laugh, and then he'd discover he was walking again. His walking never ended, not even in freedom.

Quill had other dreams, odious nightmares where he'd defecate until his insides slid out his bottom side, and then as if the ghoulish mess had a life of its own, it slithered out the camp gate possessing its own survival instincts. His intestines became a vine spreading through the trees and out into the jungle. He'd wake up screaming as a Jap grabbed his entrails and pulled on them, beating them mercilessly.

Quill was now sweating on his bed as he thought about his dreams. How could he tell anyone about his dreams? How could he tell people about Bataan? The few times he tried they didn't grasp what he said or told him to let it alone. That was the reason he got as far away from everyone as he could. The thought of being away from his small piece of life in Canada was agony.

In his mind's eye he eagerly looked for the cross in the dirt made by a boot attached to Old One Eye's Jap leg. When being transported to Japan, the ship was destroyed, and wonder of wonders, Quill had survived as had the same guard, clinging to life a wooden plank, floating in the water. In his rage, Quill shoved the small, bleeding body under the ocean swells. Old One Eye didn't come back up for air. Quill's thunderous anger fed his nightmares years after the fact. He remembered when the Americans arrived to occupy Japan after their surrender, he hardly recognized them; they seemed as apparitions. His cognitive faculties had suffered tremendously from years of poor diet, fear, and hate, to the point that his comprehension had slowed, torturously so. When he heard the word "freedom," or the clause, "soldier, you're going home," he hardly remembered that he, too, had been a soldier who had a home.

He remembered Helen and the guilt that haunted him. *She* had kept him alive. *She* had done it. *She* was the true soldier who loved him regardless. *She* forgave him. *She* breathed life into his broken body and spirit. *She* bore him children, but the children had fled when they were old enough to escape Quill's unintended tyranny. He hardly ever saw them again. He'd heard through Helen that his son Carl, and daughter, Emily, had children, but they wouldn't say where they lived. He'd seen a few pictures of his grandkids when they were young. They looked healthy, but they lived somewhere else. He'd lost his temper too often, been too unpredictable, too rigid, too this, too that. They lived in America somewhere. They begged Helen to come with them, to escape as they had done. But she would never leave Quill. *She* was the true hero. *She* gave up the prospect of ever knowing her grandchildren for his sorry hide. She also knew if she left him, he would be dead within twenty-four hours. He'd suffered for her, and she would not desert him, ever.

Quill rolled over on his side to circumvent the relentless war that followed him about like a dog does his master. True, God's grace had taken the sting and edge from the past, but so far south as he was, the past had invaded more intensely than it had in years. God would make a way of escape. In God's kingdom, what appeared to be, was truly not. And then he noticed that the room in which he lay wasn't his. Why was he *here*? It came so slowly to him. *Oh yes, Stephen.*

Other thoughts came, good thoughts, white light thoughts of warm sunny days and the cool breezes of heaven. Heaven. He was going there one day, perhaps soon. Jesus was there, and yet, He dwelled with the old soldier no matter. Jesus bore the long nights with him when his depression roared, with its python like grip compressing him until he thought he would burst. But here he lay, a hundred years from the war, maybe two hundred. And Jesus truly was the same yesterday, today, and yes, forever. Jesus was purpose personified. There could be no meaning outside of Him. Life began and ended with Him. He was Alpha and Omega. He knew all that now. And there was Chaplain Sullivan, shining like the sun, a smile as wide as the horizon. He had made the golden shore, and he waited for Quill. Helen was there too. Waiting.

From outward appearances, he was one more dead man staring skyward, the blood pooling behind his head. He'd gotten used to stepping over or walking past dead men on the march to Camp O'Donell. While in captivity, he gave little thought to them. He didn't have the strength. They had become lifeless things in his way to somewhere else. But they had left their phantom residue on him, in his nostrils, and tight around his mind.

Stephen's dead stare wasn't a look of surprise. Quill had seen the same look so many times. It was barely death to him; First Sergeant Du Pont, a walking dead man.

To his left Quill caught the scent of Susan's perfume, but how? Where? How long had he lain there immured, remembering? He looked at the clock on the table next to his bed, 11:24 p.m. Then the door opened slightly, and Susan peeked her head in to ask if he were okay. He said yes, but he couldn't hide the tears. Quill had no idea that he had been crying. Susan opened the door wider, deciding it would be okay to enter. Sensing his dismay, she stopped at his bedside.

"Quill, how are you feeling?" she inquired. She then handed him an unused tissue from her pocket.

"How am *I*? How are *you*?" Quill asked, turning her question around.

"I'm fine . . . well, I've been better. I realized I hadn't seen you for an hour, and I was a little worried. I could see your agitation on the plane. I know this is difficult on you, but what you've told me has helped me so much. You have been a God-send to me and I want . . . no, I need you. That's selfish, I know. You are a rock . . ." She reached for his hand and pulled it close, her tears were not far behind. Quill felt embarrassed at her gracious comments, and yet, he needed them at that particular moment. The Lord was near him via Susan, and he noted it.

Five minutes passed in silence. Her eyes were less puffy and red than they had been at dinner. Ridding herself of all that pent up emotion had saved her, Quill thought. Mrs. Cassalls had already cleaned the carpet in David's room. Susan almost remarked about Quill's appearance. No one except Stephen and Marcus had ever seen Quill Du Pont, so they assumed his skin's color was always that off pink, and Marcus had forgotten. When he was in Canada, Marcus was so busy arranging fishing trips and hunting parties, gabbing with clients about the spectacular view of this mountain or that peak, working around the place fixing this board or calling about that antique from Mary's Antique Shoppe in Prince George.

Marcus had been too preoccupied with what Quill had to tell him after his arrival that he looked past his old friend, not seeing his pain. Quill's hip ached more than normal. His hands and fingers throbbed, and his breathing was labored, tonight, his voice a bit more raspy.

"Oh, I'm okay, I guess." He nuzzled inwardly from the attention she gave him. He thought Susan Lloyd was the prettiest woman he'd ever seen, except for Helen, of course. And here she sat on his bed not five inches from him. He did wince when she sat, and Susan apologized.

Quill allowed Susan to talk about whatever she felt like. Finally that died. She seemed as if she wanted to *talk*, not converse, but to discuss. There was something in her look, behind her eyes, about her posture.

Quill put his broken and twisted claw on her hand, which she didn't withdraw. Lesser women would have, he thought. He knew that pain all too well. "What is it, Susan? Something's on your mind, isn't there? Stephen maybe?"

"Yes. I'm not very good at disguising it, am I?"

"Oh, that's all right. It's only natural to think about him. But I enjoy your company. You're the prettiest thing that's come through that door in the last twenty minutes."

Susan blushed, although she did need to hear these words from a man she respected. "I want to talk to you about . . ." Her spoken thoughts stopped abruptly. Susan didn't quite know how to proceed. Religious talk had always made her feel so uncomfortable. These cataclysmic events, however, had brought her to this place and she needed to broach the subject, even if she did so like a wrecking ball. Her husband was gone, and Susan wondered if she could, in all honesty, go on with her life. She was by now, beginning to feel angry with Stephen for cheating her out of a life with him. She loved him beyond what she thought possible, and he had ripped himself from her forever.

Most of all, Susan wanted to know if Quill knew where her husband was now. He suspected that this almost paralyzing question had brought her to sit on his bed. A lone tear, reflecting the light from the table lamp, slid down her cheek. These were days for tears. At least she could cry for the right reasons, Quill thought.

Susan focused on her own hands. She always did that when she was want for words. "Where—I mean—where do you think Stephen is? No—oh, I know you don't. It isn't fair of me to ask you, but, what I mean is . . . oh Quill, don't let me sound like such a fool."

"Susan. Can I ask you something personal?"

She sniffed, brought out her tissue and blew into it. "Yes."

"It's kind of personal. Are you sure?" She nodded for him to proceed.

"Okay. What were your last days like with Stephen? I mean, besides the pain you both shared?"

This *was* personal. Quill wanted her to tell him about the things that a wife values above all the gifts her man has ever given her, about particulars women share only with other women. He wanted to know about the intangible and subjective matters that husbands and wives alone keep. Her eyes scolded him for asking, yet Susan wanted or needed to reply. "They were wonderful. They were some of the sweetest, tenderest moments in our relationship. He loved me with real passion. He'd never loved me like that." Her soft, vivid blue eyes reflected, even verified her words.

"I remember those days, "Quill said. "Helen could make me forget. Oh how she loved me. I think the only thing I can offer you, Susan, and it may not help, is to say that maybe he was saying goodbye in the only way he knew how. Maybe when that Marine died in Vietnam he knew something, which he kept from all of us. I think . . . I think you have to treasure those moments for what they were, his gifts."

Quill's voice grew husky with the melancholy he felt from remembering. He had taken the time as Susan fumbled with her words to pray the small Nehemiah like prayer he'd lifted to heaven so often when words failed him, "Help, Lord." "Susan, I don't know where Stephen is right now. But God does. I can't tell you that I know for certain what his response was to the Gospel. God will do what's right. He always does. It's safest to trust His revealed character."

"But I miss my husband so much. I want him back. I want to be with him when I . . . when I die. Don't you see?" Susan broke down again. This was becoming more difficult for Quill to watch. He'd trained himself well to withdraw from such times so that he might shield himself from Susan's pain, so he couldn't feel it. In fact, Quill Du Pont lay stone faced looking up at her, because he had no other alternative, no other way of dealing with death and sorrow.

"Why can't you tell me, Quill? I know you have the answer. Where is my husband? Tell me he's in heaven!" Susan's voice grew more intense, the words striking her houseguest like boxing gloves. She knew what her church taught about its members committing suicide, and this little man was her last and best hope to reverse the outcome if she could only make him see her need for her husband. Susan detected Quill withdrawing from her into a protective shell, and that angered her all the more. "Why won't you tell me? He fought for his country," she yelled, standing erect. "Surely that must carry some weight with God. It has to. He was the finest husband and father any woman and children could want. Where is he, Quill?!" She screamed even louder than before, and then shook Quill furiously by his lapels. Try as she might, he only withdrew more circumspectively into himself. Susan seemed on the verge of hysteria when Michelle entered the room with Annika hot on her heels. Perry and Marcus were not far behind.

Susan's obvious panic prompted from Michelle, "What's wrong, dear?"

"Quill won't tell me if my husband is in heaven or not! I have a right to know. I want to know! Leave me alone, all of you. Where is my husband, Quill?" Susan shouted, beginning to pound on Quill's side, demanding answers to which the old man was not privy. David, suddenly awake from his mother's shouting, buried his head in his pillow, determined not hear his mother so upset. Margaret ventured out of her room, but held back when she observed all the adults invading the guest bedroom. Michael, from his room, put his hand over the phone; Donny waited on the other end. Michael waited for things to simmer down before he continued his train of thought. He did not want to know about what was happening. Denial was part and parcel of his mood of late.

Perry rescued Quill from Susan's fiery disposition. He led her by the arm down to her room where she collapsed, angry, confused and weeping. Perry lifted her onto her bed, and as he did so, he brushed her hair out of her face, much as he did when she was little. Watching his daughter in such obvious distress hurt him deeply, and that he did not expect. Soon, Michelle and the remaining in-laws, gathered around her bed to join father and daughter.

"Daddy, where do you think Stephen is?" Susan appeared so small, bathed in the bedside lamp's glow. Her voice had become infantile, almost innocent. Perry turned to his wife standing next to him, not knowing what to say to Susan. He'd always thought of suicide as the coward's way out, yet he remembered those darkened moments in his checkered past when those thoughts scuttled past him more than once, seductive in their lure. Annika and Michelle assured Susan that her husband was in heaven with God. Susan slammed a salvo back at them, "How do you know? Where is your *proof*? I want my husband back. And don't tell me not to question the Catholic Church!" This widow and mother appeared to be edging slowly out of her mind with grief.

Marcus phoned Dr. Lipscomb, the family doctor, informing him of the situation. Within ten minutes he stood at Susan's bedside, removing the hypodermic needle from her upper arm. "She'll rest now," He whispered. Susan was still in the throws of the sobs that had not quite run their course. It took barely two minutes before Susan Lloyd breathed heavily.

Perry returned to Quill's bed to find him packing. This was just too hard for the old man. Perry mentioned that he'd been a Marine Company commander in France in the Great War, and had seen many shell shocked Marines. Susan had reminded him of some of them just now. Quill halted his packing and said he'd been on Bataan when the Japs captured the place. That was all it took. The two men talked well into the wee hours of the morning. Two unlikely combat warriors had found each other. They spoke like thirsty men, drinking in each other's pain and experiences. Immanuel.

Fifty-Four: On the Way to the Funeral Home

>⊹∻⊹•⊙•⊹∻⊹<

Thursday, May 26, 1967

In front of the Lloyd's residence, a long, black limousine arrived, but all was not ready inside the house. Susan was holding up their trip to the funeral home to begin the vigil. Two news photographers had arrived at the Lloyds just in time to attempt to capture the grieving family for print in the next day's edition. Perry, although sixty-eight years old and in great shape for a man his age, looked menacing as he strode over to where the men stood snapping pictures. He'd found that the weight room provided him a place to vent his anger. His strength also made him more dangerous this afternoon.

Before the men could retreat, Perry Alcott latched onto one camera, threw it to the ground, smashing to pieces. The second man, aghast at anyone doing such a hideous thing to the press, attempted to take Perry's picture. Perry caught him with a hard right fist to the stomach, doubling him over, forcing him to drop his camera. Perry picked it up and heaved it well into the street where it too, crashed, separating in various sized pieces, finally skidding to a stop. Mr. Alcott turned back to the first reporter attempting to retrieve his camera. Perry reached it first and then threw it in another direction.

"Don't you ever come on this property again!"

Both men of course protested loudly of the certainty of a coming lawsuit, he could bet on that. Perry then grabbed the first cameraman

492

by the collar and tossed him to the ground. Standing over him, Perry said in an unmistakable but low voice, "I killed lesser Heine's in France than you, you piece of worthless garbage. Get out of here before I stomp your face in!"

Death and murder fueled the look in Perry's eyes. It would have been nothing for Perry to kill this reporter, and it probably would have felt good. Perry meant every word of what he said. The man on the ground scrabbled away, repeating the threat of prosecution for hampering the press from expressing their first amendment rights. "I just expressed my first amendment rights, you idiot. I fought for mine, what did you do to get yours?" Perry shouted back.

Michael couldn't believe his eyes and ears. He hustled over to where his grandpa stood glowering at the retreating cowards. "You ever come around here again, and I promise I'll kill you," Perry said, shaking in his raging anger.

Michael mistakenly touched his grandpa on the shoulder and said, "Grandpa, what . . ."

Perry turned so quickly Michael didn't have time to finish his sentence or retreat. Perry's left hand grabbed Michael's shoulder and his right fist came up hard in order to smash the thing that had startled him. That single reaction saved the lieutenant's life more than once in France.

"Grandpa!" Michael yelled. "It's me. Don't!"

Grandpa Alcott, realizing that he had reverted so quickly backward to the rolling hills and muddy trenches of France, fighting for his life, froze in place. And in that same flicker, he recognized that he wasn't in France. Here in Ft. Worth, Texas, and almost fifty years later, such behavior could have him in jail faster than he could spell Heine or Fritz. His eyes had grown twice their size when he reeled back from the brink, about to smash his grandson with a crushing right hand.

At almost the same moment, Michelle Alcott stepped out of the house to observe the finality of an unexpected commotion. There, her husband Perry, along with two disheveled and bewildered reporters, one now bloodied, and both cursing to high heavens, suddenly wheeling around to protect himself from another attacker, her grandson Michael, completely ignorant of his grandfather's mental estate. Michelle Alcott screamed, "No, Perry! It's Michael!" She'd witnessed a similar scene play out years before between Perry and another man.

Michael had not seen a man dazed to incoherence, his eyes glazed in pure hatred, in full kill mode as his grandpa now stood before him. Without his grandmother's intervention, Michael might surely have been hurt badly.

"Grandpa? It's me. Michael!"

Perry's slow comprehension turned to silence, then crimson shame. "Oh my God. Michael. I'm sorry. I . . ." The two reporters had retreated to a safe distance, licking their wounds, and making a failed attempt to repair their photographic equipment. Perry paid them no mind. "I didn't hurt you, did I?"

"No sir. I'm okay. Are *you* okay?"

Grandpa Alcott, fighting back the tears, went to one knee. Within seconds, his body wept, shaking with the same passion he'd displayed toward the reporters. Michael bent down to his grandpa, but the old man begged him off. "I'll be all right. I'm just sorry you had to see that. I'm ashamed of myself."

"I'm not. That was great, Grandpa!"

"No. No it wasn't, son."

When Michelle reached her husband and smiling grandson, Perry could barely right himself, much less stand on his own. He felt light headed, his mouth dry. *"Perry Alcott!* You could have really hurt one of those men, not to mention your grandson! *My Lord.* This is no time to be doing something like this! Our daughter needs us. She doesn't need her father in jail, for heavens *sake!"*

That was how the funeral for Stephen Lloyd began, and it would not be a good afternoon or evening for Grandpa Alcott. Michelle prayed that the anger would hopefully wear off sooner than later, but she knew the residue would leave her husband depressed, probably hostile. The whole house would feel its presence, and they would do their best to avoid him. Misunderstood castigation from his wife was the last thing Perry needed. He should talk this out, but he was not good at voicing objective truth when hell's fury whirled about him. It took him thirty minutes to quit shaking. Fortunately, Susan had not come out of the house to observe the ruckus. For that, Michelle was eternally grateful.

The trip to the Sanders-Kaufmann funeral home on Vickery Boulevard was sedated. Each man, woman and child seemed locked inside their own cell of examination. Thus, very little conversation pricked at the imposed silence. This situation was too foreign to most in the vehicle. Michael sat to the right of his mother, holding her hand. Her perfume and softness became the constants enabling him to continue. Margaret sat on Susan's left, almost crowding her. David, who tried to sneak Brit on board, huddled up near the front watching the road, content to sit in the biggest car he'd ever imagined. "Mother, isn't this neat?" he yelled back behind him. Susan attempted to focus in his direction, toward her son's immediate interests, but only recognized her name being called, not the person who had spoken it.

Susan bore the look of someone drained of sleep and understanding. She had alternately fought fatigue on Tuesday and anger on Wednesday, which led her to depression on this Thursday. The limousine's vibrating motion settled her: the children's warm bodies piled so near, their non-verbal silence, rocked her almost to sleep, but she skirmished it all aside. Ginny sat to Margaret's left, with Annika next to Ginny. Marcus moved to see about David who was pulling his yoyo out of his pocket. No one ever quite knew what was going on in David's mind. His presentation of the toy pointed to a good sign, Marcus thought.

Perry sat opposite the aforementioned passengers, shaking and interchanging his focus on the suddenly near past, all the while, struggling to stay in the present. Michelle, sitting next to Perry, attended to the care of her husband as well as her daughter. She dreaded the coming hours, but she trooped on as always. She knew that at some indeterminate place and time, Perry would "relax," as she called it, and all would be well—until the next land mine went off. Michelle had spent her entire marriage protecting Perry from the children and the children from Perry when the war invaded her home. There was so much Susan and her brothers had not seen because of Michelle Alcott.

Quill, his broken little hands, gloved for this occasion and resting on his cane, leaned over to Perry and whispered, "If they—meaning the people in the vehicle—had been in France, this would be a lot easier. Women make such lousy infantrymen." Quill said other things equally familiar and close to a combat veteran's heart. His words eased the tension and reminded Perry that they'd both seen much worse and lived long enough to sit in this car together. The words cracked Perry on the head, splitting his veneer wide. He turned to Quill, exhaled, and relaxed somewhat.

"Yeah . . ." Perry smiled for the first time in half an hour. Then he said, "We piled the boys up at Soissons, and then rolled over those Germans. Thanks Quill. I'll be all right." Both men understood so well. Michelle leaned forward and looked at Quill, who winked at her. She smiled gratefully when Perry said to her, "Honey, do you have a breath mint?"

Dolores Hernandez and her husband followed the limousine in their new Mercury. Behind them, the Wilsons followed.

Several Lloyd International employees had already arrived at the mortuary. It was impossible to miss Father McTammany. He was last seen ducking into the large front door as the limousine drove past, turned, and pulled around back, where it stopped at the covered entrance.

"Mother, it will be okay. We're right here," Michael said. Susan squeezed his hand. She knew that she was about to see her husband for the very last time. Ever.

The mortuary was as it must be, filled with the luscious smells of fresh cut flowers and the sights of well-dressed people speaking in hushed tones. These folks didn't face death often, not the kind Quill and Perry had confronted on Bataan and in the Great War, respectively, and certainly not like the dead, but honored guest, Stephen Lloyd. Quill spotted the large ficus tree and hobbled over to inspect it. His unwelcome anxiety had come for a visit. This amount of floral emotion spread around the fringes of the room exceeded Susan's expectations, and for this, she was encouraged.

Susan's gaze followed the lines of flower and ivy arrangements around the room until her eyes rested on the casket. For some strange reason she wasn't ready to look at it. It was expensive, elaborate, and bronze. The top half of it opened, exposing the man she had loved and could not possibly understand. The interior cloth was a soft pastel blue.

Despite the friends and guests attempting to speak with the widow, Susan inched her way through them to the place where her husband lay, Michael and Margaret constantly beside her. Susan noted that the bullet had done no damage to the front of her husband's face, and therefore, no one would see the exit wound. Sanders-Kaufman had done a splendid job.

Susan inhaled a bit too much air looking at Stephen, for she felt suddenly faint. The man lying there did and did not look 'natural,' and then she had to fight to keep her tears at bay and her revving emotions in check. But why? Was that not expected? Michael put his arms around his mother to protect her, and to keep her upright. "Mother," he whispered, "this is the reason we're here. We need to tell father goodbye." It was a good front, but it was all he could do to keep from screaming, despite the fact that he was becoming angrier by the day. He had quarreled with Margaret on several occasions just this morning.

Father McTammany moved cautiously through the lobby to reach the Lloyds and Susan. This was no time or venue to harm one of the smaller, more fragile old stalwart women of the church. Annika, Michelle and Perry, Ginny, Dolores and the Wilson's were also screening Susan off from anything that might swallow her, allowing only the mountain of a man, their priest, inside the circle. The family patriarch, Marcus, and his grandson, David, were busy with the yoyo about thirty feet distant. Father Ed spoke quietly into the semi-circled group of Lloyds, but mostly toward the widow, "Susan, you must . . ." He didn't finish his thought, for Ginny had turned to face him, her own look stern and maternal, as if to say, "She must what?" The flame-red haired priest backed away out of self-preservation. Grieving women could be ruthless when upset. Football was never this rough.

Father Ed retreated to a safer distance and finally spotted Marcus Lloyd. Marcus introduced Quill to Father Ed McTammany. The two men, standing opposite each other, resembled Mutt and Jeff. This priest was such an immense human, Quill thought. Certain other priests believed Father Ed was in actuality two men occupying one priest's habit. The priest extended his oversized hand to Quill. Without thinking, Quill removed his gloved hand, exposing its broken ugliness. The smaller man barely returned the grip, his hand vanishing inside the hollow of Father Ed's bear-sized paw. The priest's expression altered, from amazement, to disbelief, to questioning.

Father Ed had always dominated men by his size, if not his aggressive nature. He was well aware that people, and especially his opponents of the male gender, held him in awe and fear. He had been powerful on the field, knocking Michigan and Ohio State guards and tackles around like bowling pins at his whim. His looks came secondary. He'd had two dates in high school and four during his time at Notre Dame. Still, he liked being large, a certain power came with it. Here at the funeral home, so many of his athletic parishioners schooled about him.

Quill expected this look he was now receiving from the priest. It came repeatedly after he'd returned from captivity. The little man looked up into the giant's face, a face only a mother could really love, and said quietly, "Bataan." Nothing else need be said. An amazing thing happened, Father Ed began to weep, and little got to this behemoth. The Father knew what that single word meant. He'd had two friends that didn't return from Corregidor. The stories he'd heard made him ill. Now, he felt small, and in an inexplicable way, Quill Du Pont towered over and dominated the much larger human being standing so close to him. From that moment, Father Ed couldn't do enough for Quill. He, more than all those present this day and the next, wanted to sit and listen to whatever this brave little man had to say. Susan had requested that Quill speak at the wake *and* the Mass.

The hours dawdled along until the vigil began. Many wonderful and close friends, business associates and clients, stopped to speak with Susan and the family—as were expected, but dreaded. They said all the right things, all the necessary and expected things, or they said nothing at all. They covered their mouths with their handkerchiefs, passed by silently squeezing Susan's hand weakly or too firmly. But something unpleasant hung over it all. 'It' of course wasn't stated, but too many of these 'vultures' were wondering and whispered among themselves why Stephen had stayed in the mental hospital. They had to know how he passed. People these days didn't die, they passed to something else. Of course, very few knew what the "something else" was for certain. The Catholics supposed it to be purgatory. The Christmas/Easter Protestants hadn't a clue, nor did they care. But since he had fought for his country, surely he must pass straight into heaven. But then, there was the matter of suicide. What of that?

The rumors abounded, unwashed and unchecked. Perhaps Mr. Smith or Mrs. Jones' verbal feast might taste more appealing inside, where the casket rested, if the truth were left outside the mortuary, if the gossip mill were allowed to run a bit longer, before someone quashed it with the truth. No one dared.

Too many of these well dressed, high society women were more interested in their own opinions of the cause of death or of the family's pain than the facts. Whatever made the situation the gravest made them the more content. That was how Susan read the aftershaved and perfumed people, the coffee and cigarette breath, the murmuring conversations that burbled on in a dull drone. An occasional laugh would rise above the rest, and then be muffled: a sneeze, a cough, those staring faces, darting eyes and quick glances that just as quickly retreated lest they be caught. Susan's suspicions made her almost ill.

She *was* almost ill, fatigued beyond her capacity. She didn't want to be here, not with all these people, too many of whom she didn't know. David and some brown haired girl his age wearing new shoes ran around and among the guests, and Ginny took after the boy. When she corralled them both, Ginny scolded David and sent the girl, Andrea, to her mother. Ginny then bent down and straightened the youngest Lloyd's suit and tie, apparel so seldom worn, and which he detested wearing.

Stephen lay so silent and so handsome, frozen in time. Susan remembered the sheet spread over his body, his shoes sticking out uncovered at the end of the sheet. Her fantasy had settled on that moment, when she heard, "Mother?"

"Oh, I'm sorry, Michael. What?"

"Father McTammany said it's time to begin."

Susan sighed deeply. "Yes . . . I'll be right there." Susan turned back to contemplate the lifeless man she had loved for so many good years. "Good bye my dearest husband, my love. I will always love you." *Where are you now?* That enormous question hovered over the moment while Susan patted his folded hands. They were cold to the touch and clay-like, but they were his.

The organ began to play and this eclectic assemblage of people, gathered at the double doors leading to the auditorium, waiting for each, in his turn, to pass through and enter. Father Ed towered over the lectern speaking when Susan took her seat. "We have all come together this afternoon," he announced, "to remember our brother, Stephen Michael Lloyd."

Susan looked over at Quill, whom Michael had escorted in early to ensure he had a seat. She needed to hear him once more, and she wanted to cry so much more. His words, for better or worse, had been able to enfold her aching heart during those days in Canada.

Father Ed continued, "Mrs. Susan Lloyd has requested that a friend of hers, Mr. Quill Du Pont, say a few words. Susan Lloyd has spoken highly of Mr. Du Pont, and I learned a few hours ago that he survived the horrors of forty-two months of captivity in Bataan. I don't know what he will say to us, but I would love to hear him. Mr. Du Pont .. ?"

Quill was not a public speaker, nor did he profess to be one. He had forestalled even thinking about standing in front of this assembled and august group: bankers, C.E.O.s, the Lt. Governor, and the Texas AG, a broad spectrum of employees from Lloyd Hotels, reps from every major hotel chain in the US, doctors and lawyers, powerful women, various local mayors, a half dozen professional athletes, many military crew members from the 484th Bomb Group, including one Erik T. (Smitty) Schmitt—late of course, Gladstone board members, faculty and staff, rank and file mothers and fathers, children and infants, so few of whom the Canadian knew personally. The thought that he might say something unedifying or ignorant made him queasy. Quill sent another Nehemiah prayer skyward. He had been up early in prayer for strength. He also knew they had not come to hear him, or necessarily even Quill's God, but rather to say goodbye to a friend, church and school member, and colleague. The meaning for Quill's existence would stand with him in mere moments. He asked Michael if he would escort him to the front, which Michael did.

Quill's suit was fifteen years out of date, brown with a small stain over the breast pocket, crumpled a bit. Everyone at the Lloyd's was so preoccupied with their own preparations they had forgotten to see about Quill. His tie was also dated, short, fat, and ugly, its colors a bit faded too. His hair required but minor combing, yet the cowlick stuck up in back all the same. White bits of dandruff dotted the shoulders. He wore one black and one brown sock, because no two pairs he owned matched any longer. His shoes were scuffed.

His appearance was acceptable in Canada, among the farmers and ranchers, loggers and electricians at his church, most of whom dressed for Sunday in their bib overalls or old suits like Quill's, so he didn't stand out there. He looked more like an olive on the fruit salad plate. But he'd brushed his teeth and dabbed on his Old Spice. This was the best they would get.

Quill Du Pont embarked on his verbal journey with a slow, deliberate, and measured cadence. He almost sounded eloquent: "It would be easier and safer for me to say all the right things about my friend and employer, Mr. Stephen Lloyd. It's easier, because it doesn't hurt doing that. But if life has taught me anything, it has taught me that the easy way isn't always the best way. In fact, I'm going to end the speculation this evening. Stephen Lloyd . . . took his own life."

The audience immediately murmured and shifted in their seats. He wasn't supposed to say it openly like he did. Susan closed her eyes, her head tilted backward apiece. How she wished this away and swept clean. But suicide is not clean. Annika squeezed her husband's hand so tightly that he fussed at her and pushed her hand away. He too was caught off guard, even though he'd asked Quill to begin the way he did. That word, 'suicide,' struck him amid ships. Michelle wept openly as Quill stated the painful truth she wanted buried for her daughter's sake. Perry sat unmoved, his jaws squeezing and relaxing like a frenzied bellows, overworked by an angry blacksmith. Margaret leaned her head against her mother and wept too. David fiddled with his yoyo, and Ginny put her arm around the boy.

The family secret had just become common knowledge. Margaret believed everyone in the mortuary was looking at her, pointing accusing fingers, and wagging their tongues, thinking less of her because of her father's actions. How could Margaret face her friends now? She wished the old man, that horrible little old man, would shut up and go away. But to her chagrin, he kept speaking. "I was there. But you have to know some things first before you will *begin* to understand why, before you judge too quickly, too harshly."

"No matter what happened in Canada, Stephen Lloyd is a hero. Some of you may not know that Mr. Lloyd flew B-24 bombers in the Second World War. He probably never said anything about his experiences to you. He wasn't that kind of man. He was a decorated bomber pilot. His squadron and bomb group flew missions before the friendly fighter protection could take them all the way to their target and back. We hadn't perfected the P-51 Mustang yet, and the Germans fighters shot those huge bombers out of the sky like clay pigeons, by their hundreds. It must have been awful. He watched too many crews and friends go down or disintegrate from flak so thick you could walk on it. He lost crew member after crew member on mission after mission. That in itself makes him and all those like him genuine heroes.

"There is something else none of you know. Stephen was flying a mission in which, apparently, the bombs froze onto whatever holds them in the bomb bay, and they wouldn't release when they were supposed to let go. Well, they finally dropped off at the worst possible moment, when another damaged bomber drifted or limped directly under his airplane. And when those bombs hit the crippled airplane below his, it exploded, killing all on board. They never had a chance. Worst of all, the pilot, navigator, and co-pilot of the plane below his were good friends.

"Let me tell you why Stephen Lloyd is a hero of the greatest kind to me, personally." This little old man Margaret had wished back to Canada, had glued all the pomp and circumstance to their seats, drinking in every word. Margaret, too, listened. "Stephen Lloyd, our friend and my employer, a wonderful man, husband and father, held that incident and probably dozens more inside of him all these years. He didn't want to burden his family. He didn't want to trouble any of you. He didn't want to seem weak, and he wanted to get on with his life. But, I know from painful experience, that war never goes away. It waits. It waits until that right moment and then it strikes. Oh, it gives you clues from time to time that it's still there, but it never goes away, *never*.

"And then one day, something triggered that war of Mr. Lloyd's, and it came alive. If it hadn't been the death of one of their friends, it would have been something else. You have to believe that." Quill looked at James and Mary Ellen Wilson. James acknowledged his words. "And for the first time since that bombing mission he had to confront the men *he believes* he killed. You and I know he didn't mean to kill ten men, but he felt so very responsible for their deaths. And when *his* war finally manifested itself, he had no way to fight back, to keep it repressed any longer. Stephen was one of the most responsible, bravest men I have ever known. And that makes him a hero. He cared deeply for his fellow airmen, and he took their deaths and wounds upon himself. I'm sure he was ashamed. He, as the pilot, was responsible. War places people in unwinnable situations, and they have to live with the consequences.

At the back of the auditorium, a little man, dirty suit and scuffed boots with no polish on them, slipped in all but unnoticed. He had to stand, for there was no place for him to sit. He smelled of smoke and must. He'd come to pay his respects. He began to cough. Several of the better-dressed executives moved away a few feet. Smitty paid them no mind. He nodded his hearty agreement of the eulogy Quill rendered about their common friend, Mr. Stephen Lloyd. Smitty would slip out the back door before the little man up front finished saying the words, his goodbye's already said.

"Most of you here will never know what war does to human beings, and *I am thankful* for that. Some of you do. But if you don't, you can't imagine the situations you have to face that you could not have dreamed up in your wildest or worst nightmares. Men like Stephen Lloyd have gone out and done our dirty work so that we don't have to soil our hands. Too many of us sitting here this evening don't even give a thought to what has to be done everyday to keep the world safe, because we figure someone else will go and do it for us. I've heard some of you talk about how selfish Stephen Lloyd was for leaving his family alone. What a cowardly act his suicide was. Stephen Lloyd and men and women like him are the bravest of the brave. And they go away to war representing us when they, too, would rather stay home and have their careers like so many of you have. But they believed that *your* freedom was more important than their tomorrows were. There are no adequate words to describe such *un*selfishness.

"To my friends, the Lloyds, I can only say I know that none of my words are adequate to convey how truly honored *I am* to be able to tell everyone here that Marcus and Annika, your son, Susan, your husband, and children, your father, was and still is a great man. He was perhaps one of the strongest men I have known in my life, because he kept this tragedy and all his terrible hurts to himself so that you would not have to bear them. They were so terribly heavy. Please never think of Stephen Lloyd in any terms other than great, a man of incredible integrity, but a man whose feet, like those of our own, are made of clay. Thank you for giving me the privilege of letting me say a few words about my friend, Stephen Lloyd. . . Oh, I would like to say one last thing before I sit. I forgot. I am a Christian, and Jesus is my Savior. I have learned from the Bible that despite all the accolades and medals for heroism men accrue in their lifetimes, no matter how much power or prestige we garner over our short years on this planet, none of these things will get us into heaven. If the Lord wills, I will tell you why tomorrow." Quill walked slowly and painfully toward his seat, and Michael met him half way.

Stunned silence reigned. You could have heard a pin drop. It was eerie. No one coughed or stirred. This little man had shoved them backward into their seats. Some, he had made eat dirt. Others, he had given pause to reevaluate. Quill had set the stage, and tomorrow morning, at the Mass, he would set his closing remarks in their proper context.

Fifty-Five: A Second Funeral

Saturday, May 27, 1967

The Church of the Immaculate Conception had squatter's rights since 1904 on Camp Bowie Boulevard not far from downtown Ft. Worth. It was a large old edifice, having seen so much of Ft Worth's history pass in review before its several pointed spires, high above the pavement, pierced upward into the blue. Five buildings had been added over the past half-century. Currently, a new rectory was under construction. The music ebbed and flowed, as the huge main doors had been swung wide to receive those coming to say their final farewell.

The Lloyd's limousine pulled up in front, having come directly from the funeral home for the sealing of the casket. The driver deposited the occupants and drove to the side where he would park until the conclusion of the service. Then they would ride to the cemetery for the committal service. Stephen's service would not be a military affair, even though he, by all rights, should have had one. No one even thought to contact the VFW and start that process as had been done with Damien's service.

Susan had made them late this morning. They should have arrived forty-five minutes earlier at the mortuary, but she was having such difficulty with little things like, which brooch to wear, her hair up or down, was this the best dress, what, would Stephen have wanted her to wear? The previous day's resolve, which wasn't much, had evaporated.

Standing in front of the mirror she studied herself as if through a haze, a sad, lonely, tear-lined woman staring back at her. This cost

Susan Lloyd another ten minutes tardiness. It took everything Annika and Michelle possessed to keep her moving. But each time his name rubbed across her mind, whispering softly so that only she could hear, Susan convulsed and the dressing was halted once more, after which Annika and Michelle would rally her to restart the process. In the final analysis, Susan felt swollen and ugly, and this is not the way in which she wanted Stephen to see her for the last time. The final touch, the veil, thankfully hid her face. Her dress did not adjust well to the contour of her body this morning. It hung limp off of her shoulders. She'd lost weight the past few weeks. She felt slightly anemic. She'd almost forgotten to wear pantyhose. Susan Lloyd was really coming apart, despite Annika, her mother Michelle, and now her daughter's best resolve.

Entering the huge church building, life blurred and then slowed almost to a stop for Quill. It smelled old, traditional, and very unfamiliar. He noted the ornate gold and silver statues to Mary, the Mother of God, as well as other shiny and ornate objects, large and small, scattered around the platform well to his front. There were recesses in the walls in which the ornaments and statues were held. A priest carried the vessel forward from which smoke drifted and evaporated among the attendees. The assembled choir sang in Latin, their voices flowing, rolling, and filling the giant cathedral. It was awe-inspiring, and everything Piney Woods Church in British Canada was not. Quill felt completely out of place among the busy liturgical atmosphere, the altar boys following the priests who were genuflecting like lemmings. Occasional coughs and sneezes, and two crying babies were somewhat lost among the reverent hugeness.

When the Mass finally commenced, it was standing room only. Word had gotten around about the little man from Canada who had spoken so powerfully, if not winsomely about such a wonderful man, Stephen Lloyd. Some had left feeling guilty, even ill at ease, their feathers ruffled. Some believed Quill had attacked them with his talk about them not appreciating Stephen's service. Some thought his words very out of place, quite distasteful, they whispered. However they heard him, and they would now hear him conclude his unfinished remarks. They wanted him to say what *they* wanted him to say. They wanted him to speak kindly things, anything but what might make them uncomfortable. From the various conversations overheard by certain of the Lloyd's children, Ginny Cassalls, and the Wilson's at the wake, too many had heard of Stephen's death second and third hand.

Quill had his work cut out for him from the night before, but he had set the record straight. Sitting there in this basilica, he felt down right awkward. This grand palace was utterly contrary from the place he had come to know his God—Cheslatta Falls. Come to think of it, this cathedral could not compete with the sanctuary where God had manifested Himself to Quill.

Quill *had* honored his friend, and now he would present the solution he had foisted upon these folk. With clarity sufficient for the youngest child, Quill Du Pont would pay what he owed to his Helen. He had been silent far too long. God rest her soul, she had paid with an early death caring for the man she loved so much, and who had given her so little by comparison. It took everything she had to watch over her man who thought more about death and a dying past than making life with her good. This was for Helen, even though Susan became the aspect of his gift to Helen.

Quill stood slowly after Father Ed introduced him. His time and talk at the funeral home the day before *had* worn him out. And he felt it as he stood. His balance felt off, and Michael once again assisted him to the platform and then the lectern. He turned to face that immense sea of faces: men, women, and children. Their cold, anxious, bespectacled, curious, aristocratic, chiseled, non-committal, delicate, pain-seamed, sad, smiling features looked back at him. Several, he thought, looked friendly. The sun glinted off of eyeglasses, streaking in through the lighter colors of the huge stained glass windows. A man below him and to his right coughed. A woman sneezed seven rows back and in the middle, then apologized to those around her. A baby cried, then another tuned up in full-blown competition. Their mother's apologized, stood and pushed past those seated in their pews. Quill waited. He wanted to stop shaking from his own fear and the restlessness of his hearers. He needed the Lord to make it just right. Then he would speak.

When all felt right, as right as a brittle moment such as this can feel, he began. "Mighty big church, Father Ed." Quill heard scattered laughter. "I'm not a public . . . what? Oh, yes. I'll speak up. Sorry. I don't get many opportunities . . . is that okay?" When a few heads nodded in the affirmative from the back, Quill Du Pont trusted that he had, for the moment, found his voice that would declare the only hope he knew. He combed the audience once more until his eyes dragged across and then rested on the face of Susan, which is where he paused. She was staring off into the abyss. Would she even hear him? He couldn't help but be a little bit in love with her. She was so pretty. Helen was there too, sitting beside Susan.

"I wish Stephen Lloyd had stayed longer with us. As I said last afternoon, Stephen Lloyd's death, as unfortunate as it was, was at his own hand. I told you gathered there that despite that particular act, I count him a genuine hero. Stephen Lloyd took to himself the responsibility of the deaths of men over which he had no control. He was a remarkable man, and he will remain one of my dearest friends. I feel guilty for not being more aware of his . . ." Quill paused, all but immersed in the emotion of the moment. "Maybe I could have done or said something different. I don't know. Now I'll never really know.

"Stephen is not the only person who has looked at his past and attempted to rid himself of it. I tried to jump off a cliff not far from where I live in Canada *six* times. I'm the real coward. My guess is that for Stephen, and the war with all its death and destruction seemed to have no real or absolute meaning. So many of us on Bataan and Corregidor thought that our years in captivity were also meaningless. Stephen had asked me if the war, in the final analysis, had any real or lasting purpose. We're currently fighting a war in Southeast Asia. You see it on the nightly news. Men are still dying. Evil men are still stepping on good men. Maybe you have gone through some terrible event and you too are wondering if it had any significance, that it was senseless. And if you can't locate any logical reason behind it, maybe you too have lost your way. I have known that feeling.

"In 1942, so many of us had become prisoners of the most brutal people on earth, the Imperial Japanese. I learned quickly to hate these people. I held Roosevelt and MacArthur responsible for running out on us when we needed them the most. Just the thought of a Jap or FDR made my blood boil." Quill next told the congregation the story of 'Ole One Eye.' Susan quit staring 'out there' and was now listening. She was not necessarily lost to Quill, who seemed quite animated in his declaration of his purpose in life. When the old man spoke of the Death March, of the camps and the murder he committed, he began to cry. Public speaking and hard memories many times sabotage the best of speakers. All of those faces—the good ones and the hated—passing in front of Quill Du Pont, each with its own memories. The one blended into the other.

"Well, as I recall, it was a Sunday night in 1947. I had finally given in to my wife's begging me to go to church with her to hear this preacher that had been coming around our house to visit. Reverend Franklin fought in France in the First World War. I realize now that he was well aware of what I was going through. As Pastor Franklin preached on forgiveness that night two things happened to me. I became aware for the first time in my life that I was a sinner. When I say sinner, I don't mean like you fib once in a while or you make a mistake. I mean I suddenly knew that I was a vile, wretched lawbreaker, not just because I had killed Ole One Eye, my enemy. I cussed. I told filthy jokes and had unclean thoughts, such as hate. The Bible says that if we even so much as hate our brother, we are murderers in God's sight. I lusted and I committed adultery when I was in the Philippines. I stole supplies from the supply tent and so many other things, I'm embarrassed to say. That's what the Bible means when it says I was a sinner. I knew that hell awaited me and all those who break God's holy law. I knew that if I died right then I would go to hell forever under the just condemnation of God . . . and the prospect of that destination terrified me.

"The pastor said that I had to trust Jesus *alone* to save me, that no other person in heaven or on earth was given among men by which we must be saved, other than Jesus. Now up to that point, I had always believed if you served your country you would automatically go to heaven when you die, which, by the way, is *not* in the Bible. Everything I had believed up to that point about God and eternal things began to crumble.

"The second thing that happened to me wasn't so good either. I suddenly realized the implications of murdering a man who had done me no harm at all, the little Jap, Ole One Eye. You have to understand that in my thinking up to that point in my life, I could only think of Ole One Eye as my enemy. I think that God brought that to my memory when the Jap drew that cross in the dirt, he was telling me he was a Christian, and being an American, he naturally assumed I was, too. To make it worse, I think God had sent him to me to help keep me alive somehow. I felt as if I was sitting there on death row listening to

Pastor Franklin that night. I knew beyond the shadow of a doubt that I wasn't a Christian when I was floating in the ocean half dead, or as I sat in that church that night. I felt so guilty, I wanted to die.

"About a week later and thoroughly miserable, I started reading my wife's Bible. And the more I read it, the more it became painfully and gloriously clear to me that God delights to place the brilliant light of His saving grace against the back drop of our rebellion, our wretchedness, even the worst events we go through. I killed a defenseless man who only wanted to help me. I cheated on my wife and I still hated the Japanese for what they had done to me and so many men like me. God's grace was blinding yet winsome amid that blackness of my actions and memories.

"You know what I've discovered? Without the war, I might not have believed in Christ that day out in the pasture. I don't know. But whether I ever discover that truth completely or not, I praise and thank God for taking me through every moment of my imprisonment. No, I don't want to *ever* go through that again. But my time in the furnace of prison and captivity, if you will, began the melting process of my resistance to His free offer of grace in the Gospel, and that is just part of the overall meaning of those forty-two months of hell. Those days will never mean less, and, as I've gotten older, they only mean more."

To Susan, Quill looked like a small angel standing so high above her. He glowed. His words came to her as light personified tugging powerfully at her heart, which she realized was void of what mattered. She wanted what he had even though she'd heard him say these very things at the cabin. But she hadn't *heard* them until right then.

Quill continued. "In the Bible, Luke tells us that the Apostle Paul had put many Christian Jews in prison, men, women, the elderly, and even children, to have them beaten and killed, because they had trusted in Jesus' perfect obedient life and atoning death. You see, Paul was a murderer, too, like me. At one time he bragged about his being a Hebrew of Hebrews and a Pharisee of Pharisees. He had a violent zeal for the Law and his religion like some of us do here today. Paul believed that his zeal for God and Israel would win him God's approval.

"It was on his way to Damascus to do more of the same to the Christians there, when God knocked Paul off of his horse and shone His bright, blinding light down on him. Down on the ground and blinded, Paul heard God speak to him. In the dust and dirt, Jesus revealed His holy character to this Jew, Paul's lifelong transgressions and God's matchless saving grace to a great sinner like the Apostle Paul. He can do it for you, too.

"You see, the only work that God will accept is absolute perfection. Jesus said that you must be perfect like your heavenly Father is perfect. If we're honest, God has presented us with a humanly unsolvable problem. Only Jesus, whose character is perfect, can do perfectly all that God requires. The Apostle Paul wrote that there is no man righteous in God's sight, no, not one, and who is righteous like Jesus that can make atonement for our sin and guilt?

"After Jesus fed the five thousand and told the multitudes that He would not be their political king, He walked on water when a storm arose, which terrified His disciples. Well, all those hungry folks came looking for Jesus again the next day. So He stopped and spoke to them. He said they were looking for Him for another handout. So He told them not to work for the food which perishes, but for food that endures to eternal life, which the Son of Man would give to them, because the Father had set His seal on Jesus. So they asked Him, 'What shall we do to do the works of God?' Jesus didn't mince any words, 'This is the work of God, that you *believe* in Him whom God sent.'"

"So what does it mean to believe on Him whom sent Jesus? It means that salvation is not by *any* human works of righteousness, which we have done, but solely by *His* works and *His* mercy, by those only, *He is able to save us*. Paul told the Galatian church, 'knowing that a man is not saved by the works of law; for by the works of law no flesh shall be justified.' Moses wrote, 'and Abraham believed in the LORD, and it—his belief—was accounted to him for righteousness.' That is why last night I said that all the medals for valor a man could win in war will not put him one inch inside heaven. Not by any works *you and I* ever do can we win God's favor. In our church we have some traditions, you know, rules that someone made up along the way. Some of those traditions have become almost equal to God's law over the years. But, not even keeping church traditions will save us, no matter how good they seem. Besides, no one here is able to keep God's law or the church's traditions perfectly, anyway. Right?

"What do you think is the cruelest, most unfair thing that ever happened in all of human history? The crucifixion of God's *sinless* Son. And yet, Isaiah says that *God* was *pleased* to crush His one and only Son for sinners like you and me. Jesus, of all people, didn't deserve to die for the likes of me. Yet He chose to. He was tempted to iniquity in all points like I have been and you have been; yet He did not sin. The writer of Hebrews assures us that it is appointed for man to die *once*, only once, and after that comes judgment. There are no second chances after death, the Scripture says.

"To this day, even as a Christian, I spend too many hours and days depressed or angry because of what I suffered on Bataan. I made my wife Helen miserable because I was so miserable. My children don't want to visit me because I was so hard on them. That makes me angry, which can lead to severe depression. Then I become very sad. I thank God that after a while the sadness and pressure lets up. Jesus could take it all away if He wanted to. But He has chosen me to suffer with these symptoms for His name's sake. He knows why the pain of Bataan still lingers in me. Paul said he gloried in his *physical weaknesses* so that the *power* of Christ might be displayed in him. It hurts my pride when I realize that I am weak in so many ways. But it causes me to trust God more for His gracious strength to go one more day.

"Believe it or not, I used to play tackle for the University of Montana." There was a stirring at that comment. Quill was a small, shriveled up old man by now. His hands were broken, and he leaned on a cane to walk. "I used to love to be able to knock men my size and bigger down and then step on them. I loved football—hitting people and all. But for Bataan, but for forty-two months in captivity, but for diseases I didn't know existed that racked my body until I hoped for death, but for hunger that made me eat rats and bugs and worms ravenously, but for thirst that made me drop into stagnant pools of malaria infested water just to wet my tongue, but for the beatings so severe I couldn't stand up, my ribs were broken, and I could only breathe in short breaths, but for the pain that was excruciating, but for the loss of hope. Paul said he did not count any of his trials in this life worthy to be compared to the glory that is to be revealed one day, but that glory is only for those who repent and believe the Gospel.

"I will finish with this. I am angered at people who say that God had nothing to do with Bataan; that there was no purpose to it. To say such a thing removes any hope that my time of trial had real meaning or was in the least significant. The Bible declares that God is everywhere present at all times, and He is all-wise. If God is not intimately involved as a cosmic King in the good and bad that He has decreed for us to pass through, then Bataan had no meaning, and I am right to give up. But my past, present, and future Savior and King, Jesus Christ, was there with me during those dark days, because He eternally chose me to inherit salvation in 1947, and He is with me now. That is why my life has so much meaning, and the reason I can stand before you today. May God be praised. Amen."

Quill stopped, leaving his words to echo off the rafters. Tears pooled at the bottom of his eyes, and he pulled at his hankie to wipe his nose. He had nothing left to give. This had been for Helen, and she was here. He'd paid everything he could pay her, and it was done. He slowly gathered himself. His body ached from standing too long, and he motioned for Michael to come get him so that he might leave the stage.

Father McTammany was in tears. He'd been captivated by this 'homily.' Mr. Du Pont wasn't after all a trained theologian like himself. Father Ed had told people that God had nothing to do with their pain in any way, and in so doing, the priest had stripped their suffering of its meaning.

The committal service following was anti-climactic. Prayers were said for the dead husband and father. Bible verses read. The crowd filed by one last time. They said the things that are always expressed and mean so little, and can't be remembered until long after, if at all. Susan slumped in her seat looking through or past them. She heard only a portion of their sentiments, usually the last half of any sentence, bits and snatches of phrases. She smiled dutifully. She shook hands dutifully. She was dutiful.

The ride back to her home without Stephen lacked any real substance. She hung suspended over herself. Susan heard voices close by or next to her. Despite their proximity they made no sense. Theirs were words that came at her as incoherent things. She couldn't remember the meal that followed the service. She hated the ever-present people who wouldn't go home and leave her alone. Why were they there? What did they want?

Fifty-Six: Saying Goodbye

><⊷⊶⊙⊶⊷<

Friday, June 2, 1967

Susan awoke with a start. She felt for her husband and then remembered blearily why he wasn't lying next to her. She sensed something much deeper than her husband's absence. Something else was wrong, but Susan had no idea what. *What's wrong, Susan? I don't know. Something's wrong. I can feel it.* Panic over the unknown registered in her mind, and she shook for a few nervous minutes. It took two torturous hours before Susan could sleep again.

At 8:17, the sunlight cut through her window, in between the half drawn curtains, driving the heat of the summer and its glare into her consciousness. Gradually, Susan gained sufficient awareness to begin the process of recognizing the various familiar aspects of their bedroom: chairs, dressers, pictures, a bed made for two but occupied by one. She blinked and rolled over to stare at the ceiling. As Stephen faded from her thoughts Quill came to her mind. Then Stephen passed through her mental faculties again, and she felt her sadness return. It had been two long, dry, barren days since the funeral. Quill had left yesterday. Her daddy had driven him to the airport. Quill looked as if he was glad to return home. She heard the padding of David's feet and his ten-year-old accusatorial tones scream past her closed door, "Michael, you give me that back! Michael!" Brit added his two cents worth. *Time to get up, Susan.*

Monday, June 5, 1967

The ride to the church with its adjoining cemetery was one of quiet desperation for Susan and her two children, Michael and Margaret. The clouds promised rain; still she hoped they might abort their threat. It was cool and she wrapped the shawl around her shoulders. *I wish I'd brought a light coat. I should have remembered.* She leaned upon Michael, if only figuratively, drawing upon his ascending manhood. Margaret had come because she wanted to see . . . the place. Stephen was not there any longer to tell Susan what to do.

Nearing the cemetery, adjacent to the church—Piney Woods Church—they noticed one pickup in the gravel parking lot. It was still early, twenty-five minutes to eleven. As they pulled into the lot, a dog poked his head up from the bed of the pickup and barked. He was a large, burly mongrel of some sort, ugly brown with matted hair, the type you'd see around cattle. As the Lloyd's rental car neared the pickup, the mutt began to growl menacingly, revealing his sharp set of teeth. Michael slowed the car, deciding to park about twenty feet away from the pickup. With the possibility of intruders on the new claimed area, the dog spoke his warning. Real fear crept into the Lloyd's vehicle. "Should we get out?" Susan asked. Michael's door opened toward nearest the pickup, and the dog.

"Now *that's* a dog," Michael interjected. The dog ratcheted his warning up several levels.

"Shut up, Hank!" A voice from inside the pickup sounded just as menacing. "Shut up, you old hound!" A large man opened his side of the truck, and repeated the command, "I said, shut up, Hank!" At that, Hank's tail began to wag for all he was worth. He tucked his teeth back into his snout. Suddenly, he couldn't wait for the strangers to pet him. "He's really a friendly dog, folks. You must be the Lloyd's?" the man asked.

"Yes, that's right. This is Margaret and Michael, my children. I'm Susan."

"Hi. I'm Pete Worrells. Pleased to meet you folks. I'm a deacon here. Since we ain't got no pastor, I guess I'm elected for this morning. None of the other preachers around here was available today. Other commitments, I guess. So, if'n it'd be ok with you, I'll say some words over Quill, like I told you folks over the phone. I sure would like for you, Mrs. Lloyd, to say somethin,' too. That okay?"

Pete Worrells owned about three hundred acres. His spread began about ten miles north of the church. He raised Herefords like the ones on the Lloyd place, but quite a number less. Pete was in his late fifties, already balding. To the funeral, he wore an out of date gray suit—probably his best one—a bolero tie; his white shirt had a small stain on it. He was missing several teeth from being kicked by calves. A long, jagged scar ran down from his bottom lip, the result of his last one-sided encounter with a piece of farm machinery. His face was a leathery red from exposure to the Canadian elements. His eyes were sharp though, and his left hand missed only one finger.

He was a soft-spoken man, except when it came to Hank, the dog. Pete was married, six kids. It was just easier to come alone. Besides, Hank minded better.

"Hank, you stay in the truck." Pete and the Lloyds headed for the fenced in cemetery. Hank circled the bed, finally sat, and leaned his head over the side, his tongue hanging out as he panted.

Piney Woods Church, an interdenominational affair, was founded in 1798, the same year as the North West Company, later called the XY Company. Piney Woods had long since seen its greatest days. Maximum occupancy was a hundred four, reached in 1905, the year of the great Welsh revival and the Russo-Japanese War in Manchuria and Korea. The church needed a good coat of paint, and several boards were rotted down near the grass. It had no air conditioning; didn't need any. The wood-burning stove worked like a champ. It had a steeple with its bell connected to a rope, the usual stained glass windows, red and blue glass with angels and a Bible cut into them, the Lord's hands held together, and three body draped crosses. Inside, it had an organ, but the organist, Mrs. Jane Dally, had died five years ago. Mr. Dally didn't know how to play it, and he had been dead three years now. The dwindling congregation, now totaling sixteen, unless there was sickness, was left to sing a cappella. Services were held every quarter for the last several years, unless one of the nearby pastors could manage to visit. Any denomination would do these days.

The cemetery covered about a half-acre. One hundred ninety-seven people were buried here. Now it was one hundred ninety-eight. A huge pine tree had grown in the southwest corner. One section of fence was about to fall, and the whole sanctified enterprise was in desperate need of paint, even more so than the building. It was so difficult for these ranchers and the few that remained, mostly older folks, to take the time to see to the needed repairs. Pete kept his boys too busy, but he was expected to send them soon.

Many of the grave markers were now illegible. The oldest readable dates were Henry and Mary Pastors. Henry died Dec. 21, 1837, and she in May of the following year. He died of tuberculosis. No reason was given for her death. Their markers read, "Henry, born Feb. 12, 1788, God rest his soul," and then, "Mary, born June 23, 1795, Beloved wife of Henry."

Pete pointed the way to the freshly dug grave. Quill's casket rested on the ground next to Helen's plot. Outside the fence, a backhoe sat, its operator sitting in his truck smoking a cigarette, waiting. Pete waved and the man waved back. Another truck pulled up next to Pete's pickup. A man and a woman got out. The man patted a wagging Hank.

Beverly and Jude Smith approached the small party and the site of the burial. They, too, were an elderly couple. Beverly was heavy with age, but possessed a wonderful smile. The years had not been kind to her physically as she walked slightly bent over and her hip hurt. She wore an old dress, but it was her Sunday best. She had her well-worn Bible tucked under her right arm. Her hair was almost purple. Jude was a huge man, his best years, too, were in the distant past. His hands, thick and calloused, were large like his frame. He wore an old ball cap and his Sunday overalls. His boots were covered with various crusted debris, having seen their last polish the day he bought them. His face, too, was red and lined, leathery to a fault. When he removed his cap, his skin where the cap covered his forehead was almost white. He, too, missed a tooth, but his grin was warm and his handshake firm. His eyes were the softest blue Susan had ever seen. Their kids were all grown and gone.

An old black Lincoln, partially rust covered, next drove into the lot. Six more people exited and slammed the doors one after the other, two adults and four children. Edna and Wallace Freeburg led their four children, Sally twelve years old, Billy-ten, Carry-eight, and May-six. Each Freeburg walked or skipped up to the waiting assembly. Edna, too, was a plump woman. Wallace weighed half the amount his wife did. She was the disciplinarian of the family. As Susan took her hand, she bellowed in an unmistakable foghorn: "Billy, you let that dog go and get over here, now! Wallace, I told you not to let him out of your sight. Billy! Sorry folks. I gotta stay on these young 'uns.'"

Billy looked up—no surprise on his face—gave the dog something from his pocket, which the dog ate hungrily, and the boy scurried over to join his family. The Freeburg's introduced themselves, one after the other as they had been taught, each extending a hand to the three Lloyd's, who looked totally out of place amid these simple, but friendly country folk.

All sixteen congregants were present. Pete began the short service with a prayer. When he finished, Michael, Margaret and Susan crossed themselves in unison to the collective stare of the group. The locals were all thinking the same thing, 'Catholics.' Then Pete spoke, "Well, folks. Quill was the last Elder we had. He was a good man, and a Christian man, too. Five years ago we buried Helen. His kids ain't contacted me, so I guess I better read some from the Scriptures. It was his favorite set of verses, as I recollect. I'll be reading from Romans, chapter nine, verses six through sixteen and verses twenty and twenty-one. Pete cleared his throat.

They all spoke with that distinct Canadian shading that flavored their words and that, too, separated them from the Lloyd's southwestern introjections. "Not as though the word of God hath taken none effect. For they are not all Israel, which are Israel. Neither because they are the seed of Abraham, are they all children: but, in Isaac shall thy seed be called. That is, they which are the children of the flesh, these are not the children of God; but the children of the promise are counted for the seed. For this is the word of promise, at this time will I come, and Sara shall have a son. And not only this; but when Rebecca also had conceived by one, even by our father Isaac; (for the children being not yet born, neither having done any good or evil, that the purpose of God according to election might stand, not of works, but of him that calleth;). It was said unto her, the elder shall serve the younger. As it is written, Jacob have I loved, but Esau have I hated. What shall we say then? Is there unrighteousness with God? God forbid. For he saith to Moses, I will have mercy on whom I will have mercy, and I will have compassion on who I have compassion. So then it is not of him that willeth, nor of him that runneth, but of God that shewith mercy."

"Now verses twenty-two through twenty-four. 'What if God, willing to shew his wrath, and to make his power known, endured with much longsuffering the vessels of wrath fitted to destruction: And that he might make known the riches of his glory on the vessels of mercy, which he had afore prepared unto glory, Even us, whom he hath called, not of the Jews only, but also of the Gentiles?' Amen. May God bless His word."

Susan's mind drifted between what Quill had said in church and these verses. Certain aspects of it were beginning to take a form of cohesion. There hadn't been sufficient time yet for Susan to pull it all together. Her grief was still too raw, and Quill had died so inconveniently and too soon after she'd buried her husband. Two deaths had taken place in such terrible succession.

The small congregation surrounding Pete said, "Amen," in unison. Michael was thankful that the Freeburg's kids stood still long enough for his mother to say what she came all this distance to say. Public speaking had been his father's forte. Susan hung onto her son's arm for support. She looked so thoroughly out of place among these women. The years had proven so kind to her physically, but not so, Edna and Beverly. There were few women from which she did not stand apart. Entering a room, she would draw the air from the men. The women in the room many times literally grabbed their husbands, because they consciously stared at Susan, enmeshed in her beauty.

The gray clouds scudded past. Susan noticed that little detracted from these women's souls. Something in their eyes spoke of a kindness that Susan didn't possess in the remotest part of her being. They had both seen their share of hardship and sadness living in this wilderness separated from each other. But despite every line on their weathered faces, a joy or something distinct emanated from them. Susan was certain that Edna and Bev had their days, days that would turn any ordinary woman into a raving lunatic: long winters, hours in the kitchen unable to get outside, children always underfoot, and so forth. There was still something about Edna and Beverly. They had *something* that Susan did not.

Pete now asked Susan to say her words, and that would conclude the funeral. She bit her lip, her hesitancy palpable. This small crowd with their close informality reassured her. Margaret took her mother's other hand, and Susan looked down on her daughter, smiling up into her face. Unspoken words were exchanged.

To Susan's right, Wallace broke in upon her diffidence. "Mrs. Lloyd, it's okay. We know what you feel. It'll be okay. Go on ahead. Say the words. Quill would appreciate it." They all knew about the Lloyds, the hotels, and the vacations here for the men and their influential clients. But they didn't know, couldn't possibly know about what Stephen had been grappling with for the past several months. Stephen's death and how it occurred had been dinner table fare for several weeks around these parts.

Susan started to speak, but held her piece. Once more she attempted to say something, but halted. Susan was rarely this indecisive. Michael squeezed her arm and whispered in her ear. "Mother, it's okay. Quill would want to hear from you. It's okay. We're right here. We won't leave you."

She coughed. She was obviously fighting the tears that had suddenly begun to interfere with her practiced little speech. "I, uh, this was easier this morning," she said, managing a thin smile, which added to her own discomfort. Edna and Bev felt for her, Bev's head bobbed slightly as if trying to help Mrs. Lloyd by coaxing the words out. "Quill . . . um, Quill, well, I've known Quill for only a short time. But as Stephen and I spent hours listening to him this spring, I realized that he possessed an assurance of heaven and God that I didn't. Quill had been through so much in his life, so much pain, so much suffering, but he knew Jesus in ways that I frankly didn't understand and realize was possible. I thought I had faith. I thought I knew what faith was until I heard Quill talk about his. And I can see it in you all as well. Don't ask me how. But it's there. When he talked to me about God's love for him I knew that what he believed was more than blind hope, more than a trust that you hope is real. I'm repeating myself, I know. He kept talking about what God had done for him. All I've ever known is what I have to do for God. Quill rested in God's work on his behalf. I know now that I haven't, and I have some doubts about what I have believed all my life." Michael and Margaret both looked at their mother, surprised at her words. "I don't know if that is good or bad. Quill, too, questioned what he'd been taught. I hope I can at least ask some specific questions now. I realize that when my friend, Quill, talked about his faith, he always quoted or paraphrased the Bible. And when he did, he came alive. I may never be the same because of him.

"He went through horrible things as a prisoner of war, things that I can't possibly imagine, things that would have made most men very bitter. But he wasn't bitter. He said Jesus took all his bitterness from him. He thanked God for those trials. But, I could tell that, even though the past still hurt him, his faith in God was very real. I'm still struggling over my own loss . . . days when I'm angry, feel sorry for myself, sad . . ."

Susan's voice disappeared in the wind. She hadn't been speaking to anyone in particular the past few moments except herself. "Maybe soon I can embrace the things he believed." Susan suddenly felt Margaret and Michael's grip on her hands tighten. She stopped and surveyed her son's face. As she looked at her son and then at her daughter, she said, "Maybe we all can." Resuming her thought, "I shall miss him . . . very much."

Susan's honesty, about her lack of faith and the struggles staring back at her, rippled downward into her family. Margaret seemed the most affected; she felt life the most. So much about her was blossoming into womanhood at the very time when she needed stability. Such familial immutability was not to be. Her father's death, her brother leaving for the military to die like Damien, and now her mother's search for her own faith interfered with Margaret's native and comfortable belief system. It furrowed a line through the safety net that her parents and grandparents had weaved so meticulously for her. A tear tracked down her right cheek, which she let fall the full height of her body. Margaret tore away from the gathering and ran to the security of the car.

Strawberry blonde Carrie, all eight years of her, tugged on her mother's dress. She attempted a whispered message, "Mamma, she was crying. What's wrong with her, mamma? Why'd she run off?" Told to hush, Carrie turned a bright red when several adults stared down at her. Susan smiled, apologized for her daughter, explaining that Margaret had gone through so much lately. It was hard on her, being so young. It was difficult on them all. Everyone present understood.

Pete said a closing prayer that he'd practiced, had it written on a yellowed three x five card, and this concluded the funeral. Pete, Edna and Wallace, Beverly and Jude each shook hands with the two remaining Lloyds. They told Susan not to worry about Margaret's running off, and thanked Susan for her kind words, saying how Quill would have blushed at the fuss. Edna was soon yelling at Billy for getting his clean clothes dirty petting that dog. Billy stood in the back of Pete's truck getting Hank excited and collecting every bit of dirt and grease from the stray shingles, a rusted water pipe, some mashed chicken wire, and the Lord only knew what else Pete had collected over the years in the bed of his pickup. Susan felt the tug on her shawl. It was Carrie. "I'm sorry, ma'am. Your girl gonna be okay?" But before Susan could bend to Carrie's attenuated height, the strawberry blonde tomboy skipped away toward her mother, fully occupied in gathering her chicks into the open car door. As suddenly as they had appeared, they were all gone in a cloud of dust. Chores awaited. The wind in the top of the lone pine swirled leaving the Lloyds with a gnawing loneliness. The man on the backhoe started his machine, and in another minute, lowered the casket into the hole by several nylon straps.

"You did fine, Mother. I'm proud of you." Susan could see that Michael wanted to talk about what his mother was searching for so earnestly. Margaret sat in the back seat, her hands covering her face, sobbing. She was so young to experience these things. Susan felt her maternal instincts go into overdrive observing her daughter suffering so. Michael had his own questions and emotions to handle. Susan, although so preoccupied with her own grieving processes, had begun to notice that Michael had cried very little over the past days. This too drew a cloud over her soul. Michael was repressing this, wasn't he? *Yes*. She couldn't let that happen.

The three headed back to the cabin to pack and say goodbye to Jacques and Raymond. The chef had been kind enough to take Michael fishing, while the two women wandered about the place. Finally, when Margaret could stand it no longer, she demanded to see the place where her father died.

The lunch could not have been more wonderful. Margaret didn't eat a bite, but ran to her room to escape, as much as possible, before she was forced to face this horribly cruel world again. The airplane would probably crash. She'd live through it and be left with David to care for. Life stunk.

"Mother?" Michael asked as they pulled out onto the road leading to Vanderhoof and the 6:15 flight from Prince George to Vancouver.

"Yes? What are you thinking, Michael?"

"Mother, what is it exactly that you're searching for? We go to church. We've found God, haven't we?"

Susan let a full minute pass before she responded. "Michael, to ask the question, is to answer it."

"But I'm leaving for the Marines in a few weeks," he interjected. "I think you need to tell me what you believe Mr. Du Pont had that you don't."

Epilogue

A number of years ago, I went to an event where many different book authors were present with the books they had written. This event was as much for aspiring writers as it was for the general public who consumed these reading materials. I spoke with several writers about their works, discussed the book I was writing, asked for information about what to do or not do, how to get published, things of that nature. One of those authors asked me who my hero was?

That caused my mental "wheels" to spin. Who was my hero? Who stood out more than any other person? I was stumped. I had written hundreds of pages about the effects of PTSD, about family members, various places, not once considering who the principle character was.

On the drive home, the "whisper" I heard in my ear was—Jesus. Everything about this novel changed at that moment. Christ Jesus, more than any other person I'd written about held the place of honor. Whether I realized it or not, He had orchestrated not only the writing of the book, but all the details of my own life, my military service, too many jobs to count, my marriage and children as well. The truth is it is not by accident you have read or are holding this novel in your hand, not in the slightest. Yes, the Lord did have you pick this book up and look at it. He has already determined the next minutes as well.

I have shared the Gospel within the pages of this book. You know everything you need to know about how to be saved from the coming wrath of God. For those of you who refuse to believe, nothing I can say will make any difference now. But for those of you who are starting to ask the important questions, all you need do is to pray the prayer of the tax collector, "God, be merciful to me, the sinner!"

Acts 2:21 'AND IT SHALL BE THAT EVERYONE WHO CALLS ON THE NAME OF THE LORD WILL BE SAVED.'

Semper fi.

I wish to thank Pastor Van Lees and the congregation of Covenant of Grace church for accepting me and the bad days I brought into their settled midst. The persons and events portrayed in this book are fictitious. Any resemblance to anyone either dead or alive is purely coincidental.

Acknowledgments

On these pages you will discover the people who made the historical, technical, and medical aspects of this work possible. Each person listed below has added his or her, or some related person's life and experiences to my own database of information, which I have attempted to share with you in a readable and true form. If I have missed something, I apologize. I prefer to list these individuals in alphabetical order. I hope I have not left anyone out. Please forgive me if you should be on this list, but aren't.

Dr. Robert Andersen. Dr. Andersen was my doctor at the V. A. mental health department at Jefferson Barracks, St. Louis, MO. He has encouraged me to keep writing and given me loads of information on various diseases as well as psychiatric information about PTSD. Doc has written one book on adoption, *A Bridge Less Traveled*, and, *Second Choice, Growing Up Adopted,* both from Badger Hill Press. Thanks Doc.

Ann Bailey. Miss Ann. I love this woman. She's a Christian and loves the Lord, a real character, and a recovering alcoholic. My wife, not me, gave her a copy of my original novel to read. Well, she was ready to send it to the New York Best Seller list. I was content to keep it on my bookshelf where, I was convinced, it belonged. Miss Ann kept pestering me to let her do something with it. Finally, I gave it to her and here we are . . . again. Thank you, Miss Ann.

Jeff Bodenweiser. Jeff was my platoon Commander during the siege. Jeff was a Mustanger. Our mortar squad dropped a round right behind him when we were practicing our defensive fire procedures at Phu Bai in preparation for Khe Sanh. Fortunately for Jeff *and our squad*, the round was a dud. Jeff was awarded the Silver Star for bravery during the siege of Khe Sanh when we were overrun. He helped me with several technical issues. Jeff died several years ago. Thank you, Jeff.

Earle Breeding. Earle was the CO of Echo Company, 2nd Battalion, 26th Marine Regiment, during the siege of Khe Sanh. He answered numerous technical questions about the Corps. I've enjoyed getting to know Earle at the reunions. He was eight feet tall and breathed fire as my "boss" at Khe Sanh. It is really strange calling these two men, mentioned here by their first names. Both Jeff and Earle were enlisted Marines before I knew them. They knew what it was like to be low man on the food chain. Semper fi, Gentlemen. Earle died recently. Thanks Skipper.

Heather Elizabeth Edwards-Bruce. Heather was 1993's Miss Grand Prairie, 1994 Miss Cross Timbers Area, 1995 Miss Grapevine, 1996 Miss Burleson, 1997 Miss Crowley, 1998 Miss Gulf Coast, 1999 Miss Collin County, and ultimately first runner-up in that year's Miss Texas contest. Heather's insight was quite useful to the writing of this book. She is now married and has a daughter. Thanks Heather.

Bill Chase. I discovered Bill on a B-24 web site. His father, Robert G. Chase, was a S/Sgt assigned to the 455th Bomb Group, 742nd Bomb Squadron, of the 15th Air Force flying out of San Giovanni, Italy. Bill sent me a copy of his father's diary of many of the missions on which he flew, with notes to remind him what happened on those missions. He flew in ship no. 482 called "Fubar." Thanks for your help, Bill.

Josef and Elizabeth Doerig, owners of Nechako Lodge and Aviation. I wrote to them seeking information on that part of Canada, and Elizabeth couldn't help me enough. You can contact them on the web at Nechako Lodge or call toll free 1-877-560-0875. They live in a beautiful part of British Columbia, Canada. They have everything you need for an unforgettable adventure or vacation. Thanks much.

Seymour Gaynes. I met Seymour on a B-24 web site as well. Seymour was a navigator with the 455th Bomb Group. He was kind enough to answer my questions and he took the time to write some of his experiences down for me. He also sent me a copy of all the missions he flew, the aircraft number, flying time, sorties, and bomb loads. Thanks.

Kim Golden. Kim lived next door to us. She has had several miscarriages. It is from this wonderful lady that I was able to glean information about that troubling aspect of a woman's life. She and her husband have three great boys. I had hopes of becoming Josh's agent when he is drafted in the NFL. Kim was also kind enough to share her religious experiences with me. Thank you, Kim.

Bob Hayes. I also found Bob on a B-24 site. He too contributed to my growing wealth of information about life aboard those incredible airplanes. He was machine gunner on a B-24. Many thanks.

Dr. Van Lees. Van is my pastor, colleague, and a very good friend. We both graduated from Covenant Seminary at different times together. Dr. Dr. Van (Van has a D.Min and Ph.D, hence Dr. Dr.) helped me with the theological issues in the book. He practices the saxophone at least two hours a day. I hope to be his son's agent when Paul wins the Van Cliburn piano competition at age fifteen! He is now a masters student at the University of North Texas. Van too has had a lot to do with writing this book. He was a Historical Theology major at the Univ. of Texas, Austin. I have gone with Van to Donetsk, Ukraine, to teach Biblical Theology and other courses since 2013. I sometimes filled the pulpit for him when he went over the duck pond.

Ret Martin. Ret was a great encouragement to me during the early stages of this writing process. Ret made numerous suggestions to this work that have proven invaluable.

Reg Martin. Reg is Ret's father and my second dad. He's had as much to do with my being somewhat sane and having a book with my name on it as anyone has. There were some deep, dark holes he helped me climb out of during seminary and the years following. He is one of the godliest men I have ever met.

Larry McCartney. Larry retired as a Master Gunnery Sergeant of the Marine Corps a number of years ago. I met Larry in Vietnam, a PFC like myself when he joined Echo Company a week or two after I did. We humped the bush together, griped together on those all night, cold, and rain soaked ambushes around Phu Bai, and we survived the siege together. Larry also survived LZ Margo and hopes to have a book out about that disaster in a few years. Larry too answered a lot of technical questions for me. If he didn't know or couldn't remember something, he found it out. Semper fi, buddy.

Jim Nangle. Jim was the A-gunner on the 60 mortar when I was a lowly ammo humper. Jim helped me survive that ordeal on hill 861 Alpha during the siege. When I first met Jim, I noticed he talked funny.

That was because he was from Philadelphia, "Phiwwy," as he called it. Jim was wounded on the hand. I remember hearing that small piece of shrapnel flying through the air and catch him unawares while we were being overrun. Jim could still remember the technical nomenclature for the mortar. Outstanding, Marine!

Kathy & Tom Pellegren. I sent out a request on several B-24 web sites for information about pilots who flew the B-24, and his wife Kathy very kindly answered me. She sent me a copy of the interview she conducted with her father, Denzil Hukill, a pilot with the 49th Wing, 484th Bomb Group, 827th Bomb Squadron of the 15th Air Force, shortly before his death. Tom, her husband, shared a few anecdotes about Denzil with me.

Thomas L. Reilly. I met Thom at a Vietnam Veterans of America conference in St. Louis, where he was marketing his first book, *Next of Kin,* Brassey's, Inc. He gave me a copy and shared his experiences about writing and getting published for which I am most grateful.

Lourie Stahlschmidt. Lourie and her husband, Steve, are members of Covenant of Grace church, and were members of my Sunday school class when we lived in O'Fallon, MO. Lourie has been invaluable in helping me use the right words, put a comma here, a semi-colon there, etc. She's disgustingly happy in the morning when I have called her for help on this or that. Thank you, Miss Lourie.

Vahl Vladyka. I also met Vahl on one of the B-24 sites. He was a B-24 pilot, serving with the 49th Bomb Wing, 461st Bomb Group, 765th Bomb Squadron of the Fifteenth Air Force. Vahl gave me unfettered access to his past. What a great memory. He just opened his war chest and let me take all the time I needed—over the Internet. More than anything else, I want to say thank you to all those incredibly brave men who flew through that horrible flak and those fighters and somehow kept the bomb groups headed for the target. We are the free, because of what men like them did. Thank you and Semper fi.

Connie Wilkinson & Debbie Johnson. Maybe I saved the best for last. Connie died not long ago. She was an avid reader, several novels a week! She served with the Red Cross and was a welder, working on the Liberty ships back during the 'big one'. I conferred with her on some medical issues and both Connie and Debbie, Connie's daughter, read my manuscript for readability. Thanks ladies. Embellish, Embellish. Connie has since died. A great lady.

About the Author

Jim Carmichael, a Marine Corps veteran, served a 13 month combat tour in South Vietnam in 1967-68. He is a survivor of the 1968 Vietnamese Tet Offensive, spending 77 days on the hills surrounding the combat base at Khe Sanh. In 1997, he was diagnosed with delayed Post Traumatic Stress Disorder (PTSD).

A Long Healing Come Slowly is Jim's first historical fiction novel about a family living with a veteran who has PTSD. He intends to write a sequel in the near future. Carmichael was given the highest rating available to new writers submitting manuscripts to The Literary Agency Group and he has appeared on WATC-TV, Channel 57 in Atlanta, GA, to discuss veterans issues, PTSD, and his novel.

Jim earned his Th.G. from Pacific Coast Baptist Bible College in San Dimas, CA (1981), and an M.Div. from Covenant Theological Seminary in St. Louis, MO (1993). After his ordination he became a pastor for eight and a half years. He recently received his Ph.D. from Reformation International Theological Seminary in Fellsmere, FL.

Today, Jim is involved in several teaching ministries. He began teaching theology in 2003 in Donetsk, Ukraine, which recently had to relocate to Kiev, Ukraine due to the Russian aggression. This ministry is through the Reformed Int'l Theological Education Ministries (RITE). He has also taught in Wroclaw, Poland and Cumpina, Romania for Int'l Theological Education Ministries (ITEM). In 2013, along with Mr. Chuck Lokey and Mr. Kirk Swanson, Teaching Missions Int'l

(ITEM) was formed. Classes were added to Jim's schedule in Port au Prince, Haiti for Reformation Hope Int'l.

Jim serves as chaplain for the Advisory Council at Georgia National Cemetery in Canton, GA. He is Chairman of Friends of Veterans and has written articles for Red Clay, the magazine of the Khe Sanh Veterans Association, Inc. Jim Carmichael is married to Catherine (since 1968), has two children, five grandchildren, one dog and two cats and resides in Cumming, GA.